THE CANTERBURY TALES

Geoffrey Chaucer

Contents

PREFACE..i
LIFE OF GEOFFREY CHAUCER iv

THE CANTERBURY TALES
The Prologue 1
The Knight's Tale.. 12
The Miller's Tale. 38
The Reeve's Tale 47
The Cook's Tale. 53
The Man Of Law's Tale. 55
The Wife Of Bath's Tale. 69
The Friar's Tale. 84
The Sompnour's Tale. 89
The Clerk's Tale. 97
The Merchant's Tale. 111
The Squire's Tale. 125
The Franklin's Tale. 134
The Doctor's Tale. 145
The Pardoner's Tale. 149
The Shipman's Tale. 158
The Prioress's Tale. 164
Chaucer's Tale Of Sir Thopas 168
Chaucer's Tale Of Meliboeus. 172
The Monk's Tale 181
The Nun's Priest's Tale. 193
The Second Nun's Tale. 203
The Canon's Yeoman's Tale. 210
The Manciple's Tale 221
The Parson's Tale. 226
Preces De Chauceres.. 238

PREFACE.

THE object of this volume is to place before the general reader our two early poetic masterpieces— The Canterbury Tales and The Faerie Queen; to do so in a way that will render their "popular perusal" easy in a time of little leisure and unbounded temptations to intellectual languor; and, on the same conditions, to present a liberal and fairly representative selection from the less important and familiar poems of Chaucer and Spenser. There is, it may be said at the outset, peculiar advantage and propriety in placing the two poets side by side in the manner now attempted for the first time. Although two centuries divide them, yet Spenser is the direct and really the immediate successor to the poetical inheritance of Chaucer. Those two hundred years, eventful as they were, produced no poet at all worthy to take up the mantle that fell from Chaucer's shoulders; and Spenser does not need his affected archaisms, nor his frequent and reverent appeals to "Dan Geffrey," to vindicate for himself a place very close to his great predecessor in the literary history of England. If Chaucer is the "Well of English undefiled," Spenser is the broad and stately river that yet holds the tenure of its very life from the fountain far away in other and ruder scenes.

The Canterbury Tales, so far as they are in verse, have been printed without any abridgement or designed change in the sense. But the two Tales in prose — Chaucer's Tale of Meliboeus, and the Parson's long Sermon on Penitence — have been contracted, so as to exclude thirty pages of unattractive prose, and to admit the same amount of interesting and characteristic poetry. The gaps thus made in the prose Tales, however, are supplied by careful outlines of the omitted matter, so that the reader need be at no loss to comprehend the whole scope and sequence of the original. With The Faerie Queen a bolder course has been pursued. The great obstacle to the popularity of Spencer's splendid work has lain less in its language than in its length. If we add together the three great poems of antiquity — the twenty-four books of the Iliad, the twenty-four books of the Odyssey, and the twelve books of the Aeneid — we get at the dimensions of only one-half of The Faerie Queen. The six books, and the fragment of a seventh, which alone exist of the author's contemplated twelve, number about 35,000 verses; the sixty books of Homer and Virgil number no more than 37,000. The mere bulk of the poem, then, has opposed a formidable barrier to its popularity; to say nothing of the distracting effect produced by the numberless episodes, the tedious narrations, and the constant repetitions, which have largely swelled that bulk. In this volume the poem is compressed into two-thirds of its original space, through the expedient of representing the less interesting and more mechanical passages by a condensed prose outline, in which it has been sought as far as possible to preserve the very words of the poet. While deprecating a too critical judgement on the bare and constrained precis standing in such trying juxtaposition, it is hoped that the labour bestowed in saving the reader the trouble of wading through much that is not essential for the enjoyment of Spencer's marvellous allegory, will not be unappreciated.

As regards the manner in which the text of the two great works, especially of The Canterbury Tales, is presented, the Editor is aware that some whose judgement is weighty will differ from him. This volume has been prepared "for popular perusal;" and its very raison d'etre would have failed, if the ancient orthography had been retained. It has often been affirmed by editors of Chaucer in the old forms of the language, that a little trouble at first would render the antiquated spelling and obsolete inflections a continual source, not of difficulty, but of actual delight, for the reader coming to the study of Chaucer without any preliminary acquaintance with the English of his day — or of his copyists' days. Despite this complacent assurance, the obvious fact is, that Chaucer in the old forms has not become popular, in the true sense of the word; he is not "understood of the vulgar." In this volume, therefore, the text of Chaucer has been presented in nineteenth-century garb. But there has been not the slightest attempt to "modernise" Chaucer, in the wider meaning of the phrase; to replace his words by words which he did not use; or, following the example of some operators, to translate him into English of the modern spirit as well as the modern forms. So far from that, in every case where the old spelling or form seemed essential to metre, to rhyme, or meaning, no change has been attempted. But, wherever its preservation was not essential, the spelling of the monkish transcribers — for the most ardent purist must now despair of getting at the spelling of

GEOFFREY CHAUCER

Chaucer himself — has been discarded for that of the reader's own day. It is a poor compliment to the Father of English Poetry, to say that by such treatment the bouquet and individuality of his works must be lost. If his masterpiece is valuable for one thing more than any other, it is the vivid distinctness with which English men and women of the fourteenth century are there painted, for the study of all the centuries to follow. But we wantonly balk the artist's own purpose, and discredit his labour, when we keep before his picture the screen of dust and cobwebs which, for the English people in these days, the crude forms of the infant language have practically become. Shakespeare has not suffered by similar changes; Spencer has not suffered; it would be surprising if Chaucer should suffer, when the loss of popular comprehension and favour in his case are necessarily all the greater for his remoteness from our day. In a much smaller degree — since previous labours in the same direction had left far less to do — the same work has been performed for the spelling of Spenser; and the whole endeavour in this department of the Editor's task has been, to present a text plain and easily intelligible to the modern reader, without any injustice to the old poet. It would be presumptuous to believe that in every case both ends have been achieved together; but the laudatores temporis acti - the students who may differ most from the plan pursued in this volume — will best appreciate the difficulty of the enterprise, and most leniently regard any failure in the details of its accomplishment.

With all the works of Chaucer, outside The Canterbury Tales, it would have been absolutely impossible to deal within the scope of this volume. But nearly one hundred pages, have been devoted to his minor poems; and, by dint of careful selection and judicious abridgement — a connecting outline of the story in all such cases being given — the Editor ventures to hope that he has presented fair and acceptable specimens of Chaucer's workmanship in all styles. The preparation of this part of the volume has been a laborious task; no similar attempt on the same scale has been made; and, while here also the truth of the text in matters essential has been in nowise sacrificed to mere ease of perusal, the general reader will find opened up for him a new view of Chaucer and his works. Before a perusal of these hundred pages, will melt away for ever the lingering tradition or prejudice that Chaucer was only, or characteristically, a coarse buffoon, who pandered to a base and licentious appetite by painting and exaggerating the lowest vices of his time. In these selections — made without a thought of taking only what is to the poet's credit from a wide range of poems in which hardly a word is to his discredit — we behold Chaucer as he was; a courtier, a gallant, pure-hearted gentleman, a scholar, a philosopher, a poet of gay and vivid fancy, playing around themes of chivalric convention, of deep human interest, or broad-sighted satire. In The Canterbury Tales, we see, not Chaucer, but Chaucer's times and neighbours; the artist has lost himself in his work. To show him honestly and without disguise, as he lived his own life and sung his own songs at the brilliant Court of Edward III, is to do his memory a moral justice far more material than any wrong that can ever come out of spelling. As to the minor poems of Spenser, which follow The Faerie Queen, the choice has been governed by the desire to give at once the most interesting, and the most characteristic of the poet's several styles; and, save in the case of the Sonnets, the poems so selected are given entire. It is manifest that the endeavours to adapt this volume for popular use, have been already noticed, would imperfectly succeed without the aid of notes and glossary, to explain allusions that have become obsolete, or antiquated words which it was necessary to retain. An endeavour has been made to render each page self- explanatory, by placing on it all the glossarial and illustrative notes required for its elucidation, or — to avoid repetitions that would have occupied space — the references to the spot where information may be found. The great advantage of such a plan to the reader, is the measure of its difficulty for the editor. It permits much more flexibility in the choice of glossarial explanations or equivalents; it saves the distracting and time- consuming reference to the end or the beginning of the book; but, at the same time, it largely enhances the liability to error. The Editor is conscious that in the 12,000 or 13,000 notes, as well as in the innumerable minute points of spelling, accentuation, and rhythm, he must now and again be found tripping; he can only ask any reader who may detect all that he could himself point out as being amiss, to set off against inevitable mistakes and misjudgements, the conscientious labour bestowed on the book, and the broad consideration of its fitness for the object contemplated.

From books the Editor has derived valuable help; as from Mr Cowden Clarke's revised modern text of The Canterbury Tales, published in Mr Nimmo's Library Edition of the English Poets; from Mr Wright's scholarly edition of the same work; from the indispensable Tyrwhitt; from Mr Bell's edition of Chaucer's Poem; from Professor Craik's "Spenser and his Poetry," published twenty-five years ago by Charles Knight; and from many others. In the abridgement of the Faerie Queen, the plan may at first sight seem to be modelled on the lines of Mr Craik's painstaking condensation; but the coincidences are either inevitable or involuntary. Many of the notes, especially of those explaining classical references and those attached to the minor poems of Chaucer, have been prepared specially for this edition. The Editor leaves his task with the hope that his attempt to remove artificial obstacles to the popularity of England's earliest poets, will not altogether miscarry.

D. LAING PURVES.

LIFE OF GEOFFREY CHAUCER.

NOT in point of genius only, but even in point of time, Chaucer may claim the proud designation of "first" English poet. He wrote "The Court of Love" in 1345, and "The Romaunt of the Rose," if not also "Troilus and Cressida," probably within the next decade: the dates usually assigned to the poems of Laurence Minot extend from 1335 to 1355, while "The Vision of Piers Plowman" mentions events that occurred in 1360 and 1362 — before which date Chaucer had certainly written "The Assembly of Fowls" and his "Dream." But, though they were his contemporaries, neither Minot nor Langland (if Langland was the author of the Vision) at all approached Chaucer in the finish, the force, or the universal interest of their works and the poems of earlier writer; as Layamon and the author of the "Ormulum," are less English than Anglo-Saxon or Anglo- Norman. Those poems reflected the perplexed struggle for supremacy between the two grand elements of our language, which marked the twelfth and thirteenth centuries; a struggle intimately associated with the political relations between the conquering Normans and the subjugated Anglo-Saxons. Chaucer found two branches of the language; that spoken by the people, Teutonic in its genius and its forms; that spoken by the learned and the noble, based on the French Yet each branch had begun to borrow of the other — just as nobles and people had been taught to recognise that each needed the other in the wars and the social tasks of the time; and Chaucer, a scholar, a courtier, a man conversant with all orders of society, but accustomed to speak, think, and write in the words of the highest, by his comprehensive genius cast into the simmering mould a magical amalgamant which made the two half-hostile elements unite and interpenetrate each other. Before Chaucer wrote, there were two tongues in England, keeping alive the feuds and resentments of cruel centuries; when he laid down his pen, there was practically but one speech — there was, and ever since has been, but one people.

Geoffrey Chaucer, according to the most trustworthy traditions- for authentic testimonies on the subject are wanting — was born in 1328; and London is generally believed to have been his birth-place. It is true that Leland, the biographer of England's first great poet who lived nearest to his time, not merely speaks of Chaucer as having been born many years later than the date now assigned, but mentions Berkshire or Oxfordshire as the scene of his birth. So great uncertainty have some felt on the latter score, that elaborate parallels have been drawn between Chaucer, and Homer — for whose birthplace several cities contended, and whose descent was traced to the demigods. Leland may seem to have had fair opportunities of getting at the truth about Chaucer's birth — for Henry VIII had him, at the suppression of the monasteries throughout England, to search for records of public interest the archives of the religious houses. But it may be questioned whether he was likely to find many authentic particulars regarding the personal history of the poet in the quarters which he explored; and Leland's testimony seems to be set aside by Chaucer's own evidence as to his birthplace, and by the contemporary references which make him out an aged man for years preceding the accepted date of his death. In one of his prose works, "The Testament of Love," the poet speaks of himself in terms that strongly confirm the claim of London to the honour of giving him birth; for he there mentions "the city of London, that is to me so dear and sweet, in which I was forth growen; and more kindly love," says he, "have I to that place than to any other in earth; as every kindly creature hath full appetite to that place of his kindly engendrure, and to will rest and peace in that place to abide." This tolerably direct evidence is supported — so far as it can be at such an interval of time — by the learned Camden; in his Annals of Queen Elizabeth, he describes Spencer, who was certainly born in London, as being a fellow-citizen of Chaucer's — "Edmundus Spenserus, patria Londinensis, Musis adeo arridentibus natus, ut omnes Anglicos superioris aevi poetas, ne Chaucero quidem concive excepto, superaret."[1] The records of the time notice more than one person of the name of Chaucer, who held honourable positions about the Court; and though we cannot distinctly trace the poet's relationship with any of these namesakes or antecessors, we find excellent ground for belief that his family or friends stood well at Court, in the ease with which Chaucer made his way there, and in his subsequent career.

THE CANTERBURY TALES

Like his great successor, Spencer, it was the fortune of Chaucer to live under a splendid, chivalrous, and high-spirited reign. 1328 was the second year of Edward III; and, what with Scotch wars, French expeditions, and the strenuous and costly struggle to hold England in a worthy place among the States of Europe, there was sufficient bustle, bold achievement, and high ambition in the period to inspire a poet who was prepared to catch the spirit of the day. It was an age of elaborate courtesy, of high- paced gallantry, of courageous venture, of noble disdain for mean tranquillity; and Chaucer, on the whole a man of peaceful avocations, was penetrated to the depth of his consciousness with the lofty and lovely civil side of that brilliant and restless military period. No record of his youthful years, however, remains to us; if we believe that at the age of eighteen he was a student of Cambridge, it is only on the strength of a reference in his "Court of Love", where the narrator is made to say that his name is Philogenet, "of Cambridge clerk;" while he had already told us that when he was stirred to seek the Court of Cupid he was "at eighteen year of age." According to Leland, however, he was educated at Oxford, proceeding thence to France and the Netherlands, to finish his studies; but there remains no certain evidence of his having belonged to either University. At the same time, it is not doubted that his family was of good condition; and, whether or not we accept the assertion that his father held the rank of knighthood — rejecting the hypotheses that make him a merchant, or a vintner "at the corner of Kirton Lane" — it is plain, from Chaucer's whole career, that he had introductions to public life, and recommendations to courtly favour, wholly independent of his genius. We have the clearest testimony that his mental training was of wide range and thorough excellence, altogether rare for a mere courtier in those days: his poems attest his intimate acquaintance with the divinity, the philosophy, and the scholarship of his time, and show him to have had the sciences, as then developed and taught, "at his fingers' ends." Another proof of Chaucer's good birth and fortune would be found in the statement that, after his University career was completed, he entered the Inner Temple - - the expenses of which could be borne only by men of noble and opulent families; but although there is a story that he was once fined two shillings for thrashing a Franciscan friar in Fleet Street, we have no direct authority for believing that the poet devoted himself to the uncongenial study of the law. No special display of knowledge on that subject appears in his works; yet in the sketch of the Manciple, in the Prologue to the Canterbury Tales, may be found indications of his familiarity with the internal economy of the Inns of Court; while numerous legal phrases and references hint that his comprehensive information was not at fault on legal matters. Leland says that he quitted the University "a ready logician, a smooth rhetorician, a pleasant poet, a grave philosopher, an ingenious mathematician, and a holy divine;" and by all accounts, when Geoffrey Chaucer comes before us authentically for the first time, at the age of thirty-one, he was possessed of knowledge and accomplishments far beyond the common standard of his day.

Chaucer at this period possessed also other qualities fitted to recommend him to favour in a Court like that of Edward III. Urry describes him, on the authority of a portrait, as being then "of a fair beautiful complexion, his lips red and full, his size of a just medium, and his port and air graceful and majestic. So," continues the ardent biographer, — "so that every ornament that could claim the approbation of the great and fair, his abilities to record the valour of the one, and celebrate the beauty of the other, and his wit and gentle behaviour to converse with both, conspired to make him a complete courtier." If we believe that his "Court of Love" had received such publicity as the literary media of the time allowed in the somewhat narrow and select literary world — not to speak of "Troilus and Cressida," which, as Lydgate mentions it first among Chaucer's works, some have supposed to be a youthful production — we find a third and not less powerful recommendation to the favour of the great co- operating with his learning and his gallant bearing. Elsewhere[2] reasons have been shown for doubt whether "Troilus and Cressida" should not be assigned to a later period of Chaucer's life; but very little is positively known about the dates and sequence of his various works. In the year 1386, being called as witness with regard to a contest on a point of heraldry between Lord Scrope and Sir Robert Grosvenor, Chaucer deposed that he entered on his military career in 1359. In that year Edward III invaded France, for the third time, in pursuit of his claim to the French crown; and we may fancy that, in describing the embarkation of the knights in "Chaucer's Dream", the poet gained some of the vividness and stir of his picture from his recollections of the embarkation of the splendid and well- appointed royal host at Sandwich, on board the eleven hundred transports provided for the enterprise. In this expedition the laurels of Poitiers were flung on the ground; after vainly attempting Rheims and Paris, Edward was constrained, by cruel weather and lack of provisions, to retreat toward his ships; the fury of the elements made the retreat more disastrous than an overthrow in pitched battle; horses and men perished by thousands, or fell into the hands of the pursuing French. Chaucer, who had been made prisoner at the siege of Retters, was among the captives in the possession of France when the treaty of Bretigny — the "great peace" — was concluded, in May, 1360. Returning to England, as we may suppose, at the peace, the poet, ere long, fell into another and a pleasanter captivity; for his marriage is generally believed to have taken place shortly after his release from foreign durance. He had already gained the personal friendship and favour of John of Gaunt, Duke of Lancaster, the King's son; the Duke, while Earl of Richmond, had courted, and won to wife after a certain delay, Blanche, daughter and co-heiress of Henry Duke of Lancaster; and Chaucer is by some believed to have written "The Assembly of Fowls" to celebrate the wooing, as he wrote "Chaucer's Dream" to celebrate the wedding, of his patron. The marriage took place in 1359, the year of Chaucer's expedition to France; and as, in "The Assembly of Fowls," the formel or female eagle, who is supposed to represent the Lady Blanche, begs that her choice of a mate may be deferred for a year, 1358 and 1359 have been assigned as the respective dates of the two poems already mentioned. In the "Dream," Chaucer prominently introduces his own lady-love, to whom, after the happy union of his patron with the Lady Blanche, he is wedded amid great rejoicing; and various expressions in the same poem show that not only was the poet high in favour with the illustrious pair, but that his future wife had also peculiar claims on their regard. She was the younger daughter of Sir Payne Roet, a native of Hainault, who had, like many of his countrymen, been attracted to England by the example and patronage of Queen Philippa. The favourite attendant on the Lady Blanche was her elder sister Katherine: subsequently married to Sir Hugh Swynford, a gentleman of Lincolnshire; and destined, after the death of Blanche, to be in succession governess of her children, mistress of John of Gaunt, and lawfully-wedded Duchess of Lancaster. It is quite sufficient proof that Chaucer's position at Court was of no mean consequence, to find that his wife, the sister of the future Duchess of Lancaster, was one of the royal maids of honour, and even, as Sir Harris Nicolas conjectures, a god-daughter of the Queen — for her name also was Philippa.

Between 1359, when the poet himself testifies that he was made prisoner while bearing arms in France, and September 1366, when Queen Philippa granted to her former maid of honour, by the name of Philippa Chaucer, a yearly pension of ten marks, or L6, 13s. 4d., we have no authentic mention of Chaucer, express or indirect. It is plain from this grant that the poet's marriage with Sir Payne Roet's daughter was not celebrated later than 1366; the probability is, that it closely followed his return from the wars. In 1367, Edward III. settled upon Chaucer a life-pension of twenty marks, "for the good service which our beloved Valet — 'dilectus Valettus noster' — Geoffrey Chaucer has rendered, and will render in time to come." Camden explains 'Valettus hospitii' to signify a Gentleman of the Privy Chamber; Selden says that the designation was bestowed "upon young heirs designed to he knighted, or young gentlemen of great descent and quality." Whatever the strict meaning of the word, it is plain that the poet's position was honourable and near to the King's person, and also that his worldly circumstances were easy, if not affluent — for it need not be said that twenty marks in those days represented twelve or twenty times the sum in these. It is believed that he found powerful patronage, not merely from the Duke of Lancaster and his wife, but from Margaret Countess of Pembroke, the King's daughter. To her Chaucer is supposed to have addressed the "Goodly Ballad", in which the lady is celebrated under the image of the daisy; her he is by some understood to have represented under the title of Queen Alcestis, in the "Court of Love" and the Prologue to "The Legend of Good Women;" and in her praise we may read his charming descriptions and eulogies of the daisy — French, "Marguerite," the name of his Royal patroness. To this period of Chaucer's career we may probably attribute the elegant and courtly, if somewhat conventional, poems of "The Flower and the Leaf," "The Cuckoo and the Nightingale," &c. "The Lady Margaret," says Urry, ". . . would frequently compliment him upon his poems. But this is not to be meant of his Canterbury Tales, they being written in the latter part of his life, when the courtier and the fine gentleman gave way to solid sense and plain descriptions. In his love-pieces he was obliged to have the strictest regard to modesty and decency; the ladies at that time insisting so much upon the nicest punctilios of honour, that it was highly criminal to depreciate their sex, or do anything that might offend virtue." Chaucer, in their estimation, had sinned against the dignity and honour of womankind by his translation of the French "Roman de la Rose," and by his "Troilus and Cressida" — assuming it to have been among his less mature works; and to atone for those offences the Lady Margaret (though other and older accounts say that it was the first Queen of Richard II., Anne of

Bohemia), prescribed to him the task of writing "The Legend of Good Women" (see introductory note to that poem). About this period, too, we may place the composition of Chaucer's A. B. C., or The Prayer of Our Lady, made at the request of the Duchess Blanche, a lady of great devoutness in her private life. She died in 1369; and Chaucer, as he had allegorised her wooing, celebrated her marriage, and aided her devotions, now lamented her death, in a poem entitled "The Book of the Duchess; or, the Death of Blanche.[3]

In 1370, Chaucer was employed on the King's service abroad; and in November 1372, by the title of "Scutifer noster" — our Esquire or Shield-bearer — he was associated with "Jacobus Pronan," and "Johannes de Mari civis Januensis," in a royal commission, bestowing full powers to treat with the Duke of Genoa, his Council, and State. The object of the embassy was to negotiate upon the choice of an English port at which the Genoese might form a commercial establishment; and Chaucer, having quitted England in December, visited Genoa and Florence, and returned to England before the end of November 1373 — for on that day he drew his pension from the Exchequer in person. The most interesting point connected with this Italian mission is the question, whether Chaucer visited Petrarch at Padua. That he did, is unhesitatingly affirmed by the old biographers; but the authentic notices of Chaucer during the years 1372-1373, as shown by the researches of Sir Harris Nicolas, are confined to the facts already stated; and we are left to answer the question by the probabilities of the case, and by the aid of what faint light the poet himself affords. We can scarcely fancy that Chaucer, visiting Italy for the first time, in a capacity which opened for him easy access to the great and the famous, did not embrace the chance of meeting a poet whose works he evidently knew in their native tongue, and highly esteemed. With Mr Wright, we are strongly disinclined to believe "that Chaucer did not profit by the opportunity . . . of improving his acquaintance with the poetry, if not the poets, of the country he thus visited, whose influence was now being felt on the literature of most countries of Western Europe." That Chaucer was familiar with the Italian language appears not merely from his repeated selection as Envoy to Italian States, but by many passages in his poetry, from "The Assembly of Fowls" to "The Canterbury Tales." In the opening of the first poem there is a striking parallel to Dante's inscription on the gate of Hell. The first Song of Troilus, in "Troilus and Cressida", is a nearly literal translation of Petrarch's 88th Sonnet. In the Prologue to "The Legend of Good Women", there is a reference to Dante which can hardly have reached the poet at second- hand. And in Chaucer's great work — as in The Wife of Bath's Tale, and The Monk's Tale — direct reference by name is made to Dante, "the wise poet of Florence," "the great poet of Italy," as the source whence the author has quoted. When we consider the poet's high place in literature and at Court, which could not fail to make him free of the hospitalities of the brilliant little Lombard States; his familiarity with the tongue and the works of Italy's greatest bards, dead and living; the reverential regard which he paid to the memory of great poets, of which we have examples in "The House of Fame," and at the close of "Troilus and Cressida"[4]; along with his own testimony in the Prologue to The Clerk's Tale, we cannot fail to construe that testimony as a declaration that the Tale was actually told to Chaucer by the lips of Petrarch, in 1373, the very year in which Petrarch translated it into Latin, from Boccaccio's "Decameron."[5] Mr Bell notes the objection to this interpretation, that the words are put into the mouth, not of the poet, but of the Clerk; and meets it by the counter- objection, that the Clerk, being a purely imaginary personage, could not have learned the story at Padua from Petrarch — and therefore that Chaucer must have departed from the dramatic assumption maintained in the rest of the dialogue. Instances could be adduced from Chaucer's writings to show that such a sudden "departure from the dramatic assumption" would not be unexampled: witness the "aside" in The Wife of Bath's Prologue, where, after the jolly Dame has asserted that "half so boldly there can no man swear and lie as a woman can", the poet hastens to interpose, in his own person, these two lines:

"I say not this by wives that be wise,
  But if it be when they them misadvise."

And again, in the Prologue to the "Legend of Good Women," from a description of the daisy —

"She is the clearness and the very light,
  That in this darke world me guides and leads,"

the poet, in the very next lines, slides into an address to his lady:

"The heart within my sorrowful heart you dreads
And loves so sore, that ye be, verily,
The mistress of my wit, and nothing I," &c.

When, therefore, the Clerk of Oxford is made to say that he will tell a tale —

"The which that I
Learn'd at Padova of a worthy clerk,
As proved by his wordes and his werk.
He is now dead, and nailed in his chest,
I pray to God to give his soul good rest.
Francis Petrarc', the laureate poete,
Highte this clerk, whose rhetoric so sweet
Illumin'd all Itaile of poetry. . . .
But forth to tellen of this worthy man,
That taughte me this tale, as I began." . . .

we may without violent effort believe that Chaucer speaks in his own person, though dramatically the words are on the Clerk's lips. And the belief is not impaired by the sorrowful way in which the Clerk lingers on Petrarch's death — which would be less intelligible if the fictitious narrator had only read the story in the Latin translation, than if we suppose the news of Petrarch's death at Arqua in July 1374 to have closely followed Chaucer to England, and to have cruelly and irresistibly mingled itself with our poet's personal recollections of his great Italian contemporary. Nor must we regard as without significance the manner in which the Clerk is made to distinguish between the "body" of Petrarch's tale, and the fashion in which it was set forth in writing, with a proem that seemed "a thing impertinent", save that the poet had chosen in that way to "convey his matter" — told, or "taught," so much more directly and simply by word of mouth. It is impossible to pronounce positively on the subject; the question whether Chaucer saw Petrarch in 1373 must remain a moot-point, so long as we have only our present information; but fancy loves to dwell on the thought of the two poets conversing under the vines at Arqua; and we find in the history and the writings of Chaucer nothing to contradict, a good deal to countenance, the belief that such a meeting occurred.

Though we have no express record, we have indirect testimony, that Chaucer's Genoese mission was discharged satisfactorily; for on the 23d of April 1374, Edward III grants at Windsor to the poet, by the title of "our beloved squire" — dilecto Armigero nostro — unum pycher. vini, "one pitcher of wine" daily, to be "perceived" in the port of London; a grant which, on the analogy of more modern usage, might he held equivalent to Chaucer's appointment as Poet Laureate. When we find that soon afterwards the grant was commuted for a money payment of twenty marks per annum, we need not conclude that Chaucer's circumstances were poor; for it may be easily supposed that the daily "perception" of such an article of income was attended with considerable prosaic inconvenience. A permanent provision for Chaucer was made on the 8th of June 1374, when he was appointed Controller of the Customs in the Port of London, for the lucrative imports of wools, skins or "wool-fells," and tanned hides — on condition that he should fulfil the duties of that office in person and not by deputy, and should write out the accounts with his own hand. We have what seems evidence of Chaucer's compliance with these terms in "The House of Fame", where, in the mouth of the eagle, the poet describes himself, when he has finished his labour and made his reckonings, as not seeking rest and news in social intercourse, but going home to his own house, and there, "all so dumb as any stone," sitting "at another book," until his look is dazed; and again, in the record that in 1376 he received a grant of L731, 4s. 6d., the amount of a fine levied on one John Kent, whom Chaucer's vigilance had frustrated in the attempt to ship a quantity of wool for Dordrecht without paying the duty. The seemingly derogatory condition, that the Controller should write out the accounts or rolls ("rotulos") of his office with his own hand, appears to have been designed, or treated, as merely formal; no records in Chaucer's handwriting are known to exist — which could hardly be the case if, for the twelve years of his Controllership (1374-1386), he had duly complied with the condition; and during that period he was more than once employed abroad, so that the condition was evidently regarded as a formality even by those who had imposed it. Also in 1374, the Duke of Lancaster, whose ambitious views may well have made him anxious to retain the adhesion of a man so capable and accomplished as Chaucer, changed into a joint life-annuity remaining to the survivor, and charged on the revenues of the Savoy, a pension of L10 which two years before he settled on the poet's wife — whose sister was then the governess of the Duke's two daughters, Philippa and Elizabeth, and the Duke's own mistress. Another proof of Chaucer's personal reputation and high Court favour at this time, is his selection (1375) as ward to the son of Sir Edmond Staplegate of Bilsynton, in Kent; a charge on the surrender of which the guardian received no less a sum than L104.

We find Chaucer in 1376 again employed on a foreign mission. In 1377, the last year of Edward III., he was sent to Flanders with Sir Thomas Percy, afterwards Earl of Worcester, for the purpose of obtaining a prolongation of the truce; and in January 13738, he was associated with Sir Guichard d'Angle and other Commissioners, to pursue certain negotiations for a marriage between Princess Mary of France and the young King Richard II., which had been set on foot before the death of Edward III. The negotiation, however, proved fruitless; and in May 1378, Chaucer was selected to accompany Sir John Berkeley on a mission to the Court of Bernardo Visconti, Duke of Milan, with the view, it is supposed, of concerting military plans against the outbreak of war with France. The new King, meantime, had shown that he was not insensible to Chaucer's merit — or to the influence of his tutor and the poet's patron, the Duke of Lancaster; for Richard II. confirmed to Chaucer his pension of twenty marks, along with an equal annual sum, for which the daily pitcher of wine granted in 1374 had been commuted. Before his departure for Lombardy, Chaucer — still holding his post in the Customs — selected two representatives or trustees, to protect his estate against legal proceedings in his absence, or to sue in his name defaulters and offenders against the imposts which he was charged to enforce. One of these trustees was called Richard Forrester; the other was John Gower, the poet, the most famous English contemporary of Chaucer, with whom he had for many years been on terms of admiring friendship — although, from the strictures passed on certain productions of Gower's in the Prologue to The Man of Law's Tale,[6] it has been supposed that in the later years of Chaucer's life the friendship suffered some diminution. To the "moral Gower" and "the philosophical Strode," Chaucer "directed" or dedicated his "Troilus and Cressida;"[7] while, in the "Confessio Amantis," Gower introduces a handsome compliment to his greater contemporary, as the "disciple and the poet" of Venus, with whose glad songs and ditties, made in her praise during the flowers of his youth, the land was filled everywhere. Gower, however — a monk and a Conservative — held to the party of the Duke of Gloucester, the rival of the Wycliffite and innovating Duke of Lancaster, who was Chaucer's patron, and whose cause was not a little aided by Chaucer's strictures on the clergy; and thus it is not impossible that political differences may have weakened the old bonds of personal friendship and poetic esteem. Returning from Lombardy early in 1379, Chaucer seems to have been again sent abroad; for the records exhibit no trace of him between May and December of that year. Whether by proxy or in person, however, he received his pensions regularly until 1382, when his income was increased by his appointment to the post of Controller of Petty Customs in the port of London. In November 1384, he obtained a month's leave of absence on account of his private affairs, and a deputy was appointed to fill his place; and in February of the next year he was permitted to appoint a permanent deputy — thus at length gaining relief from that close attention to business which probably curtailed the poetic fruits of the poet's most powerful years.[8]

Chaucer is next found occupying a post which has not often been held by men gifted with his peculiar genius — that of a county member. The contest between the Dukes of Gloucester and Lancaster, and their adherents, for the control of the Government, was coming to a crisis; and when the recluse and studious Chaucer was induced to offer himself to the electors of Kent as one of the knights of their shire — where presumably he held property — we may suppose that it was with the view of supporting his patron's cause in the impending conflict. The Parliament in which the poet sat assembled at Westminster on the 1st of October, and was dissolved on the 1st of November, 1386. Lancaster was fighting and intriguing abroad, absorbed in the affairs of his Castilian succession; Gloucester and his friends at home had everything their own way; the Earl of Suffolk was dismissed from the woolsack, and impeached by the Commons; and although Richard at first stood out courageously for the friends of his uncle Lancaster, he was constrained, by the refusal of supplies, to consent to the proceedings of Gloucester. A commission was wrung from him, under protest, appointing Gloucester, Arundel, and twelve other Peers and prelates, a permanent council to inquire into the condition of all the public departments, the courts of law, and the royal household, with absolute powers of redress and dismissal. We need not ascribe to Chaucer's Parliamentary exertions in his patron's behalf, nor to any malpractices in his official conduct, the fact that he was among the earliest victims of the commission.[9] In December 1386, he was dismissed from both his offices in the port of London; but he retained his pensions, and drew them regularly twice a year at the Exchequer until 1388. In 1387, Chaucer's political reverses were aggravated by a severe domestic calamity: his wife died, and with her died the pension which had been settled on her by Queen Philippa in 1366, and confirmed to her at Richard's accession in 1377. The change made in Chaucer's pecuniary position, by the loss of his offices and his wife's pension, must have been very great. It would appear that during his prosperous times he had lived in a style quite equal to his income, and had no ample resources against a season of reverse; for, on the 1st of May 1388, less than a year and a half after being dismissed from the Customs, he was constrained to assign his pensions, by surrender in Chancery, to one John Scalby. In May 1389, Richard II., now of age, abruptly resumed the reins of government, which, for more than two years, had been ably but cruelly managed by Gloucester. The friends of Lancaster were once more supreme in the royal councils, and Chaucer speedily profited by the change. On the 12th of July he was appointed Clerk of the King's Works at the Palace of Westminster, the Tower, the royal manors of Kennington, Eltham, Clarendon, Sheen, Byfleet, Childern Langley, and Feckenham, the castle of Berkhamstead, the royal lodge of Hathenburgh in the New Forest, the lodges in the parks of Clarendon, Childern Langley, and Feckenham, and the mews for the King's falcons at Charing Cross; he received a salary of two shillings per day, and was allowed to perform the duties by deputy. For some reason unknown, Chaucer held this lucrative office[10] little more than two years, quitting it before the 16th of September 1391, at which date it had passed into the hands of one John Gedney. The next two years and a half are a blank, so far as authentic records are concerned; Chaucer is supposed to have passed them in retirement, probably devoting them principally to the composition of The Canterbury Tales. In February 1394, the King conferred upon him a grant of L20 a year for life; but he seems to have had no other source of income, and to have become embarrassed by debt, for frequent memoranda of small advances on his pension show that his circumstances were, in comparison, greatly reduced. Things appear to have grown worse and worse with the poet; for in May 1398 he was compelled to obtain from the King letters of protection against arrest, extending over a term of two years. Not for the first time, it is true — for similar documents had been issued at the beginning of Richard's reign; but at that time Chaucer's missions abroad, and his responsible duties in the port of London, may have furnished reasons for securing him against annoyance or frivolous prosecution, which were wholly wanting at the later date. In 1398, fortune began again to smile upon him; he received a royal grant of a tun of wine annually, the value being about L4. Next year, Richard II having been deposed by the son of John of Gaunt[11] — Henry of Bolingbroke, Duke of Lancaster — the new King, four days after hits accession, bestowed on Chaucer a grant of forty marks (L26, 13s. 4d.) per annum, in addition to the pension of L20 conferred by Richard II. in 1394. But the poet, now seventy-one years of age, and probably broken down by the reverses of the past few years, was not destined long to enjoy his renewed prosperity. On Christmas Eve of 1399, he entered on the possession of a house in the garden of the Chapel of the Blessed Mary of Westminster — near to the present site of Henry VII.'s Chapel — having obtained a lease from Robert Hermodesworth, a monk of the adjacent convent, for fifty-three years, at the annual rent of four marks (L2, 13s. 4d.) Until the 1st of March 1400, Chaucer drew his pensions in person; then they were received for him by another hand; and on the 25th of October, in the same year, he died, at the age of seventy-two. The only lights thrown by his poems on his closing days are furnished in the little ballad called "Good Counsel of Chaucer," — which, though said to have been written when "upon his death-bed lying in his great anguish, "breathes the very spirit of courage, resignation, and philosophic calm; and by the "Retractation" at the end of The Canterbury Tales, which, if it was not foisted in by monkish transcribers, may be supposed the effect of Chaucer's regrets and self-reproaches on that solemn review of his life-work which the close approach of death compelled. The poet was buried in Westminster Abbey;[12] and not many years after his death a slab was placed on a pillar near his grave, bearing the lines, taken from an epitaph or eulogy made by Stephanus Surigonus of Milan, at the request of Caxton:

"Galfridus Chaucer, vates, et fama poesis
Maternae, hoc sacra sum tumulatus humo."[13]

About 1555, Mr Nicholas Brigham, a gentleman of Oxford who greatly admired the genius of Chaucer, erected the present tomb, as near to the spot where the poet lay, "before the chapel of St Benet," as was then possible by reason of the "cancelli,"[14] which the Duke of Buckingham subsequently obtained leave to remove, that room might be made for the tomb of Dryden. On the structure of Mr Brigham, besides a full-length representation of Chaucer, taken from a portrait drawn by his "scholar" Thomas Occleve, was — or is, though now almost illegible — the following inscription:—

    M. S.
 QUI FUIT ANGLORUM VATES TER MAXIMUS OLIM,
 GALFRIDUS CHAUCER CONDITUR HOC TUMULO;
 ANNUM SI QUAERAS DOMINI, SI TEMPORA VITAE,
 ECCE NOTAE SUBSUNT, QUE TIBI CUNCTA NOTANT.
   25 OCTOBRIS 1400.
  AERUMNARUM REQUIES MORS.
N. BRIGHAM HOS FECIT MUSARUM NOMINE SUMPTUS
    1556.[15]

 Concerning his personal appearance and habits, Chaucer has not been reticent in his poetry. Urry sums up the traits of his aspect and character fairly thus: "He was of a middle stature, the latter part of his life inclinable to be fat and corpulent, as appears by the Host's bantering him in the journey to Canterbury, and comparing shapes with him.[16] His face was fleshy, his features just and regular, his complexion fair, and somewhat pale, his hair of a dusky yellow, short and thin; the hair of his beard in two forked tufts, of a wheat colour; his forehead broad and smooth; his eyes inclining usually to the ground, which is intimated by the Host's words; his whole face full of liveliness, a calm, easy sweetness, and a studious Venerable aspect. . . . As to his temper, he had a mixture of the gay, the modest, and the grave. The sprightliness of his humour was more distinguished by his writings than by his appearance; which gave occasion to Margaret Countess of Pembroke often to rally him upon his silent modesty in company, telling him, that his absence was more agreeable to her than his conversation, since the first was productive of agreeable pieces of wit in his writings,[17] but the latter was filled with a modest deference, and a too distant respect. We see nothing merry or jocose in his behaviour with his pilgrims, but a silent attention to their mirth, rather than any mixture of his own. . . When disengaged from public affairs, his time was entirely spent in study and reading; so agreeable to him was this exercise, that he says he preferred it to all other sports and diversions.[18] He lived within himself, neither desirous to hear nor busy to concern himself with the affairs of his neighbours. His course of living was temperate and regular; he went to rest with the sun, and rose before it; and by that means enjoyed the pleasures of the better part of the day, his morning walk and fresh contemplations. This gave him the advantage of describing the morning in so lively a manner as he does everywhere in his works. The springing sun glows warm in his lines, and the fragrant air blows cool in his descriptions; we smell the sweets of the bloomy haws, and hear the music of the feathered choir, whenever we take a forest walk with him. The hour of the day is not easier to be discovered from the reflection of the sun in Titian's paintings, than in Chaucer's morning landscapes. . . . His reading was deep and extensive, his judgement sound and discerning. . . In one word, he was a great scholar, a pleasant wit, a candid critic, a sociable companion, a steadfast friend, a grave philosopher, a temperate economist, and a pious Christian."

 Chaucer's most important poems are "Troilus and Cressida," "The Romaunt of the Rose," and "The Canterbury Tales." Of the first, containing 8246 lines, an abridgement, with a prose connecting outline of the story, is given in this volume. With the second, consisting of 7699 octosyllabic verses, like those in which "The House of Fame" is written, it was found impossible to deal in the present edition. The poem is a curtailed translation from the French "Roman de la Rose" — commenced by Guillaume de Lorris, who died in 1260, after contributing 4070 verses, and completed, in the last quarter of the thirteenth century, by Jean de Meun, who added some 18,000 verses. It is a satirical allegory, in which the vices of courts, the corruptions of the clergy, the disorders and inequalities of society in general, are unsparingly attacked, and the most revolutionary doctrines are advanced; and though, in making his translation, Chaucer softened or eliminated much of the satire of the poem, still it remained, in his verse, a caustic exposure of the abuses of the time, especially those which discredited the Church.

 The Canterbury Tales are presented in this edition with as near an approach to completeness as regard for the popular character of the volume permitted. The 17,385 verses, of which the poetical

Tales consist, have been given without abridgement or purgation — save in a single couplet; but, the main purpose of the volume being to make the general reader acquainted with the "poems" of Chaucer and Spenser, the Editor has ventured to contract the two prose Tales — Chaucer's Tale of Meliboeus, and the Parson's Sermon or Treatise on Penitence — so as to save about thirty pages for the introduction of Chaucer's minor pieces. At the same time, by giving prose outlines of the omitted parts, it has been sought to guard the reader against the fear that he was losing anything essential, or even valuable. It is almost needless to describe the plot, or point out the literary place, of the Canterbury Tales. Perhaps in the entire range of ancient and modern literature there is no work that so clearly and freshly paints for future times the picture of the past; certainly no Englishman has ever approached Chaucer in the power of fixing for ever the fleeting traits of his own time. The plan of the poem had been adopted before Chaucer chose it; notably in the "Decameron" of Boccaccio — although, there, the circumstances under which the tales were told, with the terror of the plague hanging over the merry company, lend a grim grotesqueness to the narrative, unless we can look at it abstracted from its setting. Chaucer, on the other hand, strikes a perpetual key-note of gaiety whenever he mentions the word "pilgrimage;" and at every stage of the connecting story we bless the happy thought which gives us incessant incident, movement, variety, and unclouded but never monotonous joyousness.

The poet, the evening before he starts on a pilgrimage to the shrine of St Thomas at Canterbury, lies at the Tabard Inn, in Southwark, curious to know in what companionship he is destined to fare forward on the morrow. Chance sends him "nine and twenty in a company," representing all orders of English society, lay and clerical, from the Knight and the Abbot down to the Ploughman and the Sompnour. The jolly Host of the Tabard, after supper, when tongues are loosened and hearts are opened, declares that "not this year" has he seen such a company at once under his roof-tree, and proposes that, when they set out next morning, he should ride with them and make them sport. All agree, and Harry Bailly unfolds his scheme: each pilgrim, including the poet, shall tell two tales on the road to Canterbury, and two on the way back to London; and he whom the general voice pronounces to have told the best tale, shall be treated to a supper at the common cost — and, of course, to mine Host's profit — when the cavalcade returns from the saint's shrine to the Southwark hostelry. All joyously assent; and early on the morrow, in the gay spring sunshine, they ride forth, listening to the heroic tale of the brave and gentle Knight, who has been gracefully chosen by the Host to lead the spirited competition of story-telling.

To describe thus the nature of the plan, and to say that when Chaucer conceived, or at least began to execute it, he was between sixty and seventy years of age, is to proclaim that The Canterbury Tales could never be more than a fragment. Thirty pilgrims, each telling two tales on the way out, and two more on the way back — that makes 120 tales; to say nothing of the prologue, the description of the journey, the occurrences at Canterbury, "and all the remnant of their pilgrimage," which Chaucer also undertook. No more than twenty-three of the 120 stories are told in the work as it comes down to us; that is, only twenty-three of the thirty pilgrims tell the first of the two stories on the road to Canterbury; while of the stories on the return journey we have not one, and nothing is said about the doings of the pilgrims at Canterbury — which would, if treated like the scene at the Tabard, have given us a still livelier "picture of the period." But the plan was too large; and although the poet had some reserves, in stories which he had already composed in an independent form, death cut short his labour ere he could even complete the arrangement and connection of more than a very few of the Tales. Incomplete as it is, however, the magnum opus of Chaucer was in his own time received with immense favour; manuscript copies are numerous even now — no slight proof of its popularity; and when the invention of printing was introduced into England by William Caxton, The Canterbury Tales issued from his press in the year after the first English- printed book, "The Game of the Chesse," had been struck off. Innumerable editions have since been published; and it may fairly be affirmed, that few books have been so much in favour with the reading public of every generation as this book, which the lapse of every generation has been rendering more unreadable.

Apart from "The Romaunt of the Rose," no really important poetical work of Chaucer's is omitted from or unrepresented in the present edition. Of "The Legend of Good Women," the Prologue only is given — but it is the most genuinely Chaucerian part of the poem. Of "The Court of Love," three-fourths are here presented; of "The Assembly of Fowls," "The Cuckoo and the

THE CANTERBURY TALES

Nightingale," "The Flower and the Leaf," all; of "Chaucer's Dream," one-fourth; of "The House of Fame," two-thirds; and of the minor poems such a selection as may give an idea of Chaucer's power in the "occasional" department of verse. Necessarily, no space whatever could be given to Chaucer's prose works — his translation of Boethius' Treatise on the Consolation of Philosophy; his Treatise on the Astrolabe, written for the use of his son Lewis; and his "Testament of Love," composed in his later years, and reflecting the troubles that then beset the poet. If, after studying in a simplified form the salient works of England's first great bard, the reader is tempted to regret that he was not introduced to a wider acquaintance with the author, the purpose of the Editor will have been more than attained.

The plan of the volume does not demand an elaborate examination into the state of our language when Chaucer wrote, or the nice questions of grammatical and metrical structure which conspire with the obsolete orthography to make his poems a sealed book for the masses. The most important element in the proper reading of Chaucer's verses — whether written in the decasyllabic or heroic metre, which he introduced into our literature, or in the octosyllabic measure used with such animated effect in "The House of Fame," "Chaucer's Dream," &c. — is the sounding of the terminal "e" where it is now silent. That letter is still valid in French poetry; and Chaucer's lines can be scanned only by reading them as we would read Racine's or Moliere's. The terminal "e" played an important part in grammar; in many cases it was the sign of the infinitive — the "n" being dropped from the end; at other times it pointed the distinction between singular and plural, between adjective and adverb. The pages that follow, however, being prepared from the modern English point of view, necessarily no account is taken of those distinctions; and the now silent "e" has been retained in the text of Chaucer only when required by the modern spelling, or by the exigencies of metre.

Before a word beginning with a vowel, or with the letter "h," the final "e" was almost without exception mute; and in such cases, in the plural forms and infinitives of verbs, the terminal "n" is generally retained for the sake of euphony. No reader who is acquainted with the French language will find it hard to fall into Chaucer's accentuation; while, for such as are not, a simple perusal of the text according to the rules of modern verse, should remove every difficulty.

Notes to Life of Geoffrey Chaucer

1. "Edmund Spenser, a native of London, was born with a Muse of such power, that he was superior to all English poets of preceding ages, not excepting his fellow-citizen Chaucer."
2. See introduction to "The Legend of Good Women".
3. Called in the editions before 1597 "The Dream of Chaucer". The poem, which is not included in the present edition, does indeed, like many of Chaucer's smaller works, tell the story of a dream, in which a knight, representing John of Gaunt, is found by the poet mourning the loss of his lady; but the true "Dream of Chaucer," in which he celebrates the marriage of his patron, was published for the first time by Speght in 1597. John of Gaunt, in the end of 1371, married his second wife, Constance, daughter to Pedro the Cruel of Spain; so that "The Book of the Duchess" must have been written between 1369 and 1371.
4. Where he bids his "little book"
   "Subject be unto all poesy,
   And kiss the steps, where as thou seest space,
   Of Virgil, Ovid, Homer, Lucan, Stace."
5. See note 1 to The Tale in The Clerk's Tale.
6. See note 1 to The Man of Law's Tale.
7. "Written," says Mr Wright, "in the sixteenth year of the reign of Richard II. (1392-1393);" a powerful confirmation of the opinion that this poem was really produced in Chaucer's mature age. See the introductory notes to it and to the Legend of Good Women.
8. The old biographers of Chaucer, founding on what they took to be autobiographic allusions in "The Testament of Love," assign to him between 1354 and 1389 a very different history from that here given on the strength of authentic records explored and quoted by Sir H. Nicolas. Chaucer is made to espouse the cause of John of Northampton, the Wycliffite Lord Mayor of London, whose re-election in 1384 was so vehemently opposed by the clergy, and who was imprisoned in the sequel of the grave disorders that arose. The poet, it is said, fled to the Continent, taking with him a large sum of money, which he spent in supporting companions in exile; then, returning by stealth to England

GEOFFREY CHAUCER

in quest of funds, he was detected and sent to the Tower, where he languished for three years, being released only on the humiliating condition of informing against his associates in the plot. The public records show, however, that, all the time of his alleged exile and captivity, he was quietly living in London, regularly drawing his pensions in person, sitting in Parliament, and discharging his duties in the Customs until his dismissal in 1386. It need not be said, further, that although Chaucer freely handled the errors, the ignorance, and vices of the clergy, he did so rather as a man of sense and of conscience, than as a Wycliffite — and there is no evidence that he espoused the opinions of the zealous Reformer, far less played the part of an extreme and self- regardless partisan of his old friend and college-companion.

9. "The Commissioners appear to have commenced their labours with examining the accounts of the officers employed in the collection of the revenue; and the sequel affords a strong presumption that the royal administration [under Lancaster and his friends] had been foully calumniated. We hear not of any frauds discovered, or of defaulters punished, or of grievances redressed." Such is the testimony of Lingard (chap. iv., 1386), all the more valuable for his aversion from the Wycliffite leanings of John of Gaunt. Chaucer's department in the London Customs was in those days one of the most important and lucrative in the kingdom; and if mercenary abuse of his post could have been proved, we may be sure that his and his patron's enemies would not have been content with simple dismissal, but would have heavily amerced or imprisoned him.

10. The salary was L36, 10s. per annum; the salary of the Chief Judges was L40, of the Puisne Judges about L27. Probably the Judges — certainly the Clerk of the Works — had fees or perquisites besides the stated payment.

11. Chaucer's patron had died earlier in 1399, during the exile of his son (then Duke of Hereford) in France. The Duchess Constance had died in 1394; and the Duke had made reparation to Katherine Swynford — who had already borne him four children — by marrying her in 1396, with the approval of Richard II., who legitimated the children, and made the eldest son of the poet's sister-in-law Earl of Somerset. From this long- illicit union sprang the house of Beaufort — that being the surname of the Duke's children by Katherine, after the name of the castle in Anjou (Belfort, or Beaufort) where they were born.

12. Of Chaucer's two sons by Philippa Roet, his only wife, the younger, Lewis, for whom he wrote the Treatise on the Astrolabe, died young. The elder, Thomas, married Maud, the second daughter and co-heiress of Sir John Burghersh, brother of the Bishop of Lincoln, the Chancellor and Treasurer of England. By this marriage Thomas Chaucer acquired great estates in Oxfordshire and elsewhere; and he figured prominently in the second rank of courtiers for many years. He was Chief Butler to Richard II.; under Henry IV. he was Constable of Wallingford Castle, Steward of the Honours of Wallingford and St Valery, and of the Chiltern Hundreds; and the queen of Henry IV. granted him the farm of several of her manors, a grant subsequently confirmed to him for life by the King, after the Queen's death. He sat in Parliament repeatedly for Oxfordshire, was Speaker in 1414, and in the same year went to France as commissioner to negotiate the marriage of Henry V. with the Princess Katherine. He held, before he died in 1434, various other posts of trust and distinction; but he left no heirs-male. His only child, Alice Chaucer, married twice; first Sir John Philip; and afterwards the Duke of Suffolk — attainted and beheaded in 1450. She had three children by the Duke; and her eldest son married the Princess Elizabeth, sister of Edward IV. The eldest son of this marriage, created Earl of Lincoln, was declared by Richard III heir-apparent to the throne, in case the Prince of Wales should die without issue; but the death of Lincoln himself, at the battle of Stoke in 1487, destroyed all prospect that the poet's descendants might succeed to the crown of England; and his family is now believed to be extinct.

13. "Geoffrey Chaucer, bard, and famous mother of poetry, is buried in this sacred ground."
14. Railings.
15 Translation of the epitaph: This tomb was built for Geoffrey Chaucer, who in his time was the greatest poet of the English. If you ask the year of his death, behold the words beneath, which tell you all. Death gave him rest from his toil, 25th of October 1400. N Brigham bore the cost of these words in the name of the Muses. 1556.
16. See the Prologue to Chaucer's Tale of Sir Thopas.
17. See the "Goodly Ballad of Chaucer," seventh stanza.
18. See the opening of the Prologue to "The Legend of Good Women," and the poet's account of his habits in "The House of Fame".

The Canterbury Tales

THE PROLOGUE.

WHEN that Aprilis, with his showers swoot, sweet
The drought of March hath pierced to the root,
And bathed every vein in such licour,
Of which virtue engender'd is the flower;
When Zephyrus eke with his swoote breath
Inspired hath in every holt and heath grove, forest
The tender croppes and the younge sun twigs, boughs
Hath in the Ram[1] his halfe course y-run,
And smalle fowles make melody,
That sleepen all the night with open eye,
(So pricketh them nature in their corages); hearts, inclinations
Then longe folk to go on pilgrimages,
And palmers[2] for to seeke strange strands,
To ferne hallows couth in sundry lands; distant saints known[3]
And specially, from every shire's end
Of Engleland, to Canterbury they wend,
The holy blissful Martyr for to seek,
That them hath holpen, when that they were sick. helped

Befell that, in that season on a day,
In Southwark at the Tabard[4] as I lay,
Ready to wenden on my pilgrimage
To Canterbury with devout corage,
At night was come into that hostelry
Well nine and twenty in a company
Of sundry folk, by aventure y-fall who had by chance fallen
In fellowship, and pilgrims were they all, into company.[5]
That toward Canterbury woulde ride.
The chamber, and the stables were wide,
And well we weren eased at the best. we were well provided
And shortly, when the sunne was to rest, with the best
So had I spoken with them every one,
That I was of their fellowship anon,
And made forword early for to rise, promise
To take our way there as I you devise. describe, relate

But natheless, while I have time and space,
Ere that I farther in this tale pace,
Me thinketh it accordant to reason,
To tell you alle the condition
Of each of them, so as it seemed me,
And which they weren, and of what degree;
And eke in what array that they were in:
And at a Knight then will I first begin.

A KNIGHT there was, and that a worthy man,
That from the time that he first began
To riden out, he loved chivalry,
Truth and honour, freedom and courtesy.
Full worthy was he in his Lorde's war,
And thereto had he ridden, no man farre, farther
As well in Christendom as in Heatheness,
And ever honour'd for his worthiness
At Alisandre[6] he was when it was won.
Full often time he had the board begun
Above alle nations in Prusse.[7]
In Lettowe had he reysed, and in Russe, journeyed
No Christian man so oft of his degree.
In Grenade at the siege eke had he be
Of Algesir, and ridden in Belmarie.[8]
At Leyes was he, and at Satalie,
When they were won; and in the Greate Sea
At many a noble army had he be.
At mortal battles had he been fifteen,
And foughten for our faith at Tramissene.
In listes thries, and aye slain his foe.
This ilke worthy knight had been also same[9]
Some time with the lord of Palatie,
Against another heathen in Turkie:
And evermore he had a sovereign price. He was held in very
And though that he was worthy he was wise, high esteem.
And of his port as meek as is a maid.
He never yet no villainy ne said
In all his life, unto no manner wight.
He was a very perfect gentle knight.
But for to telle you of his array,
His horse was good, but yet he was not gay.
Of fustian he weared a gipon, short doublet
Alle besmotter'd with his habergeon, soiled by his coat of mail.
For he was late y-come from his voyage,
And wente for to do his pilgrimage.

With him there was his son, a younge SQUIRE,
A lover, and a lusty bacheler,
With lockes crulle as they were laid in press. curled
Of twenty year of age he was I guess.
Of his stature he was of even length,
And wonderly deliver, and great of strength. wonderfully nimble
And he had been some time in chevachie, cavalry raids
In Flanders, in Artois, and Picardie,
And borne him well, as of so little space, in such a short time
In hope to standen in his lady's grace.

1

GEOFFREY CHAUCER

Embroider'd was he, as it were a mead
All full of freshe flowers, white and red.
Singing he was, or fluting all the day;
He was as fresh as is the month of May.
Short was his gown, with sleeves long and wide.
Well could he sit on horse, and faire ride.
He coulde songes make, and well indite,
Joust, and eke dance, and well pourtray and write.
So hot he loved, that by nightertale night-time
He slept no more than doth the nightingale.
Courteous he was, lowly, and serviceable,
And carv'd before his father at the table.[10]

A YEOMAN had he, and servants no mo'
At that time, for him list ride so it pleased him so to ride
And he was clad in coat and hood of green.
A sheaf of peacock arrows[11] bright and keen
Under his belt he bare full thriftily.
Well could he dress his tackle yeomanly:
His arrows drooped not with feathers low;
And in his hand he bare a mighty bow.
A nut-head[12] had he, with a brown visiage:
Of wood-craft coud he well all the usage: knew
Upon his arm he bare a gay bracer, small shield
And by his side a sword and a buckler,
And on that other side a gay daggere,
Harnessed well, and sharp as point of spear:
A Christopher on his breast of silver sheen.
An horn he bare, the baldric was of green:
A forester was he soothly as I guess. certainly

There was also a Nun, a PRIORESS,
That of her smiling was full simple and coy;
Her greatest oathe was but by Saint Loy;
And she was cleped Madame Eglentine. called
Full well she sang the service divine,
Entuned in her nose full seemly;
And French she spake full fair and fetisly properly
After the school of Stratford atte Bow,
For French of Paris was to her unknow.
At meate was she well y-taught withal;
She let no morsel from her lippes fall,
Nor wet her fingers in her sauce deep.
Well could she carry a morsel, and well keep,
That no droppe ne fell upon her breast.
In courtesy was set full much her lest. pleasure
Her over-lippe wiped she so clean,
That in her cup there was no farthing seen speck
Of grease, when she drunken had her draught;
Full seemely after her meat she raught: reached out her hand
And sickerly she was of great disport, surely she was of a lively
And full pleasant, and amiable of port, disposition
And pained her to counterfeite cheer took pains to assume
Of court, and be estately of mannere, a courtly disposition
And to be holden digne of reverence. worthy

But for to speaken of her conscience,
She was so charitable and so pitous, full of pity
She woulde weep if that she saw a mouse
Caught in a trap, if it were dead or bled.
Of smalle houndes had she, that she fed
With roasted flesh, and milk, and wastel bread. finest white bread
But sore she wept if one of them were dead,
Or if men smote it with a yarde smart: staff
And all was conscience and tender heart.
Full seemly her wimple y-pinched was;
Her nose tretis; her eyen gray as glass;[13] well-formed
Her mouth full small, and thereto soft and red;
But sickerly she had a fair forehead.
It was almost a spanne broad I trow;
For hardily she was not undergrow. certainly she was not small
Full fetis was her cloak, as I was ware. neat
Of small coral about her arm she bare
A pair of beades, gauded all with green;
And thereon hung a brooch of gold full sheen,
On which was first y-written a crown'd A,
And after, Amor vincit omnia. love conquers all
Another Nun also with her had she,
[That was her chapelleine, and PRIESTES three.]

A MONK there was, a fair for the mast'ry, above all others[14]
An out-rider, that loved venery; hunting
A manly man, to be an abbot able.
Full many a dainty horse had he in stable:
And when he rode, men might his bridle hear
Jingeling[15] in a whistling wind as clear,
And eke as loud, as doth the chapel bell,
There as this lord was keeper of the cell.
The rule of Saint Maur and of Saint Benet,[16]
Because that it was old and somedeal strait
This ilke monk let olde thinges pace, same
And held after the newe world the trace.
He gave not of the text a pulled hen, he cared nothing
That saith, that hunters be not holy men: for the text
Ne that a monk, when he is cloisterless;
Is like to a fish that is waterless;
This is to say, a monk out of his cloister.
This ilke text held he not worth an oyster;
And I say his opinion was good.
Why should he study, and make himselfe wood mad[17]
Upon a book in cloister always pore,
Or swinken with his handes, and labour, toil
As Austin bid? how shall the world be served?
Let Austin have his swink to him reserved.
Therefore he was a prickasour aright: hard rider
Greyhounds he had as swift as fowl of flight;
Of pricking and of hunting for the hare riding
Was all his lust, for no cost would he spare.

THE CANTERBURY TALES

pleasure
 I saw his sleeves purfil'd at the hand worked at the end with a
With gris, and that the finest of the land. fur called "gris"
And for to fasten his hood under his chin,
He had of gold y-wrought a curious pin;
A love-knot in the greater end there was.
His head was bald, and shone as any glass,
And eke his face, as it had been anoint;
He was a lord full fat and in good point;
His eyen steep, and rolling in his head, deep-set
That steamed as a furnace of a lead.
His bootes supple, his horse in great estate,
Now certainly he was a fair prelate;
He was not pale as a forpined ghost; wasted
A fat swan lov'd he best of any roast.
His palfrey was as brown as is a berry.

A FRIAR there was, a wanton and a merry,
A limitour[18], a full solemne man.
In all the orders four is none that can knows
So much of dalliance and fair language.
He had y-made full many a marriage
Of younge women, at his owen cost.
Unto his order he was a noble post;
Full well belov'd, and familiar was he
With franklins over all in his country, everywhere
And eke with worthy women of the town:
For he had power of confession,
As said himselfe, more than a curate,
For of his order he was licentiate.
Full sweetely heard he confession,
And pleasant was his absolution.
He was an easy man to give penance,
There as he wist to have a good pittance: where he know he would
For unto a poor order for to give get good payment
Is signe that a man is well y-shrive.
For if he gave, he durste make avant, dared to boast
He wiste that the man was repentant. knew
For many a man so hard is of his heart,
He may not weep although he sore smart.
Therefore instead of weeping and prayeres,
Men must give silver to the poore freres.
His tippet was aye farsed full of knives stuffed
And pinnes, for to give to faire wives;
And certainly he had a merry note:
Well could he sing and playen on a rote; from memory
Of yeddings he bare utterly the prize. songs
His neck was white as is the fleur-de-lis.
Thereto he strong was as a champion,
And knew well the taverns in every town.
And every hosteler and gay tapstere,
Better than a lazar or a beggere, leper
For unto such a worthy man as he

Accordeth not, as by his faculty,
To have with such lazars acquaintance.
It is not honest, it may not advance,
As for to deale with no such pouraille, offal, refuse
But all with rich, and sellers of vitaille. victuals
And ov'r all there as profit should arise, in every place where&
Courteous he was, and lowly of service;
There n'as no man nowhere so virtuous.
He was the beste beggar in all his house:
And gave a certain farme for the grant,[19]
None of his bretheren came in his haunt.
For though a widow hadde but one shoe,
So pleasant was his In Principio,[20]
Yet would he have a farthing ere he went;
His purchase was well better than his rent.
And rage he could and play as any whelp,
In lovedays[21]; there could he muchel help. greatly
For there was he not like a cloisterer,
With threadbare cope as is a poor scholer;
But he was like a master or a pope.
Of double worsted was his semicope, short cloak
That rounded was as a bell out of press.
Somewhat he lisped for his wantonness,
To make his English sweet upon his tongue;
And in his harping, when that he had sung,
His eyen twinkled in his head aright, eyes
As do the starres in a frosty night.
This worthy limitour[18] was call'd Huberd.

A MERCHANT was there with a forked beard,
In motley, and high on his horse he sat,
Upon his head a Flandrish beaver hat.
His bootes clasped fair and fetisly. neatly
His reasons aye spake he full solemnly,
Sounding alway th' increase of his winning.
He would the sea were kept[22] for any thing
Betwixte Middleburg and Orewell[23]
Well could he in exchange shieldes sell crown coins[24]
This worthy man full well his wit beset; employed
There wiste no wight that he was in debt, knew man
So estately was he of governance so well he managed
With his bargains, and with his chevisance. business contract
For sooth he was a worthy man withal,
But sooth to say, I n'ot how men him call. know not

A CLERK there was of Oxenford also, Oxford
That unto logic hadde long y-go. devoted himself
As leane was his horse as is a rake,
And he was not right fat, I undertake;
But looked hollow, and thereto soberly. thin; poorly
Full threadbare was his overest courtepy,

3

GEOFFREY CHAUCER

uppermost short cloak
For he had gotten him yet no benefice,
Ne was not worldly, to have an office.
For him was lever have at his bed's head rather
Twenty bookes, clothed in black or red,
Of Aristotle, and his philosophy,
Than robes rich, or fiddle, or psalt'ry.
But all be that he was a philosopher,
Yet hadde he but little gold in coffer,
But all that he might of his friendes hent, obtain
On bookes and on learning he it spent,
And busily gan for the soules pray
Of them that gave him[25] wherewith to scholay study
Of study took he moste care and heed.
Not one word spake he more than was need;
And that was said in form and reverence,
And short and quick, and full of high sentence.
Sounding in moral virtue was his speech,
And gladly would he learn, and gladly teach.

A SERGEANT OF THE LAW, wary and wise,
That often had y-been at the Parvis,[26]
There was also, full rich of excellence.
Discreet he was, and of great reverence:
He seemed such, his wordes were so wise,
Justice he was full often in assize,
By patent, and by plein commission; full
For his science, and for his high renown,
Of fees and robes had he many one.
So great a purchaser was nowhere none.
All was fee simple to him, in effect
His purchasing might not be in suspect suspicion
Nowhere so busy a man as he there was
And yet he seemed busier than he was
In termes had he case' and doomes all judgements
That from the time of King Will. were fall.
Thereto he could indite, and make a thing
There coulde no wight pinch at his writing. find fault with
And every statute coud he plain by rote knew
He rode but homely in a medley coat, multicoloured
Girt with a seint of silk, with barres small; sash
Of his array tell I no longer tale.

A FRANKELIN was in this company; Rich landowner
White was his beard, as is the daisy.
Of his complexion he was sanguine.
Well lov'd he in the morn a sop in wine.
To liven in delight was ever his won, wont
For he was Epicurus' owen son,
That held opinion, that plein delight full
Was verily felicity perfite.
An householder, and that a great, was he;
Saint Julian[27] he was in his country.
His bread, his ale, was alway after one; pressed on one
A better envined man was nowhere none; stored with wine
Withoute bake-meat never was his house,
Of fish and flesh, and that so plenteous,
It snowed in his house of meat and drink,
Of alle dainties that men coulde think.
After the sundry seasons of the year,
So changed he his meat and his soupere.
Full many a fat partridge had he in mew, cage[28]
And many a bream, and many a luce in stew[29] pike fish-pond
Woe was his cook, but if his sauce were unless
Poignant and sharp, and ready all his gear.
His table dormant in his hall alway fixed
Stood ready cover'd all the longe day.
At sessions there was he lord and sire.
Full often time he was knight of the shire Member of Parliament
An anlace, and a gipciere all of silk, dagger purse
Hung at his girdle, white as morning milk.
A sheriff had he been, and a countour[30]
Was nowhere such a worthy vavasour[31].

An HABERDASHER, and a CARPENTER,
A WEBBE, a DYER, and a TAPISER, weaver tapestry-maker
Were with us eke, cloth'd in one livery,
Of a solemn and great fraternity.
Full fresh and new their gear y-picked was. spruce
Their knives were y-chaped not with brass, mounted
But all with silver wrought full clean and well,
Their girdles and their pouches every deal. in every part
Well seemed each of them a fair burgess,
To sitten in a guild-hall, on the dais.[32]
Evereach, for the wisdom that he can, knew
Was shapely for to be an alderman. fitted
For chattels hadde they enough and rent,
And eke their wives would it well assent:
And elles certain they had been to blame.
It is full fair to be y-clep'd madame,
And for to go to vigils all before,
And have a mantle royally y-bore.[33]

A COOK they hadde with them for the nones, occasion
To boil the chickens and the marrow bones,
And powder merchant tart and galingale.
Well could he know a draught of London ale.
He could roast, and stew, and broil, and fry,
Make mortrewes, and well bake a pie.
But great harm was it, as it thoughte me,
That, on his shin a mormal hadde he. ulcer
For blanc manger, that made he with the best[34]

A SHIPMAN was there, wonned far by West: who dwelt far
For ought I wot, he was of Dartemouth. to the West
He rode upon a rouncy, as he couth, hack

THE CANTERBURY TALES

All in a gown of falding to the knee.   coarse cloth
A dagger hanging by a lace had he
About his neck under his arm adown;
The hot summer had made his hue all brown;
And certainly he was a good fellaw.
Full many a draught of wine he had y-draw
From Bourdeaux-ward, while that the chapmen sleep;
Of nice conscience took he no keep.
If that he fought, and had the higher hand,
By water he sent them home to every land.   he drowned his
But of his craft to reckon well his tides,   prisoners
His streames and his strandes him besides,
His herberow, his moon, and lodemanage,   harbourage
There was none such, from Hull unto Carthage   pilotage[35]
Hardy he was, and wise, I undertake:
With many a tempest had his beard been shake.
He knew well all the havens, as they were,
From Scotland to the Cape of Finisterre,
And every creek in Bretagne and in Spain:
His barge y-cleped was the Magdelain.

With us there was a DOCTOR OF PHYSIC;
In all this worlde was there none him like
To speak of physic, and of surgery:
For he was grounded in astronomy.
He kept his patient a full great deal
In houres by his magic natural.
Well could he fortune the ascendent make   fortunate
Of his images for his patient,.
He knew the cause of every malady,
Were it of cold, or hot, or moist, or dry,
And where engender'd, and of what humour.
He was a very perfect practisour
The cause y-know, and of his harm the root,   known
Anon he gave to the sick man his boot   remedy
Full ready had he his apothecaries,
To send his drugges and his lectuaries
For each of them made other for to win
Their friendship was not newe to begin
Well knew he the old Esculapius,
And Dioscorides, and eke Rufus;
Old Hippocras, Hali, and Gallien;
Serapion, Rasis, and Avicen;
Averrois, Damascene, and Constantin;
Bernard, and Gatisden, and Gilbertin.[36]
Of his diet measurable was he,
For it was of no superfluity,
But of great nourishing, and digestible.
His study was but little on the Bible.
In sanguine and in perse he clad was all   red blue
Lined with taffeta, and with sendall.   fine silk
And yet he was but easy of dispense: he spent very little
He kept that he won in the pestilence.   the money he made
For gold in physic is a cordial; during the plague
Therefore he loved gold in special.

A good WIFE was there OF beside BATH,
But she was somedeal deaf, and that was scath.   damage; pity
Of cloth-making she hadde such an haunt,   skill
She passed them of Ypres, and of Gaunt.[37]
In all the parish wife was there none,
That to the off'ring before her should gon,   the offering at mass
And if there did, certain so wroth was she,
That she was out of alle charity
Her coverchiefs were full fine of ground   head-dresses
I durste swear, they weighede ten pound[38]
That on the Sunday were upon her head.
Her hosen weren of fine scarlet red,
Full strait y-tied, and shoes full moist and new   fresh[39]
Bold was her face, and fair and red of hue.
She was a worthy woman all her live,
Husbands at the church door had she had five,
Withouten other company in youth;
But thereof needeth not to speak as nouth.   now
And thrice had she been at Jerusalem;
She hadde passed many a strange stream
At Rome she had been, and at Bologne,
In Galice at Saint James,[40] and at Cologne;
She coude much of wand'rng by the Way.   knew
Gat-toothed was she, soothly for to say.   Buck-toothed[41]
Upon an ambler easily she sat,
Y-wimpled well, and on her head an hat
As broad as is a buckler or a targe.
A foot-mantle about her hippes large,
And on her feet a pair of spurres sharp.
In fellowship well could she laugh and carp   jest, talk
Of remedies of love she knew perchance
For of that art she coud the olde dance.   knew

A good man there was of religion,
That was a poore PARSON of a town:
But rich he was of holy thought and werk.   work
He was also a learned man, a clerk,
That Christe's gospel truly woulde preach.
His parishens devoutly would he teach.   parishioners
Benign he was, and wonder diligent,
And in adversity full patient:
And such he was y-proved often sithes.   oftentimes
Full loth were him to curse for his tithes,
But rather would he given out of doubt,
Unto his poore parishens about,
Of his off'ring, and eke of his substance.
He could in little thing have suffisance.   he was

GEOFFREY CHAUCER

satisfied with
Wide was his parish, and houses far asunder, very little
But he ne left not, for no rain nor thunder,
In sickness and in mischief to visit
The farthest in his parish, much and lit, great and small
Upon his feet, and in his hand a staff.
This noble ensample to his sheep he gaf, gave
That first he wrought, and afterward he taught.
Out of the gospel he the wordes caught,
And this figure he added yet thereto,
That if gold ruste, what should iron do?
For if a priest be foul, on whom we trust,
No wonder is a lewed man to rust: unlearned
And shame it is, if that a priest take keep,
To see a shitten shepherd and clean sheep:
Well ought a priest ensample for to give,
By his own cleanness, how his sheep should live.
He sette not his benefice to hire,
And left his sheep eucumber'd in the mire,
And ran unto London, unto Saint Paul's,
To seeke him a chantery⁴² for souls,
Or with a brotherhood to be withold: detained
But dwelt at home, and kepte well his fold,
So that the wolf ne made it not miscarry.
He was a shepherd, and no mercenary.
And though he holy were, and virtuous,
He was to sinful men not dispitous severe
Nor of his speeche dangerous nor dign disdainful
But in his teaching discreet and benign.
To drawen folk to heaven, with fairness,
By good ensample, was his business:
But it were any person obstinate, but if it were
What so he were of high or low estate,
Him would he snibbe sharply for the nones. reprove nonce,occasion
A better priest I trow that nowhere none is.
He waited after no pomp nor reverence,
Nor maked him a spiced conscience, artificial conscience
But Christe's lore, and his apostles' twelve,
He taught, and first he follow'd it himself.

With him there was a PLOUGHMAN, was his brother,
That had y-laid of dung full many a fother. ton
A true swinker and a good was he, hard worker
Living in peace and perfect charity.
God loved he beste with all his heart
At alle times, were it gain or smart, pain, loss
And then his neighebour right as himself.
He woulde thresh, and thereto dike, and delve, dig ditches
For Christe's sake, for every poore wight,
Withouten hire, if it lay in his might.
His tithes payed he full fair and well,
Both of his proper swink, and his chattel his own labour goods
In a tabard he rode upon a mare. sleeveless jerkin

There was also a Reeve, and a Millere,
A Sompnour, and a Pardoner also,
A Manciple, and myself, there were no mo'.

The MILLER was a stout carle for the nones,
Full big he was of brawn, and eke of bones;
That proved well, for ov'r all where he came, wheresoever
At wrestling he would bear away the ram.⁴³
He was short-shoulder'd, broad, a thicke gnarr, stump of wood
There was no door, that he n'old heave off bar, could not
Or break it at a running with his head.
His beard as any sow or fox was red,
And thereto broad, as though it were a spade.
Upon the cop right of his nose he had head⁴⁴
A wart, and thereon stood a tuft of hairs
Red as the bristles of a sowe's ears.
His nose-thirles blacke were and wide. nostrils⁴⁵
A sword and buckler bare he by his side.
His mouth as wide was as a furnace.
He was a jangler, and a goliardais, buffoon⁴⁶
And that was most of sin and harlotries.
Well could he steale corn, and tolle thrice
And yet he had a thumb of gold, pardie.⁴⁷
A white coat and a blue hood weared he
A baggepipe well could he blow and soun',
And therewithal he brought us out of town.

A gentle MANCIPLE⁴⁸ was there of a temple,
Of which achatours mighte take ensample buyers
For to be wise in buying of vitaille. victuals
For whether that he paid, or took by taile, on credit
Algate he waited so in his achate, always purchase
That he was aye before in good estate.
Now is not that of God a full fair grace
That such a lewed mannes wit shall pace unlearned surpass
The wisdom of an heap of learned men?
Of masters had he more than thries ten,
That were of law expert and curious:
Of which there was a dozen in that house,
Worthy to be stewards of rent and land
Of any lord that is in Engleland,
To make him live by his proper good,
In honour debtless, but if he were wood, unless he were mad
Or live as scarcely as him list desire;
And able for to helpen all a shire
In any case that mighte fall or hap;
And yet this Manciple set their aller cap outwitted them all

The REEVE⁴⁹ was a slender choleric man
His beard was shav'd as nigh as ever he can.
His hair was by his eares round y-shorn;

His top was docked like a priest beforn
Full longe were his legges, and full lean
Y-like a staff, there was no calf y-seen
Well could he keep a garner and a bin storeplaces for grain
There was no auditor could on him win
Well wist he by the drought, and by the rain,
The yielding of his seed and of his grain
His lorde's sheep, his neat, and his dairy cattle
His swine, his horse, his store, and his poultry,
Were wholly in this Reeve's governing,
And by his cov'nant gave he reckoning,
Since that his lord was twenty year of age;
There could no man bring him in arrearage
There was no bailiff, herd, nor other hine servant
That he ne knew his sleight and his covine tricks and cheating
They were adrad of him, as of the death in dread
His wonning was full fair upon an heath abode
With greene trees y-shadow'd was his place.
He coulde better than his lord purchase
Full rich he was y-stored privily
His lord well could he please subtilly,
To give and lend him of his owen good,
And have a thank, and yet a coat and hood. also
In youth he learned had a good mistere trade
He was a well good wright, a carpentere
This Reeve sate upon a right good stot, steed
That was all pomely gray, and highte Scot. dappled called
A long surcoat of perse upon he had, sky-blue
And by his side he bare a rusty blade.
Of Norfolk was this Reeve, of which I tell,
Beside a town men clepen Baldeswell, call
Tucked he was, as is a friar, about,
And ever rode the hinderest of the rout. hindmost of the group

A SOMPNOUR was there with us in that place, summoner[50]
That had a fire-red cherubinnes face,
For sausefleme he was, with eyen narrow. red or pimply
As hot he was and lecherous as a sparrow,
With scalled browes black, and pilled beard: scanty
Of his visage children were sore afeard.
There n'as quicksilver, litharge, nor brimstone,
Boras, ceruse, nor oil of tartar none,
Nor ointement that woulde cleanse or bite,
That him might helpen of his whelkes white, pustules
Nor of the knobbes sitting on his cheeks. buttons
Well lov'd he garlic, onions, and leeks,
And for to drink strong wine as red as blood.
Then would he speak, and cry as he were wood;
And when that he well drunken had the wine,
Then would he speake no word but Latin.
A fewe termes knew he, two or three,
That he had learned out of some decree;
No wonder is, he heard it all the day.
And eke ye knowen well, how that a jay
Can clepen "Wat," as well as can the Pope. call
But whoso would in other thing him grope, search
Then had he spent all his philosophy,
Aye, Questio quid juris,[51] would he cry.

He was a gentle harlot and a kind; a low fellow[52]
A better fellow should a man not find.
He woulde suffer, for a quart of wine,
A good fellow to have his concubine
A twelvemonth, and excuse him at the full.
Full privily a finch eke could he pull. "fleece" a man
And if he found owhere a good fellaw, anywhere
He woulde teache him to have none awe
In such a case of the archdeacon's curse;
But if a manne's soul were in his purse; unless
For in his purse he should y-punished be.
"Purse is the archedeacon's hell," said he.
But well I wot, he lied right indeed:
Of cursing ought each guilty man to dread,
For curse will slay right as assoiling saveth; absolving
And also 'ware him of a significavit[53].
In danger had he at his owen guise
The younge girles of the diocese,[54]
And knew their counsel, and was of their rede. counsel
A garland had he set upon his head,
As great as it were for an alestake: The post of an alehouse sign
A buckler had he made him of a cake.

With him there rode a gentle PARDONERE[55]
Of Ronceval, his friend and his compere,
That straight was comen from the court of Rome.
Full loud he sang, "Come hither, love, to me"
This Sompnour bare to him a stiff burdoun, sang the bass
Was never trump of half so great a soun'.
This Pardoner had hair as yellow as wax,
But smooth it hung, as doth a strike of flax: strip
By ounces hung his lockes that he had,
And therewith he his shoulders oversprad.
Full thin it lay, by culpons one and one, locks, shreds
But hood for jollity, he weared none,
For it was trussed up in his wallet.
Him thought he rode all of the newe get, latest fashion[56]
Dishevel, save his cap, he rode all bare.
Such glaring eyen had he, as an hare.
A vernicle had he sew'd upon his cap. image of Christ[57]
His wallet lay before him in his lap,
Bretful of pardon come from Rome all hot. brimful

GEOFFREY CHAUCER

A voice he had as small as hath a goat.
No beard had he, nor ever one should have.
As smooth it was as it were new y-shave;
I trow he were a gelding or a mare.
But of his craft, from Berwick unto Ware,
Ne was there such another pardonere.
For in his mail he had a pillowbere, bag[58] pillowcase
Which, as he saide, was our Lady's veil:
He said, he had a gobbet of the sail piece
That Sainte Peter had, when that he went
Upon the sea, till Jesus Christ him hent. took hold of
He had a cross of latoun full of stones, copper
And in a glass he hadde pigge's bones.
But with these relics, whenne that he fond
A poore parson dwelling upon lond,
Upon a day he got him more money
Than that the parson got in moneths tway;
And thus with feigned flattering and japes, jests
He made the parson and the people his apes.
But truely to tellen at the last,
He was in church a noble ecclesiast.
Well could he read a lesson or a story,
But alderbest he sang an offertory: best of all
For well he wiste, when that song was sung,
He muste preach, and well afile his tongue, polish
To winne silver, as he right well could:
Therefore he sang full merrily and loud.

Now have I told you shortly in a clause
Th' estate, th' array, the number, and eke the cause
Why that assembled was this company
In Southwark at this gentle hostelry,
That highte the Tabard, fast by the Bell.[59]
But now is time to you for to tell
How that we baren us that ilke night, what we did that same night
When we were in that hostelry alight.
And after will I tell of our voyage,
And all the remnant of our pilgrimage.
But first I pray you of your courtesy,
That ye arette it not my villainy, count it not rudeness in me
Though that I plainly speak in this mattere.
To tellen you their wordes and their cheer;
Not though I speak their wordes properly.
For this ye knowen all so well as I,
Whoso shall tell a tale after a man,
He must rehearse, as nigh as ever he can,
Every word, if it be in his charge,
All speak he ne'er so rudely and so large; let him speak
Or elles he must tell his tale untrue,
Or feigne things, or finde wordes new.
He may not spare, although he were his brother;
He must as well say one word as another.
Christ spake Himself full broad in Holy Writ,
And well ye wot no villainy is it.
Eke Plato saith, whoso that can him read,
The wordes must be cousin to the deed.
Also I pray you to forgive it me,
All have I not set folk in their degree, although I have
Here in this tale, as that they shoulden stand:
My wit is short, ye may well understand.

Great cheere made our Host us every one,
And to the supper set he us anon:
And served us with victual of the best.
Strong was the wine, and well to drink us lest. pleased
A seemly man Our Hoste was withal
For to have been a marshal in an hall.
A large man he was with eyen steep, deep-set.
A fairer burgess is there none in Cheap[60]:
Bold of his speech, and wise and well y-taught,
And of manhoode lacked him right naught.
Eke thereto was he right a merry man,
And after supper playen he began,
And spake of mirth amonges other things,
When that we hadde made our reckonings;
And saide thus; "Now, lordinges, truly
Ye be to me welcome right heartily:
For by my troth, if that I shall not lie,
I saw not this year such a company
At once in this herberow, am is now. inn[61]
Fain would I do you mirth, an I wist how. if I knew
And of a mirth I am right now bethought.
To do you ease, and it shall coste nought. pleasure
Ye go to Canterbury; God you speed,
The blissful Martyr quite you your meed; grant you what
And well I wot, as ye go by the way, you deserve
Ye shapen you to talken and to play: intend to
For truely comfort nor mirth is none
To ride by the way as dumb as stone:
And therefore would I make you disport,
As I said erst, and do you some comfort.
And if you liketh all by one assent
Now for to standen at my judgement,
And for to worken as I shall you say
To-morrow, when ye riden on the way,
Now by my father's soule that is dead,
But ye be merry, smiteth off mine head. unless you are merry,
Hold up your hands withoute more speech. smite off my head

Our counsel was not longe for to seech: seek
Us thought it was not worth to make it wise, discuss it at length
And granted him withoute more avise, consideration
And bade him say his verdict, as him lest.
Lordings (quoth he), now hearken for the best;

THE CANTERBURY TALES

But take it not, I pray you, in disdain;
This is the point, to speak it plat and plain. flat
That each of you, to shorten with your way
In this voyage, shall tellen tales tway,
To Canterbury-ward, I mean it so,
And homeward he shall tellen other two,
Of aventures that whilom have befall.
And which of you that bear'th him best of all,
That is to say, that telleth in this case
Tales of best sentence and most solace,
Shall have a supper at your aller cost at the cost of you all
Here in this place, sitting by this post,
When that ye come again from Canterbury.
And for to make you the more merry,
I will myselfe gladly with you ride,
Right at mine owen cost, and be your guide.
And whoso will my judgement withsay,
Shall pay for all we spenden by the way.
And if ye vouchesafe that it be so,
Tell me anon withoute wordes mo', more
And I will early shape me therefore."

This thing was granted, and our oath we swore
With full glad heart, and prayed him also,
That he would vouchesafe for to do so,
And that he woulde be our governour,
And of our tales judge and reportour,
And set a supper at a certain price;
And we will ruled be at his device,
In high and low: and thus by one assent,
We be accorded to his judgement.
And thereupon the wine was fet anon. fetched.
We drunken, and to reste went each one,
Withouten any longer tarrying
A-morrow, when the day began to spring,
Up rose our host, and was our aller cock, the cock to wake us all

And gather'd us together in a flock,
And forth we ridden all a little space,
Unto the watering of Saint Thomas[62]:
And there our host began his horse arrest,
And saide; "Lordes, hearken if you lest.
Ye weet your forword, and I it record. know your promise
If even-song and morning-song accord,
Let see now who shall telle the first tale.
As ever may I drinke wine or ale,
Whoso is rebel to my judgement,
Shall pay for all that by the way is spent.
Now draw ye cuts, ere that ye farther twin. lots go
He which that hath the shortest shall begin."

"Sir Knight (quoth he), my master and my lord,
Now draw the cut, for that is mine accord.
Come near (quoth he), my Lady Prioress,
And ye, Sir Clerk, let be your shamefastness,
Nor study not: lay hand to, every man."
Anon to drawen every wight began,
And shortly for to tellen as it was,
Were it by a venture, or sort, or cas, lot chance
The sooth is this, the cut fell to the Knight,
Of which full blithe and glad was every wight;
And tell he must his tale as was reason,
By forword, and by composition,
As ye have heard; what needeth wordes mo'?
And when this good man saw that it was so,
As he that wise was and obedient
To keep his forword by his free assent,
He said; "Sithen I shall begin this game, since
Why, welcome be the cut in Godde's name.
Now let us ride, and hearken what I say."
And with that word we ridden forth our way;
And he began with right a merry cheer
His tale anon, and said as ye shall hear.

Notes to the Prologue

1. Tyrwhitt points out that "the Bull" should be read here, not "the Ram," which would place the time of the pilgrimage in the end of March; whereas, in the Prologue to the Man of Law's Tale, the date is given as the "eight and twenty day of April, that is messenger to May."
2. Dante, in the "Vita Nuova," distinguishes three classes of pilgrims: palmieri - palmers who go beyond sea to the East, and often bring back staves of palm-wood; peregrini, who go the shrine of St Jago in Galicia; Romei, who go to Rome. Sir Walter Scott, however, says that palmers were in the habit of passing from shrine to shrine, living on charity — pilgrims on the other hand, made the journey to any shrine only once, immediately returning to their ordinary avocations. Chaucer uses "palmer" of all pilgrims.
3. "Hallows" survives, in the meaning here given, in All Hallows — All-Saints — day. "Couth," past participle of "conne" to know, exists in "uncouth."
4. The Tabard — the sign of the inn — was a sleeveless coat, worn by heralds. The name of the inn was, some three centuries after Chaucer, changed to the Talbot.
5. In y-fall," "y" is a corruption of the Anglo-Saxon "ge" prefixed to participles of verbs. It is used by Chaucer merely to help the metre In German, "y-fall," or y-falle," would be "gefallen", "y-run," or "y-ronne", would be "geronnen."

GEOFFREY CHAUCER

6. Alisandre: Alexandria, in Egypt, captured by Pierre de Lusignan, king of Cyprus, in 1365 but abandoned immediately afterwards. Thirteen years before, the same Prince had taken Satalie, the ancient Attalia, in Anatolia, and in 1367 he won Layas, in Armenia, both places named just below.
7. The knight had been placed at the head of the table, above knights of all nations, in Prussia, whither warriors from all countries were wont to repair, to aid the Teutonic Order in their continual conflicts with their heathen neighbours in "Lettowe" or Lithuania (German. "Litthauen"), Russia, &c.
8. Algesiras was taken from the Moorish king of Grenada, in 1344: the Earls of Derby and Salisbury took part in the siege. Belmarie is supposed to have been a Moorish state in Africa; but "Palmyrie" has been suggested as the correct reading. The Great Sea, or the Greek sea, is the Eastern Mediterranean. Tramissene, or Tremessen, is enumerated by Froissart among the Moorish kingdoms in Africa. Palatie, or Palathia, in Anatolia, was a fief held by the Christian knights after the Turkish conquests — the holders paying tribute to the infidel. Our knight had fought with one of those lords against a heathen neighbour.
9. Ilke: same; compare the Scottish phrase "of that ilk," — that is, of the estate which bears the same name as its owner's title.
10. It was the custom for squires of the highest degree to carve at their fathers' tables.
11. Peacock Arrows: Large arrows, with peacocks' feathers.
12. A nut-head: With nut-brown hair; or, round like a nut, the hair being cut short.
13. Grey eyes appear to have been a mark of female beauty in Chaucer's time.
14. "for the mastery" was applied to medicines in the sense of "sovereign" as we now apply it to a remedy.
15. It was fashionable to hang bells on horses' bridles.
16. St. Benedict was the first founder of a spiritual order in the Roman church. Maurus, abbot of Fulda from 822 to 842, did much to re-establish the discipline of the Benedictines on a true Christian basis.
17. Wood: Mad, Scottish "wud". Felix says to Paul, "Too much learning hath made thee mad".
18. Limitour: A friar with licence or privilege to beg, or exercise other functions, within a certain district: as, "the limitour of Holderness".
19. Farme: rent; that is, he paid a premium for his licence to beg.
20. In principio: the first words of Genesis and John, employed in some part of the mass.
21. Lovedays: meetings appointed for friendly settlement of differences; the business was often followed by sports and feasting.
22. He would the sea were kept for any thing: he would for anything that the sea were guarded. "The old subsidy of tonnage and poundage," says Tyrwhitt, "was given to the king 'pour la saufgarde et custodie del mer.' — for the safeguard and keeping of the sea" (12 E. IV. C.3).
23. Middleburg, at the mouth of the Scheldt, in Holland; Orwell, a seaport in Essex.
24. Shields: Crowns, so called from the shields stamped on them; French, "ecu;" Italian, "scudo."
25. Poor scholars at the universities used then to go about begging for money to maintain them and their studies.
26. Parvis: The portico of St. Paul's, which lawyers frequented to meet their clients.
27. St Julian: The patron saint of hospitality, celebrated for supplying his votaries with good lodging and good cheer.
28. Mew: cage. The place behind Whitehall, where the king's hawks were caged was called the Mews.
29. Many a luce in stew: many a pike in his fish-pond; in those Catholic days, when much fish was eaten, no gentleman's mansion was complete without a "stew".
30. Countour: Probably a steward or accountant in the county court.
31. Vavasour: A landholder of consequence; holding of a duke, marquis, or earl, and ranking below a baron.
32. On the dais: On the raised platform at the end of the hall, where sat at meat or in judgement those high in authority, rank or honour; in our days the worthy craftsmen might have been described as "good platform men".
33. To take precedence over all in going to the evening service of the Church, or to festival meetings, to which it was the fashion to carry rich cloaks or mantles against the home-coming.
34. The things the cook could make: "marchand tart", some now unknown ingredient used in cookery; "galingale," sweet or long rooted cyprus; "mortrewes", a rich soup made by stamping flesh in a mortar; "Blanc manger", not what is now called blancmange; one part of it was the brawn of a capon.
35. Lodemanage: pilotage, from Anglo-Saxon "ladman," a leader, guide, or pilot; hence "lodestar," "lodestone."
36. The authors mentioned here were the chief medical text-books of the middle ages. The names of Galen and Hippocrates were then usually spelt "Gallien" and "Hypocras" or "Ypocras".

37. The west of England, especially around Bath, was the seat of the cloth-manufacture, as were Ypres and Ghent (Gaunt) in Flanders.
38. Chaucer here satirises the fashion of the time, which piled bulky and heavy waddings on ladies' heads.
39. Moist; here used in the sense of "new", as in Latin, "mustum" signifies new wine; and elsewhere Chaucer speaks of "moisty ale", as opposed to "old".
40. In Galice at Saint James: at the shrine of St Jago of Compostella in Spain.
41. Gat-toothed: Buck-toothed; goat-toothed, to signify her wantonness; or gap-toothed — with gaps between her teeth.
42. An endowment to sing masses for the soul of the donor.
43. A ram was the usual prize at wrestling matches.
44. Cop: Head; German, "Kopf".
45. Nose-thirles: nostrils; from the Anglo-Saxon, "thirlian," to pierce; hence the word "drill," to bore.
46. Goliardais: a babbler and a buffoon; Golias was the founder of a jovial sect called by his name.
47. The proverb says that every honest miller has a thumb of gold; probably Chaucer means that this one was as honest as his brethren.
48. A Maniciple — Latin, "manceps," a purchaser or contractor - - was an officer charged with the purchase of victuals for inns of court or colleges.
49. Reeve: A land-steward; still called "grieve" — Anglo-Saxon, "gerefa" in some parts of Scotland.
50. Sompnour: summoner; an apparitor, who cited delinquents to appear in ecclesiastical courts.
51. Questio quid juris: "I ask which law (applies)"; a cant law- Latin phrase.
52 Harlot: a low, ribald fellow; the word was used of both sexes; it comes from the Anglo-Saxon verb to hire.
53. Significavit: an ecclesiastical writ.
54. Within his jurisdiction he had at his own pleasure the young people (of both sexes) in the diocese.
55. Pardoner: a seller of pardons or indulgences.
56. Newe get: new gait, or fashion; "gait" is still used in this sense in some parts of the country.
57. Vernicle: an image of Christ; so called from St Veronica, who gave the Saviour a napkin to wipe the sweat from His face as He bore the Cross, and received it back with an impression of His countenance upon it.
58. Mail: packet, baggage; French, "malle," a trunk.
59. The Bell: apparently another Southwark tavern; Stowe mentions a "Bull" as being near the Tabard.
60. Cheap: Cheapside, then inhabited by the richest and most prosperous citizens of London.
61. Herberow: Lodging, inn; French, "Herberge."
62. The watering of Saint Thomas: At the second milestone on the old Canterbury road.

GEOFFREY CHAUCER

THE KNIGHT'S TALE.[1]

WHILOM, as olde stories tellen us, *formerly*
There was a duke that highte Theseus. *was called*[2]
Of Athens he was lord and governor,
And in his time such a conqueror
That greater was there none under the sun.
Full many a riche country had he won.
What with his wisdom and his chivalry,
He conquer'd all the regne of Feminie,[3]
That whilom was y-cleped Scythia;
And weddede the Queen Hippolyta
And brought her home with him to his country
With muchel glory and great solemnity, *great*
And eke her younge sister Emily,
And thus with vict'ry and with melody
Let I this worthy Duke to Athens ride,
And all his host, in armes him beside.

And certes, if it n'ere too long to hear, *were not*
I would have told you fully the mannere,
How wonnen was the regne of Feminie,[4] *won*
By Theseus, and by his chivalry;
And of the greate battle for the nonce
Betwixt Athenes and the Amazons;
And how assieged was Hippolyta,
The faire hardy queen of Scythia;
And of the feast that was at her wedding
And of the tempest at her homecoming.
But all these things I must as now forbear.
I have, God wot, a large field to ear *plough*[5];
And weake be the oxen in my plough;
The remnant of my tale is long enow.
I will not letten eke none of this rout. *hinder any of*
Let every fellow tell his tale about, *this company*
And let see now who shall the supper win.
There as I left, I will again begin. *where I left off*

This Duke, of whom I make mentioun,
When he was come almost unto the town,
In all his weal, and in his moste pride,
He was ware, as he cast his eye aside,
Where that there kneeled in the highe way
A company of ladies, tway and tway,
Each after other, clad in clothes black:
But such a cry and such a woe they make,
That in this world n'is creature living,
That hearde such another waimenting *lamenting*[6]
And of this crying would they never stenten, *desist*
Till they the reines of his bridle henten. *seize*
"What folk be ye that at mine homecoming
Perturben so my feaste with crying?"
Quoth Theseus; "Have ye so great envy
Of mine honour, that thus complain and cry?

Or who hath you misboden, or offended? *wronged*
Do telle me, if it may be amended;
And why that ye be clad thus all in black?"

The oldest lady of them all then spake,
When she had swooned, with a deadly cheer, *countenance*
That it was ruthe for to see or hear. *pity*
She saide; "Lord, to whom fortune hath given
Vict'ry, and as a conqueror to liven,
Nought grieveth us your glory and your honour;
But we beseechen mercy and succour.
Have mercy on our woe and our distress;
Some drop of pity, through thy gentleness,
Upon us wretched women let now fall.
For certes, lord, there is none of us all
That hath not been a duchess or a queen;
Now be we caitives, as it is well seen: *captives*
Thanked be Fortune, and her false wheel,
That none estate ensureth to be wele. *assures no continuance of*
And certes, lord, t'abiden your presence *prosperous estate*
Here in this temple of the goddess Clemence
We have been waiting all this fortenight:
Now help us, lord, since it lies in thy might.

"I, wretched wight, that weep and waile thus,
Was whilom wife to king Capaneus,
That starf at Thebes, cursed be that day: *died*[7]
And alle we that be in this array,
And maken all this lamentatioun,
We losten all our husbands at that town,
While that the siege thereabouten lay.
And yet the olde Creon, wellaway!
That lord is now of Thebes the city,
Fulfilled of ire and of iniquity,
He for despite, and for his tyranny,
To do the deade bodies villainy, *insult*
Of all our lorde's, which that been y-slaw, *slain*
Hath all the bodies on an heap y-draw,
And will not suffer them by none assent
Neither to be y-buried, nor y-brent, *burnt*
But maketh houndes eat them in despite."
And with that word, withoute more respite
They fallen groff, and cryden piteously; *grovelling*
"Have on us wretched women some mercy,
And let our sorrow sinken in thine heart."

This gentle Duke down from his courser start
With hearte piteous, when he heard them speak.
Him thoughte that his heart would all to-break,
When he saw them so piteous and so mate *abased*

12

That whilom weren of so great estate.
And in his armes he them all up hent,   raised, took
And them comforted in full good intent,
And swore his oath, as he was true knight,
He woulde do so farforthly his might   as far as his power went
Upon the tyrant Creon them to wreak,   avenge
That all the people of Greece shoulde speak,
How Creon was of Theseus y-served,
As he that had his death full well deserved.
And right anon withoute more abode   delay
His banner he display'd, and forth he rode
To Thebes-ward, and all his, host beside:
No ner Athenes would he go nor ride,   nearer
Nor take his ease fully half a day,
But onward on his way that night he lay:
And sent anon Hippolyta the queen,
And Emily her younge sister sheen   bright, lovely
Unto the town of Athens for to dwell:
And forth he rit; there is no more to tell.   rode

The red statue of Mars with spear and targe   shield
So shineth in his white banner large
That all the fieldes glitter up and down:
And by his banner borne is his pennon
Of gold full rich, in which there was y-beat   stamped
The Minotaur[8] which that he slew in Crete
Thus rit this Duke, thus rit this conqueror
And in his host of chivalry the flower,
Till that he came to Thebes, and alight
Fair in a field, there as he thought to fight.
But shortly for to speaken of this thing,
With Creon, which that was of Thebes king,
He fought, and slew him manly as a knight
In plain bataille, and put his folk to flight:
And by assault he won the city after,
And rent adown both wall, and spar, and rafter;
And to the ladies he restored again
The bodies of their husbands that were slain,
To do obsequies, as was then the guise.   custom

But it were all too long for to devise   describe
The greate clamour, and the waimenting,   lamenting
Which that the ladies made at the brenning   burning
Of the bodies, and the great honour
That Theseus the noble conqueror
Did to the ladies, when they from him went:
But shortly for to tell is mine intent.
When that this worthy Duke, this Theseus,
Had Creon slain, and wonnen Thebes thus,
Still in the field he took all night his rest,
And did with all the country as him lest.   pleased
To ransack in the tas of bodies dead,   heap
Them for to strip of harness and of weed,   armour clothes
The pillers did their business and cure,   pillagers[9]
After the battle and discomfiture.

And so befell, that in the tas they found,
Through girt with many a grievous bloody wound,
Two younge knightes ligging by and by   lying side by side
Both in one armes, wrought full richely: the same armour
Of whiche two, Arcita hight that one,
And he that other highte Palamon.
Not fully quick, nor fully dead they were,   alive
But by their coat-armour, and by their gear,
The heralds knew them well in special,
As those that weren of the blood royal
Of Thebes, and of sistren two y-born.   born of two sisters
Out of the tas the pillers have them torn,
And have them carried soft unto the tent
Of Theseus, and he full soon them sent
To Athens, for to dwellen in prison
Perpetually, he n'olde no ranson.   would take no ransom
And when this worthy Duke had thus y-done,
He took his host, and home he rit anon
With laurel crowned as a conquerour;
And there he lived in joy and in honour
Term of his life; what needeth wordes mo'?
And in a tower, in anguish and in woe,
Dwellen this Palamon, and eke Arcite,
For evermore, there may no gold them quite   set free

Thus passed year by year, and day by day,
Till it fell ones in a morn of May
That Emily, that fairer was to seen
Than is the lily upon his stalke green,
And fresher than the May with flowers new
(For with the rose colour strove her hue;
I n'ot which was the finer of them two),   know not
Ere it was day, as she was wont to do,
She was arisen, and all ready dight,   dressed
For May will have no sluggardy a-night;
The season pricketh every gentle heart,
And maketh him out of his sleep to start,
And saith, "Arise, and do thine observance."

This maketh Emily have remembrance
To do honour to May, and for to rise.
Y-clothed was she fresh for to devise;
Her yellow hair was braided in a tress,
Behind her back, a yarde long I guess.
And in the garden at the sun uprist   sunrise
She walketh up and down where as her list.
She gathereth flowers, party white and red,   mingled
To make a sotel garland for her head,   subtle, well-arranged
And as an angel heavenly she sung.
The greate tower, that was so thick and strong,
Which of the castle was the chief dungeon[10]

GEOFFREY CHAUCER

(Where as these knightes weren in prison,
Of which I tolde you, and telle shall),
Was even joinant to the garden wall, adjoining
There as this Emily had her playing.

Bright was the sun, and clear that morrowning,
And Palamon, this woful prisoner,
As was his wont, by leave of his gaoler,
Was ris'n, and roamed in a chamber on high,
In which he all the noble city sigh, saw
And eke the garden, full of branches green,
There as this fresh Emelia the sheen
Was in her walk, and roamed up and down.
This sorrowful prisoner, this Palamon
Went in his chamber roaming to and fro,
And to himself complaining of his woe:
That he was born, full oft he said, Alas!
And so befell, by aventure or cas, chance
That through a window thick of many a bar
Of iron great, and square as any spar,
He cast his eyes upon Emelia,
And therewithal he blent and cried, Ah! started aside
As though he stungen were unto the heart.
And with that cry Arcite anon up start,
And saide, "Cousin mine, what aileth thee,
That art so pale and deadly for to see?
Why cried'st thou? who hath thee done offence?
For Godde's love, take all in patience
Our prison, for it may none other be. imprisonment
Fortune hath giv'n us this adversity'.
Some wick' aspect or disposition wicked
Of Saturn[11], by some constellation,
Hath giv'n us this, although we had it sworn,
So stood the heaven when that we were born,
We must endure; this is the short and plain.

This Palamon answer'd, and said again:
"Cousin, forsooth of this opinion
Thou hast a vain imagination.
This prison caused me not for to cry;
But I was hurt right now thorough mine eye
Into mine heart; that will my bane be. destruction
The fairness of the lady that I see
Yond in the garden roaming to and fro,
Is cause of all my crying and my woe.
I n'ot wher she be woman or goddess, know not whether
But Venus is it, soothly as I guess, truly
And therewithal on knees adown he fill,
And saide: "Venus, if it be your will
You in this garden thus to transfigure
Before me sorrowful wretched creature,
Out of this prison help that we may scape.
And if so be our destiny be shape
By etern word to dien in prison,
Of our lineage have some compassion,
That is so low y-brought by tyranny."

And with that word Arcita gan espy began to look forth
Where as this lady roamed to and fro
And with that sight her beauty hurt him so,
That if that Palamon was wounded sore,
Arcite is hurt as much as he, or more.
And with a sigh he saide piteously:
"The freshe beauty slay'th me suddenly
Of her that roameth yonder in the place.
And but I have her mercy and her grace, unless
That I may see her at the leaste way,
I am but dead; there is no more to say."
This Palamon, when he these wordes heard,
Dispiteously he looked, and answer'd: angrily
"Whether say'st thou this in earnest or in play?"
"Nay," quoth Arcite, "in earnest, by my fay. faith
God help me so, me lust full ill to play." I am in no humour
This Palamon gan knit his browes tway. for jesting
"It were," quoth he, "to thee no great honour
For to be false, nor for to be traitour
To me, that am thy cousin and thy brother
Y-sworn full deep, and each of us to other,
That never for to dien in the pain[12],
Till that the death departen shall us twain,
Neither of us in love to hinder other,
Nor in none other case, my leve brother; dear
But that thou shouldest truly farther me
In every case, as I should farther thee.
This was thine oath, and mine also certain;
I wot it well, thou dar'st it not withsayn, deny
Thus art thou of my counsel out of doubt,
And now thou wouldest falsely be about
To love my lady, whom I love and serve,
And ever shall, until mine hearte sterve die
Now certes, false Arcite, thou shalt not so
I lov'd her first, and tolde thee my woe
As to my counsel, and my brother sworn
To farther me, as I have told beforn.
For which thou art y-bounden as a knight
To helpe me, if it lie in thy might,
Or elles art thou false, I dare well sayn,"

This Arcita full proudly spake again:
"Thou shalt," quoth he, "be rather false than I, sooner
And thou art false, I tell thee utterly;
For par amour I lov'd her first ere thou.
What wilt thou say? thou wist it not right now even now thou
Whether she be a woman or goddess. knowest not
Thine is affection of holiness,
And mine is love, as to a creature:
For which I tolde thee mine aventure
As to my cousin, and my brother sworn
I pose, that thou loved'st her beforn: suppose
Wost thou not well the olde clerke's saw[13],

14

THE CANTERBURY TALES

know'st
That who shall give a lover any law?
Love is a greater lawe, by my pan,
Than may be giv'n to any earthly man:
Therefore positive law, and such decree,
Is broke alway for love in each degree
A man must needes love, maugre his head.
He may not flee it, though he should be dead,
All be she maid, or widow, or else wife. whether she be
And eke it is not likely all thy life
To standen in her grace, no more than I
For well thou wost thyselfe verily,
That thou and I be damned to prison
Perpetual, us gaineth no ranson.
We strive, as did the houndes for the bone;
They fought all day, and yet their part was none.
There came a kite, while that they were so wroth,
And bare away the bone betwixt them both.
And therefore at the kinge's court, my brother,
Each man for himselfe, there is no other.
Love if thee list; for I love and aye shall
And soothly, leve brother, this is all.
Here in this prison musten we endure,
And each of us take his Aventure."

Great was the strife and long between these tway,
If that I hadde leisure for to say;
But to the effect: it happen'd on a day
(To tell it you as shortly as I may),
A worthy duke that hight Perithous[14]
That fellow was to the Duke Theseus
Since thilke day that they were children lite that little
Was come to Athens, his fellow to visite,
And for to play, as he was wont to do;
For in this world he loved no man so;
And he lov'd him as tenderly again.
So well they lov'd, as olde bookes sayn,
That when that one was dead, soothly to sayn,
His fellow went and sought him down in hell:
But of that story list me not to write.
Duke Perithous loved well Arcite,
And had him known at Thebes year by year:
And finally at request and prayere
Of Perithous, withoute ranson
Duke Theseus him let out of prison,
Freely to go, where him list over all,
In such a guise, as I you tellen shall
This was the forword, plainly to indite, promise
Betwixte Theseus and him Arcite:
That if so were, that Arcite were y-found
Ever in his life, by day or night, one stound moment[15]
In any country of this Theseus,
And he were caught, it was accorded thus,
That with a sword he shoulde lose his head;
There was none other remedy nor rede. counsel

But took his leave, and homeward he him sped;
Let him beware, his necke lieth to wed. in pledge

How great a sorrow suff'reth now Arcite!
The death he feeleth through his hearte smite;
He weepeth, waileth, crieth piteously;
To slay himself he waiteth privily.
He said; "Alas the day that I was born!
Now is my prison worse than beforn:
Now is me shape eternally to dwell it is fixed for me
Not in purgatory, but right in hell.
Alas! that ever I knew Perithous.
For elles had I dwelt with Theseus
Y-fettered in his prison evermo'.
Then had I been in bliss, and not in woe.
Only the sight of her, whom that I serve,
Though that I never may her grace deserve,
Would have sufficed right enough for me.
O deare cousin Palamon," quoth he,
"Thine is the vict'ry of this aventure,
Full blissfully in prison to endure:
In prison? nay certes, in paradise.
Well hath fortune y-turned thee the dice,
That hast the sight of her, and I th' absence.
For possible is, since thou hast her presence,
And art a knight, a worthy and an able,
That by some cas, since fortune is changeable, chance
Thou may'st to thy desire sometime attain.
But I that am exiled, and barren
Of alle grace, and in so great despair,
That there n'is earthe, water, fire, nor air,
Nor creature, that of them maked is,
That may me helpe nor comfort in this,
Well ought I sterve in wanhope and distress. die in despair
Farewell my life, my lust, and my gladness. pleasure
Alas, why plainen men so in commune why do men so often complain
Of purveyance of God, or of Fortune, of God's providence?
That giveth them full oft in many a guise
Well better than they can themselves devise?
Some man desireth for to have richess,
That cause is of his murder or great sickness.
And some man would out of his prison fain,
That in his house is of his meinie slain. servants[16]
Infinite harmes be in this mattere.
We wot never what thing we pray for here.
We fare as he that drunk is as a mouse.
A drunken man wot well he hath an house,
But he wot not which is the right way thither,
And to a drunken man the way is slither. slippery
And certes in this world so fare we.
We seeke fast after felicity,
But we go wrong full often truely.
Thus we may sayen all, and namely I, especially

That ween'd, and had a great opinion, thought
That if I might escape from prison
Then had I been in joy and perfect heal,
Where now I am exiled from my weal.
Since that I may not see you, Emily,
I am but dead; there is no remedy."

Upon that other side, Palamon,
When that he wist Arcita was agone,
Much sorrow maketh, that the greate tower
Resounded of his yelling and clamour
The pure fetters on his shinnes great very[17]
Were of his bitter salte teares wet.

"Alas!" quoth he, "Arcita, cousin mine,
Of all our strife, God wot, the fruit is thine.
Thou walkest now in Thebes at thy large,
And of my woe thou givest little charge.   takest little heed
Thou mayst, since thou hast wisdom and manhead,   manhood, courage
Assemble all the folk of our kindred,
And make a war so sharp on this country
That by some aventure, or some treaty,
Thou mayst have her to lady and to wife,
For whom that I must needes lose my life.
For as by way of possibility,
Since thou art at thy large, of prison free,
And art a lord, great is thine avantage,
More than is mine, that sterve here in a cage.
For I must weep and wail, while that I live,
With all the woe that prison may me give,
And eke with pain that love me gives also,
That doubles all my torment and my woe."

Therewith the fire of jealousy upstart
Within his breast, and hent him by the heart   seized
So woodly, that he like was to behold   madly
The box-tree, or the ashes dead and cold.
Then said; "O cruel goddess, that govern
This world with binding of your word etern   eternal
And writen in the table of adamant
Your parlement and your eternal grant,   consultation
What is mankind more unto you y-hold   by you esteemed
Than is the sheep, that rouketh in the fold!   lie huddled together
For slain is man, right as another beast;
And dwelleth eke in prison and arrest,
And hath sickness, and great adversity,
And oftentimes guiltless, pardie   by God
What governance is in your prescience,
That guiltless tormenteth innocence?
And yet increaseth this all my penance,
That man is bounden to his observance
For Godde's sake to letten of his will,   restrain his desire

Whereas a beast may all his lust fulfil.
And when a beast is dead, he hath no pain;
But man after his death must weep and plain,
Though in this worlde he have care and woe:
Withoute doubt it maye standen so.
"The answer of this leave I to divines,
But well I wot, that in this world great pine is;   pain, trouble
Alas! I see a serpent or a thief
That many a true man hath done mischief,
Go at his large, and where him list may turn.
But I must be in prison through Saturn,
And eke through Juno, jealous and eke wood,   mad
That hath well nigh destroyed all the blood
Of Thebes, with his waste walles wide.
And Venus slay'th me on that other side
For jealousy, and fear of him, Arcite."

Now will I stent of Palamon a lite,   pause little
And let him in his prison stille dwell,
And of Arcita forth I will you tell.
The summer passeth, and the nightes long
Increase double-wise the paines strong
Both of the lover and the prisonere.
I n'ot which hath the wofuller mistere.   know not condition
For, shortly for to say, this Palamon
Perpetually is damned to prison,
In chaines and in fetters to be dead;
And Arcite is exiled on his head   on peril of his head
For evermore as out of that country,
Nor never more he shall his lady see.
You lovers ask I now this question,[18]
Who lieth the worse, Arcite or Palamon?
The one may see his lady day by day,
But in prison he dwelle must alway.
The other where him list may ride or go,
But see his lady shall he never mo'.
Now deem all as you liste, ye that can,
For I will tell you forth as I began.

When that Arcite to Thebes comen was,
Full oft a day he swelt, and said, "Alas!"   fainted
For see this lady he shall never mo'.
And shortly to concluden all his woe,
So much sorrow had never creature
That is or shall be while the world may dure.
His sleep, his meat, his drink is him byraft,   taken away from him
That lean he wex, and dry as any shaft.   became
His eyen hollow, grisly to behold,
His hue sallow, and pale as ashes cold,
And solitary he was, ever alone,
And wailing all the night, making his moan.
And if he hearde song or instrument,
Then would he weepen, he might not be stent.   stopped
So feeble were his spirits, and so low,

And changed so, that no man coulde know
His speech, neither his voice, though men it heard.
And in his gear for all the world he far'd   behaviour[19]
Not only like the lovers' malady
Of Eros, but rather y-like manie madness
Engender'd of humours melancholic,
Before his head in his cell fantastic.[20]
And shortly turned was all upside down,
Both habit and eke dispositioun,
Of him, this woful lover Dan Arcite. Lord[21]
Why should I all day of his woe indite?
When he endured had a year or two
This cruel torment, and this pain and woe,
At Thebes, in his country, as I said,
Upon a night in sleep as he him laid,
Him thought how that the winged god Mercury
Before him stood, and bade him to be merry.
His sleepy yard in hand he bare upright;   rod[22]
A hat he wore upon his haires bright.
Arrayed was this god (as he took keep)   notice
As he was when that Argus[23] took his sleep;
And said him thus: "To Athens shalt thou wend;   go
There is thee shapen of thy woe an end."   fixed, prepared
And with that word Arcite woke and start.
"Now truely how sore that e'er me smart,"
Quoth he, "to Athens right now will I fare.
Nor for no dread of death shall I not spare
To see my lady that I love and serve;
In her presence I recke not to sterve."   do not care if I die
And with that word he caught a great mirror,
And saw that changed was all his colour,
And saw his visage all in other kind.
And right anon it ran him ill his mind,
That since his face was so disfigur'd
Of malady the which he had endur'd,
He mighte well, if that he bare him low,   lived in lowly fashion
Live in Athenes evermore unknow,
And see his lady wellnigh day by day.
And right anon he changed his array,
And clad him as a poore labourer.
And all alone, save only a squier,
That knew his privity and all his cas,   secrets fortune
Which was disguised poorly as he was,
To Athens is he gone the nexte way.   nearest[24]
And to the court he went upon a day,
And at the gate he proffer'd his service,
To drudge and draw, what so men would devise.   order
And, shortly of this matter for to sayn,
He fell in office with a chamberlain,
The which that dwelling was with Emily.
For he was wise, and coulde soon espy
Of every servant which that served her.
Well could he hewe wood, and water bear,
For he was young and mighty for the nones,   occasion
And thereto he was strong and big of bones
To do that any wight can him devise.

A year or two he was in this service,
Page of the chamber of Emily the bright;
And Philostrate he saide that he hight.
But half so well belov'd a man as he
Ne was there never in court of his degree.
He was so gentle of conditioun,
That throughout all the court was his renown.
They saide that it were a charity
That Theseus would enhance his degree,   elevate him in rank
And put him in some worshipful service,
There as he might his virtue exercise.
And thus within a while his name sprung
Both of his deedes, and of his good tongue,
That Theseus hath taken him so near,
That of his chamber he hath made him squire,
And gave him gold to maintain his degree;
And eke men brought him out of his country
From year to year full privily his rent.
But honestly and slyly he it spent,   discreetly, prudently
That no man wonder'd how that he it had.
And three year in this wise his life be lad,   led
And bare him so in peace and eke in werre,   war
There was no man that Theseus had so derre.   dear
And in this blisse leave I now Arcite,
And speak I will of Palamon a lite.   little

In darkness horrible, and strong prison,
This seven year hath sitten Palamon,
Forpined, what for love, and for distress.   pined, wasted away
Who feeleth double sorrow and heaviness
But Palamon? that love distraineth so,   afflicts
That wood out of his wits he went for woe,   mad
And eke thereto he is a prisonere
Perpetual, not only for a year.
Who coulde rhyme in English properly
His martyrdom? forsooth, it is not I;   truly
Therefore I pass as lightly as I may.
It fell that in the seventh year, in May
The thirde night (as olde bookes sayn,
That all this story tellen more plain),
Were it by a venture or destiny
(As when a thing is shapen it shall be),   settled, decreed
That soon after the midnight, Palamon
By helping of a friend brake his prison,
And fled the city fast as he might go,
For he had given drink his gaoler so
Of a clary[25], made of a certain wine,
With narcotise and opie of Thebes fine,   narcotics

GEOFFREY CHAUCER

and opium
That all the night, though that men would him shake,
The gaoler slept, he mighte not awake:
And thus he fled as fast as ever he may.
The night was short, and faste by the day close at hand was
That needes cast he must himself to hide. the day during which
And to a grove faste there beside he must cast about, or contrive,
With dreadful foot then stalked Palamon. to conceal himself.
For shortly this was his opinion,
That in the grove he would him hide all day,
And in the night then would he take his way
To Thebes-ward, his friendes for to pray
On Theseus to help him to warray. make war[26]
And shortly either he would lose his life,
Or winnen Emily unto his wife.
This is th' effect, and his intention plain.

Now will I turn to Arcita again,
That little wist how nighe was his care,
Till that Fortune had brought him in the snare.
The busy lark, the messenger of day,
Saluteth in her song the morning gray;
And fiery Phoebus riseth up so bright,
That all the orient laugheth at the sight,
And with his streames drieth in the greves rays groves
The silver droppes, hanging on the leaves;
And Arcite, that is in the court royal
With Theseus, his squier principal,
Is ris'n, and looketh on the merry day.
And for to do his observance to May,
Remembering the point of his desire, object
He on his courser, starting as the fire,
Is ridden to the fieldes him to play,
Out of the court, were it a mile or tway.
And to the grove, of which I have you told,
By a venture his way began to hold,
To make him a garland of the greves, groves
Were it of woodbine, or of hawthorn leaves,
And loud he sang against the sun so sheen. shining bright
"O May, with all thy flowers and thy green,
Right welcome be thou, faire freshe May,
I hope that I some green here getten may."
And from his courser, with a lusty heart, horse
Into the grove full hastily he start,
And in a path he roamed up and down,
There as by aventure this Palamon
Was in a bush, that no man might him see,
For sore afeard of his death was he.
Nothing ne knew he that it was Arcite;
God wot he would have trowed it full lite. full little believed it
But sooth is said, gone since full many years,

The field hath eyen, and the wood hath ears, eyes
It is full fair a man to bear him even, to be on his guard
For all day meeten men at unset steven. unexpected time[27]
Full little wot Arcite of his fellaw,
That was so nigh to hearken of his saw, saying, speech
For in the bush he sitteth now full still.
When that Arcite had roamed all his fill,
And sungen all the roundel lustily, sang the roundelay[28]
Into a study he fell suddenly,
As do those lovers in their quainte gears, odd fashions
Now in the crop, and now down in the breres,[29] tree-top
Now up, now down, as bucket in a well. briars
Right as the Friday, soothly for to tell,
Now shineth it, and now it raineth fast,
Right so can geary Venus overcast changeful
The heartes of her folk, right as her day
Is gearful, right so changeth she array. changeful
Seldom is Friday all the weeke like.
When Arcite had y-sung, he gan to sike, sigh
And sat him down withouten any more:
"Alas!" quoth he, "the day that I was bore!
How longe, Juno, through thy cruelty
Wilt thou warrayen Thebes the city? torment
Alas! y-brought is to confusion
The blood royal of Cadm' and Amphion:
Of Cadmus, which that was the firste man,
That Thebes built, or first the town began,
And of the city first was crowned king.
Of his lineage am I, and his offspring
By very line, as of the stock royal;
And now I am so caitiff and so thrall, wretched and enslaved
That he that is my mortal enemy,
I serve him as his squier poorely.
And yet doth Juno me well more shame,
For I dare not beknow mine owen name, acknowledge[30]
But there as I was wont to hight Arcite,
Now hight I Philostrate, not worth a mite.
Alas! thou fell Mars, and alas! Juno,
Thus hath your ire our lineage all fordo undone, ruined
Save only me, and wretched Palamon,
That Theseus martyreth in prison.
And over all this, to slay me utterly,
Love hath his fiery dart so brenningly burningly
Y-sticked through my true careful heart,
That shapen was my death erst than my shert.[31]
Ye slay me with your eyen, Emily;
Ye be the cause wherefore that I die.
Of all the remnant of mine other care
Ne set I not the mountance of a tare, value of a

18

THE CANTERBURY TALES

straw
So that I could do aught to your pleasure."

And with that word he fell down in a trance
A longe time; and afterward upstart
This Palamon, that thought thorough his heart
He felt a cold sword suddenly to glide:
For ire he quoke, no longer would he hide. quaked
And when that he had heard Arcite's tale,
As he were wood, with face dead and pale, mad
He start him up out of the bushes thick,
And said: "False Arcita, false traitor wick', wicked
Now art thou hent, that lov'st my lady so, caught
For whom that I have all this pain and woe,
And art my blood, and to my counsel sworn,
As I full oft have told thee herebeforn,
And hast bejaped here Duke Theseus, deceived, imposed upon
And falsely changed hast thy name thus;
I will be dead, or elles thou shalt die.
Thou shalt not love my lady Emily,
But I will love her only and no mo';
For I am Palamon thy mortal foe.
And though I have no weapon in this place,
But out of prison am astart by grace, escaped
I dreade not that either thou shalt die, doubt
Or else thou shalt not loven Emily.
Choose which thou wilt, for thou shalt not astart."

This Arcite then, with full dispiteous heart, wrathful
When he him knew, and had his tale heard,
As fierce as lion pulled out a swerd,
And saide thus; "By God that sitt'th above,
N'ere it that thou art sick, and wood for love, were it not
And eke that thou no weap'n hast in this place,
Thou should'st never out of this grove pace,
That thou ne shouldest dien of mine hand.
For I defy the surety and the band,
Which that thou sayest I have made to thee.
What? very fool, think well that love is free;
And I will love her maugre all thy might. despite
But, for thou art a worthy gentle knight,
And wilnest to darraine her by bataille, will reclaim her
Have here my troth, to-morrow I will not fail, by combat
Without weeting of any other wight, knowledge
That here I will be founden as a knight,
And bringe harness right enough for thee; armour and arms
And choose the best, and leave the worst for me.
And meat and drinke this night will I bring
Enough for thee, and clothes for thy bedding.
And if so be that thou my lady win,
And slay me in this wood that I am in,
Thou may'st well have thy lady as for me."

This Palamon answer'd, "I grant it thee."
And thus they be departed till the morrow,
When each of them hath laid his faith to borrow. pledged his faith

O Cupid, out of alle charity!
O Regne that wilt no fellow have with thee! queen[32]
Full sooth is said, that love nor lordship
Will not, his thanks, have any fellowship. thanks to him
Well finden that Arcite and Palamon.
Arcite is ridd anon unto the town,
And on the morrow, ere it were daylight,
Full privily two harness hath he dight, prepared
Both suffisant and meete to darraine contest
The battle in the field betwixt them twain.
And on his horse, alone as he was born,
He carrieth all this harness him beforn;
And in the grove, at time and place y-set,
This Arcite and this Palamon be met.
Then change gan the colour of their face;
Right as the hunter in the regne of Thrace kingdom
That standeth at a gappe with a spear
When hunted is the lion or the bear,
And heareth him come rushing in the greves, groves
And breaking both the boughes and the leaves,
Thinketh, "Here comes my mortal enemy,
Withoute fail, he must be dead or I;
For either I must slay him at the gap;
Or he must slay me, if that me mishap:"
So fared they, in changing of their hue
As far as either of them other knew. When they recognised each
There was no good day, and no saluting, other afar off
But straight, withoute wordes rehearsing,
Evereach of them holp to arm the other,
As friendly, as he were his owen brother.
And after that, with sharpe speares strong
They foined each at other wonder long. thrust
Thou mightest weene, that this Palamon think
In fighting were as a wood lion, mad
And as a cruel tiger was Arcite:
As wilde boars gan they together smite,
That froth as white as foam, for ire wood. mad with anger
Up to the ancle fought they in their blood.
And in this wise I let them fighting dwell,
And forth I will of Theseus you tell.

The Destiny, minister general,
That executeth in the world o'er all
The purveyance, that God hath seen beforn; foreordination
So strong it is, that though the world had sworn
The contrary of a thing by yea or nay,
Yet some time it shall fallen on a day

GEOFFREY CHAUCER

That falleth not eft in a thousand year. again
For certainly our appetites here,
Be it of war, or peace, or hate, or love,
All is this ruled by the sight above. eye, intelligence, power
This mean I now by mighty Theseus,
That for to hunten is so desirous —
And namely the greate hart in May — especially
That in his bed there dawneth him no day
That he n'is clad, and ready for to ride
With hunt and horn, and houndes him beside.
For in his hunting hath he such delight,
That it is all his joy and appetite
To be himself the greate harte's bane destruction
For after Mars he serveth now Diane.
Clear was the day, as I have told ere this,
And Theseus, with alle joy and bliss,
With his Hippolyta, the faire queen,
And Emily, y-clothed all in green,
On hunting be they ridden royally.
And to the grove, that stood there faste by,
In which there was an hart, as men him told,
Duke Theseus the straighte way doth hold,
And to the laund he rideth him full right, plain[33]
There was the hart y-wont to have his flight,
And over a brook, and so forth on his way.
This Duke will have a course at him or tway
With houndes, such as him lust to command. pleased
And when this Duke was come to the laund,
Under the sun he looked, and anon
He was ware of Arcite and Palamon,
That foughte breme, as it were bulles two. fiercely
The brighte swordes wente to and fro
So hideously, that with the leaste stroke
It seemed that it woulde fell an oak,
But what they were, nothing yet he wote. knew
This Duke his courser with his spurres smote,
And at a start he was betwixt them two, suddenly
And pulled out a sword and cried, "Ho!
No more, on pain of losing of your head.
By mighty Mars, he shall anon be dead
That smiteth any stroke, that I may see!
But tell to me what mister men ye be, manner, kind[34]
That be so hardy for to fighte here
Withoute judge or other officer,
As though it were in listes royally.[35]
This Palamon answered hastily,
And saide: "Sir, what needeth wordes mo'?
We have the death deserved bothe two,
Two woful wretches be we, and caitives,
That be accumbered of our own lives, burdened
And as thou art a rightful lord and judge,
So give us neither mercy nor refuge.
And slay me first, for sainte charity,
But slay my fellow eke as well as me.
Or slay him first; for, though thou know it lite, little

This is thy mortal foe, this is Arcite
That from thy land is banisht on his head,
For which he hath deserved to be dead.
For this is he that came unto thy gate
And saide, that he highte Philostrate.
Thus hath he japed thee full many year, deceived
And thou hast made of him thy chief esquier;
And this is he, that loveth Emily.
For since the day is come that I shall die
I make pleinly my confession, fully, unreservedly
That I am thilke woful Palamon, that same[36]
That hath thy prison broken wickedly.
I am thy mortal foe, and it am I
That so hot loveth Emily the bright,
That I would die here present in her sight.
Therefore I ask death and my jewise. judgement
But slay my fellow eke in the same wise,
For both we have deserved to be slain."

This worthy Duke answer'd anon again,
And said, "This is a short conclusion.
Your own mouth, by your own confession
Hath damned you, and I will it record;
It needeth not to pain you with the cord;
Ye shall be dead, by mighty Mars the Red.[37]

The queen anon for very womanhead
Began to weep, and so did Emily,
And all the ladies in the company.
Great pity was it as it thought them all,
That ever such a chance should befall,
For gentle men they were, of great estate,
And nothing but for love was this debate
They saw their bloody woundes wide and sore,
And cried all at once, both less and more,
"Have mercy, Lord, upon us women all."
And on their bare knees adown they fall
And would have kissed his feet there as he stood,
Till at the last aslaked was his mood his anger was
(For pity runneth soon in gentle heart); appeased
And though at first for ire he quoke and start
He hath consider'd shortly in a clause
The trespass of them both, and eke the cause:
And although that his ire their guilt accused
Yet in his reason he them both excused;
As thus; he thoughte well that every man
Will help himself in love if that he can,
And eke deliver himself out of prison.
Of women, for they wepten ever-in-one: continually
And eke his hearte had compassion
And in his gentle heart he thought anon,
And soft unto himself he saide: "Fie
Upon a lord that will have no mercy,
But be a lion both in word and deed,
To them that be in repentance and dread,
As well as-to a proud dispiteous man unpitying
That will maintaine what he first began.
That lord hath little of discretion,

THE CANTERBURY TALES

That in such case can no division: *can make no distinction*
But weigheth pride and humbless after one." *alike*
And shortly, when his ire is thus agone,
He gan to look on them with eyen light, *gentle, lenient*
And spake these same wordes all on height. *aloud*

"The god of love, ah! benedicite, *bless ye him*
How mighty and how great a lord is he!
Against his might there gaine none obstacles, *avail, conquer*
He may be called a god for his miracles
For he can maken at his owen guise
Of every heart, as that him list devise.
Lo here this Arcite, and this Palamon,
That quietly were out of my prison,
And might have lived in Thebes royally,
And weet I am their mortal enemy, *knew*
And that their death li'th in my might also,
And yet hath love, maugre their eyen two, *in spite of their eyes*
Y-brought them hither bothe for to die.
Now look ye, is not this an high folly?
Who may not be a fool, if but he love?
Behold, for Godde's sake that sits above,
See how they bleed! be they not well array'd?
Thus hath their lord, the god of love, them paid
Their wages and their fees for their service;
And yet they weene for to be full wise,
That serve love, for aught that may befall.
But this is yet the beste game of all, *joke*
That she, for whom they have this jealousy,
Can them therefor as muchel thank as me.
She wot no more of all this hote fare, *hot behaviour*
By God, than wot a cuckoo or an hare.
But all must be assayed hot or cold;
A man must be a fool, or young or old;
I wot it by myself full yore agone: *long years ago*
For in my time a servant was I one.
And therefore since I know of love's pain,
And wot how sore it can a man distrain, *distress*
As he that oft hath been caught in his last, *snare*[38]
I you forgive wholly this trespass,
At request of the queen that kneeleth here,
And eke of Emily, my sister dear.
And ye shall both anon unto me swear,
That never more ye shall my country dere *injure*
Nor make war upon me night nor day,
But be my friends in alle that ye may.
I you forgive this trespass every deal. *completely*
And they him sware his asking fair and well, *what he asked*
And him of lordship and of mercy pray'd,
And he them granted grace, and thus he said:

"To speak of royal lineage and richess,
Though that she were a queen or a princess,
Each of you both is worthy doubteless
To wedde when time is; but natheless
I speak as for my sister Emily,
For whom ye have this strife and jealousy,
Ye wot yourselves, she may not wed the two *know*
At once, although ye fight for evermo:
But one of you, all be him loth or lief, *whether or not he wishes*
He must go pipe into an ivy leaf: *"go whistle"*
This is to say, she may not have you both,
All be ye never so jealous, nor so wroth.
And therefore I you put in this degree,
That each of you shall have his destiny
As him is shape; and hearken in what wise *as is decreed for him*
Lo hear your end of that I shall devise.
My will is this, for plain conclusion
Withouten any replication, *reply*
If that you liketh, take it for the best,
That evereach of you shall go where him lest, *he pleases*
Freely without ransom or danger;
And this day fifty weekes, farre ne nerre, *neither more nor less*
Evereach of you shall bring an hundred knights,
Armed for listes up at alle rights
All ready to darraine her by bataille, *contend for*
And this behete I you withoute fail *promise*
Upon my troth, and as I am a knight,
That whether of you bothe that hath might,
That is to say, that whether he or thou
May with his hundred, as I spake of now,
Slay his contrary, or out of listes drive,
Him shall I given Emily to wive,
To whom that fortune gives so fair a grace.
The listes shall I make here in this place.
And God so wisly on my soule rue, *may God as surely have*
As I shall even judge be and true. *mercy on my soul*
Ye shall none other ende with me maken
Than one of you shalle be dead or taken.
And if you thinketh this is well y-said,
Say your advice, and hold yourselves apaid. *opinion satisfied*
This is your end, and your conclusion."
Who looketh lightly now but Palamon?
Who springeth up for joye but Arcite?
Who could it tell, or who could it indite,
The joye that is maked in the place
When Theseus hath done so fair a grace?
But down on knees went every manner wight, *kind of person*
And thanked him with all their heartes' might,
And namely these Thebans ofte sithe. *especially oftentimes*
And thus with good hope and with hearte blithe
They take their leave, and homeward gan they

ride
To Thebes-ward, with his old walles wide.

I trow men woulde deem it negligence,
If I forgot to telle the dispence expenditure
Of Theseus, that went so busily
To maken up the listes royally,
That such a noble theatre as it was,
I dare well say, in all this world there n'as. was not
The circuit a mile was about,
Walled of stone, and ditched all without.
Round was the shape, in manner of compass,
Full of degrees, the height of sixty pas see note[39]
That when a man was set on one degree
He letted not his fellow for to see. hindered
Eastward there stood a gate of marble white,
Westward right such another opposite.
And, shortly to conclude, such a place
Was never on earth made in so little space,
For in the land there was no craftes-man,
That geometry or arsmetrike can, arithmetic knew
Nor pourtrayor, nor carver of images, portrait painter
That Theseus ne gave him meat and wages
The theatre to make and to devise.
And for to do his rite and sacrifice
He eastward hath upon the gate above,
In worship of Venus, goddess of love,
Done make an altar and an oratory; caused to be made
And westward, in the mind and in memory
Of Mars, he maked hath right such another,
That coste largely of gold a fother. a great amount
And northward, in a turret on the wall,
Of alabaster white and red coral
An oratory riche for to see,
In worship of Diane of chastity,
Hath Theseus done work in noble wise.
But yet had I forgotten to devise describe
The noble carving, and the portraitures,
The shape, the countenance of the figures
That weren in there oratories three.

First in the temple of Venus may'st thou see
Wrought on the wall, full piteous to behold,
The broken sleepes, and the sikes cold, sighes
The sacred teares, and the waimentings, lamentings
The fiery strokes of the desirings,
That Love's servants in this life endure;
The oathes, that their covenants assure.
Pleasance and Hope, Desire, Foolhardiness,
Beauty and Youth, and Bawdry and Richess,
Charms and Sorc'ry, Leasings and Flattery, falsehoods
Dispence, Business, and Jealousy,
That wore of yellow goldes a garland, sunflowers[40]
And had a cuckoo sitting on her hand,
Feasts, instruments, and caroles and dances,
Lust and array, and all the circumstances
Of Love, which I reckon'd and reckon shall
In order, were painted on the wall,
And more than I can make of mention.
For soothly all the mount of Citheron,[41]
Where Venus hath her principal dwelling,
Was showed on the wall in pourtraying,
With all the garden, and the lustiness. pleasantness
Nor was forgot the porter Idleness,
Nor Narcissus the fair of yore agone, olden times
Nor yet the folly of King Solomon,
Nor yet the greate strength of Hercules,
Th' enchantments of Medea and Circes,
Nor of Turnus the hardy fierce courage,
The rich Croesus caitif in servage.[42] abased into slavery
Thus may ye see, that wisdom nor richess,
Beauty, nor sleight, nor strength, nor hardiness
Ne may with Venus holde champartie, divided possession[43]
For as her liste the world may she gie. guide
Lo, all these folk so caught were in her las snare
Till they for woe full often said, Alas!
Suffice these ensamples one or two,
Although I could reckon a thousand mo'.

The statue of Venus, glorious to see
Was naked floating in the large sea,
And from the navel down all cover'd was
With waves green, and bright as any glass.
A citole[44] in her right hand hadde she,
And on her head, full seemly for to see,
A rose garland fresh, and well smelling,
Above her head her doves flickering
Before her stood her sone Cupido,
Upon his shoulders winges had he two;
And blind he was, as it is often seen;
A bow he bare, and arrows bright and keen.

Why should I not as well eke tell you all
The portraiture, that was upon the wall
Within the temple of mighty Mars the Red?
All painted was the wall in length and brede breadth
Like to the estres of the grisly place interior chambers
That hight the great temple of Mars in Thrace,
In thilke cold and frosty region, that
There as Mars hath his sovereign mansion.
In which there dwelled neither man nor beast,
With knotty gnarry barren trees old gnarled
Of stubbes sharp and hideous to behold;
In which there ran a rumble and a sough, groaning noise
As though a storm should bursten every bough:
And downward from an hill under a bent slope
There stood the temple of Mars Armipotent,
Wrought all of burnish'd steel, of which th' entry
Was long and strait, and ghastly for to see.

And thereout came a rage and such a vise, such a furious voice
That it made all the gates for to rise.
The northern light in at the doore shone,
For window on the walle was there none
Through which men mighten any light discern.
The doors were all of adamant etern,
Y-clenched overthwart and ende-long crossways and lengthways
With iron tough, and, for to make it strong,
Every pillar the temple to sustain
Was tunne-great, of iron bright and sheen. thick as a tun (barrel)
There saw I first the dark imagining
Of felony, and all the compassing;
The cruel ire, as red as any glede, live coal
The picke-purse,45 and eke the pale dread;
The smiler with the knife under the cloak,
The shepen burning with the blacke smoke stable46
The treason of the murd'ring in the bed,
The open war, with woundes all be-bled;
Conteke with bloody knife, and sharp menace. contention, discord
All full of chirking was that sorry place. creaking, jarring noise
The slayer of himself eke saw I there,
His hearte-blood had bathed all his hair:
The nail y-driven in the shode at night, hair of the head47
The colde death, with mouth gaping upright.
Amiddes of the temple sat Mischance,
With discomfort and sorry countenance;
Eke saw I Woodness laughing in his rage, Madness
Armed Complaint, Outhees, and fierce Outrage; Outcry
The carrain in the bush, with throat y-corve, corpse slashed
A thousand slain, and not of qualm y-storve; dead of sickness
The tyrant, with the prey by force y-reft;
The town destroy'd, that there was nothing left.
Yet saw I brent the shippes hoppesteres,48 burnt
The hunter strangled with the wilde bears:
The sow freting the child right in the cradle; devouring49
The cook scalded, for all his longe ladle.
Nor was forgot, by th'infortune of Mart through the misfortune
The carter overridden with his cart; of war
Under the wheel full low he lay adown.
There were also of Mars' division,
The armourer, the bowyer, and the smith, maker of bows
That forgeth sharp swordes on his stith. anvil
And all above depainted in a tower
Saw I Conquest, sitting in great honour,
With thilke sharpe sword over his head that

Hanging by a subtle y-twined thread.
Painted the slaughter was of Julius50,
Of cruel Nero, and Antonius:
Although at that time they were yet unborn,
Yet was their death depainted there beforn,
By menacing of Mars, right by figure,
So was it showed in that portraiture,
As is depainted in the stars above,
Who shall be slain, or elles dead for love.
Sufficeth one ensample in stories old,
I may not reckon them all, though I wo'ld.

The statue of Mars upon a carte stood chariot
Armed, and looked grim as he were wood, mad
And over his head there shone two figures
Of starres, that be cleped in scriptures,
That one Puella, that other Rubeus.51
This god of armes was arrayed thus:
A wolf there stood before him at his feet
With eyen red, and of a man he eat:
With subtle pencil painted was this story,
In redouting of Mars and of his glory. reverance, fear

Now to the temple of Dian the chaste
As shortly as I can I will me haste,
To telle you all the descriptioun.
Depainted be the walles up and down
Of hunting and of shamefast chastity.
There saw I how woful Calistope,52
When that Dian aggrieved was with her,
Was turned from a woman to a bear,
And after was she made the lodestar: pole star
Thus was it painted, I can say no far; farther
Her son is eke a star as men may see.
There saw I Dane53 turn'd into a tree,
I meane not the goddess Diane,
But Peneus' daughter, which that hight Dane.
There saw I Actaeon an hart y-maked, made
For vengeance that he saw Dian all naked:
I saw how that his houndes have him caught,
And freten him, for that they knew him not. devour
Yet painted was, a little farthermore
How Atalanta hunted the wild boar;
And Meleager, and many other mo',
For which Diana wrought them care and woe.
There saw I many another wondrous story,
The which me list not drawen to memory.
This goddess on an hart full high was set, seated
With smalle houndes all about her feet,
And underneath her feet she had a moon,
Waxing it was, and shoulde wane soon.
In gaudy green her statue clothed was,
With bow in hand, and arrows in a case. quiver
Her eyen caste she full low adown,
Where Pluto hath his darke regioun.
A woman travailing was her beforn,
But, for her child so longe was unborn,
Full piteously Lucina54 gan she call,

And saide; "Help, for thou may'st best of all."
Well could he painte lifelike that it wrought;
With many a florin he the hues had bought.
Now be these listes made, and Theseus,
That at his greate cost arrayed thus
The temples, and the theatre every deal, part[55]
When it was done, him liked wonder well.

But stint I will of Theseus a lite, cease speaking little
And speak of Palamon and of Arcite.
The day approacheth of their returning,
That evereach an hundred knights should bring,
The battle to darraine as I you told; contest
And to Athens, their covenant to hold,
Hath ev'reach of them brought an hundred knights,
Well-armed for the war at alle rights.
And sickerly there trowed many a man, surely[56] believed
That never, sithen that the world began, since
For to speaken of knighthood of their hand,
As far as God hath maked sea and land,
Was, of so few, so noble a company.
For every wight that loved chivalry,
And would, his thankes, have a passant name, thanks to his own
Had prayed, that he might be of that game, efforts, have a
And well was him, that thereto chosen was. surpassing name
For if there fell to-morrow such a case,
Ye knowe well, that every lusty knight,
That loveth par amour, and hath his might
Were it in Engleland, or elleswhere,
They would, their thankes, willen to be there,
T' fight for a lady; Benedicite,
It were a lusty sighte for to see. pleasing
And right so fared they with Palamon;
With him there wente knightes many one.
Some will be armed in an habergeon,
And in a breast-plate, and in a gipon; short doublet.
And some will have a pair of plates large; back and front armour
And some will have a Prusse shield, or targe; Prussian
Some will be armed on their legges weel;
Some have an axe, and some a mace of steel.
There is no newe guise, but it was old. fashion
Armed they weren, as I have you told,
Evereach after his opinion.
There may'st thou see coming with Palamon
Licurgus himself, the great king of Thrace:
Black was his beard, and manly was his face.
The circles of his eyen in his head
They glowed betwixte yellow and red,
And like a griffin looked he about,
With kemped haires on his browes stout; combed[57]
His limbs were great, his brawns were hard and strong,
His shoulders broad, his armes round and long.
And as the guise was in his country, fashion
Full high upon a car of gold stood he,
With foure white bulles in the trace.
Instead of coat-armour on his harness,
With yellow nails, and bright as any gold,
He had a beare's skin, coal-black for old. age
His long hair was y-kempt behind his back,
As any raven's feather it shone for black.
A wreath of gold arm-great, of huge weight, thick as a man's arm
Upon his head sate, full of stones bright,
Of fine rubies and clear diamants.
About his car there wente white alauns, greyhounds[58]
Twenty and more, as great as any steer,
To hunt the lion or the wilde bear,
And follow'd him, with muzzle fast y-bound,
Collars of gold, and torettes filed round. rings
An hundred lordes had he in his rout retinue
Armed full well, with heartes stern and stout.

With Arcita, in stories as men find,
The great Emetrius the king of Ind,
Upon a steede bay trapped in steel, bay horse
Cover'd with cloth of gold diapred well, decorated
Came riding like the god of armes, Mars.
His coat-armour was of a cloth of Tars, a kind of silk
Couched with pearls white and round and great trimmed
His saddle was of burnish'd gold new beat;
A mantelet on his shoulders hanging,
Bretful of rubies red, as fire sparkling. brimful
His crispe hair like ringes was y-run,
And that was yellow, glittering as the sun.
His nose was high, his eyen bright citrine, pale yellow
His lips were round, his colour was sanguine,
A fewe fracknes in his face y-sprent, freckles sprinkled
Betwixte yellow and black somedeal y-ment mixed[59]
And as a lion he his looking cast cast about his eyes
Of five and twenty year his age I cast reckon
His beard was well begunnen for to spring;
His voice was as a trumpet thundering.
Upon his head he wore of laurel green
A garland fresh and lusty to be seen;
Upon his hand he bare, for his delight,
An eagle tame, as any lily white.
An hundred lordes had he with him there,
All armed, save their heads, in all their gear,
Full richely in alle manner things.

THE CANTERBURY TALES

For trust ye well, that earles, dukes, and kings
Were gather'd in this noble company,
For love, and for increase of chivalry.
About this king there ran on every part
Full many a tame lion and leopart.
And in this wise these lordes all and some   all and sundry
Be on the Sunday to the city come
Aboute prime[60], and in the town alight.

This Theseus, this Duke, this worthy knight
When he had brought them into his city,
And inned them, ev'reach at his degree,   lodged
He feasteth them, and doth so great labour
To easen them, and do them all honour,   make them comfortable
That yet men weene that no mannes wit   think
Of none estate could amenden it.   improve
The minstrelsy, the service at the feast,
The greate giftes to the most and least,
The rich array of Theseus' palace,
Nor who sate first or last upon the dais.[61]
What ladies fairest be, or best dancing
Or which of them can carol best or sing,
Or who most feelingly speaketh of love;
What hawkes sitten on the perch above,
What houndes liggen on the floor adown,   lie
Of all this now make I no mentioun
But of th'effect; that thinketh me the best
Now comes the point, and hearken if you lest.   please

The Sunday night, ere day began to spring,
When Palamon the larke hearde sing,
Although it were not day by houres two,
Yet sang the lark, and Palamon right tho   then
With holy heart, and with an high courage,
Arose, to wenden on his pilgrimage   go
Unto the blissful Cithera benign,
I meane Venus, honourable and digne.   worthy
And in her hour[62] he walketh forth a pace
Unto the listes, where her temple was,
And down he kneeleth, and with humble cheer   demeanour
And hearte sore, he said as ye shall hear.

"Fairest of fair, O lady mine Venus,
Daughter to Jove, and spouse of Vulcanus,
Thou gladder of the mount of Citheron![41]
For thilke love thou haddest to Adon[63]
Have pity on my bitter teares   smart,
And take mine humble prayer to thine heart.
Alas! I have no language to tell
Th'effecte, nor the torment of mine hell;
Mine hearte may mine harmes not betray;
I am so confused, that I cannot say.
But mercy, lady bright, that knowest well
My thought, and seest what harm that I feel.
Consider all this, and rue upon my sore,   take pity on

As wisly as I shall for evermore truly
Enforce my might, thy true servant to be,
And holde war alway with chastity:
That make I mine avow, so ye me help.   vow, promise
I keepe not of armes for to yelp,   boast
Nor ask I not to-morrow to have victory,
Nor renown in this case, nor vaine glory
Of prize of armes, blowing up and down,   praise for valour
But I would have fully possessioun
Of Emily, and die in her service;
Find thou the manner how, and in what wise.
I recke not but it may better be   do not know whether
To have vict'ry of them, or they of me,
So that I have my lady in mine arms.
For though so be that Mars is god of arms,
Your virtue is so great in heaven above,
That, if you list, I shall well have my love.
Thy temple will I worship evermo',
And on thine altar, where I ride or go,
I will do sacrifice, and fires bete.   make, kindle
And if ye will not so, my lady sweet,
Then pray I you, to-morrow with a spear
That Arcita me through the hearte bear
Then reck I not, when I have lost my life,
Though that Arcita win her to his wife.
This is th' effect and end of my prayere, —
Give me my love, thou blissful lady dear."
When th' orison was done of Palamon,
His sacrifice he did, and that anon,
Full piteously, with alle circumstances,
All tell I not as now his observances.   although I tell not now
But at the last the statue of Venus shook,
And made a signe, whereby that he took
That his prayer accepted was that day.
For though the signe shewed a delay,
Yet wist he well that granted was his boon;
And with glad heart he went him home full soon.

The third hour unequal[64] that Palamon
Began to Venus' temple for to gon,
Up rose the sun, and up rose Emily,
And to the temple of Dian gan hie.
Her maidens, that she thither with her lad,   led
Th' incense, the clothes, and the remnant all
That to the sacrifice belonge shall,
The hornes full of mead, as was the guise;
There lacked nought to do her sacrifice.
Smoking the temple full of clothes fair,   draping[65]
This Emily with hearte debonnair   gentle
Her body wash'd with water of a well.
But how she did her rite I dare not tell;
But it be any thing in general;   unless
And yet it were a game to hearen all   pleasure
To him that meaneth well it were no charge:
But it is good a man to be at large.   do as he will

25

GEOFFREY CHAUCER

Her bright hair combed was, untressed all.
A coronet of green oak cerriall[66]
Upon her head was set full fair and meet.
Two fires on the altar gan she bete,
And did her thinges, as men may behold
In Stace of Thebes[67], and these bookes old.
When kindled was the fire, with piteous cheer
Unto Dian she spake as ye may hear.

"O chaste goddess of the woodes green,
To whom both heav'n and earth and sea is seen,
Queen of the realm of Pluto dark and low,
Goddess of maidens, that mine heart hast know
Full many a year, and wost what I desire, knowest
To keep me from the vengeance of thine ire,
That Actaeon aboughte cruelly: earned; suffered from
Chaste goddess, well wottest thou that I
Desire to be a maiden all my life,
Nor never will I be no love nor wife.
I am, thou wost, yet of thy company, knowest
A maid, and love hunting and venery, field sports
And for to walken in the woodes wild,
And not to be a wife, and be with child.
Nought will I know the company of man.
Now help me, lady, since ye may and can,
For those three formes[68] that thou hast in thee.
And Palamon, that hath such love to me,
And eke Arcite, that loveth me so sore,
This grace I pray thee withoute more,
As sende love and peace betwixt them two:
And from me turn away their heartes so,
That all their hote love, and their desire,
And all their busy torment, and their fire,
Be queint, or turn'd into another place. quenched
And if so be thou wilt do me no grace,
Or if my destiny be shapen so
That I shall needes have one of them two,
So send me him that most desireth me.
Behold, goddess of cleane chastity,
The bitter tears that on my cheekes fall.
Since thou art maid, and keeper of us all,
My maidenhead thou keep and well conserve,
And, while I live, a maid I will thee serve.

The fires burn upon the altar clear,
While Emily was thus in her prayere:
But suddenly she saw a sighte quaint. strange
For right anon one of the fire's queint
And quick'd again, and after that anon went out and revived
That other fire was queint, and all agone:
And as it queint, it made a whisteling,
As doth a brande wet in its burning.
And at the brandes end outran anon
As it were bloody droppes many one:
For which so sore aghast was Emily,
That she was well-nigh mad, and gan to cry,
For she ne wiste what it signified;
But onely for feare thus she cried,

And wept, that it was pity for to hear.
And therewithal Diana gan appear
With bow in hand, right as an huntress,
And saide; "Daughter, stint thine heaviness. cease
Among the goddes high it is affirm'd,
And by eternal word writ and confirm'd,
Thou shalt be wedded unto one of tho those
That have for thee so muche care and woe:
But unto which of them I may not tell.
Farewell, for here I may no longer dwell.
The fires which that on mine altar brenn, burn
Shall thee declaren, ere that thou go henne, hence
Thine aventure of love, as in this case."
And with that word, the arrows in the case quiver
Of the goddess did clatter fast and ring,
And forth she went, and made a vanishing,
For which this Emily astonied was,
And saide; "What amounteth this, alas!
I put me under thy protection,
Diane, and in thy disposition."
And home she went anon the nexte way. nearest
This is th' effect, there is no more to say.

The nexte hour of Mars following this
Arcite to the temple walked is
Of fierce Mars, to do his sacrifice
With all the rites of his pagan guise.
With piteous heart and high devotion pious
Right thus to Mars he said his orison
"O stronge god, that in the regnes old realms
Of Thrace honoured art, and lord y-hold held
And hast in every regne, and every land
Of armes all the bridle in thine hand,
And them fortunest as thee list devise, send them fortune
Accept of me my piteous sacrifice. as you please
If so be that my youthe may deserve,
And that my might be worthy for to serve
Thy godhead, that I may be one of thine,
Then pray I thee to rue upon my pine, pity my anguish
For thilke pain, and thilke hote fire, that
In which thou whilom burned'st for desire
Whenne that thou usedest the beauty enjoyed
Of faire young Venus, fresh and free,
And haddest her in armes at thy will:
And though thee ones on a time misfill, were unlucky
When Vulcanus had caught thee in his las, net[69]
And found thee ligging by his wife, alas! lying
For thilke sorrow that was in thine heart,
Have ruth as well upon my paine's smart. pity
I am young and unconning, as thou know'st, ignorant, simple
And, as I trow, with love offended most believe
That e'er was any living creature:
For she, that doth me all this woe endure, causes
Ne recketh ne'er whether I sink or fleet swim
And well I wot, ere she me mercy hete, promise,

26

vouchsafe
I must with strengthe win her in the place:
And well I wot, withoute help or grace
Of thee, ne may my strengthe not avail:
Then help me, lord, to-morr'w in my bataille,
For thilke fire that whilom burned thee,
As well as this fire that now burneth me;
And do that I to-morr'w may have victory. cause
Mine be the travail, all thine be the glory.
Thy sovereign temple will I most honour
Of any place, and alway most labour
In thy pleasance and in thy craftes strong.
And in thy temple I will my banner hong, hang
And all the armes of my company,
And evermore, until that day I die,
Eternal fire I will before thee find
And eke to this my vow I will me bind:
My beard, my hair that hangeth long adown,
That never yet hath felt offension indignity
Of razor nor of shears, I will thee give,
And be thy true servant while I live.
Now, lord, have ruth upon my sorrows sore,
Give me the victory, I ask no more."

The prayer stint of Arcita the strong, ended
The ringes on the temple door that hong,
And eke the doores, clattered full fast,
Of which Arcita somewhat was aghast.
The fires burn'd upon the altar bright,
That it gan all the temple for to light;
A sweete smell anon the ground up gaf, gave
And Arcita anon his hand up haf, lifted
And more incense into the fire he cast,
With other rites more and at the last
The statue of Mars began his hauberk ring;
And with that sound he heard a murmuring
Full low and dim, that saide thus, "Victory."
For which he gave to Mars honour and glory.
And thus with joy, and hope well to fare,
Arcite anon unto his inn doth fare.
As fain as fowl is of the brighte sun. glad

And right anon such strife there is begun
For thilke granting, in the heav'n above, that
Betwixte Venus the goddess of love,
And Mars the sterne god armipotent,
That Jupiter was busy it to stent: stop
Till that the pale Saturnus the cold,[70]
That knew so many of adventures old,
Found in his old experience such an art,
That he full soon hath pleased every part.
As sooth is said, eld hath great advantage, age
In eld is bothe wisdom and usage: experience
Men may the old out-run, but not out-rede. outwit
Saturn anon, to stint the strife and drede,
Albeit that it is against his kind, nature
Of all this strife gan a remedy find.
"My deare daughter Venus," quoth Saturn,
"My course, that hath so wide for to turn, orbit[71]

Hath more power than wot any man.
Mine is the drowning in the sea so wan;
Mine is the prison in the darke cote, cell
Mine the strangling and hanging by the throat,
The murmur, and the churlish rebelling,
The groyning, and the privy poisoning. discontent
I do vengeance and plein correction, full
I dwell in the sign of the lion.
Mine is the ruin of the highe halls,
The falling of the towers and the walls
Upon the miner or the carpenter:
I slew Samson in shaking the pillar:
Mine also be the maladies cold,
The darke treasons, and the castes old: plots
My looking is the father of pestilence.
Now weep no more, I shall do diligence
That Palamon, that is thine owen knight,
Shall have his lady, as thou hast him hight. promised
Though Mars shall help his knight, yet natheless
Betwixte you there must sometime be peace:
All be ye not of one complexion,
That each day causeth such division,
I am thine ayel, ready at thy will; grandfather[72]
Weep now no more, I shall thy lust fulfil." pleasure
Now will I stenten of the gods above, cease speaking
Of Mars, and of Venus, goddess of love,
And telle you as plainly as I can
The great effect, for which that I began.

Great was the feast in Athens thilke day; that
And eke the lusty season of that May
Made every wight to be in such pleasance,
That all that Monday jousten they and dance,
And spenden it in Venus' high service.
But by the cause that they shoulde rise
Early a-morrow for to see that fight,
Unto their reste wente they at night.
And on the morrow, when the day gan spring,
Of horse and harness noise and clattering armour
There was in the hostelries all about:
And to the palace rode there many a rout train, retinue
Of lordes, upon steedes and palfreys.
There mayst thou see devising of harness decoration
So uncouth and so rich, and wrought so weel unknown, rare
Of goldsmithry, of brouding, and of steel; embroidery
The shieldes bright, the testers, and trappures helmets[73]
Gold-hewen helmets, hauberks, coat-armures; trappings
Lordes in parements on their coursers, ornamental garb[74];

GEOFFREY CHAUCER

Knightes of retinue, and eke squiers,
Nailing the spears, and helmes buckeling,
Gniding of shieldes, with lainers lacing; polishing[75]
There as need is, they were nothing idle: lanyards
The foamy steeds upon the golden bridle
Gnawing, and fast the armourers also
With file and hammer pricking to and fro;
Yeomen on foot, and knaves many one servants
With shorte staves, thick as they may gon; close walk
Pipes, trumpets, nakeres, and clariouns, drums[76]
That in the battle blowe bloody souns;
The palace full of people up and down,
There three, there ten, holding their questioun, conversation
Divining of these Theban knightes two. conjecturing
Some saiden thus, some said it shall he so;
Some helden with him with the blacke beard,
Some with the bald, some with the thick-hair'd;
Some said he looked grim, and woulde fight:
He had a sparth of twenty pound of weight. double-headed axe
Thus was the halle full of divining conjecturing
Long after that the sunne gan up spring.
The great Theseus that of his sleep is waked
With minstrelsy, and noise that was maked,
Held yet the chamber of his palace rich,
Till that the Theban knightes both y-lich alike
Honoured were, and to the palace fet. fetched
Duke Theseus is at a window set,
Array'd right as he were a god in throne:
The people presseth thitherward full soon
Him for to see, and do him reverence,
And eke to hearken his hest and his sentence. command speech
An herald on a scaffold made an O,[77]
Till the noise of the people was y-do: done
And when he saw the people of noise all still,
Thus shewed he the mighty Duke's will.
"The lord hath of his high discretion
Considered that it were destruction
To gentle blood, to fighten in the guise
Of mortal battle now in this emprise:
Wherefore to shape that they shall not die, arrange, contrive
He will his firste purpose modify.
No man therefore, on pain of loss of life,
No manner shot, nor poleaxe, nor short knife kind of
Into the lists shall send, or thither bring.
Nor short sword for to stick with point biting
No man shall draw, nor bear it by his side.
And no man shall unto his fellow ride
But one course, with a sharp y-grounden spear:
Foin if him list on foot, himself to wear. He who wishes can
And he that is at mischief shall be take, fence on foot to defend
And not slain, but be brought unto the stake,
himself, and he that
That shall be ordained on either side; is in peril shall be taken
Thither he shall by force, and there abide.
And if so fall the chieftain be take should happen
On either side, or elles slay his make, equal, match
No longer then the tourneying shall last.
God speede you; go forth and lay on fast.
With long sword and with mace fight your fill.
Go now your way; this is the lordes will.
The voice of the people touched the heaven,
So loude cried they with merry steven: sound
God save such a lord that is so good,
He willeth no destruction of blood.

Up go the trumpets and the melody,
And to the listes rode the company
By ordinance, throughout the city large, in orderly array
Hanged with cloth of gold, and not with sarge. serge[78]
Full like a lord this noble Duke gan ride,
And these two Thebans upon either side:

And after rode the queen and Emily,
And after them another company
Of one and other, after their degree.
And thus they passed thorough that city
And to the listes came they by time:
It was not of the day yet fully prime. between 6 & 9 a.m.
When set was Theseus full rich and high,
Hippolyta the queen and Emily,
And other ladies in their degrees about,
Unto the seates presseth all the rout.
And westward, through the gates under Mart,
Arcite, and eke the hundred of his part,
With banner red, is enter'd right anon;
And in the selve moment Palamon self-same
Is, under Venus, eastward in the place,
With banner white, and hardy cheer and face expression
In all the world, to seeken up and down
So even without variatioun equal
There were such companies never tway.
For there was none so wise that coulde say
That any had of other avantage
Of worthiness, nor of estate, nor age,
So even were they chosen for to guess.
And in two ranges faire they them dress. they arranged themselves
When that their names read were every one, in two rows
That in their number guile were there none, fraud
Then were the gates shut, and cried was loud;
"Do now your devoir, younge knights proud

The heralds left their pricking up and down spurring their horses
Now ring the trumpet loud and clarioun.
There is no more to say, but east and west
In go the speares sadly in the rest; steadily
In go the sharpe spurs into the side.
There see me who can joust, and who can ride.
There shiver shaftes upon shieldes thick;
He feeleth through the hearte-spoon[79] the prick.
Up spring the speares twenty foot on height;
Out go the swordes as the silver bright.
The helmes they to-hewen, and to-shred; strike in pieces[80]
Out burst the blood, with sterne streames red.
With mighty maces the bones they to-brest. burst
He[81] through the thickest of the throng gan threst. thrust
There stumble steedes strong, and down go all.
He rolleth under foot as doth a ball.
He foineth on his foe with a trunchoun, forces himself
And he him hurtleth with his horse adown.
He through the body hurt is, and sith take, afterwards captured
Maugre his head, and brought unto the stake,
As forword was, right there he must abide. covenant
Another led is on that other side.
And sometime doth them Theseus to rest, caused
Them to refresh, and drinken if them lest. pleased
Full oft a day have thilke Thebans two
Together met and wrought each other woe:
Unhorsed hath each other of them tway twice
There is no tiger in the vale of Galaphay,[82]
When that her whelp is stole, when it is lite little
So cruel on the hunter, as Arcite
For jealous heart upon this Palamon:
Nor in Belmarie[83] there is no fell lion,
That hunted is, or for his hunger wood mad
Or for his prey desireth so the blood,
As Palamon to slay his foe Arcite.
The jealous strokes upon their helmets bite;
Out runneth blood on both their sides red,
Sometime an end there is of every deed
For ere the sun unto the reste went,
The stronge king Emetrius gan hent sieze, assail
This Palamon, as he fought with Arcite,
And made his sword deep in his flesh to bite,
And by the force of twenty is he take,
Unyielding, and is drawn unto the stake.
And in the rescue of this Palamon
The stronge king Licurgus is borne down:
And king Emetrius, for all his strength
Is borne out of his saddle a sword's length,
So hit him Palamon ere he were take:
But all for nought; he was brought to the stake:
His hardy hearte might him helpe naught,
He must abide when that he was caught,
By force, and eke by composition. the bargain

Who sorroweth now but woful Palamon
That must no more go again to fight?
And when that Theseus had seen that sight
Unto the folk that foughte thus each one,
He cried, Ho! no more, for it is done!
I will be true judge, and not party.
Arcite of Thebes shall have Emily,
That by his fortune hath her fairly won."
Anon there is a noise of people gone,
For joy of this, so loud and high withal,
It seemed that the listes shoulde fall.

What can now faire Venus do above?
What saith she now? what doth this queen of love?
But weepeth so, for wanting of her will,
Till that her teares in the listes fill fall
She said: "I am ashamed doubteless."
Saturnus saide: "Daughter, hold thy peace.
Mars hath his will, his knight hath all his boon,
And by mine head thou shalt be eased soon."
The trumpeters with the loud minstrelsy,
The heralds, that full loude yell and cry,
Be in their joy for weal of Dan Arcite. Lord
But hearken me, and stinte noise a lite,
What a miracle there befell anon
This fierce Arcite hath off his helm y-done,
And on a courser for to shew his face
He pricketh endelong the large place, rides from end to end
Looking upward upon this Emily;
And she again him cast a friendly eye
(For women, as to speaken in commune, generally
They follow all the favour of fortune),
And was all his in cheer, as his in heart. countenance
Out of the ground a fire infernal start,
From Pluto sent, at request of Saturn
For which his horse for fear began to turn,
And leap aside, and founder as he leap stumble
And ere that Arcite may take any keep, care
He pight him on the pummel of his head. pitched top
That in the place he lay as he were dead.
His breast to-bursten with his saddle-bow.
As black he lay as any coal or crow,
So was the blood y-run into his face.
Anon he was y-borne out of the place
With hearte sore, to Theseus' palace.
Then was he carven out of his harness. cut
And in a bed y-brought full fair and blive quickly
For he was yet in mem'ry and alive,
And always crying after Emily.

Duke Theseus, with all his company,
Is come home to Athens his city,
With alle bliss and great solemnity.
Albeit that this aventure was fall, befallen
He woulde not discomforte them all discourage

29

GEOFFREY CHAUCER

Then said eke, that Arcite should not die,
He should be healed of his malady.
And of another thing they were as fain.   glad
That of them alle was there no one slain,
All were they sorely hurt, and namely one,   although especially
That with a spear was thirled his breast-bone.   pierced
To other woundes, and to broken arms,
Some hadden salves, and some hadden charms:
And pharmacies of herbs, and eke save sage,   Salvia officinalis
They dranken, for they would their lives have.
For which this noble Duke, as he well can,
Comforteth and honoureth every man,
And made revel all the longe night,
Unto the strange lordes, as was right.
Nor there was holden no discomforting,
But as at jousts or at a tourneying;
For soothly there was no discomfiture,
For falling is not but an aventure.   chance, accident
Nor to be led by force unto a stake
Unyielding, and with twenty knights y-take
One person all alone, withouten mo',
And harried forth by armes, foot, and toe,   dragged, hurried
And eke his steede driven forth with staves,
With footmen, bothe yeomen and eke knaves,   servants
It was aretted him no villainy: counted no disgrace to him
There may no man clepen it cowardy.   call it cowardice
For which anon Duke Theseus let cry, —   caused to be proclaimed
To stenten alle rancour and envy, —   stop
The gree as well on one side as the other,   prize, merit
And either side alike as other's brother:
And gave them giftes after their degree,
And held a feaste fully dayes three:
And conveyed the kinges worthily
Out of his town a journee   largely day's journey
And home went every man the righte way,
There was no more but "Farewell, Have good day."
Of this bataille I will no more indite
But speak of Palamon and of Arcite.

Swelleth the breast of Arcite and the sore
Increaseth at his hearte more and more.
The clotted blood, for any leache-craft   surgical skill
Corrupteth and is in his bouk y-laft   left in his body
That neither veine blood nor ventousing,   blood-letting or cupping
Nor drink of herbes may be his helping.

The virtue expulsive or animal,
From thilke virtue called natural,
Nor may the venom voide, nor expel
The pipes of his lungs began to swell
And every lacert in his breast adown   sinew, muscle
Is shent with venom and corruption.   destroyed
Him gaineth neither, for to get his life,   availeth
Vomit upward, nor downward laxative;
All is to-bursten thilke region;
Nature hath now no domination.
And certainly where nature will not wirch,   work
Farewell physic: go bear the man to chirch.   church
This all and some is, Arcite must die.
For which he sendeth after Emily,
And Palamon, that was his cousin dear,
Then said he thus, as ye shall after hear.

"Nought may the woful spirit in mine heart
Declare one point of all my sorrows' smart
To you, my lady, that I love the most:
But I bequeath the service of my ghost
To you aboven every creature,
Since that my life ne may no longer dure.
Alas the woe! alas, the paines strong
That I for you have suffered and so long!
Alas the death, alas, mine Emily!
Alas departing of our company! the severance
Alas, mine hearte's queen! alas, my wife!
Mine hearte's lady, ender of my life!
What is this world? what aske men to have?
Now with his love, now in his colde grave
Al one, withouten any company.
Farewell, my sweet, farewell, mine Emily,
And softly take me in your armes tway,
For love of God, and hearken what I say.
I have here with my cousin Palamon
Had strife and rancour many a day agone,
For love of you, and for my jealousy.
And Jupiter so wis my soule gie,   surely guides my soul
To speaken of a servant properly,
With alle circumstances truely,
That is to say, truth, honour, and knighthead,
Wisdom, humbless, estate, and high kindred,   humility
Freedom, and all that longeth to that art,
So Jupiter have of my soul part,
As in this world right now I know not one,
So worthy to be lov'd as Palamon,
That serveth you, and will do all his life.
And if that you shall ever be a wife,
Forget not Palamon, the gentle man."

And with that word his speech to fail began.
For from his feet up to his breast was come
The cold of death, that had him overnome.   overcome
And yet moreover in his armes two

THE CANTERBURY TALES

The vital strength is lost, and all ago. gone
Only the intellect, withoute more,
That dwelled in his hearte sick and sore,
Gan faile, when the hearte felte death;
Dusked his eyen two, and fail'd his breath. grew dim
But on his lady yet he cast his eye;
His laste word was; "Mercy, Emily!"
His spirit changed house, and wente there,
As I came never I cannot telle where.[84]
Therefore I stent, I am no diminister; refrain diviner
Of soules find I nought in this register.
Ne me list not th' opinions to tell
Of them, though that they writen where they dwell;
Arcite is cold, there Mars his soule gie. guide
Now will I speake forth of Emily.

Shriek'd Emily, and howled Palamon,
And Theseus his sister took anon
Swooning, and bare her from the corpse away.
What helpeth it to tarry forth the day,
To telle how she wept both eve and morrow?
For in such cases women have such sorrow,
When that their husbands be from them y-go, gone
That for the more part they sorrow so,
Or elles fall into such malady,
That at the laste certainly they die.
Infinite be the sorrows and the tears
Of olde folk, and folk of tender years,
In all the town, for death of this Theban:
For him there weepeth bothe child and man.
So great a weeping was there none certain,
When Hector was y-brought, all fresh y-slain,
To Troy: alas! the pity that was there,
Scratching of cheeks, and rending eke of hair.
"Why wouldest thou be dead?" these women cry,
"And haddest gold enough, and Emily."
No manner man might gladden Theseus,
Saving his olde father Egeus,
That knew this worlde's transmutatioun,
As he had seen it changen up and down,
Joy after woe, and woe after gladness;
And shewed him example and likeness.
"Right as there died never man," quoth he,
"That he ne liv'd in earth in some degree, rank, condition
Right so there lived never man," he said,
"In all this world, that sometime be not died.
This world is but a throughfare full of woe,
And we be pilgrims, passing to and fro:
Death is an end of every worldly sore."
And over all this said he yet much more
To this effect, full wisely to exhort
The people, that they should them recomfort.
Duke Theseus, with all his busy cure, care
Casteth about, where that the sepulture

deliberates
Of good Arcite may best y-maked be,
And eke most honourable in his degree.
And at the last he took conclusion,
That there as first Arcite and Palamon
Hadde for love the battle them between,
That in that selve grove, sweet and green, self-same
There as he had his amorous desires,
His complaint, and for love his hote fires,
He woulde make a fire, in which th' office funeral pyre
Of funeral he might all accomplice;
And let anon command to hack and hew immediately gave orders
The oakes old, and lay them on a rew in a row
In culpons, well arrayed for to brenne. logs burn
His officers with swifte feet they renne run
And ride anon at his commandement.
And after this, Duke Theseus hath sent
After a bier, and it all oversprad
With cloth of gold, the richest that he had;
And of the same suit he clad Arcite.
Upon his handes were his gloves white,
Eke on his head a crown of laurel green,
And in his hand a sword full bright and keen.
He laid him bare the visage on the bier, with face uncovered
Therewith he wept, that pity was to hear.
And, for the people shoulde see him all,
When it was day he brought them to the hall,
That roareth of the crying and the soun'.
Then came this woful Theban, Palamon,
With sluttery beard, and ruggy ashy hairs,[85]
In clothes black, y-dropped all with tears,
And (passing over weeping Emily)
The ruefullest of all the company.
And inasmuch as the service should be in order that
The more noble and rich in its degree,
Duke Theseus let forth three steedes bring,
That trapped were in steel all glittering.
And covered with the arms of Dan Arcite.
Upon these steedes, that were great and white,
There satte folk, of whom one bare his shield,
Another his spear in his handes held;
The thirde bare with him his bow Turkeis, Turkish.
Of brent gold was the case and the harness: burnished quiver
And ride forth a pace with sorrowful cheer at a foot pace
Toward the grove, as ye shall after hear. expression

The noblest of the Greekes that there were
Upon their shoulders carried the bier,
With slacke pace, and eyen red and wet,
Throughout the city, by the master street, main[86]

31

GEOFFREY CHAUCER

That spread was all with black, and wondrous high
Right of the same is all the street y-wrie. covered[87]
Upon the right hand went old Egeus,
And on the other side Duke Theseus,
With vessels in their hand of gold full fine,
All full of honey, milk, and blood, and wine;
Eke Palamon, with a great company;
And after that came woful Emily,
With fire in hand, as was that time the guise, custom
To do th' office of funeral service.

High labour, and full great appareling preparation
Was at the service, and the pyre-making,
That with its greene top the heaven raught, reached
And twenty fathom broad its armes straught: stretched
This is to say, the boughes were so broad.
Of straw first there was laid many a load.
But how the pyre was maked up on height,
And eke the names how the trees hight, were called
As oak, fir, birch, asp, alder, holm, poplere, aspen
Willow, elm, plane, ash, box, chestnut, lind, laurere, linden, lime
Maple, thorn, beech, hazel, yew, whipul tree,
How they were fell'd, shall not be told for me;
Nor how the goddes rannen up and down the forest deities
Disinherited of their habitatioun,
In which they wonned had in rest and peace, dwelt
Nymphes, Faunes, and Hamadryades;
Nor how the beastes and the birdes all
Fledden for feare, when the wood gan fall;
Nor how the ground aghast was of the light, terrified
That was not wont to see the sunne bright;
Nor how the fire was couched first with stre, laid straw
And then with dry stickes cloven in three,
And then with greene wood and spicery, spices
And then with cloth of gold and with pierrie, precious stones
And garlands hanging with full many a flower,
The myrrh, the incense with so sweet odour;
Nor how Arcita lay among all this,
Nor what richess about his body is;
Nor how that Emily, as was the guise, custom
Put in the fire of funeral service[88]; appplied the torch
Nor how she swooned when she made the fire,
Nor what she spake, nor what was her desire;
Nor what jewels men in the fire then cast
When that the fire was great and burned fast;

Nor how some cast their shield, and some their spear,
And of their vestiments, which that they wear,
And cuppes full of wine, and milk, and blood,
Into the fire, that burnt as it were wood; mad
Nor how the Greekes with a huge rout procession
Three times riden all the fire about[89]
Upon the left hand, with a loud shouting,
And thries with their speares clattering;
And thries how the ladies gan to cry;
Nor how that led was homeward Emily;
Nor how Arcite is burnt to ashes cold;
Nor how the lyke-wake was y-hold wake[90]
All thilke night, nor how the Greekes play that
The wake-plays, ne keep I not to say: funeral games care
Who wrestled best naked, with oil anoint,
Nor who that bare him best in no disjoint. in any contest
I will not tell eke how they all are gone
Home to Athenes when the play is done;
But shortly to the point now will I wend, come
And maken of my longe tale an end.

By process and by length of certain years
All stinted is the mourning and the tears ended
Of Greekes, by one general assent.
Then seemed me there was a parlement
At Athens, upon certain points and cas: cases
Amonge the which points y-spoken was
To have with certain countries alliance,
And have of Thebans full obeisance.
For which this noble Theseus anon
Let send after the gentle Palamon, caused
Unwist of him what was the cause and why: unknown
But in his blacke clothes sorrowfully
He came at his commandment on hie; in haste
Then sente Theseus for Emily.
When they were set, and hush'd was all the place seated
And Theseus abided had a space waited
Ere any word came from his wise breast
His eyen set he there as was his lest, he cast his eyes
And with a sad visage he sighed still, wherever he pleased
And after that right thus he said his will.
"The firste mover of the cause above
When he first made the faire chain of love,
Great was th' effect, and high was his intent;
Well wist he why, and what thereof he meant:
For with that faire chain of love he bond bound
The fire, the air, the water, and the lond
In certain bondes, that they may not flee:[91]
That same prince and mover eke," quoth he,
"Hath stablish'd, in this wretched world adown,
Certain of dayes and duration

32

THE CANTERBURY TALES

To all that are engender'd in this place,
Over the whiche day they may not pace, pass
All may they yet their dayes well abridge.
There needeth no authority to allege
For it is proved by experience;
But that me list declare my sentence. opinion
Then may men by this order well discern,
That thilke mover stable is and etern. the same
Well may men know, but that it be a fool,
That every part deriveth from its whole.
For nature hath not ta'en its beginning
Of no partie nor cantle of a thing, part or piece
But of a thing that perfect is and stable,
Descending so, till it be corruptable.
And therefore of His wise purveyance providence
He hath so well beset his ordinance,
That species of things and progressions
Shallen endure by successions,
And not etern, withouten any lie:
This mayst thou understand and see at eye.
Lo th' oak, that hath so long a nourishing
From the time that it 'ginneth first to spring,
And hath so long a life, as ye may see,
Yet at the last y-wasted is the tree.
Consider eke, how that the harde stone
Under our feet, on which we tread and gon, walk
Yet wasteth, as it lieth by the way.
The broade river some time waxeth drey. dry
The greate townes see we wane and wend. go, disappear
Then may ye see that all things have an end.
Of man and woman see we well also, —
That needes in one of the termes two, —
That is to say, in youth or else in age,-
He must be dead, the king as shall a page;
Some in his bed, some in the deepe sea,
Some in the large field, as ye may see:
There helpeth nought, all go that ilke way: same
Then may I say that alle thing must die.
What maketh this but Jupiter the king?
The which is prince, and cause of alle thing,
Converting all unto his proper will,
From which it is derived, sooth to tell
And hereagainst no creature alive,
Of no degree, availeth for to strive.
Then is it wisdom, as it thinketh me,
To make a virtue of necessity,
And take it well, that we may not eschew, escape
And namely what to us all is due.
And whoso grudgeth ought, he doth folly, murmurs at
And rebel is to him that all may gie. direct, guide
And certainly a man hath most honour
To dien in his excellence and flower,
When he is sicker of his goode name. certain
Then hath he done his friend, nor him, no shame himself
And gladder ought his friend be of his death,
When with honour is yielded up his breath,
Than when his name appalled is for age; decayed by old age
For all forgotten is his vassalage. valour, service
Then is it best, as for a worthy fame,
To dien when a man is best of name.
The contrary of all this is wilfulness.
Why grudge we, why have we heaviness,
That good Arcite, of chivalry the flower,
Departed is, with duty and honour,
Out of this foule prison of this life?
Why grudge here his cousin and his wife
Of his welfare, that loved him so well?
Can he them thank? nay, God wot, neverdeal, — not a jot
That both his soul and eke themselves offend, hurt
And yet they may their lustes not amend. desires control
What may I conclude of this longe serie, string of remarks
But after sorrow I rede us to be merry, counsel
And thanke Jupiter for all his grace?
And ere that we departe from this place,
I rede that we make of sorrows two
One perfect joye lasting evermo':
And look now where most sorrow is herein,
There will I first amenden and begin.
"Sister," quoth he, "this is my full assent,
With all th' advice here of my parlement,
That gentle Palamon, your owen knight,
That serveth you with will, and heart, and might,
And ever hath, since first time ye him knew,
That ye shall of your grace upon him rue, take pity
And take him for your husband and your lord:
Lend me your hand, for this is our accord.
Let see now of your womanly pity. make display
He is a kinge's brother's son, pardie. by God
And though he were a poore bachelere,
Since he hath served you so many a year,
And had for you so great adversity,
It muste be considered, 'lieveth me. believe me
For gentle mercy oweth to passen right." ought to be rightly
Then said he thus to Palamon the knight; directed
"I trow there needeth little sermoning
To make you assente to this thing.
Come near, and take your lady by the hand."
Betwixte them was made anon the band,
That hight matrimony or marriage,
By all the counsel of the baronage.
And thus with alle bliss and melody
Hath Palamon y-wedded Emily.
And God, that all this wide world hath wrought,
Send him his love, that hath it dearly bought.
For now is Palamon in all his weal,
Living in bliss, in riches, and in heal. health
And Emily him loves so tenderly,
And he her serveth all so gentilly,

33

GEOFFREY CHAUCER

That never was there worde them between
Of jealousy, nor of none other teen. cause of anger

Thus endeth Palamon and Emily
And God save all this faire company.

Notes to The Knight's Tale.

1. For the plan and principal incidents of the "Knight's Tale," Chaucer was indebted to Boccaccio, who had himself borrowed from some prior poet, chronicler, or romancer. Boccaccio speaks of the story as "very ancient;" and, though that may not be proof of its antiquity, it certainly shows that he took it from an earlier writer. The "Tale" is more or less a paraphrase of Boccaccio's "Theseida;" but in some points the copy has a distinct dramatic superiority over the original. The "Theseida" contained ten thousand lines; Chaucer has condensed it into less than one-fourth of the number. The "Knight's Tale" is supposed to have been at first composed as a separate work; it is undetermined whether Chaucer took it direct from the Italian of Boccaccio, or from a French translation.
2. Highte: was called; from the Anglo-Saxon "hatan", to bid or call; German, "Heissen", "heisst".
3. Feminie: The "Royaume des Femmes" — kingdom of the Amazons. Gower, in the "Confessio Amantis," styles Penthesilea the "Queen of Feminie."
4. Wonnen: Won, conquered; German "gewonnen."
5. Ear: To plough; Latin, "arare." "I have abundant matter for discourse." The first, and half of the second, of Boccaccio's twelve books are disposed of in the few lines foregoing.
6. Waimenting: bewailing; German, "wehklagen"
7. Starf: died; German, "sterben," "starb".
8. The Minotaur: The monster, half-man and half-bull, which yearly devoured a tribute of fourteen Athenian youths and maidens, until it was slain by Theseus.
9. Pillers: pillagers, strippers; French, "pilleurs."
10. The donjon was originally the central tower or "keep" of feudal castles; it was employed to detain prisoners of importance. Hence the modern meaning of the word dungeon.
11. Saturn, in the old astrology, was a most unpropitious star to be born under.
12. To die in the pain was a proverbial expression in the French, used as an alternative to enforce a resolution or a promise. Edward III., according to Froissart, declared that he would either succeed in the war against France or die in the pain — "Ou il mourroit en la peine." It was the fashion in those times to swear oaths of friendship and brotherhood; and hence, though the fashion has long died out, we still speak of "sworn friends."
13. The saying of the old scholar Boethius, in his treatise "De Consolatione Philosophiae", which Chaucer translated, and from which he has freely borrowed in his poetry. The words are "Quis legem det amantibus? Major lex amor est sibi." ("Who can give law to lovers? Love is a law unto himself, and greater")
14. "Perithous" and "Theseus" must, for the metre, be pronounced as words of four and three syllables respectively — the vowels at the end not being diphthongated, but enunciated separately, as if the words were printed Pe-ri-tho-us, The-se-us. The same rule applies in such words as "creature" and "conscience," which are trisyllables.
15. Stound: moment, short space of time; from Anglo-Saxon, "stund;" akin to which is German, "Stunde," an hour.
16. Meinie: servants, or menials, &c., dwelling together in a house; from an Anglo-Saxon word meaning a crowd. Compare German, "Menge," multitude.
17. The pure fetters: the very fetters. The Greeks used "katharos", the Romans "purus," in the same sense.
18. In the medieval courts of Love, to which allusion is probably made forty lines before, in the word "parlement," or "parliament," questions like that here proposed were seriously discussed.
19. Gear: behaviour, fashion, dress; but, by another reading, the word is "gyre," and means fit, trance — from the Latin, "gyro," I turn round.
20. Before his head in his cell fantastic: in front of his head in his cell of fantasy. "The division of the brain into cells, according to the different sensitive faculties," says Mr Wright, "is very ancient, and is found depicted in mediaeval manuscripts." In a manuscript in the Harleian Library, it is stated, "Certum est in prora cerebri esse fantasiam, in medio rationem discretionis, in puppi memoriam" (it is certain that in the front of the brain is imagination, in the middle reason, in the back memory) — a classification not materially differing from that of modern phrenologists.
21. Dan: Lord; Latin, "Dominus;" Spanish, "Don."
22. The "caduceus."

23. Argus was employed by Juno to watch Io with his hundred eyes but he was sent to sleep by the flute of Mercury, who then cut off his head.
24. Next: nearest; German, "naechste".
25. Clary: hippocras, wine made with spices.
26. Warray: make war; French "guerroyer", to molest; hence, perhaps, "to worry."
27. All day meeten men at unset steven: every day men meet at unexpected time. "To set a steven," is to fix a time, make an appointment.
28. Roundelay: song coming round again to the words with which it opened.
29. Now in the crop and now down in the breres: Now in the tree-top, now down in the briars. "Crop and root," top and bottom, is used to express the perfection or totality of anything.
30. Beknow: avow, acknowledge: German, "bekennen."
31. Shapen was my death erst than my shert: My death was decreed before my shirt ws shaped — that is, before any clothes were made for me, before my birth.
32. Regne: Queen; French, "Reine;" Venus is meant. The common reading, however, is "regne," reign or power.
33. Launde: plain. Compare modern English, "lawn," and French, "Landes" — flat, bare marshy tracts in the south of France.
34. Mister: manner, kind; German "muster," sample, model.
35. In listes: in the lists, prepared for such single combats between champion and accuser, &c.
36. Thilke: that, contracted from "the ilke," the same.
37. Mars the Red: referring to the ruddy colour of the planet, to which was doubtless due the transference to it of the name of the God of War. In his "Republic," enumerating the seven planets, Cicero speaks of the propitious and beneficent light of Jupiter: "Tum (fulgor) rutilis horribilisque terris, quem Martium dicitis" — "Then the red glow, horrible to the nations, which you say to be that of Mars." Boccaccio opens the "Theseida" by an invocation to "rubicondo Marte."
38. Last: lace, leash, noose, snare: from Latin, "laceus."
39. "Round was the shape, in manner of compass, Full of degrees, the height of sixty pas" The building was a circle of steps or benches, as in the ancient amphitheatre. Either the building was sixty paces high; or, more probably, there were sixty of the steps or benches.
40. Yellow goldes: The sunflower, turnsol, or girasol, which turns with and seems to watch the sun, as a jealous lover his mistress.
41. Citheron: The Isle of Venus, Cythera, in the Aegean Sea; now called Cerigo: not, as Chaucer's form of the word might imply, Mount Cithaeron, in the south-west of Boetia, which was appropriated to other deities than Venus — to Jupiter, to Bacchus, and the Muses.
42. It need not be said that Chaucer pays slight heed to chronology in this passage, where the deeds of Turnus, the glory of King Solomon, and the fate of Croesus are made memories of the far past in the time of fabulous Theseus, the Minotaur-slayer.
43. Champartie: divided power or possession; an old law-term, signifying the maintenance of a person in a law suit on the condition of receiving part of the property in dispute, if recovered.
44. Citole: a kind of dulcimer.
45. The picke-purse: The plunderers that followed armies, and gave to war a horror all their own.
46. Shepen: stable; Anglo-Saxon, "scypen;" the word "sheppon" still survives in provincial parlance.
47. This line, perhaps, refers to the deed of Jael.
48. The shippes hoppesteres: The meaning is dubious. We may understand "the dancing ships," "the ships that hop" on the waves; "steres" being taken as the feminine adjectival termination: or we may, perhaps, read, with one of the manuscripts, "the ships upon the steres" — that is, even as they are being steered, or on the open sea — a more picturesque notion.
49. Freting: devouring; the Germans use "Fressen" to mean eating by animals, "essen" by men.
50. Julius: i.e. Julius Caesar
51. Puella and Rubeus were two figures in geomancy, representing two constellations-the one signifying Mars retrograde, the other Mars direct.
52. Calistope: or Callisto, daughter of Lycaon, seduced by Jupiter, turned into a bear by Diana, and placed afterwards, with her son, as the Great Bear among the stars.
53. Dane: Daphne, daughter of the river-god Peneus, in Thessaly; she was beloved by Apollo, but to avoid his pursuit, she was, at her own prayer, changed into a laurel-tree.
54. As the goddess of Light, or the goddess who brings to light, Diana — as well as Juno — was invoked by women in childbirth: so Horace, Odes iii. 22, says:—

"Montium custos nemorumque, Virgo,
Quae laborantes utero puellas

Ter vocata audis adimisque leto,
Diva triformis."
("Virgin custodian of hills and groves, three-formed goddess who hears and saves from death young women who call upon her thrice when in childbirth")

55. Every deal: in every part; "deal" corresponds to the German "Theil" a portion.
56. Sikerly: surely; German, "sicher;" Scotch, "sikkar," certain. When Robert Bruce had escaped from England to assume the Scottish crown, he stabbed Comyn before the altar at Dumfries; and, emerging from the church, was asked by his friend Kirkpatrick if he had slain the traitor. "I doubt it," said Bruce. "Doubt," cried Kirkpatrick. "I'll mak sikkar;" and he rushed into the church, and despatched Comyn with repeated thrusts of his dagger.
57. Kemped: combed; the word survives in "unkempt."
58. Alauns: greyhounds, mastiffs; from the Spanish word "Alano," signifying a mastiff.
59. Y-ment: mixed; German, "mengen," to mix.
60. Prime: The time of early prayers, between six and nine in the morning.
61. On the dais: see note 32 to the Prologue.
62. In her hour: in the hour of the day (two hours before daybreak) which after the astrological system that divided the twenty-four among the seven ruling planets, was under the influence of Venus.
63. Adon: Adonis, a beautiful youth beloved of Venus, whose death by the tusk of a boar she deeply mourned.
64. The third hour unequal: In the third planetary hour; Palamon had gone forth in the hour of Venus, two hours before daybreak; the hour of Mercury intervened; the third hour was that of Luna, or Diana. "Unequal" refers to the astrological division of day and night, whatever their duration, into twelve parts, which of necessity varied in length with the season.
65. Smoking: draping; hence the word "smock;" "smokless," in Chaucer, means naked.
66. Cerrial: of the species of oak which Pliny, in his "Natural History," calls "cerrus."
67. Stace of Thebes: Statius, the Roman who embodied in the twelve books of his "Thebaid" the ancient legends connected with the war of the seven against Thebes.
68. Diana was Luna in heaven, Diana on earth, and Hecate in hell; hence the direction of the eyes of her statue to "Pluto's dark region." Her statue was set up where three ways met, so that with a different face she looked down each of the three; from which she was called Trivia. See the quotation from Horace, note 54.
69. Las: net; the invisible toils in which Hephaestus caught Ares and the faithless Aphrodite, and exposed them to the "inextinguishable laughter" of Olympus.
70. Saturnus the cold: Here, as in "Mars the Red" we have the person of the deity endowed with the supposed quality of the planet called after his name.
71. The astrologers ascribed great power to Saturn, and predicted "much debate" under his ascendancy; hence it was "against his kind" to compose the heavenly strife.
72. Ayel: grandfather; French "Aieul".
73. Testers: Helmets; from the French "teste", "tete", head.
74. Parements: ornamental garb, French "parer" to deck.
75. Gniding: Rubbing, polishing; Anglo-Saxon "gnidan", to rub.
76. Nakeres: Drums, used in the cavalry; Boccaccio's word is "nachere".
77. Made an O: Ho! Ho! to command attention; like "oyez", the call for silence in law-courts or before proclamations.
78. Sarge: serge, a coarse woollen cloth
79. Heart-spoon: The concave part of the breast, where the lower ribs join the cartilago ensiformis.
80. To-hewen and to-shred: "to" before a verb implies extraordinary violence in the action denoted.
81. He through the thickest of the throng etc.. "He" in this passage refers impersonally to any of the combatants.
82. Galaphay: Galapha, in Mauritania.
83. Belmarie is supposed to have been a Moorish state in Africa; but "Palmyrie" has been suggested as the correct reading.
84. As I came never I cannot telle where: Where it went I cannot tell you, as I was not there. Tyrwhitt thinks that Chaucer is sneering at Boccacio's pompous account of the passage of Arcite's soul to heaven. Up to this point, the description of the death-scene is taken literally from the "Theseida."
85. With sluttery beard, and ruggy ashy hairs: With neglected beard, and rough hair strewn with ashes. "Flotery" is the general reading; but "sluttery" seems to be more in keeping with the picture of abandonment to grief.
86. Master street: main street; so Froissart speaks of "le souverain carrefour."

87. Y-wrie: covered, hid; Anglo-Saxon, "wrigan," to veil.
88. Emily applied the funeral torch. The "guise" was, among the ancients, for the nearest relative of the deceased to do this, with averted face.
89. It was the custom for soldiers to march thrice around the funeral pile of an emperor or general; "on the left hand" is added, in reference to the belief that the left hand was propitious — the Roman augur turning his face southward, and so placing on his left hand the east, whence good omens came. With the Greeks, however, their augurs facing the north, it was just the contrary. The confusion, frequent in classical writers, is complicated here by the fact that Chaucer's description of the funeral of Arcite is taken from Statius' "Thebaid" — from a Roman's account of a Greek solemnity.
90. Lyke-wake: watching by the remains of the dead; from Anglo-Saxon, "lice," a corpse; German, "Leichnam."
91. Chaucer here borrows from Boethius, who says: "Hanc rerum seriem ligat, Terras ac pelagus regens, Et coelo imperitans, amor." (Love ties these things together: the earth, and the ruling sea, and the imperial heavens)

GEOFFREY CHAUCER

The Miller's Tale.

The Prologue.

When that the Knight had thus his tale told
In all the rout was neither young nor old,
That he not said it was a noble story,
And worthy to be drawn to memory; recorded
And namely the gentles every one. especially the gentlefolk
Our Host then laugh'd and swore, "So may I gon, prosper
This goes aright; unbuckled is the mail; the budget is opened
Let see now who shall tell another tale:
For truely this game is well begun.
Now telleth ye, Sir Monk, if that ye conne, know
Somewhat, to quiten with the Knighte's tale." match
The Miller that fordrunken was all pale,
So that unnethes upon his horse he sat, with difficulty
He would avalen neither hood nor hat, uncover
Nor abide no man for his courtesy, give way to
But in Pilate's voice[1] he gan to cry,
And swore by armes, and by blood, and bones,
"I can a noble tale for the nones occasion,
With which I will now quite the Knighte's tale." match
Our Host saw well how drunk he was of ale,
And said; "Robin, abide, my leve brother, dear
Some better man shall tell us first another:
Abide, and let us worke thriftly."
By Godde's soul," quoth he, "that will not I,
For I will speak, or elles go my way!"
Our Host answer'd; "Tell on a devil way; devil take you!
Thou art a fool; thy wit is overcome."
"Now hearken," quoth the Miller, "all and some:
But first I make a protestatioun.
That I am drunk, I know it by my soun':
And therefore if that I misspeak or say,
Wite it the ale of Southwark, I you pray: blame it on[2]
For I will tell a legend and a life
Both of a carpenter and of his wife,
How that a clerk hath set the wrighte's cap." fooled the carpenter
The Reeve answer'd and saide, "Stint thy clap, hold your tongue

Let be thy lewed drunken harlotry.
It is a sin, and eke a great folly
To apeiren any man, or him defame, injure
And eke to bringe wives in evil name.
Thou may'st enough of other thinges sayn."
This drunken Miller spake full soon again,
And saide, "Leve brother Osewold,
Who hath no wife, he is no cuckold.
But I say not therefore that thou art one;
There be full goode wives many one.
Why art thou angry with my tale now?
I have a wife, pardie, as well as thou,
Yet n'old I, for the oxen in my plough, I would not
Taken upon me more than enough,
To deemen of myself that I am one; judge
I will believe well that I am none.
An husband should not be inquisitive
Of Godde's privity, nor of his wife.
So he may finde Godde's foison there, treasure
Of the remnant needeth not to enquere."

What should I more say, but that this Millere
He would his wordes for no man forbear,
But told his churlish tale in his mannere; boorish, rude
Me thinketh, that I shall rehearse it here.
And therefore every gentle wight I pray,
For Godde's love to deem not that I say
Of evil intent, but that I must rehearse
Their tales all, be they better or worse,
Or elles falsen some of my mattere. falsify
And therefore whoso list it not to hear,
Turn o'er the leaf, and choose another tale;
For he shall find enough, both great and smale,
Of storial thing that toucheth gentiless, historical, true
And eke morality and holiness.
Blame not me, if that ye choose amiss.
The Miller is a churl, ye know well this,
So was the Reeve, with many other mo',
And harlotry they tolde bothe two. ribald tales
Avise you now, and put me out of blame; be warned
And eke men should not make earnest of game. jest, fun

Notes to the Prologue to the Miller's Tale

1. Pilate, an unpopular personage in the mystery-plays of the middle ages, was probably represented as having a gruff, harsh voice.
2. Wite: blame; in Scotland, "to bear the wyte," is to bear the blame.

THE TALE.

Whilom there was dwelling in Oxenford
A riche gnof, that guestes held to board, miser took in boarders
And of his craft he was a carpenter.
With him there was dwelling a poor scholer,
Had learned art, but all his fantasy
Was turned for to learn astrology.
He coude a certain of conclusions knew
To deeme by interrogations, determine
If that men asked him in certain hours,
When that men should have drought or elles show'rs:
Or if men asked him what shoulde fall
Of everything, I may not reckon all.

This clerk was called Hendy Nicholas; gentle, handsome
Of derne love he knew and of solace; secret, earnest
And therewith he was sly and full privy,
And like a maiden meek for to see.
A chamber had he in that hostelry
Alone, withouten any company,
Full fetisly y-dight with herbes swoot, neatly decorated
And he himself was sweet as is the root sweet
Of liquorice, or any setewall. valerian
His Almagest,[1] and bookes great and small,
His astrolabe,[2] belonging to his art,
His augrim stones,[3] layed fair apart
On shelves couched at his bedde's head, laid, set
His press y-cover'd with a falding red. coarse cloth
And all above there lay a gay psalt'ry
On which he made at nightes melody,
So sweetely, that all the chamber rang:
And Angelus ad virginem[4] he sang.
And after that he sung the kinge's note;
Full often blessed was his merry throat.
And thus this sweete clerk his time spent
After his friendes finding and his rent. Attending to his friends, and providing for the cost of his lodging
This carpenter had wedded new a wife,
Which that he loved more than his life:
Of eighteen year, I guess, she was of age.
Jealous he was, and held her narr'w in cage,
For she was wild and young, and he was old,
And deemed himself belike a cuckold. perhaps
He knew not Cato,[5] for his wit was rude,
That bade a man wed his similitude.
Men shoulde wedden after their estate,
For youth and eld are often at debate. age
But since that he was fallen in the snare,
He must endure (as other folk) his care.
Fair was this younge wife, and therewithal
As any weasel her body gent and small. slim, neat
A seint she weared, barred all of silk, girdle
A barm-cloth eke as white as morning milk apron[6]
Upon her lendes, full of many a gore. loins plait
White was her smock, and broider'd all before, robe or gown
And eke behind, on her collar about
Of coal-black silk, within and eke without.
The tapes of her white volupere head-kerchief[7]
Were of the same suit of her collere;
Her fillet broad of silk, and set full high:
And sickerly she had a likerous eye. certainly lascivious
Full small y-pulled were her browes two,
And they were bent, and black as any sloe. arched
She was well more blissful on to see pleasant to look upon
Than is the newe perjenete tree; young pear-tree
And softer than the wool is of a wether.
And by her girdle hung a purse of leather,
Tassel'd with silk, and pearled with latoun. set with brass pearls
In all this world to seeken up and down
There is no man so wise, that coude thenche fancy, think of
So gay a popelot, or such a wench. puppet[8]
Full brighter was the shining of her hue,
Than in the Tower the noble forged new. a gold coin[9]
But of her song, it was as loud and yern, lively[10]
As any swallow chittering on a bern. barn
Thereto she coulde skip, and make a game also romp
As any kid or calf following his dame.
Her mouth was sweet as braket,[11] or as methe mead
Or hoard of apples, laid in hay or heath.
Wincing she was as is a jolly colt, skittish
Long as a mast, and upright as a bolt.
A brooch she bare upon her low collere,
As broad as is the boss of a bucklere.
Her shoon were laced on her legges high;
She was a primerole, a piggesnie,[12] primrose
For any lord t' have ligging in his bed, lying
Or yet for any good yeoman to wed.

Now, sir, and eft sir, so befell the case, again
That on a day this Hendy Nicholas
Fell with this younge wife to rage and play, toy, play the rogue
While that her husband was at Oseney,[13]
As clerkes be full subtle and full quaint.
And privily he caught her by the queint, cunt
And said; "Y-wis, but if I have my will, assuredly
For derne love of thee, leman, I spill." for earnest love of thee
And helde her fast by the haunche bones, my mistress, I perish
And saide "Leman, love me well at once,

39

GEOFFREY CHAUCER

Or I will dien, all so God me save."
And she sprang as a colt doth in the trave[14];
And with her head she writhed fast away,
And said; "I will not kiss thee, by my fay. faith
Why let be," quoth she, "let be, Nicholas,
Or I will cry out harow and alas![15]
Do away your handes, for your courtesy."
This Nicholas gan mercy for to cry,
And spake so fair, and proffer'd him so fast,
That she her love him granted at the last,
And swore her oath by Saint Thomas of Kent,
That she would be at his commandement,
When that she may her leisure well espy.
"My husband is so full of jealousy,
That but ye waite well, and be privy, unless
I wot right well I am but dead," quoth she.
"Ye muste be full derne as in this case." secret
"Nay, thereof care thee nought," quoth Nicholas:
"A clerk had litherly beset his while, ill spent his time
But if he could a carpenter beguile." unless
And thus they were accorded and y-sworn
To wait a time, as I have said beforn.
When Nicholas had done thus every deal, whit
And thwacked her about the lendes well, loins
He kiss'd her sweet, and taketh his psalt'ry
And playeth fast, and maketh melody.
Then fell it thus, that to the parish church,
Of Christe's owen workes for to wirch, work
This good wife went upon a holy day;
Her forehead shone as bright as any day,
So was it washen, when she left her werk.

Now was there of that church a parish clerk,
The which that was y-cleped Absolon.
Curl'd was his hair, and as the gold it shone,
And strutted as a fanne large and broad; stretched
Full straight and even lay his jolly shode. head of hair
His rode was red, his eyen grey as goose, complexion
With Paule's windows carven on his shoes[16]
In hosen red he went full fetisly. daintily, neatly
Y-clad he was full small and properly,
All in a kirtle of a light waget; girdle sky blue
Full fair and thicke be the pointes set,
And thereupon he had a gay surplice,
As white as is the blossom on the rise. twig[17]
A merry child he was, so God me save;
Well could he letten blood, and clip, and shave,
And make a charter of land, and a quittance.
In twenty manners could he trip and dance,
After the school of Oxenforde tho,[18] then
And with his legges caste to and fro;
And playen songes on a small ribible; fiddle
Thereto he sung sometimes a loud quinible treble
And as well could he play on a gitern. guitar
In all the town was brewhouse nor tavern,
That he not visited with his solas, mirth, sport

There as that any garnard tapstere was. licentious barmaid
But sooth to say he was somedeal squaimous squeamish
Of farting, and of speeche dangerous.
This Absolon, that jolly was and gay,
Went with a censer on the holy day,
Censing the wives of the parish fast; burning incense for
And many a lovely look he on them cast,
And namely on this carpenter's wife: especially
To look on her him thought a merry life.
She was so proper, and sweet, and likerous.
I dare well say, if she had been a mouse,
And he a cat, he would her hent anon. have soon caught her
This parish clerk, this jolly Absolon,
Hath in his hearte such a love-longing!
That of no wife took he none offering;
For courtesy he said he woulde none.
The moon at night full clear and brighte shone,
And Absolon his gitern hath y-taken,
For paramours he thoughte for to waken,
And forth he went, jolif and amorous, joyous
Till he came to the carpentere's house,
A little after the cock had y-crow,
And dressed him under a shot window[19], stationed himself.
That was upon the carpentere's wall.
He singeth in his voice gentle and small;
"Now, dear lady, if thy will be,
I pray that ye will rue on me;" take pity
Full well accordant to his giterning.
This carpenter awoke, and heard him sing,
And spake unto his wife, and said anon,
What Alison, hear'st thou not Absolon,
That chanteth thus under our bower wall?" chamber
And she answer'd her husband therewithal;
"Yes, God wot, John, I hear him every deal."
This passeth forth; what will ye bet than well? better

From day to day this jolly Absolon
So wooeth her, that him is woebegone.
He waketh all the night, and all the day,
To comb his lockes broad, and make him gay.
He wooeth her by means and by brocage, by presents and by agents
And swore he woulde be her owen page.
He singeth brokking as a nightingale. quavering
He sent her piment[20], mead, and spiced ale,
And wafers piping hot out of the glede: cakes coals
And, for she was of town, he proffer'd meed.[21]
For some folk will be wonnen for richess,
And some for strokes, and some with gentiless.
Sometimes, to show his lightness and mast'ry,
He playeth Herod[22] on a scaffold high.

40

But what availeth him as in this case?
So loveth she the Hendy Nicholas,
That Absolon may blow the bucke's horn: "go whistle"
He had for all his labour but a scorn.
And thus she maketh Absolon her ape,
And all his earnest turneth to a jape. jest
Full sooth is this proverb, it is no lie;
Men say right thus alway; the nighe sly
Maketh oft time the far lief to be loth.23
For though that Absolon be wood or wroth mad
Because that he far was from her sight,
This nigh Nicholas stood still in his light.
Now bear thee well, thou Hendy Nicholas,
For Absolon may wail and sing "Alas!"

And so befell, that on a Saturday
This carpenter was gone to Oseney,
And Hendy Nicholas and Alison
Accorded were to this conclusion,
That Nicholas shall shape him a wile devise a stratagem
The silly jealous husband to beguile;
And if so were the game went aright,
She shoulde sleepen in his arms all night;
For this was her desire and his also.
And right anon, withoute wordes mo',
This Nicholas no longer would he tarry,
But doth full soft unto his chamber carry
Both meat and drinke for a day or tway.
And to her husband bade her for to say,
If that he asked after Nicholas,
She shoulde say, "She wist not where he was; knew
Of all the day she saw him not with eye;
She trowed he was in some malady, believed
For no cry that her maiden could him call
He would answer, for nought that might befall."
Thus passed forth all thilke Saturday, that
That Nicholas still in his chamber lay,
And ate, and slept, and didde what him list
Till Sunday, that the sunne went to rest. when
This silly carpenter had great marvaill wondered greatly
Of Nicholas, or what thing might him ail,
And said; "I am adrad, by Saint Thomas! afraid, in dread
It standeth not aright with Nicholas:
God shielde that he died suddenly. heaven forbid!
This world is now full fickle sickerly. certainly
I saw to-day a corpse y-borne to chirch,
That now on Monday last I saw him wirch. work
"Go up," quod he unto his knave, "anon; servant.
Clepe at his door, or knocke with a stone: call
Look how it is, and tell me boldely."
This knave went him up full sturdily,
And, at the chamber door while that he stood,
He cried and knocked as that he were wood: mad
"What how? what do ye, Master Nicholay?

How may ye sleepen all the longe day?"
But all for nought, he hearde not a word.
An hole he found full low upon the board,
Where as the cat was wont in for to creep,
And at that hole he looked in full deep,
And at the last he had of him a sight.
This Nicholas sat ever gaping upright,
As he had kyked on the newe moon. looked24
Adown he went, and told his master soon,
In what array he saw this ilke man. same

This carpenter to blissen him began, bless, cross himself
And said: "Now help us, Sainte Frideswide.25
A man wot little what shall him betide. knows
This man is fall'n with his astronomy
Into some woodness or some agony. madness
I thought aye well how that it shoulde be.
Men should know nought of Godde's privity. secrets
Yea, blessed be alway a lewed man, unlearned
That nought but only his believe can. knows no more
So far'd another clerk with astronomy: than his "credo."
He walked in the fieldes for to pry
Upon the starres, what there should befall, keep watch on
Till he was in a marle pit y-fall.26
He saw not that. But yet, by Saint Thomas!
Me rueth sore of Hendy Nicholas: I am very sorry for
He shall be rated of his studying, chidden for
If that I may, by Jesus, heaven's king!
Get me a staff, that I may underspore lever up
While that thou, Robin, heavest off the door:
He shall out of his studying, as I guess."
And to the chamber door he gan him dress apply himself.
His knave was a strong carl for the nonce,
And by the hasp he heav'd it off at once;
Into the floor the door fell down anon.
This Nicholas sat aye as still as stone,
And ever he gap'd upward into the air.
The carpenter ween'd he were in despair, thought
And hent him by the shoulders mightily, caught
And shook him hard, and cried spitously; angrily
"What, Nicholas? what how, man? look adown:
Awake, and think on Christe's passioun.
I crouche thee27 from elves, and from wights. witches
Therewith the night-spell said he anon rights, properly
On the four halves of the house about, corners
And on the threshold of the door without.
"Lord Jesus Christ, and Sainte Benedight,
Blesse this house from every wicked wight,
From the night mare, the white Pater-noster;
Where wonnest thou now, Sainte Peter's sister?"

41

dwellest
And at the last this Hendy Nicholas
Gan for to sigh full sore, and said; "Alas!
Shall all time world be lost eftsoones now?" forthwith
This carpenter answer'd; "What sayest thou?
What? think on God, as we do, men that swink." labour
This Nicholas answer'd; "Fetch me a drink;
And after will I speak in privity
Of certain thing that toucheth thee and me:
I will tell it no other man certain."

This carpenter went down, and came again,
And brought of mighty ale a large quart;
And when that each of them had drunk his part,
This Nicholas his chamber door fast shet, shut
And down the carpenter by him he set,
And saide; "John, mine host full lief and dear, loved
Thou shalt upon thy truthe swear me here,
That to no wight thou shalt my counsel wray: betray
For it is Christes counsel that I say,
And if thou tell it man, thou art forlore: lost[28]
For this vengeance thou shalt have therefor,
That if thou wraye me, thou shalt be wood." betray mad
"Nay, Christ forbid it for his holy blood!"
Quoth then this silly man; "I am no blab, talker
Nor, though I say it, am I lief to gab. fond of speech
Say what thou wilt, I shall it never tell
To child or wife, by him that harried Hell."[29]

"Now, John," quoth Nicholas, "I will not lie,
I have y-found in my astrology,
As I have looked in the moone bright,
That now on Monday next, at quarter night,
Shall fall a rain, and that so wild and wood, mad
That never half so great was Noe's flood.
This world," he said, "in less than half an hour
Shall all be dreint, so hideous is the shower: drowned
Thus shall mankinde drench, and lose their life." drown
This carpenter answer'd; "Alas, my wife!
And shall she drench? alas, mine Alisoun!"
For sorrow of this he fell almost adown,
And said; "Is there no remedy in this case?"
"Why, yes, for God," quoth Hendy Nicholas;
"If thou wilt worken after lore and rede; learning and advice
Thou may'st not worken after thine own head.
For thus saith Solomon, that was full true:
Work all by counsel, and thou shalt not rue. repent
And if thou worke wilt by good counseil,
I undertake, withoute mast or sail,
Yet shall I save her, and thee, and me.
Hast thou not heard how saved was Noe,
When that our Lord had warned him beforn,
That all the world with water should be lorn?" should perish
"Yes," quoth this carpenter," full yore ago." long since
"Hast thou not heard," quoth Nicholas, "also
The sorrow of Noe, with his fellowship,
That he had ere he got his wife to ship?[30]
Him had been lever, I dare well undertake,
At thilke time, than all his wethers black,
That she had had a ship herself alone. see note[31]
And therefore know'st thou what is best to be done?
This asketh haste, and of an hasty thing
Men may not preach or make tarrying.
Anon go get us fast into this inn house
A kneading trough, or else a kemelin, brewing-tub
For each of us; but look that they be large,
In whiche we may swim as in a barge: float
And have therein vitaille suffisant
But for one day; fie on the remenant;
The water shall aslake and go away slacken, abate
Aboute prime upon the nexte day. early morning
But Robin may not know of this, thy knave, servant
Nor eke thy maiden Gill I may not save:
Ask me not why: for though thou aske me
I will not telle Godde's privity.
Sufficeth thee, but if thy wit be mad, unless thou be
To have as great a grace as Noe had; out of thy wits
Thy wife shall I well saven out of doubt.
Go now thy way, and speed thee hereabout.
But when thou hast for her, and thee, and me,
Y-gotten us these kneading tubbes three,
Then shalt thou hang them in the roof full high,
So that no man our purveyance espy: foresight, providence
And when thou hast done thus as I have said,
And hast our vitaille fair in them y-laid,
And eke an axe to smite the cord in two
When that the water comes, that we may go,
And break an hole on high upon the gable
Into the garden-ward, over the stable,
That we may freely passe forth our way,
When that the greate shower is gone away.
Then shalt thou swim as merry, I undertake,
As doth the white duck after her drake:
Then will I clepe, 'How, Alison? How, John? call
Be merry: for the flood will pass anon.'
And thou wilt say, 'Hail, Master Nicholay,
Good-morrow, I see thee well, for it is day.'
And then shall we be lordes all our life
Of all the world, as Noe and his wife.
But of one thing I warne thee full right,
Be well advised, on that ilke night, same

THE CANTERBURY TALES

When we be enter'd into shippe's board,
That none of us not speak a single word,
Nor clepe nor cry. but be in his prayere,
For that is Godde's owen heste dear. command
Thy wife and thou must hangen far atween, asunder
For that betwixte you shall be no sin,
No more in looking than there shall in deed.
This ordinance is said: go, God thee speed
To-morrow night. when men be all asleep,
Into our kneading tubbes will we creep,
And sitte there, abiding Godde's grace.
Go now thy way, I have no longer space
To make of this no longer sermoning:
Men say thus: Send the wise, and say nothing:
Thou art so wise, it needeth thee nought teach.
Go, save our lives, and that I thee beseech."

This silly carpenter went forth his way,
Full oft he said, "Alas! and Well-a-day!,'
And to his wife he told his privity,
And she was ware, and better knew than he
What all this quainte cast was for to say. strange contrivance
But natheless she fear'd as she would dey, meant
And said: "Alas! go forth thy way anon.
Help us to scape, or we be dead each one.
I am thy true and very wedded wife;
Go, deare spouse, and help to save our life."
Lo, what a great thing is affection!
Men may die of imagination,
So deeply may impression be take.
This silly carpenter begins to quake:
He thinketh verily that he may see
This newe flood come weltering as the sea
To drenchen Alison, his honey dear. drown
He weepeth, waileth, maketh sorry cheer; dismal countenance
He sigheth, with full many a sorry sough. groan
He go'th, and getteth him a kneading trough,
And after that a tub, and a kemelin,
And privily he sent them to his inn:
And hung them in the roof full privily.
With his own hand then made he ladders three,
To climbe by the ranges and the stalks the rungs and the uprights
Unto the tubbes hanging in the balks; beams
And victualed them, kemelin, trough, and tub,
With bread and cheese, and good ale in a jub, jug
Sufficing right enough as for a day.
But ere that he had made all this array,
He sent his knave, and eke his wench also, servant maid
Upon his need to London for to go. business
And on the Monday, when it drew to night,
He shut his door withoute candle light,
And dressed every thing as it should be. prepared
And shortly up they climbed all the three.
They satte stille well a furlong way. the time it would take
"Now, Pater noster, clum,"[32] said Nicholay, to walk a furlong
And "clum," quoth John; and "clum," said Alison:
This carpenter said his devotion,
And still he sat and bidded his prayere,
Awaking on the rain, if he it hear.
The deade sleep, for weary business,
Fell on this carpenter, right as I guess,
About the curfew-time,[33] or little more,
For travail of his ghost he groaned sore, anguish of spirit
And eft he routed, for his head mislay. and then he snored,
Adown the ladder stalked Nicholay; for his head lay awry
And Alison full soft adown she sped.
Withoute wordes more they went to bed,
There as the carpenter was wont to lie: where
There was the revel, and the melody.
And thus lay Alison and Nicholas,
In business of mirth and in solace,
Until the bell of laudes gan to ring, morning service, at 3.a.m.
And friars in the chancel went to sing.

This parish clerk, this amorous Absolon,
That is for love alway so woebegone,
Upon the Monday was at Oseney
With company, him to disport and play;
And asked upon cas a cloisterer occasion monk
Full privily after John the carpenter;
And he drew him apart out of the church,
And said, "I n'ot; I saw him not here wirch know not work
Since Saturday; I trow that he be went
For timber, where our abbot hath him sent.
And dwellen at the Grange a day or two:
For he is wont for timber for to go,
Or else he is at his own house certain.
Where that he be, I cannot soothly sayn." say certainly
This Absolon full jolly was and light,
And thought, "Now is the time to wake all night,
For sickerly I saw him not stirring certainly
About his door, since day began to spring.
So may I thrive, but I shall at cock crow
Full privily go knock at his window,
That stands full low upon his bower wall: chamber
To Alison then will I tellen all
My love-longing; for I shall not miss
That at the leaste way I shall her kiss.
Some manner comfort shall I have, parfay, by my faith
My mouth hath itched all this livelong day:
That is a sign of kissing at the least.
All night I mette eke I was at a feast. dreamt
Therefore I will go sleep an hour or tway,

43

And all the night then will I wake and play."
When that the first cock crowed had, anon
Up rose this jolly lover Absolon,
And him arrayed gay, at point devise. with exact care
But first he chewed grains[34] and liquorice,
To smelle sweet, ere he had combed his hair.
Under his tongue a true love[35] he bare,
For thereby thought he to be gracious.

Then came he to the carpentere's house,
And still he stood under the shot window;
Unto his breast it raught, it was so low; reached
And soft he coughed with a semisoun'. low tone
"What do ye, honeycomb, sweet Alisoun?
My faire bird, my sweet cinamome, cinnamon, sweet spice
Awaken, leman mine, and speak to me. mistress
Full little thinke ye upon my woe,
That for your love I sweat there as I go. wherever
No wonder is that I do swelt and sweat. faint
I mourn as doth a lamb after the teat
Y-wis, leman, I have such love-longing, certainly
That like a turtle true is my mourning. turtle-dove
I may not eat, no more than a maid."
"Go from the window, thou jack fool," she said:
"As help me God, it will not be, 'come ba me.' kiss
I love another, else I were to blame",
Well better than thee, by Jesus, Absolon.
Go forth thy way, or I will cast a stone;
And let me sleep; a twenty devil way. twenty devils take ye!
"Alas!" quoth Absolon, "and well away!
That true love ever was so ill beset:
Then kiss me, since that it may be no bet, better
For Jesus' love, and for the love of me."
"Wilt thou then go thy way therewith?" , quoth she.
"Yea, certes, leman," quoth this Absolon.
"Then make thee ready," quoth she, "I come anon."
[And unto Nicholas she said full still: in a low voice
"Now peace, and thou shalt laugh anon thy fill."][36]
This Absolon down set him on his knees,
And said; "I am a lord at all degrees:
For after this I hope there cometh more;
Leman, thy grace, and, sweete bird, thine ore." favour
The window she undid, and that in haste.
"Have done," quoth she, "come off, and speed thee fast,
Lest that our neighebours should thee espy."
Then Absolon gan wipe his mouth full dry.
Dark was the night as pitch or as the coal,
And at the window she put out her hole,

And Absolon him fell ne bet ne werse,
But with his mouth he kiss'd her naked erse
Full savoury. When he was ware of this,
Aback he start, and thought it was amiss;
For well he wist a woman hath no beard.
He felt a thing all rough, and long y-hair'd,
And saide; "Fy, alas! what have I do?"
"Te he!" quoth she, and clapt the window to;
And Absolon went forth at sorry pace.
"A beard, a beard," said Hendy Nicholas;
"By God's corpus, this game went fair and well."
This silly Absolon heard every deal, word
And on his lip he gan for anger bite;
And to himself he said, "I shall thee quite. requite, be even with
Who rubbeth now, who frotteth now his lips rubs
With dust, with sand, with straw, with cloth, with chips,
But Absolon? that saith full oft, "Alas!
My soul betake I unto Sathanas,
But me were lever than all this town," quoth he rather
I this despite awroken for to be. revenged
Alas! alas! that I have been y-blent." deceived
His hote love is cold, and all y-quent. quenched
For from that time that he had kiss'd her erse,
Of paramours he sette not a kers, cared not a rush
For he was healed of his malady;
Full often paramours he gan defy,
And weep as doth a child that hath been beat.
A softe pace he went over the street
Unto a smith, men callen Dan Gerveis, master
That in his forge smithed plough-harness;
He sharped share and culter busily.
This Absolon knocked all easily,
And said; "Undo, Gerveis, and that anon."
"What, who art thou?" "It is I, Absolon."
"What? Absolon, what? Christe's sweete tree, cross
Why rise so rath? hey! Benedicite, early
What aileth you? some gay girl,[37] God it wote,
Hath brought you thus upon the viretote:[38]
By Saint Neot, ye wot well what I mean."
This Absolon he raughte not a bean recked, cared
Of all his play; no word again he gaf, spoke
For he had more tow on his distaff[39]
Than Gerveis knew, and saide; "Friend so dear,
That hote culter in the chimney here
Lend it to me, I have therewith to don: do
I will it bring again to thee full soon."
Gerveis answered; "Certes, were it gold,
Or in a poke nobles all untold, purse
Thou shouldst it have, as I am a true smith.
Hey! Christe's foot, what will ye do therewith?"
"Thereof," quoth Absolon, "be as be may;
I shall well tell it thee another day:"
And caught the culter by the colde stele. handle
Full soft out at the door he gan to steal,
And went unto the carpentere's wall

44

He coughed first, and knocked therewithal
Upon the window, light as he did ere. before[40]
This Alison answered; "Who is there
That knocketh so? I warrant him a thief."
"Nay, nay," quoth he, "God wot, my sweete lefe, love
I am thine Absolon, my own darling.
Of gold," quoth he, "I have thee brought a ring,
My mother gave it me, so God me save!
Full fine it is, and thereto well y-grave: engraved
This will I give to thee, if thou me kiss."
Now Nicholas was risen up to piss,
And thought he would amenden all the jape; improve the joke
He shoulde kiss his erse ere that he scape:
And up the window did he hastily,
And out his erse he put full privily
Over the buttock, to the haunche bone.
And therewith spake this clerk, this Absolon,
"Speak, sweete bird, I know not where thou art."
This Nicholas anon let fly a fart,
As great as it had been a thunder dent; peal, clap
That with the stroke he was well nigh y-blent; blinded
But he was ready with his iron hot,
And Nicholas amid the erse he smote.
Off went the skin an handbreadth all about.
The hote culter burned so his tout, breech
That for the smart he weened he would die; thought
As he were wood, for woe he gan to cry, mad
"Help! water, water, help for Godde's heart!"

This carpenter out of his slumber start,
And heard one cry "Water," as he were wood, mad
And thought, "Alas! now cometh Noe's flood."
He sat him up withoute wordes mo'
And with his axe he smote the cord in two;

And down went all; he found neither to sell
Nor bread nor ale, till he came to the sell, threshold[41]
Upon the floor, and there in swoon he lay.
Up started Alison and Nicholay,
And cried out an "harow!"[15] in the street.
The neighbours alle, bothe small and great
In ranne, for to gauren on this man, stare
That yet in swoone lay, both pale and wan:
For with the fall he broken had his arm.
But stand he must unto his owen harm,
For when he spake, he was anon borne down
With Hendy Nicholas and Alisoun.
They told to every man that he was wood; mad
He was aghaste so of Noe's flood, afraid
Through phantasy, that of his vanity
He had y-bought him kneading-tubbes three,
And had them hanged in the roof above;
And that he prayed them for Godde's love
To sitten in the roof for company.
The folk gan laughen at his phantasy.
Into the roof they kyken and they gape, peep, look.
And turned all his harm into a jape. jest
For whatsoe'er this carpenter answer'd,
It was for nought, no man his reason heard.
With oathes great he was so sworn adown,
That he was holden wood in all the town.
For every clerk anon right held with other;
They said, "The man was wood, my leve brother;" dear
And every wight gan laughen at his strife.
Thus swived was the carpentere's wife, enjoyed
For all his keeping and his jealousy; care
And Absolon hath kiss'd her nether eye;
And Nicholas is scalded in the tout.
This tale is done, and God save all the rout. company

Notes to the Miller's Tale

1. Almagest: The book of Ptolemy the astronomer, which formed the canon of astrological science in the middle ages.
2. Astrolabe: "Astrelagour," "astrelabore"; a mathematical instrument for taking the altitude of the sun or stars.
3. "Augrim" is a corruption of algorithm, the Arabian term for numeration; "augrim stones," therefore were probably marked with numerals, and used as counters.
4. Angelus ad virginem: The Angel's salutation to Mary; Luke i. 28. It was the "Ave Maria" of the Catholic Church service.
5. Cato: Though Chaucer may have referred to the famous Censor, more probably the reference is merely to the "Moral Distichs," which go under his name, though written after his time; and in a supplement to which the quoted passage may be found.
6. Barm-cloth: apron; from Anglo-Saxon "barme," bosom or lap.
7. Volupere: Head-gear, kerchief; from French, "envelopper," to wrap up.
8. Popelet: Puppet; but chiefly; young wench.
9. Noble: nobles were gold coins of especial purity and brightness; "Ex auro nobilissimi, unde nobilis vocatus," (made from the noblest (purest) gold, and therefore called nobles) says Vossius.
10. Yern: Shrill, lively; German, "gern," willingly, cheerfully.

GEOFFREY CHAUCER

11. Braket: bragget, a sweet drink made of honey, spices, &c. In some parts of the country, a drink made from honeycomb, after the honey is extracted, is still called "bragwort."
12. Piggesnie: a fond term, like "my duck;" from Anglo-Saxon, "piga," a young maid; but Tyrwhitt associates it with the Latin, "ocellus," little eye, a fondling term, and suggests that the "pigs- eye," which is very small, was applied in the same sense. Davenport and Butler both use the word pigsnie, the first for "darling," the second literally for "eye;" and Bishop Gardner, "On True Obedience," in his address to the reader, says: "How softly she was wont to chirpe him under the chin, and kiss him; how prettily she could talk to him (how doth my sweet heart, what saith now pig's-eye)."
13. Oseney: A once well-known abbey near Oxford.
14. Trave: travis; a frame in which unruly horses were shod.
15. Harow and Alas: Haro! was an old Norman cry for redress or aid. The "Clameur de Haro" was lately raised, under peculiar circumstances, as the prelude to a legal protest, in Jersey.
16. His shoes were ornamented like the windows of St. Paul's, especially like the old rose-window.
17. Rise: Twig, bush; German, "Reis," a twig; "Reisig," a copse.
18. Chaucer satirises the dancing of Oxford as he did the French of Stratford at Bow.
19. Shot window: A projecting or bow window, whence it was possible shoot at any one approaching the door.
20. Piment: A drink made with wine, honey, and spices.
21. Because she was town-bred, he offered wealth, or money reward, for her love.
22. Parish-clerks, like Absolon, had leading parts in the mysteries or religious plays; Herod was one of these parts, which may have been an object of competition among the amateurs of the period.
23. "The nighe sly maketh oft time the far lief to be loth": a proverb; the cunning one near at hand oft makes the loving one afar off to be odious.
24. Kyked: Looked; "keek" is still used in some parts in the sense of "peep."
25. Saint Frideswide was the patroness of a considerable priory at Oxford, and held there in high repute.
26. Plato, in his "Theatetus," tells this story of Thales; but it has since appeared in many other forms.
27. Crouche: protect by signing the sign of the cross.
28. Forlore: lost; german, "verloren."
29. Him that harried Hell: Christ who wasted or subdued hell: in the middle ages, some very active exploits against the prince of darkness and his powers were ascribed by the monkish tale- tellers to the saviour after he had "descended into hell."
30. According to the old mysteries, Noah's wife refused to come into the ark, and bade her husband row forth and get him a new wife, because he was leaving her gossips in the town to drown. Shem and his brothers got her shipped by main force; and Noah, coming forward to welcome her, was greeted with a box on the ear.
31. "Him had been lever, I dare well undertake, At thilke time, than all his wethers black, That she had had a ship herself alone." i.e. "At that time he would have given all his black wethers, if she had had an ark to herself."
32. "Clum," like "mum," a note of silence; but otherwise explained as the humming sound made in repeating prayers; from the Anglo-Saxon, "clumian," to mutter, speak in an under- tone, keep silence.
33. Curfew-time: Eight in the evening, when, by the law of William the Conqueror, all people were, on ringing of a bell, to extinguish fire and candle, and go to rest; hence the word curfew, from French, "couvre-feu," cover-fire.
34. Absolon chewed grains: these were grains of Paris, or Paradise; a favourite spice.
35. Under his tongue a true love he bare: some sweet herb; another reading, however, is "a true love-knot," which may have been of the nature of a charm.
36. The two lines within brackets are not in most of the editions: they are taken from Urry; whether he supplied them or not, they serve the purpose of a necessary explanation.
37. Gay girl: As applied to a young woman of light manners, this euphemistic phrase has enjoyed a wonderful vitality.
38. Viretote: Urry reads "meritote," and explains it from Spelman as a game in which children made themselves giddy by whirling on ropes. In French, "virer" means to turn; and the explanation may, therefore, suit either reading. In modern slang parlance, Gerveis would probably have said, "on the rampage," or "on the swing" — not very far from Spelman's rendering.
39. He had more tow on his distaff: a proverbial saying: he was playing a deeper game, had more serious business on hand.
40. Ere: before; German, "eher."
41. Sell: sill of the door, threshold; French, "seuil," Latin, "solum," the ground.

THE CANTERBURY TALES

THE REEVE'S TALE.

THE PROLOGUE.

WHEN folk had laughed all at this nice case
Of Absolon and Hendy Nicholas,
Diverse folk diversely they said,
But for the more part they laugh'd and play'd; were diverted
And at this tale I saw no man him grieve,
But it were only Osewold the Reeve.
Because he was of carpenteres craft,
A little ire is in his hearte laft; left
He gan to grudge and blamed it a lite. murmur little.
"So the I," quoth he, "full well could I him quite thrive match
With blearing of a proude miller's eye, dimming[1]
If that me list to speak of ribaldry.
But I am old; me list not play for age;[2]
Grass time is done, my fodder is now forage.
This white top writeth mine olde years; head
Mine heart is also moulded as mine hairs; grown mouldy
And I do fare as doth an open-erse; medlar[3]
That ilke fruit is ever longer werse, same
Till it be rotten in mullok or in stre. on the ground or in straw
We olde men, I dread, so fare we;
Till we be rotten, can we not be ripe;
We hop away, while that the world will pipe; dance
For in our will there sticketh aye a nail,
To have an hoary head and a green tail,
As hath a leek; for though our might be gone,
Our will desireth folly ever-in-one: continually
For when we may not do, then will we speak,
Yet in our ashes cold does fire reek. smoke[4]
Four gledes have we, which I shall devise, coals describe
Vaunting, and lying, anger, covetise. covetousness
These foure sparks belongen unto eld.
Our olde limbes well may be unweld, unwieldy

But will shall never fail us, that is sooth.
And yet have I alway a coltes tooth,[5]
As many a year as it is passed and gone
Since that my tap of life began to run;
For sickerly, when I was born, anon certainly
Death drew the tap of life, and let it gon:
And ever since hath so the tap y-run,
Till that almost all empty is the tun.
The stream of life now droppeth on the chimb.[6]
The silly tongue well may ring and chime
Of wretchedness, that passed is full yore: long
With olde folk, save dotage, is no more.[7]

When that our Host had heard this sermoning,
He gan to speak as lordly as a king,
And said; "To what amounteth all this wit?
What? shall we speak all day of holy writ?
The devil made a Reeve for to preach,
As of a souter a shipman, or a leach. cobbler[8]
Say forth thy tale, and tarry not the time: surgeon[9]
Lo here is Deptford, and 'tis half past prime:[10]
Lo Greenwich, where many a shrew is in.
It were high time thy tale to begin."

"Now, sirs," quoth then this Osewold the Reeve,
I pray you all that none of you do grieve,
Though I answer, and somewhat set his hove, hood[11]
For lawful is force off with force to shove. to repel force
This drunken miller hath y-told us here by force
How that beguiled was a carpentere,
Paraventure in scorn, for I am one: perhaps
And, by your leave, I shall him quite anon.
Right in his churlish termes will I speak,
I pray to God his necke might to-break.
He can well in mine eye see a stalk,
But in his own he cannot see a balk."[12]

Notes to the Prologue to the Reeves Tale.

1. "With blearing of a proude miller's eye": dimming his eye; playing off a joke on him.
2. "Me list not play for age": age takes away my zest for drollery.
3. The medlar, the fruit of the mespilus tree, is only edible when rotten.
4. Yet in our ashes cold does fire reek: "ev'n in our ashes live their wonted fires."
5. A colt's tooth; a wanton humour, a relish for pleasure.
6. Chimb: The rim of a barrel where the staves project beyond the head.
7. With olde folk, save dotage, is no more: Dotage is all that is left them; that is, they can only dwell fondly, dote, on the past.
8. Souter: cobbler; Scottice, "sutor;"' from Latin, "suere," to sew.
9. "Ex sutore medicus" (a surgeon from a cobbler) and "ex sutore nauclerus" (a seaman or pilot from a cobbler) were both proverbial expressions in the Middle Ages.

10. Half past prime: half-way between prime and tierce; about half-past seven in the morning.
11. Set his hove; like "set their caps;" as in the description of the Manciple in the Prologue, who "set their aller cap". "Hove" or "houfe," means "hood;" and the phrase signifies to be even with, outwit.
12. The illustration of the mote and the beam, from Matthew.

THE TALE.[1]

At Trompington, not far from Cantebrig, Cambridge
There goes a brook, and over that a brig,
Upon the whiche brook there stands a mill:
And this is very sooth that I you tell. complete truth
A miller was there dwelling many a day,
As any peacock he was proud and gay:
Pipen he could, and fish, and nettes bete, prepare
And turne cups, and wrestle well, and shete. shoot
Aye by his belt he bare a long pavade, poniard
And of his sword full trenchant was the blade.
A jolly popper bare he in his pouch; dagger
There was no man for peril durst him touch.
A Sheffield whittle bare he in his hose. small knife
Round was his face, and camuse was his nose. flat[2]
As pilled as an ape's was his skull. peeled, bald.
He was a market-beter at the full. brawler
There durste no wight hand upon him legge, lay
That he ne swore anon he should abegge. suffer the penalty

A thief he was, for sooth, of corn and meal,
And that a sly, and used well to steal.
His name was hoten deinous Simekin called "Disdainful Simkin"
A wife he hadde, come of noble kin:
The parson of the town her father was.
With her he gave full many a pan of brass,
For that Simkin should in his blood ally.
She was y-foster'd in a nunnery:
For Simkin woulde no wife, as he said,
But she were well y-nourish'd, and a maid,
To saven his estate and yeomanry:
And she was proud, and pert as is a pie. magpie
A full fair sight it was to see them two;
On holy days before her would he go
With his tippet y-bound about his head; hood
And she came after in a gite of red, gown[3]
And Simkin hadde hosen of the same.
There durste no wight call her aught but Dame:
None was so hardy, walking by that way,
That with her either durste rage or play, use freedom
But if he would be slain by Simekin unless
With pavade, or with knife, or bodekin.
For jealous folk be per'lous evermo':
Algate they would their wives wende so. unless so behave
And eke for she was somewhat smutterlich, dirty
She was as dign as water in a ditch, nasty

And all so full of hoker, and bismare. ill-nature abusive speech
Her thoughte that a lady should her spare, not judge her hardly
What for her kindred, and her nortelrie nurturing, education
That she had learned in the nunnery.

One daughter hadde they betwixt them two
Of twenty year, withouten any mo,
Saving a child that was of half year age,
In cradle it lay, and was a proper page. boy
This wenche thick and well y-grown was,
With camuse nose, and eyen gray as glass; flat
With buttocks broad, and breastes round and high;
But right fair was her hair, I will not lie.
The parson of the town, for she was fair,
In purpose was to make of her his heir
Both of his chattels and his messuage,
And strange he made it of her marriage. he made it a matter
His purpose was for to bestow her high of difficulty
Into some worthy blood of ancestry.
For holy Church's good may be dispended spent
On holy Church's blood that is descended.
Therefore he would his holy blood honour
Though that he holy Churche should devour.

Great soken hath this miller, out of doubt, toll taken for grinding
With wheat and malt, of all the land about;
And namely there was a great college especially
Men call the Soler Hall at Cantebrege,[4]
There was their wheat and eke their malt y-ground.
And on a day it happed in a stound, suddenly
Sick lay the manciple of a malady, steward[5]
Men weened wisly that he shoulde die. thought certainly
For which this miller stole both meal and corn
An hundred times more than beforn.
For theretofore he stole but courteously,
But now he was a thief outrageously.
For which the warden chid and made fare, fuss
But thereof set the miller not a tare; he cared not a rush
He crack'd his boast, and swore it was not so. talked big

Then were there younge poore scholars two,
That dwelled in the hall of which I say;

48

THE CANTERBURY TALES

Testif they were, and lusty for to play; headstrong[6]
And only for their mirth and revelry
Upon the warden busily they cry,
To give them leave for but a little stound, short time
To go to mill, and see their corn y-ground:
And hardily they durste lay their neck, boldly
The miller should not steal them half a peck
Of corn by sleight, nor them by force bereave take away
And at the last the warden give them leave:
John hight the one, and Alein hight the other,
Of one town were they born, that highte Strother,[7]
Far in the North, I cannot tell you where.
This Alein he made ready all his gear,
And on a horse the sack he cast anon:
Forth went Alein the clerk, and also John,
With good sword and with buckler by their side.
John knew the way, him needed not no guide,
And at the mill the sack adown he lay'th.

Alein spake first; "All hail, Simon, in faith,
How fares thy faire daughter, and thy wife."
"Alein, welcome," quoth Simkin, "by my life,
And John also: how now, what do ye here?"
"By God, Simon," quoth John, "need has no peer. equal
Him serve himself behoves that has no swain, servant
Or else he is a fool, as clerkes sayn.
Our manciple I hope he will be dead, expect
So workes aye the wanges in his head: cheek-teeth[8]
And therefore is I come, and eke Alein,
To grind our corn and carry it home again:
I pray you speed us hence as well ye may."
"It shall be done," quoth Simkin, "by my fay.
What will ye do while that it is in hand?"
"By God, right by the hopper will I stand,"
Quoth John, "and see how that the corn goes in.
Yet saw I never, by my father's kin,
How that the hopper wagges to and fro."
Alein answered, "John, and wilt thou so?
Then will I be beneathe, by my crown,
And see how that the meale falls adown
Into the trough, that shall be my disport: amusement
For, John, in faith I may be of your sort;
I is as ill a miller as is ye."

This miller smiled at their nicety, simplicity
And thought, "All this is done but for a wile.
They weenen that no man may them beguile, think
But by my thrift yet shall I blear their eye,[9]
For all the sleight in their philosophy.
The more quainte knackes that they make, odd little tricks

The more will I steal when that I take.
Instead of flour yet will I give them bren. bran
The greatest clerks are not the wisest men,
As whilom to the wolf thus spake the mare:[10]
Of all their art ne count I not a tare."
Out at the door he went full privily,
When that he saw his time, softly.
He looked up and down, until he found
The clerkes' horse, there as he stood y-bound
Behind the mill, under a levesell: arbour[11]
And to the horse he went him fair and well,
And stripped off the bridle right anon.
And when the horse was loose, he gan to gon
Toward the fen, where wilde mares run,
Forth, with "Wehee!" through thick and eke through thin.
This miller went again, no word he said,
But did his note, and with these clerkes play'd, business[12]
Till that their corn was fair and well y-ground.
And when the meal was sacked and y-bound,
Then John went out, and found his horse away,
And gan to cry, "Harow, and well-away!
Our horse is lost: Alein, for Godde's bones,
Step on thy feet; come off, man, all at once:
Alas! our warden has his palfrey lorn." lost
This Alein all forgot, both meal and corn;
All was out of his mind his husbandry. careful watch over
"What, which way is he gone?" he gan to cry. the corn
The wife came leaping inward at a renne, run
She said; "Alas! your horse went to the fen
With wilde mares, as fast as he could go.
Unthank come on his hand that bound him so ill luck, a curse
And his that better should have knit the rein."
"Alas!" quoth John, "Alein, for Christes pain
Lay down thy sword, and I shall mine also.
I is full wight, God wate, as is a roe. swift knows
By Godde's soul he shall not scape us bathe. both[13]
Why n' had thou put the capel in the lathe? horse[14] barn
Ill hail, Alein, by God thou is a fonne." fool
These silly clerkes have full fast y-run
Toward the fen, both Alein and eke John;
And when the miller saw that they were gone,
He half a bushel of their flour did take,
And bade his wife go knead it in a cake.
He said; I trow, the clerkes were afeard,
Yet can a miller make a clerkes beard, cheat a scholar[15]
For all his art: yea, let them go their way!
Lo where they go! yea, let the children play:
They get him not so lightly, by my crown."
These silly clerkes runnen up and down
With "Keep, keep; stand, stand; jossa, warderere. turn

49

GEOFFREY CHAUCER

Go whistle thou, and I shall keep him here." catch
But shortly, till that it was very night
They coulde not, though they did all their might,
Their capel catch, he ran alway so fast:
Till in a ditch they caught him at the last.

Weary and wet, as beastes in the rain,
Comes silly John, and with him comes Alein.
"Alas," quoth John, "the day that I was born!
Now are we driv'n till hething and till scorn. mockery
Our corn is stol'n, men will us fonnes call, fools
Both the warden, and eke our fellows all,
And namely the miller, well-away!" especially
Thus plained John, as he went by the way
Toward the mill, and Bayard in his hand. the bay horse
The miller sitting by the fire he fand. found
For it was night, and forther might they not, go their way
But for the love of God they him besought
Of herberow and ease, for their penny. lodging
The miller said again," If there be any,
Such as it is, yet shall ye have your part.
Mine house is strait, but ye have learned art;
Ye can by arguments maken a place
A mile broad, of twenty foot of space.
Let see now if this place may suffice,
Or make it room with speech, as is your guise." fashion
"Now, Simon," said this John, "by Saint Cuthberd
Aye is thou merry, and that is fair answer'd.
I have heard say, man shall take of two things,
Such as he findes, or such as he brings.
But specially I pray thee, hoste dear,
Gar[16] us have meat and drink, and make us cheer,
And we shall pay thee truly at the full:
With empty hand men may not hawkes tull. allure
Lo here our silver ready for to spend."

This miller to the town his daughter send
For ale and bread, and roasted them a goose,
And bound their horse, he should no more go loose:
And them in his own chamber made a bed.
With sheetes and with chalons fair y-spread, blankets[17]
Not from his owen bed ten foot or twelve:
His daughter had a bed all by herselve,
Right in the same chamber by and by: side by side
It might no better be, and cause why,
There was no roomer herberow in the place. roomier lodging
They suppen, and they speaken of solace,
And drinken ever strong ale at the best.
Aboute midnight went they all to rest.

Well had this miller varnished his head;
Full pale he was, fordrunken, and nought red. without his wits
He yoxed, and he spake thorough the nose, hiccuped
As he were in the quakke, or in the pose. grunting catarrh
To bed he went, and with him went his wife,
As any jay she light was and jolife, jolly
So was her jolly whistle well y-wet.
The cradle at her beddes feet was set,
To rock, and eke to give the child to suck.
And when that drunken was all in the crock pitcher[18]
To bedde went the daughter right anon,
To bedde went Alein, and also John.
There was no more; needed them no dwale.[19]
This miller had, so wisly bibbed ale, certainly
That as a horse he snorted in his sleep,
Nor of his tail behind he took no keep. heed
His wife bare him a burdoun, a full strong; bass[20]
Men might their routing hearen a furlong. snoring

The wenche routed eke for company.
Alein the clerk, that heard this melody,
He poked John, and saide: "Sleepest thou?
Heardest thou ever such a song ere now?
Lo what a compline[21] is y-mell them all. among
A wilde fire upon their bodies fall,
Who hearken'd ever such a ferly thing? strange[22]
Yea, they shall have the flow'r of ill ending!
This longe night there tides me no rest. comes to me
But yet no force, all shall be for the best. matter
For, John," said he, "as ever may I thrive,
If that I may, yon wenche will I swive. enjoy carnally
Some easement has law y-shapen us satisfaction provided
For, John, there is a law that sayeth thus,
That if a man in one point be aggriev'd,
That in another he shall be relievd.
Our corn is stol'n, soothly it is no nay,
And we have had an evil fit to-day.
And since I shall have none amendement
Against my loss, I will have easement:
By Godde's soul, it shall none, other be."
This John answer'd; Alein, avise thee: have a care
The miller is a perilous man," he said,
"And if that he out of his sleep abraid, awaked
He mighte do us both a villainy." mischief
Alein answer'd; "I count him not a fly.
And up he rose, and by the wench he crept.
This wenche lay upright, and fast she slept,
Till he so nigh was, ere she might espy,
That it had been too late for to cry:
And, shortly for to say, they were at one.
Now play, Alein, for I will speak of John.

50

This John lay still a furlong way[23] or two,
And to himself he made ruth and woe. wail
"Alas!" quoth he, "this is a wicked jape; trick
Now may I say, that I is but an ape.
Yet has my fellow somewhat for his harm;
He has the miller's daughter in his arm:
He auntred him, and hath his needes sped, adventured
And I lie as a draff-sack in my bed;
And when this jape is told another day,
I shall be held a daffe or a cockenay[24] coward
I will arise, and auntre it, by my fay: attempt
Unhardy is unsely,[25] as men say."
And up he rose, and softely he went
Unto the cradle, and in his hand it hent, took
And bare it soft unto his beddes feet.
Soon after this the wife her routing lete, stopped snoring
And gan awake, and went her out to piss
And came again and gan the cradle miss
And groped here and there, but she found none.
"Alas!" quoth she, "I had almost misgone
I had almost gone to the clerkes' bed.
Ey! Benedicite, then had I foul y-sped."
And forth she went, till she the cradle fand.
She groped alway farther with her hand
And found the bed, and thoughte not but good had no suspicion
Because that the cradle by it stood,
And wist not where she was, for it was derk;
But fair and well she crept in by the clerk,
And lay full still, and would have caught a sleep.
Within a while this John the Clerk up leap
And on this goode wife laid on full sore;
So merry a fit had she not had full yore. for a long time
He pricked hard and deep, as he were mad.

This jolly life have these two clerkes had,
Till that the thirde cock began to sing.
Alein wax'd weary in the morrowing,
For he had swonken all the longe night, laboured
And saide; "Farewell, Malkin, my sweet wight.
The day is come, I may no longer bide,
But evermore, where so I go or ride,
I is thine owen clerk, so have I hele." health
"Now, deare leman," quoth she, "go, fare wele: sweetheart
But ere thou go, one thing I will thee tell.
When that thou wendest homeward by the mill,
Right at the entry of the door behind
Thou shalt a cake of half a bushel find,
That was y-maked of thine owen meal,
Which that I help'd my father for to steal.
And goode leman, God thee save and keep."
And with that word she gan almost to weep.
Alein uprose and thought, "Ere the day daw
I will go creepen in by my fellaw:"
And found the cradle with his hand anon.

"By God!" thought he, "all wrong I have misgone:
My head is totty of my swink to-night, giddy from my labour
That maketh me that I go not aright.
I wot well by the cradle I have misgo';
Here lie the miller and his wife also."
And forth he went a twenty devil way
Unto the bed, there as the miller lay.
He ween'd t' have creeped by his fellow John, thought
And by the miller in he crept anon,
And caught him by the neck, and gan him shake,
And said; "Thou John, thou swines-head, awake
For Christes soul, and hear a noble game!
For by that lord that called is Saint Jame,
As I have thries in this shorte night
Swived the miller's daughter bolt-upright,
While thou hast as a coward lain aghast." afraid
"Thou false harlot," quoth the miller, "hast?
Ah, false traitor, false clerk," quoth he,
"Thou shalt be dead, by Godde's dignity,
Who durste be so bold to disparage disgrace
My daughter, that is come of such lineage?"
And by the throate-ball he caught Alein, Adam's apple
And he him hent dispiteously again, seized angrily
And on the nose he smote him with his fist;
Down ran the bloody stream upon his breast:
And in the floor with nose and mouth all broke
They wallow, as do two pigs in a poke.
And up they go, and down again anon,
Till that the miller spurned on a stone, stumbled
And down he backward fell upon his wife,
That wiste nothing of this nice strife:
For she was fall'n asleep a little wight while
With John the clerk, that waked had all night:
And with the fall out of her sleep she braid. woke
"Help, holy cross of Bromeholm,"[26] she said;
"In manus tuas![27] Lord, to thee I call.
Awake, Simon, the fiend is on me fall;
Mine heart is broken; help; I am but dead:
There li'th one on my womb and on mine head.
Help, Simkin, for these false clerks do fight"
This John start up as fast as e'er he might,
And groped by the walles to and fro
To find a staff; and she start up also,
And knew the estres better than this John, apartment
And by the wall she took a staff anon:
And saw a little shimmering of a light,
For at an hole in shone the moone bright,
And by that light she saw them both the two,
But sickerly she wist not who was who, certainly
But as she saw a white thing in her eye.
And when she gan this white thing espy,
She ween'd the clerk had wear'd a volupere; supposed night-cap
And with the staff she drew aye nere and nere,

51

nearer
And ween'd to have hit this Alein at the full,
And smote the miller on the pilled skull; bald
That down he went, and cried," Harow! I die."
These clerkes beat him well, and let him lie,
And greithen them, and take their horse anon, make ready, dress
And eke their meal, and on their way they gon:
And at the mill door eke they took their cake
Of half a bushel flour, full well y-bake.

Thus is the proude miller well y-beat,
And hath y-lost the grinding of the wheat;
And payed for the supper every deal every bit
Of Alein and of John, that beat him well;
His wife is swived, and his daughter als; also
Lo, such it is a miller to be false.
And therefore this proverb is said full sooth,
"Him thar not winnen well that evil do'th, he deserves not to gain
A guiler shall himself beguiled be:"
And God that sitteth high in majesty
Save all this Company, both great and smale.
Thus have I quit the Miller in my tale. made myself quits with

Notes to the Reeve's Tale

1. The incidents of this tale were much relished in the Middle Ages, and are found under various forms. Boccaccio has told them in the ninth day of his "Decameron".
2. Camuse: flat; French "camuse", snub-nosed.
3. Gite: gown or coat; French "jupe."
4. Soler Hall: the hall or college at Cambridge with the gallery or upper storey; supposed to have been Clare Hall. (Transcribers note: later commentators identify it with King's Hall, now merged with Trinity College)
5. Manciple: steward; provisioner of the hall. See also note 47 to the prologue to the Tales.
6. Testif: headstrong, wild-brained; French, "entete."
7. Strother: Tyrwhitt points to Anstruther, in Fife: Mr Wright to the Vale of Langstroth, in the West Riding of Yorkshire. Chaucer has given the scholars a dialect that may have belonged to either district, although it more immediately suggests the more northern of the two. (Transcribers note: later commentators have identified it with a now vanished village near Kirknewton in Northumberland. There was a well-known Alein of Strother in Chaucer's lifetime.)
8. Wanges: grinders, cheek-teeth; Anglo-Saxon, "Wang," the cheek; German, "Wange."
9. See note 1 to the Prologue to the Reeves Tale
10. In the "Cento Novelle Antiche," the story is told of a mule, which pretends that his name is written on the bottom of his hind foot. The wolf attempts to read it, the mule kills him with a kick in the forehead; and the fox, looking on, remarks that "every man of letters is not wise." A similar story is told in "Reynard the Fox."
11. Levesell: an arbour; Anglo-Saxon, "lefe-setl," leafy seat.
12. Noth: business; German, "Noth," necessity.
13. Bathe: both; Scottice, "baith."
14. Capel: horse; Gaelic, "capall;" French, "cheval;" Italian, "cavallo," from Latin, "caballus."
15. Make a clerkes beard: cheat a scholar; French, "faire la barbe;" and Boccaccio uses the proverb in the same sense.
16. "Gar" is Scotch for "cause;" some editions read, however, "get us some".
17. Chalons: blankets, coverlets, made at Chalons in France.
18. Crock: pitcher, cruse; Anglo-Saxon, "crocca;" German, "krug;" hence "crockery."
19. Dwale: night-shade, Solanum somniferum, given to cause sleep.
20. Burdoun: bass; "burden" of a song. It originally means the drone of a bagpipe; French, "bourdon."
21. Compline: even-song in the church service; chorus.
22. Ferly: strange. In Scotland, a "ferlie" is an unwonted or remarkable sight.
23. A furlong way: As long as it might take to walk a furlong.
24. Cockenay: a term of contempt, probably borrowed from the kitchen; a cook, in base Latin, being termed "coquinarius." compare French "coquin," rascal.
25. Unhardy is unsely: the cowardly is unlucky; "nothing venture, nothing have;" German, "unselig," unhappy.
26. Holy cross of Bromeholm: A common adjuration at that time; the cross or rood of the priory of Bromholm, in Norfolk, was said to contain part of the real cross and therefore held in high esteem.
27. In manus tuas: Latin, "in your hands".

THE COOK'S TALE.

THE PROLOGUE.

THE Cook of London, while the Reeve thus spake,
For joy he laugh'd and clapp'd him on the back:
"Aha!" quoth he, "for Christes passion,
This Miller had a sharp conclusion,
Upon this argument of herbergage. *lodging*
Well saide Solomon in his language,
Bring thou not every man into thine house,
For harbouring by night is perilous.
Well ought a man avised for to be *a man should take good heed*
Whom that he brought into his privity.
I pray to God to give me sorrow and care
If ever, since I highte Hodge of Ware, was called
Heard I a miller better set a-work; *handled*
He had a jape of malice in the derk. *trick*
But God forbid that we should stinte here, *stop*
And therefore if ye will vouchsafe to hear
A tale of me, that am a poore man,
I will you tell as well as e'er I can
A little jape that fell in our city."

Our Host answer'd and said; "I grant it thee.
Roger, tell on; and look that it be good,
For many a pasty hast thou letten blood,
And many a Jack of Dover[1] hast thou sold,
That had been twice hot and twice cold.
Of many a pilgrim hast thou Christe's curse,
For of thy parsley yet fare they the worse.
That they have eaten in thy stubble goose:
For in thy shop doth many a fly go loose.
Now tell on, gentle Roger, by thy name,
But yet I pray thee be not wroth for game; *angry with my jesting*
A man may say full sooth in game and play."
"Thou sayst full sooth," quoth Roger, "by my fay;
But sooth play quad play,[2] as the Fleming saith,
And therefore, Harry Bailly, by thy faith,
Be thou not wroth, else we departe here, *part company*
Though that my tale be of an hostelere. *innkeeper*
But natheless, I will not tell it yet,
But ere we part, y-wis thou shalt be quit."[3] *assuredly*
And therewithal he laugh'd and made cheer,[4]
And told his tale, as ye shall after hear.

Notes to the Prologue to the Cook's Tale

1. Jack of Dover: an article of cookery. (Transcriber's note: suggested by some commentators to be a kind of pie, and by others to be a fish)
2. Sooth play quad play: true jest is no jest.
3. It may be remembered that each pilgrim was bound to tell two stories; one on the way to Canterbury, the other returning.
4. Made cheer: French, "fit bonne mine;" put on a pleasant countenance.

THE TALE.

A prentice whilom dwelt in our city,
And of a craft of victuallers was he:
Galliard he was, as goldfinch in the shaw, *lively grove*
Brown as a berry, a proper short fellaw:
With lockes black, combed full fetisly. *daintily*
And dance he could so well and jollily,
That he was called Perkin Revellour.
He was as full of love and paramour,
As is the honeycomb of honey sweet;
Well was the wenche that with him might meet.
At every bridal would he sing and hop;
He better lov'd the tavern than the shop.
For when there any riding was in Cheap,[1]
Out of the shoppe thither would he leap,
And, till that he had all the sight y-seen,
And danced well, he would not come again;
And gather'd him a meinie of his sort, *company of fellows*
To hop and sing, and make such disport:
And there they sette steven for to meet *made appointment*
To playen at the dice in such a street.
For in the towne was there no prentice
That fairer coulde cast a pair of dice
Than Perkin could; and thereto he was free *he spent money liberally*
Of his dispence, in place of privity. *where he would not be seen*
That found his master well in his chaffare, *merchandise*
For oftentime he found his box full bare.

For, soothely, a prentice revellour,
That haunteth dice, riot, and paramour,
His master shall it in his shop abie, *suffer for*
All have he no part of the minstrelsy. *although*
For theft and riot they be convertible,
All can they play on gitern or ribible. *guitar or rebeck*
Revel and truth, as in a low degree,
They be full wroth all day, as men may see. *at variance*

This jolly prentice with his master bode,
Till he was nigh out of his prenticehood,
All were he snubbed both early and late, *rebuked*
And sometimes led with revel to Newgate.
But at the last his master him bethought,
Upon a day when he his paper[2] sought,
Of a proverb, that saith this same word;
Better is rotten apple out of hoard,
Than that it should rot all the remenant:
So fares it by a riotous servant;
It is well lesse harm to let him pace, *pass, go*
Than he shend all the servants in the place. *corrupt*
Therefore his master gave him a quittance,
And bade him go, with sorrow and mischance.
And thus this jolly prentice had his leve: *desire*
Now let him riot all the night, or leave. *refrain*
And, for there is no thief without a louke,[3]
That helpeth him to wasten and to souk *spend*
Of that he bribe can, or borrow may, *steal*
Anon he sent his bed and his array
Unto a compere of his owen sort, *comrade*
That loved dice, and riot, and disport;
And had a wife, that held for countenance *for appearances*
A shop, and swived for her sustenance. *prostituted herself*
. . . .[4]

Notes to the Cook's Tale

1. Cheapside, where jousts were sometimes held, and which was the great scene of city revels and processions.
2. His paper: his certificate of completion of his apprenticeship.
3. Louke: The precise meaning of the word is unknown, but it is doubtless included in the cant term "pal".
4. The Cook's Tale is unfinished in all the manuscripts; but in some, of minor authority, the Cook is made to break off his tale, because "it is so foul," and to tell the story of Gamelyn, on which Shakespeare's "As You Like It" is founded. The story is not Chaucer's, and is different in metre, and inferior in composition to the Tales. It is supposed that Chaucer expunged the Cook's Tale for the same reason that made him on his death-bed lament that he had written so much "ribaldry."

THE MAN OF LAW'S TALE.

THE PROLOGUE.

Our Hoste saw well that the brighte sun
Th' arc of his artificial day had run
The fourthe part, and half an houre more;
And, though he were not deep expert in lore,
He wist it was the eight-and-twenty day
Of April, that is messenger to May;
And saw well that the shadow of every tree
Was in its length of the same quantity
That was the body erect that caused it;
And therefore by the shadow he took his wit, knowledge
That Phoebus, which that shone so clear and bright,
Degrees was five-and-forty clomb on height;
And for that day, as in that latitude,
It was ten of the clock, he gan conclude;
And suddenly he plight his horse about. pulled[1]

"Lordings," quoth he, "I warn you all this rout, company
The fourthe partie of this day is gone.
Now for the love of God and of Saint John
Lose no time, as farforth as ye may.
Lordings, the time wasteth night and day,
And steals from us, what privily sleeping,
And what through negligence in our waking,
As doth the stream, that turneth never again,
Descending from the mountain to the plain.
Well might Senec, and many a philosopher,
Bewaile time more than gold in coffer.
For loss of chattels may recover'd be,
But loss of time shendeth us, quoth he. destroys

It will not come again, withoute dread,
No more than will Malkin's maidenhead,[2]
When she hath lost it in her wantonness.
Let us not moulde thus in idleness.
"Sir Man of Law," quoth he, "so have ye bliss,
Tell us a tale anon, as forword is. the bargain
Ye be submitted through your free assent
To stand in this case at my judgement.
Acquit you now, and holde your behest; keep your promise
Then have ye done your devoir at the least." duty
"Hoste," quoth he, "de par dieux jeo asente;[3]
To breake forword is not mine intent.
Behest is debt, and I would hold it fain,
All my behest; I can no better sayn.
For such law as a man gives another wight,

He should himselfe usen it by right.
Thus will our text: but natheless certain
I can right now no thrifty tale sayn, worthy
But Chaucer (though he can but lewedly knows but imperfectly
On metres and on rhyming craftily)
Hath said them, in such English as he can,
Of olde time, as knoweth many a man.
And if he have not said them, leve brother, dear
In one book, he hath said them in another
For he hath told of lovers up and down,
More than Ovide made of mentioun
In his Epistolae, that be full old.
Why should I telle them, since they he told?
In youth he made of Ceyx and Alcyon,[4]
And since then he hath spoke of every one
These noble wives, and these lovers eke.
Whoso that will his large volume seek
Called the Saintes' Legend of Cupid:[5]
There may he see the large woundes wide
Of Lucrece, and of Babylon Thisbe;
The sword of Dido for the false Enee;
The tree of Phillis for her Demophon;
The plaint of Diane, and of Hermion,
Of Ariadne, and Hypsipile;
The barren isle standing in the sea;
The drown'd Leander for his fair Hero;
The teares of Helene, and eke the woe
Of Briseis, and Laodamia;
The cruelty of thee, Queen Medea,
Thy little children hanging by the halse, neck
For thy Jason, that was of love so false.
Hypermnestra, Penelop', Alcest',
Your wifehood he commendeth with the best.
But certainly no worde writeth he
Of thilke wick' example of Canace, that wicked
That loved her own brother sinfully;
(Of all such cursed stories I say, Fy),
Or else of Tyrius Apollonius,
How that the cursed king Antiochus
Bereft his daughter of her maidenhead;
That is so horrible a tale to read,
When he her threw upon the pavement.
And therefore he, of full avisement, deliberately, advisedly
Would never write in none of his sermons
Of such unkind abominations; unnatural
Nor I will none rehearse, if that I may.

GEOFFREY CHAUCER

But of my tale how shall I do this day?
Me were loth to be liken'd doubteless
To Muses, that men call Pierides[6]
(Metamorphoseos[7] wot what I mean),
But natheless I recke not a bean,

Though I come after him with hawebake; lout[8]
I speak in prose, and let him rhymes make."
And with that word, he with a sober cheer
Began his tale, and said as ye shall hear.

Notes to the Prologue to The Man of Law's Tale

1. Plight: pulled; the word is an obsolete past tense from "pluck."
2. No more than will Malkin's maidenhead: a proverbial saying; which, however, had obtained fresh point from the Reeve's Tale, to which the host doubtless refers.
3. De par dieux jeo asente: "by God, I agree". It is characteristic that the somewhat pompous Sergeant of Law should couch his assent in the semi-barbarous French, then familiar in law procedure.
4. Ceyx and Alcyon: Chaucer treats of these in the introduction to the poem called "The Book of the Duchess." It relates to the death of Blanche, wife of John of Gaunt, Duke of Lancaster, the poet's patron, and afterwards his connexion by marriage.
5. The Saintes Legend of Cupid: Now called "The Legend of Good Women". The names of eight ladies mentioned here are not in the "Legend" as it has come down to us; while those of two ladies in the "legend" — Cleopatra and Philomela — are her omitted.
6. Not the Muses, who had their surname from the place near Mount Olympus where the Thracians first worshipped them; but the nine daughters of Pierus, king of Macedonia, whom he called the nine Muses, and who, being conquered in a contest with the genuine sisterhood, were changed into birds.
7. Metamorphoseos: Ovid's.
8. Hawebake: hawbuck, country lout; the common proverbial phrase, "to put a rogue above a gentleman," may throw light on the reading here, which is difficult.

THE TALE.[1]

O scatheful harm, condition of poverty,
With thirst, with cold, with hunger so confounded;
To ask help thee shameth in thine hearte;
If thou none ask, so sore art thou y-wounded,
That very need unwrappeth all thy wound hid.
Maugre thine head thou must for indigence
Or steal, or beg, or borrow thy dispence. expense

Thou blamest Christ, and sayst full bitterly,
He misdeparteth riches temporal; allots amiss
Thy neighebour thou witest sinfully, blamest
And sayst, thou hast too little, and he hath all:
"Parfay (sayst thou) sometime he reckon shall,
When that his tail shall brennen in the glede, burn in the fire
For he not help'd the needful in their need."

Hearken what is the sentence of the wise:
Better to die than to have indigence.
Thy selve neighebour will thee despise, that same
If thou be poor, farewell thy reverence.
Yet of the wise man take this sentence,
Alle the days of poore men be wick', wicked, evil
Beware therefore ere thou come to that prick. point

If thou be poor, thy brother hateth thee,
And all thy friendes flee from thee, alas!
O riche merchants, full of wealth be ye,
O noble, prudent folk, as in this case,
Your bagges be not fill'd with ambes ace, two aces
But with six-cinque, that runneth for your chance;[2] six-five
At Christenmass well merry may ye dance.

Ye seeke land and sea for your winnings,
As wise folk ye knowen all th' estate
Of regnes; ye be fathers of tidings, kingdoms
And tales, both of peace and of debate: contention, war
I were right now of tales desolate, barren, empty.
But that a merchant, gone in many a year,
Me taught a tale, which ye shall after hear.

In Syria whilom dwelt a company
Of chapmen rich, and thereto sad and true, grave, steadfast
Clothes of gold, and satins rich of hue.
That widewhere sent their spicery, to distant parts
Their chaffare was so thriftly and so new, wares advantageous
That every wight had dainty to chaffare pleasure deal
With them, and eke to selle them their ware.

Now fell it, that the masters of that sort
Have shapen them to Rome for to wend, determined, prepared
Were it for chapmanhood or for disport, trading
None other message would they thither send,
But come themselves to Rome, this is the end:
And in such place as thought them a vantage
For their intent, they took their herbergage. lodging

THE CANTERBURY TALES

Sojourned have these merchants in that town
A certain time as fell to their pleasance:
And so befell, that th' excellent renown
Of th' emperore's daughter, Dame Constance,
Reported was, with every circumstance,
Unto these Syrian merchants in such wise,
From day to day, as I shall you devise *relate*

This was the common voice of every man
"Our emperor of Rome, God him see, *look on with favour*
A daughter hath, that since the the world began,
To reckon as well her goodness and beauty,
Was never such another as is she:
I pray to God in honour her sustene, *sustain*
And would she were of all Europe the queen.

"In her is highe beauty without pride,
And youth withoute greenhood or folly: *childishness, immaturity*
To all her workes virtue is her guide;
Humbless hath slain in her all tyranny:
She is the mirror of all courtesy,
Her heart a very chamber of holiness,
Her hand minister of freedom for almess." *almsgiving*

And all this voice was sooth, as God is true;
But now to purpose let us turn again. *our tale*3
These merchants have done freight their shippes new,
And when they have this blissful maiden seen,
Home to Syria then they went full fain,
And did their needes, as they have done yore, *business formerly*
And liv'd in weal; I can you say no more. *prosperity*

Now fell it, that these merchants stood in grace *favour*
Of him that was the Soudan of Syrie: *Sultan*
For when they came from any strange place
He would of his benigne courtesy
Make them good cheer, and busily espy *inquire*
Tidings of sundry regnes, for to lear *realms learn*
The wonders that they mighte see or hear.

Amonges other things, specially
These merchants have him told of Dame Constance
So great nobless, in earnest so royally,
That this Soudan hath caught so great pleasance *pleasure*
To have her figure in his remembrance,
That all his lust, and all his busy cure, *pleasure care*
Was for to love her while his life may dure.

Paraventure in thilke large book, that
Which that men call the heaven, y-written was
With starres, when that he his birthe took,
That he for love should have his death, alas!
For in the starres, clearer than is glass,
Is written, God wot, whoso could it read,
The death of every man withoute dread. *doubt*

In starres many a winter therebeforn
Was writ the death of Hector, Achilles,
Of Pompey, Julius, ere they were born;
The strife of Thebes; and of Hercules,
Of Samson, Turnus, and of Socrates
The death; but mennes wittes be so dull,
That no wight can well read it at the full.

This Soudan for his privy council sent,
And, shortly of this matter for to pace, *to pass briefly by*
He hath to them declared his intent,
And told them certain, but he might have grace *unless*
To have Constance, within a little space,
He was but dead; and charged them in hie haste
To shape for his life some remedy. *contrive*

Diverse men diverse thinges said;
And arguments they casten up and down;
Many a subtle reason forth they laid;
They speak of magic, and abusion; *deception*
But finally, as in conclusion,
They cannot see in that none avantage,
Nor in no other way, save marriage.

Then saw they therein such difficulty
By way of reason, for to speak all plain,
Because that there was such diversity
Between their bothe lawes, that they sayn,
They trowe that no Christian prince would fain *believe willingly*
Wedden his child under our lawe sweet,
That us was given by Mahound our prophete. *Mahomet*

And he answered: "Rather than I lose
Constance, I will be christen'd doubteless
I must be hers, I may none other choose,
I pray you hold your arguments in peace,4
Save my life, and be not reckless
To gette her that hath my life in cure, *keeping*
For in this woe I may not long endure."

What needeth greater dilatation?
I say, by treaty and ambassadry,
And by the Pope's mediation,
And all the Church, and all the chivalry,
That in destruction of Mah'metry, *Mahometanism*
And in increase of Christe's lawe dear,
They be accorded so as ye may hear; *agreed*

How that the Soudan, and his baronage,
And all his lieges, shall y-christen'd be,
And he shall have Constance in marriage,
And certain gold, I n'ot what quantity, *know not*

57

GEOFFREY CHAUCER

And hereto find they suffisant surety.
The same accord is sworn on either side;
Now, fair Constance, Almighty God thee guide!

Now woulde some men waiten, as I guess,
That I should tellen all the purveyance, provision
The which the emperor of his noblesse
Hath shapen for his daughter, Dame Constance. prepared
Well may men know that so great ordinance
May no man tellen in a little clause,
As was arrayed for so high a cause.

Bishops be shapen with her for to wend,
Lordes, ladies, and knightes of renown,
And other folk enough, this is the end.
And notified is throughout all the town,
That every wight with great devotioun
Should pray to Christ, that he this marriage
Receive in gree, and speede this voyage. with good will, favour

The day is comen of her departing, —
I say the woful fatal day is come,
That there may be no longer tarrying,
But forward they them dressen all and some. prepare to set out
Constance, that was with sorrow all o'ercome,
Full pale arose, and dressed her to wend,
For well she saw there was no other end.

Alas! what wonder is it though she wept,
That shall be sent to a strange nation
From friendes, that so tenderly her kept,
And to be bound under subjection
of one, she knew not his condition?
Husbands be all good, and have been of yore, of old
That knowe wives; I dare say no more.

"Father," she said, "thy wretched child Constance,
Thy younge daughter, foster'd up so soft,
And you, my mother, my sov'reign pleasance
Over all thing, out-taken Christ on loft, except on high
Constance your child her recommendeth oft
Unto your grace; for I shall to Syrie,
Nor shall I ever see you more with eye.

"Alas! unto the barbarous nation
I must anon, since that it is your will:
But Christ, that starf for our redemption, died
So give me grace his hestes to fulfil. commands
I, wretched woman, no force though I spill! no matter though
Women are born to thraldom and penance, I perish
And to be under mannes governance."

I trow at Troy when Pyrrhus brake the wall,
Or Ilion burnt, or Thebes the city,
Nor at Rome for the harm through Hannibal,
That Romans hath y-vanquish'd times three,
Was heard such tender weeping for pity,
As in the chamber was for her parting;
But forth she must, whether she weep or sing.

O firste moving cruel Firmament,[5]
With thy diurnal sway that crowdest aye, pushest together, drivest
And hurtlest all from East till Occident
That naturally would hold another way;
Thy crowding set the heav'n in such array
At the beginning of this fierce voyage,
That cruel Mars hath slain this marriage.

Unfortunate ascendant tortuous,
Of which the lord is helpless fall'n, alas!
Out of his angle into the darkest house;
O Mars, O Atyzar,[6] as in this case;
O feeble Moon, unhappy is thy pace. progress
Thou knittest thee where thou art not receiv'd,
Where thou wert well, from thennes art thou weiv'd.[7]

Imprudent emperor of Rome, alas!
Was there no philosopher in all thy town?
Is no time bet than other in such case? better
Of voyage is there none election,
Namely to folk of high condition, especially
Not when a root is of a birth y-know? when the nativity is known
Alas! we be too lewed, or too slow. ignorant

To ship was brought this woeful faire maid
Solemnely, with every circumstance:
"Now Jesus Christ be with you all," she said.
There is no more, but "Farewell, fair Constance."
She pained her to make good countenance. made an effort
And forth I let her sail in this manner,
And turn I will again to my matter.

The mother of the Soudan, well of vices,
Espied hath her sone's plain intent,
How he will leave his olde sacrifices:
And right anon she for her council sent,
And they be come, to knowe what she meant,
And when assembled was this folk in fere, together
She sat her down, and said as ye shall hear.

"Lordes," she said, "ye knowen every one,
How that my son in point is for to lete forsake
The holy lawes of our Alkaron, Koran
Given by God's messenger Mahomete:
But one avow to greate God I hete, promise
Life shall rather out of my body start,
Than Mahomet's law go out of mine heart.

"What should us tiden of this newe law, betide, befall
But thraldom to our bodies, and penance,
And afterward in hell to be y-draw,

THE CANTERBURY TALES

For we renied Mahound our creance? denied
Mahomet our belief
But, lordes, will ye maken assurance,
As I shall say, assenting to my lore? advice
And I shall make us safe for evermore."

They sworen and assented every man
To live with her and die, and by her stand:
And every one, in the best wise he can,
To strengthen her shall all his friendes fand. endeavour[8]
And she hath this emprise taken in hand,
Which ye shall heare that I shall devise; relate
And to them all she spake right in this wise.

"We shall first feign us Christendom to take; embrace Christianity
Cold water shall not grieve us but a lite: little
And I shall such a feast and revel make,
That, as I trow, I shall the Soudan quite. requite, match
For though his wife be christen'd ne'er so white,
She shall have need to wash away the red,
Though she a fount of water with her led."

O Soudaness, root of iniquity, Sultaness
Virago thou, Semiramis the second!
O serpent under femininity,
Like to the serpent deep in hell y-bound!
O feigned woman, all that may confound
Virtue and innocence, through thy malice,
Is bred in thee, as nest of every vice!

O Satan envious! since thilke day
That thou wert chased from our heritage,
Well knowest thou to woman th' olde way.
Thou madest Eve to bring us in servage: bondage
Thou wilt fordo this Christian marriage: ruin
Thine instrument so (well-away the while!)
Mak'st thou of women when thou wilt beguile.

This Soudaness, whom I thus blame and warray, oppose, censure
Let privily her council go their way:
Why should I in this tale longer tarry?
She rode unto the Soudan on a day,
And said him, that she would reny her lay, renounce her creed
And Christendom of priestes' handes fong, take[9]
Repenting her she heathen was so long;

Beseeching him to do her that honour,
That she might have the Christian folk to feast:
"To please them I will do my labour."
The Soudan said, "I will do at your hest," desire
And kneeling, thanked her for that request;
So glad he was, he wist not what to say. knew
She kiss'd her son, and home she went her way.

Arrived be these Christian folk to land
In Syria, with a great solemne rout,
And hastily this Soudan sent his sond, message
First to his mother, and all the realm about,
And said, his wife was comen out of doubt,
And pray'd them for to ride again the queen, to meet
The honour of his regne to sustene. realm

Great was the press, and rich was the array
Of Syrians and Romans met in fere. in company
The mother of the Soudan rich and gay
Received her with all so glad a cheer face
As any mother might her daughter dear
And to the nexte city there beside
A softe pace solemnely they ride.

Nought, trow I, the triumph of Julius
Of which that Lucan maketh such a boast,
Was royaller, or more curious,
Than was th' assembly of this blissful host
But O this scorpion, this wicked ghost, spirit
The Soudaness, for all her flattering
Cast under this full mortally to sting. contrived

The Soudan came himself soon after this,
So royally, that wonder is to tell,
And welcomed her with all joy and bliss.
And thus in mirth and joy I let them dwell.
The fruit of his matter is that I tell;
When the time came, men thought it for the best
That revel stint, and men go to their rest. cease

The time is come that this old Soudaness
Ordained hath the feast of which I told,
And to the feast the Christian folk them dress
In general, yea, bothe young and old.
There may men feast and royalty behold,
And dainties more than I can you devise;
But all too dear they bought it ere they rise.

O sudden woe, that ev'r art successour
To worldly bliss! sprent is with bitterness sprinkled
Th' end of our joy, of our worldly labour;
Woe occupies the fine of our gladness. seizes the end
Hearken this counsel, for thy sickerness: security
Upon thy glade days have in thy mind
The unware woe of harm, that comes behind. unforeseen

For, shortly for to tell it at a word,
The Soudan and the Christians every one
Were all to-hewn and sticked at the board, cut to pieces
But it were only Dame Constance alone.
This olde Soudaness, this cursed crone,
Had with her friendes done this cursed deed,
For she herself would all the country lead.

Nor there was Syrian that was converted,
That of the counsel of the Soudan wot, knew
That was not all to-hewn, ere he asterted: escaped
And Constance have they ta'en anon foot-hot,

immediately
And in a ship all steereless, God wot, without rudder
They have her set, and bid her learn to sail
Out of Syria again-ward to Itale. back to Italy

A certain treasure that she thither lad, took
And, sooth to say, of victual great plenty,
They have her giv'n, and clothes eke she had
And forth she sailed in the salte sea:
O my Constance, full of benignity,
O emperores younge daughter dear,
He that is lord of fortune be thy steer! rudder, guide

She bless'd herself, and with full piteous voice
Unto the cross of Christ thus saide she;
"O dear, O wealful altar, holy cross, blessed, beneficent
Red of the Lambes blood, full of pity,
That wash'd the world from old iniquity,
Me from the fiend and from his clawes keep,
That day that I shall drenchen in the deepe. drown

"Victorious tree, protection of the true,
That only worthy were for to bear
The King of Heaven, with his woundes new,
The white Lamb, that hurt was with a spear;
Flemer of fiendes out of him and her banisher, driver out
On which thy limbes faithfully extend,[10]
Me keep, and give me might my life to mend."

Yeares and days floated this creature
Throughout the sea of Greece, unto the strait
Of Maroc, as it was her a venture: Morocco; Gibraltar
On many a sorry meal now may she bait,
After her death full often may she wait, expect
Ere that the wilde waves will her drive
Unto the place there as she shall arrive. where

Men mighten aske, why she was not slain?
Eke at the feast who might her body save?
And I answer to that demand again,
Who saved Daniel in the horrible cave,
Where every wight, save he, master or knave, servant
Was with the lion frett, ere he astart? devoured escaped
No wight but God, that he bare in his heart.

God list to shew his wonderful miracle it pleased
In her, that we should see his mighty workes:
Christ, which that is to every harm triacle, remedy, salve
By certain meanes oft, as knowe clerkes, scholars
Doth thing for certain ende, that full derk is
To manne's wit, that for our, ignorance

Ne cannot know his prudent purveyance. foresight

Now since she was not at the feast y-slaw, slain
Who kepte her from drowning in the sea?
Who kepte Jonas in the fish's maw,
Till he was spouted up at Nineveh?
Well may men know, it was no wight but he
That kept the Hebrew people from drowning,
With drye feet throughout the sea passing.

Who bade the foure spirits of tempest,[11]
That power have t' annoye land and sea,
Both north and south, and also west and east,
Annoye neither sea, nor land, nor tree?
Soothly the commander of that was he
That from the tempest aye this woman kept,
As well when she awoke as when she slept.

Where might this woman meat and drinke have?
Three year and more how lasted her vitaille? victuals
Who fed the Egyptian Mary in the cave
Or in desert? no wight but Christ sans faille. without fail
Five thousand folk it was as great marvaille
With loaves five and fishes two to feed
God sent his foison at her greate need. abundance

She drived forth into our ocean
Throughout our wilde sea, till at the last
Under an hold, that nempnen I not can, castle name
Far in Northumberland, the wave her cast
And in the sand her ship sticked so fast
That thennes would it not in all a tide:[12]
The will of Christ was that she should abide.

The Constable of the castle down did fare go
To see this wreck, and all the ship he sought, searched
And found this weary woman full of care;
He found also the treasure that she brought:
In her language mercy she besought,
The life out of her body for to twin, divide
Her to deliver of woe that she was in.

A manner Latin corrupt[13] was her speech,
But algate thereby was she understond. nevertheless
The Constable, when him list no longer seech, search
This woeful woman brought he to the lond.
She kneeled down, and thanked Godde's sond; what God had sent
But what she was she would to no man say
For foul nor fair, although that she should dey. die

She said, she was so mazed in the sea,
That she forgot her minde, by her truth.
The Constable had of her so great pity

And eke his wife, that they wept for ruth: pity
She was so diligent withoute slouth
To serve and please every one in that place,
That all her lov'd, that looked in her face.

The Constable and Dame Hermegild his wife
Were Pagans, and that country every where;
But Hermegild lov'd Constance as her life;
And Constance had so long sojourned there
In orisons, with many a bitter tear,
Till Jesus had converted through His grace
Dame Hermegild, Constabless of that place.

In all that land no Christians durste rout; assemble
All Christian folk had fled from that country
Through Pagans, that conquered all about
The plages of the North by land and sea. regions, coasts
To Wales had fled the Christianity the Old Britons who
Of olde Britons, dwelling in this isle; were Christians
There was their refuge for the meanewhile.

But yet n'ere Christian Britons so exiled, there were
That there n'ere some which in their privity not
Honoured Christ, and heathen folk beguiled;
And nigh the castle such there dwelled three:
And one of them was blind, and might not see,
But it were with thilk eyen of his mind, except those
With which men maye see when they be blind.

Bright was the sun, as in a summer's day,
For which the Constable, and his wife also,
And Constance, have y-take the righte way
Toward the sea a furlong way or two,
To playen, and to roame to and fro;
And in their walk this blinde man they met,
Crooked and old, with eyen fast y-shet. shut

"In the name of Christ," cried this blind Briton,
"Dame Hermegild, give me my sight again!"
This lady wax'd afrayed of that soun', was alarmed by that cry
Lest that her husband, shortly for to sayn,
Would her for Jesus Christe's love have slain,
Till Constance made her hold, and bade her wirch work
The will of Christ, as daughter of holy Church

The Constable wax'd abashed of that sight, astonished
And saide; "What amounteth all this fare?" what means all
Constance answered; "Sir, it is Christ's might, this ado?
That helpeth folk out of the fiendes snare:"
And so farforth she gan our law declare, with such effect

That she the Constable, ere that it were eve,
Converted, and on Christ made him believe.

This Constable was not lord of the place
Of which I speak, there as he Constance fand, found
But kept it strongly many a winter space,
Under Alla, king of Northumberland,
That was full wise, and worthy of his hand
Against the Scotes, as men may well hear;
But turn I will again to my mattere.

Satan, that ever us waiteth to beguile,
Saw of Constance all her perfectioun,
And cast anon how he might quite her while; considered how to have
And made a young knight, that dwelt in that town, revenge on her
Love her so hot of foul affectioun,
That verily him thought that he should spill perish
But he of her might ones have his will. unless

He wooed her, but it availed nought;
She woulde do no sinne by no way:
And for despite, he compassed his thought
To make her a shameful death to dey; die
He waiteth when the Constable is away,
And privily upon a night he crept
In Hermegilda's chamber while she slept.

Weary, forwaked in her orisons, having been long awake
Sleepeth Constance, and Hermegild also.
This knight, through Satanas' temptation;
All softely is to the bed y-go, gone
And cut the throat of Hermegild in two,
And laid the bloody knife by Dame Constance,
And went his way, there God give him mischance.

Soon after came the Constable home again,
And eke Alla that king was of that land,
And saw his wife dispiteously slain, cruelly
For which full oft he wept and wrung his hand;
And ill the bed the bloody knife he fand
By Dame Constance: Alas! what might she say?
For very woe her wit was all away.

To King Alla was told all this mischance
And eke the time, and where, and in what wise
That in a ship was founden this Constance,
As here before ye have me heard devise: describe
The kinges heart for pity gan agrise, to be grieved, to tremble
When he saw so benign a creature
Fall in disease and in misaventure. distress

For as the lamb toward his death is brought,
So stood this innocent before the king:
This false knight, that had this treason wrought,
Bore her in hand that she had done this thing:

accused her falsely
But natheless there was great murmuring
Among the people, that say they cannot guess
That she had done so great a wickedness.

For they had seen her ever virtuous,
And loving Hermegild right as her life:
Of this bare witness each one in that house,
Save he that Hermegild slew with his knife:
This gentle king had caught a great motife been greatly moved
Of this witness, and thought he would inquere by the evidence
Deeper into this case, the truth to lear. learn

Alas! Constance, thou has no champion,
Nor fighte canst thou not, so well-away!
But he that starf for our redemption, died
And bound Satan, and yet li'th where he lay,
So be thy stronge champion this day:
For, but Christ upon thee miracle kithe, show
Withoute guilt thou shalt be slain as swithe. immediately

She set her down on knees, and thus she said;
"Immortal God, that savedest Susanne
From false blame; and thou merciful maid,
Mary I mean, the daughter to Saint Anne,
Before whose child the angels sing Osanne, Hosanna
If I be guiltless of this felony,
My succour be, or elles shall I die."

Have ye not seen sometime a pale face
(Among a press) of him that hath been lad led
Toward his death, where he getteth no grace,
And such a colour in his face hath had,
Men mighte know him that was so bestad, bested, situated
Amonges all the faces in that rout?
So stood Constance, and looked her about.

O queenes living in prosperity,
Duchesses, and ye ladies every one,
Have some ruth on her adversity! pity
An emperor's daughter, she stood alone;
She had no wight to whom to make her moan.
O blood royal, that standest in this drede, danger
Far be thy friendes in thy greate need!

This king Alla had such compassioun,
As gentle heart is full filled of pity,
That from his eyen ran the water down
"Now hastily do fetch a book," quoth he;
"And if this knight will sweare, how that she
This woman slew, yet will we us advise consider
Whom that we will that shall be our justice."

A Briton book, written with Evangiles, the Gospels
Was fetched, and on this book he swore anon
She guilty was; and, in the meanewhiles,

An hand him smote upon the necke bone,
That down he fell at once right as a stone:
And both his eyen burst out of his face
In sight of ev'rybody in that place.

A voice was heard, in general audience,
That said; "Thou hast deslander'd guilteless
The daughter of holy Church in high presence;
Thus hast thou done, and yet hold I my peace?" shall I be silent?
Of this marvel aghast was all the press,
As mazed folk they stood every one
For dread of wreake, save Constance alone. vengeance

Great was the dread and eke the repentance
Of them that hadde wrong suspicion
Upon this sely innocent Constance; simple, harmless
And for this miracle, in conclusion,
And by Constance's mediation,
The king, and many another in that place,
Converted was, thanked be Christe's grace!

This false knight was slain for his untruth
By judgement of Alla hastily;
And yet Constance had of his death great ruth; compassion
And after this Jesus of his mercy
Made Alla wedde full solemnly
This holy woman, that is so bright and sheen,
And thus hath Christ y-made Constance a queen.

But who was woeful, if I shall not lie,
Of this wedding but Donegild, and no mo',
The kinge's mother, full of tyranny?
Her thought her cursed heart would burst in two;
She would not that her son had done so;
Her thought it a despite that he should take
So strange a creature unto his make. mate, consort

Me list not of the chaff nor of the stre straw
Make so long a tale, as of the corn.
What should I tellen of the royalty
Of this marriage, or which course goes beforn,
Who bloweth in a trump or in an horn?
The fruit of every tale is for to say;
They eat and drink, and dance, and sing, and play.

They go to bed, as it was skill and right; reasonable
For though that wives be full holy things,
They muste take in patience at night
Such manner necessaries as be pleasings kind of
To folk that have y-wedded them with rings,
And lay a lite their holiness aside a little of
As for the time, it may no better betide.

On her he got a knave child anon, male[14]
And to a Bishop and to his Constable eke
He took his wife to keep, when he is gone

THE CANTERBURY TALES

To Scotland-ward, his foemen for to seek.
Now fair Constance, that is so humble and meek,
So long is gone with childe till that still
She held her chamb'r, abiding Christe's will

The time is come, a knave child she bare;
Mauricius at the font-stone they him call.
This Constable doth forth come a messenger,
caused to come forth
And wrote unto his king that clep'd was All',
How that this blissful tiding is befall,
And other tidings speedful for to say
He hath the letter, and forth he go'th his way. i.e. the messenger

This messenger, to do his avantage, promote his own interest
Unto the kinge's mother rideth swithe, swiftly
And saluteth her full fair in his language.
"Madame," quoth he, "ye may be glad and blithe,
And thanke God an hundred thousand sithe; times
My lady queen hath child, withoute doubt,
To joy and bliss of all this realm about.

"Lo, here the letter sealed of this thing,
That I must bear with all the haste I may:
If ye will aught unto your son the king,
I am your servant both by night and day."
Donegild answer'd, "As now at this time, nay;
But here I will all night thou take thy rest,
To-morrow will I say thee what me lest." pleases

This messenger drank sadly ale and wine, steadily
And stolen were his letters privily
Out of his box, while he slept as a swine;
And counterfeited was full subtilly
Another letter, wrote full sinfully,
Unto the king, direct of this mattere
From his Constable, as ye shall after hear.

This letter said, the queen deliver'd was
Of so horrible a fiendlike creature,
That in the castle none so hardy was brave
That any while he durst therein endure:
The mother was an elf by aventure
Become, by charmes or by sorcery,
And every man hated her company.

Woe was this king when he this letter had seen,
But to no wight he told his sorrows sore,
But with his owen hand he wrote again,
"Welcome the sond of Christ for evermore will, sending
To me, that am now learned in this lore:
Lord, welcome be thy lust and thy pleasance, will, pleasure
My lust I put all in thine ordinance.

"Keepe this child, albeit foul or fair, preserve
And eke my wife, unto mine homecoming:
Christ when him list may send to me an heir
More agreeable than this to my liking."
This letter he sealed, privily weeping.
Which to the messenger was taken soon,
And forth he went, there is no more to do'n. do

O messenger full fill'd of drunkenness,
Strong is thy breath, thy limbes falter aye,
And thou betrayest alle secretness;
Thy mind is lorn, thou janglest as a jay; lost
Thy face is turned in a new array; aspect
Where drunkenness reigneth in any rout, company
There is no counsel hid, withoute doubt.

O Donegild, I have no English dign worthy
Unto thy malice, and thy tyranny:
And therefore to the fiend I thee resign,
Let him indite of all thy treachery
'Fy, mannish, fy! O nay, by God I lie; unwomanly woman
Fy, fiendlike spirit! for I dare well tell,
Though thou here walk, thy spirit is in hell.

This messenger came from the king again,
And at the kinge's mother's court he light, alighted
And she was of this messenger full fain, glad
And pleased him in all that e'er she might.
He drank, and well his girdle underpight; stowed away (liquor)
He slept, and eke he snored in his guise under his girdle
All night, until the sun began to rise.

Eft were his letters stolen every one, again
And counterfeited letters in this wise:
The king commanded his Constable anon,
On pain of hanging and of high jewise, judgement
That he should suffer in no manner wise
Constance within his regne for to abide kingdom
Three dayes, and a quarter of a tide;

But in the same ship as he her fand,
Her and her younge son, and all her gear,
He shoulde put, and crowd her from the land, push
And charge her, that she never eft come there.
O my Constance, well may thy ghost have fear, spirit
And sleeping in thy dream be in penance, pain, trouble
When Donegild cast all this ordinance. contrived plan, plot

This messenger, on morrow when he woke,
Unto the castle held the nexte way, nearest
And to the constable the letter took;
And when he this dispiteous letter sey, cruel saw
Full oft he said, "Alas, and well-away!
Lord Christ," quoth he, "how may this world

63

endure?
So full of sin is many a creature.

"O mighty God, if that it be thy will,
Since thou art rightful judge, how may it be
That thou wilt suffer innocence to spill, be destroyed
And wicked folk reign in prosperity?
Ah! good Constance, alas! so woe is me,
That I must be thy tormentor, or dey die
A shameful death, there is no other way.

Wept bothe young and old in all that place,
When that the king this cursed letter sent;
And Constance, with a deadly pale face,
The fourthe day toward her ship she went.
But natheless she took in good intent
The will of Christ, and kneeling on the strond   strand, shore
She saide, "Lord, aye welcome be thy sond   whatever thou sendest

"He that me kepte from the false blame,
While I was in the land amonges you,
He can me keep from harm and eke from shame
In the salt sea, although I see not how
As strong as ever he was, he is yet now,
In him trust I, and in his mother dere,
That is to me my sail and eke my stere."   rudder, guide

Her little child lay weeping in her arm
And, kneeling, piteously to him she said
"Peace, little son, I will do thee no harm:"
With that her kerchief off her head she braid,   took, drew
And over his little eyen she it laid,
And in her arm she lulled it full fast,
And unto heav'n her eyen up she cast.

"Mother," quoth she, "and maiden bright, Mary,
Sooth is, that through a woman's eggement   incitement, egging on
Mankind was lorn, and damned aye to die;   lost
For which thy child was on a cross y-rent: torn, pierced
Thy blissful eyen saw all his torment,
Then is there no comparison between
Thy woe, and any woe man may sustene.

"Thou saw'st thy child y-slain before thine eyen,
And yet now lives my little child, parfay: by my faith
Now, lady bright, to whom the woeful cryen,
Thou glory of womanhood, thou faire may,   maid
Thou haven of refuge, bright star of day,
Rue on my child, that of thy gentleness   take pity
Ruest on every rueful in distress.   sorrowful person

"O little child, alas! what is thy guilt,
That never wroughtest sin as yet, pardie?   par Dieu; by God
Why will thine harde father have thee spilt?   cruel   destroyed
O mercy, deare Constable," quoth she,
"And let my little child here dwell with thee:
And if thou dar'st not save him from blame,
So kiss him ones in his father's name."

Therewith she looked backward to the land,
And saide, "Farewell, husband rutheless!"
And up she rose, and walked down the strand
Toward the ship, her following all the press: multitude
And ever she pray'd her child to hold his peace,
And took her leave, and with an holy intent
She blessed her, and to the ship she went.

Victualed was the ship, it is no drede,   doubt
Abundantly for her a full long space:
And other necessaries that should need be needed
She had enough, heried be Godde's grace: praised[15]
For wind and weather, Almighty God purchase,   provide
And bring her home; I can no better say;
But in the sea she drived forth her way.

Alla the king came home soon after this
Unto the castle, of the which I told,
And asked where his wife and his child is;
The Constable gan about his heart feel cold,
And plainly all the matter he him told
As ye have heard; I can tell it no better;
And shew'd the king his seal, and eke his letter

And saide; "Lord, as ye commanded me
On pain of death, so have I done certain."
The messenger tormented was, till he tortured
Muste beknow, and tell it flat and plain,   confess[16]
From night to night in what place he had lain;
And thus, by wit and subtle inquiring,
Imagin'd was by whom this harm gan spring.

The hand was known that had the letter wrote,
And all the venom of the cursed deed;
But in what wise, certainly I know not.
Th' effect is this, that Alla, out of drede,   without doubt
His mother slew, that may men plainly read,
For that she traitor was to her liegeance: allegiance
Thus ended olde Donegild with mischance.

The sorrow that this Alla night and day
Made for his wife, and for his child also,
There is no tongue that it telle may.
But now will I again to Constance go,
That floated in the sea in pain and woe
Five year and more, as liked Christe's sond,   decree, command
Ere that her ship approached to the lond.   land

Under an heathen castle, at the last,
Of which the name in my text I not find,
Constance and eke her child the sea upcast.
Almighty God, that saved all mankind,
Have on Constance and on her child some mind,
That fallen is in heathen hand eftsoon again
In point to spill, as I shall tell you soon! in danger of perishing
Down from the castle came there many a wight
To gauren on this ship, and on Constance: gaze, stare
But shortly from the castle, on a night,
The lorde's steward, — God give him mischance, —

A thief that had renied our creance, denied our faith
Came to the ship alone, and said he would
Her leman be, whether she would or n'ould. illicit lover

Woe was this wretched woman then begone;
Her child cri'd, and she cried piteously:
But blissful Mary help'd her right anon,
For, with her struggling well and mightily,
The thief fell overboard all suddenly,
And in the sea he drenched for vengeance, drowned
And thus hath Christ unwemmed kept Constance. unblemished

O foul lust of luxury! lo thine end!
Not only that thou faintest manne's mind, weakenest
But verily thou wilt his body shend. destroy
Th' end of thy work, or of thy lustes blind,
Is complaining: how many may men find,
That not for work, sometimes, but for th' intent
To do this sin, be either slain or shent?

How may this weake woman have the strength
Her to defend against this renegate?
O Goliath, unmeasurable of length,
How mighte David make thee so mate? overthrown
So young, and of armour so desolate, devoid
How durst he look upon thy dreadful face?
Well may men see it was but Godde's grace.

Who gave Judith courage or hardiness
To slay him, Holofernes, in his tent,
And to deliver out of wretchedness
The people of God? I say for this intent
That right as God spirit of vigour sent
To them, and saved them out of mischance,
So sent he might and vigour to Constance.

Forth went her ship throughout the narrow mouth
Of Jubaltare and Septe, driving alway, Gibraltar and Ceuta
Sometime west, and sometime north and south,
And sometime east, full many a weary day:
Till Christe's mother (blessed be she aye)
Had shaped through her endless goodness resolved, arranged
To make an end of all her heaviness.

Now let us stint of Constance but a throw, cease speaking
And speak we of the Roman emperor, short time
That out of Syria had by letters know
The slaughter of Christian folk, and dishonor
Done to his daughter by a false traitor,
I mean the cursed wicked Soudaness,
That at the feast let slay both more and less. caused both high and low to be killed
For which this emperor had sent anon
His senator, with royal ordinance,
And other lordes, God wot, many a one,
On Syrians to take high vengeance:
They burn and slay, and bring them to mischance
Full many a day: but shortly this is th' end,
Homeward to Rome they shaped them to wend.

This senator repaired with victory
To Rome-ward, sailing full royally,
And met the ship driving, as saith the story,
In which Constance sat full piteously:
And nothing knew he what she was, nor why
She was in such array; nor she will say
Of her estate, although that she should dey. die

He brought her unto Rome, and to his wife
He gave her, and her younge son also:
And with the senator she led her life.
Thus can our Lady bringen out of woe
Woeful Constance, and many another mo':
And longe time she dwelled in that place,
In holy works ever, as was her grace.

The senatores wife her aunte was,
But for all that she knew her ne'er the more:
I will no longer tarry in this case,
But to King Alla, whom I spake of yore,
That for his wife wept and sighed sore,
I will return, and leave I will Constance
Under the senatores governance.

King Alla, which that had his mother slain,
Upon a day fell in such repentance;
That, if I shortly tell it shall and plain,
To Rome he came to receive his penitance,
And put him in the Pope's ordinance
In high and low, and Jesus Christ besought
Forgive his wicked works that he had wrought.

The fame anon throughout the town is borne,
How Alla king shall come on pilgrimage,
By harbingers that wente him beforn,
For which the senator, as was usage,
Rode him again, and many of his lineage, to meet him

GEOFFREY CHAUCER

As well to show his high magnificence,
As to do any king a reverence.

Great cheere did this noble senator courtesy
To King Alla and he to him also;
Each of them did the other great honor;
And so befell, that in a day or two
This senator did to King Alla go
To feast, and shortly, if I shall not lie,
Constance's son went in his company.

Some men would say,[17] at request of Constance
This senator had led this child to feast:
I may not tellen every circumstance,
Be as be may, there was he at the least:
But sooth is this, that at his mother's hest behest
Before Alla during the meates space, meal time
The child stood, looking in the kinges face.

This Alla king had of this child great wonder,
And to the senator he said anon,
"Whose is that faire child that standeth yonder?"
"I n'ot," quoth he, "by God and by Saint John; know not
A mother he hath, but father hath he none,
That I of wot:" and shortly in a stound short time[18]
He told to Alla how this child was found.

"But God wot," quoth this senator also,
"So virtuous a liver in all my life
I never saw, as she, nor heard of mo'
Of worldly woman, maiden, widow or wife:
I dare well say she hadde lever a knife rather
Throughout her breast, than be a woman wick', wicked
There is no man could bring her to that prick. point

Now was this child as like unto Constance
As possible is a creature to be:
This Alla had the face in remembrance
Of Dame Constance, and thereon mused he,
If that the childe's mother were aught she could be she
That was his wife; and privily he sight, sighed
And sped him from the table that he might. as fast as he could

"Parfay," thought he, "phantom is in mine head. by my faith
I ought to deem, of skilful judgement, a fantasy
That in the salte sea my wife is dead."
And afterward he made his argument,
"What wot I, if that Christ have hither sent
My wife by sea, as well as he her sent
To my country, from thennes that she went?"

And, after noon, home with the senator.
Went Alla, for to see this wondrous chance.
This senator did Alla great honor,
And hastily he sent after Constance:

But truste well, her liste not to dance.
When that she wiste wherefore was that sond, summons
Unneth upon her feet she mighte stand. with difficulty

When Alla saw his wife, fair he her gret, greeted
And wept, that it was ruthe for to see,
For at the firste look he on her set
He knew well verily that it was she:
And she, for sorrow, as dumb stood as a tree:
So was her hearte shut in her distress,
When she remember'd his unkindness.

Twice she swooned in his owen sight,
He wept and him excused piteously:
"Now God," quoth he, "and all his hallows bright saints
So wisly on my soule have mercy, surely
That of your harm as guilteless am I,
As is Maurice my son, so like your face,
Else may the fiend me fetch out of this place."

Long was the sobbing and the bitter pain,
Ere that their woeful hearte mighte cease;
Great was the pity for to hear them plain, lament
Through whiche plaintes gan their woe increase.
I pray you all my labour to release,
I may not tell all their woe till to-morrow,
I am so weary for to speak of sorrow.

But finally, when that the sooth is wist, truth is known
That Alla guiltless was of all her woe,
I trow an hundred times have they kiss'd,
And such a bliss is there betwixt them two,
That, save the joy that lasteth evermo',
There is none like, that any creature
Hath seen, or shall see, while the world may dure.

Then prayed she her husband meekely
In the relief of her long piteous pine, sorrow
That he would pray her father specially,
That of his majesty he would incline
To vouchesafe some day with him to dine:
She pray'd him eke, that he should by no way
Unto her father no word of her say.

Some men would say,[17] how that the child Maurice
Did this message unto the emperor:
But, as I guess, Alla was not so nice, foolish
To him that is so sovereign of honor
As he that is of Christian folk the flow'r,
Send any child, but better 'tis to deem
He went himself; and so it may well seem.

This emperor hath granted gentilly
To come to dinner, as he him besought:
And well rede I, he looked busily guess, know
Upon this child, and on his daughter thought.
Alla went to his inn, and as him ought

66

Arrayed for this feast in every wise, prepared
As farforth as his cunning may suffice. as far as his skill

The morrow came, and Alla gan him dress, make ready
And eke his wife, the emperor to meet:
And forth they rode in joy and in gladness,
And when she saw her father in the street,
She lighted down and fell before his feet.
"Father," quoth she, "your younge child Constance
Is now full clean out of your remembrance.

"I am your daughter, your Constance," quoth she,
"That whilom ye have sent into Syrie;
It am I, father, that in the salt sea
Was put alone, and damned for to die. condemned
Now, goode father, I you mercy cry,
Send me no more into none heatheness,
But thank my lord here of his kindeness."

Who can the piteous joye tellen all,
Betwixt them three, since they be thus y-met?
But of my tale make an end I shall,
The day goes fast, I will no longer let. hinder
These gladde folk to dinner be y-set;
In joy and bliss at meat I let them dwell,
A thousand fold well more than I can tell.

This child Maurice was since then emperor
Made by the Pope, and lived Christianly,
To Christe's Churche did he great honor:
But I let all his story passe by,
Of Constance is my tale especially,
In the olde Roman gestes men may find histories[19]
Maurice's life, I bear it not in mind.

This King Alla, when he his time sey, saw
With his Constance, his holy wife so sweet,
To England are they come the righte way,
Where they did live in joy and in quiet.
But little while it lasted, I you hete, promise
Joy of this world for time will not abide,
From day to night it changeth as the tide.

Who liv'd ever in such delight one day,
That him not moved either conscience,
Or ire, or talent, or some kind affray, some kind of disturbance
Envy, or pride, or passion, or offence?
I say but for this ende this sentence, judgment, opinion
That little while in joy or in pleasance
Lasted the bliss of Alla with Constance.

For death, that takes of high and low his rent,
When passed was a year, even as I guess,
Out of this world this King Alla he hent, snatched
For whom Constance had full great heaviness.
Now let us pray that God his soule bless:
And Dame Constance, finally to say,
Toward the town of Rome went her way.

To Rome is come this holy creature,
And findeth there her friendes whole and sound:
Now is she scaped all her aventure:
And when that she her father hath y-found,
Down on her knees falleth she to ground,
Weeping for tenderness in hearte blithe
She herieth God an hundred thousand sithe. praises times

In virtue and in holy almes-deed
They liven all, and ne'er asunder wend;
Till death departeth them, this life they lead:
And fare now well, my tale is at an end
Now Jesus Christ, that of his might may send
Joy after woe, govern us in his grace
And keep us alle that be in this place.

Notes to the Man of Law's Tale

1. This tale is believed by Tyrwhitt to have been taken, with no material change, from the "Confessio Amantis" of John Gower, who was contemporary with Chaucer, though somewhat his senior. In the prologue, the references to the stories of Canace, and of Apollonius Tyrius, seem to be an attack on Gower, who had given these tales in his book; whence Tyrwhitt concludes that the friendship between the two poets suffered some interruption in the latter part of their lives. Gower was not the inventor of the story, which he found in old French romances, and it is not improbable that Chaucer may have gone to the same source as Gower, though the latter undoubtedly led the way. (Transcriber's note: later commentators have identified the introduction describing the sorrows of poverty, along with the other moralising interludes in the tale, as translated from "De Contemptu Mundi" ("On the contempt of the world") by Pope Innocent.)
2. Transcriber' note: This refers to the game of hazard, a dice game like craps, in which two ("ambes ace") won, and eleven ("six-cinque") lost.
3. Purpose: discourse, tale: French "propos".
4. "Peace" rhymed with "lese" and "chese", the old forms of "lose" and "choose".
5. According to Middle Age writers there were two motions of the first heaven; one everything always from east to west above the stars; the other moving the stars against the first motion, from west to east, on two other poles.

6. Atyzar: the meaning of this word is not known; but "occifer", murderer, has been suggested instead by Urry, on the authority of a marginal reading on a manuscript. (Transcriber's note: later commentators explain it as derived from Arabic "al-ta'thir", influence - used here in an astrological sense)
7. "Thou knittest thee where thou art not receiv'd, Where thou wert well, from thennes art thou weiv'd" i.e. "Thou joinest thyself where thou art rejected, and art declined or departed from the place where thou wert well." The moon portends the fortunes of Constance.
8. Fand: endeavour; from Anglo-Saxon, "fandian," to try
9. Feng: take; Anglo-Saxon "fengian", German, "fangen".
10. Him and her on which thy limbes faithfully extend: those who in faith wear the crucifix.
11. The four spirits of tempest: the four angels who held the four winds of the earth and to whom it was given to hurt the earth and the sea (Rev. vii. 1, 2).
12. Thennes would it not in all a tide: thence would it not move for long, at all.
13. A manner Latin corrupt: a kind of bastard Latin.
14. Knave child: male child; German "Knabe".
15. Heried: honoured, praised; from Anglo-Saxon, "herian." Compare German, "herrlich," glorious, honourable.
16. Beknow: confess; German, "bekennen."
17. The poet here refers to Gower's version of the story.
18. Stound: short time; German, "stunde", hour.
19. Gestes: histories, exploits; Latin, "res gestae".

THE WIFE OF BATH'S TALE.

THE PROLOGUE.[1]

Experience, though none authority   authoritative texts
Were in this world, is right enough for me
To speak of woe that is in marriage:
For, lordings, since I twelve year was of age,
(Thanked be God that is etern on live),   lives eternally
Husbands at the church door have I had five,[2]
For I so often have y-wedded be,
And all were worthy men in their degree.
But me was told, not longe time gone is
That sithen Christe went never but ones   since
To wedding, in the Cane of Galilee,   Cana
That by that ilk example taught he me,   same
That I not wedded shoulde be but once.
Lo, hearken eke a sharp word for the nonce,   occasion
Beside a welle Jesus, God and man,
Spake in reproof of the Samaritan:
"Thou hast y-had five husbandes," said he;
"And thilke man, that now hath wedded thee,   that
Is not thine husband:"[3] thus said he certain;
What that he meant thereby, I cannot sayn.
But that I aske, why the fifthe man
Was not husband to the Samaritan?
How many might she have in marriage?
Yet heard I never tellen in mine age   in my life
Upon this number definitioun.
Men may divine, and glosen up and down;   comment
But well I wot, express without a lie,
God bade us for to wax and multiply;
That gentle text can I well understand.
Eke well I wot, he said, that mine husband
Should leave father and mother, and take to me;
But of no number mention made he,
Of bigamy or of octogamy;
Why then should men speak of it villainy?   as if it were a disgrace

Lo here, the wise king Dan Solomon,   Lord[4]
I trow that he had wives more than one;
As would to God it lawful were to me
To be refreshed half so oft as he!
What gift of God had he for all his wives!   special favour, licence
No man hath such, that in this world alive is.
God wot, this noble king, as to my wit,   as I understand
The first night had many a merry fit
With each of them, so well was him on live.   so well he lived
Blessed be God that I have wedded five!
Welcome the sixth whenever that he shall.
For since I will not keep me chaste in all,
When mine husband is from the world y-gone,
Some Christian man shall wedde me anon.
For then th' apostle saith that I am free
To wed, a' God's half, where it liketh me.   on God's part
He saith, that to be wedded is no sin;
Better is to be wedded than to brin.   burn
What recketh me though folk say villainy   care
Of shrewed Lamech, and his bigamy?   impious, wicked
I wot well Abraham was a holy man,
And Jacob eke, as far as ev'r I can.   know
And each of them had wives more than two;
And many another holy man also.
Where can ye see, in any manner age,   in any period
That highe God defended marriage   forbade[5]
By word express? I pray you tell it me;
Or where commanded he virginity?
I wot as well as you, it is no dread,   doubt
Th' apostle, when he spake of maidenhead,
He said, that precept thereof had he none:
Men may counsel a woman to be one,   a maid
But counseling is no commandement;
He put it in our owen judgement.
For, hadde God commanded maidenhead,
Then had he damned wedding out of dread;   condemned doubt
And certes, if there were no seed y-sow,   sown
Virginity then whereof should it grow?
Paul durste not commanden, at the least,
A thing of which his Master gave no hest.   command
The dart is set up for virginity;   goal[6]
Catch whoso may, who runneth best let see.
But this word is not ta'en of every wight,
But there as God will give it of his might.   except where
I wot well that th' apostle was a maid,
But natheless, although he wrote and said,
He would that every wight were such as he,
All is but counsel to virginity.
And, since to be a wife he gave me leave
Of indulgence, so is it no repreve   scandal, reproach
To wedde me, if that my make should die,   mate, husband
Without exception of bigamy;   charge, reproach

GEOFFREY CHAUCER

All were it good no woman for to touch though it might be
(He meant as in his bed or in his couch),
For peril is both fire and tow t'assemble
Ye know what this example may resemble.
This is all and some, he held virginity
More profit than wedding in frailty:
(Frailty clepe I, but if that he and she frailty I call it,
Would lead their lives all in chastity), unless
I grant it well, I have of none envy
Who maidenhead prefer to bigamy;
It liketh them t' be clean in body and ghost; soul
Of mine estate I will not make a boast. condition

For, well ye know, a lord in his household
Hath not every vessel all of gold;[7]
Some are of tree, and do their lord service.
God calleth folk to him in sundry wise,
And each one hath of God a proper gift,
Some this, some that, as liketh him to shift. appoint, distribute
Virginity is great perfection,
And continence eke with devotion:
But Christ, that of perfection is the well, fountain
Bade not every wight he should go sell
All that he had, and give it to the poor,
And in such wise follow him and his lore: doctrine
He spake to them that would live perfectly, —
And, lordings, by your leave, that am not I;
I will bestow the flower of mine age
In th' acts and in the fruits of marriage.
Tell me also, to what conclusion end, purpose
Were members made of generation,
And of so perfect wise a wight y-wrought? being
Trust me right well, they were not made for nought.
Glose whoso will, and say both up and down,
That they were made for the purgatioun
Of urine, and of other thinges smale,
And eke to know a female from a male:
And for none other cause? say ye no?
Experience wot well it is not so.
So that the clerkes be not with me wroth, scholars
I say this, that they were made for both,
That is to say, for office, and for ease for duty and
Of engendrure, there we God not displease. for pleasure
Why should men elles in their bookes set,
That man shall yield unto his wife her debt?
Now wherewith should he make his payement,
If he us'd not his silly instrument?
Then were they made upon a creature
To purge urine, and eke for engendrure.
But I say not that every wight is hold, obliged
That hath such harness as I to you told, equipment
To go and use them in engendrure;

Then should men take of chastity no cure. care
Christ was a maid, and shapen as a man, fashioned
And many a saint, since that this world began,
Yet ever liv'd in perfect chastity.
I will not vie with no virginity. contend
Let them with bread of pured wheat be fed, purified
And let us wives eat our barley bread.
And yet with barley bread, Mark tell us can,[8]
Our Lord Jesus refreshed many a man.
In such estate as God hath cleped us, called us to
I'll persevere, I am not precious, over-dainty
In wifehood I will use mine instrument
As freely as my Maker hath it sent.
If I be dangerous God give me sorrow; sparing of my favours
Mine husband shall it have, both eve and morrow,
When that him list come forth and pay his debt.
A husband will I have, I will no let, will bear no hindrance
Which shall be both my debtor and my thrall, slave
And have his tribulation withal
Upon his flesh, while that I am his wife.
I have the power during all my life
Upon his proper body, and not he;
Right thus th' apostle told it unto me,
And bade our husbands for to love us well;
All this sentence me liketh every deal. whit

Up start the Pardoner, and that anon;
"Now, Dame," quoth he, "by God and by Saint John,
Ye are a noble preacher in this case.
I was about to wed a wife, alas!
What? should I bie it on my flesh so dear? suffer for
Yet had I lever wed no wife this year." rather
"Abide," quoth she; "my tale is not begun wait in patience
Nay, thou shalt drinken of another tun
Ere that I go, shall savour worse than ale.
And when that I have told thee forth my tale
Of tribulation in marriage,
Of which I am expert in all mine age,
(This is to say, myself hath been the whip),
Then mayest thou choose whether thou wilt sip
Of thilke tunne, that I now shall broach. that tun
Beware of it, ere thou too nigh approach,
For I shall tell examples more than ten:
Whoso will not beware by other men,
By him shall other men corrected be:
These same wordes writeth Ptolemy;
Read in his Almagest, and take it there."
"Dame, I would pray you, if your will it were,"
Saide this Pardoner, "as ye began,
Tell forth your tale, and spare for no man,
And teach us younge men of your practique."

70

THE CANTERBURY TALES

"Gladly," quoth she, "since that it may you like.
But that I pray to all this company,
If that I speak after my fantasy,
To take nought agrief what I may say; to heart
For mine intent is only for to play.

Now, Sirs, then will I tell you forth my tale.
As ever may I drinke wine or ale
I shall say sooth; the husbands that I had
Three of them were good, and two were bad
The three were goode men, and rich, and old
Unnethes mighte they the statute hold they could with difficulty
In which that they were bounden unto me. obey the law
Yet wot well what I mean of this, pardie. by God
As God me help, I laugh when that I think
How piteously at night I made them swink, labour
But, by my fay, I told of it no store: by my faith, I held it
They had me giv'n their land and their treasor, of no account
Me needed not do longer diligence
To win their love, or do them reverence.
They loved me so well, by God above,
That I tolde no dainty of their love. cared nothing for
A wise woman will busy her ever-in-one constantly
To get their love, where that she hath none.
But, since I had them wholly in my hand,
And that they had me given all their land,
Why should I take keep them for to please, care
But it were for my profit, or mine ease? unless
I set them so a-worke, by my fay,
That many a night they sange, well-away!
The bacon was not fetched for them, I trow,
That some men have in Essex at Dunmow.[9]
I govern'd them so well after my law,
That each of them full blissful was and fawe fain
To bringe me gay things from the fair.
They were full glad when that I spake them fair,
For, God it wot, I chid them spiteously. rebuked them angrily
Now hearken how I bare me properly.

Ye wise wives, that can understand,
Thus should ye speak, and bear them wrong on hand, make them
For half so boldely can there no man believe falsely
Swearen and lien as a woman can.
(I say not this by wives that be wise,
But if it be when they them misadvise.) unless act unadvisedly
A wise wife, if that she can her good, knows
Shall beare them on hand the cow is wood, make them believe
And take witness of her owen maid

Of their assent: but hearken how I said.
"Sir olde kaynard,[10] is this thine array?
Why is my neigheboure's wife so gay?
She is honour'd over all where she go'th, wheresoever
I sit at home, I have no thrifty cloth. good clothes
What dost thou at my neigheboure's house?
Is she so fair? art thou so amorous?
What rown'st thou with our maid? benedicite, whisperest
Sir olde lechour, let thy japes be. tricks
And if I have a gossip, or a friend
(Withoute guilt), thou chidest as a fiend,
If that I walk or play unto his house.
Thou comest home as drunken as a mouse,
And preachest on thy bench, with evil prefe: proof
Thou say'st to me, it is a great mischief
To wed a poore woman, for costage: expense
And if that she be rich, of high parage; birth[11]
Then say'st thou, that it is a tormentry
To suffer her pride and melancholy.
And if that she be fair, thou very knave,
Thou say'st that every holour will her have; whoremonger
She may no while in chastity abide,
That is assailed upon every side.
Thou say'st some folk desire us for richess,
Some for our shape, and some for our fairness,
And some, for she can either sing or dance,
And some for gentiless and dalliance,
Some for her handes and her armes smale:
Thus goes all to the devil, by thy tale;
Thou say'st, men may not keep a castle wall
That may be so assailed over all. everywhere
And if that she be foul, thou say'st that she
Coveteth every man that she may see;
For as a spaniel she will on him leap,
Till she may finde some man her to cheap; buy
And none so grey goose goes there in the lake,
(So say'st thou) that will be without a make. mate
And say'st, it is a hard thing for to weld, wield, govern
A thing that no man will, his thankes, held. hold with his goodwill
Thus say'st thou, lorel, when thou go'st to bed, good-for-nothing
And that no wise man needeth for to wed,
Nor no man that intendeth unto heaven.
With wilde thunder dint and fiery leven stroke lightning
Mote thy wicked necke be to-broke. may
Thou say'st, that dropping houses, and eke smoke,
And chiding wives, make men to flee
Out of their owne house; ah! ben'dicite,
What aileth such an old man for to chide?
Thou say'st, we wives will our vices hide,
Till we be fast, and then we will them shew. wedded

71

GEOFFREY CHAUCER

Well may that be a proverb of a shrew. ill-tempered wretch
Thou say'st, that oxen, asses, horses, hounds,
They be assayed at diverse stounds, tested at various
Basons and lavers, ere that men them buy, seasons
Spoones, stooles, and all such husbandry,
And so be pots, and clothes, and array, raiment
But folk of wives make none assay,
Till they be wedded, — olde dotard shrew! —
And then, say'st thou, we will our vices shew.
Thou say'st also, that it displeaseth me,
But if that thou wilt praise my beauty, unless
And but thou pore alway upon my face, unless
And call me faire dame in every place;
And but thou make a feast on thilke day unless that
That I was born, and make me fresh and gay;
And but thou do to my norice honour, nurse[12]
And to my chamberere within my bow'r, chamber-maid
And to my father's folk, and mine allies; relations
Thus sayest thou, old barrel full of lies.
And yet also of our prentice Jenkin,
For his crisp hair, shining as gold so fine,
And for he squireth me both up and down,
Yet hast thou caught a false suspicioun:
I will him not, though thou wert dead to-morrow.
But tell me this, why hidest thou, with sorrow, sorrow on thee!
The keyes of thy chest away from me?
It is my good as well as thine, pardie. property
What, think'st to make an idiot of our dame?
Now, by that lord that called is Saint Jame,
Thou shalt not both, although that thou wert wood, furious
Be master of my body, and my good, property
The one thou shalt forego, maugre thine eyen. in spite of
What helpeth it of me t'inquire and spyen?
I trow thou wouldest lock me in thy chest.
Thou shouldest say, 'Fair wife, go where thee lest;
Take your disport; I will believe no tales;
I know you for a true wife, Dame Ales.' Alice
We love no man, that taketh keep or charge care
Where that we go; we will be at our large.
Of alle men most blessed may he be,
The wise astrologer Dan Ptolemy, Lord
That saith this proverb in his Almagest:[13]
'Of alle men his wisdom is highest,
That recketh not who hath the world in hand.
By this proverb thou shalt well understand,
Have thou enough, what thar thee reck or care needs, behoves
How merrily that other folkes fare?
For certes, olde dotard, by your leave,
Ye shall have [pleasure][14] right enough at eve.
He is too great a niggard that will werne forbid
A man to light a candle at his lantern;
He shall have never the less light, pardie.
Have thou enough, thee thar not plaine thee need complain
Thou say'st also, if that we make us gay
With clothing and with precious array,
That it is peril of our chastity.
And yet, — with sorrow! — thou enforcest thee,
And say'st these words in the apostle's name:
'In habit made with chastity and shame modesty
Ye women shall apparel you,' quoth he,[15]
'And not in tressed hair and gay perrie, jewels
As pearles, nor with gold, nor clothes rich.'
After thy text nor after thy rubrich
I will not work as muchel as a gnat.
Thou say'st also, I walk out like a cat;
For whoso woulde singe the catte's skin
Then will the catte well dwell in her inn; house
And if the catte's skin be sleek and gay,
She will not dwell in house half a day,
But forth she will, ere any day be daw'd,
To shew her skin, and go a caterwaw'd. caterwauling
This is to say, if I be gay, sir shrew,
I will run out, my borel for to shew. apparel, fine clothes
Sir olde fool, what helpeth thee to spyen?
Though thou pray Argus with his hundred eyen
To be my wardecorps, as he can best body-guard
In faith he shall not keep me, but me lest: unless I please
Yet could I make his beard, so may I the. make a jest of him

"Thou sayest eke, that there be thinges three, thrive
Which thinges greatly trouble all this earth,
And that no wighte may endure the ferth: fourth
O lefe sir shrew, may Jesus short thy life. pleasant shorten
Yet preachest thou, and say'st, a hateful wife
Y-reckon'd is for one of these mischances.
Be there none other manner resemblances no other kind of
That ye may liken your parables unto, comparison
But if a silly wife be one of tho? those
Thou likenest a woman's love to hell;
To barren land where water may not dwell.
Thou likenest it also to wild fire;
The more it burns, the more it hath desire
To consume every thing that burnt will be.
Thou sayest, right as wormes shend a tree, destroy
Right so a wife destroyeth her husbond;
This know they well that be to wives bond."

Lordings, right thus, as ye have understand,
Bare I stiffly mine old husbands on hand, made them believe
That thus they saiden in their drunkenness;

THE CANTERBURY TALES

And all was false, but that I took witness
On Jenkin, and upon my niece also.
O Lord! the pain I did them, and the woe,
'Full guilteless, by Godde's sweete pine;   pain
For as a horse I coulde bite and whine;
I coulde plain, an' I was in the guilt, complain even though
Or elles oftentime I had been spilt   ruined
Whoso first cometh to the nilll, first grint;   is ground
I plained first, so was our war y-stint.   stopped
They were full glad to excuse them full blive   quickly
Of things that they never aguilt their live.   were guilty in their lives
Of wenches would I beare them on hand,   falsely accuse them
When that for sickness scarcely might they stand,
Yet tickled I his hearte for that he
Ween'd that I had of him so great cherte: though affection[16]
I swore that all my walking out by night
Was for to espy wenches that he dight: adorned
Under that colour had I many a mirth.
For all such wit is given us at birth;
Deceit, weeping, and spinning, God doth give
To women kindly, while that they may live.   naturally
And thus of one thing I may vaunte me,
At th' end I had the better in each degree,
By sleight, or force, or by some manner thing,
As by continual murmur or grudging,   complaining
Namely a-bed, there hadde they mischance,   especially
There would I chide, and do them no pleasance:
I would no longer in the bed abide,
If that I felt his arm over my side,
Till he had made his ransom unto me,
Then would I suffer him do his nicety.   folly[17]
And therefore every man this tale I tell,
Win whoso may, for all is for to sell;
With empty hand men may no hawkes lure;
For winning would I all his will endure,
And make me a feigned appetite,
And yet in bacon had I never delight: i.e. of Dunmow[9]
That made me that I ever would them chide,
For, though the Pope had sitten them beside,
I would not spare them at their owen board,
For, by my troth, I quit them word for word   repaid
As help me very God omnipotent,
Though I right now should make my testament
I owe them not a word, that is not quit repaid
I brought it so aboute by my wit,
That they must give it up, as for the best
Or elles had we never been in rest.
For, though he looked as a wood lion,   furious
Yet should he fail of his conclusion.
Then would I say, "Now, goode lefe tak keep   dear heed
How meekly looketh Wilken oure sheep!
Come near, my spouse, and let me ba thy cheek   kiss[18]
Ye shoulde be all patient and meek,
And have a sweet y-spiced conscience,   tender, nice
Since ye so preach of Jobe's patience.
Suffer alway, since ye so well can preach,
And but ye do, certain we shall you teach   unless
That it is fair to have a wife in peace.
One of us two must bowe doubteless: give way
And since a man is more reasonable
Than woman is, ye must be suff'rable.
What aileth you to grudge thus and groan?   complain
Is it for ye would have my [love][14] alone?
Why, take it all: lo, have it every deal,   whit
Peter![19] shrew you but ye love it well   curse
For if I woulde sell my belle chose,   beautiful thing
I coulde walk as fresh as is a rose,
But I will keep it for your owen tooth.
Ye be to blame, by God, I say you sooth."
Such manner wordes hadde we on hand.

Now will I speaken of my fourth husband.
My fourthe husband was a revellour;
This is to say, he had a paramour,
And I was young and full of ragerie,   wantonness
Stubborn and strong, and jolly as a pie.   magpie
Then could I dance to a harpe smale,
And sing, y-wis, as any nightingale,   certainly
When I had drunk a draught of sweete wine.
Metellius, the foule churl, the swine,
That with a staff bereft his wife of life
For she drank wine, though I had been his wife,
Never should he have daunted me from drink:
And, after wine, of Venus most I think.
For all so sure as cold engenders hail,
A liquorish mouth must have a liquorish tail.
In woman vinolent is no defence,   full of wine resistance
This knowe lechours by experience.
But, lord Christ, when that it rememb'reth me
Upon my youth, and on my jollity,
It tickleth me about mine hearte-root;
Unto this day it doth mine hearte boot,   good
That I have had my world as in my time.
But age, alas! that all will envenime,   poison, embitter
Hath me bereft my beauty and my pith: vigour
Let go; farewell; the devil go therewith.
The flour is gon, there is no more to tell,
The bran, as I best may, now must I sell.
But yet to be right merry will I fand.   try
Now forth to tell you of my fourth husband,

GEOFFREY CHAUCER

I say, I in my heart had great despite,
That he of any other had delight;
But he was quit, by God and by Saint Joce:[21]   requited, paid back
I made for him of the same wood a cross;
Not of my body in no foul mannere,
But certainly I made folk such cheer,
That in his owen grease I made him fry
For anger, and for very jealousy.
By God, in earth I was his purgatory,
For which I hope his soul may be in glory.
For, God it wot, he sat full oft and sung,
When that his shoe full bitterly him wrung.   pinched
There was no wight, save God and he, that wist
In many wise how sore I did him twist.[20]
He died when I came from Jerusalem,
And lies in grave under the roode beam: cross
Although his tomb is not so curious
As was the sepulchre of Darius,
Which that Apelles wrought so subtlely.
It is but waste to bury them preciously.
Let him fare well, God give his soule rest,
He is now in his grave and in his chest.

Now of my fifthe husband will I tell:
God let his soul never come into hell.
And yet was he to me the moste shrew;   cruel, ill-tempered
That feel I on my ribbes all by rew,   in a row
And ever shall, until mine ending day.
But in our bed he was so fresh and gay,
And therewithal so well he could me glose,   flatter
When that he woulde have my belle chose,
Though he had beaten me on every bone,
Yet could he win again my love anon.
I trow, I lov'd him better, for that he
Was of his love so dangerous to me.   sparing, difficult
We women have, if that I shall not lie,
In this matter a quainte fantasy.
Whatever thing we may not lightly have,
Thereafter will we cry all day and crave.
Forbid us thing, and that desire we;
Press on us fast, and thenne will we flee.
With danger utter we all our chaffare;   difficulty merchandise
Great press at market maketh deare ware,
And too great cheap is held at little price;
This knoweth every woman that is wise.
My fifthe husband, God his soule bless,
Which that I took for love and no richess,
He some time was a clerk of Oxenford,   a scholar of Oxford
And had left school, and went at home to board
With my gossip, dwelling in oure town: godmother
God have her soul, her name was Alisoun.
She knew my heart, and all my privity,

Bet than our parish priest, so may I the.   thrive
To her betrayed I my counsel all;
For had my husband pissed on a wall,
Or done a thing that should have cost his life,
To her, and to another worthy wife,
And to my niece, which that I loved well,
I would have told his counsel every deal.   jot
And so I did full often, God it wot,
That made his face full often red and hot
For very shame, and blam'd himself, for he
Had told to me so great a privity.   secret
And so befell that ones in a Lent
(So oftentimes I to my gossip went,
For ever yet I loved to be gay,
And for to walk in March, April, and May
From house to house, to heare sundry tales),
That Jenkin clerk, and my gossip, Dame Ales,
And I myself, into the fieldes went.
Mine husband was at London all that Lent;
I had the better leisure for to play,
And for to see, and eke for to be sey   seen
Of lusty folk; what wist I where my grace   favour
Was shapen for to be, or in what place?   appointed
Therefore made I my visitations
To vigilies, and to processions,   festival-eves[22]
To preachings eke, and to these pilgrimages,
To plays of miracles, and marriages,
And weared upon me gay scarlet gites.   gowns
These wormes, nor these mothes, nor these mites
On my apparel frett them never a deal   fed whit
And know'st thou why? for they were used well.   worn
Now will I telle forth what happen'd me:
I say, that in the fieldes walked we,
Till truely we had such dalliance,
This clerk and I, that of my purveyance   foresight
I spake to him, and told him how that he,
If I were widow, shoulde wedde me.
For certainly, I say for no bobance,   boasting[23]
Yet was I never without purveyance   foresight
Of marriage, nor of other thinges eke:
I hold a mouse's wit not worth a leek,
That hath but one hole for to starte to,[24]   escape
And if that faile, then is all y-do.   done
[I bare him on hand he had enchanted me   falsely assured him
(My dame taughte me that subtilty);
And eke I said, I mette of him all night,   dreamed
He would have slain me, as I lay upright,
And all my bed was full of very blood;
But yet I hop'd that he should do me good;
For blood betoken'd gold, as me was taught.
And all was false, I dream'd of him right naught,
But as I follow'd aye my dame's lore,
As well of that as of other things more.][25]
But now, sir, let me see, what shall I sayn?
Aha! by God, I have my tale again.
When that my fourthe husband was on bier,
I wept algate and made a sorry cheer,   always

THE CANTERBURY TALES

countenance
As wives must, for it is the usage;
And with my kerchief covered my visage;
But, for I was provided with a make, mate
I wept but little, that I undertake promise
To churche was mine husband borne a-morrow
With neighebours that for him made sorrow,
And Jenkin, oure clerk, was one of tho: those
As help me God, when that I saw him go
After the bier, methought he had a pair
Of legges and of feet so clean and fair,
That all my heart I gave unto his hold. keeping
He was, I trow, a twenty winter old,
And I was forty, if I shall say sooth,
But yet I had always a colte's tooth.
Gat-toothed I was, and that became me well, see note26
I had the print of Sainte Venus' seal.
[As help me God, I was a lusty one,
And fair, and rich, and young, and well begone: in a good way
For certes I am all venerian under the influence of Venus
In feeling, and my heart is martian; under the influence of Mars
Venus me gave my lust and liquorishness,
And Mars gave me my sturdy hardiness.]25
Mine ascendant was Taure, and Mars therein: Taurus
Alas, alas, that ever love was sin!
I follow'd aye mine inclination
By virtue of my constellation:
That made me that I coulde not withdraw
My chamber of Venus from a good fellow.
[Yet have I Marte's mark upon my face,
And also in another privy place.
For God so wisly be my salvation, certainly
I loved never by discretion,
But ever follow'd mine own appetite,
All were he short, or long, or black, or white, whether
I took no keep, so that he liked me, heed
How poor he was, neither of what degree.]25
What should I say? but that at the month's end
This jolly clerk Jenkin, that was so hend, courteous
Had wedded me with great solemnity,
And to him gave I all the land and fee
That ever was me given therebefore:
But afterward repented me full sore.
He woulde suffer nothing of my list. pleasure
By God, he smote me ones with his fist,
For that I rent out of his book a leaf,
That of the stroke mine eare wax'd all deaf.
Stubborn I was, as is a lioness,
And of my tongue a very jangleress, prater
And walk I would, as I had done beforn,
From house to house, although he had it sworn: had sworn to

For which he oftentimes woulde preach prevent it
And me of olde Roman gestes teach stories
How that Sulpitius Gallus left his wife
And her forsook for term of all his
For nought but open-headed he her say bareheaded saw
Looking out at his door upon a day.
Another Roman27 told he me by name,
That, for his wife was at a summer game
Without his knowing, he forsook her eke.
And then would he upon his Bible seek
That ilke proverb of Ecclesiast, same
Where he commandeth, and forbiddeth fast,
Man shall not suffer his wife go roll about.
Then would he say right thus withoute doubt:
"Whoso that buildeth his house all of sallows, willows
And pricketh his blind horse over the fallows,
And suff'reth his wife to go seeke hallows, make pilgrimages
Is worthy to be hanged on the gallows."
But all for nought; I sette not a haw cared nothing for
Of his proverbs, nor of his olde saw;
Nor would I not of him corrected be.
I hate them that my vices telle me,
And so do more of us (God wot) than I.
This made him wood with me all utterly; furious
I woulde not forbear him in no case. endure
Now will I say you sooth, by Saint Thomas,
Why that I rent out of his book a leaf,
For which he smote me, so that I was deaf.
He had a book, that gladly night and day
For his disport he would it read alway;
He call'd it Valerie,28 and Theophrast,
And with that book he laugh'd alway full fast.
And eke there was a clerk sometime at Rome,
A cardinal, that highte Saint Jerome,
That made a book against Jovinian,
Which book was there; and eke Tertullian,
Chrysippus, Trotula, and Heloise,
That was an abbess not far from Paris;
And eke the Parables of Solomon, Proverbs
Ovide's Art,29 and bourdes many one; jests
And alle these were bound in one volume.
And every night and day was his custume
(When he had leisure and vacation
From other worldly occupation)
To readen in this book of wicked wives.
He knew of them more legends and more lives
Than be of goodde wives in the Bible.
For, trust me well, it is an impossible
That any clerk will speake good of wives,
(But if it be of holy saintes' lives) unless
Nor of none other woman never the mo'.
Who painted the lion, tell it me, who?
By God, if women haddde written stories,
As clerkes have within their oratories,

They would have writ of men more wickedness
Than all the mark of Adam[30] may redress
The children of Mercury and of Venus,[31]
Be in their working full contrarious.
Mercury loveth wisdom and science,
And Venus loveth riot and dispence. *extravagance*
And for their diverse disposition,
Each falls in other's exaltation.
As thus, God wot, Mercury is desolate
In Pisces, where Venus is exaltate,
And Venus falls where Mercury is raised.[32]
Therefore no woman by no clerk is praised.
The clerk, when he is old, and may not do
Of Venus' works not worth his olde shoe,
Then sits he down, and writes in his dotage,
That women cannot keep their marriage.
But now to purpose, why I tolde thee
That I was beaten for a book, pardie.

Upon a night Jenkin, that was our sire, *goodman*
Read on his book, as he sat by the fire,
Of Eva first, that for her wickedness
Was all mankind brought into wretchedness,
For which that Jesus Christ himself was slain,
That bought us with his hearte-blood again.
Lo here express of women may ye find
That woman was the loss of all mankind.
Then read he me how Samson lost his hairs
Sleeping, his leman cut them with her shears,
Through whiche treason lost he both his eyen.
Then read he me, if that I shall not lien,
Of Hercules, and of his Dejanire,
That caused him to set himself on fire.
Nothing forgot he of the care and woe
That Socrates had with his wives two;
How Xantippe cast piss upon his head.
This silly man sat still, as he were dead,
He wip'd his head, and no more durst he sayn,
But, "Ere the thunder stint there cometh rain." *ceases*
Of Phasiphae, that was queen of Crete,
For shrewedness he thought the tale sweet. *wickedness*
Fy, speak no more, it is a grisly thing,
Of her horrible lust and her liking.
Of Clytemnestra, for her lechery
That falsely made her husband for to die,
He read it with full good devotion.
He told me eke, for what occasion
Amphiorax at Thebes lost his life:
My husband had a legend of his wife
Eryphile, that for an ouche of gold *clasp, collar*
Had privily unto the Greekes told,
Where that her husband hid him in a place,
For which he had at Thebes sorry grace.
Of Luna told he me, and of Lucie;
They bothe made their husbands for to die,
That one for love, that other was for hate.
Luna her husband on an ev'ning late

Empoison'd had, for that she was his foe:
Lucia liquorish lov'd her husband so,
That, for he should always upon her think,
She gave him such a manner love-drink, *sort of*
That he was dead before it were the morrow:
And thus algates husbands hadde sorrow. *always*
Then told he me how one Latumeus
Complained to his fellow Arius
That in his garden growed such a tree,
On which he said how that his wives three
Hanged themselves for heart dispiteous.
"O leve brother," quoth this Arius, *dear*
"Give me a plant of thilke blessed tree,
And in my garden planted shall it be."
Of later date of wives hath he read,
That some have slain their husbands in their bed,
And let their lechour dight them all the night, *lover ride them*
While that the corpse lay on the floor upright:
And some have driven nails into their brain,
While that they slept, and thus they have them slain:
Some have them given poison in their drink:
He spake more harm than hearte may bethink.
And therewithal he knew of more proverbs,
Than in this world there groweth grass or herbs.
"Better (quoth he) thine habitation
Be with a lion, or a foul dragon,
Than with a woman using for to chide.
Better (quoth he) high in the roof abide,
Than with an angry woman in the house,
They be so wicked and contrarious:
They hate that their husbands loven aye."
He said, "A woman cast her shame away
When she cast off her smock;" and farthermo',
"A fair woman, but she be chaste also, *except*
Is like a gold ring in a sowe's nose.
Who coulde ween, or who coulde suppose *think*
The woe that in mine heart was, and the pine? *pain*
And when I saw that he would never fine *finish*
To readen on this cursed book all night,
All suddenly three leaves have I plight *plucked*
Out of his book, right as he read, and eke
I with my fist so took him on the cheek,
That in our fire he backward fell adown.
And he up start, as doth a wood lion, *furious*
And with his fist he smote me on the head,
That on the floor I lay as I were dead.
And when he saw how still that there I lay,
He was aghast, and would have fled away,
Till at the last out of my swoon I braid, *woke*
"Oh, hast thou slain me, thou false thief?" I said
"And for my land thus hast thou murder'd me?
Ere I be dead, yet will I kisse thee."
And near he came, and kneeled fair adown,
And saide", "Deare sister Alisoun,
As help me God, I shall thee never smite:
That I have done it is thyself to wite, *blame*

Forgive it me, and that I thee beseek." *beseech*
And yet eftsoons I hit him on the cheek, *immediately; again*
And saidde, "Thief, thus much am I awreak. *avenged*
Now will I die, I may no longer speak."

But at the last, with muche care and woe
We fell accorded by ourselves two: *agreed*
He gave me all the bridle in mine hand
To have the governance of house and land,
And of his tongue, and of his hand also.
I made him burn his book anon right tho. *then*
And when that I had gotten unto me
By mast'ry all the sovereignty,
And that he said, "Mine owen true wife,
Do as thee list, the term of all thy life, *as pleases thee*
Keep thine honour, and eke keep mine estate;
After that day we never had debate.
God help me so, I was to him as kind
As any wife from Denmark unto Ind,
And also true, and so was he to me:
I pray to God that sits in majesty
So bless his soule, for his mercy dear.
Now will I say my tale, if ye will hear. —

The Friar laugh'd when he had heard all this:
"Now, Dame," quoth he, "so have I joy and bliss,
This is a long preamble of a tale."
And when the Sompnour heard the Friar gale, *speak*
"Lo," quoth this Sompnour, "Godde's armes two,
A friar will intermete him evermo': *interpose*[33]
Lo, goode men, a fly and eke a frere
Will fall in ev'ry dish and eke mattere.
What speak'st thou of perambulation? *preamble*
What? amble or trot; or peace, or go sit down:
Thou lettest our disport in this mattere." *hinderesst*
"Yea, wilt thou so, Sir Sompnour?" quoth the Frere;
"Now by my faith I shall, ere that I go,
Tell of a Sompnour such a tale or two,
That all the folk shall laughen in this place."
"Now do, else, Friar, I beshrew thy face," *curse*
Quoth this Sompnour; "and I beshrewe me,
But if I telle tales two or three *unless*
Of friars, ere I come to Sittingbourne,
That I shall make thine hearte for to mourn:
For well I wot thy patience is gone."
Our Hoste cried, "Peace, and that anon;"
And saide, "Let the woman tell her tale.
Ye fare as folk that drunken be of ale. *behave*
Do, Dame, tell forth your tale, and that is best."
"All ready, sir," quoth she, "right as you lest, *please*
If I have licence of this worthy Frere."
"Yes, Dame," quoth he, "tell forth, and I will hear."

Notes to the Prologue to the Wife of Bath's Tale

1. Among the evidences that Chaucer's great work was left incomplete, is the absence of any link of connexion between the Wife of Bath's Prologue and Tale, and what goes before. This deficiency has in some editions caused the Squire's and the Merchant's Tales to be interposed between those of the Man of Law and the Wife of Bath; but in the Merchant's Tale there is internal proof that it was told after the jolly Dame's. Several manuscripts contain verses designed to serve as a connexion; but they are evidently not Chaucer's, and it is unnecessary to give them here. Of this Prologue, which may fairly be regarded as a distinct autobiographical tale, Tyrwhitt says: "The extraordinary length of it, as well as the vein of pleasantry that runs through it, is very suitable to the character of the speaker. The greatest part must have been of Chaucer's own invention, though one may plainly see that he had been reading the popular invectives against marriage and women in general; such as the 'Roman de la Rose,' 'Valerius ad Rufinum, De non Ducenda Uxore,' ('Valerius to Rufinus, on not being ruled by one's wife') and particularly 'Hieronymus contra Jovinianum.' ('Jerome against Jovinianus') St Jerome, among other things designed to discourage marriage, has inserted in his treatise a long passage from 'Liber Aureolus Theophrasti de Nuptiis.' ('Theophrastus's Golden Book of Marriage')."
2. A great part of the marriage service used to be performed in the church-porch.
3. Jesus and the Samaritan woman: John iv. 13.
4. Dan: Lord; Latin, "dominus." Another reading is "the wise man, King Solomon."
5. Defended: forbade; French, "defendre," to prohibit.
6. Dart: the goal; a spear or dart was set up to mark the point of victory.
7. "But in a great house there are not only vessels of gold and silver, but also of wood and of earth; and some to honour, and some to dishonour." — 2 Tim. ii 20.
8. Jesus feeding the multitude with barley bread: Mark vi. 41, 42.
9. At Dunmow prevailed the custom of giving, amid much merry making, a flitch of bacon to the married pair who had lived together for a year without quarrel or regret. The same custom prevailed of old in Bretagne.
10. "Cagnard," or "Caignard," a French term of reproach, originally derived from "canis," a dog.

11. Parage: birth, kindred; from Latin, "pario," I beget.
12. Norice: nurse; French, "nourrice."
13. This and the previous quotation from Ptolemy are due to the Dame's own fancy.
14. (Transcriber's note: Some Victorian censorship here. The word given in [brackets] should be "queint" i.e. "cunt".)
15. Women should not adorn themselves: see I Tim. ii. 9.
16. Cherte: affection; from French, "cher," dear.
17. Nicety: folly; French, "niaiserie."
18. Ba: kiss; from French, "baiser."
19. Peter!: by Saint Peter! a common adjuration, like Marie! from the Virgin's name.
20. St. Joce: or Judocus, a saint of Ponthieu, in France.
21. "An allusion," says Mr Wright, "to the story of the Roman sage who, when blamed for divorcing his wife, said that a shoe might appear outwardly to fit well, but no one but the wearer knew where it pinched."
22. Vigilies: festival-eves; see note 33 to the Prologue to the Tales.
23. Bobance: boasting; Ben Jonson's braggart, in "Every Man in his Humour," is named Bobadil.
24. "I hold a mouse's wit not worth a leek,
      That hath but one hole for to starte to"
    A very old proverb in French, German, and Latin.
25. The lines in brackets are only in some of the manuscripts.
26. Gat-toothed: gap-toothed; goat-toothed; or cat- or separate toothed. See note 41 to the prologue to the Tales.
27. Sempronius Sophus, of whom Valerius Maximus tells in his sixth book.
28. The tract of Walter Mapes against marriage, published under the title of "Epistola Valerii ad Rufinum."
29. "Ars Amoris."
30. All the mark of Adam: all who bear the mark of Adam i.e. all men.
31. The Children of Mercury and Venus: those born under the influence of the respective planets.
32. A planet, according to the old astrologers, was in "exaltation" when in the sign of the Zodiac in which it exerted its strongest influence; the opposite sign, in which it was weakest, was called its "dejection." Venus being strongest in Pisces, was weakest in Virgo; but in Virgo Mercury was in "exaltation."
33. Intermete: interpose; French, "entremettre."

THE TALE.[1]

In olde dayes of the king Arthour,
Of which that Britons speake great honour,
All was this land full fill'd of faerie; fairies
The Elf-queen, with her jolly company,
Danced full oft in many a green mead
This was the old opinion, as I read;
I speak of many hundred years ago;
But now can no man see none elves mo',
For now the great charity and prayeres
Of limitours, and other holy freres, begging friars[2]
That search every land and ev'ry stream
As thick as motes in the sunne-beam,
Blessing halls, chambers, kitchenes, and bowers,
Cities and burghes, castles high and towers,
Thorpes and barnes, shepens and dairies, villages[3] stables
This makes that there be now no faeries:
For there as wont to walke was an elf,
There walketh now the limitour himself,
In undermeles and in morrowings, evenings[4] mornings
And saith his matins and his holy things,
As he goes in his limitatioun. begging district
Women may now go safely up and down,
In every bush, and under every tree;

There is none other incubus[5] but he;
And he will do to them no dishonour.

And so befell it, that this king Arthour
Had in his house a lusty bacheler,
That on a day came riding from river:[6]
And happen'd, that, alone as she was born,
He saw a maiden walking him beforn,
Of which maiden anon, maugre her head, in spite of
By very force he reft her maidenhead:
For which oppression was such clamour,
And such pursuit unto the king Arthour,
That damned was this knight for to be dead condemned
By course of law, and should have lost his head;
(Paraventure such was the statute tho), then
But that the queen and other ladies mo'
So long they prayed the king of his grace,
Till he his life him granted in the place,
And gave him to the queen, all at her will
To choose whether she would him save or spill destroy
The queen thanked the king with all her might;
And, after this, thus spake she to the knight,

THE CANTERBURY TALES

When that she saw her time upon a day.
"Thou standest yet," quoth she, "in such array, a position
That of thy life yet hast thou no surety;
I grant thee life, if thou canst tell to me
What thing is it that women most desiren:
Beware, and keep thy neck-bone from the iron executioner's axe
And if thou canst not tell it me anon,
Yet will I give thee leave for to gon
A twelvemonth and a day, to seek and lear learn
An answer suffisant in this mattere. satisfactory
And surety will I have, ere that thou pace, go
Thy body for to yielden in this place."
Woe was the knight, and sorrowfully siked; sighed
But what? he might not do all as him liked.
And at the last he chose him for to wend, depart
And come again, right at the yeare's end,
With such answer as God would him purvey: provide
And took his leave, and wended forth his way.

He sought in ev'ry house and ev'ry place,
Where as he hoped for to finde grace,
To learne what thing women love the most:
But he could not arrive in any coast,
Where as he mighte find in this mattere
Two creatures according in fere. agreeing together
Some said that women loved best richess,
Some said honour, and some said jolliness,
Some rich array, and some said lust a-bed, pleasure
And oft time to be widow and be wed.
Some said, that we are in our heart most eased
When that we are y-flatter'd and y-praised.
He went full nigh the sooth, I will not lie; came very near
A man shall win us best with flattery; the truth
And with attendance, and with business
Be we y-limed, bothe more and less. caught with bird-lime
And some men said that we do love the best
For to be free, and do right as us lest, whatever we please
And that no man reprove us of our vice,
But say that we are wise, and nothing nice, foolish[7]
For truly there is none among us all,
If any wight will claw us on the gall, see note[8]
That will not kick, for that he saith us sooth:
Assay, and he shall find it, that so do'th. try
For be we never so vicious within,
We will be held both wise and clean of sin.
And some men said, that great delight have we
For to be held stable and eke secre, discreet
And in one purpose steadfastly to dwell,
And not bewray a thing that men us tell. give away
But that tale is not worth a rake-stele. rake-handle
Pardie, we women canne nothing hele, hide[9]
Witness on Midas; will ye hear the tale?
Ovid, amonges other thinges smale small
Saith, Midas had, under his longe hairs,
Growing upon his head two ass's ears;
The whiche vice he hid, as best he might,
Full subtlely from every man's sight,
That, save his wife, there knew of it no mo';
He lov'd her most, and trusted her also;
He prayed her, that to no creature
She woulde tellen of his disfigure.
She swore him, nay, for all the world to win,
She would not do that villainy or sin,
To make her husband have so foul a name:
She would not tell it for her owen shame.
But natheless her thoughte that she died,
That she so longe should a counsel hide;
Her thought it swell'd so sore about her heart
That needes must some word from her astart
And, since she durst not tell it unto man
Down to a marish fast thereby she ran,
Till she came there, her heart was all afire:
And, as a bittern bumbles in the mire, makes a humming noise
She laid her mouth unto the water down
"Bewray me not, thou water, with thy soun'"
Quoth she, "to thee I tell it, and no mo',
Mine husband hath long ass's eares two!
Now is mine heart all whole; now is it out;
I might no longer keep it, out of doubt."
Here may ye see, though we a time abide,
Yet out it must, we can no counsel hide.
The remnant of the tale, if ye will hear,
Read in Ovid, and there ye may it lear. learn

This knight, of whom my tale is specially,
When that he saw he might not come thereby,
That is to say, what women love the most,
Within his breast full sorrowful was his ghost. spirit
But home he went, for he might not sojourn,
The day was come, that homeward he must turn.
And in his way it happen'd him to ride,
In all his care, under a forest side, trouble, anxiety
Where as he saw upon a dance go
Of ladies four-and-twenty, and yet mo',
Toward this ilke dance he drew full yern, same eagerly[10]
The hope that he some wisdom there should learn;
But certainly, ere he came fully there,
Y-vanish'd was this dance, he knew not where;
No creature saw he that bare life,
Save on the green he sitting saw a wife,
A fouler wight there may no man devise. imagine, tell
Against this knight this old wife gan to rise, to

meet
And said, "Sir Knight, hereforth lieth no way. from here
Tell me what ye are seeking, by your fay.
Paraventure it may the better be:
These olde folk know muche thing." quoth she.
My leve mother," quoth this knight, "certain, dear
I am but dead, but if that I can sayn unless
What thing it is that women most desire:
Could ye me wiss, I would well quite your hire." instruct[11]
"Plight me thy troth here in mine hand," quoth she, reward you
"The nexte thing that I require of thee
Thou shalt it do, if it be in thy might,
And I will tell it thee ere it be night."
"Have here my trothe," quoth the knight; "I grant."
"Thenne," quoth she, "I dare me well avaunt, boast, affirm
Thy life is safe, for I will stand thereby,
Upon my life the queen will say as I:
Let see, which is the proudest of them all,
That wears either a kerchief or a caul,
That dare say nay to that I shall you teach.
Let us go forth withoute longer speech
Then rowned she a pistel in his ear, she whispered a secret
And bade him to be glad, and have no fear.

When they were come unto the court, this knight
Said, he had held his day, as he had hight, promised
And ready was his answer, as he said.
Full many a noble wife, and many a maid,
And many a widow, for that they be wise, —
The queen herself sitting as a justice, —
Assembled be, his answer for to hear,
And afterward this knight was bid appear.
To every wight commanded was silence,
And that the knight should tell in audience,
What thing that worldly women love the best.
This knight he stood not still, as doth a beast,
But to this question anon answer'd
With manly voice, that all the court it heard,
"My liege lady, generally," quoth he,
"Women desire to have the sovereignty
As well over their husband as their love
And for to be in mast'ry him above.
This is your most desire, though ye me kill,
Do as you list, I am here at your will."
In all the court there was no wife nor maid
Nor widow, that contraried what he said,
But said, he worthy was to have his life.
And with that word up start that olde wife
Which that the knight saw sitting on the green.

"Mercy," quoth she, "my sovereign lady queen,
Ere that your court departe, do me right.

I taughte this answer unto this knight,
For which he plighted me his trothe there,
The firste thing I would of him requere,
He would it do, if it lay in his might.
Before this court then pray I thee, Sir Knight,"
Quoth she, "that thou me take unto thy wife,
For well thou know'st that I have kept thy life. preserved
If I say false, say nay, upon thy fay." faith
This knight answer'd, "Alas, and well-away!
I know right well that such was my behest. promise
For Godde's love choose a new request
Take all my good, and let my body go."
"Nay, then," quoth she, "I shrew us bothe two, curse
For though that I be old, and foul, and poor,
I n'ould for all the metal nor the ore, would not
That under earth is grave, or lies above buried
But if thy wife I were and eke thy love."
"My love?" quoth he, "nay, my damnation,
Alas! that any of my nation
Should ever so foul disparaged be.
But all for nought; the end is this, that he
Constrained was, that needs he muste wed,
And take this olde wife, and go to bed.

Now woulde some men say paraventure
That for my negligence I do no cure take no pains
To tell you all the joy and all th' array
That at the feast was made that ilke day. same
To which thing shortly answeren I shall:
I say there was no joy nor feast at all,
There was but heaviness and muche sorrow:
For privily he wed her on the morrow;
And all day after hid him as an owl,
So woe was him, his wife look'd so foul
Great was the woe the knight had in his thought
When he was with his wife to bed y-brought;
He wallow'd, and he turned to and fro.
This olde wife lay smiling evermo',
And said, "Dear husband, benedicite,
Fares every knight thus with his wife as ye?
Is this the law of king Arthoures house?
Is every knight of his thus dangerous? fastidious, niggardly
I am your owen love, and eke your wife
I am she, which that saved hath your life
And certes yet did I you ne'er unright.
Why fare ye thus with me this firste night?
Ye fare like a man had lost his wit.
What is my guilt? for God's love tell me it,
And it shall be amended, if I may."
"Amended!" quoth this knight; "alas, nay, nay,
It will not be amended, never mo';
Thou art so loathly, and so old also,
And thereto comest of so low a kind, in addition
That little wonder though I wallow and wind;

writhe, turn about
So woulde God, mine hearte woulde brest!" burst
"Is this," quoth she, "the cause of your unrest?"
"Yea, certainly," quoth he; "no wonder is."
"Now, Sir," quoth she, "I could amend all this,
If that me list, ere it were dayes three,
So well ye mighte bear you unto me. if you could conduct
But, for ye speaken of such gentleness yourself well
As is descended out of old richess, towards me
That therefore shalle ye be gentlemen;
Such arrogancy is not worth a hen. worth nothing
Look who that is most virtuous alway,
Prive and apert, and most intendeth aye in private and public
To do the gentle deedes that he can;
And take him for the greatest gentleman.
Christ will, we claim of him our gentleness, wills, requires
Not of our elders for their old richess. ancestors
For though they gave us all their heritage,
For which we claim to be of high parage, birth, descent
Yet may they not bequeathe, for no thing,
To none of us, their virtuous living
That made them gentlemen called to be,
And bade us follow them in such degree.
Well can the wise poet of Florence,
That highte Dante, speak of this sentence: sentiment
Lo, in such manner rhyme is Dante's tale. kind of
'Full seld' upriseth by his branches smale seldom
Prowess of man, for God of his goodness
Wills that we claim of him our gentleness;'12
For of our elders may we nothing claim
But temp'ral things that man may hurt and maim.
Eke every wight knows this as well as I,
If gentleness were planted naturally
Unto a certain lineage down the line,
Prive and apert, then would they never fine cease
To do of gentleness the fair office
Then might they do no villainy nor vice.
Take fire, and bear it to the darkest house
Betwixt this and the mount of Caucasus,
And let men shut the doores, and go thenne, thence
Yet will the fire as fair and lighte brenne burn
As twenty thousand men might it behold;
Its office natural aye will it hold, it will perform its
On peril of my life, till that it die. natural duty
Here may ye see well how that gentery gentility, nobility
Is not annexed to possession,
Since folk do not their operation
Alway, as doth the fire, lo, in its kind from its very nature

For, God it wot, men may full often find
A lorde's son do shame and villainy.
And he that will have price of his gent'ry, esteem, honour
For he was boren of a gentle house, because
And had his elders noble and virtuous,
And will himselfe do no gentle deedes,
Nor follow his gentle ancestry, that dead is,
He is not gentle, be he duke or earl;
For villain sinful deedes make a churl.
For gentleness is but the renomee renown
Of thine ancestors, for their high bounte, goodness, worth
Which is a strange thing to thy person:
Thy gentleness cometh from God alone.
Then comes our very gentleness of grace; true
It was no thing bequeath'd us with our place.
Think how noble, as saith Valerius,
Was thilke Tullius Hostilius, that
That out of povert' rose to high
Read in Senec, and read eke in Boece,
There shall ye see express, that it no drede is, doubt
That he is gentle that doth gentle deedes.
And therefore, leve husband, I conclude, dear
Albeit that mine ancestors were rude,
Yet may the highe God, — and so hope I, —
Grant me His grace to live virtuously:
Then am I gentle when that I begin
To live virtuously, and waive sin. forsake

"And whereas ye of povert' me repreve, reproach
The highe God, on whom that we believe,
In wilful povert' chose to lead his life:
And certes, every man, maiden, or wife
May understand that Jesus, heaven's king,
Ne would not choose a virtuous living.
Glad povert' is an honest thing, certain; poverty cheerfully
This will Senec and other clerkes sayn endured
Whoso that holds him paid of his povert', is satisfied with
I hold him rich though he hath not a shirt.
He that coveteth is a poore wight
For he would have what is not in his might
But he that nought hath, nor coveteth to have,
Is rich, although ye hold him but a knave. slave, abject wretch
Very povert' is sinne, properly. the only true poverty is sin
Juvenal saith of povert' merrily:
The poore man, when he goes by the way
Before the thieves he may sing and play13
Povert' is hateful good,14 and, as I guess,
A full great bringer out of business; deliver from trouble
A great amender eke of sapience
To him that taketh it in patience.
Povert' is this, although it seem elenge strange15

GEOFFREY CHAUCER

Possession that no wight will challenge
Povert' full often, when a man is low,
Makes him his God and eke himself to know
Povert' a spectacle is, as thinketh me a pair of spectacles
Through which he may his very friendes see. true
And, therefore, Sir, since that I you not grieve,
Of my povert' no more me repreve. reproach
"Now, Sir, of elde ye repreve me: age
And certes, Sir, though none authority text, dictum
Were in no book, ye gentles of honour
Say, that men should an olde wight honour,
And call him father, for your gentleness;
And authors shall I finden, as I guess.
Now there ye say that I am foul and old,
Then dread ye not to be a cokewold. cuckold
For filth, and elde, all so may I the, thrive
Be greate wardens upon chastity.
But natheless, since I know your delight,
I shall fulfil your wordly appetite.
Choose now," quoth she, "one of these thinges tway,
To have me foul and old till that I dey, die
And be to you a true humble wife,
And never you displease in all my life:
Or elles will ye have me young and fair,
And take your aventure of the repair resort
That shall be to your house because of me, —
Or in some other place, it may well be?
Now choose yourselfe whether that you liketh.

This knight adviseth him and sore he siketh, considered sighed
But at the last he said in this mannere;
"My lady and my love, and wife so dear,
I put me in your wise governance,
Choose for yourself which may be most pleasance
And most honour to you and me also;
I do no force the whether of the two: care not
For as you liketh, it sufficeth me."
"Then have I got the mastery," quoth she,
"Since I may choose and govern as me lest." pleases
"Yea, certes wife," quoth he, "I hold it best."
"Kiss me," quoth she, "we are no longer wroth, at variance
For by my troth I will be to you both;
This is to say, yea, bothe fair and good.
I pray to God that I may sterve wood, die mad
But I to you be all so good and true, unless
As ever was wife since the world was new;
And but I be to-morrow as fair to seen, unless
As any lady, emperess or queen,
That is betwixt the East and eke the West
Do with my life and death right as you lest. please
Cast up the curtain, and look how it is."

And when the knight saw verily all this,
That she so fair was, and so young thereto,
For joy he hent her in his armes two: took
His hearte bathed in a bath of bliss,
A thousand times on row he gan her kiss: in succession
And she obeyed him in every thing
That mighte do him pleasance or liking.
And thus they live unto their lives' end
In perfect joy; and Jesus Christ us send
Husbandes meek and young, and fresh in bed,
And grace to overlive them that we wed.
And eke I pray Jesus to short their lives,
That will not be governed by their wives.
And old and angry niggards of dispence, expense
God send them soon a very pestilence!

Notes to the Wife of Bath's Tale

1. It is not clear whence Chaucer derived this tale. Tyrwhitt thinks it was taken from the story of Florent, in the first book of Gower's "Confessio Amantis;" or perhaps from an older narrative from which Gower himself borrowed. Chaucer has condensed and otherwise improved the fable, especially by laying the scene, not in Sicily, but at the court of our own King Arthur.
2. Limitours: begging friars. See note 18 to the prologue to the Tales.
3. Thorpes: villages. Compare German, "Dorf,"; Dutch, "Dorp."
4. Undermeles: evening-tides, afternoons; "undern" signifies the evening; and "mele," corresponds to the German "Mal" or "Mahl," time.
5. Incubus: an evil spirit supposed to do violence to women; a nightmare.
6. Where he had been hawking after waterfowl. Froissart says that any one engaged in this sport "alloit en riviere."
7. Nice: foolish; French, "niais."
8. Claw us on the gall: Scratch us on the sore place. Compare, "Let the galled jade wince." Hamlet iii. 2.
9. Hele: hide; from Anglo-Saxon, "helan," to hide, conceal.
10. Yern: eagerly; German, "gern."
11. Wiss: instruct; German, "weisen," to show or counsel.
12. Dante, "Purgatorio", vii. 121.
13. "Cantabit vacuus coram latrone viator" — "Satires," x. 22.

14. In a fabulous conference between the Emperor Adrian and the philosopher Secundus, reported by Vincent of Beauvais, occurs the passage which Chaucer here paraphrases: — "Quid est Paupertas? Odibile bonum; sanitas mater; remotio Curarum; sapientae repertrix; negotium sine damno; possessio absque calumnia; sine sollicitudinae felicitas." (What is Poverty? A hateful good; a mother of health; a putting away of cares; a discoverer of wisdom; business without injury; ownership without calumny; happiness without anxiety)
15. Elenge: strange; from French "eloigner," to remove.

GEOFFREY CHAUCER

THE FRIAR'S TALE.

THE PROLOGUE.1

This worthy limitour, this noble Frere,
He made always a manner louring cheer countenance
Upon the Sompnour; but for honesty courtesy
No villain word as yet to him spake he:
But at the last he said unto the Wife:
"Dame," quoth he, "God give you right good life,
Ye have here touched, all so may I the, thrive
In school matter a greate difficulty.
Ye have said muche thing right well, I say;
But, Dame, here as we ride by the way,
Us needeth not but for to speak of game,
And leave authorities, in Godde's name,
To preaching, and to school eke of clergy.
But if it like unto this company,
I will you of a Sompnour tell a game;
Pardie, ye may well knowe by the name,
That of a Sompnour may no good be said;
I pray that none of you be evil paid; dissatisfied
A Sompnour is a runner up and down
With mandements for fornicatioun, mandates, summonses
And is y-beat at every towne's end."
Then spake our Host; "Ah, sir, ye should be hend civil, gentle
And courteous, as a man of your estate;
In company we will have no debate:
Tell us your tale, and let the Sompnour be."
"Nay," quoth the Sompnour, "let him say by me
What so him list; when it comes to my lot,
By God, I shall him quiten every groat! pay him off
I shall him telle what a great honour
It is to be a flattering limitour
And his office I shall him tell y-wis".
Our Host answered, "Peace, no more of this."
And afterward he said unto the frere,
"Tell forth your tale, mine owen master dear."

Notes to the Prologue to the Friar's tale

1. On the Tale of the Friar, and that of the Sompnour which follows, Tyrwhitt has remarked that they "are well engrafted upon that of the Wife of Bath. The ill-humour which shows itself between these two characters is quite natural, as no two professions at that time were at more constant variance. The regular clergy, and particularly the mendicant friars, affected a total exemption from all ecclesiastical jurisdiction, except that of the Pope, which made them exceedingly obnoxious to the bishops and of course to all the inferior officers of the national hierarchy." Both tales, whatever their origin, are bitter satires on the greed and worldliness of the Romish clergy.

THE TALE.

Whilom there was dwelling in my country once on a time
An archdeacon, a man of high degree,
That boldely did execution,
In punishing of fornication,
Of witchecraft, and eke of bawdery,
Of defamation, and adultery,
Of churche-reeves, and of testaments, churchwardens
Of contracts, and of lack of sacraments,
And eke of many another manner crime, sort of
Which needeth not rehearsen at this time,
Of usury, and simony also;
But, certes, lechours did he greatest woe;
They shoulde singen, if that they were hent; caught
And smale tithers1 were foul y-shent, troubled, put to shame
If any person would on them complain;
There might astert them no pecunial pain.2
For smalle tithes, and small offering,
He made the people piteously to sing;
For ere the bishop caught them with his crook,
They weren in the archedeacon's book;
Then had he, through his jurisdiction,
Power to do on them correction.

He had a Sompnour ready to his hand,
A slier boy was none in Engleland;
For subtlely he had his espiaille, espionage
That taught him well where it might aught avail.
He coulde spare of lechours one or two,
To teache him to four and twenty mo'.
For, — though this Sompnour wood be as a hare, — furious, mad
To tell his harlotry I will not spare,
For we be out of their correction,
They have of us no jurisdiction,
Ne never shall have, term of all their lives.

THE CANTERBURY TALES

"Peter; so be the women of the stives," stews
Quoth this Sompnour, "y-put out of our cure." care

"Peace, with mischance and with misaventure,"
Our Hoste said, "and let him tell his tale.
Now telle forth, and let the Sompnour gale, whistle; bawl
Nor spare not, mine owen master dear."

This false thief, the Sompnour (quoth the Frere),
Had always bawdes ready to his hand,
As any hawk to lure in Engleland,
That told him all the secrets that they knew, —
For their acquaintance was not come of new;
They were his approvers privily. informers
He took himself at great profit thereby:
His master knew not always what he wan. won
Withoute mandement, a lewed man ignorant
He could summon, on pain of Christe's curse,
And they were inly glad to fill his purse,
And make him greate feastes at the nale. alehouse
And right as Judas hadde purses smale, small
And was a thief, right such a thief was he,
His master had but half his duety. what was owing him
He was (if I shall give him his laud)
A thief, and eke a Sompnour, and a bawd.
And he had wenches at his retinue,
That whether that Sir Robert or Sir Hugh,
Or Jack, or Ralph, or whoso that it were
That lay by them, they told it in his ear.
Thus were the wench and he of one assent;
And he would fetch a feigned mandement,
And to the chapter summon them both two,
And pill the man, and let the wenche go. plunder, pluck
Then would he say, "Friend, I shall for thy sake
Do strike thee out of oure letters blake; black
Thee thar no more as in this case travail; need
I am thy friend where I may thee avail."
Certain he knew of bribers many mo'
Than possible is to tell in yeare's two:
For in this world is no dog for the bow,[3]
That can a hurt deer from a whole know,
Bet than this Sompnour knew a sly lechour, better
Or an adult'rer, or a paramour:
And, for that was the fruit of all his rent,
Therefore on it he set all his intent.

And so befell, that once upon a day.
This Sompnour, waiting ever on his prey,
Rode forth to summon a widow, an old ribibe,[4]
Feigning a cause, for he would have a bribe.
And happen'd that he saw before him ride
A gay yeoman under a forest side:
A bow he bare, and arrows bright and keen,
He had upon a courtepy of green, short doublet
A hat upon his head with fringes blake. black

"Sir," quoth this Sompnour, "hail, and well o'ertake."
"Welcome," quoth he, "and every good fellow;
Whither ridest thou under this green shaw?" shade
Saide this yeoman; "wilt thou far to-day?"
This Sompnour answer'd him, and saide, "Nay.
Here faste by," quoth he, "is mine intent
To ride, for to raisen up a rent,
That longeth to my lorde's duety."
"Ah! art thou then a bailiff?" "Yea," quoth he.
He durste not for very filth and shame
Say that he was a Sompnour, for the name.
"De par dieux,"[5] quoth this yeoman, "leve brother, dear
Thou art a bailiff, and I am another.
I am unknown, as in this country.
Of thine acquaintance I will praye thee,
And eke of brotherhood, if that thee list. please
I have gold and silver lying in my chest;
If that thee hap to come into our shire,
All shall be thine, right as thou wilt desire."
"Grand mercy," quoth this Sompnour, "by my faith." great thanks
Each in the other's hand his trothe lay'th,
For to be sworne brethren till they dey. die[6]
In dalliance they ride forth and play.

This Sompnour, which that was as full of jangles, chattering
As full of venom be those wariangles, butcher-birds[7]
And ev'r inquiring upon every thing,
"Brother," quoth he, "where is now your dwelling,
Another day if that I should you seech?" seek, visit
This yeoman him answered in soft speech;
Brother," quoth he, "far in the North country,[8]
Where as I hope some time I shall thee see
Ere we depart I shall thee so well wiss, inform
That of mine house shalt thou never miss."
Now, brother," quoth this Sompnour, "I you pray,
Teach me, while that we ride by the way,
(Since that ye be a bailiff as am I,)
Some subtilty, and tell me faithfully
For mine office how that I most may win.
And spare not for conscience or for sin, conceal nothing
But, as my brother, tell me how do ye."
Now by my trothe, brother mine," said he,
As I shall tell to thee a faithful tale:
My wages be full strait and eke full smale;
My lord is hard to me and dangerous, niggardly
And mine office is full laborious;
And therefore by extortion I live,
Forsooth I take all that men will me give.
Algate by sleighte, or by violence, whether

85

GEOFFREY CHAUCER

From year to year I win all my dispence;
I can no better tell thee faithfully."
Now certes," quoth this Sompnour, "so fare I; do
I spare not to take, God it wot,
But if it be too heavy or too hot. unless
What I may get in counsel privily,
No manner conscience of that have I.
N'ere mine extortion, I might not live, were it not for
For of such japes will I not be shrive. tricks confessed
Stomach nor conscience know I none;
I shrew these shrifte-fathers every one. curse confessors
Well be we met, by God and by St Jame.
But, leve brother, tell me then thy name,"
Quoth this Sompnour. Right in this meane while
This yeoman gan a little for to smile.

"Brother," quoth he, "wilt thou that I thee tell?
I am a fiend, my dwelling is in hell,
And here I ride about my purchasing,
To know where men will give me any thing.
My purchase is th' effect of all my rent what I can gain is my
Look how thou ridest for the same intent sole revenue
To winne good, thou reckest never how,
Right so fare I, for ride will I now
Into the worlde's ende for a prey."

"Ah," quoth this Sompnour, "benedicite! what say y'?
I weened ye were a yeoman truly. thought
Ye have a manne's shape as well as I
Have ye then a figure determinate
In helle, where ye be in your estate?" at home
"Nay, certainly," quoth he, there have we none,
But when us liketh we can take us one,
Or elles make you seem that we be shape believe
Sometime like a man, or like an ape;
Or like an angel can I ride or go;
It is no wondrous thing though it be so,
A lousy juggler can deceive thee.
And pardie, yet can I more craft than he." skill, cunning
"Why," quoth the Sompnour, "ride ye then or gon
In sundry shapes and not always in one?"
"For we," quoth he, "will us in such form make.
As most is able our prey for to take."
"What maketh you to have all this labour?"
"Full many a cause, leve Sir Sompnour,"
Saide this fiend. "But all thing hath a time;
The day is short and it is passed prime,
And yet have I won nothing in this day;
I will intend to winning, if I may, apply myself
And not intend our things to declare:
For, brother mine, thy wit is all too bare
To understand, although I told them thee.

But for thou askest why laboure we: because
For sometimes we be Godde's instruments
And meanes to do his commandements,
When that him list, upon his creatures,
In divers acts and in divers figures:
Withoute him we have no might certain,
If that him list to stande thereagain. against it
And sometimes, at our prayer have we leave
Only the body, not the soul, to grieve:
Witness on Job, whom that we did full woe,
And sometimes have we might on both the two,
This is to say, on soul and body eke,
And sometimes be we suffer'd for to seek
Upon a man and do his soul unrest
And not his body, and all is for the best,
When he withstandeth our temptation,
It is a cause of his salvation,
Albeit that it was not our intent
He should be safe, but that we would him hent. catch
And sometimes be we servants unto man,
As to the archbishop Saint Dunstan,
And to th'apostle servant eke was I."
"Yet tell me," quoth this Sompnour, "faithfully,
Make ye you newe bodies thus alway
Of th' elements?" The fiend answered, "Nay:
Sometimes we feign, and sometimes we arise
With deade bodies, in full sundry wise,
And speak as reas'nably, and fair, and well,
As to the Pythoness[9] did Samuel:
And yet will some men say it was not he.
I do no force of your divinity. set no value upon
But one thing warn I thee, I will not jape, jest
Thou wilt algates weet how we be shape: assuredly know
Thou shalt hereafterward, my brother dear,
Come, where thee needeth not of me to lear. learn
For thou shalt by thine own experience
Conne in a chair to rede of this sentence, learn to understand
Better than Virgil, while he was alive, what I have said
Or Dante also.[10] Now let us ride blive, briskly
For I will holde company with thee,
Till it be so that thou forsake me."
"Nay," quoth this Sompnour, "that shall ne'er betide.
I am a yeoman, that is known full wide;
My trothe will I hold, as in this case;
For though thou wert the devil Satanas,
My trothe will I hold to thee, my brother,
As I have sworn, and each of us to other,
For to be true brethren in this case,
And both we go abouten our purchase. seeking what we
Take thou thy part, what that men will thee give, may pick up

86

THE CANTERBURY TALES

And I shall mine, thus may we bothe live.
And if that any of us have more than other,
Let him be true, and part it with his brother."
"I grante," quoth the devil, "by my fay."
And with that word they rode forth their way,
And right at th'ent'ring of the towne's end,
To which this Sompnour shope him for to wend, shaped go
They saw a cart, that charged was with hay,
Which that a carter drove forth on his way.
Deep was the way, for which the carte stood:
The carter smote, and cried as he were wood, mad
"Heit Scot! heit Brok! what, spare ye for the stones?
The fiend (quoth he) you fetch body and bones,
As farforthly as ever ye were foal'd, sure
So muche woe as I have with you tholed. endured[11]
The devil have all, horses, and cart, and hay."
The Sompnour said, "Here shall we have a prey,"
And near the fiend he drew, as nought ne were, as if nothing
Full privily, and rowned in his ear: were the matter
"Hearken, my brother, hearken, by thy faith, whispered
Hearest thou not, how that the carter saith?
Hent it anon, for he hath giv'n it thee, seize
Both hay and cart, and eke his capels three." horses[12]
"Nay," quoth the devil, "God wot, never a deal, whit
It is not his intent, trust thou me well;
Ask him thyself, if thou not trowest me, believest
Or elles stint a while and thou shalt see." stop
The carter thwack'd his horses on the croup,
And they began to drawen and to stoop.
"Heit now," quoth he; "there, Jesus Christ you bless,
And all his handiwork, both more and less!
That was well twight, mine owen liart, boy, pulled grey[13]
I pray God save thy body, and Saint Loy!
Now is my cart out of the slough, pardie."
"Lo, brother," quoth the fiend, "what told I thee?
Here may ye see, mine owen deare brother,
The churl spake one thing, but he thought another.
Let us go forth abouten our voyage;
Here win I nothing upon this carriage."

When that they came somewhat out of the town,
This Sompnour to his brother gan to rown;
"Brother," quoth he, "here wons an old rebeck,[14] dwells
That had almost as lief to lose her neck.
As for to give a penny of her good.
I will have twelvepence, though that she be wood, mad
Or I will summon her to our office;
And yet, God wot, of her know I no vice.
But for thou canst not, as in this country,
Winne thy cost, take here example of me."
This Sompnour clapped at the widow's gate:
"Come out," he said, "thou olde very trate; trot[15]
I trow thou hast some friar or priest with thee."
"Who clappeth?" said this wife; "benedicite,
God save you, Sir, what is your sweete will?"
"I have," quoth he, "of summons here a bill.
Up pain of cursing, looke that thou be upon
To-morrow before our archdeacon's knee,
To answer to the court of certain things."
"Now Lord," quoth she, "Christ Jesus, king of kings,
So wisly helpe me, as I not may. surely as I cannot
I have been sick, and that full many a day.
I may not go so far," quoth she, "nor ride,
But I be dead, so pricketh it my side.
May I not ask a libel, Sir Sompnour,
And answer there by my procuratour
To such thing as men would appose me?" accuse
"Yes," quoth this Sompnour, "pay anon, let see,
Twelvepence to me, and I will thee acquit.
I shall no profit have thereby but lit: little
My master hath the profit and not I.
Come off, and let me ride hastily;
Give me twelvepence, I may no longer tarry."

"Twelvepence!" quoth she; "now lady Sainte Mary
So wisly help me out of care and sin, surely
This wide world though that I should it win,
No have I not twelvepence within my hold.
Ye know full well that I am poor and old;
Kithe your almes upon me poor wretch." show your charity
"Nay then," quoth he, "the foule fiend me fetch,
If I excuse thee, though thou should'st be spilt." ruined
"Alas!" quoth she, "God wot, I have no guilt."
"Pay me," quoth he, "or, by the sweet Saint Anne,
As I will bear away thy newe pan
For debte, which thou owest me of old, —
When that thou madest thine husband cuckold, —
I paid at home for thy correction."
"Thou liest," quoth she, "by my salvation;
Never was I ere now, widow or wife,
Summon'd unto your court in all my life;
Nor never I was but of my body true.
Unto the devil rough and black of hue
Give I thy body and my pan also."
And when the devil heard her curse so
Upon her knees, he said in this mannere;
"Now, Mabily, mine owen mother dear,

Is this your will in earnest that ye say?"
"The devil," quoth she, "so fetch him ere he dey, die
And pan and all, but he will him repent." unless
"Nay, olde stoat, that is not mine intent," polecat
Quoth this Sompnour, "for to repente me
For any thing that I have had of thee;
I would I had thy smock and every cloth."
"Now, brother," quoth the devil, "be not wroth;
Thy body and this pan be mine by right.
Thou shalt with me to helle yet tonight,
Where thou shalt knowen of our privity secrets
More than a master of divinity."

And with that word the foule fiend him hent. seized
Body and soul, he with the devil went,
Where as the Sompnours have their heritage;
And God, that maked after his image
Mankinde, save and guide us all and some,
And let this Sompnour a good man become.
Lordings, I could have told you (quoth this Frere),
Had I had leisure for this Sompnour here,
After the text of Christ, and Paul, and John,
And of our other doctors many a one,
Such paines, that your heartes might agrise, be horrified
Albeit so, that no tongue may devise, — relate
Though that I might a thousand winters tell, —
The pains of thilke cursed house of hell that
But for to keep us from that cursed place
Wake we, and pray we Jesus, of his grace,
So keep us from the tempter, Satanas.
Hearken this word, beware as in this case.
The lion sits in his await alway on the watch[16]
To slay the innocent, if that he may.
Disposen aye your heartes to withstond
The fiend that would you make thrall and bond;
He may not tempte you over your might,
For Christ will be your champion and your knight;
And pray, that this our Sompnour him repent
Of his misdeeds ere that the fiend him hent. seize

Notes to the Friar's Tale

1. Small tithers: people who did not pay their full tithes. Mr Wright remarks that "the sermons of the friars in the fourteenth century were most frequently designed to impress the ahsolute duty of paying full tithes and offerings".
2. There might astert them no pecunial pain: they got off with no mere pecuniary punishment. (Transcriber's note: "Astert" means "escape". An alternative reading of this line is "there might astert him no pecunial pain" i.e. no fine ever escaped him (the archdeacon))
3. A dog for the bow: a dog attending a huntsman with bow and arrow.
4. Ribibe: the name of a musical instrument; applied to an old woman because of the shrillness of her voice.
5. De par dieux: by the gods.
6. See note 12 to the Knight's Tale.
7. Wariangles: butcher-birds; which are very noisy and ravenous, and tear in pieces the birds on which they prey; the thorn on which they do this was said to become poisonous.
8. Medieval legends located hell in the North.
9. The Pythoness: the witch, or woman, possesed with a prophesying spirit; from the Greek, "Pythia." Chaucer of course refers to the raising of Samuel's spirit by the witch of Endor.
10. Dante and Virgil were both poets who had in fancy visited Hell.
11. Tholed: suffered, endured; "thole" is still used in Scotland in the same sense.
12. Capels: horses. See note 14 to the Reeve's Tale.
13. Liart: grey; elsewhere applied by Chaucer to the hairs of an old man. So Burns, in the "Cotter's Saturday Night," speaks of the gray temples of "the sire" — "His lyart haffets wearing thin and bare."
14. Rebeck: a kind of fiddle; used like "ribibe," as a nickname for a shrill old scold.
15. Trot; a contemptuous term for an old woman who has trotted about much, or who moves with quick short steps.
16. In his await: on the watch; French, "aux aguets."

THE SOMPNOUR'S TALE.

THE PROLOGUE.

The Sompnour in his stirrups high he stood,
Upon this Friar his hearte was so wood, *furious*
That like an aspen leaf he quoke for ire: *quaked, trembled*
"Lordings," quoth he, "but one thing I desire;
I you beseech, that of your courtesy,
Since ye have heard this false Friar lie,
As suffer me I may my tale tell
This Friar boasteth that he knoweth hell,
And, God it wot, that is but little wonder,
Friars and fiends be but little asunder.
For, pardie, ye have often time heard tell,
How that a friar ravish'd was to hell
In spirit ones by a visioun,
And, as an angel led him up and down,
To shew him all the paines that there were,
In all the place saw he not a frere;
Of other folk he saw enough in woe.
Unto the angel spake the friar tho; *then*
'Now, Sir,' quoth he, 'have friars such a grace,
That none of them shall come into this place?'
'Yes' quoth the angel; 'many a millioun:'
And unto Satanas he led him down.
'And now hath Satanas,' said he, 'a tail
Broader than of a carrack[1] is the sail.
Hold up thy tail, thou Satanas,' quoth he,
'Shew forth thine erse, and let the friar see
Where is the nest of friars in this place.'
And less than half a furlong way of space immediately[2]
Right so as bees swarmen out of a hive,
Out of the devil's erse there gan to drive
A twenty thousand friars on a rout. *in a crowd*
And throughout hell they swarmed all about,
And came again, as fast as they may gon,
And in his erse they creeped every one:
He clapt his tail again, and lay full still.
This friar, when he looked had his fill
Upon the torments of that sorry place,
His spirit God restored of his grace
Into his body again, and he awoke;
But natheless for feare yet he quoke,
So was the devil's erse aye in his mind;
That is his heritage, of very kind *by his very nature*
God save you alle, save this cursed Frere;
My prologue will I end in this mannere.

Notes to the Prologue to the Sompnour's Tale

1. Carrack: A great ship of burden used by the Portuguese; the name is from the Italian, "cargare," to load
2. In less than half a furlong way of space: immediately; literally, in less time than it takes to walk half a furlong (110 yards).

THE TALE.

Lordings, there is in Yorkshire, as I guess,
A marshy country called Holderness,
In which there went a limitour about
To preach, and eke to beg, it is no doubt.
And so befell that on a day this frere
Had preached at a church in his mannere,
And specially, above every thing,
Excited he the people in his preaching
To trentals,[1] and to give, for Godde's sake,
Wherewith men mighte holy houses make,
There as divine service is honour'd,
Not there as it is wasted and devour'd,
Nor where it needeth not for to be given,
As to possessioners,[2] that may liven,
Thanked be God, in wealth and abundance.
"Trentals," said he, "deliver from penance
Their friendes' soules, as well old as young, —
Yea, when that they be hastily y-sung, —
Not for to hold a priest jolly and gay,
He singeth not but one mass in a day.
"Deliver out," quoth he, "anon the souls.
Full hard it is, with flesh-hook or with owls *awls*
To be y-clawed, or to burn or bake:[3]
Now speed you hastily, for Christe's sake."
And when this friar had said all his intent,
With qui cum patre[4] forth his way he went,
When folk in church had giv'n him what them lest; *pleased*
He went his way, no longer would he rest,
With scrip and tipped staff, y-tucked high: *with his robe tucked*
In every house he gan to pore and pry, *up high peer*
And begged meal and cheese, or elles corn.
His fellow had a staff tipped with horn,
A pair of tables all of ivory, *writing tablets*
And a pointel y-polish'd fetisly, *pencil daintily*
And wrote alway the names, as he stood;

GEOFFREY CHAUCER

Of all the folk that gave them any good,
Askaunce that he woulde for them pray. see note[5]
"Give us a bushel wheat, or malt, or rey, rye
A Godde's kichel, or a trip of cheese, little cake[6] scrap
Or elles what you list, we may not chese; choose
A Godde's halfpenny,[6] or a mass penny;
Or give us of your brawn, if ye have any;
A dagon of your blanket, leve dame, remnant
Our sister dear, — lo, here I write your name,—
Bacon or beef, or such thing as ye find."
A sturdy harlot went them aye behind, manservant[7]
That was their hoste's man, and bare a sack,
And what men gave them, laid it on his back
And when that he was out at door, anon
He planed away the names every one, rubbed out
That he before had written in his tables:
He served them with nifles and with fables. — silly tales

"Nay, there thou liest, thou Sompnour," quoth the Frere.
"Peace," quoth our Host, "for Christe's mother dear;
Tell forth thy tale, and spare it not at all."
"So thrive I," quoth this Sompnour, "so I shall."
—

So long he went from house to house, till he
Came to a house, where he was wont to be
Refreshed more than in a hundred places
Sick lay the husband man, whose that the place is,
Bed-rid upon a couche low he lay:
"Deus hic," quoth he; "O Thomas friend, good day," God be here
Said this friar, all courteously and soft.
"Thomas," quoth he, "God yield it you, full oft reward you for
Have I upon this bench fared full well,
Here have I eaten many a merry meal."
And from the bench he drove away the cat,
And laid adown his potent and his hat, staff[8]
And eke his scrip, and sat himself adown:
His fellow was y-walked into town
Forth with his knave, into that hostelry servant
Where as he shope him that night to lie. shaped, purposed

"O deare master," quoth this sicke man,
"How have ye fared since that March began?
I saw you not this fortenight and more."
"God wot," quoth he, "labour'd have I full sore;
And specially for thy salvation
Have I said many a precious orison,
And for mine other friendes, God them bless.
I have this day been at your church at mess, mass
And said sermon after my simple wit,
Not all after the text of Holy Writ;
For it is hard to you, as I suppose,

And therefore will I teach you aye the glose. gloss, comment
Glosing is a full glorious thing certain,
For letter slayeth, as we clerkes sayn. scholars
There have I taught them to be charitable,
And spend their good where it is reasonable.
And there I saw our dame; where is she?"
"Yonder I trow that in the yard she be,"
Saide this man; "and she will come anon."
"Hey master, welcome be ye by Saint John,"
Saide this wife; "how fare ye heartily?"

This friar riseth up full courteously,
And her embraceth in his armes narrow, closely
And kiss'th her sweet, and chirketh as a sparrow
With his lippes: "Dame," quoth he, "right well,
As he that is your servant every deal. whit
Thanked be God, that gave you soul and life,
Yet saw I not this day so fair a wife
In all the churche, God so save me,"
"Yea, God amend defaultes, Sir," quoth she;
"Algates welcome be ye, by my fay." always
"Grand mercy, Dame; that have I found alway.
But of your greate goodness, by your leave,
I woulde pray you that ye not you grieve,
I will with Thomas speak a little throw: a little while
These curates be so negligent and slow
To grope tenderly a conscience.
In shrift and preaching is my diligence confession
And study in Peter's wordes and in Paul's;
I walk and fishe Christian menne's souls,
To yield our Lord Jesus his proper rent;
To spread his word is alle mine intent."
"Now by your faith, O deare Sir," quoth she,
"Chide him right well, for sainte charity.
He is aye angry as is a pismire, ant
Though that he have all that he can desire,
Though I him wrie at night, and make him warm, cover
And ov'r him lay my leg and eke mine arm,
He groaneth as our boar that lies in sty:
Other disport of him right none have I,
I may not please him in no manner case."
"O Thomas, je vous dis, Thomas, Thomas, I tell you
This maketh the fiend, this must be amended. is the devil's work
Ire is a thing that high God hath defended, forbidden
And thereof will I speak a word or two."
"Now, master," quoth the wife, "ere that I go,
What will ye dine? I will go thereabout."
"Now, Dame," quoth he, "je vous dis sans doute,[9]
Had I not of a capon but the liver,
And of your white bread not but a shiver, thin slice
And after that a roasted pigge's head,
(But I would that for me no beast were dead,)

Then had I with you homely suffisance.
I am a man of little sustenance.
My spirit hath its fost'ring in the Bible.
My body is aye so ready and penible   painstaking
To wake, that my stomach is destroy'd.   watch
I pray you, Dame, that ye be not annoy'd,
Though I so friendly you my counsel shew;
By God, I would have told it but to few."
"Now, Sir," quoth she, "but one word ere I go;
My child is dead within these weeke's two,
Soon after that ye went out of this town."

"His death saw I by revelatioun,"
Said this friar, "at home in our dortour.   dormitory[10]
I dare well say, that less than half an hour
Mter his death, I saw him borne to bliss
In mine vision, so God me wiss.   direct
So did our sexton, and our fermerere,   infirmary-keeper
That have been true friars fifty year, —
They may now, God be thanked of his love,
Make their jubilee, and walk above.[12]
And up I rose, and all our convent eke,
With many a teare trilling on my cheek,
Withoute noise or clattering of bells,
Te Deum was our song, and nothing else,
Save that to Christ I bade an orison,
Thanking him of my revelation.
For, Sir and Dame, truste me right well,
Our orisons be more effectuel,
And more we see of Christe's secret things,
Than borel folk, although that they be kings.   laymen[13]
We live in povert', and in abstinence,
And borel folk in riches and dispence
Of meat and drink, and in their foul delight.
We have this worlde's lust all in despight   pleasure contempt
Lazar and Dives lived diversely,
And diverse guerdon hadde they thereby.   reward
Whoso will pray, he must fast and be clean,
And fat his soul, and keep his body lean
We fare as saith th' apostle; cloth and food   clothing
Suffice us, although they be not full good.
The cleanness and the fasting of us freres
Maketh that Christ accepteth our prayers.
Lo, Moses forty days and forty night
Fasted, ere that the high God full of might
Spake with him in the mountain of Sinai:
With empty womb of fasting many a day   stomach
Received he the lawe, that was writ
With Godde's finger; and Eli,[14] well ye wit,   know
In Mount Horeb, ere he had any speech
With highe God, that is our live's leech,   physician, healer
He fasted long, and was in contemplance.
Aaron, that had the temple in governance,

And eke the other priestes every one,
Into the temple when they shoulde gon
To praye for the people, and do service,
They woulde drinken in no manner wise
No drinke, which that might them drunken make,
But there in abstinence pray and wake,
Lest that they died: take heed what I say —
But they be sober that for the people pray —   unless
Ware that, I say — no more: for it sufficeth.
Our Lord Jesus, as Holy Writ deviseth,   narrates
Gave us example of fasting and prayeres:
Therefore we mendicants, we sely freres,   simple, lowly
Be wedded to povert' and continence,
To charity, humbless, and abstinence,
To persecution for righteousness,
To weeping, misericorde, and to cleanness.   compassion
And therefore may ye see that our prayeres
(I speak of us, we mendicants, we freres),
Be to the highe God more acceptable
Than youres, with your feastes at your table.
From Paradise first, if I shall not lie,
Was man out chased for his gluttony,
And chaste was man in Paradise certain.
But hark now, Thomas, what I shall thee sayn;
I have no text of it, as I suppose,
But I shall find it in a manner glose;   a kind of comment
That specially our sweet Lord Jesus
Spake this of friars, when he saide thus,
'Blessed be they that poor in spirit be'
And so forth all the gospel may ye see,
Whether it be liker our profession,
Or theirs that swimmen in possession;
Fy on their pomp, and on their gluttony,
And on their lewedness! I them defy.
Me thinketh they be like Jovinian,[15]
Fat as a whale, and walking as a swan;
All vinolent as bottle in the spence;   full of wine store-room
Their prayer is of full great reverence;
When they for soules say the Psalm of David,
Lo, 'Buf' they say, Cor meum eructavit.[16]
Who follow Christe's gospel and his lore   doctrine
But we, that humble be, and chaste, and pore,   poor
Workers of Godde's word, not auditours?   hearers
Therefore right as a hawk upon a sours rising
Up springs into the air, right so prayeres
Of charitable and chaste busy freres
Make their sours to Godde's eares two.   rise
Thomas, Thomas, so may I ride or go,
And by that lord that called is Saint Ive,
N'ere thou our brother, shouldest thou not thrive;   see note[17]
In our chapter pray we day and night

To Christ, that he thee sende health and might,
Thy body for to wielde hastily. soon be able to move freely

"God wot," quoth he, "nothing thereof feel I;
So help me Christ, as I in fewe years
Have spended upon divers manner freres friars of various sorts
Full many a pound, yet fare I ne'er the bet; better
Certain my good have I almost beset: spent
Farewell my gold, for it is all ago." gone
The friar answer'd, "O Thomas, dost thou so?
What needest thou diverse friars to seech? seek
What needeth him that hath a perfect leech, healer
To seeken other leeches in the town?
Your inconstance is your confusioun.
Hold ye then me, or elles our convent,
To praye for you insufficient?
Thomas, that jape it is not worth a mite; jest
Your malady is for we have too lite. because we have
Ah, give that convent half a quarter oats; too little
And give that convent four and twenty groats;
And give that friar a penny, and let him go!
Nay, nay, Thomas, it may no thing be so.
What is a farthing worth parted on twelve?
Lo, each thing that is oned in himselve made one, united
Is more strong than when it is y-scatter'd.
Thomas, of me thou shalt not be y-flatter'd,
Thou wouldest have our labour all for nought.
The highe God, that all this world hath wrought,
Saith, that the workman worthy is his hire
Thomas, nought of your treasure I desire
As for myself, but that all our convent
To pray for you is aye so diligent:
And for to builde Christe's owen church.
Thomas, if ye will learne for to wirch, work
Of building up of churches may ye learn
If it be good, in Thomas' life of Ind.[18]
Ye lie here full of anger and of ire,
With which the devil sets your heart on fire,
And chide here this holy innocent
Your wife, that is so meek and patient.
And therefore trow me, Thomas, if thee lest, believe please
Ne strive not with thy wife, as for the best.
And bear this word away now, by thy faith,
Touching such thing, lo, what the wise man saith:
'Within thy house be thou no lion;
To thy subjects do none oppression;
Nor make thou thine acquaintance for to flee.'
And yet, Thomas, eftsoones charge I thee, again
Beware from ire that in thy bosom sleeps,
Ware from the serpent, that so slily creeps
Under the grass, and stingeth subtilly.
Beware, my son, and hearken patiently,
That twenty thousand men have lost their lives

For striving with their lemans and their wives. mistresses
Now since ye have so holy and meek a wife,
What needeth you, Thomas, to make strife?
There is, y-wis, no serpent so cruel, certainly
When men tread on his tail nor half so fell, fierce
As woman is, when she hath caught an ire;
Very vengeance is then all her desire. pure, only
Ire is a sin, one of the greate seven,
Abominable to the God of heaven,
And to himself it is destruction.
This every lewed vicar and parson ignorant
Can say, how ire engenders homicide;
Ire is in sooth th' executor of pride. executioner
I could of ire you say so muche sorrow,
My tale shoulde last until to-morrow,
And therefore pray I God both day and ight,
An irous man God send him little might. passionate
It is great harm, and certes great pity
To set an irous man in high degree.

"Whilom there was an irous potestate, once judge[19]
As saith Senec, that during his estate term of office
Upon a day out rode knightes two;
And, as fortune would that it were so,
The one of them came home, the other not.
Anon the knight before the judge is brought,
That saide thus; 'Thou hast thy fellow slain,
For which I doom thee to the death certain.'
And to another knight commanded he;
'Go, lead him to the death, I charge thee.'
And happened, as they went by the way
Toward the place where as he should dey, die
The knight came, which men weened had been dead thought
Then thoughte they it was the beste rede counsel
To lead them both unto the judge again.
They saide, 'Lord, the knight hath not y-slain
His fellow; here he standeth whole alive.'
'Ye shall be dead,' quoth he, 'so may I thrive,
That is to say, both one, and two, and three.'
And to the firste knight right thus spake he:
'I damned thee, thou must algate be dead: at all events
And thou also must needes lose thine head,
For thou the cause art why thy fellow dieth.'
And to the thirde knight right thus he sayeth,
'Thou hast not done that I commanded thee.'
And thus he did do slay them alle three.

Irous Cambyses was eke dronkelew, a drunkard
And aye delighted him to be a shrew. vicious, ill-tempered
And so befell, a lord of his meinie, suite
That loved virtuous morality,
Said on a day betwixt them two right thus:
'A lord is lost, if he be vicious.

[An irous man is like a frantic beast,
In which there is of wisdom none arrest;] no control
And drunkenness is eke a foul record
Of any man, and namely of a lord. especially
There is full many an eye and many an ear
Awaiting on a lord, he knows not where. watching
For Godde's love, drink more attemperly: temperately
Wine maketh man to lose wretchedly
His mind, and eke his limbes every one.'
'The reverse shalt thou see,' quoth he, 'anon,
And prove it by thine own experience,
That wine doth to folk no such offence.
There is no wine bereaveth me my might
Of hand, nor foot, nor of mine eyen sight.'
And for despite he dranke muche more
A hundred part than he had done before, times
And right anon this cursed irous wretch
This knighte's sone let before him fetch, caused
Commanding him he should before him stand:
And suddenly he took his bow in hand,
And up the string he pulled to his ear,
And with an arrow slew the child right there.
'Now whether have I a sicker hand or non?' sure not
Quoth he; 'Is all my might and mind agone?
Hath wine bereaved me mine eyen sight?'
Why should I tell the answer of the knight?
His son was slain, there is no more to say.
Beware therefore with lordes how ye play, use freedom
Sing placebo;[20] and I shall if I can,
But if it be unto a poore man: unless
To a poor man men should his vices tell,
But not t' a lord, though he should go to hell.
Lo, irous Cyrus, thilke Persian, that
How he destroy'd the river of Gisen,[21]
For that a horse of his was drowned therein,
When that he wente Babylon to win:
He made that the river was so small,
That women mighte wade it over all. everywhere
Lo, what said he, that so well teache can,
'Be thou no fellow to an irous man,
Nor with no wood man walke by the way, furious
Lest thee repent;' I will no farther say.

"Now, Thomas, leve brother, leave thine ire, dear
Thou shalt me find as just as is as squire;
Hold not the devil's knife aye at thine heart;
Thine anger doth thee all too sore smart; pain
But shew to me all thy confession."
"Nay," quoth the sicke man, "by Saint Simon
I have been shriven this day of my curate; confessed
I have him told all wholly mine estate.
Needeth no more to speak of it, saith he,
But if me list of mine humility."
"Give me then of thy good to make our cloister,"
Quoth he, "for many a mussel and many an oyster,
When other men have been full well at ease,
Hath been our food, our cloister for to rese: raise, build
And yet, God wot, unneth the foundement scarcely foundation
Performed is, nor of our pavement
Is not a tile yet within our wones: habitation
By God, we owe forty pound for stones.
Now help, Thomas, for him that harrow'd hell, Christ[22]
For elles must we oure bookes sell,
And if ye lack our predication,
Then goes this world all to destruction.
For whoso from this world would us bereave,
So God me save, Thomas, by your leave,
He would bereave out of this world the sun
For who can teach and worken as we conne? know how to do
And that is not of little time (quoth he),
But since Elijah was, and Elisee, Elisha
Have friars been, that find I of record,
In charity, y-thanked be our Lord.
Now, Thomas, help for sainte charity."
And down anon he set him on his knee,
The sick man waxed well-nigh wood for ire, mad
He woulde that the friar had been a-fire
With his false dissimulation.
"Such thing as is in my possession,"
Quoth he, "that may I give you and none other:
Ye say me thus, how that I am your brother."
"Yea, certes," quoth this friar, "yea, truste well;
I took our Dame the letter of our seal"[23]
"Now well," quoth he, "and somewhat shall I give
Unto your holy convent while I live;
And in thine hand thou shalt it have anon,
On this condition, and other none,
That thou depart it so, my deare brother, divide
That every friar have as much as other:
This shalt thou swear on thy profession,
Withoute fraud or cavillation." quibbling
"I swear it," quoth the friar, "upon my faith."
And therewithal his hand in his he lay'th;
"Lo here my faith, in me shall be no lack."
"Then put thine hand adown right by my back,"
Saide this man, "and grope well behind,
Beneath my buttock, there thou shalt find
A thing, that I have hid in privity."
"Ah," thought this friar, "that shall go with me."
And down his hand he launched to the clift, cleft
In hope for to finde there a gift.
And when this sicke man felte this frere
About his taile groping there and here,
Amid his hand he let the friar a fart;
There is no capel drawing in a cart, horse

That might have let a fart of such a soun'.
The friar up start, as doth a wood lioun: fierce
"Ah, false churl," quoth he, "for Godde's bones,
This hast thou in despite done for the nones: on purpose
Thou shalt abie this fart, if that I may." suffer for
His meinie, which that heard of this affray, servants
Came leaping in, and chased out the frere,
And forth he went with a full angry cheer countenance
And fetch'd his fellow, there as lay his store:
He looked as it were a wilde boar,
And grounde with his teeth, so was he wroth.
A sturdy pace down to the court he go'th,
Where as there wonn'd a man of great honour, dwelt
To whom that he was always confessour:
This worthy man was lord of that village.
This friar came, as he were in a rage,
Where as this lord sat eating at his board:
Unnethes might the friar speak one word, with difficulty
Till at the last he saide, "God you see." save

This lord gan look, and said, "Ben'dicite!
What? Friar John, what manner world is this?
I see well that there something is amiss;
Ye look as though the wood were full of thieves.
Sit down anon, and tell me what your grieve is, grievance, grief
And it shall be amended, if I may."
"I have," quoth he, "had a despite to-day,
God yielde you, adown in your village, reward you
That in this world is none so poor a page,
That would not have abominatioun
Of that I have received in your town:
And yet ne grieveth me nothing so sore,
As that the olde churl, with lockes hoar,
Blasphemed hath our holy convent eke."
"Now, master," quoth this lord, "I you beseek"

"No master, Sir," quoth he, "but servitour,
Though I have had in schoole that honour.[24]
God liketh not, that men us Rabbi call
Neither in market, nor in your large hall."
"No force," quoth he; "but tell me all your grief." no matter
Sir," quoth this friar, "an odious mischief
This day betid is to mine order and me, befallen
And so par consequence to each degree
Of holy churche, God amend it soon."
"Sir," quoth the lord, "ye know what is to doon: do
Distemp'r you not, ye be my confessour. be not impatient
Ye be the salt of th' earth, and the savour;
For Godde's love your patience now hold;

Tell me your grief." And he anon him told
As ye have heard before, ye know well what.
The lady of the house aye stiller sat,
Till she had hearde what the friar said,
"Hey, Godde's mother;" quoth she, "blissful maid,
Is there ought elles? tell me faithfully."
"Madame," quoth he, "how thinketh you thereby?"
"How thinketh me?" quoth she; "so God me speed,
I say, a churl hath done a churlish deed,
What should I say? God let him never the; thrive
His sicke head is full of vanity;
I hold him in a manner phrenesy." a sort of frenzy
"Madame," quoth he, "by God, I shall not lie,
But I in other wise may be awreke, revenged
I shall defame him ov'r all there I speak; wherever
This false blasphemour, that charged me
To parte that will not departed be,
To every man alike, with mischance."

The lord sat still, as he were in a trance,
And in his heart he rolled up and down,
"How had this churl imaginatioun
To shewe such a problem to the frere.
Never ere now heard I of such mattere;
I trow the Devil put it in his mind. believe
In all arsmetrik shall there no man find, arithmetic
Before this day, of such a question.
Who shoulde make a demonstration,
That every man should have alike his part
As of the sound and savour of a fart?
O nice proude churl, I shrew his face. foolish curse
Lo, Sires," quoth the lord, "with harde grace,
Who ever heard of such a thing ere now?
To every man alike? tell me how.
It is impossible, it may not be.
Hey nice churl, God let him never the. foolish thrive
The rumbling of a fart, and every soun',
Is but of air reverberatioun,
And ever wasteth lite and lite away; little
There is no man can deemen, by my fay, judge, decide
If that it were departed equally. divided
What? lo, my churl, lo yet how shrewedly impiously, wickedly
Unto my confessour to-day he spake;
I hold him certain a demoniac.
Now eat your meat, and let the churl go play,
Let him go hang himself a devil way!"

Now stood the lorde's squier at the board,
That carv'd his meat, and hearde word by word
Of all this thing, which that I have you said.
"My lord," quoth he, "be ye not evil paid, displeased
I coulde telle, for a gowne-cloth, cloth for a gown

To you, Sir Friar, so that ye be not wrot,
How that this fart should even dealed be equally
Among your convent, if it liked thee."
"Tell," quoth the lord, "and thou shalt have anon
A gowne-cloth, by God and by Saint John."
"My lord," quoth he, "when that the weather is fair,
Withoute wind, or perturbing of air,
Let bring a cart-wheel here into this hall, cause
But looke that it have its spokes all;
Twelve spokes hath a cart-wheel commonly;
And bring me then twelve friars, know ye why?
For thirteen is a convent as I guess;25
Your confessor here, for his worthiness,
Shall perform up the number of his convent. complete
Then shall they kneel adown by one assent,
And to each spoke's end, in this mannere,
Full sadly lay his nose shall a frere; carefully, steadily
Your noble confessor there, God him save,
Shall hold his nose upright under the nave.
Then shall this churl, with belly stiff and tought tight
As any tabour, hither be y-brought; drum
And set him on the wheel right of this cart
Upon the nave, and make him let a fart,
And ye shall see, on peril of my life,
By very proof that is demonstrative,
That equally the sound of it will wend, go
And eke the stink, unto the spokes' end,
Save that this worthy man, your confessour'
(Because he is a man of great honour),
Shall have the firste fruit, as reason is;
The noble usage of friars yet it is,
The worthy men of them shall first be served,
And certainly he hath it well deserved;
He hath to-day taught us so muche good
With preaching in the pulpit where he stood,
That I may vouchesafe, I say for me,
He had the firste smell of fartes three;
And so would all his brethren hardily;
He beareth him so fair and holily."

The lord, the lady, and each man, save the frere,
Saide, that Jankin spake in this mattere
As well as Euclid, or as Ptolemy.
Touching the churl, they said that subtilty
And high wit made him speaken as he spake;
He is no fool, nor no demoniac.
And Jankin hath y-won a newe gown;
My tale is done, we are almost at town.

Notes to the Sompnour's Tale

1. Trentals: The money given to the priests for performing thirty masses for the dead, either in succession or on the anniversaries of their death; also the masses themselves, which were very profitable to the clergy.
2. Possessioners: The regular religious orders, who had lands and fixed revenues; while the friars, by their vows, had to depend on voluntary contributions, though their need suggested many modes of evading the prescription.
3. In Chaucer's day the most material notions about the tortures of hell prevailed, and were made the most of by the clergy, who preyed on the affection and fear of the survivors, through the ingenious doctrine of purgatory. Old paintings and illuminations represent the dead as torn by hooks, roasted in fires, boiled in pots, and subjected to many other physical torments.
4. Qui cum patre: "Who with the father"; the closing words of the final benediction pronounced at Mass.
5. Askaunce: The word now means sideways or asquint; here it means "as if;" and its force is probably to suggest that the second friar, with an ostentatious stealthiness, noted down the names of the liberal, to make them believe that they would be remembered in the holy beggars' orisons.
6. A Godde's kichel/halfpenny: a little cake/halfpenny, given for God's sake.
7. Harlot: hired servant; from Anglo-Saxon, "hyran," to hire; the word was commonly applied to males.
8. Potent: staff; French, "potence," crutch, gibbet.
9. Je vous dis sans doute: French; "I tell you without doubt."
10. Dortour: dormitory; French, "dortoir."
12. The Rules of St Benedict granted peculiar honours and immunities to monks who had lived fifty years — the jubilee period — in the order. The usual reading of the words ending the two lines is "loan" or "lone," and "alone;" but to walk alone does not seem to have been any peculiar privilege of a friar, while the idea of precedence, or higher place at table and in processions, is suggested by the reading in the text.
13. Borel folk: laymen, people who are not learned; "borel" was a kind of coarse cloth.
14. Eli: Elijah (1 Kings, xix.)
15. An emperor Jovinian was famous in the mediaeval legends for his pride and luxury

16. Cor meum eructavit: literally, "My heart has belched forth;" in our translation, (i.e. the Authorised "King James" Version - Transcriber) "My heart is inditing a goodly matter." (Ps. xlv. 1.). "Buf" is meant to represent the sound of an eructation, and to show the "great reverence" with which "those in possession," the monks of the rich monasteries, performed divine service,
17. N'ere thou our brother, shouldest thou not thrive: if thou wert not of our brotherhood, thou shouldst have no hope of recovery.
18. Thomas' life of Ind: The life of Thomas of India - i.e. St. Thomas the Apostle, who was said to have travelled to India.
19. Potestate: chief magistrate or judge; Latin, "potestas;" Italian, "podesta." Seneca relates the story of Cornelius Piso; "De Ira," i. 16.
20. Placebo: An anthem of the Roman Church, from Psalm cxvi. 9, which in the Vulgate reads, "Placebo Domino in regione vivorum" — "I will please the Lord in the land of the living"
21. The Gysen: Seneca calls it the Gyndes; Sir John Mandeville tells the story of the Euphrates. "Gihon," was the name of one of the four rivers of Eden (Gen. ii, 13).
22. Him that harrowed Hell: Christ. See note 14 to the Reeve's Tale.
23. Mr. Wright says that "it was a common practice to grant under the conventual seal to benefactors and others a brotherly participation in the spiritual good works of the convent, and in their expected reward after death."
24. The friar had received a master's degree.
25. The regular number of monks or friars in a convent was fixed at twelve, with a superior, in imitation of the apostles and their Master; and large religious houses were held to consist of so many convents.

The Clerk's Tale.

The Prologue.

"SIR Clerk of Oxenford," our Hoste said,
"Ye ride as still and coy, as doth a maid
That were new spoused, sitting at the board:
This day I heard not of your tongue a word.
I trow ye study about some sophime: sophism
But Solomon saith, every thing hath time.
For Godde's sake, be of better cheer, livelier mien
It is no time for to study here.
Tell us some merry tale, by your fay;   faith
For what man that is entered in a play,
He needes must unto that play assent.
But preache not, as friars do in Lent,
To make us for our olde sinnes weep,
Nor that thy tale make us not to sleep.
Tell us some merry thing of aventures.
Your terms, your coloures, and your figures,
Keep them in store, till so be ye indite
High style, as when that men to kinges write.
Speake so plain at this time, I you pray,
That we may understande what ye say."

This worthy Clerk benignely answer'd;
"Hoste," quoth he, "I am under your yerd,   rod[1]
Ye have of us as now the governance,
And therefore would I do you obeisance,
As far as reason asketh, hardily: boldly, truly
I will you tell a tale, which that I
Learn'd at Padova of a worthy clerk,
As proved by his wordes and his werk.
He is now dead, and nailed in his chest,
I pray to God to give his soul good rest.
Francis Petrarc', the laureate poet,[2]
Highte this clerk, whose rhetoric so sweet was called
Illumin'd all Itale of poetry,
As Linian[3] did of philosophy,
Or law, or other art particulere:
But death, that will not suffer us dwell here
But as it were a twinkling of an eye,
Them both hath slain, and alle we shall die.

"But forth to tellen of this worthy man,
That taughte me this tale, as I began,
I say that first he with high style inditeth
(Ere he the body of his tale writeth)
A proem, in the which describeth he
Piedmont, and of Saluces[4] the country,
And speaketh of the Pennine hilles high,
That be the bounds of all West Lombardy:
And of Mount Vesulus in special,
Where as the Po out of a welle small
Taketh his firste springing and his source,
That eastward aye increaseth in his course
T'Emilia-ward,[5] to Ferraro, and Venice,
The which a long thing were to devise.   narrate
And truely, as to my judgement,
Me thinketh it a thing impertinent,   irrelevant
Save that he would conveye his mattere:
But this is the tale, which that ye shall hear."

Notes to the Prologue to the Clerk's Tale

1. Under your yerd: under your rod; as the emblem of government or direction.
2. Francesco Petrarca, born 1304, died 1374; for his Latin epic poem on the carer of Scipio, called "Africa," he was solemnly crowned with the poetic laurel in the Capitol of Rome, on Easter-day of 1341.
3. Linian: An eminent jurist and philosopher, now almost forgotten, who died four or five years after Petrarch.
4. Saluces: Saluzzo, a district of Savoy; its marquises were celebrated during the Middle Ages.
5. Emilia: The region called Aemilia, across which ran the Via Aemilia — made by M. Aemilius Lepidus, who was consul at Rome B.C. 187. It continued the Flaminian Way from Ariminum (Rimini) across the Po at Placentia (Piacenza) to Mediolanum (Milan), traversing Cisalpine Gaul.

GEOFFREY CHAUCER

THE TALE.[1]

Pars Prima. First Part

There is, right at the west side of Itale,
Down at the root of Vesulus[2] the cold,
A lusty plain, abundant of vitaille; pleasant victuals
There many a town and tow'r thou may'st behold,
That founded were in time of fathers old,
And many another delectable sight;
And Saluces this noble country hight.

A marquis whilom lord was of that land,
As were his worthy elders him before, ancestors
And obedient, aye ready to his hand,
Were all his lieges, bothe less and more:
Thus in delight he liv'd, and had done yore, long
Belov'd and drad, through favour of fortune, held in reverence
Both of his lordes and of his commune. commonalty

Therewith he was, to speak of lineage,
The gentilest y-born of Lombardy,
A fair person, and strong, and young of age,
And full of honour and of courtesy:
Discreet enough his country for to gie, guide, rule
Saving in some things that he was to blame;
And Walter was this younge lordes name.

I blame him thus, that he consider'd not
In time coming what might him betide,
But on his present lust was all his thought, pleasure
And for to hawk and hunt on every side;
Well nigh all other cares let he slide,
And eke he would (that was the worst of all)
Wedde no wife for aught that might befall.

Only that point his people bare so sore,
That flockmel on a day to him they went, in a body
And one of them, that wisest was of lore
(Or elles that the lord would best assent
That he should tell him what the people meant,
Or elles could he well shew such mattere),
He to the marquis said as ye shall hear.

"O noble Marquis! your humanity
Assureth us and gives us hardiness,
As oft as time is of necessity,
That we to you may tell our heaviness:
Accepte, Lord, now of your gentleness,
What we with piteous heart unto you plain, complain of
And let your ears my voice not disdain.

"All have I nought to do in this mattere although
More than another man hath in this place,
Yet forasmuch as ye, my Lord so dear,
Have always shewed me favour and grace,
I dare the better ask of you a space
Of audience, to shewen our request,
And ye, my Lord, to do right as you lest. as pleaseth you

"For certes, Lord, so well us like you
And all your work, and ev'r have done, that we
Ne coulde not ourselves devise how
We mighte live in more felicity:
Save one thing, Lord, if that your will it be,
That for to be a wedded man you lest;
Then were your people in sovereign hearte's rest. completely

"Bowe your neck under the blissful yoke
Of sovereignty, and not of service,
Which that men call espousal or wedlock:
And thinke, Lord, among your thoughtes wise,
How that our dayes pass in sundry wise;
For though we sleep, or wake, or roam, or ride,
Aye fleeth time, it will no man abide.

"And though your greene youthe flow'r as yet,
In creepeth age always as still as stone,
And death menaceth every age, and smit smiteth
In each estate, for there escapeth none:
And all so certain as we know each one
That we shall die, as uncertain we all
Be of that day when death shall on us fall.

"Accepte then of us the true intent, mind, desire
That never yet refused youre hest, command
And we will, Lord, if that ye will assent,
Choose you a wife, in short time at the lest, least
Born of the gentilest and of the best
Of all this land, so that it ought to seem
Honour to God and you, as we can deem.

"Deliver us out of all this busy dread, doubt
And take a wife, for highe Godde's sake:
For if it so befell, as God forbid,
That through your death your lineage should slake, become extinct
And that a strange successor shoulde take
Your heritage, oh! woe were us on live: alive
Wherefore we pray you hastily to wive."

Their meeke prayer and their piteous cheer
Made the marquis for to have pity.
"Ye will," quoth he, "mine owen people dear,
To that I ne'er ere thought constraine me. before
I me rejoiced of my liberty,
That seldom time is found in rnarriage;
Where I was free, I must be in servage! servitude

"But natheless I see your true intent,
And trust upon your wit, and have done aye:
Wherefore of my free will I will assent
To wedde me, as soon as e'er I may.
But whereas ye have proffer'd me to-day

THE CANTERBURY TALES

To choose me a wife, I you release
That choice, and pray you of that proffer cease.

"For God it wot, that children often been
Unlike their worthy elders them before,
Bounte comes all of God, not of the strene goodness
Of which they be engender'd and y-bore: stock, race
I trust in Godde's bounte, and therefore
My marriage, and mine estate and rest,
I him betake; he may do as him lest. commend to him

"Let me alone in choosing of my wife;
That charge upon my back I will endure:
But I you pray, and charge upon your life,
That what wife that I take, ye me assure
To worship her, while that her life may dure, honour
In word and work both here and elleswhere,
As she an emperore's daughter were.

"And farthermore this shall ye swear, that ye
Against my choice shall never grudge nor strive. murmur
For since I shall forego my liberty
At your request, as ever may I thrive,
Where as mine heart is set, there will I live
And but ye will assent in such mannere, unless
I pray you speak no more of this mattere."

With heartly will they sworen and assent
To all this thing, there said not one wight nay:
Beseeching him of grace, ere that they went,
That he would grante them a certain day
Of his espousal, soon as e'er he may,
For yet always the people somewhat dread were in fear or doubt
Lest that the marquis woulde no wife wed.

He granted them a day, such as him lest,
On which he would be wedded sickerly, certainly
And said he did all this at their request;
And they with humble heart full buxomly, obediently[3]
Kneeling upon their knees full reverently,
Him thanked all; and thus they have an end
Of their intent, and home again they wend.

And hereupon he to his officers
Commanded for the feaste to purvey. provide
And to his privy knightes and squiers
Such charge he gave, as him list on them lay:
And they to his commandement obey,
And each of them doth all his diligence
To do unto the feast all reverence.

Pars Secunda Second Part

Not far from thilke palace honourable, that
Where as this marquis shope his marriage, prepared; resolved on
There stood a thorp, of sighte delectable, hamlet
In which the poore folk of that village
Hadde their beastes and their harbourage, dwelling
And of their labour took their sustenance,
After the earthe gave them abundance.

Among this poore folk there dwelt a man
Which that was holden poorest of them all;
But highe God sometimes sende can
His grace unto a little ox's stall;
Janicola men of that thorp him call.
A daughter had he, fair enough to sight,
And Griseldis this younge maiden hight.

But for to speak of virtuous beauty,
Then was she one the fairest under sun:
Full poorely y-foster'd up was she;
No likerous lust was in her heart y-run; luxurious pleasure
Well ofter of the well than of the tun
She drank,[4] and, for she woulde virtue please because
She knew well labour, but no idle ease.

But though this maiden tender were of age;
Yet in the breast of her virginity
There was inclos'd a sad and ripe corage; steadfast and mature
And in great reverence and charity spirit
Her olde poore father foster'd she.
A few sheep, spinning, on the field she kept,
She woulde not be idle till she slept.

And when she homeward came, she would bring
Wortes, and other herbes, times oft, plants, cabbages
The which she shred and seeth'd for her living,
And made her bed full hard, and nothing soft:
And aye she kept her father's life on loft up, aloft
With ev'ry obeisance and diligence,
That child may do to father's reverence.

Upon Griselda, this poor creature,
Full often sithes this marquis set his eye, times
As he on hunting rode, paraventure: by chance
And when it fell that he might her espy,
He not with wanton looking of folly
His eyen cast on her, but in sad wise serious
Upon her cheer he would him oft advise; countenance consider

99

GEOFFREY CHAUCER

Commending in his heart her womanhead,
And eke her virtue, passing any wight
Of so young age, as well in cheer as deed.
For though the people have no great insight
In virtue, he considered full right
Her bounte, and disposed that he would goodness
Wed only her, if ever wed he should.

The day of wedding came, but no wight can
Telle what woman that it shoulde be;
For which marvail wonder'd many a man,
And saide, when they were in privity,
"Will not our lord yet leave his vanity?
Will he not wed? Alas, alas the while!
Why will he thus himself and us beguile?"

But natheless this marquis had done make caused to be made
Of gemmes, set in gold and in azure,
Brooches and ringes, for Griselda's sake,
And of her clothing took he the measure
Of a maiden like unto her stature,
And eke of other ornamentes all
That unto such a wedding shoulde fall. befit

The time of undern of the same day evening⁵
Approached, that this wedding shoulde be,
And all the palace put was in array,
Both hall and chamber, each in its degree,
Houses of office stuffed with plenty
There may'st thou see of dainteous vitaille, victuals, provisions
That may be found, as far as lasts Itale.

This royal marquis, richely array'd,
Lordes and ladies in his company,
The which unto the feaste were pray'd,
And of his retinue the bach'lery,
With many a sound of sundry melody,
Unto the village, of the which I told,
In this array the right way did they hold.

Griseld' of this (God wot) full innocent,
That for her shapen was all this array, prepared
To fetche water at a well is went,
And home she came as soon as e'er she may.
For well she had heard say, that on that day
The marquis shoulde wed, and, if she might,
She fain would have seen somewhat of that sight.

She thought, "I will with other maidens stand,
That be my fellows, in our door, and see
The marchioness; and therefore will I fand strive
To do at home, as soon as it may be,
The labour which belongeth unto me,
And then I may at leisure her behold,
If she this way unto the castle hold."

And as she would over the threshold gon,
The marquis came and gan for her to call,
And she set down her water-pot anon
Beside the threshold, in an ox's stall,
And down upon her knees she gan to fall,
And with sad countenance kneeled still, steady
Till she had heard what was the lorde's will.

The thoughtful marquis spake unto the maid
Full soberly, and said in this mannere:
"Where is your father, Griseldis?" he said.
And she with reverence, in humble cheer, with humble air
Answered, "Lord, he is all ready here."
And in she went withoute longer let delay
And to the marquis she her father fet. fetched

He by the hand then took the poore man,
And saide thus, when he him had aside:
"Janicola, I neither may nor can
Longer the pleasance of mine hearte hide;
If that thou vouchesafe, whatso betide,
Thy daughter will I take, ere that I wend, go
As for my wife, unto her life's end.

"Thou lovest me, that know I well certain,
And art my faithful liegeman y-bore, born
And all that liketh me, I dare well sayn
It liketh thee; and specially therefore
Tell me that point, that I have said before, —
If that thou wilt unto this purpose draw,
To take me as for thy son-in-law."

This sudden case the man astonied so, event
That red he wax'd, abash'd, and all quaking amazed
He stood; unnethes said he wordes mo', scarcely
But only thus; "Lord," quoth he, "my willing
Is as ye will, nor against your liking
I will no thing, mine owen lord so dear;
Right as you list governe this mattere."

"Then will I," quoth the marquis softely,
"That in thy chamber I, and thou, and she,
Have a collation; and know'st thou why? conference
For I will ask her, if her will it be
To be my wife, and rule her after me:
And all this shall be done in thy presence,
I will not speak out of thine audience." hearing

And in the chamber while they were about
The treaty, which ye shall hereafter hear,
The people came into the house without,
And wonder'd them in how honest mannere
And tenderly she kept her father dear;
But utterly Griseldis wonder might,
For never erst ne saw she such a sight. before

No wonder is though that she be astoned, astonished
To see so great a guest come in that place,
She never was to no such guestes woned; accustomed, wont
For which she looked with full pale face.
But shortly forth this matter for to chase, push on,

100

THE CANTERBURY TALES

pursue
These are the wordes that the marquis said
To this benigne, very, faithful maid. true[6]

"Griseld'," he said, "ye shall well understand,
It liketh to your father and to me
That I you wed, and eke it may so stand,
As I suppose ye will that it so be:
But these demandes ask I first," quoth he,
"Since that it shall be done in hasty wise;
Will ye assent, or elles you advise? consider

"I say this, be ye ready with good heart
To all my lust, and that I freely may, pleasure
As me best thinketh, do you laugh or smart, cause you to
And never ye to grudge, night nor day, murmur
And eke when I say Yea, ye say not Nay,
Neither by word, nor frowning countenance?
Swear this, and here I swear our alliance."

Wond'ring upon this word, quaking for dread,
She saide; "Lord, indigne and unworthy
Am I to this honour that ye me bede, offer
But as ye will yourself, right so will I:
And here I swear, that never willingly
In word or thought I will you disobey,
For to be dead; though me were loth to dey." die

"This is enough, Griselda mine," quoth he.
And forth he went with a full sober cheer,
Out at the door, and after then came she,
And to the people he said in this mannere:
"This is my wife," quoth he, "that standeth here.
Honoure her, and love her, I you pray,
Whoso me loves; there is no more to say."

And, for that nothing of her olde gear
She shoulde bring into his house, he bade
That women should despoile her right there; strip
Of which these ladies were nothing glad
To handle her clothes wherein she was clad:
But natheless this maiden bright of hue
From foot to head they clothed have all new.

Her haires have they comb'd that lay untress'd loose
Full rudely, and with their fingers small
A crown upon her head they have dress'd,
And set her full of nouches[7] great and small:
Of her array why should I make a tale?
Unneth the people her knew for her fairness, scarcely
When she transmuted was in such richess.

The marquis hath her spoused with a ring
Brought for the same cause, and then her set
Upon a horse snow-white, and well ambling,
And to his palace, ere he longer let delayed
With joyful people, that her led and met,
Conveyed her; and thus the day they spend
In revel, till the sunne gan descend.

And, shortly forth this tale for to chase,
I say, that to this newe marchioness
God hath such favour sent her of his grace,
That it ne seemed not by likeliness
That she was born and fed in rudeness, —
As in a cot, or in an ox's stall, —
But nourish'd in an emperore's hall.

To every wight she waxen is so dear grown
And worshipful, that folk where she was born,
That from her birthe knew her year by year,
Unnethes trowed they, but durst have sworn, scarcely believed
That to Janicol' of whom I spake before,
She was not daughter, for by conjecture
Them thought she was another creature.

For though that ever virtuous was she,
She was increased in such excellence
Of thewes good, y-set in high bounte, qualities
And so discreet, and fair of eloquence,
So benign, and so digne of reverence, worthy
And coulde so the people's heart embrace,
That each her lov'd that looked on her face.

Not only of Saluces in the town
Published was the bounte of her name,
But eke besides in many a regioun;
If one said well, another said the same:
So spread of here high bounte the fame,
That men and women, young as well as old,
Went to Saluces, her for to behold.

Thus Walter lowly, — nay, but royally,-
Wedded with fortn'ate honestete, virtue
In Godde's peace lived full easily
At home, and outward grace enough had he:
And, for he saw that under low degree
Was honest virtue hid, the people him held
A prudent man, and that is seen full seld'. seldom

Not only this Griseldis through her wit
Couth all the feat of wifely homeliness, knew all the duties
But eke, when that the case required it,
The common profit coulde she redress:
There n'as discord, rancour, nor heaviness
In all the land, that she could not appease,
And wisely bring them all in rest and ease

Though that her husband absent were or non, not
If gentlemen or other of that country,
Were wroth, she woulde bringe them at one, at feud
So wise and ripe wordes hadde she,
And judgement of so great equity,
That she from heaven sent was, as men wend, weened, imagined
People to save, and every wrong t'amend

Not longe time after that this Griseld'
Was wedded, she a daughter had y-bore;

GEOFFREY CHAUCER

All she had lever borne a knave child, rather boy
Glad was the marquis and his folk therefore;
For, though a maiden child came all before,
She may unto a knave child attain
By likelihood, since she is not barren.

   Pars Tertia. Third Part

There fell, as falleth many times mo',
When that his child had sucked but a throw,   little while
This marquis in his hearte longed so
To tempt his wife, her sadness for to know,   steadfastness
That he might not out of his hearte throw
This marvellous desire his wife t'asssay;   try
Needless, God wot, he thought her to affray.   without cause alarm, disturb
He had assayed her anough before,
And found her ever good; what needed it
Her for to tempt, and always more and more?
Though some men praise it for a subtle wit,
But as for me, I say that evil it sit   it ill became him
T'assay a wife when that it is no need,
And putte her in anguish and in dread.

For which this marquis wrought in this mannere:
He came at night alone there as she lay,
With sterne face and with full troubled cheer,
And saide thus; "Griseld'," quoth he "that day
That I you took out of your poor array,
And put you in estate of high nobless,
Ye have it not forgotten, as I guess.

"I say, Griseld', this present dignity,
In which that I have put you, as I trow   believe
Maketh you not forgetful for to be
That I you took in poor estate full low,
For any weal you must yourselfe know.
Take heed of every word that I you say,
There is no wight that hears it but we tway.   two

"Ye know yourself well how that ye came here
Into this house, it is not long ago;
And though to me ye be right lefe and dear,   loved
Unto my gentles ye be nothing so: nobles, gentlefolk
They say, to them it is great shame and woe
For to be subject, and be in servage,
To thee, that born art of small lineage.

"And namely since thy daughter was y-bore   especially
These wordes have they spoken doubteless;
But I desire, as I have done before,
To live my life with them in rest and peace:
I may not in this case be reckeless;
I must do with thy daughter for the best,
Not as I would, but as my gentles lest.   please

"And yet, God wot, this is full loth to me: odious
But natheless withoute your weeting   knowing
I will nought do; but this will I," quoth he,
"That ye to me assenten in this thing.
Shew now your patience in your working,
That ye me hight and swore in your village   promised
The day that maked was our marriage."

When she had heard all this, she not amev'd   changed
Neither in word, in cheer, nor countenance
(For, as it seemed, she was not aggriev'd);
She saide; "Lord, all lies in your pleasance,
My child and I, with hearty obeisance
Be youres all, and ye may save or spill   destroy
Your owen thing: work then after your will.

"There may no thing, so God my soule save,
Like to you, that may displease me: be pleasing
Nor I desire nothing for to have,
Nor dreade for to lose, save only ye:
This will is in mine heart, and aye shall be,
No length of time, nor death, may this deface,
Nor change my corage to another place."   spirit, heart

Glad was the marquis for her answering,
But yet he feigned as he were not so;
All dreary was his cheer and his looking
When that he should out of the chamber go.
Soon after this, a furlong way or two,[8]
He privily hath told all his intent
Unto a man, and to his wife him sent.

A manner sergeant was this private man,   kind of squire
The which he faithful often founden had   discreet
In thinges great, and eke such folk well can
Do execution in thinges bad:
The lord knew well, that he him loved and drad.   dreaded
And when this sergeant knew his lorde's will,
Into the chamber stalked he full still.

"Madam," he said, "ye must forgive it me,
Though I do thing to which I am constrain'd;
Ye be so wise, that right well knowe ye
That lordes' hestes may not be y-feign'd;   see note[9]
They may well be bewailed and complain'd,
But men must needs unto their lust obey;   pleasure
And so will I, there is no more to say.

"This child I am commanded for to take."
And spake no more, but out the child he hent   seized
Dispiteously, and gan a cheer to make   unpityingly show, aspect
As though he would have slain it ere he went.
Griseldis must all suffer and consent:

And as a lamb she sat there meek and still,
And let this cruel sergeant do his will

Suspicious was the diffame of this man, ominous evil reputation
Suspect his face, suspect his word also,
Suspect the time in which he this began:
Alas! her daughter, that she loved so,
She weened he would have it slain right tho, thought then
But natheless she neither wept nor siked, sighed
Conforming her to what the marquis liked.

But at the last to speake she began,
And meekly she unto the sergeant pray'd,
So as he was a worthy gentle man,
That she might kiss her child, ere that it died:
And in her barme this little child she laid, lap, bosom
With full sad face, and gan the child to bless, cross
And lulled it, and after gan it kiss.

And thus she said in her benigne voice:
Farewell, my child, I shall thee never see;
But since I have thee marked with the cross,
Of that father y-blessed may'st thou be
That for us died upon a cross of tree:
Thy soul, my little child, I him betake, commit unto him
For this night shalt thou dien for my sake.

I trow that to a norice in this case believe nurse
It had been hard this ruthe for to see: pitiful sight
Well might a mother then have cried, "Alas!"
But natheless so sad steadfast was she,
That she endured all adversity,
And to the sergeant meekely she said,
"Have here again your little younge maid.

"Go now," quoth she, "and do my lord's behest.
And one thing would I pray you of your grace,
But if my lord forbade you at the least, unless
Bury this little body in some place,
That neither beasts nor birdes it arace." tear[10]
But he no word would to that purpose say,
But took the child and went upon his way.

The sergeant came unto his lord again,
And of Griselda's words and of her cheer demeanour
He told him point for point, in short and plain,
And him presented with his daughter dear.
Somewhat this lord had ruth in his mannere,
But natheless his purpose held he still,
As lordes do, when they will have their will;

And bade this sergeant that he privily
Shoulde the child full softly wind and wrap,
With alle circumstances tenderly,
And carry it in a coffer, or in lap;
But, upon pain his head off for to swap, strike

That no man shoulde know of his intent,
Nor whence he came, nor whither that he went;

But at Bologna, to his sister dear,
That at that time of Panic' was Countess, Panico
He should it take, and shew her this mattere,
Beseeching her to do her business
This child to foster in all gentleness,
And whose child it was he bade her hide
From every wight, for aught that might betide.

The sergeant went, and hath fulfill'd this thing.
But to the marquis now returne we;
For now went he full fast imagining
If by his wife's cheer he mighte see,
Or by her wordes apperceive, that she
Were changed; but he never could her find,
But ever-in-one alike sad and kind. constantly steadfast

As glad, as humble, as busy in service,
And eke in love, as she was wont to be,
Was she to him, in every manner wise; sort of way
And of her daughter not a word spake she;
No accident for no adversity no change of humour resulting
Was seen in her, nor e'er her daughter's name from her affliction
She named, or in earnest or in game.

Pars Quarta Fourth Part

In this estate there passed be four year
Ere she with childe was; but, as God wo'ld,
A knave child she bare by this Waltere, boy
Full gracious and fair for to behold;
And when that folk it to his father told,
Not only he, but all his country, merry
Were for this child, and God they thank and hery. praise

When it was two year old, and from the breast
Departed of the norice, on a day taken, weaned
This marquis caughte yet another lest was seized by yet
To tempt his wife yet farther, if he may. another desire
Oh! needless was she tempted in as say; trial
But wedded men not connen no measure, know no moderation
When that they find a patient creature.

"Wife," quoth the marquis, "ye have heard ere this
My people sickly bear our marriage; regard with displeasure
And namely since my son y-boren is, especially
Now is it worse than ever in all our age:
The murmur slays mine heart and my corage,
For to mine ears cometh the voice so smart,

painfully
That it well nigh destroyed hath mine heart.

"Now say they thus, 'When Walter is y-gone,
Then shall the blood of Janicol' succeed,
And be our lord, for other have we none:'
Such wordes say my people, out of drede. doubt
Well ought I of such murmur take heed,
For certainly I dread all such sentence, expression of opinion
Though they not plainen in mine audience. complain in my hearing

"I woulde live in peace, if that I might;
Wherefore I am disposed utterly,
As I his sister served ere by night, before
Right so think I to serve him privily.
This warn I you, that ye not suddenly
Out of yourself for no woe should outraie; become outrageous, rave
Be patient, and thereof I you pray."

"I have," quoth she, "said thus, and ever shall,
I will no thing, nor n'ill no thing, certain,
But as you list; not grieveth me at all
Though that my daughter and my son be slain
At your commandement; that is to sayn,
I have not had no part of children twain,
But first sickness, and after woe and pain.

"Ye be my lord, do with your owen thing
Right as you list, and ask no rede of me:
For, as I left at home all my clothing
When I came first to you, right so," quoth she,
"Left I my will and all my liberty,
And took your clothing: wherefore I you pray,
Do your pleasance, I will your lust obey. will

"And, certes, if I hadde prescience
Your will to know, ere ye your lust me told, will
I would it do withoute negligence:
But, now I know your lust, and what ye wo'ld,
All your pleasance firm and stable I hold;
For, wist I that my death might do you ease,
Right gladly would I dien you to please.

"Death may not make no comparisoun
Unto your love." And when this marquis say saw
The constance of his wife, he cast adown
His eyen two, and wonder'd how she may
In patience suffer all this array;
And forth he went with dreary countenance;
But to his heart it was full great pleasance.

This ugly sergeant, in the same wise
That he her daughter caught, right so hath he
(Or worse, if men can any worse devise,)
Y-hent her son, that full was of beauty: seized
And ever-in-one so patient was she, unvaryingly
That she no cheere made of heaviness,
But kiss'd her son, and after gan him bless.

Save this she prayed him, if that he might,
Her little son he would in earthe grave, bury
His tender limbes, delicate to sight,
From fowles and from beastes for to save.
But she none answer of him mighte have;
He went his way, as him nothing ne raught, cared
But to Bologna tenderly it brought.

The marquis wonder'd ever longer more
Upon her patience; and, if that he
Not hadde soothly knowen therebefore
That perfectly her children loved she,
He would have ween'd that of some subtilty, thought
And of malice, or for cruel corage, disposition
She hadde suffer'd this with sad visage. steadfast, unmoved

But well he knew, that, next himself, certain
She lov'd her children best in every wise.
But now of women would I aske fain,
If these assayes mighte not suffice?
What could a sturdy husband more devise stern
To prove her wifehood and her steadfastness,
And he continuing ev'r in sturdiness?

But there be folk of such condition,
That, when they have a certain purpose take,
Thiey cannot stint of their intention, cease
But, right as they were bound unto a stake,
They will not of their firste purpose slake: slacken, abate
Right so this marquis fully hath purpos'd
To tempt his wife, as he was first dispos'd.

He waited, if by word or countenance
That she to him was changed of corage: spirit
But never could he finde variance,
She was aye one in heart and in visage,
And aye the farther that she was in age,
The more true (if that it were possible)
She was to him in love, and more penible. painstaking in devotion

For which it seemed thus, that of them two
There was but one will; for, as Walter lest, pleased
The same pleasance was her lust also; pleasure
And, God be thanked, all fell for the best.
She shewed well, for no worldly unrest,
A wife as of herself no thinge should
Will, in effect, but as her husbaud would.

The sland'r of Walter wondrous wide sprad,
That of a cruel heart he wickedly,
For he a poore woman wedded had, because
Had murder'd both his children privily:
Such murmur was among them commonly.
No wonder is: for to the people's ear
There came no word, but that they murder'd were.

For which, whereas his people therebefore
Had lov'd him well, the sland'r of his diffame infamy
Made them that they him hated therefore.
To be a murd'rer is a hateful name.
But natheless, for earnest or for game,
He of his cruel purpose would not stent;
To tempt his wife was set all his intent.

When that his daughter twelve year was of age,
He to the Court of Rome, in subtle wise
Informed of his will, sent his message, messenger
Commanding him such bulles to devise
As to his cruel purpose may suffice,
How that the Pope, for his people's rest,
Bade him to wed another, if him lest. wished

I say he bade they shoulde counterfeit
The Pope's bulles, making mention
That he had leave his firste wife to lete, leave
To stinte rancour and dissension put an end to
Betwixt his people and him: thus spake the bull,
The which they have published at full.

The rude people, as no wonder is,
Weened full well that it had been right so: thought, believed
But, when these tidings came to Griseldis.
I deeme that her heart was full of woe;
But she, alike sad for evermo', steadfast
Disposed was, this humble creature,
Th' adversity of fortune all t' endure;

Abiding ever his lust and his pleasance,
To whom that she was given, heart and all,
As to her very worldly suffisance. to the utmost extent
But, shortly if this story tell I shall, of her power
The marquis written hath in special
A letter, in which he shewed his intent,
And secretly it to Bologna sent.

To th' earl of Panico, which hadde tho there
Wedded his sister, pray'd he specially
To bringe home again his children two
In honourable estate all openly:
But one thing he him prayed utterly,
That he to no wight, though men would inquere,
Shoulde not tell whose children that they were,

But say, the maiden should y-wedded be
Unto the marquis of Saluce anon.
And as this earl was prayed, so did he,
For, at day set, he on his way is gone
Toward Saluce, and lorde's many a one
In rich array, this maiden for to guide, —
Her younge brother riding her beside.

Arrayed was toward her marriage as if for
This freshe maiden, full of gemmes clear;
Her brother, which that seven year was of age,
Arrayed eke full fresh in his mannere:

And thus, in great nobless, and with glad cheer,
Toward Saluces shaping their journey,
From day to day they rode upon their way.

Pars Quinta. Fifth Part

Among all this, after his wick' usage, while all this was
The marquis, yet his wife to tempte more going on
To the uttermost proof of her corage,
Fully to have experience and lore knowledge
If that she were as steadfast as before,
He on a day, in open audience,
Full boisterously said her this sentence:

"Certes, Griseld', I had enough pleasance
To have you to my wife, for your goodness,
And for your truth, and for your obeisance,
Not for your lineage, nor for your richess;
But now know I, in very soothfastness,
That in great lordship, if I well advise,
There is great servitude in sundry wise.

"I may not do as every ploughman may:
My people me constraineth for to take
Another wife, and cryeth day by day;
And eke the Pope, rancour for to slake,
Consenteth it, that dare I undertake:
And truely, thus much I will you say,
My newe wife is coming by the way.

"Be strong of heart, and void anon her place; immediately vacate
And thilke dower that ye brought to me, that
Take it again, I grant it of my grace.
Returne to your father's house," quoth he;
"No man may always have prosperity;
With even heart I rede you to endure counsel
The stroke of fortune or of aventure."

And she again answer'd in patience:
"My Lord," quoth she, "I know, and knew alway,
How that betwixte your magnificence
And my povert' no wight nor can nor may
Make comparison, it is no nay; cannot be denied
I held me never digne in no mannere worthy
To be your wife, nor yet your chamberere. chamber-maid

"And in this house, where ye me lady made,
(The highe God take I for my witness,
And all so wisly he my soule glade), surely gladdened
I never held me lady nor mistress,
But humble servant to your worthiness,
And ever shall, while that my life may dure,
Aboven every worldly creature.

"That ye so long, of your benignity,
Have holden me in honour and nobley, nobility
Where as I was not worthy for to be,

That thank I God and you, to whom I pray
Foryield it you; there is no more to say: reward
Unto my father gladly will I wend, go
And with him dwell, unto my lifes end,

"Where I was foster'd as a child full small,
Till I be dead my life there will I lead,
A widow clean in body, heart, and all.
For since I gave to you my maidenhead,
And am your true wife, it is no dread, doubt
God shielde such a lordes wife to take forbid
Another man to husband or to make. mate

"And of your newe wife, God of his grace
So grant you weal and all prosperity:
For I will gladly yield to her my place,
In which that I was blissful wont to be.
For since it liketh you, my Lord," quoth she,
"That whilom weren all mine hearte's rest,
That I shall go, I will go when you lest.

"But whereas ye me proffer such dowaire
As I first brought, it is well in my mind,
It was my wretched clothes, nothing fair,
The which to me were hard now for to find.
O goode God! how gentle and how kind
Ye seemed by your speech and your visage,
The day that maked was our marriage!

"But sooth is said, — algate I find it true, at all events
For in effect it proved is on me, —
Love is not old as when that it is new.
But certes, Lord, for no adversity,
To dien in this case, it shall not be
That e'er in word or work I shall repent
That I you gave mine heart in whole intent.

"My Lord, ye know that in my father's place
Ye did me strip out of my poore weed, raiment
And richely ye clad me of your grace;
To you brought I nought elles, out of dread,
But faith, and nakedness, and maidenhead;
And here again your clothing I restore,
And eke your wedding ring for evermore.

"The remnant of your jewels ready be
Within your chamber, I dare safely sayn:
Naked out of my father's house," quoth she,
"I came, and naked I must turn again.
All your pleasance would I follow fain: cheerfully
But yet I hope it be not your intent
That smockless I out of your palace went. naked

"Ye could not do so dishonest a thing, dishonourable
That thilke womb, in which your children lay, that
Shoulde before the people, in my walking,
Be seen all bare: and therefore I you pray,
Let me not like a worm go by the way:
Remember you, mine owen Lord so dear,
I was your wife, though I unworthy were.

"Wherefore, in guerdon of my maidenhead, reward
Which that I brought and not again I bear,
As vouchesafe to give me to my meed reward
But such a smock as I was wont to wear,
That I therewith may wrie the womb of her cover
That was your wife: and here I take my leave
Of you, mine owen Lord, lest I you grieve."

"The smock," quoth he, "that thou hast on thy back,
Let it be still, and bear it forth with thee."
But well unnethes thilke word he spake, with difficulty
But went his way for ruth and for pity.
Before the folk herselfe stripped she,
And in her smock, with foot and head all bare,
Toward her father's house forth is she fare. gone

The folk her follow'd weeping on her way,
And fortune aye they cursed as they gon: go
But she from weeping kept her eyen drey, dry
Nor in this time worde spake she none.
Her father, that this tiding heard anon,
Cursed the day and time, that nature
Shope him to be a living creature. formed, ordained

For, out of doubt, this olde poore man
Was ever in suspect of her marriage:
For ever deem'd he, since it first began,
That when the lord fulfill'd had his corage, had gratified his whim
He woulde think it were a disparage disparagement
To his estate, so low for to alight,
And voide her as soon as e'er he might. dismiss

Against his daughter hastily went he to meet
(For he by noise of folk knew her coming),
And with her olde coat, as it might be,
He cover'd her, full sorrowfully weeping:
But on her body might he it not bring,
For rude was the cloth, and more of age
By dayes fele than at her marriage. many[11]

Thus with her father for a certain space
Dwelled this flow'r of wifely patience,
That neither by her words nor by her face,
Before the folk nor eke in their absence,
Ne shewed she that her was done offence,
Nor of her high estate no remembrance
Ne hadde she, as by her countenance. to judge from

No wonder is, for in her great estate
Her ghost was ever in plein humility; spirit full
No tender mouth, no hearte delicate,

THE CANTERBURY TALES

No pomp, and no semblant of royalty;
But full of patient benignity,
Discreet and prideless, aye honourable,
And to her husband ever meek and stable.

Men speak of Job, and most for his humbless,
As clerkes, when them list, can well indite,
Namely of men; but, as in soothfastness, *particularly*
Though clerkes praise women but a lite, *little*
There can no man in humbless him acquite
As women can, nor can be half so true
As women be, but it be fall of new. *unless it has lately come to pass*

Pars Sexta *Sixth Part*

From Bologn' is the earl of Panic' come,
Of which the fame up sprang to more and less;
And to the people's eares all and some
Was know'n eke, that a newe marchioness
He with him brought, in such pomp and richess
That never was there seen with manne's eye
So noble array in all West Lombardy.

The marquis, which that shope and knew all this, *arranged*
Ere that the earl was come, sent his message *messenger*
For thilke poore sely Griseldis; *innocent*
And she, with humble heart and glad visage,
Nor with no swelling thought in her corage, *mind*
Came at his hest, and on her knees her set, *command*
And rev'rently and wisely she him gret. *greeted*

"Griseld'," quoth he, "my will is utterly,
This maiden, that shall wedded be to me,
Received be to-morrow as royally
As it possible is in my house to be;
And eke that every wight in his degree
Have his estate in sitting and service, what befits his
And in high pleasance, as I can devise. *condition*

"I have no women sufficient, certain,
The chambers to array in ordinance
After my lust; and therefore would I fain *pleasure*
That thine were all such manner governance:
Thou knowest eke of old all my pleasance;
Though thine array be bad, and ill besey, *poor to look on*
Do thou thy devoir at the leaste way." *do your duty in the quickest manner*
"Not only, Lord, that I am glad," quoth she,
"To do your lust, but I desire also
You for to serve and please in my degree,
Withoute fainting, and shall evermo':
Nor ever for no weal, nor for no woe,
Ne shall the ghost within mine hearte stent *spirit cease*
To love you best with all my true intent."

And with that word she gan the house to dight, *arrange*
And tables for to set, and beds to make,
And pained her to do all that she might, *she took pains*
Praying the chambereres for Godde's sake *chamber-maids*
To hasten them, and faste sweep and shake,
And she the most serviceable of all
Hath ev'ry chamber arrayed, and his hall.

Aboute undern gan the earl alight, *afternoon*[5]
That with him brought these noble children tway;
For which the people ran to see the sight
Of their array, so richely besey; *rich to behold*
And then at erst amonges them they say, *for the first time*
That Walter was no fool, though that him lest pleased
To change his wife; for it was for the best.

For she is fairer, as they deemen all, *think*
Than is Griseld', and more tender of age,
And fairer fruit between them shoulde fall,
And more pleasant, for her high lineage:
Her brother eke so fair was of visage,
That them to see the people hath caught pleasance,
Commending now the marquis' governance.

"O stormy people, unsad and ev'r untrue, *variable*
And undiscreet, and changing as a vane,
Delighting ev'r in rumour that is new,
For like the moon so waxe ye and wane:
Aye full of clapping, dear enough a jane, *worth nothing*[12]
Your doom is false, your constance evil preveth, *judgment proveth*
A full great fool is he that you believeth."

Thus saide the sad folk in that city, *sedate*
When that the people gazed up and down;
For they were glad, right for the novelty,
To have a newe lady of their town.
No more of this now make I mentioun,
But to Griseld' again I will me dress,
And tell her constancy and business.

Full busy was Griseld' in ev'ry thing
That to the feaste was appertinent;
Right nought was she abash'd of her clothing, *ashamed*
Though it were rude, and somedeal eke to-rent; *tattered*
But with glad cheer unto the gate she went *expression*

107

With other folk, to greet the marchioness,
And after that did forth her business.

With so glad cheer his guestes she receiv'd *expression*
And so conningly each in his degree, *cleverly, skilfully*
That no defaulte no man apperceiv'd,
But aye they wonder'd what she mighte be
That in so poor array was for to see,
And coude such honour and reverence; *knew, understood*
And worthily they praise her prudence.

In all this meane while she not stent *ceased*
This maid, and eke her brother, to commend
With all her heart in full benign intent,
So well, that no man could her praise amend:
But at the last, when that these lordes wend go
To sitte down to meat, he gan to call
Griseld', as she was busy in the hall.

"Griseld'," quoth he, as it were in his play,
"How liketh thee my wife, and her beauty?"
"Right well, my Lord," quoth she, "for, in good fay, *faith*
A fairer saw I never none than she:
I pray to God give you prosperity;
And so I hope, that he will to you send
Pleasance enough unto your lives end.

"One thing beseech I you, and warn also,
That ye not pricke with no tormenting
This tender maiden, as ye have done mo: *me*[13]
For she is foster'd in her nourishing
More tenderly, and, to my supposing,
She mighte not adversity endure
As could a poore foster'd creature."

And when this Walter saw her patience,
Her gladde cheer, and no malice at all,
And he so often had her done offence, *although*
And she aye sad and constant as a wall, *steadfast*
Continuing ev'r her innocence o'er all,
The sturdy marquis gan his hearte dress *prepare*
To rue upon her wifely steadfastness.

"This is enough, Griselda mine," quoth he,
"Be now no more aghast, nor evil paid, *afraid, nor displeased*
I have thy faith and thy benignity
As well as ever woman was, assay'd,
In great estate and poorely array'd:
Now know I, deare wife, thy steadfastness;"
And her in arms he took, and gan to kiss.

And she for wonder took of it no keep; *notice*
She hearde not what thing he to her said:
She far'd as she had start out of a sleep,
Till she out of her mazedness abraid. *awoke*
"Griseld'," quoth he, "by God that for us died,

Thou art my wife, none other I have,
Nor ever had, as God my soule save.

"This is thy daughter, which thou hast suppos'd
To be my wife; that other faithfully
Shall be mine heir, as I have aye dispos'd;
Thou bare them of thy body truely:
At Bologna kept I them privily:
Take them again, for now may'st thou not say
That thou hast lorn none of thy children tway. *lost*

"And folk, that otherwise have said of me,
I warn them well, that I have done this deed
For no malice, nor for no cruelty,
But to assay in thee thy womanhead:
And not to slay my children (God forbid),
But for to keep them privily and still,
Till I thy purpose knew, and all thy will."

When she this heard, in swoon adown she falleth
For piteous joy; and after her swooning,
She both her younge children to her calleth,
And in her armes piteously weeping
Embraced them, and tenderly kissing,
Full like a mother, with her salte tears
She bathed both their visage and their hairs.

O, what a piteous thing it was to see
Her swooning, and her humble voice to hear!
"Grand mercy, Lord, God thank it you," quoth she,
That ye have saved me my children dear;
Now reck I never to be dead right here; *care*
Since I stand in your love, and in your grace,
No force of death, nor when my spirit pace. *no matter for pass*

"O tender, O dear, O young children mine,
Your woeful mother weened steadfastly *believed firmly*
That cruel houndes, or some foul vermine,
Had eaten you; but God of his mercy,
And your benigne father tenderly
Have done you keep:" and in that same stound *caused you to be preserved hour fell*
All suddenly she swapt down to the ground.
And in her swoon so sadly holdeth she *firmly*
Her children two, when she gan them embrace,
That with great sleight and great *difficulty art*
The children from her arm they can arace, *pull away*
O! many a tear on many a piteous face
Down ran of them that stoode her beside,
Unneth' aboute her might they abide. *scarcely*

Walter her gladdeth, and her sorrow slaketh: *assuages*
She riseth up abashed from her trance, *astonished*
And every wight her joy and feaste maketh,

Till she hath caught again her countenance.
Walter her doth so faithfully pleasance,
That it was dainty for to see the cheer
Betwixt them two, since they be met in fere. together

The ladies, when that they their time sey, saw
Have taken her, and into chamber gone,
And stripped her out of her rude array,
And in a cloth of gold that brightly shone,
And with a crown of many a riche stone
Upon her head, they into hall her brought:
And there she was honoured as her ought.

Thus had this piteous day a blissful end;
For every man and woman did his might
This day in mirth and revel to dispend,
Till on the welkin shone the starres bright: firmament
For more solemn in every mannes sight
This feaste was, and greater of costage, expense
Than was the revel of her marriage.

Full many a year in high prosperity
Lived these two in concord and in rest;
And richely his daughter married he
Unto a lord, one of the worthiest
Of all Itale; and then in peace and rest
His wife's father in his court he kept,
Till that the soul out of his body crept.

His son succeeded in his heritage,
In rest and peace, after his father's day:
And fortunate was eke in marriage,
All he put not his wife in great assay: although
This world is not so strong, it is no nay, not to be denied
As it hath been in olde times yore;
And hearken what this author saith, therefore;

This story is said,[14] not for that wives should
Follow Griselda in humility,
For it were importable though they would; not to be borne
But for that every wight in his degree
Shoulde be constant in adversity,
As was Griselda; therefore Petrarch writeth
This story, which with high style he inditeth.

For, since a woman was so patient
Unto a mortal man, well more we ought
Receiven all in gree that God us sent. good-will
For great skill is he proved that he wrought: see note[15]
But he tempteth no man that he hath bought,
As saith Saint James, if ye his 'pistle read;
He proveth folk all day, it is no dread. doubt

And suffereth us, for our exercise,
With sharpe scourges of adversity
Full often to be beat in sundry wise;
Not for to know our will, for certes he,

Ere we were born, knew all our frailty;
And for our best is all his governance;
Let us then live in virtuous sufferance.

But one word, lordings, hearken, ere I go:
It were full hard to finde now-a-days
In all a town Griseldas three or two:
For, if that they were put to such assays,
The gold of them hath now so bad allays alloys
With brass, that though the coin be fair at eye, to see
It woulde rather break in two than ply. bend

For which here, for the Wife's love of Bath, —
Whose life and all her sex may God maintain
In high mast'ry, and elles were it scath, — damage, pity
I will, with lusty hearte fresh and green,
Say you a song to gladden you, I ween:
And let us stint of earnestful mattere.
Hearken my song, that saith in this mannere.

    L'Envoy of Chaucer.

"Griseld' is dead, and eke her patience,
And both at once are buried in Itale:
For which I cry in open audience,
No wedded man so hardy be t' assail
His wife's patience, in trust to find
Griselda's, for in certain he shall fail.

"O noble wives, full of high prudence,
Let no humility your tongues nail;
Nor let no clerk have cause or diligence
To write of you a story of such marvail,
As of Griselda patient and kind,
Lest Chichevache[16] you swallow in her entrail.

"Follow Echo, that holdeth no silence,
But ever answereth at the countertail; counter-tally[17]
Be not bedaffed for your innocence, befooled
But sharply take on you the governail; helm
Imprinte well this lesson in your mind,
For common profit, since it may avail.

"Ye archiwives, stand aye at defence, wives of rank
Since ye be strong as is a great camail, camel
Nor suffer not that men do you offence.
And slender wives, feeble in battail,
Be eager as a tiger yond in Ind;
Aye clapping as a mill, I you counsail.

"Nor dread them not, nor do them reverence;
For though thine husband armed be in mail,
The arrows of thy crabbed eloquence
Shall pierce his breast, and eke his aventail;[18]
In jealousy I rede eke thou him bind, advise
And thou shalt make him couch as doth a quail. submit, shrink

"If thou be fair, where folk be in presence
Shew thou thy visage and thine apparail:
If thou be foul, be free of thy dispence;
To get thee friendes aye do thy travail:
Be aye of cheer as light as leaf on lind, linden, lime-tree
And let him care, and weep, and wring, and wail."

Notes to the Clerk's Tale

1. Petrarch, in his Latin romance, "De obedientia et fide uxoria Mythologia," (Of obedient and faithful wives in Mythology) translated the charming story of "the patient Grizel" from the Italian of Bocaccio's "Decameron;" and Chaucer has closely followed Petrarch's translation, made in 1373, the year before that in which he died. The fact that the embassy to Genoa, on which Chaucer was sent, took place in 1372-73, has lent countenance to the opinion that the English poet did actually visit the Italian bard at Padua, and hear the story from his own lips. This, however, is only a probability; for it is a moot point whether the two poets ever met.
2. Vesulus: Monte Viso, a lofty peak at the junction of the Maritime and Cottian Alps; from two springs on its east side rises the Po.
3. Buxomly: obediently; Anglo-Saxon, "bogsom," old English, "boughsome," that can be easily bent or bowed; German, "biegsam," pliant, obedient.
4. Well ofter of the well than of the tun she drank: she drank water much more often than wine.
5. Undern: afternoon, evening, though by some "undern" is understood as dinner-time — 9 a. m. See note 4 to the Wife of Bath's Tale.
6. Very: true; French "vrai".
7. Nouches: Ornaments of some kind not precisely known; some editions read "ouches," studs, brooches. (Transcriber's note: The OED gives "nouches" as a form of "ouches," buckles)
8. A furlong way or two: a short time; literally, as long as it takes to walk one or two furlongs (a furlong is 220 yards)
9. Lordes' hestes may not be y-feign'd: it will not do merely to feign compliance with a lord's commands.
10. Arace: tear; French, "arracher."
11. Fele: many; German, "viel."
12. Dear enough a jane: worth nothing. A jane was a small coin of little worth, so the meaning is "not worth a red cent".
13. Mo: me. "This is one of the most licentious corruptions of orthography," says Tyrwhitt, "that I remember to have observed in Chaucer;" but such liberties were common among the European poets of his time, when there was an extreme lack of certainty in orthography.
14. The fourteen lines that follow are translated almost literally from Petrarch's Latin.
15. For great skill is he proved that he wrought: for it is most reasonable that He should prove or test that which he made.
16. Chichevache, in old popular fable, was a monster that fed only on good women, and was always very thin from scarcity of such food; a corresponding monster, Bycorne, fed only on obedient and kind husbands, and was always fat. The origin of the fable was French; but Lydgate has a ballad on the subject. "Chichevache" literally means "niggardly" or "greedy cow."
17. Countertail: Counter-tally or counter-foil; something exactly corresponding.
18. Aventail: forepart of a helmet, vizor.

THE MERCHANT'S TALE.

THE PROLOGUE.1

"Weeping and wailing, care and other sorrow,
I have enough, on even and on morrow,"
Quoth the Merchant, "and so have other mo',   other
That wedded be; I trow that it be so;   believe
For well I wot it fareth so by me.
I have a wife, the worste that may be,
For though the fiend to her y-coupled were,
She would him overmatch, I dare well swear.
Why should I you rehearse in special
Her high malice? she is a shrew at all.   thoroughly,
                                                  in
There is a long and large difference   everything
                                                  wicked
Betwixt Griselda's greate patience,
And of my wife the passing cruelty.
Were I unbounden, all so may I the, thrive
I woulde never eft come in the snare.   again
We wedded men live in sorrow and care;
Assay it whoso will, and he shall find
That I say sooth, by Saint Thomas of Ind,2
As for the more part; I say not all, —
God shielde that it shoulde so befall.   forbid
Ah! good Sir Host, I have y-wedded be
These monethes two, and more not, pardie;
And yet I trow that he that all his life   believe
Wifeless hath been, though that men would him   rive wound
Into the hearte, could in no mannere
Telle so much sorrow, as I you here
Could tellen of my wife's cursedness."   wickedness

"Now," quoth our Host, "Merchant, so God you bless,
Since ye so muche knowen of that art,
Full heartily I pray you tell us part."
"Gladly," quoth he; "but of mine owen sore,
For sorry heart, I telle may no more."

Notes to the Prologue to the Merchant's Tale

1. Though the manner in which the Merchant takes up the closing words of the Envoy to the Clerk's Tale, and refers to the patience of Griselda, seems to prove beyond doubt that the order of the Tales in the text is the right one, yet in some manuscripts of good authority the Franklin's Tale follows the Clerk's, and the Envoy is concluded by this stanza: — "This worthy Clerk when ended was his tale, Our Hoste said, and swore by cocke's bones 'Me lever were than a barrel of ale My wife at home had heard this legend once; This is a gentle tale for the nonce; As, to my purpose, wiste ye my will. But thing that will not be, let it be still.'"
In other manuscripts of less authority the Host proceeds, in two similar stanzas, to impose a Tale on the Franklin; but Tyrwhitt is probably right in setting them aside as spurious, and in admitting the genuineness of the first only, if it be supposed that Chaucer forgot to cancel it when he had decided on another mode of connecting the Merchant's with the Clerk's Tale.
2. Saint Thomas of Ind: St. Thomas the Apostle, who was believed to have travelled in India.

THE TALE.1

Whilom there was dwelling in Lombardy
A worthy knight, that born was at Pavie,
In which he liv'd in great prosperity;
And forty years a wifeless man was he,
And follow'd aye his bodily delight
On women, where as was his appetite,
As do these fooles that be seculeres.2
And, when that he was passed sixty years,
Were it for holiness, or for dotage,
I cannot say, but such a great corage   inclination
Hadde this knight to be a wedded man,
That day and night he did all that he can
To espy where that he might wedded be;
Praying our Lord to grante him, that he
Mighte once knowen of that blissful life
That is betwixt a husband and his wife,
And for to live under that holy bond
With which God firste man and woman bond.
"None other life," said he, "is worth a bean;
For wedlock is so easy, and so clean,
That in this world it is a paradise."
Thus said this olde knight, that was so wise.
And certainly, as sooth as God is king,   true
To take a wife it is a glorious thing,
And namely when a man is old and hoar,   especially
Then is a wife the fruit of his treasor;
Then should he take a young wife and a fair,
On which he might engender him an heir,
And lead his life in joy and in solace;   mirth,
                                                  delight
Whereas these bachelors singen "Alas!"

When that they find any adversity
In love, which is but childish vanity.
And truely it sits well to be so, *becomes, befits*
That bachelors have often pain and woe:
On brittle ground they build, and brittleness
They finde when they weene sickerness: *think that there*
They live but as a bird or as a beast, *is security*
In liberty, and under no arrest; *check, control*
Whereas a wedded man in his estate
Liveth a life blissful and ordinate,
Under the yoke of marriage y-bound;
Well may his heart in joy and bliss abound.
For who can be so buxom as a wife? *obedient*
Who is so true, and eke so attentive
To keep him, sick and whole, as is his make? *care for mate*
For weal or woe she will him not forsake:
She is not weary him to love and serve,
Though that he lie bedrid until he sterve. *die*
And yet some clerkes say it is not so;
Of which he, Theophrast, is one of tho: *those*
What force though Theophrast list for to lie? *what matter*

"Take no wife," quoth he,³ "for husbandry, *thrift*
As for to spare in household thy dispence;
A true servant doth more diligence
Thy good to keep, than doth thine owen wife,
For she will claim a half part all her life.
And if that thou be sick, so God me save,
Thy very friendes, or a true knave, *servant*
Will keep thee bet than she, that waiteth aye *ahways waits to*
After thy good, and hath done many a day." *inherit your property*
This sentence, and a hundred times worse,
Writeth this man, there God his bones curse.
But take no keep of all such vanity, *notice*
Defy Theophrast, and hearken to me. *distrust*

A wife is Godde's gifte verily;
All other manner giftes hardily, *truly*
As handes, rentes, pasture, or commune, *common land*
Or mebles, all be giftes of fortune, *furniture*⁴
That passen as a shadow on the wall:
But dread thou not, if plainly speak I shall, *doubt*
A wife will last, and in thine house endure,
Well longer than thee list, paraventure. *perhaps*
Marriage is a full great sacrament;
He which that hath no wife, I hold him shent; *ruined*
He liveth helpless, and all desolate
(I speak of folk in secular estate): *who are not*
And hearken why, I say not this for nought, — *of the clergy*
That woman is for manne's help y-wrought.
The highe God, when he had Adam maked,
And saw him all alone belly naked,

God of his greate goodness saide then,
Let us now make a help unto this man
Like to himself; and then he made him Eve.
Here may ye see, and hereby may ye preve, *prove*
That a wife is man's help and his comfort,
His paradise terrestre and his disport.
So buxom and so virtuous is she, *obedient, complying*
They muste needes live in unity;
One flesh they be, and one blood, as I guess,
With but one heart in weal and in distress.
A wife? Ah! Saint Mary, ben'dicite,
How might a man have any adversity
That hath a wife? certes I cannot say
The bliss the which that is betwixt them tway,
There may no tongue it tell, or hearte think.
If he be poor, she helpeth him to swink; *labour*
She keeps his good, and wasteth never a deal; *whit*
All that her husband list, her liketh well; *pleaseth*
She saith not ones Nay, when he saith Yea;
"Do this," saith he; "All ready, Sir," saith she.
O blissful order, wedlock precious!
Thou art so merry, and eke so virtuous,
And so commended and approved eke,
That every man that holds him worth a leek
Upon his bare knees ought all his life
To thank his God, that him hath sent a wife;
Or elles pray to God him for to send
A wife, to last unto his life's end.
For then his life is set in sickerness, *security*
He may not be deceived, as I guess,
So that he work after his wife's rede; *counsel*
Then may he boldely bear up his head,
They be so true, and therewithal so wise.
For which, if thou wilt worken as the wise,
Do alway so as women will thee rede. *counsel*
Lo how that Jacob, as these clerkes read,
By good counsel of his mother Rebecc'
Bounde the kiddes skin about his neck;
For which his father's benison he wan. *benediction*
Lo Judith, as the story telle can,
By good counsel she Godde's people kept,
And slew him, Holofernes, while he slept.
Lo Abigail, by good counsel, how she
Saved her husband Nabal, when that he
Should have been slain. And lo, Esther also
By counsel good deliver'd out of woe
The people of God, and made him, Mardoche,
Of Assuere enhanced for to be. *advanced in dignity*
There is nothing in gree superlative *of higher esteem*
(As saith Senec) above a humble wife.
Suffer thy wife's tongue, as Cato bit; *bid*
She shall command, and thou shalt suffer it,
And yet she will obey of courtesy.
A wife is keeper of thine husbandry:

THE CANTERBURY TALES

Well may the sicke man bewail and weep,
There as there is no wife the house to keep.
I warne thee, if wisely thou wilt wirch,   work
Love well thy wife, as Christ loveth his church:
Thou lov'st thyself, if thou lovest thy wife.
No man hateth his flesh, but in his life
He fost'reth it; and therefore bid I thee
Cherish thy wife, or thou shalt never the.   thrive
Husband and wife, what so men jape or play,   although men joke
Of worldly folk holde the sicker way; and   jeer certain
They be so knit there may no harm betide,
And namely upon the wife's side.   especially

For which this January, of whom I told,
Consider'd hath within his dayes old,
The lusty life, the virtuous quiet,
That is in marriage honey-sweet.
And for his friends upon a day he sent
To tell them the effect of his intent.
With face sad, his tale he hath them told: grave, earnest
He saide, "Friendes, I am hoar and old,
And almost (God wot) on my pitte's brink,   grave's
Upon my soule somewhat must I think.
I have my body foolishly dispended,
Blessed be God that it shall be amended;
For I will be certain a wedded man,
And that anon in all the haste I can,
Unto some maiden, fair and tender of age;
I pray you shape for my marriage   arrange, contrive
All suddenly, for I will not abide:
And I will fond to espy, on my side,   try
To whom I may be wedded hastily.
But forasmuch as ye be more than,
Ye shalle rather such a thing espy
Than I, and where me best were to ally.
But one thing warn I you, my friendes dear,
I will none old wife have in no mannere:
She shall not passe sixteen year certain.
Old fish and younge flesh would I have fain.
Better," quoth he, "a pike than a pickerel,   young pike
And better than old beef is tender veal.
I will no woman thirty year of age,
It is but beanestraw and great forage.
And eke these olde widows (God it wot)
They conne so much craft on Wade's boat,[5]   know
So muche brooke harm when that them lest,   they can do so much
That with them should I never live in rest.   harm when they wish
For sundry schooles make subtle clerkes;
Woman of many schooles half a clerk is.
But certainly a young thing men may guy,   guide
Right as men may warm wax with handes ply.   bend, mould
Wherefore I say you plainly in a clause,
I will none old wife have, right for this cause.
For if so were I hadde such mischance,
That I in her could have no pleasance,
Then should I lead my life in avoutrie,   adultery
And go straight to the devil when I die.
Nor children should I none upon her getten:
Yet were me lever houndes had me eaten   I would rather
Than that mine heritage shoulde fall
In strange hands: and this I tell you all.
I doubte not I know the cause why
Men shoulde wed: and farthermore know I
There speaketh many a man of marriage
That knows no more of it than doth my page,
For what causes a man should take a wife.
If he ne may not live chaste his life,
Take him a wife with great devotion,
Because of lawful procreation
Of children, to th' honour of God above,
And not only for paramour or love;
And for they shoulde lechery eschew,
And yield their debte when that it is due:
Or for that each of them should help the other
In mischief, as a sister shall the brother,   trouble
And live in chastity full holily.
But, Sires, by your leave, that am not I,
For, God be thanked, I dare make avaunt,   boast
I feel my limbes stark and suffisant strong
To do all that a man belongeth to:
I wot myselfe best what I may do.
Though I be hoar, I fare as doth a tree,
That blossoms ere the fruit y-waxen be;   grown
The blossomy tree is neither dry nor dead;
I feel me now here hoar but on my head.
Mine heart and all my limbes are as green
As laurel through the year is for to seen.   see
And, since that ye have heard all mine intent,
I pray you to my will ye would assent."

Diverse men diversely him told
Of marriage many examples old;
Some blamed it, some praised it, certain;
But at the haste, shortly for to sayn
(As all day falleth altercation constantly,   every day
Betwixte friends in disputation),
There fell a strife betwixt his brethren two,
Of which that one was called Placebo,
Justinus soothly called was that other.

Placebo said; "O January, brother,
Full little need have ye, my lord so dear,
Counsel to ask of any that is here:
But that ye be so full of sapience,
That you not liketh, for your high prudence,
To waive from the word of Solomon.   depart, deviate
This word said he unto us every one;
Work alle thing by counsel, — thus said he, —

And thenne shalt thou not repente thee
But though that Solomon spake such a word,
Mine owen deare brother and my lord,
So wisly God my soule bring at rest, surely
I hold your owen counsel is the best.
For, brother mine, take of me this motive; advice, encouragement
I have now been a court-man all my life,
And, God it wot, though I unworthy be,
I have standen in full great degree
Aboute lordes of full high estate;
Yet had I ne'er with none of them debate;
I never them contraried truely.
I know well that my lord can more than I; knows
What that he saith I hold it firm and stable,
I say the same, or else a thing semblable.
A full great fool is any counsellor
That serveth any lord of high honour
That dare presume, or ones thinken it;
That his counsel should pass his lorde's wit.
Nay, lordes be no fooles by my fay.
Ye have yourselfe shewed here to day
So high sentence, so holily and well judgment, sentiment
That I consent, and confirm every deal in every point
Your wordes all, and your opinioun
By God, there is no man in all this town
Nor in Itale, could better have y-said.
Christ holds him of this counsel well apaid. satisfied
And truely it is a high courage
Of any man that stopen is in age, advanced[6]
To take a young wife, by my father's kin;
Your hearte hangeth on a jolly pin.
Do now in this matter right as you lest,
For finally I hold it for the best."

Justinus, that aye stille sat and heard,
Right in this wise to Placebo answer'd.
"Now, brother mine, be patient I pray,
Since ye have said, and hearken what I say.
Senec, among his other wordes wise,
Saith, that a man ought him right well advise, consider
To whom he gives his hand or his chattel.
And since I ought advise me right well
To whom I give my good away from me,
Well more I ought advise me, pardie,
To whom I give my body: for alway
I warn you well it is no childe's play
To take a wife without advisement.
Men must inquire (this is mine assent)
Whe'er she be wise, or sober, or dronkelew, given to drink
Or proud, or any other ways a shrew,
A chidester, or a waster of thy good, a scold
Or rich or poor; or else a man is wood. mad
Albeit so, that no man finde shall
None in this world, that trotteth whole in all, is sound in
No man, nor beast, such as men can devise, every point describe
But nathehess it ought enough suffice
With any wife, if so were that she had
More goode thewes than her vices bad: qualities
And all this asketh leisure to inquere.
For, God it wot, I have wept many a tear
Full privily, since I have had a wife.
Praise whoso will a wedded manne's life,
Certes, I find in it but cost and care,
And observances of all blisses bare.
And yet, God wot, my neighebours about,
And namely of women many a rout, especially company
Say that I have the moste steadfast wife,
And eke the meekest one, that beareth life.
But I know best where wringeth me my shoe, pinches
Ye may for me right as you like do
Advise you, ye be a man of age,
How that ye enter into marriage;
And namely with a young wife and a fair, especially
By him that made water, fire, earth, air,
The youngest man that is in all this rout company
Is busy enough to bringen it about
To have his wife alone, truste me:
Ye shall not please her fully yeares three,
This is to say, to do her full pleasance.
A wife asketh full many an observance.
I pray you that ye be not evil apaid." displeased

"Well," quoth this January, "and hast thou said?
Straw for thy Senec, and for thy proverbs,
I counte not a pannier full of herbs
Of schoele termes; wiser men than thou,
As thou hast heard, assented here right now
To my purpose: Placebo, what say ye?"
"I say it is a cursed man," quoth he, ill-natured, wicked
"That letteth matrimony, sickerly." hindereth
And with that word they rise up suddenly,
And be assented fully, that he should
Be wedded when him list, and where he would.

High fantasy and curious business
From day to day gan in the soul impress imprint themselves
Of January about his marriage
Many a fair shape, and many a fair visage
There passed through his hearte night by night.
As whoso took a mirror polish'd bright,
And set it in a common market-place,
Then should he see many a figure pace
By his mirror; and in the same wise
Gan January in his thought devise
Of maidens, which that dwelte him beside:
He wiste not where that he might abide. stay, fix

THE CANTERBURY TALES

his choice
For if that one had beauty in her face,
Another stood so in the people's grace
For her sadness and her benignity, sedateness
That of the people greatest voice had she:
And some were rich and had a badde name.
But natheless, betwixt earnest and game,
He at the last appointed him on one,
And let all others from his hearte gon,
And chose her of his own authority;
For love is blind all day, and may not see.
And when that he was into bed y-brought,
He pourtray'd in his heart and in his thought
Her freshe beauty, and her age tender,
Her middle small, her armes long and slender,
Her wise governance, her gentleness.
Her womanly bearing, and her sadness. sedateness
And when that he on her was condescended, had selected her
He thought his choice might not be amended;
For when that he himself concluded had,
He thought each other manne's wit so bad,
That impossible it were to reply
Against his choice; this was his fantasy.
His friendes sent he to, at his instance,
And prayed them to do him that pleasance,
That hastily they would unto him come;
He would abridge their labour all and some:
Needed no more for them to go nor ride,[7]
He was appointed where he would abide. he had definitively

Placebo came, and eke his friendes soon, made his choice
And alderfirst he bade them all a boon, first of all he asked
That none of them no arguments would make a favour of them
Against the purpose that he had y-take:
Which purpose was pleasant to God, said he,
And very ground of his prosperity.
He said, there was a maiden in the town,
Which that of beauty hadde great renown;
All were it so she were of small degree, although
Sufficed him her youth and her beauty;
Which maid, he said, he would have to his wife,
To lead in ease and holiness his life;
And thanked God, that he might have her all,
That no wight with his blisse parte shall; have a share
And prayed them to labour in this need,
And shape that he faile not to speed:
For then, he said, his spirit was at ease.
"Then is," quoth he, "nothing may me displease,
Save one thing pricketh in my conscience,
The which I will rehearse in your presence.
I have," quoth he, "heard said, full yore ago, long
There may no man have perfect blisses two,
This is to say, on earth and eke in heaven.

For though he keep him from the sinne's seven,
And eke from every branch of thilke tree,[8]
Yet is there so perfect felicity,
And so great ease and lust, in marriage, comfort and pleasure
That ev'r I am aghast, now in mine age ashamed, afraid
That I shall head now so merry a life,
So delicate, withoute woe or strife,
That I shall have mine heav'n on earthe here.
For since that very heav'n is bought so dear,
With tribulation and great penance,
How should I then, living in such pleasance
As alle wedded men do with their wives,
Come to the bliss where Christ etern on live is? lives eternally
This is my dread; and ye, my brethren tway, doubt
Assoile me this question, I you pray." resolve, answer

Justinus, which that hated his folly,
Answer'd anon right in his japery; mockery, jesting way
And, for he would his longe tale abridge,
He woulde no authority allege, written texts
But saide; "Sir, so there be none obstacle
Other than this, God of his high miracle,
And of his mercy, may so for you wirch, work
That, ere ye have your rights of holy church,
Ye may repent of wedded manne's life,
In which ye say there is no woe nor strife:
And elles God forbid, but if he sent unless
A wedded man his grace him to repent
Well often, rather than a single man.
And therefore, Sir, the beste rede I can, this is the best counsel
Despair you not, but have in your memory, that I know
Paraventure she may be your purgatory;
She may be Godde's means, and Godde's whip;
And then your soul shall up to heaven skip
Swifter than doth an arrow from a bow.
I hope to God hereafter ye shall know
That there is none so great felicity
In marriage, nor ever more shall be,
That you shall let of your salvation; hinder
So that ye use, as skill is and reason,
The lustes of your wife attemperly, pleasures moderately
And that ye please her not too amorously,
And that ye keep you eke from other sin.
My tale is done, for my wit is but thin.
Be not aghast hereof, my brother dear, aharmed, afraid
But let us waden out of this mattere,
The Wife of Bath, if ye have understand,
Of marriage, which ye have now in hand,

115

GEOFFREY CHAUCER

Declared hath full well in little space;
Fare ye now well, God have you in his grace."

And with this word this Justin' and his brother
Have ta'en their leave, and each of them of other.
And when they saw that it must needes be,
They wroughte so, by sleight and wise treaty,
That she, this maiden, which that Maius hight, was named May
As hastily as ever that she might,
Shall wedded be unto this January.
I trow it were too longe you to tarry,
If I told you of every script and band written bond
By which she was feoffed in his hand;
Or for to reckon of her rich array
But finally y-comen is the day
That to the churche bothe be they went,
For to receive the holy sacrament,
Forth came the priest, with stole about his neck,
And bade her be like Sarah and Rebecc'
In wisdom and in truth of marriage;
And said his orisons, as is usage,
And crouched them, and prayed God should them bless, crossed
And made all sicker enough with holiness. certain

Thus be they wedded with solemnity;
And at the feaste sat both he and she,
With other worthy folk, upon the dais.
All full of joy and bliss is the palace,
And full of instruments, and of vitaille, victuals, food
The moste dainteous of all Itale. delicate
Before them stood such instruments of soun',
That Orpheus, nor of Thebes Amphioun,
Ne made never such a melody.
At every course came in loud minstrelsy,
That never Joab trumped for to hear,
Nor he, Theodomas, yet half so clear
At Thebes, when the city was in doubt.
Bacchus the wine them skinked all about. poured[9]
And Venus laughed upon every wight
(For January was become her knight,
And woulde both assaye his courage
In liberty, and eke in marriage),
And with her firebrand in her hand about
Danced before the bride and all the rout.
And certainly I dare right well say this,
Hymeneus, that god of wedding is,
Saw never his life so merry a wedded man.
Hold thou thy peace, thou poet Marcian,[10]
That writest us that ilke wedding merry same
Of her Philology and him Mercury,
And of the songes that the Muses sung;
Too small is both thy pen, and eke thy tongue
For to describen of this marriage.
When tender youth hath wedded stooping age,
There is such mirth that it may not be writ;

Assay it youreself, then may ye wit know
If that I lie or no in this mattere.

Maius, that sat with so benign a cheer, countenance
Her to behold it seemed faerie;
Queen Esther never look'd with such an eye
On Assuere, so meek a look had she;
I may you not devise all her beauty;
But thus much of her beauty tell I may,
That she was like the bright morrow of May
Full filled of all beauty and pleasance.
This January is ravish'd in a trance,
At every time he looked in her face;
But in his heart he gan her to menace,
That he that night in armes would her strain
Harder than ever Paris did Helene.
But natheless yet had he great pity
That thilke night offende her must he,
And thought, "Alas, O tender creature,
Now woulde God ye mighte well endure
All my courage, it is so sharp and keen;
I am aghast ye shall it not sustene. afraid
But God forbid that I did all my might.
Now woulde God that it were waxen night,
And that the night would lasten evermo'.
I would that all this people were y-go." gone away
And finally he did all his labour,
As he best mighte, saving his honour,
To haste them from the meat in subtle wise.

The time came that reason was to rise;
And after that men dance, and drinke fast,
And spices all about the house they cast,
And full of joy and bliss is every man,
All but a squire, that highte Damian,
Who carv'd before the knight full many a day;
He was so ravish'd on his lady May,
That for the very pain he was nigh wood; mad
Almost he swelt and swooned where he stood, fainted
So sore had Venus hurt him with her brand,
As that she bare it dancing in her hand.
And to his bed he went him hastily;
No more of him as at this time speak I;
But there I let him weep enough and plain, bewail
Till freshe May will rue upon his pain.
O perilous fire, that in the bedstraw breedeth!
O foe familiar, that his service bedeth! domestic[11] offers
O servant traitor, O false homely hewe, servant[12]
Like to the adder in bosom shy untrue,
God shield us alle from your acquaintance!
O January, drunken in pleasance
Of marriage, see how thy Damian,
Thine owen squier and thy boren man, born[13]
Intendeth for to do thee villainy: dishonour, outrage

116

God grante thee thine homehy foe t' espy. enemy
in the household
For in this world is no worse pestilence
Than homely foe, all day in thy presence.

Performed hath the sun his arc diurn, daily
No longer may the body of him sojourn
On the horizon, in that latitude:
Night with his mantle, that is dark and rude,
Gan overspread the hemisphere about:
For which departed is this lusty rout pleasant
company
From January, with thank on every side.
Home to their houses lustily they ride,
Where as they do their thinges as them lest,
And when they see their time they go to rest.
Soon after that this hasty January eager
Will go to bed, he will no longer tarry.
He dranke hippocras, clarre, and vernage[14]
Of spices hot, to increase his courage;
And many a lectuary had he full fine, potion
Such as the cursed monk Dan Constantine[15]
Hath written in his book de Coitu; of sexual
intercourse
To eat them all he would nothing eschew:
And to his privy friendes thus said he:
"For Godde's love, as soon as it may be,
Let voiden all this house in courteous wise."
everyone leave
And they have done right as he will devise.
Men drinken, and the travers draw anon; curtains
The bride is brought to bed as still as stone;
And when the bed was with the priest y-bless'd,
Out of the chamber every wight him dress'd,
And January hath fast in arms y-take
His freshe May, his paradise, his make. mate
He lulled her, he kissed her full oft;
With thicke bristles of his beard unsoft,
Like to the skin of houndfish, sharp as brere
dogfish briar
(For he was shav'n all new in his mannere),
He rubbed her upon her tender face,
And saide thus; "Alas! I must trespace
To you, my spouse, and you greatly offend,
Ere time come that I will down descend.
But natheless consider this," quoth he,
"There is no workman, whatsoe'er he be,
That may both worke well and hastily:
This will be done at leisure perfectly.
It is no force how longe that we play; no matter
In true wedlock coupled be we tway;
And blessed be the yoke that we be in,
For in our actes may there be no sin.
A man may do no sinne with his wife,
Nor hurt himselfe with his owen knife;
For we have leave to play us by the law."

Thus labour'd he, till that the day gan daw,
And then he took a sop in fine clarre,
And upright in his bedde then sat he.

And after that he sang full loud and clear,
And kiss'd his wife, and made wanton cheer.
He was all coltish, full of ragerie wantonness
And full of jargon as a flecked pie.[16]
The slacke skin about his necke shaked,
While that he sang, so chanted he and craked.
quavered
But God wot what that May thought in her heart,
When she him saw up sitting in his shirt
In his night-cap, and with his necke lean:
She praised not his playing worth a bean.
Then said he thus; "My reste will I take
Now day is come, I may no longer wake;
And down he laid his head and slept till prime.
And afterward, when that he saw his time,
Up rose January, but freshe May
Helde her chamber till the fourthe day,
As usage is of wives for the best.
For every labour some time must have rest,
Or elles longe may he not endure;
This is to say, no life of creature,
Be it of fish, or bird, or beast, or man.

Now will I speak of woeful Damian,
That languisheth for love, as ye shall hear;
Therefore I speak to him in this manneare.
I say. "O silly Damian, alas!
Answer to this demand, as in this case,
How shalt thou to thy lady, freshe May,
Telle thy woe? She will alway say nay;
Eke if thou speak, she will thy woe bewray;
betray
God be thine help, I can no better say.
This sicke Damian in Venus' fire
So burned that he died for desire;
For which he put his life in aventure, at risk
No longer might he in this wise endure;
But privily a penner gan he borrow, writing-case
And in a letter wrote he all his sorrow,
In manner of a complaint or a lay,
Unto his faire freshe lady May.
And in a purse of silk, hung on his shirt,
He hath it put, and laid it at his heart.

The moone, that at noon was thilke day that
That January had wedded freshe May,
In ten of Taure, was into Cancer glided;[17]
So long had Maius in her chamber abided,
As custom is unto these nobles all.
A bride shall not eaten in the ball
Till dayes four, or three days at the least,
Y-passed be; then let her go to feast.
The fourthe day complete from noon to noon,
When that the highe masse was y-done,
In halle sat this January, and May,
As fresh as is the brighte summer's day.
And so befell, how that this goode man
Remember'd him upon this Damian.
And saide; "Saint Mary, how may this be,
That Damian attendeth not to me?

Is he aye sick? or how may this betide?"
His squiers, which that stoode there beside,
Excused him, because of his sickness,
Which letted him to do his business: hindered
None other cause mighte make him tarry.
"That me forthinketh," quoth this January, grieves,
causes
"He is a gentle squier, by my truth; uneasiness
If that he died, it were great harm and ruth.
He is as wise, as discreet, and secre', secret, trusty
As any man I know of his degree,
And thereto manly and eke serviceble,
And for to be a thrifty man right able.
But after meat, as soon as ever I may
I will myself visit him, and eke May,
To do him all the comfort that I can."
And for that word him blessed every man,
That of his bounty and his gentleness
He woulde so comforten in sickness
His squier, for it was a gentle deed.

"Dame," quoth this January, "take good heed,
At after meat, ye with your women all
(When that ye be in chamb'r out of this hall),
That all ye go to see this Damian:
Do him disport, he is a gentle man;
And telle him that I will him visite,
Have I nothing but rested me a lite: when only I
have rested
And speed you faste, for I will abide me a little
Till that ye sleepe faste by my side."
And with that word he gan unto him call
A squier, that was marshal of his hall,
And told him certain things that he wo'ld.
This freshe May hath straight her way y-hold,
With all her women, unto Damian.
Down by his beddes side sat she than, then
Comforting him as goodly as she may.
This Damian, when that his time he say, saw
In secret wise his purse, and eke his bill,
In which that he y-written had his will,
Hath put into her hand withoute more,
Save that he sighed wondrous deep and sore,
And softely to her right thus said he:
"Mercy, and that ye not discover me:
For I am dead if that this thing be kid."
discovered[18]
The purse hath she in her bosom hid,
And went her way; ye get no more of me;
But unto January come is she,
That on his bedde's side sat full soft.
He took her, and he kissed her full oft,
And laid him down to sleep, and that anon.
She feigned her as that she muste gon
There as ye know that every wight must need;
And when she of this bill had taken heed,
She rent it all to cloutes at the last, fragments
And in the privy softely it cast.
Who studieth now but faire freshe May? is
thoughtful
Adown by olde January she lay,
That slepte, till the cough had him awaked:
Anon he pray'd her strippe her all naked,
He would of her, he said, have some pleasance;
And said her clothes did him incumbrance.
And she obey'd him, be her lefe or loth. willing
or unwilling
But, lest that precious folk be with me wroth,
over-nice[19]
How that he wrought I dare not to you tell,
Or whether she thought it paradise or hell;
But there I let them worken in their wise
Till evensong ring, and they must arise.

Were it by destiny, or aventure, chance
Were it by influence, or by nature,
Or constellation, that in such estate
The heaven stood at that time fortunate
As for to put a bill of Venus' works
(For alle thing hath time, as say these clerks),
To any woman for to get her love,
I cannot say; but greate God above,
That knoweth that none act is causeless,
He deem of all, for I will hold my peace. let him
judge
But sooth is this, how that this freshe May
Hath taken such impression that day
Of pity on this sicke Damian,
That from her hearte she not drive can
The remembrance for to do him ease. to satisfy
"Certain," thought she, "whom that this thing
displease his desire
I recke not, for here I him assure,
To love him best of any creature,
Though he no more haddee than his shirt."
Lo, pity runneth soon in gentle heart.
Here may ye see, how excellent franchise
generosity
In women is when they them narrow advise.
closely consider
Some tyrant is, — as there be many a one, —
That hath a heart as hard as any stone,
Which would have let him sterven in the place
die
Well rather than have granted him her grace;
And then rejoicen in her cruel pride.
And reckon not to be a homicide.
This gentle May, full filled of pity,
Right of her hand a letter maked she,
In which she granted him her very grace;
There lacked nought, but only day and place,
Where that she might unto his lust suffice:
For it shall be right as he will devise.
And when she saw her time upon a day
To visit this Damian went this May,
And subtilly this letter down she thrust
Under his pillow, read it if him lust. pleased
She took him by the hand, and hard him twist

THE CANTERBURY TALES

So secretly, that no wight of it wist,
And bade him be all whole; and forth she went
To January, when he for her sent.
Up rose Damian the nexte morrow,
All passed was his sickness and his sorrow.
He combed him, he proined[20] him and picked,
He did all that unto his lady liked;
And eke to January he went as low
As ever did a dogge for the bow.[21]
He is so pleasant unto every man
(For craft is all, whoso that do it can),
Every wight is fain to speak him good;
And fully in his lady's grace he stood.
Thus leave I Damian about his need,
And in my tale forth I will proceed.

Some clerke holde that felicity   writers, scholars
Stands in delight; and therefore certain he,
This noble January, with all his might
In honest wise as longeth to a knight, belongeth
Shope him to live full deliciously: prepared, arranged
His housing, his array, as honestly   honourably, suitably
To his degree was maked as a king's.
Amonges other of his honest things
He had a garden walled all with stone;
So fair a garden wot I nowhere none.
For out of doubt I verily suppose
That he that wrote the Romance of the Rose[22]
Could not of it the beauty well devise; describe
Nor Priapus[23] mighte not well suffice,
Though he be god of gardens, for to tell
The beauty of the garden, and the well fountain
That stood under a laurel always green.
Full often time he, Pluto, and his queen
Proserpina, and all their faerie,
Disported them and made melody
About that well, and danced, as men told.
This noble knight, this January old
Such dainty had in it to walk and play, pleasure
That he would suffer no wight to bear the key,
Save he himself, for of the small wicket
He bare always of silver a cliket, key
With which, when that him list, he it unshet. opened
And when that he would pay his wife's debt,
In summer season, thither would he go,
And May his wife, and no wight but they two;
And thinges which that were not done in bed,
He in the garden them perform'd and sped.
And in this wise many a merry day
Lived this January and fresh May,
But worldly joy may not always endure
To January, nor to no creatucere.

O sudden hap! O thou fortune unstable!
Like to the scorpion so deceivable, deceitful
That fhatt'rest with thy head when thou wilt sting;

Thy tail is death, through thine envenoming.
O brittle joy! O sweete poison quaint! strange
O monster, that so subtilly canst paint
Thy giftes, under hue of steadfastness,
That thou deceivest bothe more and less! great and small
Why hast thou January thus deceiv'd,
That haddest him for thy full friend receiv'd?
And now thou hast bereft him both his eyen,
For sorrow of which desireth he to dien.
Alas! this noble January free,
Amid his lust and his prosperity pleasure
Is waxen blind, and that all suddenly.
He weeped and he wailed piteously;
And therewithal the fire of jealousy
(Lest that his wife should fall in some folly)
So burnt his hearte, that he woulde fain,
That some man bothe him and her had slain;
For neither after his death, nor in his life,
Ne would he that she were no love nor wife,
But ever live as widow in clothes black,
Sole as the turtle that hath lost her make. mate
But at the last, after a month or tway,
His sorrow gan assuage, soothe to say.
For, when he wist it might none other be,
He patiently took his adversity:
Save out of doubte he may not foregon
That he was jealous evermore-in-one: continually
Which jealousy was so outrageous,
That neither in hall, nor in none other house,
Nor in none other place never the mo'
He woulde suffer her to ride or go,
But if that he had hand on her alway. unless
For which full often wepte freshe May,
That loved Damian so burningly
That she must either dien suddenly,
Or elles she must have him as her lest: pleased
She waited when her hearte woulde brest. expected burst
Upon that other side Damian
Becomen is the sorrowfullest man
That ever was; for neither night nor day
He mighte speak a word to freshe May,
As to his purpose, of no such mattere,
But if that January must it hear, unless
That had a hand upon her evermo'.
But natheless, by writing to and fro,
And privy signes, wist he what she meant,
And she knew eke the fine of his intent. end, aim

O January, what might it thee avail,
Though thou might see as far as shippes sail?
For as good is it blind deceiv'd to be,
As be deceived when a man may see.
Lo, Argus, which that had a hundred eyen,[24]
For all that ever he could pore or pryen,
Yet was he blent; and, God wot, so be mo', deceived
That weene wisly that it be not so: think

confidently
Pass over is an ease, I say no more.
This freshe May, of which I spake yore, previously
In warm wax hath imprinted the cliket taken an impression
That January bare of the small wicket of the key
By which into his garden oft he went;
And Damian, that knew all her intent,
The cliket counterfeited privily;
There is no more to say, but hastily
Some wonder by this cliket shall betide,
Which ye shall hearen, if ye will abide.

O noble Ovid, sooth say'st thou, God wot,
What sleight is it, if love be long and hot,
That he'll not find it out in some mannere?
By Pyramus and Thisbe may men lear; learn
Though they were kept full long and strait o'er all,
They be accorded, rowning through a wall, agreed whispering
Where no wight could have found out such a sleight.
But now to purpose; ere that dayes eight
Were passed of the month of July, fill it befell
That January caught so great a will,
Through egging of his wife, him for to play inciting
In his garden, and no wight but they tway,
That in a morning to this May said he:25
"Rise up, my wife, my love, my lady free;
The turtle's voice is heard, mine owen sweet;
The winter is gone, with all his raines weet. wet
Come forth now with thine eyen columbine eyes like the doves
Well fairer be thy breasts than any wine.
The garden is enclosed all about;
Come forth, my white spouse; for, out of doubt,
Thou hast me wounded in mine heart, O wife:
No spot in thee was e'er in all thy life.
Come forth, and let us taken our disport;
I choose thee for my wife and my comfort."
Such olde lewed wordes used he. foolish, ignorant
On Damian a signe made she,
That he should go before with his cliket.
This Damian then hath opened the wicket,
And in he start, and that in such mannere
That no wight might him either see or hear;
And still he sat under a bush. Anon
This January, as blind as is a stone,
With Maius in his hand, and no wight mo',
Into this freshe garden is y-go,
And clapped to the wicket suddenly.
"Now, wife," quoth he, "here is but thou and I;
Thou art the creature that I beste love:
For, by that Lord that sits in heav'n above,
Lever I had to dien on a knife, rather

Than thee offende, deare true wife.
For Godde's sake, think how I thee chees, chose
Not for no covetise doubteless, covetousness
But only for the love I had to thee.
And though that I be old, and may not see,
Be to me true, and I will tell you why.
Certes three things shall ye win thereby:
First, love of Christ, and to yourself honour,
And all mine heritage, town and tow'r.
I give it you, make charters as you lest;
This shall be done to-morrow ere sun rest,
So wisly God my soule bring to bliss! surely
I pray you, on this covenant me kiss.
And though that I be jealous, wite me not; blame
Ye be so deep imprinted in my thought,
That when that I consider your beauty,
And therewithal th'unlikely eld of me, dissimilar age
I may not, certes, though I shoulde die,
Forbear to be out of your company,
For very love; this is withoute doubt:
Now kiss me, wife, and let us roam about."

This freshe May, when she these wordes heard,
Benignely to January answer'd;
But first and forward she began to weep:
"I have," quoth she, "a soule for to keep
As well as ye, and also mine honour,
And of my wifehood thilke tender flow'r that same
Which that I have assured in your hond,
When that the priest to you my body bond:
Wherefore I will answer in this mannere,
With leave of you mine owen lord so dear.
I pray to God, that never dawn the day
That I no sterve, as foul as woman may, do not die
If e'er I do unto my kin that shame,
Or elles I impaire so my name,
That I bee false; and if I do that lack,
Do strippe me, and put me in a sack,
And in the nexte river do me drench: drown
I am a gentle woman, and no wench.
Why speak ye thus? but men be e'er untrue,
And women have reproof of you aye new.
Ye know none other dalliance, I believe,
But speak to us of untrust and repreve." reproof

And with that word she saw where Damian
Sat in the bush, and coughe she began;
And with her finger signe made she,
That Damian should climb upon a tree
That charged was with fruit; and up he went:
For verily he knew all her intent,
And every signe that she coulde make,
Better than January her own make. mate
For in a letter she had told him all
Of this matter, how that he worke shall.
And thus I leave him sitting in the perry, pear-

120

tree
And January and May roaming full merry.

Bright was the day, and blue the firmament;
Phoebus of gold his streames down had sent
To gladden every flow'r with his warmness;
He was that time in Geminis, I guess,
But little from his declination
Of Cancer, Jove's exaltation.
And so befell, in that bright morning-tide,
That in the garden, on the farther side,
Pluto, that is the king of Faerie,
And many a lady in his company
Following his wife, the queen Proserpina, —
Which that he ravished out of Ethna,26
While that she gather'd flowers in the mead
(In Claudian ye may the story read,
How in his grisly chariot he her fet), — fetched
This king of Faerie adown him set
Upon a bank of turfes fresh and green,
And right anon thus said he to his queen.
"My wife," quoth he, "there may no wight say nay, —
Experience so proves it every day, —
The treason which that woman doth to man.
Ten hundred thousand stories tell I can
Notable of your untruth and brittleness inconstancy
O Solomon, richest of all richess,
Full fill'd of sapience and worldly glory,
Full worthy be thy wordes of memory
To every wight that wit and reason can. knows
Thus praised he yet the bounte of man: goodness
'Among a thousand men yet found I one,
But of all women found I never none.'27
Thus said this king, that knew your wickedness;
And Jesus, Filius Sirach,28 as I guess,
He spake of you but seldom reverence.
A wilde fire and corrupt pestilence
So fall upon your bodies yet to-night!
Ne see ye not this honourable knight?
Because, alas! that he is blind and old,
His owen man shall make him cuckold.
Lo, where he sits, the lechour, in the tree.
Now will I granten, of my majesty,
Unto this olde blinde worthy knight,
That he shall have again his eyen sight,
When that his wife will do him villainy;
Then shall be knowen all her harlotry,
Both in reproof of her and other mo'."
"Yea, Sir," quoth Proserpine," and will ye so?
Now by my mother Ceres' soul I swear
That I shall give her suffisant answer,
And alle women after, for her sake;
That though they be in any guilt y-take,
With face bold they shall themselves excuse,
And bear them down that woulde them accuse.
For lack of answer, none of them shall dien.

All had ye seen a thing with both your eyen, although
Yet shall we visage it so hardily, confront it
And weep, and swear, and chide subtilly,
That ye shall be as lewed as be geese. ignorant, confounded
What recketh me of your authorities?
I wot well that this Jew, this Solomon,
Found of us women fooles many one:
But though that he founde no good woman,
Yet there hath found many another man
Women full good, and true, and virtuous;
Witness on them that dwelt in Christes house;
With martyrdom they proved their constance.
The Roman gestes29 make remembrance
Of many a very true wife also.
But, Sire, be not wroth, albeit so,
Though that he said he found no good woman,
I pray you take the sentence of the man: opinion, real meaning
He meant thus, that in sovereign bounte perfect goodness
Is none but God, no, neither he nor she. man nor woman
Hey, for the very God that is but one,
Why make ye so much of Solomon?
What though he made a temple, Godde's house?
What though he were rich and glorious?
So made he eke a temple of false goddes;
How might he do a thing that more forbode is? forbidden
Pardie, as fair as ye his name emplaster, plaster over, "whitewash"
He was a lechour, and an idolaster, idol hater
And in his eld he very God forsook. the true
And if that God had not (as saith the book)
Spared him for his father's sake, he should
Have lost his regne rather than he would. kingdom sooner
I sette not of all the villainy value not
That he of women wrote, a butterfly.
I am a woman, needes must I speak,
Or elles swell until mine hearte break.
For since he said that we be jangleresses, chatterers
As ever may I brooke whole my tresses, preserve
I shall not spare for no courtesy
To speak him harm, that said us villainy."
"Dame," quoth this Pluto, "be no longer wroth;
I give it up: but, since I swore mine oath
That I would grant to him his sight again,
My word shall stand, that warn I you certain:
I am a king; it sits me not to lie." becomes, befits
"And I," quoth she, "am queen of Faerie.
Her answer she shall have, I undertake,
Let us no more wordes of it make.
Forsooth, I will no longer you contrary."

Now let us turn again to January,
That in the garden with his faire May
Singeth well merrier than the popinjay: parrot
"You love I best, and shall, and other none."
So long about the alleys is he gone,
Till he was come to that ilke perry, the same pear-tree
Where as this Damian satte full merry
On high, among the freshe leaves green.
This freshe May, that is so bright and sheen,
Gan for to sigh, and said, "Alas my side!
Now, Sir," quoth she, "for aught that may betide,
I must have of the peares that I see,
Or I must die, so sore longeth me
To eaten of the smalle peares green;
Help, for her love that is of heaven queen!
I tell you well, a woman in my plight[30]
May have to fruit so great an appetite,
That she may dien, but she of it have. " unless
"Alas!" quoth he, "that I had here a knave servant
That coulde climb; alas! alas!" quoth he,
"For I am blind." "Yea, Sir, no force," quoth she; no matter
"But would ye vouchesafe, for Godde's sake,
The perry in your armes for to take
(For well I wot that ye mistruste me),
Then would I climbe well enough," quoth she,
"So I my foot might set upon your back."
"Certes," said he, "therein shall be no lack,
Might I you helpe with mine hearte's blood."
He stooped down, and on his back she stood,
And caught her by a twist, and up she go'th. twig, bough
(Ladies, I pray you that ye be not wroth,
I cannot glose, I am a rude man): mince matters
And suddenly anon this Damian
Gan pullen up the smock, and in he throng. rushed[31]
And when that Pluto saw this greate wrong,
To January he gave again his sight,
And made him see as well as ever he might.
And when he thus had caught his sight again,
Was never man of anything so fain:
But on his wife his thought was evermo'.
Up to the tree he cast his eyen two,
And saw how Damian his wife had dress'd,
In such mannere, it may not be express'd,
But if I woulde speak uncourteously. unless
And up he gave a roaring and a cry,
As doth the mother when the child shall die;
"Out! help! alas! harow!" he gan to cry;
"O stronge, lady, stowre![32] what doest thou?"

And she answered: "Sir, what aileth you?
Have patience and reason in your mind,
I have you help'd on both your eyen blind.
On peril of my soul, I shall not lien,
As me was taught to helpe with your eyen,
Was nothing better for to make you see,
Than struggle with a man upon a tree:
God wot, I did it in full good intent."
"Struggle!" quoth he, "yea, algate in it went. whatever way
God give you both one shame's death to dien!
He swived thee; I saw it with mine eyen; enjoyed carnally
And elles be I hanged by the halse." neck
"Then is," quoth she, "my medicine all false;
For certainly, if that ye mighte see,
Ye would not say these wordes unto me.
Ye have some glimpsing, and no perfect sight." glimmering
"I see," quoth he, "as well as ever I might,
(Thanked be God!) with both mine eyen two,
And by my faith me thought he did thee so."
"Ye maze, ye maze, goode Sir," quoth she; rave, are confused
"This thank have I for I have made you see:
Alas!" quoth she, "that e'er I was so kind."
"Now, Dame," quoth he, "let all pass out of mind;
Come down, my lefe, and if I have missaid, love
God help me so, as I am evil apaid. dissatisfied
But, by my father's soul, I ween'd have seen
How that this Damian had by thee lain,
And that thy smock had lain upon his breast."
"Yea, Sir," quoth she, "ye may ween as ye lest: think as you
But, Sir, a man that wakes out of his sleep, please
He may not suddenly well take keep notice
Upon a thing, nor see it perfectly,
Till that he be adawed verily. awakened
Right so a man, that long hath blind y-be,
He may not suddenly so well y-see,
First when his sight is newe come again,
As he that hath a day or two y-seen.
Till that your sight establish'd be a while,
There may full many a sighte you beguile.
Beware, I pray you, for, by heaven's king,
Full many a man weeneth to see a thing,
And it is all another than it seemeth;
He which that misconceiveth oft misdeemeth."
And with that word she leapt down from the tree.
This January, who is glad but he?
He kissed her, and clipped her full oft, embraced
And on her womb he stroked her full soft;
And to his palace home he hath her lad. led
Now, goode men, I pray you to be glad.
Thus endeth here my tale of January,
God bless us, and his mother, Sainte Mary.

THE CANTERBURY TALES

Notes to The Merchant's Tale

1. If, as is probable, this Tale was translated from the French, the original is not now extant. Tyrwhitt remarks that the scene "is laid in Italy, but none of the names, except Damian and Justin, seem to be Italian, but rather made at pleasure; so that I doubt whether the story be really of Italian growth. The adventure of the pear-tree I find in a small collection of Latin fables, written by one Adoiphus, in elegiac verses of his fashion, in the year 1315. . . . Whatever was the real origin of the Tale, the machinery of the fairies, which Chaucer has used so happily, was probably added by himself; and, indeed, I cannot help thinking that his Pluto and Proserpina were the true progenitors of Oberon and Titania; or rather, that they themselves have, once at least, deigned to revisit our poetical system under the latter names."
2. Seculeres: of the laity; but perhaps, since the word is of two- fold meaning, Chaucer intends a hit at the secular clergy, who, unlike the regular orders, did not live separate from the world, but shared in all its interests and pleasures — all the more easily and freely, that they had not the civil restraint of marriage.
3. This and the next eight lines are taken from the "Liber aureolus Theophrasti de nuptiis," ("Theophrastus's Golden Book of Marriage") quoted by Hieronymus, "Contra Jovinianum," ("Against Jovinian") and thence again by John of Salisbury.
4. Mebles: movables, furniture, &c.; French, "meubles."
5. "Wade's boat" was called Guingelot; and in it, according to the old romance, the owner underwent a long series of wild adventures, and performed many strange exploits. The romance is lost, and therefore the exact force of the phrase in the text is uncertain; but Mr Wright seems to be warranted in supposing that Wade's adventures were cited as examples of craft and cunning — that the hero, in fact, was a kind of Northern Ulysses, It is possible that to the same source we may trace the proverbial phrase, found in Chaucer's "Remedy of Love," to "bear Wattis pack" signifying to be duped or beguiled.
6. Stopen: advanced; past participle of "step." Elsewhere "y-stept in age" is used by Chaucer.
7. They did not need to go in quest of a wife for him, as they had promised.
8. Thilke tree: that tree of original sin, of which the special sins are the branches.
9. Skinked: poured out; from Anglo-Saxon, "scencan."
10. Marcianus Capella, who wrote a kind of philosophical romance, "De Nuptiis Mercurii et Philologiae" (Of the Marriage of Mercury and Philology) . "Her" and "him," two lines after, like "he" applied to Theodomas, are prefixed to the proper names for emphasis, according to the Anglo- Saxon usage.
11. Familiar: domestic; belonging to the "familia," or household.
12. Hewe: domestic servant; from Anglo-Saxon, "hiwa." Tyrwhitt reads "false of holy hue;" but Mr Wright has properly restored the reading adopted in the text.
13. Boren man: born; owing to January faith and loyalty because born in his household.
14. Hippocras: spiced wine. Clarre: also a kind of spiced wine. Vernage: a wine believed to have come from Crete, although its name — Italian, "Vernaccia" — seems to be derived from Verona.
15. Dan Constantine: a medical author who wrote about 1080; his works were printed at Basle in 1536.
16. Full of jargon as a flecked pie: he chattered like a magpie
17. Nearly all the manuscripts read "in two of Taure;" but Tyrwhitt has shown that, setting out from the second degree of Taurus, the moon, which in the four complete days that Maius spent in her chamber could not have advanced more than fifty- three degrees, would only have been at the twenty-fifth degree of Gemini — whereas, by reading "ten," she is brought to the third degree of Cancer.
18. Kid; or "kidde," past participle of "kythe" or "kithe," to show or discover.
19. Precious: precise, over-nice; French, "precieux," affected.
20. Proined: or "pruned;" carefully trimmed and dressed himself. The word is used in falconry of a hawk when she picks and trims her feathers.
21. A dogge for the bow: a dog attending a hunter with the bow.
22 The Romance of the Rose: a very popular mediaeval romance, the English version of which is partly by Chaucer. It opens with a description of a beautiful garden.
23. Priapus: Son of Bacchus and Venus: he was regarded as the promoter of fertility in all agricultural life, vegetable and animal; while not only gardens, but fields, flocks, bees — and even fisheries — were supposed to be under his protection.
24. Argus was employed by Juno to watch Io with his hundred eyes but he was sent to sleep by the flute of Mercury, who then cut off his head.

25. "My beloved spake, and said unto me, Rise up, my love, my fair one, and come away. For lo, the winter is past, the rain is over and gone: The flowers appear on the earth, the time of the singing of the birds is come, and the voice of the turtle is heard in our land." — Song of Solomon, ii. 10-12.
26. "That fair field,
    Of Enna, where Proserpine, gath'ring flowers,
    Herself a fairer flow'r, by gloomy Dis
    Was gather'd."
    — Milton, Paradise Lost, iv. 268
27. "Behold, this have I found, saith the preacher, counting one by one, to find out the account: Which yet my soul seeketh, but I find not: one man amongst a thousand have I found, but a woman among all those I have not found. Lo, this only have I found, that God hath made man upright." Ecclesiastes vii. 27-29.
28. Jesus, the son of Sirach, to whom is ascribed one of the books of the Apochrypha — that called the "Wisdom of Jesus the Son of Sirach, or Ecclesiasticus;" in which, especially in the ninth and twenty-fifth chapters, severe cautions are given against women.
29. Roman gestes: histories; such as those of Lucretia, Porcia, &c.
30. May means January to believe that she is pregnant, and that she has a craving for unripe pears.
31. At this point, and again some twenty lines below, several verses of a very coarse character had been inserted in later manuscripts; but they are evidently spurious, and are omitted in the best editions.
32. "Store" is the general reading here, but its meaning is not obvious. "Stowre" is found in several manuscripts; it signifies "struggle" or "resist;" and both for its own appropriateness, and for the force which it gives the word "stronge," the reading in the text seems the better.

The Squire's Tale.

The Prologue.

"HEY! Godde's mercy!" said our Hoste tho, then
"Now such a wife I pray God keep me fro'.
Lo, suche sleightes and subtilities
In women be; for aye as busy as bees
Are they us silly men for to deceive,
And from the soothe will they ever weive, *truth swerve, depart*
As this Merchante's tale it proveth well.
But natheless, as true as any steel,
I have a wife, though that she poore be;
But of her tongue a labbing shrew is she; *chattering*
And yet she hath a heap of vices mo'. *moreover*
Thereof no force; let all such thinges go. *no matter*
But wit ye what? in counsel be it said, *know secret, confidence*
Me rueth sore I am unto her tied;
For, an' I shoulde reckon every vice if
Which that she hath, y-wis I were too nice; *certainly foolish*
And cause why, it should reported be
And told her by some of this company
(By whom, it needeth not for to declare,
Since women connen utter such chaffare[1]),
And eke my wit sufficeth not thereto
To tellen all; wherefore my tale is do. *done*
Squier, come near, if it your wille be,
And say somewhat of love, for certes ye
Conne thereon as much as any man." *know about it*
"Nay, Sir," quoth he; "but such thing as I can,
With hearty will, — for I will not rebel
Against your lust, — a tale will I tell. *pleasure*
Have me excused if I speak amiss;
My will is good; and lo, my tale is this."

Notes to the Prologue to the Squire's Tale

1. Women connen utter such chaffare: women are adepts at giving circulation to such wares. The Host evidently means that his wife would be sure to hear of his confessions from some female member of the company.

THE TALE.[1]

Pars Prima. *First part*

At Sarra, in the land of Tartary,
There dwelt a king that warrayed Russie,[2] *made war on*
Through which there died many a doughty man;
This noble king was called Cambuscan,[3]
Which in his time was of so great renown,
That there was nowhere in no regioun
So excellent a lord in alle thing:
Him lacked nought that longeth to a king,
As of the sect of which that he was born.
He kept his law to which he was y-sworn,
And thereto he was hardy, wise, and rich, *moreover, besides*
And piteous and just, always y-lich; *alike, even-tempered*
True of his word, benign and honourable;
Of his corage as any centre stable; *firm, immovable of spirit*
Young, fresh, and strong, in armes desirous
As any bachelor of all his house.
A fair person he was, and fortunate,
And kept alway so well his royal estate,
That there was nowhere such another man.
This noble king, this Tartar Cambuscan,
Hadde two sons by Elfeta his wife,
Of which the eldest highte Algarsife,
The other was y-called Camballo.
A daughter had this worthy king also,
That youngest was, and highte Canace:
But for to telle you all her beauty,
It lies not in my tongue, nor my conning; *skill*
I dare not undertake so high a thing:
Mine English eke is insufficient,
It muste be a rhetor excellent, *orator*
That couth his colours longing for that art, *see*[4]
If he should her describen any part;
I am none such, I must speak as I can.

And so befell, that when this Cambuscan
Had twenty winters borne his diadem,
As he was wont from year to year, I deem,
He let the feast of his nativity *his birthday party*
Do crye, throughout Sarra his city, *be proclaimed*
The last Idus of March, after the year.
Phoebus the sun full jolly was and clear,
For he was nigh his exaltation
In Marte's face, and in his mansion[5]
In Aries, the choleric hot sign:
Full lusty was the weather and benign; *pleasant*
For which the fowls against the sunne sheen,

GEOFFREY CHAUCER

bright
What for the season and the younge green,
Full loude sange their affections:
Them seemed to have got protections
Against the sword of winter keen and cold.
This Cambuscan, of which I have you told,
In royal vesture, sat upon his dais,
With diadem, full high in his palace;
And held his feast so solemn and so rich,
That in this worlde was there none it lich. like
Of which if I should tell all the array,
Then would it occupy a summer's day;
And eke it needeth not for to devise describe
At every course the order of service.
I will not tellen of their strange sewes, dishes[6]
Nor of their swannes, nor of their heronsews. young herons[7]
Eke in that land, as telle knightes old,
There is some meat that is full dainty hold,
That in this land men reck of it full small: care for
There is no man that may reporten all.
I will not tarry you, for it is prime,
And for it is no fruit, but loss of time;
Unto my purpose I will have recourse. story[8]
And so befell that, after the third course,
While that this king sat thus in his nobley, noble array
Hearing his ministreles their thinges play
Before him at his board deliciously,
In at the halle door all suddenly
There came a knight upon a steed of brass,
And in his hand a broad mirror of glass;
Upon his thumb he had of gold a ring,
And by his side a naked sword hanging:
And up he rode unto the highe board.
In all the hall was there not spoke a word,
For marvel of this knight; him to behold
Full busily they waited, young and old. watched

This strange knight, that came thus suddenly,
All armed, save his head, full richly,
Saluted king, and queen, and lordes all,
By order as they satten in the hall,
With so high reverence and observance,
As well in speech as in his countenance,
That Gawain[9] with his olde courtesy,
Though he were come again out of Faerie,
Him coulde not amende with a word. could not better him
And after this, before the highe board, by one word
He with a manly voice said his message,
After the form used in his language,
Withoute vice of syllable or letter. fault
And, for his tale shoulde seem the better,
Accordant to his worde's was his cheer, demeanour
As teacheth art of speech them that it lear. learn
Albeit that I cannot sound his style,
Nor cannot climb over so high a stile,
Yet say I this, as to commune intent, general sense or meaning
Thus much amounteth all that ever he meant, this is the sum of
If it so be that I have it in mind.
He said; "The king of Araby and Ind,
My liege lord, on this solemne day
Saluteth you as he best can and may,
And sendeth you, in honour of your feast,
By me, that am all ready at your hest, command
This steed of brass, that easily and well
Can in the space of one day naturel
(This is to say, in four-and-twenty hours),
Whereso you list, in drought or else in show'rs,
Beare your body into every place
To which your hearte willeth for to pace, pass, go
Withoute wem of you, through foul or fair. hurt, injury
Or if you list to fly as high in air
As doth an eagle, when him list to soar,
This same steed shall bear you evermore
Withoute harm, till ye be where you lest it pleases you
(Though that ye sleepen on his back, or rest),
And turn again, with writhing of a pin. twisting
He that it wrought, he coude many a gin; knew contrivance[10]
He waited in any a constellation, observed
Ere he had done this operation,
And knew full many a seal[11] and many a bond
This mirror eke, that I have in mine hond,
Hath such a might, that men may in it see
When there shall fall any adversity
Unto your realm, or to yourself also,
And openly who is your friend or foe.
And over all this, if any lady bright
Hath set her heart on any manner wight,
If he be false, she shall his treason see,
His newe love, and all his subtlety,
So openly that there shall nothing hide.
Wherefore, against this lusty summer-tide,
This mirror, and this ring that ye may see,
He hath sent to my lady Canace,
Your excellente daughter that is here.
The virtue of this ring, if ye will hear,
Is this, that if her list it for to wear
Upon her thumb, or in her purse it bear,
There is no fowl that flyeth under heaven,
That she shall not well understand his steven, speech, sound
And know his meaning openly and plain,
And answer him in his language again:
And every grass that groweth upon root
She shall eke know, to whom it will do boot, remedy
All be his woundes ne'er so deep and wide.
This naked sword, that hangeth by my side,
Such virtue hath, that what man that it smite,

Throughout his armour it will carve and bite,
Were it as thick as is a branched oak:
And what man is y-wounded with the stroke
Shall ne'er be whole, till that you list, of grace,
To stroke him with the flat in thilke place the same
Where he is hurt; this is as much to sayn,
Ye muste with the flatte sword again
Stroke him upon the wound, and it will close.
This is the very sooth, withoute glose; deceit
It faileth not, while it is in your hold."

And when this knight had thus his tale told,
He rode out of the hall, and down he light.
His steede, which that shone as sunne bright,
Stood in the court as still as any stone.
The knight is to his chamber led anon,
And is unarmed, and to meat y-set. seated
These presents be full richely y-fet, — fetched
This is to say, the sword and the mirrour, —
And borne anon into the highe tow'r,
With certain officers ordain'd therefor;
And unto Canace the ring is bore
Solemnely, where she sat at the table;
But sickerly, withouten any fable,
The horse of brass, that may not be remued. removed[12]
It stood as it were to the ground y-glued;
There may no man out of the place it drive
For no engine of windlass or polive; pulley
And cause why, for they can not the craft; know not the cunning
And therefore in the place they have it laft, of the mechanism
Till that the knight hath taught them the mannere
To voide him, as ye shall after hear. remove

Great was the press, that swarmed to and fro
To gauren on this horse that stoode so: gaze
For it so high was, and so broad and long,
So well proportioned for to be strong,
Right as it were a steed of Lombardy;
Therewith so horsely, and so quick of eye,
As it a gentle Poileis[13] courser were:
For certes, from his tail unto his ear
Nature nor art ne could him not amend
In no degree, as all the people wend. weened, thought
But evermore their moste wonder was
How that it coulde go, and was of brass;
It was of Faerie, as the people seem'd.
Diverse folk diversely they deem'd;
As many heads, as many wittes been.
They murmured, as doth a swarm of been, bees
And made skills after their fantasies, reasons
Rehearsing of the olde poetries,
And said that it was like the Pegasee, Pegasus
The horse that hadde winges for to flee; fly
Or else it was the Greeke's horse Sinon,[14]
That broughte Troye to destruction,

As men may in the olde gestes read. tales of adventures
Mine heart," quoth one, "is evermore in dread;
I trow some men of armes be therein,
That shape them this city for to win: design, prepare
It were right good that all such thing were know."
Another rowned to his fellow low, whispered
And said, "He lies; for it is rather like
An apparence made by some magic,
As jugglers playen at these feastes great."
Of sundry doubts they jangle thus and treat.
As lewed people deeme commonly ignorant
Of thinges that be made more subtilly
Than they can in their lewdness comprehend;
They deeme gladly to the badder end. are ready to think
And some of them wonder'd on the mirrour, the worst
That borne was up into the master tow'r, chief[15]
How men might in it suche thinges see.
Another answer'd and said, it might well be
Naturally by compositions
Of angles, and of sly reflections;
And saide that in Rome was such a one.
They speak of Alhazen and Vitellon,[16]
And Aristotle, that wrote in their lives
Of quainte mirrors, and of prospectives, curious
As knowe they that have their bookes heard.
And other folk have wonder'd on the swerd, sword
That woulde pierce throughout every thing;
And fell in speech of Telephus the king,
And of Achilles for his quainte spear,[17]
For he could with it bothe heal and dere, wound
Right in such wise as men may with the swerd
Of which right now ye have yourselves heard.
They spake of sundry hard'ning of metal,
And spake of medicines therewithal,
And how, and when, it shoulde harden'd be,
Which is unknowen algate unto me. however
Then spake they of Canacee's ring,
And saiden all, that such a wondrous thing
Of craft of rings heard they never none,
Save that he, Moses, and King Solomon,
Hadden a name of conning in such art. a reputation for
Thus said the people, and drew them apart. knowledge
Put natheless some saide that it was
Wonder to maken of fern ashes glass,
And yet is glass nought like ashes of fern;
But for they have y-knowen it so ferne because before[18]
Therefore ceaseth their jangling and their wonder.
As sore wonder some on cause of thunder,
On ebb and flood, on gossamer and mist,

And on all things, till that the cause is *wist.* known
Thus jangle they, and deemen and devise,
Till that the king gan from his board arise.

Phoebus had left the angle meridional,
And yet ascending was the beast royal,
The gentle Lion, with his Aldrian,[19]
When that this Tartar king, this Cambuscan,
Rose from the board, there as he sat full high
Before him went the loude minstrelsy,
Till he came to his chamber of parements,[20]
There as they sounded diverse instruments,
That it was like a heaven for to hear.
Now danced lusty Venus' children dear:
For in the Fish their lady sat full Pisces
And looked on them with a friendly eye.[21]
This noble king is set upon his throne;
This strange knight is fetched to him full *sone,* soon
And on the dance he goes with Canace.
Here is the revel and the jollity,
That is not able a dull man to *devise:* describe
He must have knowen love and his service,
And been a feastly man, as fresh as May, *merry,* gay
That shoulde you devise such array.
Who coulde telle you the form of dances
So uncouth, and so freshe *countenances* unfamliar gestures
Such subtle lookings and dissimulances,
For dread of jealous men's apperceivings?
No man but Launcelot,[22] and he is dead.
Therefore I pass o'er all this *lustihead* pleasantness
I say no more, but in this jolliness
I leave them, till to supper men them dress.
The steward bids the spices for to *hie* haste
And eke the wine, in all this melody;
The ushers and the squiers be y-gone,
The spices and the wine is come anon;
They eat and drink, and when this hath an end,
Unto the temple, as reason was, they wend;
The service done, they suppen all by day
What needeth you rehearse their array?
Each man wot well, that at a kinge's feast
Is plenty, to the most, and to the *least,* highest
And dainties more than be in my knowing.

At after supper went this noble king
To see the horse of brass, with all a rout
Of lordes and of ladies him about.
Such wond'ring was there on this horse of brass,
That, since the great siege of Troye was,
There as men wonder'd on a horse also,
Ne'er was there such a wond'ring as was *tho.* there
But finally the king asked the knight
The virtue of this courser, and the might,
And prayed him to tell his governance. *mode of managing him*

The horse anon began to trip and dance,
When that the knight laid hand upon his rein,
And saide, "Sir, there is no more to sayn,
But when you list to riden anywhere,
Ye muste trill a pin, stands in his ear, *turn*[23]
Which I shall telle you betwixt us two;
Ye muste name him to what place also,
Or to what country that you list to ride.
And when ye come where you list abide,
Bid him descend, and trill another pin
(For therein lies th' effect of all the gin), *contrivance*[10]
And he will down descend and do your will,
And in that place he will abide still;
Though all the world had the contrary swore,
He shall not thence be throwen nor be bore.
Or, if you list to bid him thennes gon,
Trill this pin, and he will vanish anon
Out of the sight of every manner wight,
And come again, be it by day or night,
When that you list to clepe him again *call*
In such a guise, as I shall to you sayn
Betwixte you and me, and that full soon.
Ride[24] when you list, there is no more to do'n.'
Informed when the king was of the knight,
And had conceived in his wit aright
The manner and the form of all this thing,
Full glad and blithe, this noble doughty king
Repaired to his revel as beforn.
The bridle is into the tower borne,
And kept among his jewels *lefe* and dear; cherished
The horse vanish'd, I n'ot in what mannere, *know not*
Out of their sight; ye get no more of me:
But thus I leave in lust and jollity
This Cambuscan his lordes *feastying,* entertaining[25]
Until well nigh the day began to spring.

Pars Secunda. Second Part

The norice of digestion, the sleep, *nurse*
Gan on them wink, and bade them take *keep,* heed
That muche mirth and labour will have rest.
And with a gaping mouth he all them *kest,* yawning kissed
And said, that it was time to lie down,
For blood was in his dominatioun:[26]
"Cherish the blood, nature's friend," quoth he.
They thanked him gaping, by two and three;
And every wight gan draw him to his rest;
As sleep them bade, they took it for the best.
Their dreames shall not now be told for me;
Full are their heades of fumosity,[27]
That caused dreams of which there is no charge: *of no significance*
They slepte; till that, it was prime *large,* late morning

THE CANTERBURY TALES

The moste part, but it was Canace; except
She was full measurable, as women be: moderate
For of her father had she ta'en her leave
To go to rest, soon after it was eve;
Her liste not appalled for to be; to look pale
Nor on the morrow unfeastly for to see; to look sad, depressed
And slept her firste sleep; and then awoke.
For such a joy she in her hearte took
Both of her quainte a ring and her mirrour,.
That twenty times she changed her colour;
And in her sleep, right for th' impression
Of her mirror, she had a vision.
Wherefore, ere that the sunne gan up glide,
She call'd upon her mistress' her beside, governesses
And saide, that her liste for to rise.

These olde women, that be gladly wise
As are her mistresses answer'd anon,
And said; "Madame, whither will ye gon
Thus early? for the folk be all in rest."
"I will," quoth she, "arise; for me lest
No longer for to sleep, and walk about."
Her mistresses call'd women a great rout,
And up they rose, well a ten or twelve;
Up rose freshe Canace herselve,
As ruddy and bright as is the yonnge sun
That in the Ram is four degrees y-run;
No higher was he, when she ready was;
And forth she walked easily a pace,
Array'd after the lusty season swoot, pleasant sweet
Lightely for to play, and walk on foot,
Nought but with five or six of her meinie;
And in a trench forth in the park went she. sunken path
The vapour, which up from the earthe glode, glided
Made the sun to seem ruddy and broad:
But, natheless, it was so fair a sight
That it made all their heartes for to light, be lightened, glad
What for the season and the morrowning,
And for the fowles that she hearde sing.
For right anon she wiste what they meant knew
Right by their song, and knew all their intent.
The knotte, why that every tale is told, nucleus, chief matter
If it be tarried till the list be cold delayed inclination
Of them that have it hearken'd after yore, for a long time
The savour passeth ever longer more;
For fulsomness of the prolixity:
And by that same reason thinketh me.
I shoulde unto the knotte condescend,
And maken of her walking soon an end.

Amid a tree fordry, as white as chalk, thoroughly dried up
There sat a falcon o'er her head full high,
That with a piteous voice so gan to cry;
That all the wood resounded of her cry,
And beat she had herself so piteously
With both her winges, till the redde blood
Ran endelong the tree, there as she stood from top to bottom
And ever-in-one alway she cried and shright; incessantly shrieked
And with her beak herselfe she so pight, wounded
That there is no tiger, nor cruel beast,
That dwelleth either in wood or in forest;
But would have wept, if that he weepe could,
For sorrow of her; she shriek'd alway so loud.
For there was never yet no man alive,
If that he could a falcon well descrive; describe
That heard of such another of fairness
As well of plumage, as of gentleness;
Of shape, of all that mighte reckon'd be.
A falcon peregrine seemed she,
Of fremde land; and ever as she stood foreign[28]
She swooned now and now for lack of blood;
Till well-nigh is she fallen from the tree.

This faire kinge's daughter Canace,
That on her finger bare the quainte ring,
Through which she understood well every thing
That any fowl may in his leden sayn, language[29]
And could him answer in his leden again;
Hath understoode what this falcon said,
And well-nigh for the ruth almost she died;. pity
And to the tree she went, full hastily,
And on this falcon looked piteously;
And held her lap abroad; for well she wist
The falcon muste falle from the twist twig, bough
When that she swooned next, for lack of blood.
A longe while to waite her she stood;
Till at the last she apake in this mannere
Unto the hawk, as ye shall after hear:
"What is the cause, if it be for to tell,
That ye be in this furial pain of hell?" raging, furious
Quoth Canace unto this hawk above;
"Is this for sorrow of of death; or loss of love?
For; as I trow, these be the causes two; believe
That cause most a gentle hearte woe:
Of other harm it needeth not to speak.
For ye yourself upon yourself awreak; inflict
Which proveth well, that either ire or dread fear
Must be occasion of your cruel deed,
Since that I see none other wight you chase:
For love of God, as do yourselfe grace; have mercy on
Or what may be your help? for, west nor east, yourself
I never saw ere now no bird nor beast
That fared with himself so piteously

129

GEOFFREY CHAUCER

Ye slay me with your sorrow verily;
I have of you so great compassioun.
For Godde's love come from the tree adown
And, as I am a kinge's daughter true,
If that I verily the causes knew
Of your disease, if it lay in my might, distress
I would amend it, ere that it were night,
So wisly help me the great God of kind. surely nature
And herbes shall I right enoughe find,
To heale with your hurtes hastily."
Then shriek'd this falcon yet more piteously
Than ever she did, and fell to ground anon,
And lay aswoon, as dead as lies a stone,
Till Canace had in her lap her take,
Unto that time she gan of swoon awake:
And, after that she out of swoon abraid, awoke
Right in her hawke's leden thus she said:

"That pity runneth soon in gentle heart
(Feeling his simil'tude in paines smart),
Is proved every day, as men may see,
As well by work as by authority; by experience as by doctrine
For gentle hearte kitheth gentleness. sheweth
I see well, that ye have on my distress
Compassion, my faire Canace,
Of very womanly benignity
That nature in your princples hath set.
But for no hope for to fare the bet, better
But for t' obey unto your hearte free,
And for to make others aware by me,
As by the whelp chastis'd is the lion, instructed, corrected
Right for that cause and that conclusion,
While that I have a leisure and a space,
Mine harm I will confessen ere I pace." depart
And ever while the one her sorrow told,
The other wept, as she to water wo'ld, as if she would dissolve
Till that the falcon bade her to be still, into water
And with a sigh right thus she said her till: to her
"Where I was bred (alas that ilke day!) same
And foster'd in a rock of marble gray
So tenderly, that nothing ailed me,
I wiste not what was adversity, knew
Till I could flee full high under the sky. fly
Then dwell'd a tercelet[30] me faste by,
That seem'd a well of alle gentleness;
All were he full of treason and falseness, although he was
It was so wrapped under humble cheer, under an aspect
And under hue of truth, in such mannere, of humility
Under pleasance, and under busy pain,
That no wight weened that he coulde feign,
So deep in grain he dyed his colours.
Right as a serpent hides him under flow'rs,
Till he may see his time for to bite,
Right so this god of love's hypocrite
Did so his ceremonies and obeisances,
And kept in semblance all his observances,
That sounden unto gentleness of love. are consonant to
As on a tomb is all the fair above,
And under is the corpse, which that ye wet,
Such was this hypocrite, both cold and hot;
And in this wise he served his intent,
That, save the fiend, none wiste what he meant:
Till he so long had weeped and complain'd,
And many a year his service to me feign'd,
Till that mine heart, too piteous and too nice, foolish, simple
All innocent of his crowned malice,
Forfeared of his death, as thoughte me, greatly afraid lest
Upon his oathes and his surety he should die
Granted him love, on this conditioun,
That evermore mine honour and renown
Were saved, bothe privy and apert; privately and in public
This is to say, that, after his desert,
I gave him all my heart and all my thought
(God wot, and he, that other wayes nought), in no other way
And took his heart in change of mine for aye.
But sooth is said, gone since many a day,
A true wight and a thiefe think not one. do not think alike
And when he saw the thing so far y-gone,
That I had granted him fully my love,
In such a wise as I have said above,
And given him my true heart as free
As he swore that he gave his heart to me,
Anon this tiger, full of doubleness,
Fell on his knees with so great humbleness,
With so high reverence, as by his cheer, mien
So like a gentle lover in mannere,
So ravish'd, as it seemed, for the joy,
That never Jason, nor Paris of Troy, —
Jason? certes, nor ever other man,
Since Lamech[31] was, that alderfirst began first of all
To love two, as write folk beforn,
Nor ever since the firste man was born,
Coulde no man, by twenty thousand
Counterfeit the sophimes of his art; sophistries, beguilements
Where doubleness of feigning should approach,
Nor worthy were t'unbuckle his galoche, shoe[32]
Nor could so thank a wight, as he did me.
His manner was a heaven for to see
To any woman, were she ne'er so wise;
So painted he and kempt, at point devise, combed, studied
As well his wordes as his countenance. with perfect precision

And I so lov'd him for his obeisance,
And for the truth I deemed in his heart,
That, if so were that any thing him smart, pained
All were it ne'er so lite, and I it wist, little
Methought I felt death at my hearte twist.
And shortly, so farforth this thing is went, gone
That my will was his wille's instrument;
That is to say, my will obey'd his will
In alle thing, as far as reason fill, fell; allowed
Keeping the boundes of my worship ever;
And never had I thing so lefe, or lever, so dear, or dearer
As him, God wot, nor never shall no mo'.

"This lasted longer than a year or two,
That I supposed of him naught but good.
But finally, thus at the last it stood,
That fortune woulde that he muste twin depart, separate
Out of that place which that I was in.
Whe'er me was woe, it is no question; whether
I cannot make of it description.
For one thing dare I telle boldely,
I know what is the pain of death thereby;
Such harm I felt, for he might not byleve. stay[33]
So on a day of me he took his leave,
So sorrowful eke, that I ween'd verily,
That he had felt as muche harm as I,
When that I heard him speak, and saw his hue.
But natheless, I thought he was so true,
And eke that he repaire should again
Within a little while, sooth to sayn,
And reason would eke that he muste go
For his honour, as often happ'neth so,
That I made virtue of necessity,
And took it well, since that it muste be.
As I best might, I hid from him my sorrow,
And took him by the hand, Saint John to borrow, witness, pledge
And said him thus; 'Lo, I am youres all;
Be such as I have been to you, and shall.'
What he answer'd, it needs not to rehearse;
Who can say bet than he, who can do worse? better
When he had all well said, then had he done.
Therefore behoveth him a full long spoon,
That shall eat with a fiend; thus heard I say.
So at the last he muste forth his way,
And forth he flew, till he came where him lest.
When it came him to purpose for to rest,
I trow that he had thilke text in mind,
That alle thing repairing to his kind
Gladdeth himself;[34] thus say men, as I guess;
Men love of [proper] kind newfangleness, see note[35]
As birdes do, that men in cages feed.
For though thou night and day take of them heed,
And strew their cage fair and soft as silk,

And give them sugar, honey, bread, and milk,
Yet, right anon as that his door is up, immediately on his
He with his feet will spurne down his cup, door being opened
And to the wood he will, and wormes eat;
So newefangle be they of their meat,
And love novelties, of proper kind;
No gentleness of bloode may them bind.
So far'd this tercelet, alas the day!
Though he were gentle born, and fresh, and gay,
And goodly for to see, and humble, and free,
He saw upon a time a kite flee, fly
And suddenly he loved this kite so,
That all his love is clean from me y-go:
And hath his trothe falsed in this wise.
Thus hath the kite my love in her service,
And I am lorn withoute remedy." lost, undone

And with that word this falcon gan to cry,
And swooned eft in Canacee's barme again lap
Great was the sorrow, for that hawke's harm,
That Canace and all her women made;
They wist not how they might the falcon glade. gladden
But Canace home bare her in her lap,
And softely in plasters gan her wrap,
There as she with her beak had hurt herself.
Now cannot Canace but herbes delve
Out of the ground, and make salves new
Of herbes precious and fine of hue,
To heale with this hawk; from day to night
She did her business, and all her might.
And by her bedde's head she made a mew, bird cage
And cover'd it with velouettes blue,[36] velvets
In sign of truth that is in woman seen;
And all without the mew is painted green,
In which were painted all these false fowls,
As be these tidifes, tercelets, and owls; titmice
And pies, on them for to cry and chide,
Right for despite were painted them beside.

Thus leave I Canace her hawk keeping.
I will no more as now speak of her ring,
Till it come eft to purpose for to sayn again
How that this falcon got her love again
Repentant, as the story telleth us,
By mediation of Camballus,
The kinge's son of which that I you told.
But henceforth I will my process hold
To speak of aventures, and of battailes,
That yet was never heard so great marvailles.
First I will telle you of Cambuscan,
That in his time many a city wan;
And after will I speak of Algarsife,
How he won Theodora to his wife,
For whom full oft in great peril he was,
N'had he been holpen by the horse of brass. had he not

And after will I speak of Camballo,[37]
That fought in listes with the brethren two
For Canace, ere that he might her win;

And where I left I will again begin.
. . . .[38]

Notes to the Squire's Tale

1. The Squire's Tale has not been found under any other form among the literary remains of the Middle Ages; and it is unknown from what original it was derived, if from any. The Tale is unfinished, not because the conclusion has been lost, but because the author left it so.
2. The Russians and Tartars waged constant hostilities between the thirteenth and sixteenth centuries.
3. In the best manuscripts the name is "Cambynskan," and thus, no doubt, it should strictly be read. But it is a most pardonable offence against literal accuracy to use the word which Milton has made classical, in "Il Penseroso," speaking of

"him that left half-told
    The story of Cambuscan bold,
    Of Camball, and of Algarsife,
    And who had Canace to wife,
    That owned the virtuous Ring and Glass,
    And of the wondrous Horse of Brass,
    On which the Tartar King did ride"

Surely the admiration of Milton might well seem to the spirit of Chaucer to condone a much greater transgression on his domain than this verbal change — which to both eye and ear is an unquestionable improvement on the uncouth original.
4. Couth his colours longing for that art: well skilled in using the colours — the word-painting — belonging to his art.
5. Aries was the mansion of Mars — to whom "his" applies. Leo was the mansion of the Sun.
6. Sewes: Dishes, or soups. The precise force of the word is uncertain; but it may be connected with "seethe," to boil, and it seems to describe a dish in which the flesh was served up amid a kind of broth or gravy. The "sewer," taster or assayer of the viands served at great tables, probably derived his name from the verb to "say" or "assay;" though Tyrwhitt would connect the two words, by taking both from the French, "asseoir," to place — making the arrangement of the table the leading duty of the "sewer," rather than the testing of the food.
7. Heronsews: young herons; French, "heronneaux."
8. Purpose: story, discourse; French, "propos."
9. Gawain was celebrated in mediaeval romance as the most courteous among King Arthur's knights.
10. Gin: contrivance; trick; snare. Compare Italian, "inganno," deception; and our own "engine."
11. Mr Wright remarks that "the making and arrangement of seals was one of the important operations of mediaeval magic."
12. Remued: removed; French, "remuer," to stir.
13. Polies: Apulian. The horses of Apulia — in old French "Poille," in Italian "Puglia" — were held in high value.
14. The Greeke's horse Sinon: the wooden horse of the Greek Sinon, introduced into Troy by the stratagem of its maker.
15. Master tower: chief tower; as, in the Knight's Tale, the principal street is called the "master street." See note 86 to the Knight's Tale.
16. Alhazen and Vitellon: two writers on optics — the first supposed to have lived about 1100, the other about 1270. Tyrwhitt says that their works were printed at Basle in 1572, under the title "Alhazeni et Vitellonis Opticae."
17. Telephus, a son of Hercules, reigned over Mysia when the Greeks came to besiege Troy, and he sought to prevent their landing. But, by the art of Dionysus, he was made to stumble over a vine, and Achilles wounded him with his spear. The oracle informed Telephus that the hurt could be healed only by him, or by the weapon, that inflicted it; and the king, seeking the Grecian camp, was healed by Achilles with the rust of the charmed spear.
18. Ferne: before; a corruption of "forne," from Anglo-Saxon, "foran."
19. Aldrian: or Aldebaran; a star in the neck of the constellation Leo.
20. Chamber of parements: Presence-chamber, or chamber of state, full of splendid furniture and ornaments. The same expression is used in French and Italian.

THE CANTERBURY TALES

21. In Pisces, Venus was said to be at her exaltation or greatest power. A planet, according to the old astrologers, was in "exaltation" when in the sign of the Zodiac in which it exerted its strongest influence; the opposite sign, in which it was weakest, was called its "dejection."
22. Launcelot: Arthur's famous knight, so accomplished and courtly, that he was held the very pink of chivalry.
23. Trill: turn; akin to "thirl", "drill."
24. Ride: another reading is "bide," alight or remain.
25. Feastying: entertaining; French, "festoyer," to feast.
26. The old physicians held that blood dominated in the human body late at night and in the early morning. Galen says that the domination lasts for seven hours.
27. Fumosity: fumes of wine rising from the stomach to the head.
28. Fremde: foreign, strange; German, "fremd" in the northern dialects, "frem," or "fremmed," is used in the same sense.
29. Leden: Language, dialect; from Anglo-Saxon, "leden" or "laeden," a corruption from "Latin."
30. Tercelet: the "tassel," or male of any species of hawk; so called, according to Cotgrave, because he is one third ("tiers") smaller than the female.
31. "And Lamech took unto him two wives: the name of the one Adah, and the name of the other Zillah" (Gen. iv. 19).
32. Galoche: shoe; it seems to have been used in France, of a "sabot," or wooden shoe. The reader cannot fail to recall the same illustration in John i. 27, where the Baptist says of Christ: "He it is, who coming after me is preferred before me; whose shoe's latchet I am not worthy to unloose."
33. Byleve; stay; another form is "bleve;" from Anglo-Saxon, "belitan," to remain. Compare German, "bleiben."
34. This sentiment, as well as the illustration of the bird which follows, is taken from the third book of Boethius, "De Consolatione Philosophiae," metrum 2. It has thus been rendered in Chaucer's translation: "All things seek aye to their proper course, and all things rejoice on their returning again to their nature."
35. Men love of proper kind newfangleness: Men, by their own — their very — nature, are fond of novelty, and prone to inconstancy.
36. Blue was the colour of truth, as green was that of inconstancy. In John Stowe's additions to Chaucer's works, printed in 1561, there is "A balade whiche Chaucer made against women inconstaunt," of which the refrain is, "In stead of blue, thus may ye wear all green."
37. Unless we suppose this to be a namesake of the Camballo who was Canace's brother — which is not at all probable — we must agree with Tyrwhitt that there is a mistake here; which no doubt Chaucer would have rectified, if the tale had not been "left half-told," One manuscript reads "Caballo;" and though not much authority need be given to a difference that may be due to mere omission of the mark of contraction over the "a," there is enough in the text to show that another person than the king's younger son is intended. The Squire promises to tell the adventures that befell each member of Cambuscan's family; and in thorough consistency with this plan, and with the canons of chivalric story, would be "the marriage of Canace to some knight who was first obliged to fight for her with her two brethren; a method of courtship," adds Tyrwhitt, "very consonant to the spirit of ancient chivalry."
38. (Trancriber's note) In some manuscripts the following two lines, being the beginning of the third part, are found: -

Apollo whirleth up his chair so high,
    Till that Mercurius' house, the sly…

GEOFFREY CHAUCER

THE FRANKLIN'S TALE.

THE PROLOGUE.[1]

"IN faith, Squier, thou hast thee well acquit,
And gentilly; I praise well thy wit,"
Quoth the Franklin; "considering thy youthe
So feelingly thou speak'st, Sir, I aloue thee,   *allow, approve*
As to my doom, there is none that is here   *as far as my judgment*
Of eloquence that shall be thy peer,   *goes*
If that thou live; God give thee goode chance,
And in virtue send thee continuance,
For of thy speaking I have great dainty.   *value, esteem*
I have a son, and, by the Trinity;
It were me lever than twenty pound worth land,   *I would rather*
Though it right now were fallen in my hand,
He were a man of such discretion
As that ye be: fy on possession,
But if a man be virtuous withal.   *unless*
I have my sone snibbed and yet shall,   *rebuked; "snubbed."*
For he to virtue listeth not   *t'intend, does not wish to*
But for to play at dice, and to dispend,   *apply himself*
And lose all that he hath, is his usage;
And he had lever talke with a page,
Than to commune with any gentle wight,
There he might learen gentilless aright."

Straw for your gentillesse!" quoth our Host.
"What? Frankelin, pardie, Sir, well thou wost   *knowest*
That each of you must tellen at the least
A tale or two, or breake his behest."   *promise*
"That know I well, Sir," quoth the Frankelin;
"I pray you have me not in disdain,
Though I to this man speak a word or two."
"Tell on thy tale, withoute wordes mo'."
"Gladly, Sir Host," quoth he, "I will obey
Unto your will; now hearken what I say;
I will you not contrary in no wise,   *disobey*
As far as that my wittes may suffice.
I pray to God that it may please you,
Then wot I well that it is good enow.

"These olde gentle Bretons, in their days,
Of divers aventures made lays,[2]
Rhymeden in their firste Breton tongue;
Which layes with their instruments they sung,
Or elles reade them for their pleasance;
And one of them have I in remembrance,
Which I shall say with good will as I can.
But, Sirs, because I am a borel man,   *rude, unlearned*
At my beginning first I you beseech
Have me excused of my rude speech.
I learned never rhetoric, certain;
Thing that I speak, it must be bare and plain.
I slept never on the mount of Parnasso,
Nor learned Marcus Tullius Cicero.
Coloures know I none, withoute dread,   *doubt*
But such colours as growen in the mead,
Or elles such as men dye with or paint;
Colours of rhetoric be to me quaint;   *strange*
My spirit feeleth not of such mattere.
But, if you list, my tale shall ye hear."

Notes to the Prologue to the Franklin's Tale

1. In the older editions, the verses here given as the prologue were prefixed to the Merchant's Tale, and put into his mouth. Tyrwhitt was abundantly justified, by the internal evidence afforded by the lines themselves, in transferring them to their present place.
2. The "Breton Lays" were an important and curious element in the literature of the Middle Ages; they were originally composed in the Armorican language, and the chief collection of them extant was translated into French verse by a poetess calling herself "Marie," about the middle of the thirteenth century. But though this collection was the most famous, and had doubtless been read by Chaucer, there were other British or Breton lays, and from one of those the Franklin's Tale is taken. Boccaccio has dealt with the same story in the "Decameron" and the "Philocopo," altering the circumstances to suit the removal of its scene to a southern clime.

THE CANTERBURY TALES

THE TALE.

In Armoric', that called is Bretagne,
There was a knight, that lov'd and did his pain   devoted himself,
To serve a lady in his beste wise; strove
And many a labour, many a great emprise,   enterprise
He for his lady wrought, ere she were won:
For she was one the fairest under sun,
And eke thereto come of so high kindred,
That well unnethes durst this knight for dread, see note[1]
Tell her his woe, his pain, and his distress
But, at the last, she for his worthiness,
And namely for his meek obeisance,   especially
Hath such a pity caught of his penance, suffering, distress
That privily she fell of his accord
To take him for her husband and her lord
(Of such lordship as men have o'er their wives);
And, for to lead the more in bliss their lives,
Of his free will he swore her as a knight,
That never in all his life he day nor night
Should take upon himself no mastery
Against her will, nor kithe her jealousy,   show
But her obey, and follow her will in all,
As any lover to his lady shall;
Save that the name of sovereignty
That would he have, for shame of his degree.
She thanked him, and with full great humbless
She saide; "Sir, since of your gentleness
Ye proffer me to have so large a reign,
Ne woulde God never betwixt us twain,
As in my guilt, were either war or strife: see note[2]
Sir, I will be your humble true wife,
Have here my troth, till that my hearte brest." burst
Thus be they both in quiet and in rest.

For one thing, Sires, safely dare I say,
That friends ever each other must obey,
If they will longe hold in company.
Love will not be constrain'd by mastery.
When mast'ry comes, the god of love anon
Beateth[3] his wings, and, farewell, he is gone.
Love is a thing as any spirit free.
Women of kind desire liberty, by nature
And not to be constrained as a thrall,   slave
And so do men, if soothly I say shall.
Look who that is most patient in love,
He is at his advantage all above.   enjoys the highest
Patience is a high virtue certain,   advantages of all
For it vanquisheth, as these clerkes sayn,
Thinges that rigour never should attain.
For every word men may not chide or plain.
Learne to suffer, or, so may I go,   prosper
Ye shall it learn whether ye will or no.
For in this world certain no wight there is,
That he not doth or saith sometimes amiss.

Ire, or sickness, or constellation, the influence of
Wine, woe, or changing of complexion,   the planets
Causeth full oft to do amiss or speaken:
On every wrong a man may not be wreaken. revenged
After the time must be temperance according to
To every wight that can of governance.   is capable of
And therefore hath this worthy wise knight
(To live in ease) sufferance her behight;   promised
And she to him full wisly gan to swear   surely
That never should there be default in her.
Here may men see a humble wife accord;
Thus hath she ta'en her servant and her lord,
Servant in love, and lord in marriage.
Then was he both in lordship and servage?
Servage? nay, but in lordship all above,
Since he had both his lady and his love:
His lady certes, and his wife also,
The which that law of love accordeth to.
And when he was in this prosperrity,
Home with his wife he went to his country,
Not far from Penmark,[4] where his dwelling was,
And there he liv'd in bliss and in solace.   delight
Who coulde tell, but he had wedded be, unless
The joy, the ease, and the prosperity,
That is betwixt a husband and his wife?
A year and more lasted this blissful life,
Till that this knight, of whom I spake thus,
That of Cairrud[5] was call'd Arviragus,
Shope him to go and dwell a year or twain   prepared, arranged
In Engleland, that call'd was eke Britain,
To seek in armes worship and honour
(For all his lust he set in such labour);   pleasure
And dwelled there two years; the book saith thus.

Now will I stint of this Arviragus,   cease speaking
And speak I will of Dorigen his wife,
That lov'd her husband as her hearte's life.
For his absence weepeth she and siketh,   sigheth
As do these noble wives when them liketh;
She mourneth, waketh, waileth, fasteth, plaineth;
Desire of his presence her so distraineth,
That all this wide world she set at nought.
Her friendes, which that knew her heavy thought,
Comforte her in all that ever they may;
They preache her, they tell her night and day,
That causeless she slays herself, alas!
And every comfort possible in this case
They do to her, with all their business,   assiduity
And all to make her leave her heaviness.
By process, as ye knowen every one,
Men may so longe graven in a stone,
Till some figure therein imprinted be:
So long have they comforted her, till she

135

Received hath, by hope and by reason,
Th' imprinting of their consolation,
Through which her greate sorrow gan assuage;
She may not always duren in such rage.
And eke Arviragus, in all this care,
Hath sent his letters home of his welfare,
And that he will come hastily again,
Or elles had this sorrow her hearty-slain.
Her friendes saw her sorrow gin to slake,   slacken, diminish
And prayed her on knees for Godde's sake
To come and roamen in their company,
Away to drive her darke fantasy;
And finally she granted that request,
For well she saw that it was for the best.

Now stood her castle faste by the sea,
And often with her friendes walked she,
Her to disport upon the bank on high,
There as many a ship and barge sigh,   saw
Sailing their courses, where them list to go.
But then was that a parcel of her woe,   part
For to herself full oft, "Alas!" said she,
Is there no ship, of so many as I see,
Will bringe home my lord? then were my heart
All warish'd of this bitter paine's smart."   cured[6]
Another time would she sit and think,
And cast her eyen downward from the brink;
But when she saw the grisly rockes blake,   black
For very fear so would her hearte quake,
That on her feet she might her not sustene   sustain
Then would she sit adown upon the green,
And piteously into the sea behold,   look out on the sea
And say right thus, with careful sikes cold: painful sighs
"Eternal God! that through thy purveyance
Leadest this world by certain governance,
In idle, as men say, ye nothing make;   idly, in vain
But, Lord, these grisly fiendly rockes blake,
That seem rather a foul confusion
Of work, than any fair creation
Of such a perfect wise God and stable,
Why have ye wrought this work unreasonable?
For by this work, north, south, or west, or east,
There is not foster'd man, nor bird, nor beast:
It doth no good, to my wit, but annoyeth.   works mischief[7]
See ye not, Lord, how mankind it destroyeth?
A hundred thousand bodies of mankind
Have rockes slain, all be they not in mind;   though they are
Which mankind is so fair part of thy work,   forgotten
Thou madest it like to thine owen mark.   image
Then seemed it ye had a great cherte   love, affection
Toward mankind; but how then may it be
That ye such meanes make it to destroy?
Which meanes do no good, but ever annoy.
I wot well, clerkes will say as them lest,   please
By arguments, that all is for the best,
Although I can the causes not y-know;
But thilke God that made the wind to blow, that
As keep my lord, this is my conclusion:
To clerks leave I all disputation:
But would to God that all these rockes blake
Were sunken into helle for his sake
These rockes slay mine hearte for the fear."
Thus would she say, with many a piteous tear.

Her friendes saw that it was no disport
To roame by the sea, but discomfort,
And shope them for to playe somewhere else.   arranged
They leade her by rivers and by wells,
And eke in other places delectables;
They dancen, and they play at chess and tables.   backgammon
So on a day, right in the morning-tide,
Unto a garden that was there beside,
In which that they had made their ordinance   provision, arrangement
Of victual, and of other purveyance,
They go and play them all the longe day:
And this was on the sixth morrow of May,
Which May had painted with his softe showers
This garden full of leaves and of flowers:
And craft of manne's hand so curiously
Arrayed had this garden truely,
That never was there garden of such price,   value, praise
But if it were the very Paradise.   unless
Th'odour of flowers, and the freshe sight,
Would have maked any hearte light
That e'er was born, but if too great sickness   unless
Or too great sorrow held it in distress;
So full it was of beauty and pleasance.
And after dinner they began to dance
And sing also, save Dorigen alone
Who made alway her complaint and her moan,
For she saw not him on the dance go
That was her husband, and her love also;
But natheless she must a time abide
And with good hope let her sorrow slide.

Upon this dance, amonge other men,
Danced a squier before Dorigen
That fresher was, and jollier of array
As to my doom, than is the month of May.   in my judgment
He sang and danced, passing any man,
That is or was since that the world began;
Therewith he was, if men should him descrive,
One of the beste faring men alive,   most accomplished
Young, strong, and virtuous, and rich, and wise,
And well beloved, and holden in great price.   esteem, value

And, shortly if the sooth I telle shall,
Unweeting of this Dorigen at all, unknown to
This lusty squier, servant to Venus,
Which that y-called was Aurelius,
Had lov'd her best of any creature
Two year and more, as was his aventure; fortune
But never durst he tell her his grievance;
Withoute cup he drank all his penance.
He was despaired, nothing durst he say,
Save in his songes somewhat would he wray betray
His woe, as in a general complaining;
He said, he lov'd, and was belov'd nothing.
Of suche matter made he many lays,
Songes, complaintes, roundels, virelays[8]
How that he durste not his sorrow tell,
But languished, as doth a Fury in hell;
And die he must, he said, as did Echo
For Narcissus, that durst not tell her woe.
In other manner than ye hear me say,
He durste not to her his woe bewray,
Save that paraventure sometimes at dances,
Where younge folke keep their observances,
It may well be he looked on her face
In such a wise, as man that asketh grace,
But nothing wiste she of his intent.
Nath'less it happen'd, ere they thennes went, thence (from the
Because that he was her neighebour, garden)
And was a man of worship and honour,
And she had known him of time yore, for a long time
They fell in speech, and forth aye more and more
Unto his purpose drew Aurelius;
And when he saw his time, he saide thus:
Madam," quoth he, "by God that this world made,
So that I wist it might your hearte glade, gladden
I would, that day that your Arviragus
Went over sea, that I, Aurelius,
Had gone where I should never come again;
For well I wot my service is in vain.
My guerdon is but bursting of mine heart. reward
Madame, rue upon my paine's smart,
For with a word ye may me slay or save.
Here at your feet God would that I were grave.
I have now no leisure more to say:
Have mercy, sweet, or you will do me dey." cause me to die

She gan to look upon Aurelius;
"Is this your will," quoth she, "and say ye thus?
Ne'er erst," quoth she, "I wiste what ye meant: before
But now, Aurelius, I know your intent.
By thilke God that gave me soul and life, that
Never shall I be an untrue wife
In word nor work, as far as I have wit;
I will be his to whom that I am knit;

Take this for final answer as of me."
But after that in play thus saide she. playfully, in jest
"Aurelius," quoth she, "by high God above,
Yet will I grante you to be your love
(Since I you see so piteously complain);
Looke, what day that endelong Bretagne from end to end of
Ye remove all the rockes, stone by stone,
That they not lette ship nor boat to gon, prevent
I say, when ye have made this coast so clean
Of rockes, that there is no stone seen,
Then will I love you best of any man;
Have here my troth, in all that ever I can;
For well I wot that it shall ne'er betide.
Let such folly out of your hearte glide.
What dainty should a man have in his life value, pleasure
For to go love another manne's wife,
That hath her body when that ever him liketh?"
Aurelius full often sore siketh; sigheth
Is there none other grace in you?" quoth he,
"No, by that Lord," quoth she, "that maked me.
Woe was Aurelius when that he this heard,
And with a sorrowful heart he thus answer'd.
"Madame, quoth he, "this were an impossible.
Then must I die of sudden death horrible."
And with that word he turned him anon.

Then came her other friends many a one,
And in the alleys roamed up and down,
And nothing wist of this conclusion,
But suddenly began to revel new,
Till that the brighte sun had lost his hue,
For th' horizon had reft the sun his light
(This is as much to say as it was night);
And home they go in mirth and in solace;
Save only wretch'd Aurelius, alas
He to his house is gone with sorrowful heart.
He said, he may not from his death astart. escape
Him seemed, that he felt his hearte cold.
Up to the heav'n his handes gan he hold,
And on his knees bare he set him down.
And in his raving said his orisoun. prayer
For very woe out of his wit he braid; wandered
He wist not what he spake, but thus he said;
With piteous heart his plaint hath he begun
Unto the gods, and first unto the Sun.
He said; "Apollo God and governour
Of every plante, herbe, tree, and flower,
That giv'st, after thy declination,
To each of them his time and his season,
As thine herberow changeth low and high; dwelling, situation
Lord Phoebus: cast thy merciable eye
On wretched Aurelius, which that am but lorn. undone
Lo, lord, my lady hath my death y-sworn,
Withoute guilt, but thy benignity unless

GEOFFREY CHAUCER

Upon my deadly heart have some pity.
For well I wot, Lord Phoebus, if you lest, please
Ye may me helpe, save my lady, best.
Now vouchsafe, that I may you devise tell, explain
How that I may be holp, and in what wise. helped
Your blissful sister, Lucina the sheen,[9]
That of the sea is chief goddess and queen, —
Though Neptunus have deity in the sea,
Yet emperess above him is she; —
Ye know well, lord, that, right as her desire
Is to be quick'd and lighted of your fire, quickened
For which she followeth you full busily,
Right so the sea desireth naturally
To follow her, as she that is goddess
Both in the sea and rivers more and less.
Wherefore, Lord Phoebus, this is my request,
Do this miracle, or do mine hearte brest; cause my heart
That flow, next at this opposition, to burst
Which in the sign shall be of the Lion,
As praye her so great a flood to bring,
That five fathom at least it overspring
The highest rock in Armoric Bretagne,
And let this flood endure yeares twain:
Then certes to my lady may I say,
"Holde your hest," the rockes be away.
Lord Phoebus, this miracle do for me,
Pray her she go no faster course than ye;
I say this, pray your sister that she go
No faster course than ye these yeares two:
Then shall she be even at full alway,
And spring-flood laste bothe night and day.
And but she vouchesafe in such mannere if she do not
To grante me my sov'reign lady dear,
Pray her to sink every rock adown
Into her owen darke regioun
Under the ground, where Pluto dwelleth in
Or nevermore shall I my lady win.
Thy temple in Delphos will I barefoot seek.
Lord Phoebus! see the teares on my cheek
And on my pain have some compassioun."
And with that word in sorrow he fell down,
And longe time he lay forth in a trance.
His brother, which that knew of his penance, distress
Up caught him, and to bed he hath him brought,
Despaired in this torment and this thought
Let I this woeful creature lie;
Choose he for me whe'er he will live or die. whether

Arviragus with health and great honour
(As he that was of chivalry the flow'r)
Is come home, and other worthy men.
Oh, blissful art thou now, thou Dorigen!

Thou hast thy lusty husband in thine arms,
The freshe knight, the worthy man of arms,
That loveth thee as his own hearte's life:
Nothing list him to be imaginatif he cared not to fancy
If any wight had spoke, while he was out,
To her of love; he had of that no doubt; fear, suspicion
He not intended to no such mattere, occupied himself with
But danced, jousted, and made merry cheer.
And thus in joy and bliss I let them dwell,
And of the sick Aurelius will I tell
In languor and in torment furious
Two year and more lay wretch'd Aurelius,
Ere any foot on earth he mighte gon;
Nor comfort in this time had he none,
Save of his brother, which that was a clerk. scholar
He knew of all this woe and all this work;
For to none other creature certain
Of this matter he durst no worde sayn;
Under his breast he bare it more secree
Than e'er did Pamphilus for Galatee.[10]
His breast was whole withoute for to seen,
But in his heart aye was the arrow keen,
And well ye know that of a sursanure[11]
In surgery is perilous the cure,
But men might touch the arrow or come thereby. except
His brother wept and wailed privily,
Till at the last him fell in remembrance,
That while he was at Orleans[12] in France, —
As younge clerkes, that be likerous — eager
To readen artes that be curious,
Seeken in every halk and every hern nook and corner[13]
Particular sciences for to learn,—
He him remember'd, that upon a day
At Orleans in study a book he say saw
Of magic natural, which his fellaw,
That was that time a bachelor of law
All were he there to learn another craft, though
Had privily upon his desk y-laft;
Which book spake much of operations
Touching the eight and-twenty mansions
That longe to the Moon, and such folly
As in our dayes is not worth a fly;
For holy church's faith, in our believe, belief, creed
Us suff'reth none illusion to grieve.
And when this book was in his remembrance
Anon for joy his heart began to dance,
And to himself he saide privily;
"My brother shall be warish'd hastily cured
For I am sicker that there be sciences, certain
By which men make divers apparences,
Such as these subtle tregetoures play. tricksters[14]
For oft at feaste's have I well heard say,

That tregetours, within a halle large,
Have made come in a water and a barge,
And in the halle rowen up and down.
Sometimes hath seemed come a grim lioun,
And sometimes flowers spring as in a mead;
Sometimes a vine, and grapes white and red;
Sometimes a castle all of lime and stone;
And, when them liked, voided it anon: vanished
Thus seemed it to every manne's sight.
Now then conclude I thus; if that I might
At Orleans some olde fellow find,
That hath these Moone's mansions in mind,
Or other magic natural above.
He should well make my brother have his love.
For with an appearance a clerk may make, learned man
To manne's sight, that all the rockes blake
Of Bretagne were voided every one, removed
And shippes by the brinke come and gon,
And in such form endure a day or two;
Then were my brother warish'd of his woe, cured
Then must she needes holde her behest, keep her promise
Or elles he shall shame her at the least."
Why should I make a longer tale of this?
Unto his brother's bed he comen is,
And such comfort he gave him, for to gon
To Orleans, that he upstart anon,
And on his way forth-ward then is he fare, gone
In hope for to be lissed of his care. eased of[15]

When they were come almost to that city,
But if it were a two furlong or three, all but
A young clerk roaming by himself they met,
Which that in Latin thriftily them gret. greeted them
And after that he said a wondrous thing; civilly
I know," quoth he, "the cause of your coming;"
Aud ere they farther any foote went,
He told them all that was in their intent.
The Breton clerk him asked of fellows
The which he hadde known in olde daws, days
And he answer'd him that they deade were,
For which he wept full often many a tear.
Down off his horse Aurelius light anon,
And forth with this magician is be gone
Home to his house, and made him well at ease;
Them lacked no vitail that might them please. victuals, food
So well-array'd a house as there was one,
Aurelius in his life saw never none.
He shewed him, ere they went to suppere,
Forestes, parkes, full of wilde deer.
There saw he hartes with their hornes high,
The greatest that were ever seen with eye.
He saw of them an hundred slain with hounds,
And some with arrows bleed of bitter wounds.
He saw, when voided were the wilde deer, passed away

These falconers upon a fair rivere,
That with their hawkes have the heron slain.
Then saw he knightes jousting in a plain.
And after this he did him such pleasance,
That he him shew'd his lady on a dance,
In which himselfe danced, as him thought.
And when this master, that this magic wrought,
Saw it was time, he clapp'd his handes two,
And farewell, all the revel is y-go. gone, removed
And yet remov'd they never out of the house,
While they saw all the sightes marvellous;
But in his study, where his bookes be,
They satte still, and no wight but they three.
To him this master called his squier,
And said him thus, "May we go to supper?
Almost an hour it is, I undertake,
Since I you bade our supper for to make,
When that these worthy men wente with me
Into my study, where my bookes be."
"Sir," quoth this squier, "when it liketh you.
It is all ready, though ye will right now."
"Go we then sup," quoth he, "as for the best;
These amorous folk some time must have rest."
At after supper fell they in treaty
What summe should this master's guerdon be, reward
To remove all the rockes of Bretagne,
And eke from Gironde[16] to the mouth of Seine.
He made it strange, and swore, so God him save, a matter of
Less than a thousand pound he would not have, difficulty
Nor gladly for that sum he would not gon. see note[17]
Aurelius with blissful heart anon
Answered thus; "Fie on a thousand pound!
This wide world, which that men say is round,
I would it give, if I were lord of it.
This bargain is full-driv'n, for we be knit; agreed
Ye shall be payed truly by my troth.
But looke, for no negligence or sloth,
Ye tarry us here no longer than to-morrow."
"Nay," quoth the clerk, "have here my faith to borrow." I pledge my
To bed is gone Aurelius when him lest, faith on it
And well-nigh all that night he had his rest,
What for his labour, and his hope of bliss,
His woeful heart of penance had a liss. had a respite from suffering
Upon the morrow, when that it was day,
Unto Bretagne they took the righte way,
Aurelius and this magician beside,
And be descended where they would abide:
And this was, as the bookes me remember,
The colde frosty season of December.
Phoebus wax'd old, and hued like latoun, brass
That in his hote declinatioun
Shone as the burned gold, with streames bright;

beams
But now in Capricorn adown he light,
Where as he shone full pale, I dare well sayn.
The bitter frostes, with the sleet and rain,
Destroyed have the green in every yard. courtyard, garden
Janus sits by the fire with double beard,
And drinketh of his bugle horn the wine:
Before him stands the brawn of tusked swine
And "nowel" crieth every lusty man Noel[18]
Aurelius, in all that ev'r he can,
Did to his master cheer and reverence,
And prayed him to do his diligence
To bringe him out of his paines smart,
Or with a sword that he would slit his heart.
This subtle clerk such ruth had on this man, pity
That night and day he sped him, that he can,
To wait a time of his conclusion;
This is to say, to make illusion,
By such an appearance of jugglery
(I know no termes of astrology),
That she and every wight should ween and say,
That of Bretagne the rockes were away,
Or else they were sunken under ground.
So at the last he hath a time found
To make his japes and his wretchedness tricks
Of such a superstitious cursedness. detestable villainy
His tables Toletanes[19] forth he brought,
Full well corrected, that there lacked nought,
Neither his collect, nor his expanse years,
Neither his rootes, nor his other gears,
As be his centres, and his arguments,
And his proportional conveniens
For his equations in everything.
And by his eighte spheres in his working,
He knew full well how far Alnath[20] was shove
From the head of that fix'd Aries above,
That in the ninthe sphere consider'd is.
Full subtily he calcul'd all this.
When he had found his firste mansion,
He knew the remnant by proportion;
And knew the rising of his moone well,
And in whose face, and term, and every deal;
And knew full well the moone's mansion
Accordant to his operation;
And knew also his other observances,
For such illusions and such meschances, wicked devices
As heathen folk used in thilke days.
For which no longer made he delays;
But through his magic, for a day or tway,[21]
It seemed all the rockes were away.

Aurelius, which yet despaired is
Whe'er he shall have his love, or fare amiss, whether
Awaited night and day on this miracle:
And when he knew that there was none obstacle,
That voided were these rockes every one, removed
Down at his master's feet he fell anon,
And said; "I, woeful wretch'd Aurelius,
Thank you, my Lord, and lady mine Venus,
That me have holpen from my cares cold."
And to the temple his way forth hath he hold,
Where as he knew he should his lady see.
And when he saw his time, anon right he
With dreadful heart and with full humble cheer fearful mien
Saluteth hath his sovereign lady dear.
"My rightful Lady," quoth this woeful man,
"Whom I most dread, and love as I best can,
And lothest were of all this world displease,
Were't not that I for you have such disease, distress, affliction
That I must die here at your foot anon,
Nought would I tell how me is woebegone.
But certes either must I die or plain; bewail
Ye slay me guilteless for very pain.
But of my death though that ye have no ruth,
Advise you, ere that ye break your truth:
Repente you, for thilke God above,
Ere ye me slay because that I you love.
For, Madame, well ye wot what ye have hight; promised
Not that I challenge anything of right
Of you, my sovereign lady, but of grace:
But in a garden yond', in such a place,
Ye wot right well what ye behighte me, promised
And in mine hand your trothe plighted ye,
To love me best; God wot ye saide so,
Albeit that I unworthy am thereto;
Madame, I speak it for th' honour of you,
More than to save my hearte's life right now;
I have done so as ye commanded me,
And if ye vouchesafe, ye may go see.
Do as you list, have your behest in mind,
For, quick or dead, right there ye shall me find;
In you hes all to do me live or dey; cause me to
But well I wot the rockes be away." live or die

He took his leave, and she astonish'd stood;
In all her face was not one drop of blood:
She never ween'd t'have come in such a trap.
"Alas!" quoth she, "that ever this should hap!
For ween'd I ne'er, by possibility,
That such a monster or marvail might be;
It is against the process of nature."
And home she went a sorrowful creature;
For very fear unnethes may she go. scarcely
She weeped, wailed, all a day or two,
And swooned, that it ruthe was to see:
But why it was, to no wight tolde she,
For out of town was gone Arviragus.
But to herself she spake, and saide thus,
With face pale, and full sorrowful cheer,
In her complaint, as ye shall after hear.

"Alas!" quoth she, "on thee, Fortune, I plain, complain
That unware hast me wrapped in thy chain,
From which to scape, wot I no succour,
Save only death, or elles dishonour;
One of these two behoveth me to choose.
But natheless, yet had I lever lose sooner, rather
My life, than of my body have shame,
Or know myselfe false, or lose my name;
And with my death I may be quit y-wis. I may certainly purchase
Hath there not many a noble wife, ere this, my exemption
And many a maiden, slain herself, alas!
Rather than with her body do trespass?
Yes, certes; lo, these stories bear witness.22
When thirty tyrants full of cursedness wickedness
Had slain Phidon in Athens at the feast,
They commanded his daughters to arrest,
And bringe them before them, in despite,
All naked, to fulfil their foul delight;
And in their father's blood they made them dance
Upon the pavement, — God give them mischance.
For which these woeful maidens, full of dread,
Rather than they would lose their maidenhead,
They privily be start into a well, suddenly leaped
And drowned themselves, as the bookes tell.
They of Messene let inquire and seek
Of Lacedaemon fifty maidens eke,
On which they woulde do their lechery:
But there was none of all that company
That was not slain, and with a glad intent
Chose rather for to die, than to assent
To be oppressed of her maidenhead. forcibly bereft
Why should I then to dien be in dread?
Lo, eke the tyrant Aristoclides,
That lov'd a maiden hight Stimphalides,
When that her father slain was on a night,
Unto Diana's temple went she right,
And hent the image in her handes two, caught, clasped
From which image she woulde never go;
No wight her handes might off it arace, pluck away by force
Till she was slain right in the selfe place. same
Now since that maidens hadde such despite
To be defouled with man's foul delight,
Well ought a wife rather herselfe to sle, slay
Than be defouled, as it thinketh me.
What shall I say of Hasdrubale's wife,
That at Carthage bereft herself of life?
For, when she saw the Romans win the town,
She took her children all, and skipt adown
Into the fire, and rather chose to die,
Than any Roman did her villainy.
Hath not Lucretia slain herself, alas!
At Rome, when that she oppressed was ravished
Of Tarquin? for her thought it was a shame
To live, when she hadde lost her name.
The seven maidens of Milesie also
Have slain themselves for very dread and woe,
Rather than folk of Gaul them should oppress.
More than a thousand stories, as I guess,
Could I now tell as touching this mattere.
When Abradate was slain, his wife so dear23
Herselfe slew, and let her blood to glide
In Abradate's woundes, deep and wide,
And said, 'My body at the leaste way
There shall no wight defoul, if that I may.'
Why should I more examples hereof sayn?
Since that so many have themselves slain,
Well rather than they would defouled be,
I will conclude that it is bet for me better
To slay myself, than be defouled thus.
I will be true unto Arviragus,
Or elles slay myself in some mannere,
As did Demotione's daughter dear,
Because she woulde not defouled be.
O Sedasus, it is full great pity
To reade how thy daughters died, alas!
That slew themselves for suche manner cas. in circumstances of
As great a pity was it, or well more, the same kind
The Theban maiden, that for Nicanor
Herselfe slew, right for such manner woe.
Another Theban maiden did right so;
For one of Macedon had her oppress'd,
She with her death her maidenhead redress'd. vindicated
What shall I say of Niceratus' wife,
That for such case bereft herself her life?
How true was eke to Alcibiades
His love, that for to dien rather chese, chose
Than for to suffer his body unburied be?
Lo, what a wife was Alceste?" quoth she.
"What saith Homer of good Penelope?
All Greece knoweth of her chastity.
Pardie, of Laedamia is written thus,
That when at Troy was slain Protesilaus,24
No longer would she live after his day.
The same of noble Porcia tell I may;
Withoute Brutus coulde she not live,
To whom she did all whole her hearte give.25
The perfect wifehood of Artemisie26
Honoured is throughout all Barbarie.
O Teuta27 queen, thy wifely chastity
To alle wives may a mirror be."28

Thus plained Dorigen a day or tway,
Purposing ever that she woulde dey; die
But natheless upon the thirde night
Home came Arviragus, the worthy knight,
And asked her why that she wept so sore.
And she gan weepen ever longer more.
"Alas," quoth she, "that ever I was born!
Thus have I said," quoth she; "thus have I

GEOFFREY CHAUCER

sworn."
And told him all, as ye have heard before:
It needeth not rehearse it you no more.
This husband with glad cheer, in friendly wise, demeanour
Answer'd and said, as I shall you devise. relate
"Is there aught elles, Dorigen, but this?"
"Nay, nay," quoth she, "God help me so, as wis assuredly
This is too much, an it were Godde's will." if
"Yea, wife," quoth he, "let sleepe what is still,
It may be well par'venture yet to-day.
Ye shall your trothe holde, by my fay.
For, God so wisly have mercy on me, certainly
I had well lever sticked for to be, I had rather be slain
For very love which I to you have,
But if ye should your trothe keep and save.
Truth is the highest thing that man may keep."
But with that word he burst anon to weep,
And said; "I you forbid, on pain of death,
That never, while you lasteth life or breath,
To no wight tell ye this misaventure;
As I may best, I will my woe endure,
Nor make no countenance of heaviness,
That folk of you may deeme harm, or guess."
And forth he call'd a squier and a maid.
"Go forth anon with Dorigen," he said,
"And bringe her to such a place anon."
They take their leave, and on their way they gon:
But they not wiste why she thither went;
He would to no wight telle his intent.

This squier, which that hight Aurelius,
On Dorigen that was so amorous,
Of aventure happen'd her to meet
Amid the town, right in the quickest street, nearest
As she was bound to go the way forthright prepared, going[29]
Toward the garden, there as she had hight. promised
And he was to the garden-ward also;
For well he spied when she woulde go
Out of her house, to any manner place;
But thus they met, of aventure or grace,
And he saluted her with glad intent,
And asked of her whitherward she went.
And she answered, half as she were mad,
"Unto the garden, as my husband bade,
My trothe for to hold, alas! alas!"
Aurelius gan to wonder on this case,
And in his heart had great compassion
Of her, and of her lamentation,
And of Arviragus, the worthy knight,
That bade her hold all that she hadde hight;
So loth him was his wife should break her truth troth, pledged word
And in his heart he caught of it great ruth, pity

Considering the best on every side,
That from his lust yet were him lever abide, see note[30]
Than do so high a churlish wretchedness wickedness
Against franchise, and alle gentleness; generosity
For which in fewe words he saide thus;
"Madame, say to your lord Arviragus,
That since I see the greate gentleness
Of him, and eke I see well your distress,
That him were lever have shame (and that were ruth) rather pity
Than ye to me should breake thus your truth,
I had well lever aye to suffer woe, forever
Than to depart the love betwixt you two. sunder, split up
I you release, Madame, into your hond,
Quit ev'ry surement and ev'ry bond, surety
That ye have made to me as herebeforn,
Since thilke time that ye were born.
Have here my truth, I shall you ne'er repreve reproach
Of no behest; and here I take my leave, of no (breach of)
As of the truest and the beste wife promise
That ever yet I knew in all my life.
But every wife beware of her behest;
On Dorigen remember at the least.
Thus can a squier do a gentle deed,
As well as can a knight, withoute drede." doubt

She thanked him upon her knees bare,
And home unto her husband is she fare, gone
And told him all, as ye have hearde said;
And, truste me, he was so well apaid, satisfied
That it were impossible me to write.
Why should I longer of this case indite?
Arviragus and Dorigen his wife
In sov'reign blisse ledde forth their life;
Ne'er after was there anger them between;
He cherish'd her as though she were a queen,
And she was to him true for evermore;
Of these two folk ye get of me no more.

Aurelius, that his cost had all forlorn, utterly lost
Cursed the time that ever he was born.
"Alas!" quoth he, "alas that I behight promised
Of pured gold a thousand pound of weight refined
To this philosopher! how shall I do?
I see no more, but that I am fordo. ruined, undone
Mine heritage must I needes sell,
And be a beggar; here I will not dwell,
And shamen all my kindred in this place,
But I of him may gette better grace. unless
But natheless I will of him assay
At certain dayes year by year to pay,
And thank him of his greate courtesy.
My trothe will I keep, I will not he."

With hearte sore he went unto his coffer,
And broughte gold unto this philosopher,
The value of five hundred pound, I guess,
And him beseeched, of his gentleness,
To grant him dayes of the remenant; time to pay up
And said; "Master, I dare well make avaunt,
I failed never of my truth as yet.
For sickerly my debte shall be quit
Towardes you how so that e'er I fare
To go a-begging in my kirtle bare:
But would ye vouchesafe, upon surety,
Two year, or three, for to respite me,
Then were I well, for elles must I sell
Mine heritage; there is no more to tell."

This philosopher soberly answer'd, gravely
And saide thus, when he these wordes heard;
"Have I not holden covenant to thee?"
"Yes, certes, well and truely," quoth he.
"Hast thou not had thy lady as thee liked?"
"No, no," quoth he, and sorrowfully siked. sighed
"What was the cause? tell me if thou can."
Aurelius his tale anon began,
And told him all as ye have heard before,
It needeth not to you rehearse it more.
He said, "Arviragus of gentleness
Had lever die in sorrow and distress, rather
Than that his wife were of her trothe false."
The sorrow of Dorigen he told him als', also
How loth her was to be a wicked wife,
And that she lever had lost that day her life;
And that her troth she swore through innocence;
She ne'er erst had heard speak of apparence before see note31
That made me have of her so great pity,
And right as freely as he sent her to me,
As freely sent I her to him again:
This is all and some, there is no more to sayn."

The philosopher answer'd; "Leve brother, dear
Evereach of you did gently to the other;
Thou art a squier, and he is a knight,
But God forbidde, for his blissful might,
But if a clerk could do a gentle deed
As well as any of you, it is no drede doubt
Sir, I release thee thy thousand pound,
As thou right now were crept out of the ground,
Nor ever ere now haddest knowen me.
For, Sir, I will not take a penny of thee
For all my craft, nor naught for my travail; labour, pains
Thou hast y-payed well for my vitaille;
It is enough; and farewell, have good day."
And took his horse, and forth he went his way.
Lordings, this question would I ask now,
Which was the moste free, as thinketh you? generous32
Now telle me, ere that ye farther wend.
I can no more, my tale is at an end. know, can tell

Notes to The Franklin's Tale

1. Well unnethes durst this knight for dread: This knight hardly dared, for fear (that she would not entertain his suit.)
2. "Ne woulde God never betwixt us twain, As in my guilt, were either war or strife" Would to God there may never be war or strife between us, through my fault.
3. Perhaps the true reading is "beteth" — prepares, makes ready, his wings for flight.
4. Penmark: On the west coast of Brittany, between Brest and L'Orient. The name is composed of two British words, "pen," mountain, and "mark," region; it therefore means the mountainous country
5. Cairrud: "The red city;" it is not known where it was situated.
6. Warished: cured; French, "guerir," to heal, or recover from sickness.
7. Annoyeth: works mischief; from Latin, "nocco," I hurt.
8. Virelays: ballads; the "virelai" was an ancient French poem of two rhymes.
9. Lucina the sheen: Diana the bright. See note 54 to the Knight's Tale.
10. In a Latin poem, very popular in Chaucer's time, Pamphilus relates his amour with Galatea, setting out with the idea adopted by our poet in the lines that follow.
11. Sursanure: A wound healed on the surface, but festering beneath.
12. Orleans: Where there was a celebrated and very famous university, afterwards eclipsed by that of Paris. It was founded by Philip le Bel in 1312.
13. Every halk and every hern: Every nook and corner, Anglo-Saxon, "healc," a nook; "hyrn," a corner.
14. Tregetoures: tricksters, jugglers. The word is probably derived — in "treget," deceit or imposture — from the French "trebuchet," a military machine; since it is evident that much and elaborate machinery must have been employed to produce the effects afterwards described. Another derivation is from the Low Latin, "tricator," a deceiver.
15. Lissed of: eased of; released from; another form of "less" or "lessen."
16. Gironde: The river, formed by the union of the Dordogne and Garonne, on which Bourdeaux stands.

17. Nor gladly for that sum he would not gon: And even for that sum he would not willingly go to work.
18. "Noel," the French for Christmas — derived from "natalis," and signifying that on that day Christ was born — came to be used as a festive cry by the people on solemn occasions.
19. Tables Toletanes: Toledan tables; the astronomical tables composed by order Of Alphonso II, King of Castile, about 1250 and so called because they were adapted to the city of Toledo.
20. "Alnath," Says Mr Wright, was "the first star in the horns of Aries, whence the first mansion of the moon is named."
21. Another and better reading is "a week or two."
22. These stories are all taken from the book of St Jerome "Contra Jovinianum," from which the Wife of Bath drew so many of her ancient instances. See note 1 to the prologue to the Wife of Bath's Tale.
23. Panthea. Abradatas, King of Susa, was an ally of the Assyrians against Cyrus; and his wife was taken at the conquest of the Assyrian camp. Struck by the honourable treatment she received at the captors hands, Abradatas joined Cyrus, and fell in battle against his former alhes. His wife, inconsolable at his loss, slew herself immediately.
24. Protesilaus was the husband of Laedamia. She begged the gods, after his death, that but three hours' converse with him might be allowed her; the request was granted; and when her dead husband, at the expiry of the time, returned to the world of shades, she bore him company.
25. The daughter of Cato of Utica, Porcia married Marcus Brutus, the friend and the assassin of Julius Caesar; when her husband died by his own hand after the battle of Philippi, she committed suicide, it is said, by swallowing live coals — all other means having been removed by her friends.
26. Artemisia, Queen of Caria, who built to her husband Mausolus, the splendid monument which was accounted among the wonders of the world; and who mingled her husband's ashes with her daily drink. "Barbarie" is used in the Greek sense, to designate the non-Hellenic peoples of Asia.
27. Teuta: Queen of Illyria, who, after her husband's death, made war on and was conquered by the Romans, B.C 228.
28. At this point, in some manuscripts, occur thefollowing two
   lines: —
   "The same thing I say of Bilia,
   Of Rhodegone and of Valeria."
29. Bound: prepared; going. To "boun" or "bown" is a good old word, whence comes our word "bound," in the sense of "on the way."
30. That from his lust yet were him lever abide: He would rather do without his pleasure.
31. Such apperence: such an ocular deception, or apparition — more properly, disappearance — as the removal of the rocks.
32. The same question is stated a the end of Boccaccio's version of the story in the "Philocopo," where the queen determines in favour of Aviragus. The question is evidently one of those which it was the fashion to propose for debate in the mediaeval "courts of love."

THE DOCTOR'S TALE.

THE PROLOGUE.[1]

["YEA, let that passe," quoth our Host, "as now.
Sir Doctor of Physik, I praye you,
Tell us a tale of some honest mattere."
"It shall be done, if that ye will it hear,"
Said this Doctor; and his tale gan anon.
"Now, good men," quoth he, "hearken everyone."]

Notes to the Prologue to the Doctor's Tale

1. The authenticity of the prologue is questionable. It is found in one manuscript only; other manuscripts give other prologues, more plainly not Chaucer's than this; and some manuscripts have merely a colophon to the effect that "Here endeth the Franklin's Tale and beginneth the Physician's Tale without a prologue." The Tale itself is the well-known story of Virginia, with several departures from the text of Livy. Chaucer probably followed the "Romance of the Rose" and Gower's "Confessio Amantis," in both of which the story is found.

THE TALE.

There was, as telleth Titus Livius,[1]
A knight, that called was Virginius,
Full filled of honour and worthiness,
And strong of friendes, and of great richess.
This knight one daughter hadde by his wife;
No children had he more in all his life.
Fair was this maid in excellent beauty
Aboven ev'ry wight that man may see:
For nature had with sov'reign diligence
Y-formed her in so great excellence,
As though she woulde say, "Lo, I, Nature,
Thus can I form and paint a creature,
When that me list; who can me counterfeit?
Pygmalion? not though he aye forge and beat,
Or grave or painte: for I dare well sayn,
Apelles, Zeuxis, shoulde work in vain,
Either to grave, or paint, or forge, or beat,
If they presumed me to counterfeit.
For he that is the former principal,
Hath made me his vicar-general
To form and painten earthly creatures
Right as me list, and all thing in my cure is,   *care*
Under the moone, that may wane and wax.
And for my work right nothing will I ax   *ask*
My lord and I be full of one accord.
I made her to the worship of my lord;
So do I all mine other creatures,
What colour that they have, or what figures."
Thus seemeth me that Nature woulde say.

This maiden was of age twelve year and tway,   *two*
In which that Nature hadde such delight.
For right as she can paint a lily white,
And red a rose, right with such painture
She painted had this noble creature,
Ere she was born, upon her limbes free,
Where as by right such colours shoulde be:
And Phoebus dyed had her tresses great,
Like to the streames of his burned heat.   *beams, rays*
And if that excellent was her beauty,
A thousand-fold more virtuous was she.
In her there lacked no condition,
That is to praise, as by discretion.
As well in ghost as body chaste was she: *mind, spirit*
For which she flower'd in virginity,
With all humility and abstinence,
With alle temperance and patience,
With measure eke of bearing and array.   *moderation*
Discreet she was in answering alway,
Though she were wise as Pallas, dare I sayn;
Her faconde eke full womanly and plain,   *speech*[2]
No counterfeited termes hadde she
To seeme wise; but after her degree
She spake, and all her worde's more and less
Sounding in virtue and in gentleness.
Shamefast she was in maiden's shamefastness,
Constant in heart, and ever in business diligent,   *eager*
To drive her out of idle sluggardy:
Bacchus had of her mouth right no mast'ry.
For wine and slothe[3] do Venus increase,
As men in fire will casten oil and grease.
And of her owen virtue, unconstrain'd,
She had herself full often sick y-feign'd,
For that she woulde flee the company,

GEOFFREY CHAUCER

Where likely was to treaten of folly,
As is at feasts, at revels, and at dances,
That be occasions of dalliances.
Such thinges make children for to be
Too soone ripe and bold, as men may see,
Which is full perilous, and hath been yore; of old
For all too soone may she learne lore
Of boldeness, when that she is a wife.

And ye mistresses, in your olde life governesses,
  duennas
That lordes' daughters have in governance,
Take not of my wordes displeasance
Thinke that ye be set in governings
Of lordes' daughters only for two things;
Either for ye have kept your honesty,
Or else for ye have fallen in frailty
And knowe well enough the olde dance,
And have forsaken fully such meschance
  wickedness[4]
For evermore; therefore, for Christe's sake,
To teach them virtue look that ye not slake. be
  slack, fail
A thief of venison, that hath forlaft forsaken, left
His lik'rousness, and all his olde craft, gluttony
Can keep a forest best of any man;
Now keep them well, for if ye will ye can.
Look well, that ye unto no vice assent,
Lest ye be damned for your wick' intent, wicked,
  evil
For whoso doth, a traitor is certain;
And take keep of that I shall you sayn; heed
Of alle treason, sov'reign pestilence
Is when a wight betrayeth innocence.
Ye fathers, and ye mothers eke also,
Though ye have children, be it one or mo',
Yours is the charge of all their surveyance,
  supervision
While that they be under your governance.
Beware, that by example of your living,
Or by your negligence in chastising,
That they not perish for I dare well say,
If that they do, ye shall it dear abeye. pay for,
  suffer for
Under a shepherd soft and negligent
The wolf hath many a sheep and lamb to-rent.
Suffice this example now as here,
For I must turn again to my mattere.

This maid, of which I tell my tale express,
She kept herself, her needed no mistress;
For in her living maidens mighte read,
As in a book, ev'ry good word and deed
That longeth to a maiden virtuous;
She was so prudent and so bounteous.
For which the fame out sprang on every side
Both of her beauty and her bounte wide:
  goodness
That through the land they praised her each one
That loved virtue, save envy alone,

That sorry is of other manne's weal,
And glad is of his sorrow and unheal —
  misfortune
The Doctor maketh this descriptioun. —[5]
This maiden on a day went in the town
Toward a temple, with her mother dear,
As is of younge maidens the mannere.
Now was there then a justice in that town,
That governor was of that regioun:
And so befell, this judge his eyen cast
Upon this maid, avising her full fast, observing
As she came forth by where this judge stood;
Anon his hearte changed and his mood,
So was he caught with beauty of this maid
And to himself full privily he said,
"This maiden shall be mine for any man." despite
  what any
Anon the fiend into his hearte ran, man may do
And taught him suddenly, that he by sleight
This maiden to his purpose winne might.
For certes, by no force, nor by no meed, bribe,
  reward
Him thought he was not able for to speed;
For she was strong of friendes, and eke she
Confirmed was in such sov'reign bounte,
That well he wist he might her never win,
As for to make her with her body sin.
For which, with great deliberatioun,
He sent after a clerk[6] was in the town,
The which he knew for subtle and for bold.
This judge unto this clerk his tale told
In secret wise, and made him to assure
He shoulde tell it to no creature,
And if he did, he shoulde lose his head.
And when assented was this cursed rede, counsel,
  plot
Glad was the judge, and made him greate cheer,
And gave him giftes precious and dear.
When shapen was all their conspiracy arranged
From point to point, how that his lechery
Performed shoulde be full subtilly,
As ye shall hear it after openly,
Home went this clerk, that highte Claudius.
This false judge, that highte Appius, —
(So was his name, for it is no fable,
But knowen for a storial thing notable; historical,
  authentic
The sentence of it sooth is out of doubt); —
  account true
This false judge went now fast about
To hasten his delight all that he may.
And so befell, soon after on a day,
This false judge, as telleth us the story,
As he was wont, sat in his consistory,
And gave his doomes upon sundry case';
  judgments
This false clerk came forth a full great pace, in
  haste
And saide; Lord, if that it be your will,

As do me right upon this piteous bill, petition
In which I plain upon Virginius.
And if that he will say it is not thus,
I will it prove, and finde good witness,
That sooth is what my bille will express."
The judge answer'd, "Of this, in his absence,
I may not give definitive sentence.
Let do him call, and I will gladly hear; cause
Thou shalt have alle right, and no wrong here."
Virginius came to weet the judge's will, know, learn
And right anon was read this cursed bill;
The sentence of it was as ye shall hear
"To you, my lord, Sir Appius so clear,
Sheweth your poore servant Claudius,
How that a knight called Virginius,
Against the law, against all equity,
Holdeth, express against the will of me,
My servant, which that is my thrall by right, slave
Which from my house was stolen on a night,
While that she was full young; I will it preve prove
By witness, lord, so that it you not grieve; be not displeasing
She is his daughter not, what so he say.
Wherefore to you, my lord the judge, I pray,
Yield me my thrall, if that it be your will."
Lo, this was all the sentence of the bill.
Virginius gan upon the clerk behold;
But hastily, ere he his tale told,
And would have proved it, as should a knight,
And eke by witnessing of many a wight,
That all was false that said his adversary,
This cursed judge would no longer tarry,
Nor hear a word more of Virginius,
But gave his judgement, and saide thus:
"I deem anon this clerk his servant have; pronounce, determine
Thou shalt no longer in thy house her save.
Go, bring her forth, and put her in our ward
The clerk shall have his thrall: thus I award."

And when this worthy knight, Virginius,
Through sentence of this justice Appius,
Muste by force his deare daughter give
Unto the judge, in lechery to live,
He went him home, and sat him in his hall,
And let anon his deare daughter call;
And with a face dead as ashes cold
Upon her humble face he gan behold,
With father's pity sticking through his heart, piercing
All would he from his purpose not convert. although turn aside
"Daughter," quoth he, "Virginia by name,
There be two wayes, either death or shame,
That thou must suffer, — alas that I was bore! born
For never thou deservedest wherefore

To dien with a sword or with a knife,
O deare daughter, ender of my life,
Whom I have foster'd up with such pleasance
That thou were ne'er out of my remembrance;
O daughter, which that art my laste woe,
And in this life my laste joy also,
O gem of chastity, in patience
Take thou thy death, for this is my sentence:
For love and not for hate thou must be dead;
My piteous hand must smiten off thine head.
Alas, that ever Appius thee say! saw
Thus hath he falsely judged thee to-day."
And told her all the case, as ye before
Have heard; it needeth not to tell it more.

"O mercy, deare father," quoth the maid.
And with that word she both her armes laid
About his neck, as she was wont to do,
(The teares burst out of her eyen two),
And said, "O goode father, shall I die?
Is there no grace? is there no remedy?"
"No, certes, deare daughter mine," quoth he.
"Then give me leisure, father mine, quoth she,
"My death for to complain a little space bewail
For, pardie, Jephthah gave his daughter grace
For to complain, ere he her slew, alas![7]
And, God it wot, nothing was her trespass, offence
But for she ran her father first to see,
To welcome him with great solemnity."
And with that word she fell a-swoon anon;
And after, when her swooning was y-gone,
She rose up, and unto her father said:
"Blessed be God, that I shall die a maid.
Give me my death, ere that I have shame;
Do with your child your will, in Godde's name."
And with that word she prayed him full oft
That with his sword he woulde smite her soft;
And with that word, a-swoon again she fell.
Her father, with full sorrowful heart and fell, stern, cruel
Her head off smote, and by the top it hent, took
And to the judge he went it to present,
As he sat yet in doom in consistory. judgment

And when the judge it saw, as saith the story,
He bade to take him, and to hang him fast.
But right anon a thousand people in thrast rushed in
To save the knight, for ruth and for pity
For knowen was the false iniquity.
The people anon had suspect in this thing, suspicion
By manner of the clerke's challenging,
That it was by th'assent of Appius;
They wiste well that he was lecherous.
For which unto this Appius they gon,
And cast him in a prison right anon,
Where as he slew himself: and Claudius,
That servant was unto this Appius,

Was doomed for to hang upon a tree;
But that Virginius, of his pity,
So prayed for him, that he was exil'd;
And elles certes had he been beguil'd; see note[8]
The remenant were hanged, more and less,
That were consenting to this cursedness. *villainy*
Here men may see how sin hath his merite: *deserts*
Beware, for no man knows how God will smite
In no degree, nor in which manner wise

The worm of conscience may agrise *frighten, horrify*
Of wicked life, though it so privy be,
That no man knows thereof, save God and he;
For be he lewed man or elles lear'd, *ignorant learned*
He knows not how soon he shall be afear'd;
Therefore I rede you this counsel take, *advise*
Forsake sin, ere sinne you forsake.

Notes to the Doctor's Tale

1. Livy, Book iii. cap. 44, et seqq.
2. Faconde: utterance, speech; from Latin, "facundia," eloquence.
3. Slothe: other readings are "thought" and "youth."
4. Meschance: wickedness; French, "mechancete."
5. This line seems to be a kind of aside thrown in by Chaucer himself.
6. The various readings of this word are "churl," or "cherl," in the best manuscripts; "client" in the common editions, and "clerk" supported by two important manuscripts. "Client" would perhaps be the best reading, if it were not awkward for the metre; but between "churl" and "clerk" there can be little doubt that Mr Wright chose wisely when he preferred the second.
7. Judges xi. 37, 38. "And she said unto her father, Let . . . me alone two months, that I may go up and down upon the mountains, and bewail my virginity, I and my fellows. And he said, go."
8. Beguiled: "cast into gaol," according to Urry's explanation; though we should probably understand that, if Claudius had not been sent out of the country, his death would have been secretly contrived through private detestation.

THE PARDONER'S TALE.

THE PROLOGUE.

OUR Hoste gan to swear as he were wood;
"Harow!" quoth he, "by nailes and by blood,[1]
This was a cursed thief, a false justice.
As shameful death as hearte can devise
Come to these judges and their advoca's.   *advocates, counsellors*
Algate this sely maid is slain, alas!   *nevertheless innocent*
Alas! too deare bought she her beauty.
Wherefore I say, that all day man may see
That giftes of fortune and of nature
Be cause of death to many a creature.
Her beauty was her death, I dare well sayn;
Alas! so piteously as she was slain.
[Of bothe giftes, that I speak of now
Men have full often more harm than prow,]   *profit*
But truely, mine owen master dear,
This was a piteous tale for to hear;
But natheless, pass over; 'tis no force.   *no matter*
I pray to God to save thy gentle corse,   *body*
And eke thine urinals, and thy jordans,
Thine Hippocras, and eke thy Galliens,[2]
And every boist full of thy lectuary,   *box*[3]
God bless them, and our lady Sainte Mary.
So may I the', thou art a proper man,   *thrive*
And like a prelate, by Saint Ronian;
Said I not well? Can I not speak in term? in set form
But well I wot thou dost mine heart to erme,   *makest grieve*[4]
That I have almost caught a cardiacle: *heartache*[5]
By corpus Domini[6], but I have triacle,   *unless a remedy*
Or else a draught of moist and corny[7] ale,
Or but I hear anon a merry tale, unless
Mine heart is brost for pity of this maid.   *burst, broken*
Thou bel ami, thou Pardoner," he said,   *good friend*
"Tell us some mirth of japes right anon."   *jokes*
"It shall be done," quoth he, "by Saint Ronion.
But first," quoth he, "here at this ale-stake   *ale-house sign*[8]
I will both drink, and biten on a cake."
But right anon the gentles gan to cry,
"Nay, let him tell us of no ribaldry.
Tell us some moral thing, that we may lear   *learn*
Some wit, and thenne will we gladly hear."   *wisdom, sense*
"I grant y-wis," quoth he; "but I must think   *surely*
Upon some honest thing while that I drink."

Notes to the Prologue to the Pardoner's Tale

1. The nails and blood of Christ, by which it was then a fashion to swear.
2. Mediaeval medical writers; see note 36 to the Prologue to the Tales.
3. Boist: box; French "boite," old form "boiste."
4. Erme: grieve; from Anglo-Saxon, "earme," wretched.
5. Cardiacle: heartache; from Greek, "kardialgia."
6. Corpus Domini: God's body.
7. Corny ale: New and strong, nappy. As to "moist," see note 39 to the Prologue to the Tales.
8. (Transcriber's Note)In this scene the pilgrims are refreshing themselves at tables in front of an inn. The pardoner is drunk, which explains his boastful and revealing confession of his deceits.

THE TALE.[1]

Lordings (quoth he), in churche when I preach,
I paine me to have an hautein speech,   *take pains loud*[2]
And ring it out, as round as doth a bell,
For I know all by rote that I tell.
My theme is always one, and ever was;
Radix malorum est cupiditas.[3]
First I pronounce whence that I come,
And then my bulles shew I all and some;
Our liege lorde's seal on my patent,
That shew I first, my body to warrent,   *for the protection*
That no man be so hardy, priest nor clerk,   *of my person*
Me to disturb of Christe's holy werk.
And after that then tell I forth my tales.
Bulles of popes, and of cardinales,
Of patriarchs, and of bishops I shew,
And in Latin I speak a wordes few,
To savour with my predication,
And for to stir men to devotion
Then show I forth my longe crystal stones,

GEOFFREY CHAUCER

Y-crammed fall of cloutes and of bones; *rags, fragments*
Relics they be, as weene they each one. *as my listeners think*
Then have I in latoun a shoulder-bone *brass*
Which that was of a holy Jewe's sheep.
"Good men," say I, "take of my wordes keep; *heed*
If that this bone be wash'd in any well,
If cow, or calf, or sheep, or oxe swell,
That any worm hath eat, or worm y-stung,
Take water of that well, and wash his tongue,
And it is whole anon; and farthermore
Of pockes, and of scab, and every sore
Shall every sheep be whole, that of this well
Drinketh a draught; take keep of that I tell. *heed*

"If that the goodman, that the beastes oweth, *owneth*
Will every week, ere that the cock him croweth,
Fasting, y-drinken of this well a draught,
As thilke holy Jew our elders taught,
His beastes and his store shall multiply.
And, Sirs, also it healeth jealousy;
For though a man be fall'n in jealous rage,
Let make with this water his pottage,
And never shall he more his wife mistrist, *mistrust*
Though he the sooth of her defaulte wist; *though he truly*
All had she taken priestes two or three.[4] *knew her sin*
Here is a mittain eke, that ye may see; *glove, mitten*
He that his hand will put in this mittain,
He shall have multiplying of his grain,
When he hath sowen, be it wheat or oats,
So that he offer pence, or elles groats.
And, men and women, one thing warn I you;
If any wight be in this churche now
That hath done sin horrible, so that he
Dare not for shame of it y-shriven be; *confessed*
Or any woman, be she young or old,
That hath y-made her husband cokewold, *cuckold*
Such folk shall have no power nor no grace
To offer to my relics in this place.
And whoso findeth him out of such blame,
He will come up and offer in God's name;
And I assoil him by the authority *absolve*
Which that by bull y-granted was to me."

By this gaud have I wonne year by year *jest, trick*
A hundred marks, since I was pardonere.
I stande like a clerk in my pulpit,
And when the lewed people down is set, *ignorant*
I preache so as ye have heard before,
And telle them a hundred japes more. *jests, deceits*
Then pain I me to stretche forth my neck,
And east and west upon the people I beck,
As doth a dove, sitting on a bern; *barn*
My handes and my tongue go so yern, *briskly*
That it is joy to see my business.
Of avarice and of such cursedness *wickedness*
Is all my preaching, for to make them free
To give their pence, and namely unto me. *especially*
For mine intent is not but for to win,
And nothing for correction of sin.
I recke never, when that they be buried,
Though that their soules go a blackburied.[5]
For certes many a predication *preaching is often inspired*
Cometh oft-time of evil intention; *by evil motives*
Some for pleasance of folk, and flattery,
To be advanced by hypocrisy;
And some for vainglory, and some for hate.
For, when I dare not otherwise debate,
Then will I sting him with my tongue smart *sharply*
In preaching, so that he shall not astart *escape*
To be defamed falsely, if that he
Hath trespass'd to my brethren or to me. *offended*
For, though I telle not his proper name,
Men shall well knowe that it is the same
By signes, and by other circumstances.
Thus quite I folk that do us displeasances: *I am revenged on*
Thus spit I out my venom, under hue
Of holiness, to seem holy and true.
But, shortly mine intent I will devise,
I preach of nothing but of covetise.
Therefore my theme is yet, and ever was, —
Radix malorum est cupiditas.[3]
Thus can I preach against the same vice
Which that I use, and that is avarice.
But though myself be guilty in that sin,
Yet can I maken other folk to twin *depart*
From avarice, and sore them repent.
But that is not my principal intent;
I preache nothing but for covetise.
Of this mattere it ought enough suffice.
Then tell I them examples many a one,
Of olde stories longe time gone;
For lewed people love tales old; *unlearned*
Such thinges can they well report and hold.
What? trowe ye, that whiles I may preach
And winne gold and silver for I teach, *because*
That I will live in povert' wilfully?
Nay, nay, I thought it never truely.
For I will preach and beg in sundry lands;
I will not do no labour with mine hands,
Nor make baskets for to live thereby,
Because I will not beggen idly.
I will none of the apostles counterfeit; *imitate (in poverty)*
I will have money, wool, and cheese, and wheat,
All were it given of the poorest page, *even if*

Or of the pooreste widow in a village:
All should her children sterve for famine. die
Nay, I will drink the liquor of the vine,
And have a jolly wench in every town.
But hearken, lordings, in conclusioun;
Your liking is, that I shall tell a tale
Now I have drunk a draught of corny ale,
By God, I hope I shall you tell a thing
That shall by reason be to your liking;
For though myself be a full vicious man,
A moral tale yet I you telle can,
Which I am wont to preache, for to win.
Now hold your peace, my tale I will begin.

In Flanders whilom was a company
Of younge folkes, that haunted folly,
As riot, hazard, stewes, and taverns; brothels
Where as with lutes, harpes, and giterns, guitars
They dance and play at dice both day and night,
And eat also, and drink over their might;
Through which they do the devil sacrifice
Within the devil's temple, in cursed wise,
By superfluity abominable.
Their oathes be so great and so damnable,
That it is grisly for to hear them swear. dreadful[6]
Our blissful Lorde's body they to-tear; tore to pieces[7]
Them thought the Jewes rent him not enough,
And each of them at other's sinne lough. laughed
And right anon in come tombesteres[8]
Fetis and small, and younge fruitesteres. dainty fruit-girls
Singers with harpes, baudes, waferers, revellers cake-sellers
Which be the very devil's officers,
To kindle and blow the fire of lechery,
That is annexed unto gluttony.
The Holy Writ take I to my witness,
That luxury is in wine and drunkenness.[9]
Lo, how that drunken Lot unkindely unnaturally
Lay by his daughters two unwittingly,
So drunk he was he knew not what he wrought.
Herodes, who so well the stories sought,[10]
When he of wine replete was at his feast,
Right at his owen table gave his hest command
To slay the Baptist John full guilteless.
Seneca saith a good word, doubteless:
He saith he can no difference find
Betwixt a man that is out of his mind,
And a man whiche that is drunkelew: a drunkard[11]
But that woodness, y-fallen in a shrew, madness one evil-tempered
Persevereth longer than drunkenness.

O gluttony, full of all cursedness;
O cause first of our confusion,
Original of our damnation,
Till Christ had bought us with his blood again!
Looke, how deare, shortly for to sayn,
Abought was first this cursed villainy: atoned for
Corrupt was all this world for gluttony.
Adam our father, and his wife also,
From Paradise, to labour and to woe,
Were driven for that vice, it is no dread. doubt
For while that Adam fasted, as I read,
He was in Paradise; and when that he
Ate of the fruit defended of the tree, forbidden[12]
Anon he was cast out to woe and pain.
O gluttony! well ought us on thee plain.
Oh! wist a man how many maladies
Follow of excess and of gluttonies,
He woulde be the more measurable moderate
Of his diete, sitting at his table.
Alas! the shorte throat, the tender mouth,
Maketh that east and west, and north and south,
In earth, in air, in water, men do swink labour
To get a glutton dainty meat and drink.
Of this mattere, O Paul! well canst thou treat
Meat unto womb, and womb eke unto meat, belly
Shall God destroye both, as Paulus saith.[13]
Alas! a foul thing is it, by my faith,
To say this word, and fouler is the deed,
When man so drinketh of the white and red, i.e. wine
That of his throat he maketh his privy
Through thilke cursed superfluity
The apostle saith,[14] weeping full piteously,
There walk many, of which you told have I, —
I say it now weeping with piteous voice, —
That they be enemies of Christe's crois; cross
Of which the end is death; womb is their God. belly
O womb, O belly, stinking is thy cod, bag[15]
Full fill'd of dung and of corruptioun;
At either end of thee foul is the soun.
How great labour and cost is thee to find! supply
These cookes how they stamp, and strain, and grind,
And turne substance into accident,
To fulfill all thy likerous talent!
Out of the harde bones knocke they
The marrow, for they caste naught away
That may go through the gullet soft and swoot sweet
Of spicery and leaves, of bark and root,
Shall be his sauce y-maked by delight,
To make him have a newer appetite.
But, certes, he that haunteth such delices
Is dead while that he liveth in those vices.

A lecherous thing is wine, and drunkenness
Is full of striving and of wretchedness.
O drunken man! disfgur'd is thy face,[16]
Sour is thy breath, foul art thou to embrace:
And through thy drunken nose sowneth the soun',
As though thous saidest aye, Samsoun! Samsoun!

And yet, God wot, Samson drank never wine.
Thou fallest as it were a sticked swine;
Thy tongue is lost, and all thine honest cure; care
For drunkenness is very sepulture tomb
Of manne's wit and his discretion.
In whom that drink hath domination,
He can no counsel keep, it is no dread. doubt
Now keep you from the white and from the red,
And namely from the white wine of Lepe,[17] especially
That is to sell in Fish Street[18] and in Cheap.
This wine of Spaine creepeth subtilly —
In other wines growing faste by,
Of which there riseth such fumosity,
That when a man hath drunken draughtes three,
And weeneth that he be at home in Cheap,
He is in Spain, right at the town of Lepe,
Not at the Rochelle, nor at Bourdeaux town;
And thenne will he say, Samsoun! Samsoun!
But hearken, lordings, one word, I you pray,
That all the sovreign actes, dare I say,
Of victories in the Old Testament,
Through very God that is omnipotent,
Were done in abstinence and in prayere:
Look in the Bible, and there ye may it lear. learn
Look, Attila, the greate conqueror,
Died in his sleep,[19] with shame and dishonour,
Bleeding aye at his nose in drunkenness:
A captain should aye live in soberness
And o'er all this, advise you right well consider, bethink
What was commanded unto Lemuel;[20]
Not Samuel, but Lemuel, say I.
Reade the Bible, and find it expressly
Of wine giving to them that have justice.
No more of this, for it may well suffice.

And, now that I have spoke of gluttony,
Now will I you defende hazardry. forbid gambling
Hazard is very mother of leasings, lies
And of deceit, and cursed forswearings:
Blasphem' of Christ, manslaughter, and waste also
Of chattel and of time; and furthermo' property
It is repreve, and contrar' of honour, reproach
For to be held a common hazardour.
And ever the higher he is of estate,
The more he is holden desolate. undone, worthless
If that a prince use hazardry,
In alle governance and policy
He is, as by common opinion,
Y-hold the less in reputation.

Chilon, that was a wise ambassador,
Was sent to Corinth with full great honor
From Lacedemon,[21] to make alliance;
And when he came, it happen'd him, by chance,
That all the greatest that were of that land,
Y-playing atte hazard he them fand. found
For which, as soon as that it mighte be,
He stole him home again to his country
And saide there, "I will not lose my name,
Nor will I take on me so great diffame, reproach
You to ally unto no hazardors. gamblers
Sende some other wise ambassadors,
For, by my troth, me were lever die, rather
Than I should you to hazardors ally.
For ye, that be so glorious in honours,
Shall not ally you to no hazardours,
As by my will, nor as by my treaty."
This wise philosopher thus said he.
Look eke how to the King Demetrius
The King of Parthes, as the book saith us,
Sent him a pair of dice of gold in scorn,
For he had used hazard therebeforn:
For which he held his glory and renown
At no value or reputatioun.
Lordes may finden other manner play
Honest enough to drive the day away.

Now will I speak of oathes false and great
A word or two, as olde bookes treat.
Great swearing is a thing abominable,
And false swearing is more reprovable.
The highe God forbade swearing at all;
Witness on Matthew:[22] but in special
Of swearing saith the holy Jeremie,[23]
Thou thalt swear sooth thine oathes, and not lie:
And swear in doom and eke in righteousness; judgement
But idle swearing is a cursedness. wickedness
Behold and see, there in the firste table
Of highe Godde's hestes honourable, commandments
How that the second best of him is this,
Take not my name in idle or amiss. in vain
Lo, rather him forbiddeth such swearing, sooner
Than homicide, or many a cursed thing;
I say that as by order thus it standeth;
This knoweth he that his hests understandeth, commandments
How that the second hest of God is that.
And farthermore, I will thee tell all plat, flatly, plainly
That vengeance shall not parte from his house,
That of his oathes is outrageous.
"By Godde's precious heart, and by his nails,[24]
And by the blood of Christ, that is in Hailes,[25]
Seven is my chance, and thine is cinque and trey:
By Godde's armes, if thou falsely play,
This dagger shall throughout thine hearte go."
This fruit comes of the bicched bones two, two cursed bones (dice)
Forswearing, ire, falseness, and homicide.
Now, for the love of Christ that for us died,
Leave your oathes, bothe great and smale.
But, Sirs, now will I ell you forth my tale.

THE CANTERBURY TALES

These riotoures three, of which I tell,
Long erst than prime rang of any bell, before
Were set them in a tavern for to drink;
And as they sat, they heard a belle clink
Before a corpse, was carried to the grave.
That one of them gan calle to his knave, servant
"Go bet,"[26] quoth he, "and aske readily
What corpse is this, that passeth here forth by;
And look that thou report his name well."
"Sir," quoth the boy, "it needeth never a deal; whit
It was me told ere ye came here two hours;
He was, pardie, an old fellow of yours,
And suddenly he was y-slain to-night;
Fordrunk as he sat on his bench upright, completely drunk
There came a privy thief, men clepe Death,
That in this country all the people slay'th,
And with his spear he smote his heart in two,
And went his way withoute wordes mo'.
He hath a thousand slain this pestilence;
And, master, ere you come in his presence,
Me thinketh that it were full necessary
For to beware of such an adversary;
Be ready for to meet him evermore.
Thus taughte me my dame; I say no more."
"By Sainte Mary," said the tavernere,
"The child saith sooth, for he hath slain this year,
Hence ov'r a mile, within a great village,
Both man and woman, child, and hind, and page;
I trow his habitation be there;
To be advised great wisdom it were, watchful, on one's guard
Ere that he did a man a dishonour." lest

"Yea, Godde's armes," quoth this riotour,
"Is it such peril with him for to meet?
I shall him seek, by stile and eke by street.
I make a vow, by Godde's digne bones." worthy
Hearken, fellows, we three be alle ones: at one
Let each of us hold up his hand to other,
And each of us become the other's brother,
And we will slay this false traitor Death;
He shall be slain, he that so many slay'th,
By Godde's dignity, ere it be night."
Together have these three their trothe plight
To live and die each one of them for other
As though he were his owen sworen brother.
And up they start, all drunken, in this rage,
And forth they go towardes that village
Of which the taverner had spoke beforn,
And many a grisly oathe have they sworn, dreadful
And Christe's blessed body they to-rent; tore to pieces[7]
"Death shall be dead, if that we may him hent." catch
When they had gone not fully half a mile,
Right as they would have trodden o'er a stile,

An old man and a poore with them met.
This olde man full meekely them gret, greeted
And saide thus; "Now, lordes, God you see!" look on graciously
The proudest of these riotoures three
Answer'd again; "What? churl, with sorry grace,
Why art thou all forwrapped save thy face? closely wrapt up
Why livest thou so long in so great age?"
This olde man gan look on his visage,
And saide thus; "For that I cannot find
A man, though that I walked unto Ind,
Neither in city, nor in no village go,
That woulde change his youthe for mine age;
And therefore must I have mine age still
As longe time as it is Godde's will.
And Death, alas! he will not have my life.
Thus walk I like a resteless caitife, miserable wretch
And on the ground, which is my mother's gate,
I knocke with my staff, early and late,
And say to her, 'Leve mother, let me in. dear
Lo, how I wane, flesh, and blood, and skin;
Alas! when shall my bones be at rest?
Mother, with you I woulde change my chest,
That in my chamber longe time hath be,
Yea, for an hairy clout to wrap in me.' wrap myself in
But yet to me she will not do that grace,
For which fall pale and welked is my face. withered
But, Sirs, to you it is no courtesy
To speak unto an old man villainy,
But he trespass in word or else in deed. except
In Holy Writ ye may yourselves read;
'Against an old man, hoar upon his head, to meet
Ye should arise:' therefore I you rede, advise
Ne do unto an old man no harm now,
No more than ye would a man did you
In age, if that ye may so long abide.
And God be with you, whether ye go or ride
I must go thither as I have to go."

"Nay, olde churl, by God thou shalt not so,"
Saide this other hazardor anon;
"Thou partest not so lightly, by Saint John.
Thou spakest right now of that traitor Death,
That in this country all our friendes slay'th;
Have here my troth, as thou art his espy; spy
Tell where he is, or thou shalt it abie, suffer for
By God and by the holy sacrament;
For soothly thou art one of his assent
To slay us younge folk, thou false thief."
"Now, Sirs," quoth he, "if it be you so lief desire
To finde Death, turn up this crooked way,
For in that grove I left him, by my fay,
Under a tree, and there he will abide;
Nor for your boast he will him nothing hide.
See ye that oak? right there ye shall him find.

God save you, that bought again mankind,
And you amend!" Thus said this olde man;
And evereach of these riotoures ran,
Till they came to the tree, and there they found
Of florins fine, of gold y-coined round,
Well nigh a seven bushels, as them thought.
No longer as then after Death they sought;
But each of them so glad was of the sight,
For that the florins were so fair and bright,
That down they sat them by the precious hoard.
The youngest of them spake the firste word:
"Brethren," quoth he, "take keep what I shall say; heed
My wit is great, though that I bourde and play joke, frolic
This treasure hath Fortune unto us given
In mirth and jollity our life to liven;
And lightly as it comes, so will we spend.
Hey! Godde's precious dignity! who wend weened, thought
Today that we should have so fair a grace?
But might this gold be carried from this place
Home to my house, or elles unto yours
(For well I wot that all this gold is ours),
Then were we in high felicity.
But truely by day it may not be;
Men woulde say that we were thieves strong,
And for our owen treasure do us hong. have us hanged
This treasure muste carried be by night,
As wisely and as slily as it might.
Wherefore I rede, that cut among us all advise lots
We draw, and let see where the cut will fall:
And he that hath the cut, with hearte blithe
Shall run unto the town, and that full swithe, quickly
And bring us bread and wine full privily:
And two of us shall keepe subtilly
This treasure well: and if he will not tarry,
When it is night, we will this treasure carry,
By one assent, where as us thinketh best."
Then one of them the cut brought in his fist,
And bade them draw, and look where it would fall;
And it fell on the youngest of them all;
And forth toward the town he went anon.
And all so soon as that he was y-gone,
The one of them spake thus unto the other;
"Thou knowest well that thou art my sworn brother,
Thy profit will I tell thee right anon. what is for thine
Thou knowest well that our fellow is gone, advantage
And here is gold, and that full great plenty,
That shall departed be among us three. divided
But natheless, if I could shape it so contrive
That it departed were among us two,
Had I not done a friende's turn to thee?"

Th' other answer'd, "I n'ot how that may be; know not
He knows well that the gold is with us tway.
What shall we do? what shall we to him say?"
"Shall it be counsel?" said the firste shrew; secret wretch
"And I shall tell to thee in wordes few
What we shall do, and bring it well about."
"I grante," quoth the other, "out of doubt,
That by my truth I will thee not bewray." betray
"Now," quoth the first, "thou know'st well we be tway,
And two of us shall stronger be than one.
Look; when that he is set, thou right anon sat down
Arise, as though thou wouldest with him play;
And I shall rive him through the sides tway, stab
While that thou strugglest with him as in game;
And with thy dagger look thou do the same.
And then shall all this gold departed be, divided
My deare friend, betwixte thee and me:
Then may we both our lustes all fulfil, pleasures
And play at dice right at our owen will."
And thus accorded be these shrewes tway agreed wretches
To slay the third, as ye have heard me say.

The youngest, which that wente to the town,
Full oft in heart he rolled up and down
The beauty of these florins new and bright.
"O Lord!" quoth he, "if so were that I might
Have all this treasure to myself alone,
There is no man that lives under the throne
Of God, that shoulde have so merry as I."
And at the last the fiend our enemy
Put in his thought, that he should poison buy,
With which he mighte slay his fellows twy. two
For why, the fiend found him in such living, leading such a
That he had leave to sorrow him to bring. (bad) life
For this was utterly his full intent
To slay them both, and never to repent.
And forth he went, no longer would he tarry,
Into the town to an apothecary,
And prayed him that he him woulde sell
Some poison, that he might his rattes quell, kill his rats
And eke there was a polecat in his haw, farm-yard, hedge[27]
That, as he said, his capons had y-slaw: slain
And fain he would him wreak, if that he might, revenge
Of vermin that destroyed him by night.
Th'apothecary answer'd, "Thou shalt have
A thing, as wisly God my soule save, surely
In all this world there is no creature
That eat or drank hath of this confecture,
Not but the mountance of a corn of wheat,

amount
That he shall not his life anon forlete; immediately lay down
Yea, sterve he shall, and that in lesse while die
Than thou wilt go apace nought but a mile: quickly
This poison is so strong and violent."
This cursed man hath in his hand y-hent taken
This poison in a box, and swift he ran
Into the nexte street, unto a man,
And borrow'd of him large bottles three;
And in the two the poison poured he;
The third he kepte clean for his own drink,
For all the night he shope him for to swink purposed labour
In carrying off the gold out of that place.
And when this riotour, with sorry grace,
Had fill'd with wine his greate bottles three,

To his fellows again repaired he.
What needeth it thereof to sermon more? talk, discourse
For, right as they had cast his death before, plotted
Right so they have him slain, and that anon.
And when that this was done, thus spake the one;
"Now let us sit and drink, and make us merry,
And afterward we will his body bury."
And with that word it happen'd him par cas by chance
To take the bottle where the poison was,
And drank, and gave his fellow drink also,
For which anon they sterved both the two. died
But certes I suppose that Avicen
Wrote never in no canon, nor no fen,[28]
More wondrous signes of empoisoning,
Than had these wretches two ere their ending.
Thus ended be these homicides two,
And eke the false empoisoner also.

O cursed sin, full of all cursedness!
O trait'rous homicide! O wickedness!
O glutt'ny, luxury, and hazardry!
Thou blasphemer of Christ with villany, outrage, impiety
And oathes great, of usage and of pride!
Alas! mankinde, how may it betide,
That to thy Creator, which that thee wrought,
And with his precious hearte-blood thee bought,
Thou art so false and so unkind, alas! unnatural
Now, good men, God forgive you your trespass,
And ware you from the sin of avarice. keep
Mine holy pardon may you all warice, heal
So that ye offer nobles or sterlings, gold or silver coins
Or elles silver brooches, spoons, or rings.
Bowe your head under this holy bull.
Come up, ye wives, and offer of your will;
Your names I enter in my roll anon;
Into the bliss of heaven shall ye gon;

I you assoil by mine high powere, absolve[29]
You that will offer, as clean and eke as clear
As ye were born. Lo, Sires, thus I preach;
And Jesus Christ, that is our soules' leech, healer
So grante you his pardon to receive;
For that is best, I will not deceive.

But, Sirs, one word forgot I in my tale;
I have relics and pardon in my mail,
As fair as any man in Engleland,
Which were me given by the Pope's hand.
If any of you will of devotion
Offer, and have mine absolution,
Come forth anon, and kneele here adown
And meekely receive my pardoun.
Or elles take pardon, as ye wend, go
All new and fresh at every towne's end,
So that ye offer, always new and new,
Nobles or pence which that be good and true.
'Tis an honour to evereach that is here, each one
That ye have a suffisant pardonere suitable
T'assoile you in country as ye ride, absolve
For aventures which that may betide.
Paraventure there may fall one or two
Down of his horse, and break his neck in two.
Look, what a surety is it to you all,
That I am in your fellowship y-fall,
That may assoil you bothe more and lass, absolve
When that the soul shall from the body pass. great and small
I rede that our Hoste shall begin, advise
For he is most enveloped in sin.
Come forth, Sir Host, and offer first anon,
And thou shalt kiss; the relics every one,
Yea, for a groat; unbuckle anon thy purse.

"Nay, nay," quoth he, "then have I Christe's curse!
Let be," quoth he, "it shall not be, so the'ch. so may I thrive
Thou wouldest make me kiss thine olde breech,
And swear it were a relic of a saint,
Though it were with thy fundament depaint'. stained by your bottom
But, by the cross which that Saint Helen fand, found[30]
I would I had thy coilons in mine hand, testicles
Instead of relics, or of sanctuary.
Let cut them off, I will thee help them carry;
They shall be shrined in a hogge's turd."
The Pardoner answered not one word;
So wroth he was, no worde would he say.

"Now," quoth our Host, "I will no longer play
With thee, nor with none other angry man."
But right anon the worthy Knight began
(When that he saw that all the people lough), laughed
"No more of this, for it is right enough.
Sir Pardoner, be merry and glad of cheer;

And ye, Sir Host, that be to me so dear,
I pray you that ye kiss the Pardoner;
And, Pardoner, I pray thee draw thee ner, nearer
And as we didde, let us laugh and play."
Anon they kiss'd, and rode forth their way.

Notes to the Pardoner's Tale

1. The outline of this Tale is to be found in the "Cento Novelle Antiche," but the original is now lost. As in the case of the Wife of Bath's Tale, there is a long prologue, but in this case it has been treated as part of the Tale.
2. Hautein: loud, lofty; from French, "hautain."
3. Radix malorum est cupiditas: "the love of money is the root of all evil" (1 Tim.vi. 10)
4. All had she taken priestes two or three: even if she had committed adultery with two or three priests.
5. Blackburied: The meaning of this is not very clear, but it is probably a periphrastic and picturesque way of indicating damnation.
6. Grisly: dreadful; fitted to "agrise" or horrify the listener.
7. Mr Wright says: "The common oaths in the Middle Ages were by the different parts of God's body; and the popular preachers represented that profane swearers tore Christ's body by their imprecations." The idea was doubtless borrowed from the passage in Hebrews (vi. 6), where apostates are said to "crucify to themselves the Son of God afresh, and put Him to an open shame."
8. Tombesteres: female dancers or tumblers; from Anglo-Saxon, "tumban," to dance.
9. "Be not drunk with wine, wherein is excess." Eph. v.18.
10. The reference is probably to the diligent inquiries Herod made at the time of Christ's birth. See Matt. ii. 4-8
11. A drunkard. "Perhaps," says Tyrwhitt, "Chaucer refers to Epist. LXXXIII., 'Extende in plures dies illum ebrii habitum; nunquid de furore dubitabis? nunc quoque non est minor sed brevior.'" ("Prolong the drunkard's condition to several days; will you doubt his madness? Even as it is, the madness is no less; merely shorter.")
12. Defended: forbidden; French, "defendu." St Jerome, in his book against Jovinian, says that so long as Adam fasted, he was in Paradise; he ate, and he was thrust out.
13. "Meats for the belly, and the belly for meats; but God shall destroy both it and them." 1 Cor. vi. 13.
14. "For many walk, of whom I have told you often, and now tell you even weeping, that they are the enemies of the cross of Christ: Whose end is destruction, whose God is their belly, and whose glory is in their shame, who mind earthly things." Phil. iii. 18, 19.
15. Cod: bag; Anglo-Saxon, "codde;" hence peas-cod, pin-cod (pin-cushion), &c.
16. Compare with the lines which follow, the picture of the drunken messenger in the Man of Law's Tale.
17. Lepe: A town near Cadiz, whence a stronger wine than the Gascon vintages afforded was imported to England. French wine was often adulterated with the cheaper and stronger Spanish.
18. Another reading is "Fleet Street."
19. Attila was suffocated in the night by a haemorrhage, brought on by a debauch, when he was preparing a new invasion of Italy, in 453.
20. "It is not for kings, O Lemuel, it is not for kings to drink wine, nor for princes strong drink; lest they drink, and forget the law, and pervert the judgment of any of the afflicted." Prov. xxxi. 4, 5.
21. Most manuscripts, evidently in error, have "Stilbon" and "Calidone" for Chilon and Lacedaemon. Chilon was one of the seven sages of Greece, and flourished about B.C. 590. According to Diogenes Laertius, he died, under the pressure of age and joy, in the arms of his son, who had just been crowned victor at the Olympic games.
22. "Swear not at all;" Christ's words in Matt. v. 34.
23. "And thou shalt swear, the lord liveth in truth, in judgement, and in righteousness." Jeremiah iv. 2
24. The nails that fastened Christ on the cross, which were regarded with superstitious reverence.
25. Hailes: An abbey in Gloucestershire, where, under the designation of "the blood of Hailes," a portion of Christ's blood was preserved.
26. Go bet: a hunting phrase; apparently its force is, "go beat up the game."
27. Haw; farm-yard, hedge Compare the French, "haie."
28. Avicen, or Avicenna, was among the distinguished physicians of the Arabian school in the eleventh century, and very popular in the Middle Ages. His great work was called "Canon Medicinae," and was divided into "fens," "fennes," or sections.
29. Assoil: absolve. compare the Scotch law-term "assoilzie," to acquit.

30. Saint Helen, according to Sir John Mandeville, found the cross of Christ deep below ground, under a rock, where the Jews had hidden it; and she tested the genuineness of the sacred tree, by raising to life a dead man laid upon it.

GEOFFREY CHAUCER

THE SHIPMAN'S TALE.[1]

THE PROLOGUE

Our Host upon his stirrups stood anon,
And saide; "Good men, hearken every one,
This was a thrifty tale for the nones. *discreet, profitable*
Sir Parish Priest," quoth he, "for Godde's bones,
Tell us a tale, as was thy forword yore: *promise formerly*
I see well that ye learned men in lore
Can muche good, by Godde's dignity." *know*
The Parson him answer'd, "Ben'dicite!
What ails the man, so sinfully to swear?"
Our Host answer'd, "O Jankin, be ye there?
Now, good men," quoth our Host, "hearken to me.
I smell a Lollard[2] in the wind," quoth he.
"Abide, for Godde's digne passion, worthy
For we shall have a predication:
This Lollard here will preachen us somewhat."
"Nay, by my father's soul, that shall he not,
Saide the Shipman; "Here shall he not preach,
He shall no gospel glose here nor teach. *comment upon*
We all believe in the great God," quoth he.
"He woulde sowe some difficulty,
Or springe cockle[3] in our cleane corn.
And therefore, Host, I warne thee beforn,
My jolly body shall a tale tell,
And I shall clinke you so merry a bell,
That I shall waken all this company;
But it shall not be of philosophy,
Nor of physic, nor termes quaint of law;
There is but little Latin in my maw." *belly*

Notes to the Prologue to the Shipman's Tale

1. The Prologue here given was transferred by Tyrwhitt from the place, preceding the Squire's Tale, which it had formerly occupied; the Shipman's Tale having no Prologue in the best manuscripts.
2. Lollard: A contemptuous name for the followers of Wyckliffe; presumably derived from the Latin, "lolium," tares, as if they were the tares among the Lord's wheat; so, a few lines below, the Shipman intimates his fear lest the Parson should "spring cockle in our clean corn."
3. Cockle: A weed, the "Agrostemma githago" of Linnaeus; perhaps named from the Anglo-Saxon, "ceocan," because it chokes the corn. (Transcriber's note: It is also possible Chaucer had in mind Matthew 13:25, where in some translations, an enemy sowed "cockle" amongst the wheat. (Other translations have "tares" and "darnel".))

THE TALE.[1]

A Merchant whilom dwell'd at Saint Denise,
That riche was, for which men held him wise.
A wife he had of excellent beauty,
And companiable and revellous was she, *fond of society and merry making*
Which is a thing that causeth more dispence
Than worth is all the cheer and reverence
That men them do at feastes and at dances.
Such salutations and countenances
Passen, as doth the shadow on the wall;
Put woe is him that paye must for all.
The sely husband algate he must pay, *innocent always*
He must us[2] clothe and he must us array
All for his owen worship richely:
In which array we dance jollily.
And if that he may not, paraventure,
Or elles list not such dispence endure,
But thinketh it is wasted and y-lost,
Then must another paye for our cost,
Or lend us gold, and that is perilous.

This noble merchant held a noble house;
For which he had all day so great repair, *resort of visitors*
For his largesse, and for his wife was fair,
That wonder is; but hearken to my tale.
Amonges all these guestes great and smale,
There was a monk, a fair man and a bold,
I trow a thirty winter he was old,
That ever-in-one was drawing to that place. *constantly*
This younge monk, that was so fair of face,
Acquainted was so with this goode man,
Since that their firste knowledge began,
That in his house as familiar was he
As it is possible any friend to be.
And, for as muchel as this goode man,
And eke this monk of which that I began,
Were both the two y-born in one village,

THE CANTERBURY TALES

The monk him claimed, as for cousinage, claimed kindred
And he again him said not once nay, with him
But was as glad thereof as fowl of day;
"For to his heart it was a great pleasance.
Thus be they knit with etern' alliance,
And each of them gan other to assure
Of brotherhood while that their life may dure.
Free was Dan[3] John, and namely of dispence, especially spending
As in that house, and full of diligence
To do pleasance, and also great costage; liberal outlay
He not forgot to give the leaste page
In all that house; but, after their degree,
He gave the lord, and sithen his meinie, afterwards servants
When that he came, some manner honest thing;
For which they were as glad of his coming
As fowl is fain when that the sun upriseth.
No more of this as now, for it sufficeth.

But so befell, this merchant on a day
Shope him to make ready his array, resolved, arranged
Toward the town of Bruges[4] for to fare,
To buye there a portion of ware; merchandise
For which he hath to Paris sent anon
A messenger, and prayed hath Dan John
That he should come to Saint Denis, and play enjoy himself
With him, and with his wife, a day or tway,
Ere he to Bruges went, in alle wise.
This noble monk, of which I you devise, tell
Had of his abbot, as him list, licence,
(Because he was a man of high prudence,
And eke an officer out for to ride,
To see their granges and their barnes wide);[5]
And unto Saint Denis he came anon.
Who was so welcome as my lord Dan John,
Our deare cousin, full of courtesy?
With him he brought a jub of malvesie, jug
And eke another full of fine vernage,[6]
And volatile, as aye was his usage: wild-fowl
And thus I let them eat, and drink, and play,
This merchant and this monk, a day or tway.
The thirde day the merchant up ariseth,
And on his needeis sadly him adviseth;
And up into his countour-house went he, counting-house[7]
To reckon with himself as well may be,
Of thilke year, how that it with him stood,
And how that he dispended had his good,
And if that he increased were or non.
His bookes and his bagges many a one
He laid before him on his counting-board.
Full riche was his treasure and his hoard;
For which full fast his countour door he shet;
And eke he would that no man should him let hinder
Of his accountes, for the meane time:
And thus he sat, till it was passed prime.

Dan John was risen in the morn also,
And in the garden walked to and fro,
And had his thinges said full courteously.
The good wife came walking full privily
Into the garden, where he walked soft,
And him saluted, as she had done oft;
A maiden child came in her company,
Which as her list she might govern and gie, guide
For yet under the yarde was the maid. rod[8]
"O deare cousin mine, Dan John," she said,
"What aileth you so rath for to arise?" early
"Niece," quoth he, "it ought enough suffice
Five houres for to sleep upon a night;'
But it were for an old appalled wight, unless pallid, wasted
As be these wedded men, that lie and dare, stare
As in a forme sits a weary hare,
Alle forstraught with houndes great and smale; distracted, confounded
But, deare niece, why be ye so pale?
I trowe certes that our goode man
Hath you so laboured, since this night began,
That you were need to reste hastily."
And with that word he laugh'd full merrily,
And of his owen thought he wax'd all red.
This faire wife gan for to shake her head,
And saide thus; "Yea, God wot all" quoth she.
"Nay, cousin mine, it stands not so with me;
For by that God, that gave me soul and life,
In all the realm of France is there no wife
That lesse lust hath to that sorry play;
For I may sing alas and well-away!
That I was born; but to no wight," quoth she,
"Dare I not tell how that it stands with me.
Wherefore I think out of this land to wend,
Or elles of myself to make an end,
So full am I of dread and eke of care."

This monk began upon this wife to stare,
And said, "Alas! my niece, God forbid
That ye for any sorrow, or any dread,
Fordo yourself: but telle me your grief, destroy
Paraventure I may, in your mischief, distress
Counsel or help; and therefore telle me
All your annoy, for it shall be secre.
For on my portos here I make an oath, breviary
That never in my life, for lief nor loth, willing or unwilling
Ne shall I of no counsel you bewray."
"The same again to you," quoth she, "I say.
By God and by this portos I you swear,
Though men me woulden all in pieces tear,
Ne shall I never, for to go to hell, though I should
Bewray one word of thing that ye me tell, betray
For no cousinage, nor alliance,

But verily for love and affiance." confidence, promise
Thus be they sworn, and thereupon they kiss'd,
And each of them told other what them list.
"Cousin," quoth she, "if that I hadde space,
As I have none, and namely in this place, specially
Then would I tell a legend of my life,
What I have suffer'd since I was a wife
With mine husband, all be he your cousin. although
"Nay," quoth this monk, "by God and Saint Martin,
He is no more cousin unto me,
Than is the leaf that hangeth on the tree;
I call him so, by Saint Denis of France,
To have the more cause of acquaintance
Of you, which I have loved specially
Aboven alle women sickerly, surely
This swear I you on my professioun; by my vows of religion
Tell me your grief, lest that he come adown,
And hasten you, and go away anon."

"My deare love," quoth she, "O my Dan John,
Full lief were me this counsel for to hide, pleasant
But out it must, I may no more abide.
My husband is to me the worste man
That ever was since that the world began;
But since I am a wife, it sits not me becomes
To telle no wight of our privity,
Neither in bed, nor in none other place;
God shield I shoulde tell it for his grace; forbid
A wife shall not say of her husband
But all honour, as I can understand;
Save unto you thus much I telle shall;
As help me God, he is nought worth at all
In no degree, the value of a fly.
But yet me grieveth most his niggardy. stinginess
And well ye wot, that women naturally
Desire thinges six, as well as I.
They woulde that their husbands shoulde be
Hardy, and wise, and rich, and thereto free, brave
And buxom to his wife, and fresh in bed. yielding, obedient
But, by that ilke Lord that for us bled, same
For his honour myself for to array,
On Sunday next I muste needes pay
A hundred francs, or elles am I lorn. ruined, undone
Yet were me lever that I were unborn, I would rather
Than me were done slander or villainy.
And if mine husband eke might it espy,
I were but lost; and therefore I you pray,
Lend me this sum, or elles must I dey. die
Dan John, I say, lend me these hundred francs;
Pardie, I will not faile you, my thanks, if I can help it
If that you list to do that I you pray;

For at a certain day I will you pay,
And do to you what pleasance and service
That I may do, right as you list devise.
And but I do, God take on me vengeance, unless
As foul as e'er had Ganilion[9] of France."

This gentle monk answer'd in this mannere;
"Now truely, mine owen lady dear,
I have," quoth he, "on you so greate ruth, pity
That I you swear, and plighte you my truth,
That when your husband is to Flanders fare, gone
I will deliver you out of this care,
For I will bringe you a hundred francs."
And with that word he caught her by the flanks,
And her embraced hard, and kissed her oft.
"Go now your way," quoth he, "all still and soft,
And let us dine as soon as that ye may,
For by my cylinder 'tis prime of day; portable sundial
Go now, and be as true as I shall be ."
"Now elles God forbidde, Sir," quoth she;
And forth she went, as jolly as a pie,
And bade the cookes that they should them hie, make haste
So that men mighte dine, and that anon.
Up to her husband is this wife gone,
And knocked at his contour boldely.
"Qui est la?" quoth he. "Peter! it am I," who is there?
Quoth she; "What, Sir, how longe all will ye fast?
How longe time will ye reckon and cast
Your summes, and your bookes, and your things?
The devil have part of all such reckonings!
Ye have enough, pardie, of Godde's sond. sending, gifts
Come down to-day, and let your bagges stond. stand
Ne be ye not ashamed, that Dan John
Shall fasting all this day elenge gon? see note[10]
What? let us hear a mass, and go we dine."
"Wife," quoth this man, "little canst thou divine
The curious businesse that we have;
For of us chapmen, all so God me save, merchants
And by that lord that cleped is Saint Ive,
Scarcely amonges twenty, ten shall thrive
Continually, lasting unto our age.
We may well make cheer and good visage,
And drive forth the world as it may be,
And keepen our estate in privity,
Till we be dead, or elles that we play
A pilgrimage, or go out of the way.
And therefore have I great necessity
Upon this quaint world to advise me. strange consider
For evermore must we stand in dread
Of hap and fortune in our chapmanhead. trading
To Flanders will I go to-morrow at day,
And come again as soon as e'er I may:
For which, my deare wife, I thee beseek beseech

THE CANTERBURY TALES

As be to every wight buxom and meek, civil,
courteous
And for to keep our good be curious,
And honestly governe well our house.
Thou hast enough, in every manner wise,
That to a thrifty household may suffice.
Thee lacketh none array, nor no vitail;
Of silver in thy purse thou shalt not fail."

And with that word his contour door he shet, shut
And down he went; no longer would he let; delay, hinder
And hastily a mass was there said,
And speedily the tables were laid,
And to the dinner faste they them sped,
And richely this monk the chapman fed.
And after dinner Dan John soberly
This chapman took apart, and privily
He said him thus: "Cousin, it standeth so,
That, well I see, to Bruges ye will go;
God and Saint Austin speede you and guide.
I pray you, cousin, wisely that ye ride:
Governe you also of your diet
Attemperly, and namely in this heat. moderately
Betwixt us two needeth no strange fare; ado, ceremony
Farewell, cousin, God shielde you from care.
If any thing there be, by day or night,
If it lie in my power and my might,
That ye me will command in any wise,
It shall be done, right as ye will devise.
But one thing ere ye go, if it may be;
I woulde pray you for to lend to me
A hundred frankes, for a week or twy,
For certain beastes that I muste buy,
To store with a place that is ours
(God help me so, I would that it were yours);
I shall not faile surely of my day,
Not for a thousand francs, a mile way.
But let this thing be secret, I you pray;
For yet to-night these beastes must I buy.
And fare now well, mine owen cousin dear;
Grand mercy of your cost and of your cheer." great thanks

This noble merchant gentilly anon like a gentleman
Answer'd and said, "O cousin mine, Dan John,
Now sickerly this is a small request:
My gold is youres, when that it you lest,
And not only my gold, but my chaffare; merchandise
Take what you list, God shielde that ye spare.
God forbid that you
But one thing is, ye know it well enow should take too little
Of chapmen, that their money is their plough.
We may creance while we have a name, obtain credit
But goldless for to be it is no game.
Pay it again when it lies in your ease;
After my might full fain would I you please."

These hundred frankes set he forth anon,
And privily he took them to Dan John;
No wight in all this world wist of this loan,
Saving the merchant and Dan John alone.
They drink, and speak, and roam a while, and play,
Till that Dan John rode unto his abbay.
The morrow came, and forth this merchant rideth
To Flanders-ward, his prentice well him guideth,
Till he came unto Bruges merrily.
Now went this merchant fast and busily
About his need, and buyed and creanced; got credit
He neither played at the dice, nor danced;
But as a merchant, shortly for to tell,
He led his life; and there I let him dwell.

The Sunday next the merchant was y-gone, after
To Saint Denis y-comen is Dan John,
With crown and beard all fresh and newly shave,
In all the house was not so little a knave, servant-boy
Nor no wight elles that was not full fain
For that my lord Dan John was come again.
And shortly to the point right for to gon,
The faire wife accorded with Dan John,
That for these hundred francs he should all night
Have her in his armes bolt upright;
And this accord performed was in deed.
In mirth all night a busy life they lead,
Till it was day, that Dan John went his way,
And bade the meinie "Farewell; have good day." servants
For none of them, nor no wight in the town,
Had of Dan John right no suspicioun;
And forth he rode home to his abbay,
Or where him list; no more of him I say.

The merchant, when that ended was the fair,
To Saint Denis he gan for to repair,
And with his wife he made feast and cheer,
And tolde her that chaffare was so dear, merchandise
That needes must he make a chevisance; loan[11]
For he was bound in a recognisance
To paye twenty thousand shields anon. crowns, ecus
For which this merchant is to Paris gone,
To borrow of certain friendes that he had
A certain francs, and some with him he lad. took
And when that he was come into the town,
For great cherte and great affectioun love
Unto Dan John he wente first to play;
Not for to borrow of him no money,
Bat for to weet and see of his welfare, know
And for to telle him of his chaffare,

As friendes do, when they be met in fere. *company*
Dan John him made feast and merry cheer;
And he him told again full specially,
How he had well y-bought and graciously
(Thanked be God) all whole his merchandise;
Save that he must, in alle manner wise,
Maken a chevisance, as for his best;
And then he shoulde be in joy and rest.
Dan John answered, "Certes, I am fain glad
That ye in health be come borne again:
And if that I were rich, as have I bliss,
Of twenty thousand shields should ye not miss,
For ye so kindely the other day
Lente me gold, and as I can and may
I thank you, by God and by Saint Jame.
But natheless I took unto our Dame,
Your wife at home, the same gold again,
Upon your bench; she wot it well, certain,
By certain tokens that I can her tell
Now, by your leave, I may no longer dwell;
Our abbot will out of this town anon,
And in his company I muste gon.
Greet well our Dame, mine owen niece sweet,
And farewell, deare cousin, till we meet.

This merchant, which that was full ware and wise,
Creanced hath, and paid eke in Paris *had obtained credit*
To certain Lombards ready in their hond
The sum of gold, and got of them his bond,
And home he went, merry as a popinjay. *parrot*
For well he knew he stood in such array
That needes must he win in that voyage
A thousand francs, above all his costage. *expenses*
His wife full ready met him at the gate,
As she was wont of old usage algate *always*
And all that night in mirthe they beset; *spent*
For he was rich, and clearly out of debt.
When it was day, the merchant gan embrace
His wife all new, and kiss'd her in her face,
And up he went, and maked it full tough.

"No more," quoth she, "by God ye have enough;"
And wantonly again with him she play'd,
Till at the last this merchant to her said.
"By God," quoth he, "I am a little wroth
With you, my wife, although it be me loth;
And wot ye why? by God, as that I guess,
That ye have made a manner strangeness *a kind of estrangement*
Betwixte me and my cousin, Dan John.
Ye should have warned me, ere I had gone,
That he you had a hundred frankes paid
By ready token; he had him evil apaid *was displeased*
For that I to him spake of chevisance, *borrowing*
(He seemed so as by his countenance);
But natheless, by God of heaven king,
I thoughte not to ask of him no thing.
I pray thee, wife, do thou no more so.
Tell me alway, ere that I from thee go,
If any debtor hath in mine absence
Y-payed thee, lest through thy negligence
I might him ask a thing that he hath paid."

This wife was not afeared nor afraid,
But boldely she said, and that anon;
"Mary! I defy that false monk Dan John,
I keep not of his tokens never a deal: *care whit*
He took me certain gold, I wot it well. —
What? evil thedom on his monke's snout! — *thriving*
For, God it wot, I ween'd withoute doubt
That he had given it me, because of you,
To do therewith mine honour and my prow, *profit*
For cousinage, and eke for belle cheer
That he hath had full often here.
But since I see I stand in such disjoint, *awkward position*
I will answer you shortly to the point.
Ye have more slacke debtors than am I;
For I will pay you well and readily,
From day to day, and if so be I fail,
I am your wife, score it upon my tail,
And I shall pay as soon as ever I may.
For, by my troth, I have on mine array,
And not in waste, bestow'd it every deal.
And, for I have bestowed it so well,
For your honour, for Godde's sake I say,
As be not wroth, but let us laugh and play.
Ye shall my jolly body have to wed; *in pledge*
By God, I will not pay you but in bed;
Forgive it me, mine owen spouse dear;
Turn hitherward, and make better cheer."

The merchant saw none other remedy;
And for to chide, it were but a folly,
Since that the thing might not amended be.
"Now, wife," he said, "and I forgive it thee;
But by thy life be no more so large; *liberal, lavish*
Keep better my good, this give I thee in charge."
Thus endeth now my tale; and God us send
Taling enough, until our lives' end!

THE CANTERBURY TALES

Notes to the Shipman's Tale

1. In this Tale Chaucer seems to have followed an old French story, which also formed the groundwork of the first story in the eighth day of the "Decameron."
2. "He must us clothe": So in all the manuscripts and from this and the following lines, it must be inferred that Chaucer had intended to put the Tale in the mouth of a female speaker.
3. Dan: a title bestowed on priests and scholars; from "Dominus," like the Spanish "Don".
4. Bruges was in Chaucer's time the great emporium of European commerce.
5. The monk had been appointed by his abbot to inspect and manage the rural property of the monastery.
6. Malvesie or Malmesy wine derived its name from Malvasia, a region of the Morea near Cape Malea, where it was made, as it also was on Chios and some other Greek islands. Vernage was "vernaccia", a sweet Italian wine.
7. Contour-house: counting-house; French, "comptoir."
8. Under the yarde: under the rod; in pupillage; a phrase properly used of children, but employed by the Clerk in the prologue to his tale. See note 1 to the Prologue to the Clerk's Tale.
9. Genelon, Ganelon, or Ganilion; one of Charlemagne's officers, whose treachery was the cause of the disastrous defeat of the Christians by the Saracens at Roncevalles; he was torn to pieces by four horses.
10. Elenge: From French, "eloigner," to remove; it may mean either the lonely, cheerless condition of the priest, or the strange behaviour of the merchant in leaving him to himself.
11. Make a chevisance: raise money by means of a borrowing agreement; from French, "achever," to finish; the general meaning of the word is a bargain, an agreement.

GEOFFREY CHAUCER

THE PRIORESS'S TALE.

THE PROLOGUE.

"WELL said, by corpus Domini," quoth our Host; the Lord's body
"Now longe may'st thou saile by the coast,
Thou gentle Master, gentle Marinere.
God give the monk a thousand last quad year! ever so much evil[1]
Aha! fellows, beware of such a jape. trick
The monk put in the manne's hood an ape, fooled him
And in his wife's eke, by Saint Austin.
Drawe no monkes more into your inn.

But now pass over, and let us seek about,
Who shall now telle first of all this rout
Another tale;" and with that word he said,
As courteously as it had been a maid;
"My Lady Prioresse, by your leave,
So that I wist I shoulde you not grieve, offend
I woulde deeme that ye telle should judge, decide
A tale next, if so were that ye would.
Now will ye vouchesafe, my lady dear?"
"Gladly," quoth she; and said as ye shall hear.

Notes to the Prologue to the Prioress's Tale.

1. A thousand last quad year: ever so much evil. "Last" means a load, "quad," bad; and literally we may read "a thousand weight of bad years." The Italians use "mal anno" in the same sense.

THE TALE.[1]

O Lord our Lord! thy name how marvellous
Is in this large world y-spread![2] (quoth she)
For not only thy laude precious praise
Performed is by men of high degree,
But by the mouth of children thy bounte goodness
Performed is, for on the breast sucking
Sometimes showe they thy herying.[3] glory

Wherefore in laud, as I best can or may
Of thee, and of the white lily flow'r
Which that thee bare, and is a maid alway,
To tell a story I will do my labour;
Not that I may increase her honour,
For she herselven is honour and root
Of bounte, next her son, and soules' boot. help

O mother maid, O maid and mother free! bounteous
O bush unburnt, burning in Moses' sight,
That ravished'st down from the deity,
Through thy humbless, the ghost that in thee light;[4]
Of whose virtue, when he thine hearte light, lightened, gladdened
Conceived was the Father's sapience;
Help me to tell it to thy reverence.

Lady! thy bounty, thy magnificence,
Thy virtue, and thy great humility,
There may no tongue express in no science:
For sometimes, Lady! ere men pray to thee,
Thou go'st before, of thy benignity,
And gettest us the light, through thy prayere,
To guiden us unto thy son so dear.

My conning is so weak, O blissful queen, skill, ability
For to declare thy great worthiness,
That I not may the weight of it sustene;
But as a child of twelvemonth old, or less,
That can unnethes any word express, scarcely
Right so fare I; and therefore, I you pray,
Guide my song that I shall of you say.

There was in Asia, in a great city,
Amonges Christian folk, a Jewery,[5]
Sustained by a lord of that country,
For foul usure, and lucre of villainy,
Hateful to Christ, and to his company;
And through the street men mighte ride and wend, go, walk
For it was free, and open at each end.

A little school of Christian folk there stood
Down at the farther end, in which there were
Children an heap y-come of Christian blood,
That learned in that schoole year by year
Such manner doctrine as men used there;
This is to say, to singen and to read,
As smalle children do in their childhead.

Among these children was a widow's son,
A little clergion, seven year of age, young clerk or scholar
That day by day to scholay was his won, study wont
And eke also, whereso he saw th' image
Of Christe's mother, had he in usage,
As him was taught, to kneel adown, and say
Ave Maria as he went by the way.

164

THE CANTERBURY TALES

Thus had this widow her little son y-taught
Our blissful Lady, Christe's mother dear,
To worship aye, and he forgot it not;
For sely child will always soone lear.   innocent learn
But aye when I remember on this mattere,
Saint Nicholas[6] stands ever in my presence;
For he so young to Christ did reverence.

This little child his little book learning,
As he sat in the school at his primere,
He Alma redemptoris[7] hearde sing,
As children learned their antiphonere;[8]
And as he durst, he drew him nere and nere,   nearer
And hearken'd aye the wordes and the note,
Till he the firste verse knew all by rote.

Nought wist he what this Latin was to say,   meant
For he so young and tender was of age;
But on a day his fellow gan he pray
To expound him this song in his language,
Or tell him why this song was in usage:
This pray'd he him to construe and declare,
Full oftentime upon his knees bare.

His fellow, which that elder was than he,
Answer'd him thus: "This song, I have heard say,
Was maked of our blissful Lady free,
Her to salute, and eke her to pray
To be our help and succour when we dey.   die
I can no more expound in this mattere:
I learne song, I know but small grammere."

"And is this song y-made in reverence
Of Christe's mother?" said this innocent;
Now certes I will do my diligence
To conne it all, ere Christmas be went;   learn; con
Though that I for my primer shall be shent,   disgraced
And shall be beaten thries in an hour,
I will it conne, our Lady to honour."

His fellow taught him homeward privily on the way home
From day to day, till he coud it by rote,   knew
And then he sang it well and boldely
From word to word according with the note;
Twice in a day it passed through his throat;
To schoole-ward, and homeward when he went;
On Christ's mother was set all his intent.

As I have said, throughout the Jewery,
This little child, as he came to and fro,
Full merrily then would he sing and cry,
O Alma redemptoris, evermo';
The sweetness hath his hearte pierced so
Of Christe's mother, that to her to pray
He cannot stint of singing by the way.   cease

Our firste foe, the serpent Satanas,
That hath in Jewes' heart his waspe's nest,
Upswell'd and said, "O Hebrew people, alas!
Is this to you a thing that is honest,   creditable, becoming
That such a boy shall walken as him lest
In your despite, and sing of such sentence,
Which is against your lawe's reverence?"

From thenceforth the Jewes have conspired
This innocent out of the world to chase;
A homicide thereto have they hired,
That in an alley had a privy place,
And, as the child gan forth by for to pace,
This cursed Jew him hent, and held him fast   seized
And cut his throat, and in a pit him cast.

I say that in a wardrobe he him threw,   privy
Where as the Jewes purged their entrail.
O cursed folk! O Herodes all new!
What may your evil intente you avail?
Murder will out, certain it will not fail,
And namely where th' honour of God shall spread;   especially
The blood out crieth on your cursed deed.

O martyr souded to virginity, confirmed[9]
Now may'st thou sing, and follow ever-in-one   continually
The white Lamb celestial (quoth she),
Of which the great Evangelist Saint John
In Patmos wrote, which saith that they that gon
Before this Lamb, and sing a song all new,
That never fleshly woman they ne knew.[10]

This poore widow waited all that night
After her little child, but he came not;
For which, as soon as it was daye's light,
With face pale, in dread and busy thought,
She hath at school and elleswhere him sought,
Till finally she gan so far espy,
That he was last seen in the Jewery.

With mother's pity in her breast enclosed,
She went, as she were half out of her mind,
To every place, where she hath supposed
By likelihood her little child to find:
And ever on Christ's mother meek and kind
She cried, and at the laste thus she wrought,
Among the cursed Jewes she him sought.

She freined, and she prayed piteously asked[11]
To every Jew that dwelled in that place,
To tell her, if her childe went thereby;
They saide, "Nay;" but Jesus of his grace
Gave in her thought, within a little space,
That in that place after her son she cried,
Where he was cast into a pit beside.

O greate God, that preformest thy laud
By mouth of innocents, lo here thy might!

165

This gem of chastity, this emeraud, emerald
And eke of martyrdom the ruby bright,
Where he with throat y-carven lay upright, cut
He Alma Redemptoris gan to sing
So loud, that all the place began to ring.

The Christian folk, that through the streete went,
In came, for to wonder on this thing:
And hastily they for the provost sent.
He came anon withoute tarrying,
And heried Christ, that is of heaven king, praised
And eke his mother, honour of mankind;
And after that the Jewes let he bind. caused

With torment, and with shameful death each one
The provost did these Jewes for to sterve caused die
That of this murder wist, and that anon;
He woulde no such cursedness observe overlook
Evil shall have that evil will deserve;
Therefore with horses wild he did them draw,
And after that he hung them by the law.

The child, with piteous lamentation,
Was taken up, singing his song alway:
And with honour and great procession,
They crry him unto the next abbay.
His mother swooning by the biere lay;
Unnethes might the people that were there scarcely
This newe Rachel bringe from his bier.

Upon his biere lay this innocent
Before the altar while the masses last'; lasted
And, after that, th' abbot with his convent
Have sped them for to bury him full fast;
And when they holy water on him cast,
Yet spake this child, when sprinkled was the water,
And sang, O Alma redemptoris mater!

This abbot, which that was a holy man,
As monkes be, or elles ought to be,
This younger child to conjure he began,
And said; "O deare child! I halse thee, implore[12]
In virtue of the holy Trinity;
Tell me what is thy cause for to sing,
Since that thy throat is cut, to my seeming."

"My throat is cut unto my necke-bone,"
Saide this child, "and, as by way of kind, in course of nature
I should have died, yea long time agone;
But Jesus Christ, as ye in bookes find,
Will that his glory last and be in mind;
And, for the worship of his mother dear, glory
Yet may I sing O Alma loud and clear.

"This well of mercy, Christe's mother sweet, fountain
I loved alway, after my conning: knowledge
And when that I my life should forlete, leave
To me she came, and bade me for to sing
This anthem verily in my dying,
As ye have heard; and, when that I had sung,
Me thought she laid a grain upon my tongue.

"Wherefore I sing, and sing I must certain,
In honour of that blissful maiden free,
Till from my tongue off taken is the grain.
And after that thus saide she to me;
'My little child, then will I fetche thee,
When that the grain is from thy tongue take:
Be not aghast, I will thee not forsake.'" afraid

This holy monk, this abbot him mean I,
His tongue out caught, and took away the grain;
And he gave up the ghost full softely.
And when this abbot had this wonder seen,
His salte teares trickled down as rain:
And groff he fell all flat upon the ground, prostrate, grovelling
And still he lay, as he had been y-bound.

The convent lay eke on the pavement all the monks
Weeping, and herying Christ's mother dear. praising
And after that they rose, and forth they went,
And took away this martyr from his bier,
And in a tomb of marble stones clear
Enclosed they his little body sweet;
Where he is now, God lene us for to meet. grant

O younge Hugh of Lincoln![13] slain also
With cursed Jewes, — as it is notable,
For it is but a little while ago, —
Pray eke for us, we sinful folk unstable,
That, of his mercy, God so merciable merciful
On us his greate mercy multiply,
For reverence of his mother Mary.

Notes to the Prioress's Tale

1. Tales of the murder of children by Jews were frequent in the Middle Ages, being probably designed to keep up the bitter feeling of the Christians against the Jews. Not a few children were canonised on this account; and the scene of the misdeeds was laid anywhere and everywhere, so that Chaucer could be at no loss for material.
2. This is from Psalm viii. 1, "Domine, dominus noster, quam admirabile est nomen tuum in universa terra."
3. "Out of the mouths of babes and sucklings hast Thou ordained strength." — Psalms viii. 2.

4. The ghost that in thee light: the spirit that on thee alighted; the Holy Ghost through whose power Christ was conceived.
5. Jewery: A quarter which the Jews were permitted to inhabit; the Old Jewry in London got its name in this way.
6. St. Nicholas, even in his swaddling clothes — so says the "Breviarium Romanum" —gave promise of extraordinary virtue and holiness; for, though he sucked freely on other days, on Wednesdays and Fridays he applied to the breast only once, and that not until the evening.
7. "O Alma Redemptoris Mater," ("O soul mother of the Redeemer") — the beginning of a hymn to the Virgin.
8. Antiphonere: A book of anthems, or psalms, chanted in the choir by alternate verses.
9. Souded; confirmed; from French, "soulde;" Latin, "solidatus."
10. "And they sung as it were a new song before the throne, and before the four beasts, and the elders: and no man could learn that song but the hundred and forty and four thousand, which were redeemed from the earth. These are they which were not defiled with women; for they are virgins. These are they which follow the Lamb whithersoever he goeth. These were redeemed from among men, being the firstfruits unto God and to the Lamb." — Revelations xiv. 3, 4.
11. Freined: asked, inquired; from Anglo-Saxon, "frinan," "fraegnian." Compare German, "fragen."
12. Halse: embrace or salute; implore: from Anglo-Saxon "hals," the neck.
14 A boy said to have been slain by the Jews at Lincoln in 1255, according to Matthew Paris. Many popular ballads were made about the event, which the diligence of the Church doubtless kept fresh in mind at Chaucer's day.

GEOFFREY CHAUCER

CHAUCER'S TALE OF SIR THOPAS.

THE PROLOGUE.[1]

WHEN said was this miracle, every man
As sober was, that wonder was to see, serious
Till that our Host to japen he began, talk lightly
And then at erst he looked upon me, for the first time
And saide thus; "What man art thou?" quoth he;
"Thou lookest as thou wouldest find an hare,
For ever on the ground I see thee stare.

"Approach near, and look up merrily.
Now ware you, Sirs, and let this man have place.
He in the waist is shapen as well as I;[2]
This were a puppet in an arm t'embrace

For any woman small and fair of face.
He seemeth elvish by his countenance, surly, morose
For unto no wight doth he dalliance.

"Say now somewhat, since other folk have said;
Tell us a tale of mirth, and that anon."
"Hoste," quoth I, "be not evil apaid, dissatisfied
For other tale certes can I none, know
Eut of a rhyme I learned yore agone." long
"Yea, that is good," quoth he; "now shall we hear
Some dainty thing, me thinketh by thy cheer."
expression, mien

Notes to the Prologue to Chaucer's Tale of Sir Thopas

1. This prologue is interesting, for the picture which it gives of Chaucer himself; riding apart from and indifferent to the rest of the pilgrims, with eyes fixed on the ground, and an "elvish", morose, or rather self-absorbed air; portly, if not actually stout, in body; and evidently a man out of the common, as the closing words of the Host imply.
2. Referring to the poet's corpulency.

THE TALE[1]

The First Fit part

Listen, lordings, in good intent,
And I will tell you verrament truly
Of mirth and of solas, delight, solace
All of a knight was fair and gent, gentle
In battle and in tournament,
His name was Sir Thopas.

Y-born he was in far country,
In Flanders, all beyond the sea,
At Popering[2] in the place;
His father was a man full free,
And lord he was of that country,
As it was Godde's grace.[3]

Sir Thopas was a doughty swain,
White was his face as paindemain,[4]
His lippes red as rose.
His rode is like scarlet in grain, complexion
And I you tell in good certain
He had a seemly nose.

His hair, his beard, was like saffroun,
That to his girdle reach'd adown,
His shoes of cordewane:[5]
Of Bruges were his hosen brown;
His robe was of ciclatoun,[6]
That coste many a jane.[7]

He coulde hunt at the wild deer,
And ride on hawking for rivere by the river
With gray goshawk on hand:[8]
Thereto he was a good archere,
Of wrestling was there none his peer,
Where any ram[9] should stand.

Full many a maiden bright in bow'r
They mourned for him par amour,
When them were better sleep;
But he was chaste, and no lechour,
And sweet as is the bramble flow'r
That beareth the red heep. hip

And so it fell upon a day,
For sooth as I you telle may,
Sir Thopas would out ride;
He worth upon his steede gray, mounted
And in his hand a launcegay, spear[10]
A long sword by his side.

He pricked through a fair forest,
Wherein is many a wilde beast,
Yea, bothe buck and hare;
And as he pricked north and east,
I tell it you, him had almost almost
Betid a sorry care. befallen

There sprange herbes great and small,
The liquorice and the setewall, valerian

THE CANTERBURY TALES

And many a clove-gilofre,[12]
And nutemeg to put in ale,
Whether it be moist or stale, new
Or for to lay in coffer.

The birdes sang, it is no nay,
The sperhawk and the popinjay, sparrowhawk parrot[13]
That joy it was to hear;
The throstle-cock made eke his lay,
The woode-dove upon the spray
She sang full loud and clear.

Sir Thopas fell in love-longing
All when he heard the throstle sing,
And prick'd as he were wood; rode as if he
His faire steed in his pricking were mad
So sweated, that men might him wring,
His sides were all blood.

Sir Thopas eke so weary was
For pricking on the softe grass,
So fierce was his corage, inclination, spirit
That down he laid him in that place,
To make his steed some solace,
And gave him good forage.

"Ah, Saint Mary, ben'dicite,
What aileth thilke love at me
To binde me so sore?
Me dreamed all this night, pardie,
An elf-queen shall my leman be, mistress
And sleep under my gore. shirt

An elf-queen will I love, y-wis, assuredly
For in this world no woman is
Worthy to be my make mate
In town;
All other women I forsake,
And to an elf-queen I me take
By dale and eke by down."[14]

Into his saddle he clomb anon,
And pricked over stile and stone
An elf-queen for to spy,
Till he so long had ridden and gone,
That he found in a privy wonne haunt
The country of Faery,
So wild;
For in that country was there none
That to him durste ride or gon,
Neither wife nor child.

Till that there came a great giaunt,
His name was Sir Oliphaunt,[15]
A perilous man of deed;
He saide, "Child, by Termagaunt,[16] young man
But if thou prick out of mine haunt, unless
Anon I slay thy steed
With mace.
Here is the Queen of Faery,
With harp, and pipe, and symphony,
Dwelling in this place."

The Child said, "All so may I the, thrive
To-morrow will I meete thee,
When I have mine armor;
And yet I hope, par ma fay, by my faith
That thou shalt with this launcegay
Abyen it full sore; suffer for
Thy maw belly
Shall I pierce, if I may,
Ere it be fully prime of day,
For here thou shalt be slaw." slain

Sir Thopas drew aback full fast;
This giant at him stones cast
Out of a fell staff sling:
But fair escaped Child Thopas,
And all it was through Godde's grace,
And through his fair bearing.[17]

Yet listen, lordings, to my tale,
Merrier than the nightingale,
For now I will you rown, whisper
How Sir Thopas, with sides smale, small[18]
Pricking over hill and dale,
Is come again to town.

His merry men commanded he
To make him both game and glee;
For needes must he fight
With a giant with heades three,
For paramour and jollity
Of one that shone full bright.

"Do come," he saide, "my minstrales summon
And gestours for to telle tales. story-tellers
Anon in mine arming,
Of romances that be royales,[19]
Of popes and of cardinales,
And eke of love-longing."

They fetch'd him first the sweete wine,
And mead eke in a maseline, drinking-bowl
And royal spicery; of maple wood[20]
Of ginger-bread that was full fine,
And liquorice and eke cumin,
With sugar that is trie. refined

He didde, next his white lere, put on skin
Of cloth of lake fine and clear, fine linen
A breech and eke a shirt;
And next his shirt an haketon, cassock
And over that an habergeon, coat of mail
For piercing of his heart;

And over that a fine hauberk, plate-armour
Was all y-wrought of Jewes' werk, magicians'
Full strong it was of plate;
And over that his coat-armour, knight's surcoat
As white as is the lily flow'r,[21]
In which he would debate. fight

His shield was all of gold so red
And therein was a boare's head,
A charboucle beside; carbuncle[22]
And there he swore on ale and bread,
How that the giant should be dead,
Betide whatso betide.

His jambeaux were of cuirbouly,[23] boots
His sworde's sheath of ivory,
His helm of latoun bright, brass
His saddle was of rewel[24] bone,
His bridle as the sunne shone,
Or as the moonelight.

His speare was of fine cypress,
That bodeth war, and nothing peace;
The head full sharp y-ground.
His steede was all dapple gray,
It went an amble in the way
Full softely and round
In land.

Lo, Lordes mine, here is a fytt;
If ye will any more of it,
To tell it will I fand. try

The Second Fit

Now hold your mouth for charity,
Bothe knight and lady free,
And hearken to my spell; tale[25]
Of battle and of chivalry,
Of ladies' love and druerie, gallantry
Anon I will you tell.

Men speak of romances of price worth, esteem
Of Horn Child, and of Ipotis,
Of Bevis, and Sir Guy,[26]
Of Sir Libeux,[27] and Pleindamour,
But Sir Thopas, he bears the flow'r
Of royal chivalry.

His goode steed he all bestrode,
And forth upon his way he glode, shone
As sparkle out of brand; torch
Upon his crest he bare a tow'r,
And therein stick'd a lily flow'r;[28]
God shield his corse from shand! body harm

And, for he was a knight auntrous, adventurous
He woulde sleepen in none house,
But liggen in his hood, lie
His brighte helm was his wanger, pillow[29]
And by him baited his destrer fed horse[30]
Of herbes fine and good.

Himself drank water of the well,
As did the knight Sir Percivel,[31]
So worthy under weed;
Till on a day – . . .

Notes to Chaucer's Tale of Sir Thopas

1. "The Rhyme of Sir Thopas," as it is generally called, is introduced by Chaucer as a satire on the dull, pompous, and prolix metrical romances then in vogue. It is full of phrases taken from the popular rhymesters in the vein which he holds up to ridicule; if, indeed — though of that there is no evidence — it be not actually part of an old romance which Chaucer selected and reproduced to point his assault on the prevailing taste in literature. Transcriber's note: The Tale is full of incongruities of every kind, which Purves does not refer to; I point some of them out in the notes which follow - marked TN.
2. Poppering, or Poppeling, a parish in the marches of Calais of which the famous antiquary Leland was once Rector. TN: The inhabitants of Popering had a reputation for stupidity.
3. TN: The lord of Popering was the abbot of the local monastery - who could, of course, have no legitimate children.
4. Paindemain: Either "pain de matin," morning bread, or "pain de Maine," because it was made best in that province; a kind of fine white bread.
5. Cordewane: Cordovan; fine Spanish leather, so called from the name of the city where it was prepared
6. Ciclatoun: A rich Oriental stuff of silk and gold, of which was made the circular robe of state called a "ciclaton," from the Latin, "cyclas." The word is French.
7. Jane: a Genoese coin, of small value; in our old statutes called "gallihalpens," or galley half-pence.
8. TN: In Mediaeval falconry the goshawk was not regarded as a fit bird for a knight. It was the yeoman's bird.
9. A ram was the usual prize of wrestling contests. TN: Wrestling and archery were sports of the common people, not knightly accomplishments.
10. Launcegay: spear; "azagay" is the name of a Moorish weapon, and the identity of termination is singular.
12. Clove-gilofre: clove-gilliflower; "Caryophyllus hortensis."
13. TN: The sparrowhawk and parrot can only squawk unpleasantly.
14. TN: The sudden and pointless changes in the stanza form are of course part of Chaucer's parody.
15. Sir Oliphaunt: literally, "Sir Elephant;" Sir John Mandeville calls those animals "Olyfauntes."

THE CANTERBURY TALES

16. Termagaunt: A pagan or Saracen deity, otherwise named Tervagan, and often mentioned in Middle Age literature. His name has passed into our language, to denote a ranter or blusterer, as be was represented to be.
17. TN: His "fair bearing" would not have been much defence against a sling-stone.
18. TN: "Sides small": a conventional description for a woman, not a man.
19. Romances that be royal: so called because they related to Charlemagne and his family.
20. TN: A knight would be expected to have a gold or silver drinking vessel.
21. TN: The coat-armour or coat of arms should have had his heraldic emblems on it, not been pure white
22. Charboucle: Carbuncle; French, "escarboucle;" a heraldic device resembling a jewel.
23. Cuirbouly: "Cuir boulli," French, boiled or prepared leather; also used to cover shields, &c.
24. Rewel bone: No satisfactory explanation has been furnished of this word, used to describe some material from which rich saddles were made. TN: The OED defines it as narwhal ivory.
25. Spell: Tale, discourse, from Anglo-Saxon, "spellian," to declare, tell a story.
26. Sir Bevis of Hampton, and Sir Guy of Warwick, two knights of great renown.
27. Libeux: One of Arthur's knights, called "Ly beau desconus," "the fair unknown."
28. TN: The crest was a small emblem worn on top of a knight's helmet. A tower with a lily stuck in it would have been unwieldy and absurd.
29. Wanger: pillow; from Anglo-Saxon, "wangere," because the "wanges;" or cheeks, rested on it.
30. Destrer: "destrier," French, a war-horse; in Latin, "dextrarius," as if led by the right hand.
31. Sir Percival de Galois, whose adventures were written in more than 60,000 verses by Chretien de Troyes, one of the oldest and best French romancers, in 1191.

Chaucer's Tale Of Meliboeus.

THE PROLOGUE.

"No more of this, for Godde's dignity!"
Quoth oure Hoste; "for thou makest me
So weary of thy very lewedness, stupidity, ignorance[1]
That, all so wisly God my soule bless, surely
Mine eares ache for thy drafty speech. worthless[2]
Now such a rhyme the devil I beteche: commend to
This may well be rhyme doggerel," quoth he.
"Why so?" quoth I; "why wilt thou lette me prevent
More of my tale than any other man,
Since that it is the best rhyme that I can?" know
"By God!" quoth he, "for, plainly at one word,
Thy drafty rhyming is not worth a tord:
Thou dost naught elles but dispendest time. wastest
Sir, at one word, thou shalt no longer rhyme.
Let see whether thou canst tellen aught in gest, by way of
Or tell in prose somewhat, at the least, narrative
In which there be some mirth or some doctrine."
"Gladly," quoth I, "by Godde's sweete pine, suffering
I will you tell a little thing in prose,
That oughte like you, as I suppose, please
Or else certes ye be too dangerous. fastidious
It is a moral tale virtuous,
All be it told sometimes in sundry wise although it be
By sundry folk, as I shall you devise.
As thus, ye wot that ev'ry Evangelist,
That telleth us the pain of Jesus Christ, passion
He saith not all thing as his fellow doth;
But natheless their sentence is all soth, true
And all accorden as in their sentence, meaning
All be there in their telling difference;
For some of them say more, and some say less,
When they his piteous passion express;
I mean of Mark and Matthew, Luke and John;
But doubteless their sentence is all one.
Therefore, lordinges all, I you beseech,
If that ye think I vary in my speech,
As thus, though that I telle somedeal more
Of proverbes, than ye have heard before
Comprehended in this little treatise here,
T'enforce with the effect of my mattere, with which to
And though I not the same wordes say enforce
As ye have heard, yet to you all I pray
Blame me not; for as in my sentence
Shall ye nowhere finde no difference
From the sentence of thilke treatise lite, this little
After the which this merry tale I write.
And therefore hearken to what I shall say,
And let me tellen all my tale, I pray."

Notes to the Prologue to Chaucer's Tale of Meliboeus.

1. Chaucer crowns the satire on the romanticists by making the very landlord of the Tabard cry out in indignant disgust against the stuff which he had heard recited — the good Host ascribing to sheer ignorance the string of pompous platitudes and prosaic details which Chaucer had uttered.
2. Drafty: worthless, vile; no better than draff or dregs; from the Anglo-Saxon, "drifan" to drive away, expel.

THE TALE.[1]

    A young man called Meliboeus, mighty and rich, begat upon his wife, that called was Prudence, a daughter which that called was Sophia. Upon a day befell, that he for his disport went into the fields him to play. His wife and eke his daughter hath he left within his house, of which the doors were fast shut. Three of his old foes have it espied, and set ladders to the walls of his house, and by the windows be entered, and beaten his wife, and wounded his daughter with five mortal wounds, in five sundry places; that is to say, in her feet, in her hands, in her ears, in her nose, and in her mouth; and left her for dead, and went away. When Meliboeus returned was into his house, and saw all this mischief, he, like a man mad, rending his clothes, gan weep and cry. Prudence his wife, as farforth as she durst, besought him of his weeping for to stint: but not forthy [notwithstanding] he gan to weep and cry ever longer the more.

    This noble wife Prudence remembered her upon the sentence of Ovid, in his book that called is the "Remedy of Love,"[2] where he saith: He is a fool that disturbeth the mother to weep in the death of her child, till she have wept her fill, as for a certain time; and then shall a man do his diligence with amiable words her to recomfort and pray her of her weeping for to stint [cease]. For which reason this noble wife Prudence suffered her husband for to weep and cry, as for a certain space; and when she saw her time, she said to him in this wise: "Alas! my lord," quoth she, "why make ye yourself for to be like a fool? For sooth it appertaineth not to a wise man to make such a sorrow. Your daughter, with the grace of God, shall warish [be cured] and escape. And all [although] were it so that she right now were dead, ye ought not for her death yourself to destroy. Seneca saith, 'The wise man shall not take too great discomfort for the death of his children, but certes he should suffer it in patience, as well as he abideth the death of his own proper person.'"

Meliboeus answered anon and said: "What man," quoth he, "should of his weeping stint, that hath so great a cause to weep? Jesus Christ, our Lord, himself wept for the death of Lazarus his friend." Prudence answered, "Certes, well I wot, attempered [moderate] weeping is nothing defended [forbidden] to him that sorrowful is, among folk in sorrow but it is rather granted him to weep. The Apostle Paul unto the Romans writeth, 'Man shall rejoice with them that make joy, and weep with such folk as weep.' But though temperate weeping be granted, outrageous weeping certes is defended. Measure of weeping should be conserved, after the lore [doctrine] that teacheth us Seneca. 'When that thy friend is dead,' quoth he, 'let not thine eyes too moist be of tears, nor too much dry: although the tears come to thine eyes, let them not fall. And when thou hast forgone [lost] thy friend, do diligence to get again another friend: and this is more wisdom than to weep for thy friend which that thou hast lorn [lost] for therein is no boot [advantage]. And therefore if ye govern you by sapience, put away sorrow out of your heart. Remember you that Jesus Sirach saith, 'A man that is joyous and glad in heart, it him conserveth flourishing in his age: but soothly a sorrowful heart maketh his bones dry.' He said eke thus, 'that sorrow in heart slayth full many a man.' Solomon saith 'that right as moths in the sheep's fleece annoy [do injury] to the clothes, and the small worms to the tree, right so annoyeth sorrow to the heart of man.' Wherefore us ought as well in the death of our children, as in the loss of our goods temporal, have patience. Remember you upon the patient Job, when he had lost his children and his temporal substance, and in his body endured and received full many a grievous tribulation, yet said he thus: 'Our Lord hath given it to me, our Lord hath bereft it me; right as our Lord would, right so be it done; blessed be the name of our Lord.'"

To these foresaid things answered Meliboeus unto his wife Prudence: "All thy words," quoth he, "be true, and thereto [also] profitable, but truly mine heart is troubled with this sorrow so grievously, that I know not what to do." "Let call," quoth Prudence, "thy true friends all, and thy lineage, which be wise, and tell to them your case, and hearken what they say in counselling, and govern you after their sentence [opinion]. Solomon saith, 'Work all things by counsel, and thou shall never repent.'" Then, by counsel of his wife Prudence, this Meliboeus let call [sent for] a great congregation of folk, as surgeons, physicians, old folk and young, and some of his old enemies reconciled (as by their semblance) to his love and to his grace; and therewithal there come some of his neighbours, that did him reverence more for dread than for love, as happeneth oft. There come also full many subtle flatterers, and wise advocates learned in the law. And when these folk together assembled were, this Meliboeus in sorrowful wise showed them his case, and by the manner of his speech it seemed that in heart he bare a cruel ire, ready to do vengeance upon his foes, and suddenly desired that the war should begin, but nevertheless yet asked he their counsel in this matter. A surgeon, by licence and assent of such as were wise, up rose, and to Meliboeus said as ye may hear. "Sir," quoth he, "as to us surgeons appertaineth, that we do to every wight the best that we can, where as we be withholden, [employed] and to our patient that we do no damage; wherefore it happeneth many a time and oft, that when two men have wounded each other, one same surgeon healeth them both; wherefore unto our art it is not pertinent to nurse war, nor parties to support [take sides]. But certes, as to the warishing [healing] of your daughter, albeit so that perilously she be wounded, we shall do so attentive business from day to night, that, with the grace of God, she shall be whole and sound, as soon as is possible." Almost right in the same wise the physicians answered, save that they said a few words more: that right as maladies be cured by their contraries, right so shall man warish war (by peace). His neighbours full of envy, his feigned friends that seemed reconciled, and his flatterers, made semblance of weeping, and impaired and agregged [aggravated] much of this matter, in praising greatly Meliboeus of might, of power, of riches, and of friends, despising the power of his adversaries: and said utterly, that he anon should wreak him on his foes, and begin war.

Up rose then an advocate that was wise, by leave and by counsel of other that were wise, and said, "Lordings, the need [business] for which we be assembled in this place, is a full heavy thing, and an high matter, because of the wrong and of the wickedness that hath been done, and eke by reason of the great damages that in time coming be possible to fall for the same cause, and eke by reason of the great riches and power of the parties both; for which reasons, it were a full great peril to err in this matter. Wherefore, Meliboeus, this is our sentence [opinion]; we counsel you, above all things, that right anon thou do thy diligence in keeping of thy body, in such a wise that thou want no espy nor watch thy body to save. And after that, we counsel that in thine house thou set sufficient garrison, so that they may as well thy body as thy house defend. But, certes, to move war or suddenly to do vengeance, we may not deem [judge] in so little time that it were profitable. Wherefore we ask leisure and space to have deliberation in this case to deem; for the common proverb saith thus; 'He that soon deemeth soon shall repent.' And eke men say, that that judge is wise, that soon understandeth a matter, and judgeth by leisure. For albeit so that all tarrying be annoying, algates [nevertheless] it is no reproof [subject for reproach] in giving of judgement, nor in vengeance taking, when it is sufficient and, reasonable. And that shewed our Lord Jesus Christ by example; for when that the woman that was taken in adultery was brought in his presence to know what should be done with her person, albeit that he wist well himself what he would answer, yet would he not answer suddenly, but he would have deliberation, and in the ground he wrote twice. And by these causes we ask deliberation and we shall then by the grace of God counsel the thing that shall be profitable."

Up started then the young folk anon at once, and the most part of that company have scorned these old wise men and begun to make noise and said, "Right as while that iron is hot men should smite, right so men should wreak their wrongs while that they be fresh and new:" and with loud voice they cried. "War! War!" Up rose then one of these old wise, and with his hand made countenance [a sign, gesture] that men should hold them still, and give him audience. "Lordings," quoth he, "there is full many a man that crieth, 'War! war!' that wot full little what war amounteth. War at his beginning hath so great an entering and so large, that every wight may enter when him liketh, and lightly [easily] find war: but certes what end shall fall thereof it is not light to know. For soothly when war is once begun, there is full many a child unborn of his mother, that shall sterve [die] young by cause of that war, or else live in sorrow and die in wretchedness; and therefore, ere that any war be begun, men must have great counsel and great deliberation." And when this old man weened [thought, intended] to enforce his tale by reasons, well-nigh all at once began they to rise for to break his tale, and bid him full oft his words abridge. For soothly he that preacheth to them that list not hear his words, his sermon them annoyeth. For Jesus Sirach saith, that music in weeping is a noyous [troublesome] thing. This is to say, as much availeth to speak before folk to whom his speech annoyeth, as to sing before him that weepeth. And when this wise man saw that him wanted audience, all shamefast he sat him down again. For Solomon saith, 'Where as thou mayest have no audience, enforce thee not to speak.' "I see well," quoth this wise man, "that the common proverb is sooth, that good counsel wanteth, when it is most need." Yet [besides, further] had this Meliboeus in his council many folk, that privily in his ear counselled him certain thing, and counselled him the contrary in general audience. When Meliboeus had heard that the greatest part of his council were accorded [in agreement] that he should make war, anon he consented to their counselling, and fully affirmed their sentence [opinion, judgement].

(Dame Prudence, seeing her husband's resolution thus taken, in full humble wise, when she saw her time, begins to counsel him against war, by a warning against haste in requital of either good or evil. Meliboeus tells her that he will not work by her counsel, because he should be held a fool if he rejected for her advice the opinion of so many wise men; because all women are bad; because it would seem that he had given her the mastery over him; and because she could not keep his secret, if he resolved to follow her advice. To these reasons Prudence answers that it is no folly to change counsel when things, or men's judgements of them, change — especially to alter a resolution taken on the impulse of a great multitude of folk, where every man crieth and clattereth what him liketh; that if all women had been wicked, Jesus Christ would never have descended to be born of a woman, nor have showed himself first to a woman after his resurrection and that when Solomon said he had found no good woman, he meant that God alone was supremely good;[3] that her husband would not seem to give her the mastery by following her counsel, for he had his own free choice in following or rejecting it; and that he knew well and had often tested her great silence, patience, and secrecy. And whereas he had quoted a saying, that in wicked counsel women vanquish men, she reminds him that she would counsel him against doing a wickedness on which he had set his mind, and cites instances to show that many women have been and yet are full good, and their counsel wholesome and profitable. Lastly, she quotes the words of God himself, when he was about to make woman as an help meet for man; and promises that, if her husband will trust her counsel, she will restore to him his daughter whole and sound, and make him have honour in this case. Meliboeus answers that because of his wife's sweet words, and also because he has proved and assayed her great wisdom and her great truth, he will govern him by her counsel in all things. Thus encouraged, Prudence enters on a long discourse, full of learned citations, regarding the manner in which counsellors should be chosen and consulted, and the times and reasons for changing a counsel. First, God must be besought for guidance. Then a man must well examine his own thoughts, of such things as he holds to be best for his own profit; driving out of his heart anger, covetousness, and hastiness, which perturb and pervert the judgement. Then he must keep his counsel secret, unless confiding it to another shall be more profitable; but, in so confiding it, he shall say nothing to bias the mind of the counsellor toward flattery or subserviency. After that he should consider his friends and his enemies, choosing of the former such as be most faithful and wise, and eldest and most approved in counselling; and even of these only a few. Then he must eschew the counselling of fools, of flatterers, of his old enemies that be reconciled, of servants who bear him great reverence and fear, of folk that be drunken and can hide no counsel, of such as counsel one thing privily and the contrary openly; and of young folk, for their counselling is not ripe. Then, in examining his counsel, he must truly tell his tale; he must consider whether the thing he proposes to do be reasonable, within his power, and acceptable to the more part and the better part of his counsellors; he must look at the things that may follow from that counselling, choosing the best and waiving all besides; he must consider the root whence the matter of his counsel is engendered, what fruits it may bear, and from what causes they be sprung. And having thus examined his counsel and approved it by many wise folk and old, he shall consider if he may perform it and make of it a good end; if he be in doubt, he shall choose rather to suffer than to begin; but otherwise he shall prosecute his resolution steadfastly till the enterprise be at an end. As to changing his counsel, a man may do so without reproach, if the cause cease, or when a new case betides, or if he find that by error or otherwise harm or damage may result, or if his counsel be dishonest or come of dishonest cause, or if it be impossible or may not properly be kept; and he must take it for a general rule, that every counsel which is affirmed so strongly, that it may not be changed for any condition that may betide, that counsel is wicked. Meliboeus, admitting that his wife had spoken well and suitably as to counsellors and counsel in general, prays her to tell him in especial what she thinks of the counsellors whom they have chosen in their present need. Prudence replies that his counsel in this case could not properly be called a counselling, but a movement of folly; and points out that he has erred in sundry wise against the rules which he had just laid down. Granting that he has erred, Meliboeus says that he is all ready to change his counsel right as she will devise; for, as the proverb runs, to do sin is human, but to persevere long in sin is work of the Devil. Prudence then minutely recites, analyses, and criticises the counsel given to her husband in the assembly of his friends. She commends the advice of the physicians and surgeons, and urges that they should be well rewarded for their noble speech and their services in healing Sophia; and she asks Meliboeus how he understands their proposition that one contrary must be cured by another contrary. Meliboeus answers, that he should do vengeance on his enemies, who had done him wrong. Prudence, however, insists that vengeance is not the contrary of vengeance, nor wrong of wrong, but the like; and that wickedness should be healed by goodness, discord by accord, war by peace. She proceeds to deal with the counsel of the lawyers and wise folk that advised Meliboeus to take prudent measures for the security of his body and of his house. First, she would have her husband pray for the protection and aid of Christ; then commit the keeping of his person to his true friends; then suspect and avoid all strange folk, and liars, and such people as she had already warned him against; then beware of presuming on his strength, or the weakness of his adversary, and neglecting to guard his person — for every wise man dreadeth his enemy; then he should evermore be on the watch against ambush and all espial, even in what seems a place of safety; though he should not be so cowardly, as to fear where is no cause for dread; yet he should dread to be poisoned, and therefore shun scorners, and fly their words as venom. As to the fortification of his house, she points out that towers and great edifices are costly and laborious, yet useless unless defended by true friends that be old and wise; and the greatest and strongest garrison that a rich man may have, as well to keep his person as his goods, is, that he be beloved by his subjects and by his neighbours. Warmly approving the counsel that in all this business Meliboeus should proceed with great diligence and deliberation, Prudence goes on to examine the advice given by his neighbours that do him reverence without love, his old enemies reconciled, his flatterers that counselled him certain things privily and openly counselled him the contrary, and the young folk that counselled him to avenge himself and make war at once. She reminds him that he stands alone against three powerful enemies, whose kindred are numerous and close, while his are fewer and remote in relationship; that only the judge who has jurisdiction in a case may take sudden vengeance on any man; that her husband's power does not accord with his desire; and that, if he did take vengeance, it would only breed fresh wrongs and contests. As to the causes of the wrong done to him, she holds that God, the causer of all things, has permitted him to suffer because he has drunk so much honey[4] of sweet temporal riches, and delights, and honours of this world, that he is drunken, and has forgotten Jesus Christ his Saviour; the three enemies of mankind, the flesh, the fiend, and the world, have entered his heart by the windows of his body, and wounded his soul in five places — that is to say, the deadly sins that have entered into his heart by the five senses; and in the same manner Christ has suffered his three enemies to enter his house by the windows, and wound his daughter in the five places before specified. Meliboeus demurs, that if his wife's objections prevailed, vengeance would never be taken, and thence great mischiefs would arise; but Prudence replies that the taking of vengeance lies with the judges, to whom the private individual must have recourse. Meliboeus declares that such vengeance does not please him, and that, as Fortune has nourished and helped him from his childhood, he will now assay her, trusting, with God's help, that she will aid him to avenge his shame. Prudence warns him against trusting to Fortune, all the less because she has hitherto favoured him, for just on that account she is the more likely to fail him; and she calls on him to leave his vengeance with the Sovereign Judge, that avengeth all villainies and wrongs. Meliboeus argues that if he refrains from taking vengeance he will invite his enemies to do him further wrong, and he will be put and held over low; but Prudence contends that such a result can be brought about only by the neglect of the judges, not by the patience of the individual. Supposing that he had leave to avenge himself, she repeats that he is not strong enough, and quotes the common saw, that it is madness for a man to strive with a stronger than himself, peril to strive with one of equal strength, and folly to strive with a weaker. But, considering his own defaults and demerits, — remembering the patience of Christ and the undeserved tribulations of the saints, the brevity of this life with all its trouble and sorrow, the discredit thrown on the wisdom and training of a man who cannot bear wrong with patience — he should refrain wholly from taking vengeance. Meliboeus submits that he is not at all a perfect man, and his heart will never be at peace until he is avenged; and that as his enemies disregarded the peril when they attacked him, so he might, without reproach, incur some peril in attacking them in return, even though he did a great excess in avenging one wrong by another. Prudence strongly deprecates all outrage or excess; but Meliboeus insists that he cannot see that it might greatly harm him though he took a vengeance, for he is richer and mightier than his enemies, and all things obey money. Prudence thereupon launches into a long dissertation on the advantages of riches, the evils of poverty, the means by which wealth should be gathered, and the manner in which it should be used; and concludes by counselling her husband not to move war and battle through trust in his riches, for they suffice not to maintain war, the battle is not always to the strong or the numerous, and the perils of conflict are many. Meliboeus then curtly asks her for her counsel how he shall do in this need; and she answers that certainly she counsels him to agree with his adversaries and have peace with them. Meliboeus on this cries out that plainly she loves not his honour or his worship, in counselling him to go and humble himself before his enemies, crying mercy to them that, having done him so grievous wrong, ask him not to be reconciled. Then Prudence, making semblance of wrath, retorts that she loves his honour and profit as she loves her own, and ever has done; she cites the Scriptures in support of her counsel to seek peace; and says she will leave him to his own courses, for she knows well he is so stubborn, that he will do nothing for her. Meliboeus then relents; admits that he is angry and cannot judge aright; and puts himself wholly in her hands, promising to do just as she desires, and admitting that he is the more held to love and praise her, if she reproves him of his folly)

Then Dame Prudence discovered all her counsel and her will unto him, and said: "I counsel you," quoth she, "above all things, that ye make peace between God and you, and be reconciled unto Him and to his grace; for, as I have said to you herebefore, God hath suffered you to have this tribulation and disease [distress, trouble] for your sins; and if ye do as I say you, God will send your adversaries unto you, and make them fall at your feet, ready to do your will and your commandment. For Solomon saith, 'When the condition of man is pleasant and liking to God, he changeth the hearts of the man's adversaries, and constraineth them to beseech him of peace of grace.' And I pray you let me speak with your adversaries in privy place, for they shall not know it is by your will or your assent; and then, when I know their will and their intent, I may counsel you the more surely." "'Dame," quoth Meliboeus, "'do your will and your liking, for I put me wholly in your disposition and ordinance."

Then Dame Prudence, when she saw the goodwill of her husband, deliberated and took advice in herself, thinking how she might bring this need [affair, emergency] unto a good end. And when she saw her time, she sent for these adversaries to come into her into a privy place, and showed wisely into them the great goods that come of peace, and the great harms and perils that be in war; and said to them, in goodly manner, how that they ought have great repentance of the injuries and wrongs that they had done to Meliboeus her Lord, and unto her and her daughter. And when they heard the goodly words of Dame Prudence, then they were surprised and ravished, and had so great joy of her, that wonder was to tell. "Ah lady!" quoth they, "ye have showed unto us the blessing of sweetness, after the saying of David the prophet; for the reconciling which we be not worthy to have in no manner, but we ought require it with great contrition and humility, ye of your great goodness have presented unto us. Now see we well, that the science and conning [knowledge] of Solomon is full true; for he saith, that sweet words multiply and increase friends, and make shrews [the ill-natured or angry] to be debonair [gentle, courteous] and meek. Certes we put our deed, and all our matter and cause, all wholly in your goodwill, and be ready to obey unto the speech and commandment of my lord Meliboeus. And therefore, dear and benign lady, we pray you and beseech you as meekly as we can and may, that it like unto your great goodness to fulfil in deed your goodly words. For we consider and acknowledge that we have offended and grieved my lord Meliboeus out of measure, so far forth that we be not of power to make him amends; and therefore we oblige and bind us and our friends to do all his will and his commandment. But peradventure he hath such heaviness and such wrath to usward, [towards us] because of our offence, that he will enjoin us such a pain [penalty] as we may not bear nor sustain; and therefore, noble lady, we beseech to your womanly pity to take such advisement [consideration] in this need, that we, nor our friends, be not disinherited and destroyed through our folly."

"Certes," quoth Prudence, "it is an hard thing, and right perilous, that a man put him all utterly in the arbitration and judgement and in the might and power of his enemy. For Solomon saith, 'Believe me, and give credence to that that I shall say: to thy son, to thy wife, to thy friend, nor to thy brother, give thou never might nor mastery over thy body, while thou livest.' Now, since he defendeth [forbiddeth] that a man should not give to his brother, nor to his friend, the might of his body, by a stronger reason he defendeth and forbiddeth a man to give himself to his enemy. And nevertheless, I counsel you that ye mistrust not my lord: for I wot well and know verily, that he is debonair and meek, large, courteous and nothing desirous nor envious of good nor riches: for there is nothing in this world that he desireth save only worship and honour. Furthermore I know well, and am right sure, that he shall nothing do in this need without counsel of me; and I shall so work in this case, that by the grace of our Lord God ye shall be reconciled unto us."

Then said they with one voice, ""Worshipful lady, we put us and our goods all fully in your will and disposition, and be ready to come, what day that it like unto your nobleness to limit us or assign us, for to make our obligation and bond, as strong as it liketh unto your goodness, that we may fulfil the will of you and of my lord Meliboeus."

When Dame Prudence had heard the answer of these men, she bade them go again privily, and she returned to her lord Meliboeus, and told him how she found his adversaries full repentant, acknowledging full lowly their sins and trespasses, and how they were ready to suffer all pain, requiring and praying him of mercy and pity. Then said Meliboeus, "He is well worthy to have pardon and forgiveness of his sin, that excuseth not his sin, but acknowledgeth, and repenteth him, asking indulgence. For Seneca saith, 'There is the remission and forgiveness, where the confession is; for confession is neighbour to innocence.' And therefore I assent and confirm me to have peace, but it is good that we do naught without the assent and will of our friends." Then was Prudence right glad and joyful, and said, "Certes, Sir, ye be well and goodly advised; for right as by the counsel, assent, and help of your friends ye have been stirred to avenge you and make war, right so without their counsel shall ye not accord you, nor have peace with your adversaries. For the law saith, 'There is nothing so good by way of kind, [nature] as a thing to be unbound by him that it was bound.'"

And then Dame Prudence, without delay or tarrying, sent anon her messengers for their kin and for their old friends, which were true and wise; and told them by order, in the presence of Meliboeus, all this matter, as it is above expressed and declared; and prayed them that they would give their advice and counsel what were best to do in this need. And when Meliboeus' friends had taken their advice and deliberation of the foresaid matter, and had examined it by great business and great diligence, they gave full counsel for to have peace and rest, and that Meliboeus should with good heart receive his adversaries to forgiveness and mercy. And when Dame Prudence had heard the assent of her lord Meliboeus, and the counsel of his friends, accord with her will and her intention, she was wondrous glad in her heart, and said: "There is an old proverb that saith, 'The goodness that thou mayest do this day, do it, and abide not nor delay it not till to-morrow:' and therefore I counsel you that ye send your messengers, such as be discreet and wise, unto your adversaries, telling them on your behalf, that if they will treat of peace and of accord, that they shape [prepare] them, without delay or tarrying, to come unto us." Which thing performed was indeed. And when these trespassers and repenting folk of their follies, that is to say, the adversaries of Meliboeus, had heard what these messengers said unto them, they were right glad and joyful, and answered full meekly and benignly, yielding graces and thanks to their lord Meliboeus, and to all his company; and shaped them without delay to go with the messengers, and obey to the commandment of their lord Meliboeus. And right anon they took their way to the court of Meliboeus, and took with them some of their true friends, to make faith for them, and for to be their borrows [sureties].

And when they were come to the presence of Meliboeus, he said to them these words; "It stands thus," quoth Meliboeus, "and sooth it is, that ye causeless, and without skill and reason, have done great injuries and wrongs to me, and to my wife Prudence, and to my daughter also; for ye have entered into my house by violence, and have done such outrage, that all men know well that ye have deserved the death: and therefore will I know and weet of you, whether ye will put the punishing and chastising, and the vengeance of this outrage, in the will of me and of my wife, or ye will not?" Then the wisest of them three answered for them all, and said; "Sir," quoth he, "we know well, that we be I unworthy to come to the court of so great a lord and so worthy as ye be, for we have so greatly mistaken us, and have offended and aguilt [incurred guilt] in such wise against your high lordship, that truly we have deserved the death. But yet for the great goodness and debonairte [courtesy, gentleness] that all the world witnesseth of your person, we submit us to the excellence and benignity of your gracious lordship, and be ready to obey to all your commandments, beseeching you, that of your merciable [merciful] pity ye will consider our great repentance and low submission, and grant us forgiveness of our outrageous trespass and offence; for well we know, that your liberal grace and mercy stretch them farther into goodness, than do our outrageous guilt and trespass into wickedness; albeit that cursedly [wickedly] and damnably we have aguilt [incurred guilt] against your high lordship." Then Meliboeus took them up from the ground full benignly, and received their obligations and their bonds, by their oaths upon their pledges and borrows, [sureties] and assigned them a certain day to return unto his court for to receive and accept sentence and judgement, that Meliboeus would command to be done on them, by the causes aforesaid; which things ordained, every man returned home to his house.

And when that Dame Prudence saw her time she freined [inquired] and asked her lord Meliboeus, what vengeance he thought to take of his adversaries. To which Meliboeus answered, and said; "Certes," quoth he, "I think and purpose me fully to disinherit them of all that ever they have, and for to put them in exile for evermore." "Certes," quoth Dame Prudence, "this were a cruel sentence, and much against reason. For ye be rich enough, and have no need of other men's goods; and ye might lightly [easily] in this wise get you a covetous name, which is a vicious thing, and ought to be eschewed of every good man: for, after the saying of the Apostle, covetousness is root of all harms. And therefore it were better for you to lose much good of your own, than for to take of their good in this manner. For better it is to lose good with worship [honour], than to win good with villainy and shame. And every man ought to do his diligence and his business to get him a good name. And yet [further] shall he not only busy him in keeping his good name, but he shall also enforce him alway to do some thing by which he may renew his good name; for it is written, that the old good los [reputation5] of a man is soon gone and passed, when it is not renewed. And as touching that ye say, that ye will exile your adversaries, that thinketh ye much against reason, and out of measure, [moderation] considered the power that they have given you upon themselves. And it is written, that he is worthy to lose his privilege, that misuseth the might and the power that is given him. And I set case [if I assume] ye might enjoin them that pain by right and by law (which I trow ye may not do), I say, ye might not put it to execution peradventure, and then it were like to return to the war, as it was before. And therefore if ye will that men do you obeisance, ye must deem [decide] more courteously, that is to say, ye must give more easy sentences and judgements. For it is written, 'He that most courteously commandeth, to him men most obey.' And therefore I pray you, that in this necessity and in this need ye cast you [endeavour, devise a way] to overcome your heart. For Seneca saith, that he that overcometh his heart, overcometh twice. And Tullius saith, 'There is nothing so commendable in a great lord, as when he is debonair and meek, and appeaseth him lightly [easily].' And I pray you, that ye will now forbear to do vengeance, in such a manner, that your good name may be kept and conserved, and that men may have cause and matter to praise you of pity and of mercy; and that ye have no cause to repent you of thing that ye do. For Seneca saith, 'He overcometh in an evil manner, that repenteth him of his victory.' Wherefore I pray you let mercy be in your heart, to the effect and intent that God Almighty have mercy upon you in his last judgement; for Saint James saith in his Epistle, 'Judgement without mercy shall be done to him, that hath no mercy of another wight.'"

When Meliboeus had heard the great skills [arguments, reasons] and reasons of Dame Prudence, and her wise information and teaching, his heart gan incline to the will of his wife, considering her true intent, he conformed him anon and assented fully to work after her counsel, and thanked God, of whom proceedeth all goodness and all virtue, that him sent a wife of so great discretion. And when the day came that his adversaries should appear in his presence, he spake to them full goodly, and said in this wise; "Albeit so, that of your pride and high presumption and folly, an of your negligence and unconning, [ignorance] ye have misborne [misbehaved] you, and trespassed [done injury] unto me, yet forasmuch as I see and behold your great humility, and that ye be sorry and repentant of your guilts, it constraineth me to do you grace and mercy. Wherefore I receive you into my grace, and forgive you utterly all the offences, injuries, and wrongs, that ye have done against me and mine, to this effect and to this end, that God of his endless mercy will at the time of our dying forgive us our guilts, that we have trespassed to him in this wretched world; for doubtless, if we be sorry and repentant of the sins and guilts which we have trespassed in the sight of our Lord God, he is so free and so merciable [merciful], that he will forgive us our guilts, and bring us to the bliss that never hath end." Amen.

Notes to Chaucer's Tale of Meliboeus.

1. The Tale of Meliboeus is literally translated from a French story, or rather "treatise," in prose, entitled "Le Livre de Melibee et de Dame Prudence," of which two manuscripts, both dating from the fifteenth century, are preserved in the British Museum. Tyrwhitt, justly enough, says of it that it is indeed, as Chaucer called it in the prologue, "'a moral tale virtuous,' and was probably much esteemed in its time; but, in this age of levity, I doubt some readers will be apt to regret that he did not rather give us the remainder of Sir Thopas." It has been remarked that in the earlier portion of the Tale, as it left the hand of the poet, a number of blank verses were intermixed; though this peculiarity of style, noticeable in any case only in the first 150 or 200 lines, has necessarily all but disappeared by the changes of spelling made in the modern editions. The Editor's purpose being to present to the public not "The Canterbury Tales" merely, but "The Poems of Chaucer," so far as may be consistent with the limits of this volume, he has condensed the long reasonings and learned quotations of Dame Prudence into a mere outline, connecting those portions of the Tale wherein lies so much of story as it actually possesses, and the general reader will probably not regret the sacrifice, made in the view of retaining so far as possible the completeness of the Tales, while lessening the intrusion of prose into a volume or poems. The good wife of Meliboeus literally overflows with quotations from David, Solomon, Jesus the Son of Sirach, the Apostles, Ovid, Cicero, Seneca, Cassiodorus, Cato, Petrus Alphonsus — the converted Spanish Jew, of the twelfth century, who wrote the "Disciplina Clericalis" — and other authorities; and in some passages, especially where husband and wife debate the merits or demerits of women, and where Prudence dilates on the evils of poverty, Chaucer only reproduces

much that had been said already in the Tales that preceded — such as the Merchant's and the Man of Law's.
2. The lines which follow are a close translation of the original Latin, which reads:
> "Quis matrem, nisi mentis inops, in funere nati
> Flere vetet? non hoc illa monenda loco.
> Cum dederit lacrymas, animumque expleverit aegrum,
> Ille dolor verbis emoderandus erit."

Ovid, "Remedia Amoris," 127-131.
3. See the conversation between Pluto and Proserpine, in the Merchant's Tale.
4. "Thy name," she says, "is Meliboeus; that is to say, a man that drinketh honey."
5. Los: reputation; from the past participle of the Anglo-Saxon, "hlisan" to celebrate. Compare Latin, "laus."

ous tale of Melibee,
THE MONK'S TALE.
THE PROLOGUE

WHEN ended was my tale of Melibee,
And of Prudence and her benignity,
Our Hoste said, "As I am faithful man,
And by the precious corpus Madrian,[1]
I had lever than a barrel of ale, rather
That goode lefe my wife had heard this tale; dear
For she is no thing of such patience
As was this Meliboeus' wife Prudence.
By Godde's bones! when I beat my knaves
She bringeth me the greate clubbed staves,
And crieth, 'Slay the dogges every one,
And break of them both back and ev'ry bone.'
And if that any neighebour of mine
Will not in church unto my wife incline,
Or be so hardy to her to trespace, offend
When she comes home she rampeth in my face, springs
And crieth, 'False coward, wreak thy wife avenge
By corpus Domini, I will have thy knife,
And thou shalt have my distaff, and go spin.'
From day till night right thus she will begin.
'Alas!' she saith, 'that ever I was shape destined
To wed a milksop, or a coward ape,
That will be overlad with every wight! imposed on
Thou darest not stand by thy wife's right.'

"This is my life, but if that I will fight; unless
And out at door anon I must me dight, betake myself
Or elles I am lost, but if that I
Be, like a wilde lion, fool-hardy.
I wot well she will do me slay some day make
Some neighebour and thenne go my way; take to flight
For I am perilous with knife in hand,
Albeit that I dare not her withstand;
For she is big in armes, by my faith!
That shall he find, that her misdoth or saith.[2]
But let us pass away from this mattere.
My lord the Monk," quoth he, "be merry of cheer,
For ye shall tell a tale truely.
Lo, Rochester stands here faste by.
Ride forth, mine owen lord, break not our game.
But by my troth I cannot tell your name;
Whether shall I call you my lord Dan John,
Or Dan Thomas, or elles Dan Albon?
Of what house be ye, by your father's kin?
I vow to God, thou hast a full fair skin;
It is a gentle pasture where thou go'st;
Thou art not like a penant or a ghost. penitent
Upon my faith thou art some officer,
Some worthy sexton, or some cellarer.
For by my father's soul, as to my dome, in my judgement
Thou art a master when thou art at home;
No poore cloisterer, nor no novice,
But a governor, both wily and wise,
And therewithal, of brawnes and of bones, sinews
A right well-faring person for the nonce.
I pray to God give him confusion
That first thee brought into religion.
Thou would'st have been a treade-fowl aright; cock
Hadst thou as greate leave, as thou hast might,
To perform all thy lust in engendrure, generation, begettting
Thou hadst begotten many a creature.
Alas! why wearest thou so wide a cope?[3]
God give me sorrow, but, an I were pope, if
Not only thou, but every mighty man,
Though he were shorn full high upon his pan,[4] crown
Should have a wife; for all this world is lorn; undone, ruined
Religion hath ta'en up all the corn
Of treading, and we borel men be shrimps: lay
Of feeble trees there come wretched imps. shoots[5]
This maketh that our heires be so slender
And feeble, that they may not well engender.
This maketh that our wives will assay
Religious folk, for they may better pay
Of Venus' payementes than may we:
God wot, no lusheburghes[6] paye ye.
But be not wroth, my lord, though that I play;
Full oft in game a sooth have I heard say."

This worthy Monk took all in patience,
And said, "I will do all my diligence,
As far as souneth unto honesty, agrees with good manners
To telle you a tale, or two or three.
And if you list to hearken hitherward,
I will you say the life of Saint Edward;
Or elles first tragedies I will tell,
Of which I have an hundred in my cell.
Tragedy is to say a certain story, means
As olde bookes maken us memory,
Of him that stood in great prosperity,
And is y-fallen out of high degree
In misery, and endeth wretchedly.
And they be versified commonly
Of six feet, which men call hexametron;
In prose eke be indited many a one, also
And eke in metre, in many a sundry wise.

GEOFFREY CHAUCER

Lo, this declaring ought enough suffice.
Now hearken, if ye like for to hear.
But first I you beseech in this mattere,
Though I by order telle not these things,
Be it of popes, emperors, or kings,
After their ages, as men written find, in chronological order
But tell them some before and some behind,
As it now cometh to my remembrance,
Have me excused of mine ignorance."

Notes to the Prologue to The Monk's Tale

1. The Corpus Madrian: the body of St. Maternus, of Treves.
2. That her misdoth or saith: that does or says any thing to offend her.
3. Cope: An ecclesiastcal vestment covering all the body like a cloak.
4. Though he were shorn full high upon his pan: though he were tonsured, as the clergy are.
5. Imps: shoots, branches; from Anglo-Saxon, "impian," German, "impfen," to implant, ingraft. The word is now used in a very restricted sense, to signify the progeny, children, of the devil.
6. Lusheburghes: base or counterfeit coins; so called because struck at Luxemburg. A great importation of them took place during the reigns of the earlier Edwards, and they caused much annoyance and complaint, till in 1351 it was declared treason to bring them into the country.

THE TALE.[1]

I will bewail, in manner of tragedy,
The harm of them that stood in high degree,
And felle so, that there was no remedy
To bring them out of their adversity.
For, certain, when that Fortune list to flee,
There may no man the course of her wheel hold:
Let no man trust in blind prosperity;
Beware by these examples true and old.

At LUCIFER, though he an angel were,
And not a man, at him I will begin.
For though Fortune may no angel dere, *hurt*
From high degree yet fell he for his sin
Down into hell, where as he yet is in.
O Lucifer! brightest of angels all,
Now art thou Satanas, that may'st not twin *depart*
Out of the misery in which thou art fall.

Lo ADAM, in the field of Damascene[2]
With Godde's owen finger wrought was he,
And not begotten of man's sperm unclean;
And welt all Paradise saving one tree: *commanded*
Had never worldly man so high degree
As Adam, till he for misgovernance *misbehaviour*
Was driven out of his prosperity
To labour, and to hell, and to mischance.

Lo SAMPSON, which that was annunciate
By the angel, long ere his nativity;[3]
And was to God Almighty consecrate,
And stood in nobless while that he might see;
Was never such another as was he,
To speak of strength, and thereto hardiness; *courage*
But to his wives told he his secre,
Through which he slew himself for wretchedness.

Sampson, this noble and mighty champion,
Withoute weapon, save his handes tway,
He slew and all to-rente the lion, *tore to pieces*
Toward his wedding walking by the way.
His false wife could him so please, and pray,
Till she his counsel knew; and she, untrue,
Unto his foes his counsel gan bewray,
And him forsook, and took another new.

Three hundred foxes Sampson took for ire,
And all their tailes he together band,
And set the foxes' tailes all on fire,
For he in every tail had knit a brand,
And they burnt all the combs of that lend,
And all their oliveres and vines eke. *olive trees*[4]
A thousand men he slew eke with his hand,
And had no weapon but an ass's cheek.

When they were slain, so thirsted him, that he
Was well-nigh lorn, for which he gan to pray *near to perishing*
That God would on his pain have some pity,
And send him drink, or elles must he die;

And of this ass's check, that was so dry,
Out of a wang-tooth sprang anon a well, *cheek-tooth*
Of which, he drank enough, shortly to say.
Thus help'd him God, as Judicum[5] can tell.

By very force, at Gaza, on a night,
Maugre the Philistines of that city, *in spite of*
The gates of the town he hath up plight, *plucked, wrenched*
And on his back y-carried them hath he
High on an hill, where as men might them see.
O noble mighty Sampson, lefe and dear, *loved*
Hadst thou not told to women thy secre,
In all this world there had not been thy peer.

This Sampson never cider drank nor wine,
Nor on his head came razor none nor shear,
By precept of the messenger divine;
For all his strengthes in his haires were;
And fully twenty winters, year by year,
He had of Israel the governance;
But soone shall he weepe many a tear,
For women shall him bringe to mischance.

Unto his leman Dalila he told, *mistress*
That in his haires all his strengthe lay;
And falsely to his foemen she him sold,
And sleeping in her barme upon a day *lap*
She made to clip or shear his hair away,
And made his foemen all his craft espien.
And when they founde him in this array,
They bound him fast, and put out both his eyen.

But, ere his hair was clipped or y-shave,
There was no bond with which men might him bind;
But now is he in prison in a cave,
Where as they made him at the querne grind. *mill*[6]
O noble Sampson, strongest of mankind!
O whilom judge in glory and richess!
Now may'st thou weepe with thine eyen blind,
Since thou from weal art fall'n to wretchedness.

Th'end of this caitiff was as I shall say; *wretched man*
His foemen made a feast upon a day,
And made him as their fool before them play;
And this was in a temple of great array.
But at the last he made a foul affray,
For he two pillars shook, and made them fall,
And down fell temple and all, and there it lay,
And slew himself and eke his foemen all;

This is to say, the princes every one;
And eke three thousand bodies were there slain
With falling of the great temple of stone.
Of Sampson now will I no more sayn;
Beware by this example old and plain,

That no man tell his counsel to his wife
Of such thing as he would have secret *fain, wish
to be secret*
If that it touch his limbes or his life.

Of HERCULES the sov'reign conquerour
Singe his workes' land and high renown;
For in his time of strength he bare the flow'r.
He slew and reft the skin of the lion
He of the Centaurs laid the boast adown;
He Harpies[7] slew, the cruel birdes fell;
He golden apples reft from the dragon
He drew out Cerberus the hound of hell.

He slew the cruel tyrant Busirus.[8]
And made his horse to fret him flesh and bone; *devour*
He slew the fiery serpent venomous;
Of Achelous' two hornes brake he one.
And he slew Cacus in a cave of stone;
He slew the giant Antaeus the strong;
He slew the grisly boar, and that anon;
And bare the heav'n upon his necke long.[9]

Was never wight, since that the world began,
That slew so many monsters as did he;
Throughout the wide world his name ran,
What for his strength, and for his high bounte;
And every realme went he for to see;
He was so strong that no man might him let; *withstand*
At both the worlde's ends, as saith Trophee,[10]
Instead of boundes he a pillar set.

A leman had this noble champion,
That highte Dejanira, fresh as May;
And, as these clerkes make mention,
She hath him sent a shirte fresh and gay;
Alas! this shirt, alas and well-away!
Envenomed was subtilly withal,
That ere that he had worn it half a day,
It made his flesh all from his bones fall.

But natheless some clerkes her excuse
By one, that highte Nessus, that it maked;
Be as he may, I will not her accuse;
But on his back this shirt he wore all naked,
Till that his flesh was for the venom blaked. *blackened*
And when he saw none other remedy,
In hote coals he hath himselfe raked,
For with no venom deigned he to die.

Thus sterf this worthy mighty Hercules. *died*
Lo, who may trust on Fortune any throw? *for a moment*
For him that followeth all this world of pres, *near*[11]
Ere he be ware, is often laid full low;
Full wise is he that can himselfe know.
Beware, for when that Fortune list to glose

Then waiteth she her man to overthrow,
By such a way as he would least suppose.

The mighty throne, the precious treasor,
The glorious sceptre, and royal majesty,
That had the king NABUCHODONOSOR
With tongue unnethes may described be. *scarcely*
He twice won Jerusalem the city,
The vessels of the temple he with him lad; *took away*
At Babylone was his sov'reign see, *seat*
In which his glory and delight he had.

The fairest children of the blood royal
Of Israel he did do geld anon, *caused to be castrated*
And maked each of them to be his thrall. *slave*
Amonges others Daniel was one,
That was the wisest child of every one;
For he the dreames of the king expounded,
Where in Chaldaea clerkes was there none
That wiste to what fine his dreames sounded. *end*

This proude king let make a statue of gold
Sixty cubites long, and seven in bread',
To which image hathe young and old
Commanded he to lout, and have in dread, *bow down to*
Or in a furnace, full of flames red,
He should be burnt that woulde not obey:
But never would assente to that deed
Daniel, nor his younge fellows tway.

This king of kinges proud was and elate; *lofty*
He ween'd that God, that sits in majesty, *thought*
Mighte him not bereave of his estate;
But suddenly he lost his dignity,
And like a beast he seemed for to be,
And ate hay as an ox, and lay thereout
In rain, with wilde beastes walked he,
Till certain time was y-come about.

And like an eagle's feathers wax'd his hairs,
His nailes like a birde's clawes were,
Till God released him at certain years,
And gave him wit; and then with many a tear
He thanked God, and ever his life in fear
Was he to do amiss, or more trespace:
And till that time he laid was on his bier,
He knew that God was full of might and grace.

His sone, which that highte BALTHASAR,
That held the regne after his father's day, *possessed the kingdom*
He by his father coulde not beware,
For proud he was of heart and of array;
And eke an idolaster was he aye.
His high estate assured him in pride; *confirmed*
But Fortune cast him down, and there he lay,
And suddenly his regne gan divide.

THE CANTERBURY TALES

A feast he made unto his lordes all
Upon a time, and made them blithe be,
And then his officeres gan he call;
"Go, bringe forth the vessels," saide he,
"Which that my father in his prosperity
Out of the temple of Jerusalem reft,
And to our highe goddes thanks we
Of honour, that our elders with us left."
   forefathers

His wife, his lordes, and his concubines
Aye dranke, while their appetites did last,
Out of these noble vessels sundry wines.
And on a wall this king his eyen cast,
And saw an hand, armless, that wrote full fast;
For fear of which he quaked, and sighed sore.
This hand, that Balthasar so sore aghast,   dismayed
Wrote Mane, tekel, phares, and no more.

In all that land magician was there none
That could expounde what this letter meant.
But Daniel expounded it anon,
And said, "O King, God to thy father lent
Glory and honour, regne, treasure, rent;   revenue
And he was proud, and nothing God he drad;
   dreaded
And therefore God great wreche upon him sent,
   vengeance
And him bereft the regne that he had.

"He was cast out of manne's company;
With asses was his habitation
And ate hay, as a beast, in wet and dry,
Till that he knew by grace and by reason
That God of heaven hath domination
O'er every regne, and every creature;
And then had God of him compassion,
And him restor'd his regne and his figure.

"Eke thou, that art his son, art proud also,
And knowest all these things verily;
And art rebel to God, and art his foe.
Thou drankest of his vessels boldely;
Thy wife eke, and thy wenches, sinfully
Drank of the same vessels sundry wines,
And heried false goddes cursedly;   praised
Therefore to thee y-shapen full great pine is.   great
   punishment is   prepared for thee
"This hand was sent from God, that on the wall
Wrote Mane, tekel, phares, truste me;
Thy reign is done; thou weighest naught at all;
Divided is thy regne, and it shall be
To Medes and to Persians giv'n," quoth he.
And thilke same night this king was slaw   slain
And Darius occupied his degree,
Though he thereto had neither right nor law.

Lordings, example hereby may ye take,
How that in lordship is no sickerness;   security
For when that Fortune will a man forsake,
She bears away his regne and his richess,
And eke his friendes bothe more and less,
For what man that hath friendes through fortune,
Mishap will make them enemies, I guess;
This proverb is full sooth, and full commune.

ZENOBIA, of Palmyrie the queen,[12]
As write Persians of her nobless,
So worthy was in armes, and so keen,
That no wight passed her in hardiness,
Nor in lineage, nor other gentleness.   noble
   qualities
Of the king's blood of Perse is she descended;
   Persia
I say not that she hadde most fairness,
But of her shape she might not be amended.

From her childhood I finde that she fled
Office of woman, and to woods she went,
And many a wilde harte's blood she shed
With arrows broad that she against them sent;
She was so swift, that she anon them hent.   caught
And when that she was older, she would kill
Lions, leopards, and beares all to-rent,   torn to
   pieces
And in her armes wield them at her will.

She durst the wilde beastes' dennes seek,
And runnen in the mountains all the night,
And sleep under a bush; and she could eke
Wrestle by very force and very might
With any young man, were he ne'er so wight;
   active, nimble
There mighte nothing in her armes stond.
She kept her maidenhood from every wight,
To no man deigned she for to be bond.

But at the last her friendes have her married
To Odenate,[13] a prince of that country;
All were it so, that she them longe tarried.
And ye shall understande how that he
Hadde such fantasies as hadde she;
But natheless, when they were knit in fere,
   together
They liv'd in joy, and in felicity,
For each of them had other lefe and dear.   loved

Save one thing, that she never would assent,
By no way, that he shoulde by her lie
But ones, for it was her plain intent
To have a child, the world to multiply;
And all so soon as that she might espy
That she was not with childe by that deed,
Then would she suffer him do his fantasy
Eftsoon, and not but ones, out of dread.   again
   without doubt

And if she were with child at thilke cast,   that
No more should he playe thilke game
Till fully forty dayes were past;
Then would she once suffer him do the same.
All were this Odenatus wild or tame,   whether

185

He got no more of her; for thus she said,
It was to wives lechery and shame
In other case if that men with them play'd.   on other terms

Two sones, by this Odenate had she,
The which she kept in virtue and lettrure.   learning
But now unto our tale turne we;
I say, so worshipful a creature,
And wise therewith, and large with measure,   bountiful moderation
So penible in the war, and courteous eke,   laborious
Nor more labour might in war endure,
Was none, though all this worlde men should seek.

Her rich array it mighte not be told,
As well in vessel as in her clothing:
She was all clad in pierrie and in gold,   jewellery
And eke she lefte not, for no hunting,   did not neglect
To have of sundry tongues full knowing,
When that she leisure had, and for t'intend   apply
To learne bookes was all her liking,
How she in virtue might her life dispend.

And, shortly of this story for to treat,
So doughty was her husband and eke she,
That they conquered many regnes great
In th'Orient, with many a fair city
Appertinent unto the majesty
Of Rome, and with strong hande held them fast,
Nor ever might their foemen do them flee,   make
Aye while that Odenatus' dayes last'.

Her battles, whoso list them for to read,
Against Sapor the king,[14] and other mo',
And how that all this process fell in deed,
Why she conquer'd, and what title thereto,
And after of her mischief and her woe,   misfortune
How that she was besieged and y-take,
Let him unto my master Petrarch go,
That writes enough of this, I undertake.

When Odenate was dead, she mightily
The regne held, and with her proper hand
Against her foes she fought so cruelly,
That there n'as king nor prince in all that land,   was not
That was not glad, if be that grace fand
That she would not upon his land warray;   make war
With her they maden alliance by bond,
To be in peace, and let her ride and play.

The emperor of Rome, Claudius,
Nor, him before, the Roman Gallien,
Durste never be so courageous,
Nor no Armenian, nor Egyptien,
Nor Syrian, nor no Arabien,
Within the fielde durste with her fight,
Lest that she would them with her handes slen,   slay
Or with her meinie putte them to flight.   troops

In kinges' habit went her sones two,
As heires of their father's regnes all;
And Heremanno and Timolao
Their names were, as Persians them call
But aye Fortune hath in her honey gall;
This mighty queene may no while endure;
Fortune out of her regne made her fall
To wretchedness and to misadventure.

Aurelian, when that the governance
Of Rome came into his handes tway,[15]
He shope upon this queen to do vengeance;   prepared
And with his legions he took his way
Toward Zenobie, and, shortly for to say,
He made her flee, and at the last her hent,   took
And fetter'd her, and eke her children tway,
And won the land, and home to Rome he went.

Amonges other things that he wan,
Her car, that was with gold wrought and pierrie,   jewels
This greate Roman, this Aurelian
Hath with him led, for that men should it see.
Before in his triumphe walked she
With gilte chains upon her neck hanging;
Crowned she was, as after her degree,   according to
And full of pierrie her clothing.

Alas, Fortune! she that whilom was
Dreadful to kinges and to emperours,
Now galeth all the people on her, alas!   yelleth
And she that helmed was in starke stowres,   wore a helmet in
And won by force townes strong and tow'rs,   obstinate battles
Shall on her head now wear a vitremite;[16]
And she that bare the sceptre full of flow'rs
Shall bear a distaff, her cost for to quite.   to make her living

Although that NERO were so vicious
As any fiend that lies full low adown,
Yet he, as telleth us Suetonius,[17]
This wide world had in subjectioun,
Both East and West, South and Septentrioun.
Of rubies, sapphires, and of pearles white
Were all his clothes embroider'd up and down,
For he in gemmes greatly gan delight.

More delicate, more pompous of array,
More proud, was never emperor than he;
That ilke cloth that he had worn one day,   same robe

After that time he would it never see;
Nettes of gold thread had he great plenty,
To fish in Tiber, when him list to play;
His lustes were as law, in his degree,   pleasures
For Fortune as his friend would him obey.

He Rome burnt for his delicacy;   pleasure
The senators he slew upon a day,
To heare how that men would weep and cry;
And slew his brother, and by his sister lay.
His mother made he in piteous array;
For he her wombe slitte, to behold
Where he conceived was; so well-away!
That he so little of his mother told.   valued

No tear out of his eyen for that sight
Came; but he said, a fair woman was she.
Great wonder is, how that he could or might
Be doomesman of her deade beauty: judge
The wine to bringe him commanded he,
And drank anon; none other woe he made,
When might is joined unto cruelty,
Alas! too deepe will the venom wade.

In youth a master had this emperour,
To teache him lettrure and courtesy;   literature, learning
For of morality he was the flow'r,
As in his time, but if bookes lie.   unless
And while this master had of him mast'ry,
He made him so conning and so souple,   subtle
That longe time it was ere tyranny,
Or any vice, durst in him uncouple.   be let loose

This Seneca, of which that I devise,   tell
Because Nero had of him suche dread,
For he from vices would him aye chastise
Discreetly, as by word, and not by deed;
"Sir," he would say, "an emperor must need
Be virtuous, and hate tyranny."
For which he made him in a bath to bleed
On both his armes, till he muste die.

This Nero had eke of a custumance   habit
In youth against his master for to rise;   stand in his presence
Which afterward he thought a great grievance;
Therefore he made him dien in this wise.
But natheless this Seneca the wise
Chose in a bath to die in this mannere,
Rather than have another tormentise;   torture
And thus hath Nero slain his master dear.

Now fell it so, that Fortune list no longer
The highe pride of Nero to cherice;   cherish
For though he were strong, yet was she stronger.
She thoughte thus; "By God, I am too nice   foolish
To set a man, that is full fill'd of vice,
In high degree, and emperor him call!
By God, out of his seat I will him trice!   thrust[18]

When he least weeneth, soonest shall he fall."   expecteth

The people rose upon him on a night,
For his default; and when he it espied,
Out of his doors anon he hath him dight   betaken himself
Alone, and where he ween'd t'have been allied,   regarded with
He knocked fast, and aye the more he cried   friendship
The faster shutte they their doores all;
Then wist he well he had himself misgied,   misled
And went his way, no longer durst he call.

The people cried and rumbled up and down,
That with his eares heard he how they said;
"Where is this false tyrant, this Neroun?"
For fear almost out of his wit he braid, went
And to his goddes piteously he pray'd
For succour, but it mighte not betide
For dread of this he thoughte that died,
And ran into a garden him to hide.

And in this garden found he churles tway,
That satte by a fire great and red;
And to these churles two he gan to pray
To slay him, and to girdon off his head,   strike
That to his body, when that he were dead,
Were no despite done for his defame.   infamy
Himself he slew, he coud no better rede;   he knew no better
Of which Fortune laugh'd and hadde game.   counsel

Was never capitain under a king,
That regnes more put in subjectioun,
Nor stronger was in field of alle thing
As in his time, nor greater of renown,
Nor more pompous in high presumptioun,
Than HOLOFERNES, whom Fortune aye kiss'd
So lik'rously, and led him up and down,
Till that his head was off ere that he wist.   before he knew it

Not only that this world had of him awe,
For losing of richess and liberty;
But he made every man reny his law.   renounce his religion[19]
Nabuchodonosor was God, said he;
None other Godde should honoured be.
Against his hest there dare no wight trespace,   command
Save in Bethulia, a strong city,
Where Eliachim priest was of that place.

But take keep of the death of Holofern;   notice
Amid his host he drunken lay at night
Within his tente, large as is a bern;   barn
And yet, for all his pomp and all his might,
Judith, a woman, as he lay upright

Sleeping, his head off smote, and from his tent
Full privily she stole from every wight,
And with his head unto her town she went.

What needeth it of king ANTIOCHUS[20]
To tell his high and royal majesty,
His great pride, and his workes venomous?
For such another was there none as he;
Reade what that he was in Maccabee.
And read the proude wordes that he said,
And why he fell from his prosperity,
And in an hill how wretchedly he died.

Fortune him had enhanced so in pride,
That verily he ween'd he might attain
Unto the starres upon every side,
And in a balance weighen each mountain,
And all the floodes of the sea restrain.
And Godde's people had he most in hate
Them would he slay in torment and in pain,
Weening that God might not his pride abate.

And for that Nicanor and Timothee
With Jewes were vanquish'd mightily,[21]
Unto the Jewes such an hate had he,
That he bade graith his car full hastily,   prepare his chariot
And swore and saide full dispiteously,
Unto Jerusalem he would eftsoon,   immediately
To wreak his ire on it full cruelly
But of his purpose was he let full soon.   prevented

God for his menace him so sore smote,
With invisible wound incurable,
That in his guttes carf it so and bote,   cut gnawed
Till that his paines were importable;   unendurable
And certainly the wreche was reasonable,   vengeance
For many a manne's guttes did he pain;
But from his purpose, curs'd and damnable,   impious
For all his smart he would him not restrain;
But bade anon apparaile his host.   prepare

And suddenly, ere he was of it ware,
God daunted all his pride, and all his boast
For he so sore fell out of his chare,   chariot
That it his limbes and his skin to-tare,
So that he neither mighte go nor ride
But in a chaire men about him bare,
Alle forbruised bothe back and side.

The wreche of God him smote so cruelly,   vengeance
That through his body wicked wormes crept,
And therewithal he stank so horribly
That none of all his meinie that him kept,   servants
Whether so that he woke or elles slept,
Ne mighte not of him the stink endure.
In this mischief he wailed and eke wept,
And knew God Lord of every creature.

To all his host, and to himself also,
Full wlatsem was the stink of his carrain;   loathsome body
No manne might him beare to and fro.
And in this stink, and this horrible pain,
He starf full wretchedly in a mountain.   dies
Thus hath this robber, and this homicide,
That many a manne made to weep and plain,
Such guerdon as belongeth unto pride.   reward

The story of ALEXANDER is so commune,
That ev'ry wight that hath discretion
Hath heard somewhat or all of his fortune.
This wide world, as in conclusion,
He won by strength; or, for his high renown,
They were glad for peace to him to send.
The pride and boast of man he laid adown,
Whereso he came, unto the worlde's end.

Comparison yet never might be maked
Between him and another conqueror;
For all this world for dread of him had quaked
He was of knighthood and of freedom flow'r:
Fortune him made the heir of her honour.
Save wine and women, nothing might assuage
His high intent in arms and labour,
So was he full of leonine courage.

What praise were it to him, though I you told
Of Darius, and a hundred thousand mo',
Of kinges, princes, dukes, and earles bold,
Which he conquer'd, and brought them into woe?
I say, as far as man may ride or go,
The world was his, why should I more devise?   tell
For, though I wrote or told you evermo',
Of his knighthood it mighte not suffice.

Twelve years he reigned, as saith Maccabee
Philippe's son of Macedon he was,
That first was king in Greece the country.
O worthy gentle Alexander, alas   noble
That ever should thee falle such a case!
Empoison'd of thine owen folk thou were;
Thy six[22] fortune hath turn'd into an ace,
And yet for thee she wepte never a tear.

Who shall me give teares to complain
The death of gentiless, and of franchise,   generosity
That all this worlde had in his demaine,   dominion
And yet he thought it mighte not suffice,
So full was his corage of high emprise?   spirit
Alas! who shall me helpe to indite
False Fortune, and poison to despise?
The whiche two of all this woe I wite.   blame

By wisdom, manhood, and by great labour,
From humbleness to royal majesty
Up rose he, JULIUS the Conquerour,

That won all th' Occident, by land and sea, West
By strength of hand or elles by treaty,
And unto Rome made them tributary;
And since of Rome the emperor was he, afterwards
Till that Fortune wax'd his adversary.

O mighty Caesar, that in Thessaly
Against POMPEIUS, father thine in law,[23]
That of th' Orient had all the chivalry,
As far as that the day begins to daw,
That through thy knighthood hast them take and slaw, slain
Save fewe folk that with Pompeius fled;
Through which thou put all th' Orient in awe;[24]
Thanke Fortune that so well thee sped.

But now a little while I will bewail
This Pompeius, this noble governor
Of Rome, which that fled at this battaile
I say, one of his men, a false traitor,
His head off smote, to winne him favor
Of Julius, and him the head he brought;
Alas! Pompey, of th' Orient conqueror,
That Fortune unto such a fine thee brought! end

To Rome again repaired Julius,
With his triumphe laureate full high;
But on a time Brutus and Cassius,
That ever had of his estate envy,
Full privily have made conspiracy
Against this Julius in subtle wise
And cast the place in which he shoulde die, arranged
With bodekins, as I shall you devise. daggers tell

This Julius to the Capitole went
Upon a day, as he was wont to gon;
And in the Capitol anon him hent seized
This false Brutus, and his other fone, foes
And sticked him with bodekins anon
With many a wound, and thus they let him lie.
But never groan'd he at no stroke but one,
Or else at two, but if the story lie. unless

So manly was this Julius of heart,
And so well loved estately honesty dignified propriety
That, though his deadly woundes sore smart, pained him
His mantle o'er his hippes caste he,
That ne man shoulde see his privity
And as he lay a-dying in a trance,
And wiste verily that dead was he,
Of honesty yet had he remembrance.

Lucan, to thee this story I recommend,
And to Sueton', and Valerie also,
That of this story write word and end the whole[25]
How that to these great conquerores two
Fortune was first a friend, and since a foe.

No manne trust upon her favour long,
But have her in await for evermo'; ever be watchful against her
Witness on all these conquerores strong.

The riche CROESUS,[26] whilom king of Lyde,
Of which Croesus Cyrus him sore drad, — dreaded
Yet was he caught amiddes all his pride,
And to be burnt men to the fire him lad;
But such a rain down from the welkin shad, poured from the sky
That slew the fire, and made him to escape:
But to beware no grace yet he had,
Till fortune on the gallows made him gape.

When he escaped was, he could not stint refrain
For to begin a newe war again;
He weened well, for that Fortune him sent
Such hap, that he escaped through the rain,
That of his foes he mighte not be slain.
And eke a sweven on a night he mette, dream dreamed
Of which he was so proud, and eke so fain, glad
That he in vengeance all his hearte set.

Upon a tree he was set, as he thought,
Where Jupiter him wash'd, both back and side,
And Phoebus eke a fair towel him brought
To dry him with; and therefore wax'd his pride.
And to his daughter that stood him beside,
Which he knew in high science to abound,
He bade her tell him what it signified;
And she his dream began right thus expound.

"The tree," quoth she, "the gallows is to mean,
And Jupiter betokens snow and rain,
And Phoebus, with his towel clear and clean,
These be the sunne's streames sooth to sayn; rays
Thou shalt y-hangeth be, father, certain;
Rain shall thee wash, and sunne shall thee dry."
Thus warned him full plat and eke full plain
His daughter, which that called was Phanie.

And hanged was Croesus the proude king;
His royal throne might him not avail.
Tragedy is none other manner thing,
Nor can in singing crien nor bewail,
But for that Fortune all day will assail
With unware stroke the regnes that be proud:[27] kingdoms
For when men truste her, then will she fail,
And cover her bright face with a cloud.

O noble, O worthy PEDRO,[28] glory OF SPAIN,
Whem Fortune held so high in majesty,
Well oughte men thy piteous death complain.
Out of thy land thy brother made thee flee,
And after, at a siege, by subtlety,

Thou wert betray'd, and led unto his tent,
Where as he with his owen hand slew thee,
Succeeding in thy regne and in thy rent. *kingdom
revenues*

The field of snow, with th' eagle of black therein,
Caught with the lion, red-colour'd as the glede, *burning coal*
He brew'd this cursedness, and all this sin; *wickedness, villainy*
The wicked nest was worker of this deed;
Not Charles' Oliver,[29] that took aye heed
Of truth and honour, but of Armorike
Ganilien Oliver, corrupt for meed, *reward, bribe*
Broughte this worthy king in such a brike. *breach, ruin*

O worthy PETRO, King of CYPRE[30] also,
That Alexandre won by high mast'ry,
Full many a heathnen wroughtest thou full woe,
Of which thine owen lieges had envy;
And, for no thing but for thy chivalry,
They in thy bed have slain thee by the morrow;
Thus can Fortune her wheel govern and gie, *guide*
And out of joy bringe men into sorrow.

Of Milan greate BARNABO VISCOUNT,[30]
God of delight, and scourge of Lombardy,
Why should I not thine clomben wert so high? *climbed*
Thy brother's son, that was thy double ally,
For he thy nephew was and son-in-law,
Within his prison made thee to die,
But why, nor how, n'ot I that thou were slaw. *I know not slain*

Of th' Earl HUGOLIN OF PISE the languour *agony*
There may no tongue telle for pity.
But little out of Pisa stands a tow'r,
In whiche tow'r in prison put was he,
Aud with him be his little children three;
The eldest scarcely five years was of age;
Alas! Fortune, it was great cruelty
Such birdes for to put in such a cage.

Damned was he to die in that prison;
For Roger, which that bishop was of Pise,
Had on him made a false suggestion,
Through which the people gan upon him rise,
And put him in prison, in such a wise
As ye have heard; and meat and drink he had
So small, that well unneth it might suffice, *scarcely*
And therewithal it was full poor and bad.

And on a day befell, that in that hour
When that his meate wont was to be brought,
The jailor shut the doores of the tow'r;
He heard it right well, but he spake nought.
And in his heart anon there fell a thought,
That they for hunger woulde do him dien; *cause him to die*
"Alas!" quoth he, "alas that I was wrought!" *made, born*
Therewith the teares fell from his eyen.

His youngest son, that three years was of age,
Unto him said, "Father, why do ye weep?
When will the jailor bringen our pottage?
Is there no morsel bread that ye do keep?
I am so hungry, that I may not sleep.
Now woulde God that I might sleepen ever!
Then should not hunger in my wombe creep; *stomach*
There is no thing, save bread, that one were lever." *dearer*

Thus day by day this child begun to cry,
Till in his father's barme adown he lay, *lap*
And saide, "Farewell, father, I must die;"
And kiss'd his father, and died the same day.
And when the woeful father did it sey, *see*
For woe his armes two he gan to bite,
And said, "Alas! Fortune, and well-away!
To thy false wheel my woe all may I wite." *blame*

His children ween'd that it for hunger was
That he his armes gnaw'd, and not for woe,
And saide, "Father, do not so, alas!
But rather eat the flesh upon us two.
Our flesh thou gave us, our flesh take us fro',
And eat enough;" right thus they to him said.
And after that, within a day or two,
They laid them in his lap adown, and died.

Himself, despaired, eke for hunger starf. *died*
Thus ended is this Earl of Pise;
From high estate Fortune away him carf. *cut off*
Of this tragedy it ought enough suffice
Whoso will hear it in a longer wise, *at greater length*
Reade the greate poet of ltale,
That Dante hight, for he can it devise[32]
From point to point, not one word will he fail.

Notes to the Monk's Tale

1. The Monk's Tale is founded in its main features on Bocccacio's work, "De Casibus Virorum Illustrium;" ("Stories of Illustrious Men") but Chaucer has taken the separate stories of which it is composed from different authors, and dealt with them after his own fashion.

THE CANTERBURY TALES

2. Boccaccio opens his book with Adam, whose story is told at much greater length than here. Lydgate, in his translation from Boccaccio, speaks of Adam and Eve as made "of slime of the erth in Damascene the felde."
3. Judges xiii. 3. Boccaccio also tells the story of Samson; but Chaucer seems, by his quotation a few lines below, to have taken his version direct from the sacred book.
4. Oliveres: olive trees; French, "oliviers."
5. "Liber Judicum," the Book of Judges; chap. xv.
6. Querne: mill; from Anglo-Saxon, "cyrran," to turn, "cweorn," a mill,
7. Harpies: the Stymphalian Birds, which fed on human flesh.
8. Busiris, king of Egypt, was wont to sacrifice all foreigners coming to his dominions. Hercules was seized, bound, and led to the altar by his orders, but the hero broke his bonds and slew the tyrant.
9. The feats of Hercules here recorded are not all these known as the "twelve labours;" for instance, the cleansing of the Augean stables, and the capture of Hippolyte's girdle are not in this list — other and less famous deeds of the hero taking their place. For this, however, we must accuse not Chaucer, but Boethius, whom he has almost literally translated, though with some change of order.
10. Trophee: One of the manuscripts has a marginal reference to "Tropheus vates Chaldaeorum" ("Tropheus the prophet of the Chaldees"); but it is not known what author Chaucer meant — unless the reference is to a passage in the "Filostrato" of Boccaccio, on which Chaucer founded his "Troilus and Cressida," and which Lydgate mentions, under the name of "Trophe," as having been translated by Chaucer.
11. Pres: near; French, "pres;" the meaning seems to be, this nearer, lower world.
12 Chaucer has taken the story of Zenobia from Boccaccio's work "De Claris Mulieribus." ("Of Illustrious Women")
13. Odenatus, who, for his services to the Romans, received from Gallienus the title of "Augustus;" he was assassinated in A.D. 266 — not, it was believed, without the connivance of Zenobia, who succeeded him on the throne.
14. Sapor was king of Persia, who made the Emperor Valerian prisoner, conquered Syria, and was pressing triumphantly westward when he was met and defeated by Odenatus and Zenobia.
15. Aurelain became Emperor in A.D. 270.
16. Vitremite: The signification of this word, which is spelled in several ways, is not known. Skinner's explanation, "another attire," founded on the spelling "autremite," is obviously insufficient.
17. Great part of this "tragedy" of Nero is really borrowed, however, from the "Romance of the Rose."
18. Trice: thrust; from Anglo-Saxon, "thriccan."
19. So, in the Man of Law's Tale, the Sultaness promises her son that she will "reny her lay."
20. As the "tragedy" of Holofernes is founded on the book of Judith, so is that of Antiochus on the Second Book of the Maccabees, chap. ix.
21. By the insurgents under the leadership of Judas Maccabeus; 2 Macc. chap. viii.
22. Six: the highest cast on a dicing-cube; here representing the highest favour of fortune.
23. Pompey had married his daughter Julia to Caesar; but she died six years before Pompey's final overthrow.
24. At the battle of Pharsalia, B.C. 48.
25. Word and end: apparently a corruption of the Anglo-Saxon phrase, "ord and end," meaning the whole, the beginning and the end.
26. At the opening of the story of Croesus, Chaucer has copied from his own translation of Boethius; but the story is mainly taken from the "Romance of the Rose"
27. "This reflection," says Tyrwhttt, "seems to have been suggested by one which follows soon after the mention of Croesus in the passage just cited from Boethius. 'What other thing bewail the cryings of tragedies but only the deeds of fortune, that with an awkward stroke, overturneth the realms of great nobley?'" — in some manuscripts the four "tragedies" that follow are placed between those of Zenobia and Nero; but although the general reflection with which the "tragedy" of Croesus closes might most appropriately wind up the whole series, the general chronological arrangement which is observed in the other cases recommends the order followed in the text. Besides, since, like several other Tales, the Monk's tragedies were cut short by the impatience of the auditors, it is more natural that the Tale should close abruptly, than by such a rhetorical finish as these lines afford.
28. Pedro the Cruel, King of Aragon, against whom his brother Henry rebelled. He was by false pretences inveigled into his brother's tent, and treacherously slain. Mr Wright has remarked that "the cause of Pedro, though he was no better than a cruel and reckless tyrant, was popular in England from the very circumstance that Prince Edward (the Black Prince) had embarked in it."

29. Not the Oliver of Charlemagne — but a traitorous Oliver of Armorica, corrupted by a bribe. Ganilion was the betrayer of the Christian army at Roncevalles (see note 9 to the Shipman's Tale); and his name appears to have been for a long time used in France to denote a traitor. Duguesclin, who betrayed Pedro into his brother's tent, seems to be intended by the term "Ganilion Oliver," but if so, Chaucer has mistaken his name, which was Bertrand — perhaps confounding him, as Tyrwhttt suggests, with Oliver du Clisson, another illustrious Breton of those times, who was also Constable of France, after Duguesclin. The arms of the latter are supposed to be described a little above
30. Pierre de Lusignan, King of Cyprus, who captured Alexandria in 1363 (see note 6 to the Prologue to the Tales). He was assassinated in 1369.
31. Bernabo Visconti, Duke of Milan, was deposed and imprisoned by his nephew, and died a captive in 1385. His death is the latest historical fact mentioned in the Tales; and thus it throws the date of their composition to about the sixtieth year of Chaucer's age.
32. The story of Ugolino is told in the 33rd Canto of the "Inferno."

THE NUN'S PRIEST'S TALE.

THE PROLOGUE.

"Ho!" quoth the Knight, "good sir, no more of this;
That ye have said is right enough, y-wis, of a surety
And muche more; for little heaviness
Is right enough to muche folk, I guess.
I say for me, it is a great disease, source of distress, annoyance
Where as men have been in great wealth and ease,
To hearen of their sudden fall, alas!
And the contrary is joy and great solas, delight, comfort
As when a man hath been in poor estate,
And climbeth up, and waxeth fortunate,
And there abideth in prosperity;
Such thing is gladsome, as it thinketh me,
And of such thing were goodly for to tell."

"Yea," quoth our Hoste, "by Saint Paule's bell.
Ye say right sooth; this monk hath clapped loud; talked
He spake how Fortune cover'd with a cloud
I wot not what, and als' of a tragedy
Right now ye heard: and pardie no remedy
It is for to bewaile, nor complain
That that is done, and also it is pain,
As ye have said, to hear of heaviness.
Sir Monk, no more of this, so God you bless;
Your tale annoyeth all this company;
Such talking is not worth a butterfly,
For therein is there no sport nor game;
Therefore, Sir Monke, Dan Piers by your name,
I pray you heart'ly, tell us somewhat else,

For sickerly, n'ere clinking of your bells, were it not for the
That on your bridle hang on every side,
By heaven's king, that for us alle died,
I should ere this have fallen down for sleep,
Although the slough had been never so deep;
Then had your tale been all told in vain.
For certainly, as these clerkes sayn,
Where as a man may have no audience,
Nought helpeth it to telle his sentence.
And well I wot the substance is in me,
If anything shall well reported be.
Sir, say somewhat of hunting,[1] I you pray."

"Nay," quoth the Monk, "I have no lust to play; no fondness for
Now let another tell, as I have told." jesting
Then spake our Host with rude speech and bold,
And said unto the Nunne's Priest anon,
"Come near, thou Priest, come hither, thou Sir John,[2]
Tell us such thing as may our heartes glade. gladden
Be blithe, although thou ride upon a jade.
What though thine horse be bothe foul and lean?
If he will serve thee, reck thou not a bean;
Look that thine heart be merry evermo'."

"Yes, Host," quoth he, "so may I ride or go,
But I be merry, y-wis I will be blamed." unless
And right anon his tale he hath attamed commenced[3]
And thus he said unto us every one,
This sweete priest, this goodly man, Sir John.

Notes to the Prologue to the Nun's Priest's Tale

1. The request is justified by the description of Monk in the Prologue as "an out-rider, that loved venery."
2. On this Tyrwhitt remarks; "I know not how it has happened, that in the principal modern languages, John, or its equivalent, is a name of contempt or at least of slight. So the Italians use 'Gianni,' from whence 'Zani;' the Spaniards 'Juan,' as 'Bobo Juan,' a foolish John; the French 'Jean,' with various additions; and in English, when we call a man 'a John,' we do not mean it as a title of honour." The title of "Sir" was usually given by courtesy to priests.
3. Attamed: commenced, broached. Compare French, "entamer", to cut the first piece off a joint; thence to begin.

THE TALE.[1]

A poor widow, somedeal y-stept in age, somewhat advanced
Was whilom dwelling in a poor cottage,
Beside a grove, standing in a dale.

This widow, of which I telle you my tale,
Since thilke day that she was last a wife,
In patience led a full simple life,
For little was her chattel and her rent. her goods

and her income
By husbandry of such as God her sent, thrifty management
She found herself, and eke her daughters two. maintained
Three large sowes had she, and no mo';
Three kine, and eke a sheep that highte Mall.
Full sooty was her bow'r, and eke her hall, chamber
In which she ate full many a slender meal.
Of poignant sauce knew she never a deal. whit
No dainty morsel passed through her throat;
Her diet was accordant to her cote. in keeping with her cottage
Repletion her made never sick;
Attemper diet was all her physic, moderate
And exercise, and hearte's suffisance. contentment of heart
The goute let her nothing for to dance, did not prevent her
Nor apoplexy shente not her head. from dancing hurt
No wine drank she, neither white nor red:
Her board was served most with white and black,
Milk and brown bread, in which she found no lack,
Seind bacon, and sometimes an egg or tway; singed
For she was as it were a manner dey. kind of day labourer[2]
A yard she had, enclosed all about
With stickes, and a drye ditch without,
In which she had a cock, hight Chanticleer;
In all the land of crowing n'as his peer. was not his equal
His voice was merrier than the merry orgon, organ[3]
On masse days that in the churches gon.
Well sickerer was his crowing in his lodge, more punctual
Than is a clock, or an abbay horloge. clock[4]
By nature he knew each ascension
Of th' equinoctial in thilke town;
For when degrees fiftene were ascended,
Then crew he, that it might not be amended.
His comb was redder than the fine coral,
Embattell'd[5] as it were a castle wall.
His bill was black, and as the jet it shone;
Like azure were his legges and his tone; toes
His nailes whiter than the lily flow'r,
And like the burnish'd gold was his colour,
This gentle cock had in his governance
Sev'n hennes, for to do all his pleasance,
Which were his sisters and his paramours,
And wondrous like to him as of colours.
Of which the fairest-hued in the throat
Was called Damoselle Partelote,
Courteous she was, discreet, and debonair,
And companiable, and bare herself so fair, sociable

Since the day that she sev'n night was old,
That truely she had the heart in hold
Of Chanticleer, locked in every lith; limb
He lov'd her so, that well was him therewith,
But such a joy it was to hear them sing,
When that the brighte sunne gan to spring,
In sweet accord, "My lefe is fare in land."[6] my love is
For, at that time, as I have understand, gone abroad
Beastes and birdes coulde speak and sing.

And so befell, that in a dawening,
As Chanticleer among his wives all
Sat on his perche, that was in the hall,
And next him sat this faire Partelote,
This Chanticleer gan groanen in his throat,
As man that in his dream is dretched sore, oppressed
And when that Partelote thus heard him roar,
She was aghast, and saide, "Hearte dear, afraid
What aileth you to groan in this mannere?
Ye be a very sleeper, fy for shame!"
And he answer'd and saide thus; "Madame,
I pray you that ye take it not agrief; amiss, in umbrage
By God, me mette I was in such mischief, I dreamed trouble
Right now, that yet mine heart is sore affright'.
Now God," quoth he, "my sweven read aright dream, vision.
And keep my body out of foul prisoun.
Me mette, how that I roamed up and down I dreamed
Within our yard, where as I saw a beast
Was like an hound, and would have made arrest siezed
Upon my body, and would have had me dead.
His colour was betwixt yellow and red;
And tipped was his tail, and both his ears,
With black, unlike the remnant of his hairs.
His snout was small, with glowing eyen tway;
Yet of his look almost for fear I dey; died
This caused me my groaning, doubteless."

"Away,"[7] quoth she, "fy on you, heartless! coward
Alas!" quoth she, "for, by that God above!
Now have ye lost my heart and all my love;
I cannot love a coward, by my faith.
For certes, what so any woman saith,
We all desiren, if it mighte be,
To have husbandes hardy, wise, and free,
And secret, and no niggard nor no fool, discreet
Nor him that is aghast of every tool, afraid rag, trifle
Nor no avantour, by that God above! braggart
How durste ye for shame say to your love
That anything might make you afear'd?
Have ye no manne's heart, and have a beard?

THE CANTERBURY TALES

Alas! and can ye be aghast of swevenes? dreams
Nothing but vanity, God wot, in sweven is,
Swevens engender of repletions, are caused by over-eating
And oft of fume, and of complexions, drunkenness
When humours be too abundant in a wight.
Certes this dream, which ye have mette tonight,
Cometh of the great supefluity
Of youre rede cholera, pardie, bile
Which causeth folk to dreaden in their dreams
Of arrows, and of fire with redde beams,
Of redde beastes, that they will them bite,
Of conteke, and of whelpes great and lite; contention little
Right as the humour of melancholy
Causeth full many a man in sleep to cry,
For fear of bulles, or of beares blake,
Or elles that black devils will them take,
Of other humours could I tell also,
That worke many a man in sleep much woe;
That I will pass as lightly as I can.
Lo, Cato, which that was so wise a man,
Said he not thus, 'Ne do no force of dreams,'[8] attach no weight to
Now, Sir," quoth she, "when we fly from these beams,
For Godde's love, as take some laxatife;
On peril of my soul, and of my life,
I counsel you the best, I will not lie,
That both of choler, and melancholy,
Ye purge you; and, for ye shall not tarry,
Though in this town is no apothecary,
I shall myself two herbes teache you,
That shall be for your health, and for your prow; profit
And in our yard the herbes shall I find,
The which have of their property by kind nature
To purge you beneath, and eke above.
Sire, forget not this for Godde's love;
Ye be full choleric of complexion;
Ware that the sun, in his ascension,
You finde not replete of humours hot;
And if it do, I dare well lay a groat,
That ye shall have a fever tertiane,
Or else an ague, that may be your bane,
A day or two ye shall have digestives
Of wormes, ere ye take your laxatives,
Of laurel, centaury,[9] and fumeterere,[10]
Or else of elder-berry, that groweth there,
Of catapuce,[11] or of the gaitre-berries,[12]
Or herb ivy growing in our yard, that merry is:
Pick them right as they grow, and eat them in,
Be merry, husband, for your father's kin;
Dreade no dream; I can say you no more."

"Madame," quoth he, "grand mercy of your lore,
But natheless, as touching Dan Catoun, Cato
That hath of wisdom such a great renown,
Though that he bade no dreames for to dread,
By God, men may in olde bookes read
Of many a man more of authority
Than ever Cato was, so may I the, thrive
That all the reverse say of his sentence, opinion
And have well founden by experience
That dreames be significations
As well of joy, as tribulations
That folk enduren in this life present.
There needeth make of this no argument;
The very preve sheweth it indeed. trial, experience
One of the greatest authors that men read[13]
Saith thus, that whilom two fellowes went
On pilgrimage in a full good intent;
And happen'd so, they came into a town
Where there was such a congregatioun
Of people, and eke so strait of herbergage, without lodging
That they found not as much as one cottage
In which they bothe might y-lodged be:
Wherefore they musten of necessity,
As for that night, departe company;
And each of them went to his hostelry, inn
And took his lodging as it woulde fall.
The one of them was lodged in a stall,
Far in a yard, with oxen of the plough;
That other man was lodged well enow,
As was his aventure, or his fortune,
That us governeth all, as in commune.
And so befell, that, long ere it were day,
This man mette in his bed, there: as he lay, dreamed
How that his fellow gan upon him call,
And said, 'Alas! for in an ox's stall
This night shall I be murder'd, where I lie
Now help me, deare brother, or I die;
In alle haste come to me,' he said.
This man out of his sleep for fear abraid; started
But when that he was wak'd out of his sleep,
He turned him, and took of this no keep; paid this no attention
He thought his dream was but a vanity.
Thus twies in his sleeping dreamed he, twice
And at the thirde time yet his fellow again
Came, as he thought, and said, 'I am now slaw; slain
Behold my bloody woundes, deep and wide.
Arise up early, in the morning, tide,
And at the west gate of the town,' quoth he,
'A carte full of dung there shalt: thou see,
In which my body is hid privily.
Do thilke cart arroste boldely. stop
My gold caused my murder, sooth to sayn.'
And told him every point how he was slain,
With a full piteous face, and pale of hue.

"And, truste well, his dream he found full true;
For on the morrow, as soon as it was day,

GEOFFREY CHAUCER

To his fellowes inn he took his way;
And when that he came to this ox's stall,
After his fellow he began to call.
The hostelere answered him anon,
And saide, 'Sir, your fellow is y-gone,
As soon as day he went out of the town.'
This man gan fallen in suspicioun,
Rememb'ring on his dreames that he mette, dreamed
And forth he went, no longer would he let, delay
Unto the west gate of the town, and fand found
A dung cart, as it went for to dung land,
That was arrayed in the same wise
As ye have heard the deade man devise; describe
And with an hardy heart he gan to cry,
'Vengeance and justice of this felony:
My fellow murder'd in this same night
And in this cart he lies, gaping upright.
I cry out on the ministers,' quoth he.
'That shoulde keep and rule this city;
Harow! alas! here lies my fellow slain.'
What should I more unto this tale sayn?
The people out start, and cast the cart to ground
And in the middle of the dung they found
The deade man, that murder'd was all new.
O blissful God! that art so good and true,
Lo, how that thou bewray'st murder alway.
Murder will out, that see we day by day.
Murder is so wlatsom and abominable loathsome
To God, that is so just and reasonable,
That he will not suffer it heled be; concealed[14]
Though it abide a year, or two, or three,
Murder will out, this is my conclusioun,
And right anon, the ministers of the town
Have hent the carter, and so sore him pined, seized tortured
And eke the hostelere so sore engined, racked
That they beknew their wickedness anon, confessed
And were hanged by the necke bone.

"Here may ye see that dreames be to dread.
And certes in the same book I read,
Right in the nexte chapter after this
(I gabbe not, so have I joy and bliss), talk idly
Two men that would, have passed over sea,
For certain cause, into a far country,
If that the wind not hadde been contrary,
That made them in a city for to tarry,
That stood full merry upon an haven side;
But on a day, against the even-tide,
The wind gan change, and blew right as them lest. as they wished
Jolly and glad they wente to their rest,
And caste them full early for to sail. resolved
But to the one man fell a great marvail
That one of them, in sleeping as he lay,
He mette a wondrous dream, against the day: dreamed

He thought a man stood by his bedde's side,
And him commanded that he should abide;
And said him thus; 'If thou to-morrow wend,
Thou shalt be drown'd; my tale is at an end.'
He woke, and told his follow what he mette,
And prayed him his voyage for to let; delay
As for that day, he pray'd him to abide.
His fellow, that lay by his bedde's side,
Gan for to laugh, and scorned him full fast.
'No dream,' quoth he, 'may so my heart aghast, frighten
That I will lette for to do my things. delay
I sette not a straw by thy dreamings,
For swevens be but vanities and japes. dreams jokes, deceits
Men dream all day of owles and of apes,
And eke of many a maze therewithal; wild imagining
Men dream of thing that never was, nor shall.
But since I see, that thou wilt here abide,
And thus forslothe wilfully thy tide, idle away time
God wot, it rueth me; and have good day.' I am sorry for it
And thus he took his leave, and went his way.
But, ere that he had half his course sail'd,
I know not why, nor what mischance it ail'd,
But casually the ship's bottom rent, by accident
And ship and man under the water went,
In sight of other shippes there beside
That with him sailed at the same tide.

"And therefore, faire Partelote so dear,
By such examples olde may'st thou lear, learn
That no man shoulde be too reckless
Of dreames, for I say thee doubteless,
That many a dream full sore is for to dread.
Lo, in the life of Saint Kenelm[15] I read,
That was Kenulphus' son, the noble king
Of Mercenrike,[16] how Kenelm mette a thing.
A little ere he was murder'd on a day,
His murder in his vision he say. saw
His norice him expounded every deal nurse part
His sweven, and bade him to keep him well guard
For treason; but he was but seven years old,
And therefore little tale hath he told he attached little
Of any dream, so holy was his heart. significance to
By God, I hadde lever than my shirt
That ye had read his legend, as have I.
Dame Partelote, I say you truely,
Macrobius, that wrote the vision
In Afric' of the worthy Scipion,[17]
Affirmeth dreames, and saith that they be
'Warnings of thinges that men after see.
And furthermore, I pray you looke well
In the Old Testament, of Daniel,

THE CANTERBURY TALES

If he held dreames any vanity.
Read eke of Joseph, and there shall ye see
Whether dreames be sometimes (I say not all)
Warnings of thinges that shall after fall.
Look of Egypt the king, Dan Pharaoh,
His baker and his buteler also,
Whether they felte none effect in dreams. significance
Whoso will seek the acts of sundry remes realms
May read of dreames many a wondrous thing.
Lo Croesus, which that was of Lydia king,
Mette he not that he sat upon a tree,
Which signified he shoulde hanged be?[18]
Lo here, Andromache, Hectore's wife,[19]
That day that Hector shoulde lose his life,
She dreamed on the same night beforn,
How that the life of Hector should be lorn, lost
If thilke day he went into battaile;
She warned him, but it might not avail;
He wente forth to fighte natheless,
And was y-slain anon of Achilles.
But thilke tale is all too long to tell;
And eke it is nigh day, I may not dwell.
Shortly I say, as for conclusion,
That I shall have of this avision
Adversity; and I say furthermore,
That I ne tell of laxatives no store, hold laxatives
For they be venomous, I wot it well; of no value
I them defy, I love them never a del. distrust whit

"But let us speak of mirth, and stint all this; cease
Madame Partelote, so have I bliss,
Of one thing God hath sent me large grace; liberal
For when I see the beauty of your face,
Ye be so scarlet-hued about your eyen,
I maketh all my dreade for to dien,
For, all so sicker as In principio,[20] certain
Mulier est hominis confusio.[21]
Madam, the sentence of of this Latin is, meaning
Woman is manne's joy and manne's bliss.
For when I feel at night your softe side, —
Albeit that I may not on you ride,
For that our perch is made so narrow, Alas!
I am so full of joy and of solas, delight
That I defy both sweven and eke dream."
And with that word he flew down from the beam,
For it was day, and eke his hennes all;
And with a chuck he gan them for to call,
For he had found a corn, lay in the yard.
Royal he was, he was no more afear'd;
He feather'd Partelote twenty time,
And as oft trode her, ere that it was prime.
He looked as it were a grim lion,
And on his toes he roamed up and down;
He deigned not to set his feet to ground;
He chucked, when he had a corn y-found,
And to him ranne then his wives all.

Thus royal, as a prince is in his hall,
Leave I this Chanticleer in his pasture;
And after will I tell his aventure.

When that the month in which the world began,
That highte March, when God first maked man,
Was complete, and y-passed were also,
Since March ended, thirty days and two,
Befell that Chanticleer in all his pride,
His seven wives walking him beside,
Cast up his eyen to the brighte sun,
That in the sign of Taurus had y-run
Twenty degrees and one, and somewhat more;
He knew by kind, and by none other lore, nature learning
That it was prime, and crew with blissful steven. voice
"The sun," he said, "is clomben up in heaven
Twenty degrees and one, and more y-wis. assuredly
Madame Partelote, my worlde's bliss,
Hearken these blissful birdes how they sing,
And see the freshe flowers how they spring;
Full is mine heart of revel and solace."
But suddenly him fell a sorrowful case; casualty
For ever the latter end of joy is woe:
God wot that worldly joy is soon y-go:
And, if a rhetor coulde fair indite, orator
He in a chronicle might it safely write,
As for a sov'reign notability a thing supremely notable
Now every wise man, let him hearken me;
This story is all as true, I undertake,
As is the book of Launcelot du Lake,
That women hold in full great reverence.
Now will I turn again to my sentence.

A col-fox,[22] full of sly iniquity,
That in the grove had wonned yeares three, dwelt
By high imagination forecast,
The same night thorough the hedges brast burst
Into the yard, where Chanticleer the fair
Was wont, and eke his wives, to repair;
And in a bed of wortes still he lay, cabbages
Till it was passed undern[23] of the day,
Waiting his time on Chanticleer to fall:
As gladly do these homicides all,
That in awaite lie to murder men.
O false murd'rer! Rouking in thy den! crouching, lurking
O new Iscariot, new Ganilion![24]
O false dissimuler, O Greek Sinon,[25]
That broughtest Troy all utterly to sorrow!
O Chanticleer! accursed be the morrow
That thou into thy yard flew from the beams; rafters
Thou wert full well y-warned by thy dreams
That thilke day was perilous to thee.
But what that God forewot must needes be, foreknows

GEOFFREY CHAUCER

After th' opinion of certain clerkes.
Witness on him that any perfect clerk is,
That in school is great altercation
In this matter, and great disputation,
And hath been of an hundred thousand men.
But I ne cannot boult it to the bren, examine it thoroughly[26]
As can the holy doctor Augustine,
Or Boece, or the bishop Bradwardine,[27]
Whether that Godde's worthy foreweeting foreknowledge
Straineth me needly for to do a thing forces me
(Needly call I simple necessity),
Or elles if free choice be granted me
To do that same thing, or do it not,
Though God forewot it ere that it was wrought; knew in advance
Or if his weeting straineth never a deal, his knowing constrains
But by necessity conditionel. not at all
I will not have to do of such mattere;
My tale is of a cock, as ye may hear,
That took his counsel of his wife, with sorrow,
To walken in the yard upon the morrow
That he had mette the dream, as I you told.
Womane's counsels be full often cold; mischievous, unwise
Womane's counsel brought us first to woe,
And made Adam from Paradise to go,
There as he was full merry and well at ease.
But, for I n'ot to whom I might displease know not
If I counsel of women woulde blame,
Pass over, for I said it in my game. jest
Read authors, where they treat of such mattere
And what they say of women ye may hear.
These be the cocke's wordes, and not mine;
I can no harm of no woman divine. conjecture, imagine
Fair in the sand, to bathe her merrily, bask
Lies Partelote, and all her sisters by,
Against the sun, and Chanticleer so free
Sang merrier than the mermaid in the sea;
For Physiologus saith sickerly, certainly
How that they singe well and merrily.[28]
And so befell that, as he cast his eye
Among the wortes, on a butterfly, cabbages
He was ware of this fox that lay full low.
Nothing ne list him thenne for to crow, he had no inclination
But cried anon "Cock! cock!" and up he start,
As man that was affrayed in his heart.
For naturally a beast desireth flee
From his contrary, if be may it see, enemy
Though he ne'er erst had soon it with his eye never before
This Chanticleer, when he gan him espy,
He would have fled, but that the fox anon
Said, "Gentle Sir, alas! why will ye gon?

Be ye afraid of me that am your friend?
Now, certes, I were worse than any fiend,
If I to you would harm or villainy.
I am not come your counsel to espy.
But truely the cause of my coming
Was only for to hearken how ye sing;
For truely ye have as merry a steven, voice
As any angel hath that is in heaven;
Therewith ye have of music more feeling,
Than had Boece, or any that can sing.
My lord your father (God his soule bless)
And eke your mother of her gentleness,
Have in mnine house been, to my great ease: satisfaction
And certes, Sir, full fain would I you please.
But, for men speak of singing, I will say,
So may I brooke well mine eyen tway, enjoy, possess, or use
Save you, I hearde never man so sing
As did your father in the morrowning.
Certes it was of heart all that he sung.
And, for to make his voice the more strong,
He would so pain him, that with both his eyen make such an exertion
He muste wink, so loud he woulde cryen,
And standen on his tiptoes therewithal,
And stretche forth his necke long and small.
And eke he was of such discretion,
That there was no man, in no region,
That him in song or wisdom mighte pass.
I have well read in Dan Burnel the Ass,[29]
Among his verse, how that there was a cock
That, for a prieste's son gave him a knock because
Upon his leg, while he was young and nice, foolish
He made him for to lose his benefice.
But certain there is no comparison
Betwixt the wisdom and discretion
Of youre father, and his subtilty.
Now singe, Sir, for sainte charity,
Let see, can ye your father counterfeit?"

This Chanticleer his wings began to beat,
As man that could not his treason espy,
So was he ravish'd with his flattery.
Alas! ye lordes, many a false flattour flatterer[30]
Is in your court, and many a losengeour, deceiver[31]
That please you well more, by my faith,
Than he that soothfastness unto you saith. truth
Read in Ecclesiast' of flattery;
Beware, ye lordes, of their treachery.
This Chanticleer stood high upon his toes,
Stretching his neck, and held his eyen close,
And gan to crowe loude for the nonce
And Dan Russel[32] the fox start up at once,
And by the gorge hente Chanticleer, seized by the throat
And on his back toward the wood him bare.

For yet was there no man that him pursu'd.
O destiny, that may'st not be eschew'd! escaped
Alas, that Chanticleer flew from the beams!
Alas, his wife raughte nought of dreams! regarded
And on a Friday fell all this mischance.
O Venus, that art goddess of pleasance,
Since that thy servant was this Chanticleer
And in thy service did all his powere,
More for delight, than the world to multiply,
Why wilt thou suffer him on thy day to die?
O Gaufrid, deare master sovereign,[33]
That, when thy worthy king Richard was slain
With shot, complainedest his death so sore,
Why n'had I now thy sentence and thy lore,
The Friday for to chiden, as did ye?
(For on a Friday, soothly, slain was he),
Then would I shew you how that I could plain lament
For Chanticleere's dread, and for his pain.

Certes such cry nor lamentation
Was ne'er of ladies made, when Ilion
Was won, and Pyrrhus with his straighte sword,
When he had hent king Priam by the beard, seized
And slain him (as saith us Eneidos),[34] The Aeneid
As maden all the hennes in the close, yard
When they had seen of Chanticleer the sight.
But sov'reignly Dame Partelote shright, above all others
Full louder than did Hasdrubale's wife, shrieked
When that her husband hadde lost his life,
And that the Romans had y-burnt Carthage;
She was so full of torment and of rage,
That wilfully into the fire she start,
And burnt herselfe with a steadfast heart.
O woeful hennes! right so cried ye,
As, when that Nero burned the city
Of Rome, cried the senators' wives,
For that their husbands losten all their lives;
Withoute guilt this Nero hath them slain.
Now will I turn unto my tale again;

The sely widow, and her daughters two, simple, honest
Hearde these hennes cry and make woe,
And at the doors out started they anon,
And saw the fox toward the wood is gone,
And bare upon his back the cock away:
They cried, "Out! harow! and well-away!
Aha! the fox!" and after him they ran,
And eke with staves many another man
Ran Coll our dog, and Talbot, and Garland;
And Malkin, with her distaff in her hand
Ran cow and calf, and eke the very hogges
So fear'd they were for barking of the dogges,
And shouting of the men and women eke.
They ranne so, them thought their hearts would break.
They yelled as the fiendes do in hell;
The duckes cried as men would them quell; kill, destroy
The geese for feare flewen o'er the trees,
Out of the hive came the swarm of bees,
So hideous was the noise, ben'dicite!
Certes he, Jacke Straw,[35] and his meinie, followers
Ne made never shoutes half so shrill
When that they woulden any Fleming kill,
As thilke day was made upon the fox.
Of brass they broughte beames and of box, trumpets[36]
Of horn and bone, in which they blew and pooped, tooted
And therewithal they shrieked and they hooped;
It seemed as the heaven shoulde fall

Now, goode men, I pray you hearken all;
Lo, how Fortune turneth suddenly
The hope and pride eke of her enemy.
This cock, that lay upon the fox's back,
In all his dread unto the fox he spake,
And saide, "Sir, if that I were as ye,
Yet would I say (as wisly God help me), surely
'Turn ye again, ye proude churles all;
A very pestilence upon you fall.
Now am I come unto the woode's side,
Maugre your head, the cock shall here abide;
I will him eat, in faith, and that anon.'"
The fox answer'd, "In faith it shall be done:"
And, as he spake the word, all suddenly
The cock brake from his mouth deliverly, nimbly
And high upon a tree he flew anon.
And when the fox saw that the cock was gone,
"Alas!" quoth he, "O Chanticleer, alas!
I have," quoth he, "y-done to you trespass, offence
Inasmuch as I maked you afear'd,
When I you hent, and brought out of your yard; took
But, Sir, I did it in no wick' intent;
Come down, and I shall tell you what I meant.
I shall say sooth to you, God help me so."
"Nay then," quoth he, "I shrew us both the two, curse
And first I shrew myself, both blood and bones,
If thou beguile me oftener than once.
Thou shalt no more through thy flattery
Do me to sing and winke with mine eye; cause
For he that winketh when he shoulde see,
All wilfully, God let him never the." thrive
"Nay," quoth the fox; "but God give him mischance
That is so indiscreet of governance,
That jangleth when that he should hold his peace." chatters

Lo, what it is for to be reckeless
And negligent, and trust on flattery.
But ye that holde this tale a folly,

As of a fox, or of a cock or hen,
Take the morality thereof, good men.
For Saint Paul saith, That all that written is,
To our doctrine it written is y-wis.[37] is surely written for

Take the fruit, and let the chaff be still. our instruction

Now goode God, if that it be thy will,
As saith my Lord,[38] so make us all good men;
And bring us all to thy high bliss. Amen.

Notes to the Nun's Priest's Tale

1. The Tale of the Nun's Priest is founded on the fifth chapter of an old French metrical "Romance of Renard;" the same story forming one of the fables of Marie, the translator of the Breton Lays. (See note 2 to the Prologue to the Franklin's Tale.) Although Dryden was in error when he ascribed the Tale to Chaucer's own invention, still the materials on which he had to operate were out of comparison more trivial than the result.
2. Tyrwhitt quotes two statutes of Edward III, in which "deys" are included among the servants employed in agricultural pursuits; the name seems to have originally meant a servant who gave his labour by the day, but afterwards to have been appropriated exclusively to one who superintended or worked in a dairy.
3. Orgon: here licentiously used for the plural, "organs" or "orgons," corresponding to the plural verb "gon" in the next line.
4. Horloge: French, "clock."
5. Embattell'd: indented on the upper edge like the battlements of a castle.
6. My lefe is fare in land: This seems to have been the refrain of some old song, and its precise meaning is uncertain. It corresponds in cadence with the morning salutation of the cock; and may be taken as a greeting to the sun, which is beloved of Chanticleer, and has just come upon the earth — or in the sense of a more local boast, as vaunting the fairness of his favourite hen above all others in the country round.

    Transcriber's note: Later commentators explain "fare in land" as "gone abroad" and have identified the song:

    My lefe is fare in lond
    Alas! Why is she so?
    And I am so sore bound
    I may not come her to.
    She hath my heart in hold
    Where ever she ride or go
    With true love a thousand-fold.

(Printed in The Athenaeum, 1896, Vol II, p. 566).

7. "Avoi!" is the word here rendered "away!" It was frequently used in the French fabliaux, and the Italians employ the word "via!" in the same sense.
8. "Ne do no force of dreams:" "Somnia ne cares;" — Cato "De Moribus," 1 ii, dist. 32
9. Centaury: the herb so called because by its virtue the centaur Chiron was healed when the poisoned arrow of Hercules had accidentally wounded his foot.
10. Fumetere: the herb "fumitory."
11. Catapuce: spurge; a plant of purgative qualities. To its name in the text correspond the Italian "catapuzza," and French "catapuce" — words the origin of which is connected with the effects of the plant.
12. Gaitre-berries: dog-wood berries.
13. One of the greatest authors that men read: Cicero, who in his book "De Divinatione" tells this and the following story, though in contrary order and with many differences.
14. Haled or hylled; from Anglo-Saxon "helan" hid, concealed
15. Kenelm succeeded his father as king of the Saxon realm of Mercia in 811, at the age of seven years; but he was slain by his ambitious aunt Quendrada. The place of his burial was miraculously discovered, and he was subsequently elevated to the rank of a saint and martyr. His life is in the English "Golden Legend."
16. Mercenrike: the kingdom of Mercia; Anglo-Saxon, Myrcnarice. Compare the second member of the compound in the German, "Frankreich," France; "Oesterreich," Austria.
17. Cicero ("De Republica," lib. vi.) wrote the Dream of Scipio, in which the Younger relates the appearance of the Elder Africanus, and the counsels and exhortations which the shade addressed to

the sleeper. Macrobius wrote an elaborate "Commentary on the Dream of Scipio," — a philosophical treatise much studied and relished during the Middle Ages.
18. See the Monk's Tale for this story.
19. Andromache's dream will not be found in Homer; It is related in the book of the fictitious Dares Phrygius, the most popular authority during the Middle Ages for the history of the Trojan War.
20. In principio: In the beginning; the first words of Genesis and of the Gospel of John.
21. Mulier est hominis confusio: This line is taken from the same fabulous conference between the Emperor Adrian and the philosopher Secundus, whence Chaucer derived some of the arguments in praise of poverty employed in the Wife of Bath's Tale proper. See note 14 to the Wife of Bath's tale. The passage transferred to the text is the commencement of a description of woman. "Quid est mulier? hominis confusio," &c. ("What is Woman? A union with man", &c.)
22. Col-fox: a blackish fox, so called because of its likeness to coal, according to Skinner; though more probably the prefix has a reproachful meaning, and is in some way connected with the word "cold" as, some forty lines below, it is applied to the prejudicial counsel of women, and as frequently it is used to describe "sighs" and other tokens of grief, and "cares" or "anxieties."
23. Undern: In this case, the meaning of "evening" or "afternoon" can hardly be applied to the word, which must be taken to signify some early hour of the forenoon. See also note 4 to the Wife of Bath's tale and note 5 to the Clerk's Tale.
24. Ganilion: a traitor. See note 9 to the Shipman's Tale and note 28 to the Monk's Tale.
25. Greek Sinon: The inventor of the Trojan Horse. See note 14 to the Squire's Tale
26. Boult it from the bren: Examine the matter thoroughly; a metaphor taken from the sifting of meal, to divide the fine flour from the bran.
27. Thomas Bradwardine, Archbishop of Canterbury in the thirteenth century, who wrote a book, "De Causa Dei," in controversy with Pelagius; and also numerous other treatises, among them some on predestination.
28. In a popular mediaeval Latin treatise by one Theobaldus, entitled "Physiologus de Naturis XII. Animalium" ("A description of the nature of twelve animals"), sirens or mermaids are described as skilled in song, and drawing unwary mariners to destruction by the sweetness of their voices.
29. "Nigellus Wireker," says Urry's Glossary, "a monk and precentor of Canterbury, wrote a Latin poem intituled 'Speculum Speculorum,' ('The mirror of mirrors') dedicated to William Longchamp, Bishop of Ely, and Lord Chancellor; wherein, under the fable of an Ass (which he calls 'Burnellus') that desired a longer tail, is represented the folly of such as are not content with their own condition. There is introduced a tale of a cock, who having his leg broke by a priest's son (called Gundulfus) watched an opportunity to be revenged; which at last presented itself on this occasion: A day was appointed for Gundulfus's being admitted into holy orders at a place remote from his father's habitation; he therefore orders the servants to call him at first cock-crowing, which the cock overhearing did not crow at all that morning. So Gundulfus overslept himself, and was thereby disappointed of his ordination, the office being quite finished before he came to the place." Wireker's satire was among the most celebrated and popular Latin poems of the Middle Ages. The Ass was probably as Tyrwhitt suggests, called "Burnel" or "Brunel," from his brown colour; as, a little below, a reddish fox is called "Russel."
30. Flattour: flatterer; French, "flatteur."
31. Losengeour: deceiver, cozener; the word had analogues in the French "losengier," and the Spanish "lisongero." It is probably connected with "leasing," falsehood; which has been derived from Anglo-Saxon "hlisan," to celebrate — as if it meant the spreading of a false renown
32. Dan Russel: Master Russet; a name given to the fox, from his reddish colour.
33. Geoffrey de Vinsauf was the author of a well-known mediaeval treatise on composition in various poetical styles of which he gave examples. Chaucer's irony is therefore directed against some grandiose and affected lines on the death of Richard I., intended to illustrate the pathetic style, in which Friday is addressed as "O Veneris lachrymosa dies" ("O tearful day of Venus").
34. "Priamum altaria ad ipsa trementem Traxit, et in multo lapsantem sanguine nati Implicuitque comam laeva, dextraque coruscum Extulit, ac lateri capulo tenus abdidit ensem. Haec finis Priami fatorum." ("He dragged Priam trembling to his own altar, slipping on the blood of his child; He took his hair in his left hand, and with the right drew the flashing sword, and hid it to the hilt [in his body]. Thus an end was made of Priam") — Virgil, Aeneid. ii. 550.
35. Jack Straw: The leader of a Kentish rising, in the reign of Richard II, in 1381, by which the Flemish merchants in London were great sufferers.
36. Beams: trumpets; Anglo-Saxon, "bema."

37. "All scripture is given by inspiration of God, and is profitable for doctrine, for reproof, for correction, for instruction in righteousness: that the man of God may be perfect, throughly furnished unto all good works." — 2 Tim. iii. 16.

THE EPILOGUE[1]

"Sir Nunne's Priest," our hoste said anon,
"Y-blessed be thy breech, and every stone;
This was a merry tale of Chanticleer.
But by my truth, if thou wert seculere, a layman
Thou wouldest be a treadefowl aright; cock
For if thou have courage as thou hast might,
Thee were need of hennes, as I ween,
Yea more than seven times seventeen.
See, whate brawnes hath this gentle priest,
muscles, sinews
So great a neck, and such a large breast
He looketh as a sperhawk with his eyen
Him needeth not his colour for to dyen
With Brazil, nor with grain of Portugale.
But, Sir, faire fall you for your tale'."
And, after that, he with full merry cheer
Said to another, as ye shall hear.

Notes to the Epilogue to the Nun's Priest's Tale

1. The sixteen lines appended to the Tale of the Nun's Priest seem, as Tyrwhitt observes, to commence the prologue to the succeeding Tale — but the difficulty is to determine which that Tale should be. In earlier editions, the lines formed the opening of the prologue to the Manciple's Tale; but most of the manuscripts acknowledge themselves defective in this part, and give the Nun's Tale after that of the Nun's Priest. In the Harleian manuscript, followed by Mr Wright, the second Nun's Tale, and the Canon's Yeoman's Tale, are placed after the Franklin's tale; and the sixteen lines above are not found — the Manciple's prologue coming immediately after the "Amen" of the Nun's Priest. In two manuscripts, the last line of the sixteen runs thus: "Said unto the Nun as ye shall hear;" and six lines more evidently forged, are given to introduce the Nun's Tale. All this confusion and doubt only strengthen the certainty, and deepen the regret, that "The Canterbury Tales" were left at Chaucer's, death not merely very imperfect as a whole, but destitute of many finishing touches that would have made them complete so far as the conception had actually been carried into performance.

THE SECOND NUN'S TALE[1]

The minister and norice unto vices, nurse
Which that men call in English idleness,
The porter at the gate is of delices; delights
T'eschew, and by her contrar' her oppress, —
That is to say, by lawful business, — occupation, activity
Well oughte we to do our all intent apply ourselves
Lest that the fiend through idleness us hent. seize

For he, that with his thousand cordes sly
Continually us waiteth to beclap, entangle, bind
When he may man in idleness espy,
He can so lightly catch him in his trap,
Till that a man be hent right by the lappe, seize hem
He is not ware the fiend hath him in hand;
Well ought we work, and idleness withstand.

And though men dreaded never for to die,
Yet see men well by reason, doubteless,
That idleness is root of sluggardy,
Of which there cometh never good increase;
And see that sloth them holdeth in a leas, leash[2]
Only to sleep, and for to eat and drink,
And to devouren all that others swink. labour

And, for to put us from such idleness,
That cause is of so great confusion,
I have here done my faithful business,
After the Legend, in translation
Right of thy glorious life and passion, —
Thou with thy garland wrought of rose and lily,
Thee mean I, maid and martyr, Saint Cecilie.

And thou, thou art the flow'r of virgins all,
Of whom that Bernard list so well to write,[3]
To thee at my beginning first I call;
Thou comfort of us wretches, do me indite
Thy maiden's death, that won through her merite
Th' eternal life, and o'er the fiend victory,
As man may after readen in her story.

Thou maid and mother, daughter of thy Son,
Thou well of mercy, sinful soules' cure,
In whom that God of bounte chose to won; dwell
Thou humble and high o'er every creature,
Thou nobilest, so far forth our nature, as far as our nature admits
That no disdain the Maker had of kind, nature
His Son in blood and flesh to clothe and wind. wrap

Within the cloister of thy blissful sides
Took manne's shape th' eternal love and peace,
That of the trine compass Lord and guide is the trinity
Whom earth, and sea, and heav'n, out of release, unceasingly
Aye hery; and thou, Virgin wemmeless, forever praise immaculate
Bare of thy body, and dweltest maiden pure,
The Creator of every creature.

Assembled is in thee magnificence[4]
With mercy, goodness, and with such pity,
That thou, that art the sun of excellence,
Not only helpest them that pray to thee,
But oftentime, of thy benignity,
Full freely, ere that men thine help beseech,
Thou go'st before, and art their lives' leech. healer, saviour.

Now help, thou meek and blissful faire maid,
Me, flemed wretch, in this desert of gall; banished, outcast
Think on the woman Cananee that said
That whelpes eat some of the crumbes all
That from their Lorde's table be y-fall;[5]
And though that I, unworthy son of Eve,[6]
Be sinful, yet accepte my believe. faith

And, for that faith is dead withoute werkes,
For to worke give me wit and space,
That I be quit from thennes that most derk is; freed from the most
O thou, that art so fair and full of grace, dark place (Hell)
Be thou mine advocate in that high place,
Where as withouten end is sung Osanne,
Thou Christe's mother, daughter dear of Anne.

And of thy light my soul in prison light,
That troubled is by the contagion
Of my body, and also by the weight
Of earthly lust and false affection;
O hav'n of refuge, O salvation
Of them that be in sorrow and distress,
Now help, for to my work I will me dress.

Yet pray I you, that reade what I write,[6]
Forgive me that I do no diligence
This ilke story subtilly t' indite. same
For both have I the wordes and sentence
Of him that at the sainte's reverence
The story wrote, and follow her legend;
And pray you that you will my work amend.

First will I you the name of Saint Cecilie
Expound, as men may in her story see.
It is to say in English, Heaven's lily,[7]
For pure chasteness of virginity;
Or, for she whiteness had of honesty, purity

And green of conscience, and of good fame
The sweete savour, Lilie was her name.

Or Cecilie is to say, the way of blind;[7]
For she example was by good teaching;
Or else Cecilie, as I written find,
Is joined by a manner conjoining
Of heaven and Lia,[7] and herein figuring
The heaven is set for thought of holiness,
And Lia for her lasting business.

Cecilie may eke be said in this mannere,
Wanting of blindness, for her greate light
Of sapience, and for her thewes clear. *qualities*
Or elles, lo, this maiden's name bright
Of heaven and Leos[7] comes, for which by right
Men might her well the heaven of people call,
Example of good and wise workes all;

For Leos people in English is to say;
And right as men may in the heaven see
The sun and moon, and starres every way,
Right so men ghostly, in this maiden free, *spiritually*
Sawen of faith the magnanimity,
And eke the clearness whole of sapience,
And sundry workes bright of excellence.

And right so as these philosophers write,
That heav'n is swift and round, and eke burning,
Right so was faire Cecilie the white
Full swift and busy in every good working,
And round and whole in good persevering,[8]
And burning ever in charity full bright;
Now have I you declared what she hight. *why she had her name*

This maiden bright Cecile, as her life saith,
Was come of Romans, and of noble kind,
And from her cradle foster'd in the faith
Of Christ, and bare his Gospel in her mind:
She never ceased, as I written find,
Of her prayere, and God to love and dread,
Beseeching him to keep her maidenhead.

And when this maiden should unto a man
Y-wedded be, that was full young of age,
Which that y-called was Valerian,
And come was the day of marriage,
She, full devout and humble in her corage, *heart*
Under her robe of gold, that sat full fair,
Had next her flesh y-clad her in an hair. *garment of hair-cloth*

And while the organs made melody,
To God alone thus in her heart sang she;
"O Lord, my soul and eke my body gie *guide*
Unwemmed, lest that I confounded be." *unblemished*
And, for his love that died upon the tree,
Every second or third day she fast',
Aye bidding in her orisons full fast. *praying*

The night came, and to bedde must she gon
With her husband, as it is the mannere;
And privily she said to him anon;
"O sweet and well-beloved spouse dear,
There is a counsel, an' ye will it hear, *secret if*
Which that right fain I would unto you say,
So that ye swear ye will it not bewray." *betray*

Valerian gan fast unto her swear
That for no case nor thing that mighte be,
He never should to none bewrayen her;
And then at erst thus to him saide she; *for the first time*
"I have an angel which that loveth me,
That with great love, whether I wake or sleep,
Is ready aye my body for to keep;

"And if that he may feelen, out of dread, *without doubt*
That ye me touch or love in villainy,
He right anon will slay you with the deed,
And in your youthe thus ye shoulde die.
And if that ye in cleane love me gie," *guide*
He will you love as me, for your cleanness,
And shew to you his joy and his brightness."

Valerian, corrected as God wo'ld,
Answer'd again, "If I shall truste thee,
Let me that angel see, and him behold;
And if that it a very angel be,
Then will I do as thou hast prayed me;
And if thou love another man, forsooth
Right with this sword then will I slay you both."

Cecile answer'd anon right in this wise;
"If that you list, the angel shall ye see,
So that ye trow Of Christ, and you baptise; *know*
Go forth to Via Appia," quoth she,
That from this towne stands but miles three,
And to the poore folkes that there dwell
Say them right thus, as that I shall you tell,

"Tell them, that I, Cecile, you to them sent
To shewe you the good Urban the old,
For secret needes, and for good intent; *business*
And when that ye Saint Urban have behold,
Tell him the wordes which I to you told
And when that he hath purged you from sin,
Then shall ye see that angel ere ye twin *depart*

Valerian is to the place gone;
And, right as he was taught by her learning
He found this holy old Urban anon
Among the saintes' burials louting; *lying concealed*[9]
And he anon, withoute tarrying,
Did his message, and when that he it told,
Urban for joy his handes gan uphold.

The teares from his eyen let he fall;
"Almighty Lord, O Jesus Christ,"
Quoth he, "Sower of chaste counsel, herd of us

THE CANTERBURY TALES

The fruit of thilke seed of chastity that all; shepherd
That thou hast sown in Cecile, take to thee
Lo, like a busy bee, withoute guile,
Thee serveth aye thine owen thrall Cicile, servant

"For thilke spouse, that she took but now, lately
Full like a fierce lion, she sendeth here,
As meek as e'er was any lamb to owe."
And with that word anon there gan appear
An old man, clad in white clothes clear,
That had a book with letters of gold in hand,
And gan before Valerian to stand.

Valerian, as dead, fell down for dread,
When he him saw; and he up hent him tho, took there
And on his book right thus he gan to read;
"One Lord, one faith, one God withoute mo',
One Christendom, one Father of all also,
Aboven all, and over all everywhere."
These wordes all with gold y-written were.

When this was read, then said this olde man,
"Believ'st thou this or no? say yea or nay."
"I believe all this," quoth Valerian,
"For soother thing than this, I dare well say, truer
Under the Heaven no wight thinke may."
Then vanish'd the old man, he wist not where
And Pope Urban him christened right there.

Valerian went home, and found Cecilie
Within his chamber with an angel stand;
This angel had of roses and of lily
Corones two, the which he bare in hand, crowns
And first to Cecile, as I understand,
He gave the one, and after gan he take
The other to Valerian her make. mate, husband

"With body clean, and with unwemmed thought, unspotted, blameless
Keep aye well these corones two," quoth he;
"From Paradise to you I have them brought,
Nor ever more shall they rotten be,
Nor lose their sweet savour, truste me,
Nor ever wight shall see them with his eye,
But he be chaste, and hate villainy.

"And thou, Valerian, for thou so soon
Assented hast to good counsel, also
Say what thee list, and thou shalt have thy boon." wish desire
"I have a brother," quoth Valerian tho, then
"That in this world I love no man so;
I pray you that my brother may have grace
To know the truth, as I do in this place."

The angel said, "God liketh thy request,
And bothe, with the palm of martyrdom,
Ye shalle come unto this blissful rest."
And, with that word, Tiburce his brother came.
And when that he the savour undernome perceived
Which that the roses and the lilies cast,
Within his heart he gan to wonder fast;

And said; "I wonder, this time of the year,
Whence that sweete savour cometh so
Of rose and lilies, that I smelle here;
For though I had them in mine handes two,
The savour might in me no deeper go;
The sweete smell, that in my heart I find,
Hath changed me all in another kind."

Valerian said, "Two crownes here have we,
Snow-white and rose-red, that shine clear,
Which that thine eyen have no might to see;
And, as thou smellest them through my prayere,
So shalt thou see them, leve brother dear, beloved
If it so be thou wilt withoute sloth
Believe aright, and know the very troth. "

Tiburce answered, "Say'st thou this to me
In soothness, or in dreame hear I this?"
"In dreames," quoth Valorian, "have we be
Unto this time, brother mine, y-wis
But now at erst in truth our dwelling is." for the first time
How know'st thou this," quoth Tiburce; "in what wise?"
Quoth Valerian, "That shall I thee devise describe

"The angel of God hath me the truth y-taught,
Which thou shalt see, if that thou wilt reny renounce
The idols, and be clean, and elles nought."
[And of the miracle of these crownes tway
Saint Ambrose in his preface list to say;
Solemnely this noble doctor dear
Commendeth it, and saith in this mannere

"The palm of martyrdom for to receive,
Saint Cecilie, full filled of God's gift,
The world and eke her chamber gan to weive; forsake
Witness Tiburce's and Cecilie's shrift, confession
To which God of his bounty woulde shift
Corones two, of flowers well smelling,
And made his angel them the crownes bring.

"The maid hath brought these men to bliss above;
The world hath wist what it is worth, certain,
Devotion of chastity to love."][10]
Then showed him Cecilie all open and plain,
That idols all are but a thing in vain,
For they be dumb, and thereto they be deave; therefore deaf
And charged him his idols for to leave.

"Whoso that troweth not this, a beast he is," believeth
Quoth this Tiburce, "if that I shall not lie."
And she gan kiss his breast when she heard this,
And was full glad he could the truth espy:

"This day I take thee for mine ally." chosen friend
Saide this blissful faire maiden dear;
And after that she said as ye may hear.

"Lo, right so as the love of Christ," quoth she,
"Made me thy brother's wife, right in that wise
Anon for mine ally here take I thee,
Since that thou wilt thine idoles despise.
Go with thy brother now and thee baptise,
And make thee clean, so that thou may'st behold
The angel's face, of which thy brother told."

Tiburce answer'd, and saide, "Brother dear,
First tell me whither I shall, and to what man?"
"To whom?" quoth he, "come forth with goode cheer,
I will thee lead unto the Pope Urban."
"To Urban? brother mine Valerian,"
Quoth then Tiburce; "wilt thou me thither lead?
Me thinketh that it were a wondrous deed.

"Meanest thou not that Urban," quoth he tho, then
"That is so often damned to be dead,
And wons in halkes always to and fro, dwells corners
And dare not ones putte forth his head?
Men should him brennen in a fire so red, burn
If he were found, or if men might him spy:
And us also, to bear him company.

"And while we seeke that Divinity
That is y-hid in heaven privily,
Algate burnt in this world should we be." nevertheless
To whom Cecilie answer'd boldely;
"Men mighte dreade well and skilfully reasonably
This life to lose, mine owen deare brother,
If this were living only, and none other.

"But there is better life in other place,
That never shall be loste, dread thee nought;
Which Godde's Son us tolde through his grace
That Father's Son which alle thinges wrought;
And all that wrought is with a skilful thought, reasonable
The Ghost, that from the Father gan proceed, Holy Spirit
Hath souled them, withouten any drede. endowed them with a soul doubt
By word and by miracle, high God's Son,
When he was in this world, declared here.
That there is other life where men may won." dwell
To whom answer'd Tiburce, "O sister dear,
Saidest thou not right now in this mannere,
There was but one God, Lord in soothfastness, truth
And now of three how may'st thou bear witness?"

"That shall I tell," quoth she, "ere that I go.
Right as a man hath sapiences three, mental faculties
Memory, engine, and intellect also, wit[11]
So in one being of divinity
Three persones there maye right well be."
Then gan she him full busily to preach
Of Christe's coming, and his paines teach,

And many pointes of his passion;
How Godde's Son in this world was withhold employed
To do mankinde plein remission, full
That was y-bound in sin and cares cold. wretched[12]
All this thing she unto Tiburce told,
And after that Tiburce, in good intent,
With Valerian to Pope Urban he went.

That thanked God, and with glad heart and light
He christen'd him, and made him in that place
Perfect in his learning, and Godde's knight.
And after this Tiburce got such grace,
That every day he saw in time and space
Th' angel of God, and every manner boon request, favour
That be God asked, it was sped full anon. granted, successful

It were full hard by order for to sayn
How many wonders Jesus for them wrought,
But at the last, to telle short and plain,
The sergeants of the town of Rome them sought,
And them before Almach the Prefect brought,
Which them apposed, and knew all their intent, questioned
And to th'image of Jupiter them sent.

And said, "Whoso will not do sacrifice,
Swap off his head, this is my sentence here." strike
Anon these martyrs, that I you devise, of whom I tell you
One Maximus, that was an officere
Of the prefect's, and his corniculere[13]
Them hent, and when he forth the saintes lad, seized led
Himself he wept for pity that he had.

When Maximus had heard the saintes lore, doctrine, teaching
He got him of the tormentores leave, torturers
And led them to his house withoute more;
And with their preaching, ere that it were eve,
They gonnen from the tormentors to reave, began wrest, root out
And from Maxim', and from his folk each one,
The false faith, to trow in God alone. believe

Cecilia came, when it was waxen night,
With priestes, that them christen'd all in fere; in a

company
And afterward, when day was waxen light,
Cecile them said with a full steadfast cheer, mien
"Now, Christe's owen knightes lefe and dear, beloved
Cast all away the workes of darkness,
And arme you in armour of brightness.

Ye have forsooth y-done a great battaile,
Your course is done, your faith have ye conserved;[14]
O to the crown of life that may not fail;
The rightful Judge, which that ye have served
Shall give it you, as ye have it deserved."
And when this thing was said, as I devise, relate
Men led them forth to do the sacrifice.

But when they were unto the place brought
To telle shortly the conclusion,
They would incense nor sacrifice right nought
But on their knees they sette them adown,
With humble heart and sad devotion, steadfast
And loste both their headed in the place;
Their soules wente to the King of grace.

This Maximus, that saw this thing betide,
With piteous teares told it anon right,
That he their soules saw to heaven glide
With angels, full of clearness and of light
Andt with his word converted many a wight.
For which Almachius did him to-beat see note[15]
With whip of lead, till he his life gan lete. quit

Cecile him took, and buried him anon
By Tiburce and Valerian softely,
Within their burying-place, under the stone.
And after this Almachius hastily
Bade his ministers fetchen openly
Cecile, so that she might in his presence
Do sacrifice, and Jupiter incense. burn incense to

But they, converted at her wise lore, teaching
Wepte full sore, and gave full credence
Unto her word, and cried more and more;
"Christ, Godde's Son, withoute difference,
Is very God, this is all our sentence, opinion
That hath so good a servant him to serve
Thus with one voice we trowe, though we sterve. believe die

Almachius, that heard of this doing,
Bade fetch Cecilie, that he might her see;
And alderfirst, lo, this was his asking; first of all
"What manner woman arte thou?" quoth he,
"I am a gentle woman born," quoth she.
"I aske thee," quoth he,"though it thee grieve,
Of thy religion and of thy believe."

"Ye have begun your question foolishly,"
Quoth she, "that wouldest two answers conclude
In one demand? ye aske lewedly." ignorantly
Almach answer'd to that similitude,

"Of whence comes thine answering so rude?"
"Of whence?" quoth she, when that she was freined, asked
"Of conscience, and of good faith unfeigned."

Almachius saide; "Takest thou no heed
Of my power?" and she him answer'd this;
"Your might," quoth she, "full little is to dread;
For every mortal manne's power is
But like a bladder full of wind, y-wis; certainly
For with a needle's point, when it is blow',
May all the boast of it be laid full low."

"Full wrongfully begunnest thou," quoth he,
"And yet in wrong is thy perseverance.
Know'st thou not how our mighty princes free
Have thus commanded and made ordinance,
That every Christian wight shall have penance, punishment
But if that he his Christendom withsay, deny
And go all quit, if he will it renay?" renounce

"Your princes erren, as your nobley doth," nobility
Quoth then Cecile, "and with a wood sentence mad judgment
Ye make us guilty, and it is not sooth: true
For ye that knowe well our innocence,
Forasmuch as we do aye reverence
To Christ, and for we bear a Christian name,
Ye put on us a crime and eke a blame.

"But we that knowe thilke name so
For virtuous, we may it not withsay."
Almach answered, "Choose one of these two,
Do sacrifice, or Christendom renay,
That thou may'st now escape by that way."
At which the holy blissful faire maid
Gan for to laugh, and to the judge said;

"O judge, confused in thy nicety, confounded in thy folly
Wouldest thou that I reny innocence?
To make me a wicked wight," quoth she,
"Lo, he dissimuleth here in audience; dissembles
He stareth and woodeth in his advertence." grows furious thought
To whom Almachius said, "Unsely wretch, unhappy
Knowest thou not how far my might may stretch?

"Have not our mighty princes to me given
Yea bothe power and eke authority
To make folk to dien or to liven?
Why speakest thou so proudly then to me?"
"I speake not but steadfastly," quoth she,
Not proudly, for I say, as for my side,
We hate deadly thilke vice of pride. mortally

"And, if thou dreade not a sooth to hear, truth
Then will I shew all openly by right,
That thou hast made a full great leasing here.

falsehood
Thou say'st thy princes have thee given might
Both for to slay and for to quick a wight, — give life to
Thou that may'st not but only life bereave;
Thou hast none other power nor no leave.

"But thou may'st say, thy princes have thee maked
Minister of death; for if thou speak of mo',
Thou liest; for thy power is full naked."
"Do away thy boldness," said Almachius tho, then
"And sacrifice to our gods, ere thou go.
I recke not what wrong that thou me proffer,
For I can suffer it as a philosopher.

"But those wronges may I not endure,
That thou speak'st of our goddes here," quoth he.
Cecile answer'd, "O nice creature, foolish
Thou saidest no word, since thou spake to me,
That I knew not therewith thy nicety, folly
And that thou wert in every manner wise every sort of way
A lewed officer, a vain justice. ignorant

"There lacketh nothing to thine outward eyen
That thou art blind; for thing that we see all
That it is stone, that men may well espyen,
That ilke stone a god thou wilt it call. very, selfsame
I rede thee let thine hand upon it fall, advise
And taste it well, and stone thou shalt it find; examine, test
Since that thou see'st not with thine eyen blind.

"It is a shame that the people shall
So scorne thee, and laugh at thy folly;
For commonly men wot it well over all, know it everywhere
That mighty God is in his heaven high;
And these images, well may'st thou espy,
To thee nor to themselves may not profite,
For in effect they be not worth a mite."

These wordes and such others saide she,
And he wax'd wroth, and bade men should her lead
Home to her house; "And in her house," quoth he,
"Burn her right in a bath, with flames red."
And as he bade, right so was done the deed;
For in a bath they gan her faste shetten, shut, confine
And night and day great fire they under betten. kindled, applied

The longe night, and eke a day also,
For all the fire, and eke the bathe's heat,
She sat all cold, and felt of it no woe,
It made her not one droppe for to sweat;
But in that bath her life she must lete. leave
For he, Almachius, with full wick' intent,
To slay her in the bath his sonde sent. message, order

Three strokes in the neck he smote her tho, there
The tormentor, but for no manner chance executioner
He might not smite her faire neck in two:
And, for there was that time an ordinance
That no man should do man such penance, severity, torture
The fourthe stroke to smite, soft or sore,
This tormentor he durste do no more;

But half dead, with her necke carven there gashed
He let her lie, and on his way is went.
The Christian folk, which that about her were,
With sheetes have the blood full fair y-hent; taken up
Three dayes lived she in this torment,
And never ceased them the faith to teach,
That she had foster'd them, she gan to preach.

And them she gave her mebles and her thing, goods
And to the Pope Urban betook them tho; commended then
And said, "I aske this of heaven's king,
To have respite three dayes and no mo',
To recommend to you, ere that I go,
These soules, lo; and that I might do wirch cause to be made
Here of mine house perpetually a church."

Saint Urban, with his deacons, privily
The body fetch'd, and buried it by night
Among his other saintes honestly;
Her house the church of Saint Cecilie hight; is called
Saint Urban hallow'd it, as he well might;
In which unto this day, in noble wise,
Men do to Christ and to his saint service.

Notes to the Nun's Priest's Tale

1. This Tale was originally composed by Chaucer as a separate work, and as such it is mentioned in the "Legend of Good Women" under the title of "The Life of Saint Cecile". Tyrwhitt quotes the line in which the author calls himself an "unworthy son of Eve," and that in which he says, "Yet pray I you, that reade what I write", as internal evidence that the insertion of the poem in the Canterbury Tales was the result of an afterthought; while the whole tenor of the introduction confirms the belief that Chaucer composed it as a writer or translator — not, dramatically, as a speaker. The story is almost literally translated from the Life of St Cecilia in the "Legenda Aurea."

2. Leas: leash, snare; the same as "las," oftener used by Chaucer.
3. The nativity and assumption of the Virgin Mary formed the themes of some of St Bernard's most eloquent sermons.
4. Compare with this stanza the fourth stanza of the Prioress's Tale, the substance of which is the same.
5. "But he answered and said, it is not meet to take the children's bread, and cast it to dogs. And she said, Truth, Lord: yet the dogs eat of the crumbs which fall from their master's table." — Matthew xv. 26, 27.
6. See note 1.
7. These are Latin puns: Heaven's lily - "Coeli lilium"; The way of blind - "Caeci via"; Heaven and Lia - from "Coeli", heaven, and "Ligo," to bind; Heaven and Leos - from Coeli and "Laos," (Ionian Greek) or "Leos" (Attic Greek), the people. Such punning derivations of proper names were very much in favour in the Middle Ages. The explanations of St Cecilia's name are literally taken from the prologue to the Latin legend.
8. This passage suggests Horace's description of the wise man, who, among other things, is "in se ipse totus, teres, atque rotundus." ("complete in himself, polished and rounded") — Satires, 2, vii. 80.
9. Louting: lingering, or lying concealed; the Latin original has "Inter sepulchra martyrum latiantem" ("hiding among the tombs of martyrs")
10. The fourteen lines within brackets are supposed to have been originally an interpolation in the Latin legend, from which they are literally translated. They awkwardly interrupt the flow of the narration.
11. Engine: wit; the devising or constructive faculty; Latin, "ingenium."
12. Cold: wretched, distressful; see note 22 to the Nun's Priest's Tale.
13. Corniculere: The secretary or registrar who was charged with publishing the acts, decrees and orders of the prefect.
14. "I have fought a good fight, I have finished my course, I have kept the faith: Henceforth there is laid up for me a crown of righteousness" — 2 Tim. iv. 7, 8.
15. Did him to-beat: Caused him to be cruelly or fatally beaten; the force of the "to" is intensive.

GEOFFREY CHAUCER

THE CANON'S YEOMAN'S TALE.[1]

THE PROLOGUE.

WHEN ended was the life of Saint Cecile,
Ere we had ridden fully five mile,[2]
At Boughton-under-Blee us gan o'ertake
A man, that clothed was in clothes black,
And underneath he wore a white surplice.
His hackenay, which was all pomely-gris,   nag dapple-gray
So sweated, that it wonder was to see;
It seem'd as he had pricked miles three.   spurred
The horse eke that his yeoman rode upon
So sweated, that unnethes might he gon.   hardly go
About the peytrel[3] stood the foam full high;
He was of foam, as flecked as a pie.   spotted like a magpie
A maile twyfold[4] on his crupper lay;
It seemed that he carried little array;
All light for summer rode this worthy man.
And in my heart to wonder I began
What that he was, till that I understood
How that his cloak was sewed to his hood;
For which, when I had long advised me,   considered
I deemed him some Canon for to be.
His hat hung at his back down by a lace,   cord
For he had ridden more than trot or pace;
He hadde pricked like as he were wood.   mad
A clote-leaf he had laid under his hood,   burdock-leaf
For sweat, and for to keep his head from heat.
But it was joye for to see him sweat;
His forehead dropped as a stillatory   still
Were full of plantain or of paritory.   wallflower
And when that he was come, he gan to cry,
"God save," quoth he, "this jolly company.
Fast have I pricked," quoth he, "for your sake,
Because that I would you overtake,
To riden in this merry company."
His Yeoman was eke full of courtesy,
And saide, "Sirs, now in the morning tide
Out of your hostelry I saw you ride,
And warned here my lord and sovereign,
Which that to ride with you is full fain,
For his disport; he loveth dalliance."
"Friend, for thy warning God give thee good chance,"   fortune
Said oure Host; "certain it woulde seem
Thy lord were wise, and so I may well deem;
He is full jocund also, dare I lay;
Can he aught tell a merry tale or tway,
With which he gladden may this company?"
"Who, Sir? my lord? Yea, Sir, withoute lie,

He can of mirth and eke of jollity knows
Not but enough; also, Sir, truste me, not less than
An ye him knew all so well as do I, if
Ye would wonder how well and craftily
He coulde work, and that in sundry wise.
He hath take on him many a great emprise,   task, undertaking
Which were full hard for any that is here
To bring about, but they of him it lear.   unless learn
As homely as he rides amonges you,
If ye him knew, it would be for your prow: advantage
Ye woulde not forego his acquaintance
For muche good, I dare lay in balance
All that I have in my possession.
He is a man of high discretion.
I warn you well, he is a passing man."   surpassing, extraordinary
Well," quoth our Host, "I pray thee tell me than,
Is he a clerk, or no? Tell what he is."   scholar, priest
"Nay, he is greater than a clerk, y-wis,"   certainly
Saide this Yeoman; "and, in wordes few,
Host, of his craft somewhat I will you shew,
I say, my lord can such a subtlety knows
(But all his craft ye may not weet of me,   learn
And somewhat help I yet to his working),
That all the ground on which we be riding
Till that we come to Canterbury town,
He could all cleane turnen up so down,
And pave it all of silver and of gold."
And when this Yeoman had this tale told
Unto our Host, he said; "Ben'dicite!
This thing is wonder marvellous to me,
Since that thy lord is of so high prudence,
Because of which men should him reverence,
That of his worship recketh he so lite;   honour little
His overest slop it is not worth a mite   upper garment
As in effect to him, so may I go;
It is all baudy and to-tore also.   slovenly
Why is thy lord so sluttish, I thee pray,
And is of power better clothes to bey,   buy
If that his deed accordeth with thy speech?
Telle me that, and that I thee beseech."

"Why?" quoth this Yeoman, "whereto ask ye me?
God help me so, for he shall never the thrive
(But I will not avowe that I say,   admit
And therefore keep it secret, I you pray);
He is too wise, in faith, as I believe.

210

THE CANTERBURY TALES

Thing that is overdone, it will not preve stand the test
Aright, as clerkes say; it is a vice;
Wherefore in that I hold him lewd and nice." ignorant and foolish
For when a man hath over great a wit,
Full oft him happens to misusen it;
So doth my lord, and that me grieveth sore.
God it amend; I can say now no more."

"Thereof no force, good Yeoman, "quoth our Host; no matter
"Since of the conning of thy lord, thou know'st, knowledge
Tell how he doth, I pray thee heartily,
Since that be is so crafty and so sly. wise
Where dwelle ye, if it to telle be?"
"In the suburbes of a town," quoth he,
"Lurking in hernes and in lanes blind, corners
Where as these robbers and these thieves by kind nature
Holde their privy fearful residence,
As they that dare not show their presence,
So fare we, if I shall say the soothe." truth
"Yet," quoth our Hoste, "let me talke to thee;
Why art thou so discolour'd of thy face?"
"Peter!" quoth he, "God give it harde grace,
I am so us'd the hote fire to blow,
That it hath changed my colour, I trow;
I am not wont in no mirror to pry,
But swinke sore, and learn to multiply.[5] labour
We blunder ever, and poren in the fire, toil peer
And, for all that, we fail of our desire
For ever we lack our conclusion
To muche folk we do illusion,
And borrow gold, be it a pound or two,
Or ten or twelve, or many summes mo',
And make them weenen, at the leaste way, fancy
That of a pounde we can make tway.
Yet is it false; and aye we have good hope
It for to do, and after it we grope: search, strive
But that science is so far us beforn,
That we may not, although we had it sworn,

It overtake, it slides away so fast;
It will us make beggars at the last."
While this Yeoman was thus in his talking,
This Canon drew him near, and heard all thing
Which this Yeoman spake, for suspicion
Of menne's speech ever had this Canon:
For Cato saith, that he that guilty is,[6]
Deemeth all things be spoken of him y-wis; surely
Because of that he gan so nigh to draw
To his Yeoman, that he heard all his saw;
And thus he said unto his Yeoman tho then
"Hold thou thy peace,and speak no wordes mo':
For if thou do, thou shalt it dear abie. pay dearly for it
Thou slanderest me here in this company
And eke discoverest that thou shouldest hide."
"Yea," quoth our Host, "tell on, whatso betide;
Of all his threatening reck not a mite."
"In faith," quoth he, "no more do I but lite." little
And when this Canon saw it would not be
But his Yeoman would tell his privity, secrets
He fled away for very sorrow and shame.

"Ah!" quoth the Yeoman, "here shall rise a game; some diversion
All that I can anon I will you tell,
Since he is gone; the foule fiend him quell! destroy
For ne'er hereafter will I with him meet,
For penny nor for pound, I you behete. promise
He that me broughte first unto that game,
Ere that he die, sorrow have he and shame.
For it is earnest to me, by my faith; a serious matter
That feel I well, what so any man saith;
And yet for all my smart, and all my grief,
For all my sorrow, labour, and mischief, trouble
I coulde never leave it in no wise.
Now would to God my witte might suffice
To tellen all that longeth to that art!
But natheless yet will I telle part;
Since that my lord is gone, I will not spare;
Such thing as that I know, I will declare."

Notes to the Prologue to the Canon's Yeoman's Tale

1. "The introduction," says Tyrwhitt, "of the Canon's Yeoman to tell a Tale at a time when so many of the original characters remain to be called upon, appears a little extraordinary. It should seem that some sudden resentment had determined Chaucer to interrupt the regular course of his work, in order to insert a satire against the alchemists. That their pretended science was much cultivated about this time, and produced its usual evils, may fairly be inferred from the Act, which was passed soon after, 5 H. IV. c. iv., to make it felony 'to multiply gold or silver, or to use the art of multiplication.'" Tyrwhitt finds in the prologue some colour for the hypothesis that this Tale was intended by Chaucer to begin the return journey from Canterbury; but against this must be set the fact that the Yeoman himself expressly speaks of the distance to Canterbury yet to be ridden.
2. Fully five mile: From some place which the loss of the Second Nun's Prologue does not enable us to identify.
3. Peytrel: the breast-plate of a horse's harness; French, "poitrail."
4. A maile twyfold: a double valise; a wallet hanging across the crupper on either side of the horse.

5. Multiply: transmute metals, in the attempt to multiply gold and silver by alchemy.
6. "Conscius ipse sibi de se putat omnia dici" ("The conspirator believes that everything spoken refers to himself") — "De Moribus," I. i. dist. 17.

THE TALE.[1]

With this Canon I dwelt have seven year,
And of his science am I ne'er the near *nearer*
All that I had I have lost thereby,
And, God wot, so have many more than I.
Where I was wont to be right fresh and gay
Of clothing, and of other good array
Now may I wear an hose upon mine head;
And where my colour was both fresh and red,
Now is it wan, and of a leaden hue
(Whoso it useth, sore shall he it rue);
And of my swink yet bleared is mine eye; *labour*
Lo what advantage is to multiply!
That sliding science hath me made so bare, *slippery, deceptive*
That I have no good, where that ever I fare; *property*
And yet I am indebted so thereby
Of gold, that I have borrow'd truely,
That, while I live, I shall it quite never; *repay*
Let every man beware by me for ever.
What manner man that casteth him thereto, *betaketh*
If he continue, I hold his thrift y-do; *prosperity at an end*
So help me God, thereby shall he not win,
But empty his purse, and make his wittes thin.
And when he, through his madness and folly,
Hath lost his owen good through jupartie, *hazard*[2]
Then he exciteth other men thereto,
To lose their good as he himself hath do'.
For unto shrewes joy it is and ease *wicked folk*
To have their fellows in pain and disease. *trouble*
Thus was I ones learned of a clerk;
Of that no charge; I will speak of our work. *matter*

When we be there as we shall exercise
Our elvish craft, we seeme wonder wise, *fantastic, wicked*
Our termes be so clergial and quaint. *learned and strange*
I blow the fire till that mine hearte faint.
Why should I tellen each proportion
Of thinges, whiche that we work upon,
As on five or six ounces, may well be,
Of silver, or some other quantity?
And busy me to telle you the names,
As orpiment, burnt bones, iron squames, *scales*[3]
That into powder grounden be full small?
And in an earthen pot how put is all,
And, salt y-put in, and also peppere,
Before these powders that I speak of here,
And well y-cover'd with a lamp of glass?
And of much other thing which that there was?
And of the pots and glasses engluting, *sealing up*
That of the air might passen out no thing?
And of the easy fire, and smart also, *slow quick*
Which that was made? and of the care and woe
That we had in our matters subliming,
And in amalgaming, and calcining
Of quicksilver, called mercury crude?
For all our sleightes we can not conclude.
Our orpiment, and sublim'd mercury,
Our ground litharge eke on the porphyry, *white lead*
Of each of these of ounces a certain, *certain proportion*
Not helpeth us, our labour is in vain.
Nor neither our spirits' ascensioun,
Nor our matters that lie all fix'd adown,
May in our working nothing us avail;
For lost is all our labour and travail,
And all the cost, a twenty devil way,
Is lost also, which we upon it lay.

There is also full many another thing
That is unto our craft appertaining,
Though I by order them not rehearse can,
Because that I am a lewed man; *unlearned*
Yet will I tell them as they come to mind,
Although I cannot set them in their kind,
As sal-armoniac, verdigris, borace;
And sundry vessels made of earth and glass;[4]
Our urinales, and our descensories,
Phials, and croslets, and sublimatories,
Cucurbites, and alembikes eke,
And other suche, dear enough a leek, *worth less than a leek*
It needeth not for to rehearse them all.
Waters rubifying, and bulles' gall,
Arsenic, sal-armoniac, and brimstone,
And herbes could I tell eke many a one,
As egremoine, valerian, and lunary, *agrimony moon-wort*
And other such, if that me list to tarry;
Our lampes burning bothe night and day,
To bring about our craft if that we may;
Our furnace eke of calcination,
And of waters albification,
Unslaked lime, chalk, and glair of an ey, *egg-white*
Powders diverse, ashes, dung, piss, and clay,
Seared pokettes,[5] saltpetre, and vitriol;
And divers fires made of wood and coal;
Sal-tartar, alkali, salt preparate,
And combust matters, and coagulate;

THE CANTERBURY TALES

Clay made with horse and manne's hair, and oil
Of tartar, alum, glass, barm, wort, argoil, potter's clay[6]
Rosalgar, and other matters imbibing; flowers of antimony
And eke of our matters encorporing,   incorporating
And of our silver citrination,[7]
Our cementing, and fermentation,
Our ingots, tests, and many thinges mo'.   moulds[8]
I will you tell, as was me taught also,
The foure spirits, and the bodies seven,
By order, as oft I heard my lord them neven.   name
The first spirit Quicksilver called is;
The second Orpiment; the third, y-wis,
Sal-Armoniac, and the fourth Brimstone.
The bodies sev'n eke, lo them here anon.
Sol gold is, and Luna silver we threpe   name[9]
Mars iron, Mercury quicksilver we clepe;   call
Saturnus lead, and Jupiter is tin,
And Venus copper, by my father's kin.

This cursed craft whoso will exercise,
He shall no good have that him may suffice;
For all the good he spendeth thereabout,
He lose shall, thereof have I no doubt.
Whoso that list to utter his folly,   display
Let him come forth and learn to multiply:
And every man that hath aught in his coffer,
Let him appear, and wax a philosopher;
Ascaunce that craft is so light to lear.   as if learn
Nay, nay, God wot, all be he monk or frere,
Priest or canon, or any other wight;
Though he sit at his book both day and night;
In learning of this elvish nice lore,   fantastic, foolish
All is in vain; and pardie muche more,
Is to learn a lew'd man this subtlety;   ignorant
Fie! speak not thereof, for it will not be.
And conne he letterure, or conne he none,   if he knows learning
As in effect, he shall it find all one;
For bothe two, by my salvation,
Concluden in multiplication   transmutation by alchemy
Alike well, when they have all y-do;
This is to say, they faile bothe two.
Yet forgot I to make rehearsale
Of waters corrosive, and of limaile,   metal filings
And of bodies' mollification,
And also of their induration,
Oiles, ablutions, metal fusible,
To tellen all, would passen any Bible
That owhere is; wherefore, as for the best,   anywhere
Of all these names now will I me rest;
For, as I trow, I have you told enough
To raise a fiend, all look he ne'er so rough.

Ah! nay, let be; the philosopher's stone,
Elixir call'd, we seeke fast each one;
For had we him, then were we sicker enow;   secure
But unto God of heaven I make avow,   confession
For all our craft, when we have all y-do,
And all our sleight, he will not come us to.
He hath y-made us spende muche good,
For sorrow of which almost we waxed wood,   mad
But that good hope creeped in our heart,
Supposing ever, though we sore smart,
To be relieved by him afterward.
Such supposing and hope is sharp and hard.
I warn you well it is to seeken ever.
That future temps hath made men dissever,   time part from
In trust thereof, from all that ever they had,
Yet of that art they cannot waxe sad,   repentant
For unto them it is a bitter sweet;
So seemeth it; for had they but a sheet
Which that they mighte wrap them in at night,
And a bratt to walk in by dayelight,   cloak[10]
They would them sell, and spend it on this craft;
They cannot stint, until no thing be laft.   cease
And evermore, wherever that they gon,
Men may them knowe by smell of brimstone;
For all the world they stinken as a goat;
Their savour is so rammish and so hot,
That though a man a mile from them be,
The savour will infect him, truste me.
Lo, thus by smelling and threadbare array,
If that men list, this folk they knowe may.
And if a man will ask them privily,
Why they be clothed so unthriftily,   shabbily
They right anon will rownen in his ear,   whisper
And sayen, if that they espied were,
Men would them slay, because of their science:
Lo, thus these folk betrayen innocence!

Pass over this; I go my tale unto.
Ere that the pot be on the fire y-do   placed
Of metals, with a certain quantity
My lord them tempers, and no man but he   adjusts the proportions
(Now he is gone, I dare say boldely);
For as men say, he can do craftily,
Algate I wot well he hath such a name,   although
And yet full oft he runneth into blame;
And know ye how? full oft it happ'neth so,
The pot to-breaks, and farewell! all is go'.   gone
These metals be of so great violence,
Our walles may not make them resistence,
But if they were wrought of lime and stone;   unless
They pierce so, that through the wall they gon;
And some of them sink down into the ground
(Thus have we lost by times many a pound),
And some are scatter'd all the floor about;

213

GEOFFREY CHAUCER

Some leap into the roof withoute doubt.
Though that the fiend not in our sight him show,
I trowe that he be with us, that shrew;   impious wretch
In helle, where that he is lord and sire,
Is there no more woe, rancour, nor ire.
When that our pot is broke, as I have said,
Every man chides, and holds him evil apaid.   dissatisfied
Some said it was long on the fire-making;   because of [1]
Some saide nay, it was on the blowing
(Then was I fear'd, for that was mine office);
"Straw!" quoth the third, "ye be lewed and nice,   ignorant foolish
It was not temper'd as it ought to be."   mixed in due proportions
"Nay," quoth the fourthe, "stint and hearken me;   stop
Because our fire was not y-made of beech,
That is the cause, and other none, so the'ch.   so may I thrive
I cannot tell whereon it was along,
But well I wot great strife is us among."
"What?" quoth my lord, "there is no more to do'n,
Of these perils I will beware eftsoon.   another time
I am right sicker that the pot was crazed.   sure cracked
Be as be may, be ye no thing amazed.   confounded
As usage is, let sweep the floor as swithe;   quickly
Pluck up your heartes and be glad and blithe."

The mullok on a heap y-sweeped was,   rubbish
And on the floor y-cast a canevas,
And all this mullok in a sieve y-throw,
And sifted, and y-picked many a throw.   time
"Pardie," quoth one, "somewhat of our metal
Yet is there here, though that we have not all.
And though this thing mishapped hath as now,   has gone amiss
Another time it may be well enow.   at present
We muste put our good in adventure;   risk our property
A merchant, pardie, may not aye endure,
Truste me well, in his prosperity:
Sometimes his good is drenched in the sea,   drowned, sunk
And sometimes comes it safe unto the land."
"Peace," quoth my lord; "the next time I will fand   endeavour
To bring our craft all in another plight,   to a different conclusion
And but I do, Sirs, let me have the wite;   blame
There was default in somewhat, well I wot."
Another said, the fire was over hot.
But be it hot or cold, I dare say this,
That we concluden evermore amiss;
We fail alway of that which we would have;
And in our madness evermore we rave.
And when we be together every one,
Every man seemeth a Solomon.
But all thing, which that shineth as the gold,
It is not gold, as I have heard it told;
Nor every apple that is fair at eye,
It is not good, what so men clap or cry.   assert
Right so, lo, fareth it amonges us.
He that the wisest seemeth, by Jesus,
Is most fool, when it cometh to the prefe;   proof, test
And he that seemeth truest, is a thief.
That shall ye know, ere that I from you wend;
By that I of my tale have made an end.

There was a canon of religioun
Amonges us, would infect all a town,   deceive
Though it as great were as was Nineveh,
Rome, Alisandre, Troy, or other three.   Alexandria
His sleightes and his infinite falseness   cunning tricks
There coulde no man writen, as I guess,
Though that he mighte live a thousand year;
In all this world of falseness n'is his peer.   there is not
For in his termes he will him so wind,
And speak his wordes in so sly a kind,
When he commune shall with any wight,
That he will make him doat anon aright,   become foolishly
But it a fiende be, as himself is.   fond of him
Full many a man hath he beguil'd ere this,
And will, if that he may live any while;
And yet men go and ride many a mile
Him for to seek, and have his acquaintance,
Not knowing of his false governance.   deceitful conduct
And if you list to give me audience,
I will it telle here in your presence.
But, worshipful canons religious,
Ne deeme not that I slander your house,
Although that my tale of a canon be.
Of every order some shrew is, pardie;
And God forbid that all a company
Should rue a singular manne's folly.   individual
To slander you is no thing mine intent;
But to correct that is amiss I meant.
This tale was not only told for you,
But eke for other more; ye wot well how
That amonges Christe's apostles twelve
There was no traitor but Judas himself;
Then why should all the remenant have blame,
That guiltless were? By you I say the same.
Save only this, if ye will hearken me,
If any Judas in your convent be,
Remove him betimes, I you rede,   counsel
If shame or loss may causen any dread.

214

And be no thing displeased, I you pray;
But in this case hearken what I say.

In London was a priest, an annualere,[12]
That therein dwelled hadde many a year,
Which was so pleasant and so serviceable
Unto the wife, where as he was at table,
That she would suffer him no thing to pay
For board nor clothing, went he ne'er so gay;
And spending silver had he right enow;
Thereof no force; will proceed as now, no matter
And telle forth my tale of the canon,
That brought this prieste to confusion.
This false canon came upon a day
Unto the prieste's chamber, where he lay,
Beseeching him to lend him a certain
Of gold, and he would quit it him again.
"Lend me a mark," quoth he, "but dayes three,
And at my day I will it quite thee.
And if it so be that thou find me false,
Another day hang me up by the halse." neck
This priest him took a mark, and that as swithe, quickly
And this canon him thanked often sithe, times
And took his leave, and wente forth his way;
And at the thirde day brought his money,
And to the priest he took his gold again,
Whereof this priest was wondrous glad and fain. pleased
"Certes," quoth he, "nothing annoyeth me I am not unwiling
To lend a man a noble, or two, or three,
Or what thing were in my possession,
When he so true is of condition,
That in no wise he breake will his day;
To such a man I never can say nay."
"What," quoth this canon, "should I be untrue?
Nay, that were thing y-fallen all of new! a new thing to happen
Truth is a thing that I will ever keep,
Unto the day in which that I shall creep
Into my grave; and elles God forbid;
Believe this as sicker as your creed. sure
God thank I, and in good time be it said,
That there was never man yet evil apaid displeased, dissatisfied
For gold nor silver that he to me lent,
Nor ever falsehood in mine heart I meant.
And Sir," quoth he, "now of my privity,
Since ye so goodly have been unto me,
And kithed to me so great gentleness, shown
Somewhat, to quite with your kindeness,
I will you shew, and if you list to lear, learn
I will you teache plainly the mannere
How I can worken in philosophy.
Take good heed, ye shall well see at eye with your own eye
That I will do a mas'try ere I go."
"Yea," quoth the priest; "yea, Sir, and will ye so?

Mary! thereof I pray you heartily."
"At your commandement, Sir, truely,"
Quoth the canon, "and elles God forbid."
Lo, how this thiefe could his service bede! offer

Full sooth it is that such proffer'd service
Stinketh, as witnesse these olde wise; those wise folk of old
And that full soon I will it verify
In this canon, root of all treachery,
That evermore delight had and gladness
(Such fiendly thoughtes in his heart impress) press into his heart
How Christe's people he may to mischief bring.
God keep us from his false dissimuling!
What wiste this priest with whom that he dealt?
Nor of his harm coming he nothing felt.
O sely priest, O sely innocent! simple
With covetise anon thou shalt be blent; blinded; beguiled
O graceless, full blind is thy conceit!
For nothing art thou ware of the deceit
Which that this fox y-shapen hath to thee; contrived
His wily wrenches thou not mayest flee. snares
Wherefore, to go to the conclusioun
That referreth to thy confusion,
Unhappy man, anon I will me hie hasten
To telle thine unwit and thy folly, stupidity
And eke the falseness of that other wretch,
As farforth as that my conning will stretch. knowledge
This canon was my lord, ye woulde ween; imagine
Sir Host, in faith, and by the heaven's queen,
It was another canon, and not he,
That can an hundred fold more subtlety. knows
He hath betrayed folkes many a time;
Of his falseness it doleth me to rhyme. paineth
And ever, when I speak of his falsehead,
For shame of him my cheekes waxe red;
Algates they beginne for to glow, at least
For redness have I none, right well I know,
In my visage; for fumes diverse
Of metals, which ye have me heard rehearse,
Consumed have and wasted my redness.
Now take heed of this canon's cursedness. villainy

"Sir," quoth he to the priest, "let your man gon
For quicksilver, that we it had anon;
And let him bringen ounces two or three;
And when he comes, as faste shall ye see
A wondrous thing, which ye saw ne'er ere this."
"Sir," quoth the priest, "it shall be done, y-wis." certainly
He bade his servant fetche him this thing,
And he all ready was at his bidding,
And went him forth, and came anon again
With this quicksilver, shortly for to sayn;
And took these ounces three to the canoun;

And he them laide well and fair adown,
And bade the servant coales for to bring,
That he anon might go to his working.
The coales right anon weren y-fet, fetched
And this canon y-took a crosselet crucible
Out of his bosom, and shew'd to the priest.
"This instrument," quoth he, "which that thou seest,
Take in thine hand, and put thyself therein
Of this quicksilver an ounce, and here begin,
In the name of Christ, to wax a philosopher.
There be full few, which that I woulde proffer
To shewe them thus much of my science;
For here shall ye see by experience
That this quicksilver I will mortify,[13]
Right in your sight anon withoute lie,
And make it as good silver, and as fine,
As there is any in your purse, or mine,
Or ellesswhere; and make it malleable,
And elles holde me false and unable
Amonge folk for ever to appear.
I have a powder here that cost me dear,
Shall make all good, for it is cause of all
My conning, which that I you shewe shall. knowledge
Voide your man, and let him be thereout; send away
And shut the doore, while we be about
Our privity, that no man us espy,
While that we work in this phiosophy."
All, as he bade, fulfilled was in deed.
This ilke servant right anon out yede, went
And his master y-shut the door anon,
And to their labour speedily they gon.

This priest, at this cursed canon's bidding,
Upon the fire anon he set this thing,
And blew the fire, and busied him full fast.
And this canon into the croslet cast
A powder, I know not whereof it was
Y-made, either of chalk, either of glass,
Or somewhat elles, was not worth a fly,
To blinden with this priest; and bade him hie deceive make haste
The coales for to couchen all above lay in order
The croslet; "for, in token I thee love,"
Quoth this canon, "thine owen handes two
Shall work all thing that here shall be do'."
"Grand mercy," quoth the priest, and was full glad, great thanks
And couch'd the coales as the canon bade.
And while he busy was, this fiendly wretch,
This false canon (the foule fiend him fetch),
Out of his bosom took a beechen coal,
In which full subtifly was made a hole,
And therein put was of silver limaile filings
An ounce, and stopped was withoute fail
The hole with wax, to keep the limaile in.
And understande, that this false gin contrivance
Was not made there, but it was made before;
And other things I shall tell you more,
Hereafterward, which that he with him brought;
Ere he came there, him to beguile he thought,
And so he did, ere that they went atwin; separated
Till he had turned him, could he not blin. cease[14]
It doleth me, when that I of him speak; paineth
On his falsehood fain would I me awreak, revenge myself
If I wist how, but he is here and there;
He is so variant, he abides nowhere. changeable

But take heed, Sirs, now for Godde's love.
He took his coal, of which I spake above,
And in his hand he bare it privily,
And while the prieste couched busily
The coales, as I tolde you ere this,
This canon saide, "Friend, ye do amiss;
This is not couched as it ought to be,
But soon I shall amenden it," quoth he.
"Now let me meddle therewith but a while,
For of you have I pity, by Saint Gile.
Ye be right hot, I see well how ye sweat;
Have here a cloth, and wipe away the wet."
And while that the prieste wip'd his face,
This canon took his coal, — with sorry grace, — evil fortune
And layed it above on the midward attend him!
Of the croslet, and blew well afterward,
Till that the coals beganne fast to brenn. burn
"Now give us drinke," quoth this canon then,
"And swithe all shall be well, I undertake. quickly
Sitte we down, and let us merry make."
And whenne that this canon's beechen coal
Was burnt, all the limaile out of the hole
Into the crosselet anon fell down;
And so it muste needes, by reasoun,
Since it above so even couched was; exactly laid
But thereof wist the priest no thing, alas!
He deemed all the coals alike good,
For of the sleight he nothing understood.

And when this alchemister saw his time,
"Rise up, Sir Priest," quoth he, "and stand by me;
And, for I wot well ingot have ye none; mould
Go, walke forth, and bring me a chalk stone;
For I will make it of the same shape
That is an ingot, if I may have hap.
Bring eke with you a bowl, or else a pan,
Full of water, and ye shall well see than then
How that our business shall hap and preve succeed
And yet, for ye shall have no misbeleve mistrust
Nor wrong conceit of me, in your absence,
I wille not be out of your presence,
But go with you, and come with you again."
The chamber-doore, shortly for to sayn,
They opened and shut, and went their way,
And forth with them they carried the key;

THE CANTERBURY TALES

And came again without any delay.
Why should I tarry all the longe day?
He took the chalk, and shap'd it in the wise
Of an ingot, as I shall you devise; describe
I say, he took out of his owen sleeve
A teine of silver (evil may he cheve!) little piece prosper
Which that ne was but a just ounce of weight.
And take heed now of his cursed sleight;
He shap'd his ingot, in length and in brede breadth
Of this teine, withouten any drede, doubt
So slily, that the priest it not espied;
And in his sleeve again he gan it hide;
And from the fire he took up his mattere,
And in th' ingot put it with merry cheer;
And in the water-vessel he it cast,
When that him list, and bade the priest as fast
Look what there is; "Put in thine hand and grope;
There shalt thou finde silver, as I hope."
What, devil of helle! should it elles be?
Shaving of silver, silver is, pardie.
He put his hand in, and took up a teine
Of silver fine; and glad in every vein
Was this priest, when he saw that it was so.
"Godde's blessing, and his mother's also,
And alle hallows, have ye, Sir Canon!" saints
Saide this priest, "and I their malison curse
But, an' ye vouchesafe to teache me if
This noble craft and this subtility,
I will be yours in all that ever I may."
Quoth the canon, "Yet will I make assay
The second time, that ye may take heed,
And be expert of this, and, in your need,
Another day assay in mine absence
This discipline, and this crafty science.
Let take another ounce," quoth he tho, then
"Of quicksilver, withoute wordes mo',
And do therewith as ye have done ere this
With that other, which that now silver is."

The priest him busied, all that e'er he can,
To do as this canon, this cursed man,
Commanded him, and fast he blew the fire
For to come to th' effect of his desire.
And this canon right in the meanewhile
All ready was this priest eft to beguile, again
and, for a countenance, in his hande bare stratagem
An hollow sticke (take keep and beware); heed
Of silver limaile put was, as before
Was in his coal, and stopped with wax well
For to keep in his limaile every deal. particle
And while this priest was in his business,
This canon with his sticke gan him dress apply
To him anon, and his powder cast in,
As he did erst (the devil out of his skin
Him turn, I pray to God, for his falsehead,
For he was ever false in thought and deed),

And with his stick, above the crosselet,
That was ordained with that false get, provided contrivance
He stirr'd the coales, till relente gan
The wax against the fire, as every man,
But he a fool be, knows well it must need.
And all that in the sticke was out yede, went
And in the croslet hastily it fell. quickly
Now, goode Sirs, what will ye bet than well? better
When that this priest was thus beguil'd again,
Supposing naught but truthe, sooth to sayn,
He was so glad, that I can not express
In no mannere his mirth and his gladness;
And to the canon he proffer'd eftsoon forthwith; again
Body and good. "Yea," quoth the canon soon,
"Though poor I be, crafty thou shalt me find; skilful
I warn thee well, yet is there more behind.
Is any copper here within?" said he.
"Yea, Sir," the prieste said, "I trow there be."
"Elles go buy us some, and that as swithe. swiftly
Now, goode Sir, go forth thy way and hie thee." hasten
He went his way, and with the copper came,
And this canon it in his handes name, took[15]
And of that copper weighed out an ounce.
Too simple is my tongue to pronounce,
As minister of my wit, the doubleness
Of this canon, root of all cursedness.
He friendly seem'd to them that knew him not;
But he was fiendly, both in work and thought.
It wearieth me to tell of his falseness;
And natheless yet will I it express,
To that intent men may beware thereby,
And for none other cause truely.
He put this copper in the crosselet,
And on the fire as swithe he hath it set, swiftly
And cast in powder, and made the priest to blow,
And in his working for to stoope low,
As he did erst, and all was but a jape; before trick
Right as him list the priest he made his ape. befooled him
And afterward in the ingot he it cast,
And in the pan he put it at the last
Of water, and in he put his own hand;
And in his sleeve, as ye beforehand
Hearde me tell, he had a silver teine; small piece
He silly took it out, this cursed heine wretch
(Unweeting this priest of his false craft), unsuspecting
And in the panne's bottom he it laft left
And in the water rumbleth to and fro,
And wondrous privily took up also
The copper teine (not knowing thilke priest),
And hid it, and him hente by the breast, took
And to him spake, and thus said in his game;
"Stoop now adown; by God, ye be to blame;

217

Helpe me now, as I did you whilere; before
Put in your hand, and looke what is there."

This priest took up this silver teine anon;
And thenne said the canon, "Let us gon,
With these three teines which that we have wrought,
To some goldsmith, and weet if they be aught: find out if they are
For, by my faith, I would not for my hood worth anything
But if they were silver fine and good, unless
And that as swithe well proved shall it be." quickly
Unto the goldsmith with these teines three
They went anon, and put them in assay proof
To fire and hammer; might no man say nay,
But that they weren as they ought to be.
This sotted priest, who gladder was than he? stupid, besotted
Was never bird gladder against the day;
Nor nightingale in the season of May
Was never none, that better list to sing;
Nor lady lustier in carolling,
Or for to speak of love and womanhead;
Nor knight in arms to do a hardy deed,
To standen in grace of his lady dear,
Than had this priest this crafte for to lear;
And to the canon thus he spake and said;
"For love of God, that for us alle died,
And as I may deserve it unto you,
What shall this receipt coste? tell me now."
"By our Lady," quoth this canon, "it is dear.
I warn you well, that, save I and a frere,
In Engleland there can no man it make."
"No force," quoth he; "now, Sir, for Godde's sake, no matter
What shall I pay? telle me, I you pray."
"Y-wis," quoth he, "it is full dear, I say. certainly
Sir, at one word, if that you list it have,
Ye shall pay forty pound, so God me save;
And n'ere the friendship that ye did ere this were it not for
To me, ye shoulde paye more, y-wis."
This priest the sum of forty pound anon
Of nobles fet, and took them every one fetched
To this canon, for this ilke receipt.
All his working was but fraud and deceit.
"Sir Priest," he said, "I keep to have no los care praise[16]
Of my craft, for I would it were kept close;
And as ye love me, keep it secre:
For if men knewen all my subtlety,
By God, they woulde have so great envy
To me, because of my philosophy,
I should be dead, there were no other way."
"God it forbid," quoth the priest, "what ye say.
Yet had I lever spenden all the good rather
Which that I have (and elles were I wood), mad
Than that ye shoulde fall in such mischief."
"For your good will, Sir, have ye right good prefe," results of your
Quoth the canon; "and farewell, grand mercy." experiments
He went his way, and never the priest him sey saw
After that day; and when that this priest should
Maken assay, at such time as he would,
Of this receipt, farewell! it would not be.
Lo, thus bejaped and beguil'd was he; tricked
Thus made he his introduction
To bringe folk to their destruction.

Consider, Sirs, how that in each estate
Betwixte men and gold there is debate,
So farforth that unnethes is there none. scarcely is there any
This multiplying blint so many a one, blinds, deceive
That in good faith I trowe that it be
The cause greatest of such scarcity.
These philosophers speak so mistily
In this craft, that men cannot come thereby,
For any wit that men have how-a-days.
They may well chatter, as do these jays,
And in their termes set their lust and pain, pleasure and exertion
But to their purpose shall they ne'er attain.
A man may lightly learn, if he have aught, easily
To multiply, and bring his good to naught.
Lo, such a lucre is in this lusty game; profit pleasant
A manne's mirth it will turn all to grame, sorrow[17]
And empty also great and heavy purses,
And make folke for to purchase curses
Of them that have thereto their good y-lent.
Oh, fy for shame! they that have been brent, burnt
Alas! can they not flee the fire's heat?
Ye that it use, I rede that ye it lete, advise leave
Lest ye lose all; for better than never is late;
Never to thrive, were too long a date.
Though ye prowl aye, ye shall it never find;
Ye be as bold as is Bayard the blind,
That blunders forth, and peril casteth none; perceives no danger
He is as bold to run against a stone,
As for to go beside it in the way:
So fare ye that multiply, I say.
If that your eyen cannot see aright,
Look that your minde lacke not his sight.
For though you look never so broad, and stare,
Ye shall not win a mite on that chaffare, traffic, commerce
But wasten all that ye may rape and renn. get by hook or crook
Withdraw the fire, lest it too faste brenn; burn

Meddle no more with that art, I mean;
For if ye do, your thrift is gone full clean. prosperity
And right as swithe I will you telle here quickly
What philosophers say in this mattere.

Lo, thus saith Arnold of the newe town,[18]
As his Rosary maketh mentioun,
He saith right thus, withouten any lie;
"There may no man mercury mortify,[13]
But it be with his brother's knowleding." except
Lo, how that he, which firste said this thing,
Of philosophers father was, Hermes;[19]
He saith, how that the dragon doubteless
He dieth not, but if that he be slain
With his brother. And this is for to sayn,
By the dragon, Mercury, and none other,
He understood, and Brimstone by his brother,
That out of Sol and Luna were y-draw. drawn, derived
"And therefore," said he, "take heed to my saw. saying
Let no man busy him this art to seech, study, explore
But if that he th'intention and speech unless
Of philosophers understande can;
And if he do, he is a lewed man. ignorant, foolish
For this science and this conning," quoth he, knowledge
"Is of the secret of secrets[20] pardie."
Also there was a disciple of Plato,
That on a time said his master to,
As his book, Senior,[21] will bear witness,
And this was his demand in soothfastness:
"Tell me the name of thilke privy stone." that
secret
And Plato answer'd unto him anon;
"Take the stone that Titanos men name."
"Which is that?" quoth he. "Magnesia is the same,"
Saide Plato. "Yea, Sir, and is it thus?
This is ignotum per ignotius.[22]
What is Magnesia, good Sir, I pray?"
"It is a water that is made, I say,
Of th' elementes foure," quoth Plato.
"Tell me the roote, good Sir," quoth he tho, then
"Of that water, if that it be your will."
"Nay, nay," quoth Plato, "certain that I n'ill. will not
The philosophers sworn were every one,
That they should not discover it to none,
Nor in no book it write in no mannere;
For unto God it is so lefe and dear, precious
That he will not that it discover'd be,
But where it liketh to his deity
Man for to inspire, and eke for to defend' protect
Whom that he liketh; lo, this is the end."

Then thus conclude I, since that God of heaven
Will not that these philosophers neven name
How that a man shall come unto this stone,
I rede as for the best to let it gon. counsel
For whoso maketh God his adversary,
As for to work any thing in contrary
Of his will, certes never shall he thrive,
Though that he multiply term of his live.[23]
And there a point; for ended is my tale. end
God send ev'ry good man boot of his bale.
remedy for his sorrow

Note to the Canon's Yeoman's Tale

1. The Tale of the Canon's Yeoman, like those of the Wife of Bath and the Pardoner, is made up of two parts; a long general introduction, and the story proper. In the case of the Wife of Bath, the interruptions of other pilgrims, and the autobiographical nature of the discourse, recommend the separation of the prologue from the Tale proper; but in the other cases the introductory or merely connecting matter ceases wholly where the opening of "The Tale" has been marked in the text.
2. Jupartie: Jeopardy, hazard. In Froissart's French, "a jeu partie" is used to signify a game or contest in which the chances were exactly equal for both sides.
3. Squames: Scales; Latin, "squamae."
4. Descensories: vessels for distillation "per descensum;" they were placed under the fire, and the spirit to be extracted was thrown downwards. Croslets: crucibles; French, "creuset.". Cucurbites: retorts; distilling-vessels; so called from their likeness in shape to a gourd — Latin, "cucurbita." Alembikes:stills, limbecs.
5. Seared pokettes: the meaning of this phrase is obscure; but if we take the reading "cered poketts," from the Harleian manuscript, we are led to the supposition that it signifies receptacles — bags or pokes — prepared with wax for some process. Latin, "cera," wax.
6. Argoil: potter's clay, used for luting or closing vessels in the laboratories of the alchemists; Latin, "argilla;" French, "argile."
7. Citrination: turning to a citrine colour, or yellow, by chemical action; that was the colour which proved the philosopher's stone.
8. Ingots: not, as in its modern meaning, the masses of metal shaped by pouring into moulds; but the moulds themslves into which the fused metal was poured. Compare Dutch, "ingieten," part. "inghehoten," to infuse; German, "eingiessen," part. "eingegossen," to pour in.

9. Threpe: name; from Anglo-Saxon, "threapian."
10. Bratt: coarse cloak; Anglo-Saxon, "bratt." The word is still used in Lincolnshire, and some parts of the north, to signify a coarse kind of apron.
11. Long on: in consequence of; the modern vulgar phrase "all along of," or "all along on," best conveys the force of the words in the text.
12. Annualere: a priest employed in singing "annuals" or anniversary masses for the dead, without any cure of souls; the office was such as, in the Prologue to the Tales, Chaucer praises the Parson for not seeking: Nor "ran unto London, unto Saint Poul's, to seeke him a chantery for souls."
13. Mortify: a chemical phrase, signifying the dissolution of quicksilver in acid.
14. Blin: cease; from Anglo-Saxon, "blinnan," to desist.
15. Name: took; from Anglo-Saxon, "niman," to take. Compare German, "nehmen," "nahm."
16. Los: praise, reputataion. See note 5 to Chaucer's tale of Meliboeus.
17. Grame: sorrow; Anglo-Saxon, "gram;" German, "Gram."
18. Arnaldus Villanovanus, or Arnold de Villeneuve, was a distinguished French chemist and physician of the fourteenth century; his "Rosarium Philosophorum" was a favourite text-book with the alchemists of the generations that succeeded.
19. Hermes Trismegistus, counsellor of Osiris, King of Egypt, was credited with the invention of writing and hieroglyphics, the drawing up of the laws of the Egyptians, and the origination of many sciences and arts. The Alexandrian school ascribed to him the mystic learning which it amplified; and the scholars of the Middle Ages regarded with enthusiasm and reverence the works attributed to him — notably a treatise on the philosopher's stone.
20. Secret of secrets: "Secreta Secretorum;" a treatise, very popular in the Middle Ages, supposed to contain the sum of Aristotle's instructions to Alexander. Lydgate translated about half of the work, when his labour was interrupted by his death about 1460; and from the same treatise had been taken most of the seventh book of Gower's "Confessio Amantis."
21. Tyrwhitt says that this book was printed in the "Theatrum Chemicum," under the title, "Senioris Zadith fi. Hamuelis tabula chymica" ("The chemical tables of Senior Zadith, son of Hamuel"); and the story here told of Plato and his disciple was there related of Solomon, but with some variations.
22. Ignotum per ignotius: To explain the unknown by the more unknown.
23. Though he multiply term of his live: Though he pursue the alchemist's art all his days.

The Manciple's Tale.

The Prologue.

WEET ye not where there stands a little town, know
Which that y-called is Bob-up-and-down,[1]
Under the Blee, in Canterbury way?
There gan our Hoste for to jape and play,
And saide, "Sirs, what? Dun is in the mire.[2]
Is there no man, for prayer nor for hire,
That will awaken our fellow behind?
A thief him might full rob and bind easily
See how he nappeth, see, for cocke's bones,
As he would falle from his horse at ones.
Is that a Cook of London, with mischance?[3]
Do him come forth, he knoweth his penance; make
For he shall tell a tale, by my fay, faith
Although it be not worth a bottle hay.

Awake, thou Cook," quoth he; "God give thee sorrow
What aileth thee to sleepe by the morrow? in the day time
Hast thou had fleas all night, or art drunk?
Or had thou with some quean all night y-swunk, whore laboured
So that thou mayest not hold up thine head?"
The Cook, that was full pale and nothing red,
Said to Host, "So God my soule bless,
As there is fall'n on me such heaviness,
I know not why, that me were lever sleep, rather
Than the best gallon wine that is in Cheap."
"Well," quoth the Manciple, "if it may do ease
To thee, Sir Cook, and to no wight displease
Which that here rideth in this company,
And that our Host will of his courtesy,
I will as now excuse thee of thy tale;
For in good faith thy visage is full pale:
Thine eyen daze, soothly as me thinketh, are dim
And well I wot, thy breath full soure stinketh,
That sheweth well thou art not well disposed;
Of me certain thou shalt not be y-glosed. flattered
See how he yawneth, lo, this drunken wight,
As though he would us swallow anon right.
Hold close thy mouth, man, by thy father's kin;
The devil of helle set his foot therein!
Thy cursed breath infecte will us all:
Fy! stinking swine, fy! foul may thee befall.
Ah! take heed, Sirs, of this lusty man.
Now, sweete Sir, will ye joust at the fan?[4]
Thereto, me thinketh, ye be well y-shape.
I trow that ye have drunken wine of ape,[5]
And that is when men playe with a straw."

And with this speech the Cook waxed all wraw, wrathful
And on the Manciple he gan nod fast
For lack of speech; and down his horse him cast,
Where as he lay, till that men him up took.
This was a fair chevachie of a cook: cavalry expedition
Alas! that he had held him by his ladle!
And ere that he again were in the saddle
There was great shoving bothe to and fro
To lift him up, and muche care and woe,
So unwieldy was this silly paled ghost.
And to the Manciple then spake our Host:
"Because that drink hath domination
Upon this man, by my salvation
I trow he lewedly will tell his tale. stupidly
For were it wine, or old or moisty ale, new
That he hath drunk, he speaketh in his nose,
And sneezeth fast, and eke he hath the pose[6]
He also hath to do more than enough
To keep him on his capel out of the slough; horse
And if he fall from off his capel eftsoon, again
Then shall we alle have enough to do'n
In lifting up his heavy drunken corse.
Tell on thy tale, of him make I no force. I take no account
But yet, Manciple, in faith thou art too nice foolish
Thus openly to reprove him of his vice;
Another day he will paraventure
Reclaime thee, and bring thee to the lure;[7]
I mean, he speake will of smalle things,
As for to pinchen at thy reckonings, pick flaws in
That were not honest, if it came to prefe." test, proof
Quoth the Manciple, "That were a great mischief;
So might he lightly bring me in the snare.
Yet had I lever paye for the mare rather
Which he rides on, than he should with me strive.
I will not wrathe him, so may I thrive)
That that I spake, I said it in my bourde. jest
And weet ye what? I have here in my gourd
A draught of wine, yea, of a ripe grape,
And right anon ye shall see a good jape. trick
This Cook shall drink thereof, if that I may;
On pain of my life he will not say nay."
And certainly, to tellen as it was,
Of this vessel the cook drank fast (alas!
What needed it? he drank enough beforn),
And when he hadde pouped in his horn, belched
To the Manciple he took the gourd again.

GEOFFREY CHAUCER

And of that drink the Cook was wondrous fain,
And thanked him in such wise as he could.

Then gan our Host to laughe wondrous loud,
And said, "I see well it is necessary
Where that we go good drink with us to carry;
For that will turne rancour and disease *trouble,*
annoyance

T'accord and love, and many a wrong appease.
O Bacchus, Bacchus, blessed be thy name,
That so canst turnen earnest into game!
Worship and thank be to thy deity.
Of that mattere ye get no more of me.
Tell on thy tale, Manciple, I thee pray."
"Well, Sir," quoth he, "now hearken what I say."

Notes to the Prologue to the Manciple's Tale

1. Bob-up-and-down: Mr Wright supposes this to be the village of Harbledown, near Canterbury, which is situated on a hill, and near which there are many ups and downs in the road. Like Boughton, where the Canon and his Yeoman overtook the pilgrims, it stood on the skirts of the Kentish forest of Blean or Blee.
2. Dun is in the mire: a proverbial saying. "Dun" is a name for an ass, derived from his colour.
3. The mention of the Cook here, with no hint that he had already told a story, confirms the indication given by the imperfect condition of his Tale, that Chaucer intended to suppress the Tale altogether, and make him tell a story in some other place.
4. The quintain; called "fan" or "vane," because it turned round like a weather-cock.
5. Referring to the classification of wine, according to its effects on a man, given in the old "Calendrier des Bergiers," The man of choleric temperament has "wine of lion;" the sanguine, "wine of ape;" the phlegmatic, "wine of sheep;" the melancholic, "wine of sow." There is a Rabbinical tradition that, when Noah was planting vines, Satan slaughtered beside them the four animals named; hence the effect of wine in making those who drink it display in turn the characteristics of all the four.
6. The pose: a defluxion or rheum which stops the nose and obstructs the voice.
7. Bring thee to his lure: A phrase in hawking — to recall a hawk to the fist; the meaning here is, that the Cook may one day bring the Manciple to account, or pay him off, for the rebuke of his drunkenness.

THE TALE.1

When Phoebus dwelled here in earth adown,
As olde bookes make mentioun,
He was the moste lusty bacheler pleasant
Of all this world, and eke the best archer. *also*
He slew Python the serpent, as he lay
Sleeping against the sun upon a day;
And many another noble worthy deed
He with his bow wrought, as men maye read.
Playen he could on every minstrelsy,
And singe, that it was a melody
To hearen of his cleare voice the soun'.
Certes the king of Thebes, Amphioun,
That with his singing walled the city,
Could never singe half so well as he.
Thereto he was the seemlieste man
That is, or was since that the world began;
What needeth it his features to descrive?
For in this world is none so fair alive.
He was therewith full fill'd of gentleness,
Of honour, and of perfect worthiness.

This Phoebus, that was flower of bach'lery,
As well in freedom as in chivalry, *generosity*
For his disport, in sign eke of victory
Of Python, so as telleth us the story,
Was wont to bearen in his hand a bow.
Now had this Phoebus in his house a crow,
Which in a cage he foster'd many a day,

And taught it speaken, as men teach a jay.
White was this crow, as is a snow-white swan,
And counterfeit the speech of every man
He coulde, when he shoulde tell a tale.
Therewith in all this world no nightingale
Ne coulde by an hundred thousand deal part
Singe so wondrous merrily and well.
Now had this Phoebus in his house a wife;
Which that he loved more than his life.
And night and day did ever his diligence
Her for to please, and do her reverence:
Save only, if that I the sooth shall sayn,
Jealous he was, and would have kept her fain.
For him were loth y-japed for to be; *tricked,*
deceived
And so is every wight in such degree;
But all for nought, for it availeth nought.
A good wife, that is clean of work and thought,
Should not be kept in none await certain: *observation*
And truely the labour is in vain
To keep a shrewe, for it will not be. *ill-disposed*
woman
This hold I for a very nicety, *sheer folly*
To spille labour for to keepe wives; *lose*

Thus writen olde clerkes in their lives.
But now to purpose, as I first began.

222

This worthy Phoebus did all that he can
To please her, weening, through such pleasance,
And for his manhood and his governance,
That no man should have put him from her grace;
But, God it wot, there may no man embrace
As to distrain a thing, which that nature succeed in constraining
Hath naturally set in a creature.
Take any bird, and put it in a cage,
And do all thine intent, and thy corage, what thy heart prompts
To foster it tenderly with meat and drink
Of alle dainties that thou canst bethink,
And keep it all so cleanly as thou may;
Although the cage of gold be never so gay,
Yet had this bird, by twenty thousand fold,
Lever in a forest, both wild and cold, rather
Go eate wormes, and such wretchedness.
For ever this bird will do his business
T'escape out of his cage when that he may:
His liberty the bird desireth aye.[2]
Let take a cat, and foster her with milk
And tender flesh, and make her couch of silk,
And let her see a mouse go by the wall,
Anon she weiveth milk, and flesh, and all, forsaketh
And every dainty that is in that house,
Such appetite hath she to eat the mouse.
Lo, here hath kind her domination, nature
And appetite flemeth discretion. drives out
A she-wolf hath also a villain's kind
The lewedeste wolf that she may find,
Or least of reputation, will she take
In time when her lust to have a make. she desires mate
All these examples speak I by these men with reference to
That be untrue, and nothing by women.
For men have ever a lik'rous appetite
On lower things to perform their delight
Than on their wives, be they never so fair,
Never so true, nor so debonair. gentle, mild
Flesh is so newefangled, with mischance, ill luck to it
That we can in no thinge have pleasance
That souneth unto virtue any while. accords with

This Phoebus, which that thought upon no guile,
Deceived was for all his jollity;
For under him another hadde she,
A man of little reputation,
Nought worth to Phoebus in comparison.
The more harm is; it happens often so,
Of which there cometh muche harm and woe.
And so befell, when Phoebus was absent,
His wife anon hath for her leman sent. unlawful lover
Her leman! certes that is a knavish speech.

Forgive it me, and that I you beseech.
The wise Plato saith, as ye may read,
The word must needs accorde with the deed;
If men shall telle properly a thing,
The word must cousin be to the working.
I am a boistous man, right thus I say. rough-spoken, downright
There is no difference truely
Betwixt a wife that is of high degree
(If of her body dishonest she be),
And any poore wench, other than this
(If it so be they worke both amiss),
But, for the gentle is in estate above, because
She shall be call'd his lady and his love;
And, for that other is a poor woman,
She shall be call'd his wench and his leman:
And God it wot, mine owen deare brother,
Men lay the one as low as lies the other.
Right so betwixt a titleless tyrant usurper
And an outlaw, or else a thief errant, wandering
The same I say, there is no difference
(To Alexander told was this sentence),
But, for the tyrant is of greater might
By force of meinie for to slay downright, followers
And burn both house and home, and make all plain, level
Lo, therefore is he call'd a captain;
And, for the outlaw hath but small meinie,
And may not do so great an harm as he,
Nor bring a country to so great mischief,
Men calle him an outlaw or a thief.
But, for I am a man not textuel, learned in texts
I will not tell of texts never a deal; whit
I will go to my tale, as I began.

When Phoebus' wife had sent for her leman,
Anon they wroughten all their lust volage. light or rash pleasure
This white crow, that hung aye in the cage,
Beheld their work, and said never a word;
And when that home was come Phoebus the lord,
This crowe sung, "Cuckoo, cuckoo, cuckoo!"
"What? bird," quoth Phoebus, "what song sing'st thou now?
Wert thou not wont so merrily to sing,
That to my heart it was a rejoicing
To hear thy voice? alas! what song is this?"
"By God," quoth he, "I singe not amiss.
Phoebus," quoth he, "for all thy worthiness,
For all thy beauty, and all thy gentleness,
For all thy song, and all thy minstrelsy,
For all thy waiting, bleared is thine eye despite all thy watching,
With one of little reputation, thou art befooled
Not worth to thee, as in comparison,
The mountance of a gnat, so may I thrive; value
For on thy bed thy wife I saw him swive."

What will ye more? the crow anon him told,
By sade tokens, and by wordes bold,   grave, trustworthy
How that his wife had done her lechery,
To his great shame and his great villainy;
And told him oft, he saw it with his eyen.
This Phoebus gan awayward for to wrien;   turn aside
Him thought his woeful hearte burst in two.
His bow he bent, and set therein a flo,   arrow
And in his ire he hath his wife slain;
This is th' effect, there is no more to sayn.
For sorrow of which he brake his minstrelsy,
Both harp and lute, gitern and psaltery;   guitar
And eke he brake his arrows and his bow;
And after that thus spake he to the crow.

"Traitor," quoth he, "with tongue of scorpion,
Thou hast me brought to my confusion;
Alas that I was wrought! why n'ere I dead?   made was not
O deare wife, O gem of lustihead,   pleasantness
That wert to me so sad, and eke so true,   steadfast
Now liest thou dead, with face pale of hue,
Full guilteless, that durst I swear y-wis!   certainly
O rakel hand, to do so foul amiss   rash, hasty
O troubled wit, O ire reckeless,
That unadvised smit'st the guilteless!
O wantrust, full of false suspicion!   distrust[3]
Where was thy wit and thy discretion?
O! every man beware of rakelness,   rashness
Nor trow no thing withoute strong witness.   believe
Smite not too soon, ere that ye weete why,   know
And be advised well and sickerly   consider surely
Ere ye do any execution   take any action
Upon your ire for suspicion.   upon your anger
Alas! a thousand folk hath rakel ire
Foully fordone, and brought them in the mire.
Alas! for sorrow I will myself slee   slay
And to the crow, "O false thief," said he,
"I will thee quite anon thy false tale.
Thou sung whilom like any nightingale,   once on a time
Now shalt thou, false thief, thy song foregon,   lose
And eke thy white feathers every one,
Nor ever in all thy life shalt thou speak;
Thus shall men on a traitor be awreak.   revenged
Thou and thine offspring ever shall be blake,   black
Nor ever sweete noise shall ye make,
But ever cry against tempest and rain,   before, in warning of
In token that through thee my wife is slain."
And to the crow he start, and that anon,   sprang
And pull'd his white feathers every one,
And made him black, and reft him all his song,
And eke his speech, and out at door him flung
Unto the devil, which I him betake;   to whom I commend him
And for this cause be all crowes blake.
Lordings, by this ensample, I you pray,
Beware, and take keep what that ye say;   heed
Nor telle never man in all your life
How that another man hath dight his wife;
He will you hate mortally certain.
Dan Solomon, as wise clerkes sayn,
Teacheth a man to keep his tongue well;
But, as I said, I am not textuel.
But natheless thus taughte me my dame;
"My son, think on the crow, in Godde's name.
My son, keep well thy tongue, and keep thy friend;
A wicked tongue is worse than is a fiend:
My sone, from a fiend men may them bless.   defend by crossing themselves
My son, God of his endeless goodness
Walled a tongue with teeth, and lippes eke,
For man should him advise, what he speak.   because consider
My son, full often for too muche speech
Hath many a man been spilt, as clerkes teach;   destroyed
But for a little speech advisedly
Is no man shent, to speak generally.   ruined
My son, thy tongue shouldest thou restrain
At alle time, but when thou dost thy pain   except when you do
To speak of God in honour and prayere.   your best effort
The firste virtue, son, if thou wilt lear,   learn
Is to restrain and keepe well thy tongue;[4]
Thus learne children, when that they be young.
My son, of muche speaking evil advis'd,
Where lesse speaking had enough suffic'd,
Cometh much harm; thus was me told and taught;
In muche speeche sinne wanteth not.
Wost thou whereof a rakel tongue serveth?   knowest hasty
Right as a sword forcutteth and forcarveth
An arm in two, my deare son, right so
A tongue cutteth friendship all in two.
A jangler is to God abominable.   prating man
Read Solomon, so wise and honourable;
Read David in his Psalms, and read Senec'.
My son, speak not, but with thine head thou beck,   nod
Dissimule as thou wert deaf, if that thou hear
A jangler speak of perilous mattere.
The Fleming saith, and learn if that thee lest,   if it please thee
That little jangling causeth muche rest.
My son, if thou no wicked word hast said,
Thee thar not dreade for to be bewray'd;   thou hast no need to
But he that hath missaid, I dare well sayn,   fear to be betrayed

He may by no way call his word again.
Thing that is said is said, and forth it go'th,5
Though him repent, or be he ne'er so loth;
He is his thrall, to whom that he hath said
A tale, of which he is now evil apaid. which he now regrets
My son, beware, and be no author new
Of tidings, whether they be false or true;6
Whereso thou come, amonges high or low,
Keep well thy tongue, and think upon the crow."

Notes to the Manciple's Tale

1. "The fable of 'The Crow,' says Tyrwhitt, "which is the subject of the Manciple's Tale, has been related by so many authors, from Ovid down to Gower, that it is impossible to say whom Chaucer principally followed. His skill in new dressing an old story was never, perhaps, more successfully exerted."
2. See the parallel to this passage in the Squire's Tale, and note 34 to that tale.
3. Wantrust: distrust — want of trust; so "wanhope," despair - - want of hope.
4. This is quoted in the French "Romance of the Rose," from Cato "De Moribus," 1. i., dist. 3: "Virtutem primam esse puta compescere linguam." ("The first virtue is to be able to control the tongue")
5. "Semel emissum volat irrevocabile verbum." ("A word once uttered flies away and cannot be called back") — Horace, Epist. 1., 18, 71.
6. This caution is also from Cato "De Moribus," 1. i., dist. 12: "Rumoris fuge ne incipias novus auctor haberi." ("Do not pass on rumours or be the author of new ones")

GEOFFREY CHAUCER

THE PARSON'S TALE.

THE PROLOGUE.

By that the Manciple his tale had ended,
The sunne from the south line was descended
So lowe, that it was not to my sight
Degrees nine-and-twenty as in height.
Four of the clock it was then, as I guess,
For eleven foot, a little more or less,
My shadow was at thilke time, as there,
Of such feet as my lengthe parted were
In six feet equal of proportion.
Therewith the moone's exaltation, rising
In meane Libra, gan alway ascend, in the middle of
As we were ent'ring at a thorpe's end. village's
For which our Host, as he was wont to gie, govern
As in this case, our jolly company,
Said in this wise; "Lordings every one,
Now lacketh us no more tales than one.
Fulfill'd is my sentence and my decree;
I trow that we have heard of each degree. from each class or rank
Almost fulfilled is mine ordinance; in the company
I pray to God so give him right good chance
That telleth us this tale lustily.
Sir Priest," quoth he, "art thou a vicary? vicar
Or art thou a Parson? say sooth by thy fay. faith
Be what thou be, breake thou not our play;
For every man, save thou, hath told his tale.
Unbuckle, and shew us what is in thy mail. wallet
For truely me thinketh by thy cheer
Thou shouldest knit up well a great mattere.
Tell us a fable anon, for cocke's bones."

This Parson him answered all at ones;
"Thou gettest fable none y-told for me,
For Paul, that writeth unto Timothy,
Reproveth them that weive soothfastness, forsake truth
And telle fables, and such wretchedness.
Why should I sowe draff out of my fist, chaff, refuse
When I may sowe wheat, if that me list?

For which I say, if that you list to hear
Morality and virtuous mattere,
And then that ye will give me audience,
I would full fain at Christe's reverence
Do you pleasance lawful, as I can.
But, truste well, I am a southern man,
I cannot gest, rom, ram, ruf,[1] by my letter; relate stories
And, God wot, rhyme hold I but little better.
And therefore if you list, I will not glose, mince matters
I will you tell a little tale in prose,
To knit up all this feast, and make an end.
And Jesus for his grace wit me send
To shewe you the way, in this voyage,
Of thilke perfect glorious pilgrimage,[2]
That hight Jerusalem celestial.
And if ye vouchesafe, anon I shall
Begin upon my tale, for which I pray
Tell your advice, I can no better say. opinion
But natheless this meditation
I put it aye under correction
Of clerkes, for I am not textuel; scholars
I take but the sentence, trust me well. meaning, sense
Therefore I make a protestation,
That I will stande to correction."
Upon this word we have assented soon;
For, as us seemed, it was for to do'n, a thing worth doing
To enden in some virtuous sentence, discourse
And for to give him space and audience;
And bade our Host he shoulde to him say
That alle we to tell his tale him pray.
Our Hoste had. the wordes for us all:
"Sir Priest," quoth he, "now faire you befall;
Say what you list, and we shall gladly hear."
And with that word he said in this mannere;
"Telle," quoth he, "your meditatioun,
But hasten you, the sunne will adown.
Be fructuous, and that in little space; fruitful; profitable
And to do well God sende you his grace."

Notes to the Prologue to the Parson's Tale

1. Rom, ram, ruf: a contemptuous reference to the alliterative poetry which was at that time very popular, in preference even, it would seem, to rhyme, in the northern parts of the country, where the language was much more barbarous and unpolished than in the south.
2. Perfect glorious pilgrimage: the word is used here to signify the shrine, or destination, to which pilgrimage is made.

THE CANTERBURY TALES
THE TALE.[1]

[The Parson begins his "little treatise" –(which, if given at length, would extend to about thirty of these pages, and which cannot by any stretch of courtesy or fancy be said to merit the title of a "Tale") in these words: —]

Our sweet Lord God of Heaven, that no man will perish, but will that we come all to the knowledge of him, and to the blissful life that is perdurable [everlasting], admonishes us by the prophet Jeremiah, that saith in this wise: "Stand upon the ways, and see and ask of old paths, that is to say, of old sentences, which is the good way, and walk in that way, and ye shall find refreshing for your souls,"[2] &c. Many be the spiritual ways that lead folk to our Lord Jesus Christ, and to the reign of glory; of which ways there is a full noble way, and full convenable, which may not fail to man nor to woman, that through sin hath misgone from the right way of Jerusalem celestial; and this way is called penitence. Of which men should gladly hearken and inquire with all their hearts, to wit what is penitence, and whence it is called penitence, and in what manner, and in how many manners, be the actions or workings of penitence, and how many species there be of penitences, and what things appertain and behove to penitence, and what things disturb penitence.

[Penitence is described, on the authority of Saints Ambrose, Isidore, and Gregory, as the bewailing of sin that has been wrought, with the purpose never again to do that thing, or any other thing which a man should bewail; for weeping and not ceasing to do the sin will not avail — though it is to be hoped that after every time that a man falls, be it ever so often, he may find grace to arise through penitence. And repentant folk that leave their sin ere sin leave them, are accounted by Holy Church sure of their salvation, even though the repentance be at the last hour. There are three actions of penitence; that a man be baptized after he has sinned; that he do no deadly sin after receiving baptism; and that he fall into no venial sins from day to day. "Thereof saith St Augustine, that penitence of good and humble folk is the penitence of every day." The species of penitence are three: solemn, when a man is openly expelled from Holy Church in Lent, or is compelled by Holy Church to do open penance for an open sin openly talked of in the country; common penance, enjoined by priests in certain cases, as to go on pilgrimage naked or barefoot; and privy penance, which men do daily for private sins, of which they confess privately and receive private penance. To very perfect penitence are behoveful and necessary three things: contrition of heart, confession of mouth, and satisfaction; which are fruitful penitence against delight in thinking, reckless speech, and wicked sinful works.

Penitence may be likened to a tree, having its root in contrition, biding itself in the heart as a tree-root does in the earth; out of this root springs a stalk, that bears branches and leaves of confession, and fruit of satisfaction. Of this root also springs a seed of grace, which is mother of all security, and this seed is eager and hot; and the grace of this seed springs of God, through remembrance on the day of judgment and on the pains of hell. The heat of this seed is the love of God, and the desire of everlasting joy; and this heat draws the heart of man to God, and makes him hate his sin. Penance is the tree of life to them that receive it. In penance or contrition man shall understand four things: what is contrition; what are the causes that move a man to contrition; how he should be contrite; and what contrition availeth to the soul. Contrition is the heavy and grievous sorrow that a man receiveth in his heart for his sins, with earnest purpose to confess and do penance, and never more to sin. Six causes ought to move a man to contrition: 1. He should remember him of his sins; 2. He should reflect that sin putteth a man in great thraldom, and all the greater the higher is the estate from which he falls; 3. He should dread the day of doom and the horrible pains of hell; 4. The sorrowful remembrance of the good deeds that man hath omitted to do here on earth, and also the good that he hath lost, ought to make him have contrition; 5. So also ought the remembrance of the passion that our Lord Jesus Christ suffered for our sins; 6. And so ought the hope of three things, that is to say, forgiveness of sin, the gift of grace to do well, and the glory of heaven with which God shall reward man for his good deeds. — All these points the Parson illustrates and enforces at length; waxing especially eloquent under the third head, and plainly setting forth the sternly realistic notions regarding future punishments that were entertained in the time of Chaucer:-][3]

Certes, all the sorrow that a man might make from the beginning of the world, is but a little thing, at retard of [in comparison with] the sorrow of hell. The cause why that Job calleth hell the land of darkness;[4] understand, that he calleth it land or earth, for it is stable and never shall fail, and dark, for he that is in hell hath default [is devoid] of light natural; for certes the dark light, that shall come out of the fire that ever shall burn, shall turn them all to pain that be in hell, for it sheweth them the horrible devils that them torment. Covered with the darkness of death; that is to say, that he that is in hell shall have default of the sight of God; for certes the sight of God is the life perdurable [everlasting]. The darkness of death, be the sins that the wretched man hath done, which that disturb [prevent] him to see the face of God, right as a dark cloud doth between us and the sun. Land of misease, because there be three manner of defaults against three things that folk of this world have in this present life; that is to say, honours, delights, and riches. Against honour have they in hell shame and confusion: for well ye wot, that men call honour the reverence that man doth to man; but in hell is no honour nor reverence; for certes no more reverence shall be done there to a king than to a knave [servant]. For which God saith by the prophet Jeremiah; "The folk that me despise shall be in despite." Honour is also called great lordship. There shall no wight serve other, but of harm and torment. Honour is also called great dignity and highness; but in hell shall they be all fortrodden [trampled under foot] of devils. As God saith, "The horrible devils shall go and come upon the heads of damned folk;" and this is, forasmuch as the higher that they were in this present life, the more shall they be abated [abased] and defouled in hell. Against the riches of this world shall they have misease [trouble, torment] of poverty, and this poverty shall be in four things: in default [want] of treasure; of which David saith, "The rich folk that embraced and oned [united] all their heart to treasure of this world, shall sleep in the sleeping of death, and nothing shall they find in their hands of all their treasure." And moreover, the misease of hell shall be in default of meat and drink. For God saith thus by Moses, "They shall be wasted with hunger, and the birds of hell shall devour them with bitter death, and the gall of the dragon shall be their drink, and the venom of the dragon their morsels." And furthermore, their misease shall be in default of clothing, for they shall be naked in body, as of clothing, save the fire in which they burn, and other filths; and naked shall they be in soul, of all manner virtues, which that is the clothing of the soul. Where be then the gay robes, and the soft sheets, and the fine shirts? Lo, what saith of them the prophet Isaiah, that under them shall be strewed moths, and their covertures shall be of worms of hell. And furthermore, their misease shall be in default of friends, for he is not poor that hath good friends: but there is no friend; for neither God nor any good creature shall be friend to them, and evereach of them shall hate other with deadly hate. The Sons and the daughters shall rebel against father and mother, and kindred against kindred, and chide and despise each other, both day and night, as God saith by the prophet Micah. And the loving children, that whom loved so fleshly each other, would each of them eat the other if they might. For how should they love together in the pains of hell, when they hated each other in the prosperity of this life? For trust well, their fleshly love was deadly hate; as saith the prophet David; "Whoso loveth wickedness, he hateth his own soul:" and whoso hateth his own soul, certes he may love none other wight in no manner: and therefore in hell is no solace nor no friendship, but ever the more kindreds that be in hell, the more cursing, the more chiding, and the more deadly hate there is among them. And furtherover, they shall have default of all manner delights; for certes delights be after the appetites of the five wits [senses]; as sight, hearing, smelling, savouring [tasting], and touching. But in hell their sight shall be full of darkness and of smoke, and their eyes full of tears; and their hearing full of waimenting [lamenting] and grinting [gnashing] of teeth, as saith Jesus Christ; their nostrils shall be full of stinking; and, as saith Isaiah the prophet, their savouring [tasting] shall be full of bitter gall; and touching of all their body shall be covered with fire that never shall quench, and with worms that never shall die, as God saith by the mouth of Isaiah. And forasmuch as they shall not ween that they may die for pain, and by death flee from pain, that may they understand in the word of Job, that saith, "There is the shadow of death." Certes a shadow hath the likeness of the thing of which it is shadowed, but the shadow is not the same thing of which it is shadowed: right so fareth the pain of hell; it is like death, for the horrible anguish; and why? for it paineth them ever as though they should die anon; but certes they shall not die. For, as saith Saint Gregory, "To wretched caitiffs shall be given death without death, and end without end, and default without failing; for their death shall always live, and their end shall evermore begin, and their default shall never fail." And therefore saith Saint John the Evangelist, "They shall follow death, and they shall not find him, and they shall desire to die, and death shall flee from them." And eke Job saith, that in hell is no order of rule. And albeit that God hath created all things in right order, and nothing without order, but all things be ordered and numbered, yet nevertheless they that be damned be not in order, nor hold no order. For the earth shall bear them no fruit (for, as the prophet David saith, "God shall destroy the fruit of the earth, as for them"); nor water shall give them no moisture, nor the air no refreshing, nor the fire no light. For as saith Saint Basil, "The burning of the fire of this world shall God give in hell to them that be damned, but the light and the clearness shall be given in heaven to his children; right as the good man giveth flesh to his children, and bones to his hounds." And for they shall have no hope to escape, saith Job at last, that there shall horror and grisly dread dwell without end. Horror is always dread of harm that is to come, and this dread shall ever dwell in the hearts of them that be damned. And therefore have they lost all their hope for seven causes. First, for God that is their judge shall be without mercy to them; nor they may not please him; nor none of his hallows [saints]; nor they may give nothing for their ransom; nor they have no voice to speak to him; nor they may not flee from pain; nor they have no goodness in them that they may shew to deliver them from pain.

[Under the fourth head, of good works, the Parson says: —]

The courteous Lord Jesus Christ will that no good work be lost, for in somewhat it shall avail. But forasmuch as the good works that men do while they be in good life be all amortised [killed, deadened] by sin following, and also since all the good works that men do while they be in deadly sin be utterly dead, as for to have the life perdurable [everlasting], well may that man that no good works doth, sing that new French song, J'ai tout perdu — mon temps et mon labour[5]. For certes, sin bereaveth a man both the goodness of nature, and eke the goodness of grace. For soothly the grace of the Holy Ghost fareth like fire, that may not be idle; for fire faileth anon as it forleteth [leaveth] its working, and right so grace faileth anon as it forleteth its working. Then loseth the sinful man the goodness of glory, that only is to good men that labour and work. Well may he be sorry then, that oweth all his life to God, as long as he hath lived, and also as long as he shall live, that no goodness hath to pay with his debt to God, to whom he oweth all his life: for trust well he shall give account, as saith Saint Bernard, of all the goods that have been given him in his present life, and how he hath them dispended, insomuch that there shall not perish an hair of his head, nor a moment of an hour shall not perish of his time, that he shall not give thereof a reckoning.

[Having treated of the causes, the Parson comes to the manner, of contrition — which should be universal and total, not merely of outward deeds of sin, but also of wicked delights and thoughts and words; "for certes Almighty God is all good, and therefore either he forgiveth all, or else right naught." Further, contrition should be "wonder sorrowful and anguishous," and also continual, with steadfast purpose of confession and amendment. Lastly, of what contrition availeth, the Parson says, that sometimes it delivereth man from sin; that without it neither confession nor satisfaction is of any worth; that it "destroyeth the prison of hell, and maketh weak and feeble all the strengths of the devils, and restoreth the gifts of the Holy Ghost and of all good virtues, and cleanseth the soul of sin, and delivereth it from the pain of hell, and from the company of the devil, and from the servage [slavery] of sin, and restoreth it to all goods spiritual, and to the company and communion of Holy Church." He who should set his intent to these things, would no longer be inclined to sin, but would give his heart and body to the service of Jesus Christ, and thereof do him homage. "For, certes, our Lord Jesus Christ hath spared us so benignly in our follies, that if he had not pity on man's soul, a sorry song might we all sing."

The Second Part of the Parson's Tale or Treatise opens with an explanation of what is confession — which is termed "the second part of penitence, that is, sign of contrition;" whether it ought needs be done or not; and what things be convenable to true confession. Confession is true shewing of sins to the priest, without excusing, hiding, or forwrapping [disguising] of anything, and without vaunting of good works. "Also, it is necessary to understand whence that sins spring, and how they increase, and which they be." From Adam we took original sin; "from him fleshly descended be we all, and engendered of vile and corrupt matter;" and the penalty of Adam's transgression dwelleth with us as to temptation, which penalty is called concupiscence. "This concupiscence, when it is wrongfully disposed or ordained in a man, it maketh him covet, by covetise of flesh, fleshly sin by sight of his eyes, as to earthly things, and also covetise of highness by pride of heart." The Parson proceeds to shew how man is tempted in his flesh to sin; how, after his natural concupiscence, comes suggestion of the devil, that is to say the devil's bellows, with which he bloweth in man the fire of con cupiscence; and how man then bethinketh him whether he will do or no the thing to which he is tempted. If he flame up into pleasure at the thought, and give way, then is he all dead in soul; "and thus is sin accomplished, by temptation, by delight, and by consenting; and then is the sin actual." Sin is either venial, or deadly; deadly, when a man loves any creature more than Jesus Christ our Creator, venial, if he love Jesus Christ less than he ought. Venial sins diminish man's love to God more and more, and may in this wise skip into deadly sin; for many small make a great. "And hearken this example: A great wave of the sea cometh sometimes with so great a violence, that it drencheth [causes to sink] the ship: and the same harm do sometimes the small drops, of water that enter through a little crevice in the thurrok [hold, bilge], and in the bottom of the ship, if men be so negligent that they discharge them not betimes. And therefore, although there be difference betwixt these two causes of drenching, algates [in any case] the ship is dreint [sunk]. Right so fareth it sometimes of deadly sin," and of venial sins when they multiply in a man so greatly as to make him love worldly things more than God. The Parson then enumerates specially a number of sins which many a man peradventure deems no sins, and confesses them not, and yet nevertheless they are truly sins: —]

This is to say, at every time that a man eateth and drinketh more than sufficeth to the sustenance of his body, in certain he doth sin; eke when he speaketh more than it needeth, he doth sin; eke when he heareth not benignly the complaint of the poor; eke when he is in health of body, and will not fast when other folk fast, without cause reasonable; eke when he sleepeth more than needeth, or when he cometh by that occasion too late to church, or to other works of charity; eke when he useth his wife without sovereign desire of engendrure, to the honour of God, or for the intent to yield his wife his debt of his body; eke when he will not visit the sick, or the prisoner, if he may; eke if he love wife, or child, or other worldly thing, more than reason requireth; eke if he flatter or blandish more than he ought for any necessity; eke if he minish or withdraw the alms of the poor; eke if he apparail [prepare] his meat more deliciously than need is, or eat it too hastily by likerousness [gluttony]; eke if he talk vanities in the church, or at God's service, or that he be a talker of idle words of folly or villainy, for he shall yield account of them at the day of doom; eke when he behighteth [promiseth] or assureth to do things that he may not perform; eke when that by lightness of folly he missayeth or scorneth his neighbour; eke when he hath any wicked suspicion of thing, that he wot of it no soothfastness: these things, and more without number, be sins, as saith Saint Augustine.

[No earthly man may eschew all venial sins; yet may he refrain him, by the burning love that he hath to our Lord Jesus Christ, and by prayer and confession, and other good works, so that it shall but little grieve. "Furthermore, men may also refrain and put away venial sin, by receiving worthily the precious body of Jesus Christ; by receiving eke of holy water; by alms-deed; by general confession of Confiteor at mass, and at prime, and at compline [evening service]; and by blessing of bishops and priests, and by other good works." The Parson then proceeds to weightier matters:—]

Now it is behovely [profitable, necessary] to tell which be deadly sins, that is to say, chieftains of sins; forasmuch as all they run in one leash, but in diverse manners. Now be they called chieftains, forasmuch as they be chief, and of them spring all other sins. The root of these sins, then, is pride, the general root of all harms. For of this root spring certain branches: as ire, envy, accidie[6] or sloth, avarice or covetousness (to common understanding), gluttony, and lechery: and each of these sins hath his branches and his twigs, as shall be declared in their chapters following. And though so be, that no man can tell utterly the number of the twigs, and of the harms that come of pride, yet will I shew a part of them, as ye shall understand. There is inobedience, vaunting, hypocrisy, despite, arrogance, impudence, swelling of hearte, insolence, elation, impatience, strife, contumacy, presumption, irreverence, pertinacity, vain- glory and many another twig that I cannot tell nor declare. . . .]

And yet [moreover] there is a privy species of pride that waiteth first to be saluted ere he will salute, all [although] be he less worthy than that other is; and eke he waiteth [expecteth] or desireth to sit or to go above him in the way, or kiss the pax,[7] or be incensed, or go to offering before his neighbour, and such semblable [like] things, against his duty peradventure, but that he hath his heart and his intent in such a proud desire to be magnified and honoured before the people. Now be there two manner of prides; the one of them is within the heart of a man, and the other is without. Of which soothly these foresaid things, and more than I have said, appertain to pride that is within the heart of a man and there be other species of pride that be without: but nevertheless, the one of these species of pride is sign of the other, right as the gay levesell [bush] at the tavern is sign of the wine that is in the cellar. And this is in many things: as in speech and countenance, and outrageous array of clothing; for certes, if there had been no sin in clothing, Christ would not so soon have noted and spoken of the clothing of that rich man in the gospel. And Saint Gregory saith, that precious clothing is culpable for the dearth [dearness] of it, and for its softness, and for its strangeness and disguising, and for the superfluity or for the inordinate scantness of it; alas! may not a man see in our days the sinful costly array of clothing, and namely [specially] in too much superfluity, or else in too disordinate scantness? As to the first sin, in superfluity of clothing, which that maketh it so dear, to the harm of the people, not only the cost of the embroidering, the disguising, indenting or barring, ounding, paling,[8] winding, or banding, and semblable [similar] waste of cloth in vanity; but there is also the costly furring [lining or edging with fur] in their gowns, so much punching of chisels to make holes, so much dagging [cutting] of shears, with the superfluity in length of the foresaid gowns, trailing in the dung and in the mire, on horse and eke on foot, as well of man as of woman, that all that trailing is verily (as in effect) wasted, consumed, threadbare, and rotten with dung, rather than it is given to the poor, to great damage of the foresaid poor folk, and that in sundry wise: this is to say, the more that cloth is wasted, the more must it cost to the poor people for the scarceness; and furthermore, if so be that they would give such punched and dagged clothing to the poor people, it is not convenient to wear for their estate, nor sufficient to boot [help, remedy] their necessity, to keep them from the distemperance [inclemency] of the firmament. Upon the other side, to speak of the horrible disordinate scantness of clothing, as be these cutted slops or hanselines [breeches], that through their shortness cover not the shameful member of man, to wicked intent alas! some of them shew the boss and the shape of the horrible swollen members, that seem like to the malady of hernia, in the wrapping of their hosen, and eke the buttocks of them, that fare as it were the hinder part of a she-ape in the full of the moon. And more over the wretched swollen members that they shew through disguising, in departing [dividing] of their hosen in white and red, seemeth that half their shameful privy members were flain [flayed]. And if so be that they depart their hosen in other colours, as is white and blue, or white and black, or black and red, and so forth; then seemeth it, by variance of colour, that the half part of their privy members be corrupt by the fire of Saint Anthony, or by canker, or other such mischance. And of the hinder part of their buttocks it is full horrible to see, for certes, in that part of their body where they purge their stinking ordure, that foul part shew they to the people proudly in despite of honesty [decency], which honesty Jesus Christ and his friends observed to shew in his life. Now as of the outrageous array of women, God wot, that though the visages of some of them seem full chaste and debonair [gentle], yet notify they, in their array of attire, likerousness and pride. I say not that honesty [reasonable and appropriate style] in clothing of man or woman unconvenable but, certes, the superfluity or disordinate scarcity of clothing is reprovable. Also the sin of their ornament, or of apparel, as in things that appertain to riding, as in too many delicate horses, that be holden for delight, that be so fair, fat, and costly; and also in many a vicious knave, [servant] that is sustained because of them; in curious harness, as in saddles, cruppers, peytrels, [breast-plates] and bridles, covered with precious cloth and rich bars and plates of gold and silver. For which God saith by Zechariah the prophet, "I will confound the riders of such horses." These folk take little regard of the riding of God's Son of heaven, and of his harness, when he rode upon an ass, and had no other harness but the poor clothes of his disciples; nor we read not that ever he rode on any other beast. I speak this for the sin of superfluity, and not for reasonable honesty [seemliness], when reason it requireth. And moreover, certes, pride is greatly notified in holding of great meinie [retinue of servants], when they be of little profit or of right no profit, and namely [especially] when that meinie is felonous [violent] and damageous [harmful] to the people by hardiness [arrogance] of high lordship, or by way of office; for certes, such lords sell then their lordship to the devil of hell, when they sustain the wickedness of their meinie. Or else, when these folk of low degree, as they that hold hostelries, sustain theft of their hostellers, and that is in many manner of deceits: that manner of folk be the flies that follow the honey, or else the hounds that follow the carrion. Such foresaid folk strangle spiritually their lordships; for which thus saith David the prophet, "Wicked death may come unto these lordships, and God give that they may descend into hell adown; for in their houses is iniquity and shrewedness, [impiety] and not God of heaven." And certes, but if [unless] they do amendment, right as God gave his benison [blessing] to Laban by the service of Jacob, and to Pharaoh by the service of Joseph; right so God will give his malison [condemnation] to such lordships as sustain the wickedness of their servants, but [unless] they come to amendment. Pride of the table apaireth [worketh harm] eke full oft; for, certes, rich men be called to feasts, and poor folk be put away and rebuked; also in excess of divers meats and drinks, and namely [specially] such manner bake-meats and dish-meats burning of wild fire, and painted and castled with paper, and semblable [similar] waste, so that it is abuse to think. And eke in too great preciousness of vessel, [plate] and curiosity of minstrelsy, by which a man is stirred more to the delights of luxury, if so be that he set his heart the less upon our Lord Jesus Christ, certain it is a sin; and certainly the delights might be so great in this case, that a man might lightly [easily] fall by them into deadly sin.

[The sins that arise of pride advisedly and habitually are deadly; those that arise by frailty unadvised suddenly, and suddenly withdraw again, though grievous, are not deadly. Pride itself springs sometimes of the goods of nature, sometimes of the goods of fortune, sometimes of the goods of grace; but the Parson, enumerating and examining all these in turn, points out how little security they possess and how little ground for pride they furnish, and goes on to enforce the remedy against pride — which is humility or meekness, a virtue through which a man hath true knowledge of himself, and holdeth no high esteem of himself in regard of his deserts, considering ever his frailty.]

Now be there three manners [kinds] of humility; as humility in heart, and another in the mouth, and the third in works. The humility in the heart is in four manners: the one is, when a man holdeth himself as nought worth before God of heaven; the second is, when he despiseth no other man; the third is, when he recketh not though men hold him nought worth; the fourth is, when he is not sorry of his humiliation. Also the humility of mouth is in four things: in temperate speech; in humility of speech; and when he confesseth with his own mouth that he is such as he thinketh that he is in his heart; another is, when he praiseth the bounte [goodness] of another man and nothing thereof diminisheth. Humility eke in works is in four manners: the first is, when he putteth other men before him; the second is, to choose the lowest place of all; the third is, gladly to assent to good counsel; the fourth is, to stand gladly by the award [judgment] of his sovereign, or of him that is higher in degree: certain this is a great work of humility.

[The Parson proceeds to treat of the other cardinal sins, and their remedies: (2.) Envy, with its remedy, the love of God principally and of our neighbours as ourselves: (3.) Anger, with all its fruits in revenge, rancour, hate, discord, manslaughter, blasphemy, swearing, falsehood, flattery, chiding and reproving, scorning, treachery, sowing of strife, doubleness of tongue, betraying of counsel to a man's disgrace, menacing, idle words, jangling, japery or buffoonery, &c. — and its remedy in the virtues called mansuetude, debonairte, or gentleness, and patience or sufferance: (4.) Sloth, or "Accidie," which comes after the sin of Anger, because Envy blinds the eyes of a man, and Anger troubleth a man, and Sloth maketh him heavy, thoughtful, and peevish. It is opposed to every estate of man — as unfallen, and held to work in praising and adoring God; as sinful, and held to labour in praying for deliverance from sin; and as in the state of grace, and held to works of penitence. It resembles the heavy and sluggish condition of those in hell; it will suffer no hardness and no penance; it prevents any beginning of good works; it causes despair of God's mercy, which is the sin against the Holy Ghost; it induces somnolency and neglect of communion in prayer with God; and it breeds negligence or recklessness, that cares for nothing, and is the nurse of all mischiefs, if ignorance is their mother. Against Sloth, and these and other branches and fruits of it, the remedy lies in the virtue of fortitude or strength, in its various species of magnanimity or great courage; faith and hope in God and his saints; surety or sickerness, when a man fears nothing that can oppose the good works he has under taken; magnificence, when he carries out great works of goodness begun; constancy or stableness of heart; and other incentives to energy and laborious service: (5.) Avarice, or Covetousness, which is the root of all harms, since its votaries are idolaters, oppressors and enslavers of men, deceivers of their equals in business, simoniacs, gamblers, liars, thieves, false swearers, blasphemers, murderers, and sacrilegious. Its remedy lies in compassion and pity largely exercised, and in reasonable liberality — for those who spend on "fool-largesse," or ostentation of worldly estate and luxury, shall receive the malison [condemnation] that Christ shall give at the day of doom to them that shall be damned: (6.) Gluttony; — of which the Parson treats so briefly that the chapter may be given in full: —]

After Avarice cometh Gluttony, which is express against the commandment of God. Gluttony is unmeasurable appetite to eat or to drink; or else to do in aught to the unmeasurable appetite and disordered covetousness [craving] to eat or drink. This sin corrupted all this world, as is well shewed in the sin of Adam and of Eve. Look also what saith Saint Paul of gluttony: "Many," saith he, "go, of which I have oft said to you, and now I say it weeping, that they be enemies of the cross of Christ, of which the end is death, and of which their womb [stomach] is their God and their glory;" in confusion of them that so savour [take delight in] earthly things. He that is usant [accustomed, addicted] to this sin of gluttony, he may no sin withstand, he must be in servage [bondage] of all vices, for it is the devil's hoard, [lair, lurking-place] where he hideth him in and resteth. This sin hath many species. The first is drunkenness, that is the horrible sepulture of man's reason: and therefore when a man is drunken, he hath lost his reason; and this is deadly sin. But soothly, when that a man is not wont to strong drink, and peradventure knoweth not the strength of the drink, or hath feebleness in his head, or hath travailed [laboured], through which he drinketh the more, all [although] be he suddenly caught with drink, it is no deadly sin, but venial. The second species of gluttony is, that the spirit of a man waxeth all troubled for drunkenness, and bereaveth a man the discretion of his wit. The third species of gluttony is, when a man devoureth his meat, and hath no rightful manner of eating. The fourth is, when, through the great abundance of his meat, the humours of his body be distempered. The fifth is, forgetfulness by too much drinking, for which a man sometimes forgetteth by the morrow what be did at eve. In other manner be distinct the species of gluttony, after Saint Gregory. The first is, for to eat or drink before time. The second is, when a man getteth him too delicate meat or drink. The third is, when men take too much over measure [immoderately]. The fourth is curiosity [nicety] with great intent [application, pains] to make and apparel [prepare] his meat. The fifth is, for to eat too greedily. These be the five fingers of the devil's hand, by which he draweth folk to the sin.

Against gluttony the remedy is abstinence, as saith Galen; but that I hold not meritorious, if he do it only for the health of his body. Saint Augustine will that abstinence be done for virtue, and with patience. Abstinence, saith he, is little worth, but if [unless] a man have good will thereto, and but it be enforced by patience and by charity, and that men do it for God's sake, and in hope to have the bliss in heaven. The fellows of abstinence be temperance, that holdeth the mean in all things; also shame, that eschewth all dishonesty [indecency, impropriety], sufficiency, that seeketh no rich meats nor drinks, nor doth no force of [sets no value on] no outrageous apparelling of meat; measure [moderation] also, that restraineth by reason the unmeasurable appetite of eating; soberness also, that restraineth the outrage of drink; sparing also, that restraineth the delicate ease to sit long at meat, wherefore some folk stand of their own will to eat, because they will eat at less leisure.

[At great length the Parson then points out the many varieties of the sin of (7.) Lechery, and its remedy in chastity and continence, alike in marriage and in widowhood; also in the abstaining from all such indulgences of eating, drinking, and sleeping as inflame the passions, and from the company of all who may tempt to the sin. Minute guidance is given as to the duty of confessing fully and faithfully the circumstances that attend and may aggravate this sin; and the Treatise then passes to the consideration of the conditions that are essential to a true and profitable confession of sin in general. First, it must be in sorrowful bitterness of spirit; a condition that has five signs — shamefastness, humility in heart and outward sign, weeping with the bodily eyes or in the heart, disregard of the shame that might curtail or garble confession, and obedience to the penance enjoined. Secondly, true confession must be promptly made, for dread of death, of increase of sinfulness, of forgetfulness of what should be confessed, of Christ's refusal to hear if it be put off to the last day of life; and this condition has four terms; that confession be well pondered beforehand, that the man confessing have comprehended in his mind the number and greatness of his sins and how long he has lain in sin, that he be contrite for and eschew his sins, and that he fear and flee the occasions for that sin to which he is inclined. — What follows under this head is of some interest for the light which it throws on the rigorous government wielded by the Romish Church in those days —]

Also thou shalt shrive thee of all thy sins to one man, and not a parcel [portion] to one man, and a parcel to another; that is to understand, in intent to depart [divide] thy confession for shame or dread; for it is but strangling of thy soul. For certes Jesus Christ is entirely all good, in him is none imperfection, and therefore either he forgiveth all perfectly, or else never a deal [not at all]. I say not that if thou be assigned to thy penitencer[9] for a certain sin, that thou art bound to shew him all the remnant of thy sins, of which thou hast been shriven of thy curate, but if it like thee [unless thou be pleased] of thy humility; this is no departing [division] of shrift. And I say not, where I speak of division of confession, that if thou have license to shrive thee to a discreet and an honest priest, and where thee liketh, and by the license of thy curate, that thou mayest not well shrive thee to him of all thy sins: but let no blot be behind, let no sin be untold as far as thou hast remembrance. And when thou shalt be shriven of thy curate, tell him eke all the sins that thou hast done since thou wert last shriven. This is no wicked intent of division of shrift. Also, very shrift [true confession] asketh certain conditions. First, that thou shrive thee by thy free will, not constrained, nor for shame of folk, nor for malady [sickness], or such things: for it is reason, that he that trespasseth by his free will, that by his free will he confess his trespass; and that no other man tell his sin but himself; nor he shall not nay nor deny his sin, nor wrath him against the priest for admonishing him to leave his sin. The second condition is, that thy shrift be lawful, that is to say, that thou that shrivest thee, and eke the priest that heareth thy confession, be verily in the faith of Holy Church, and that a man be not despaired of the mercy of Jesus Christ, as Cain and Judas were. And eke a man must accuse himself of his own trespass, and not another: but he shall blame and wite [accuse] himself of his own malice and of his sin, and none other: but nevertheless, if that another man be occasion or else enticer of his sin, or the estate of the person be such by which his sin is aggravated, or else that be may not plainly shrive him but [unless] he tell the person with which he hath sinned, then may he tell, so that his intent be not to backbite the person, but only to declare his confession. Thou shalt not eke make no leasings [falsehoods] in thy confession for humility, peradventure, to say that thou hast committed and done such sins of which that thou wert never guilty. For Saint Augustine saith, "If that thou, because of humility, makest a leasing on thyself, though thou were not in sin before, yet art thou then in sin through thy leasing." Thou must also shew thy sin by thine own proper mouth, but [unless] thou be dumb, and not by letter; for thou that hast done the sin, thou shalt have the shame of the confession. Thou shalt not paint thy confession with fair and subtle words, to cover the more thy sin; for then beguilest thou thyself, and not the priest; thou must tell it plainly, be it never so foul nor so horrible. Thou shalt eke shrive thee to a priest that is discreet to counsel thee; and eke thou shalt not shrive thee for vain-glory, nor for hypocrisy, nor for no cause but only for the doubt [fear] of Jesus' Christ and the health of thy soul. Thou shalt not run to the priest all suddenly, to tell him lightly thy sin, as who telleth a jape [jest] or a tale, but advisedly and with good devotion; and generally shrive thee oft; if thou oft fall, oft arise by confession. And though thou shrive thee oftener than once of sin of which thou hast been shriven, it is more merit; and, as saith Saint Augustine, thou shalt have the more lightly [easily] release and grace of God, both of sin and of pain. And certes, once a year at the least way, it is lawful to be houseled,[10] for soothly once a year all things in the earth renovelen [renew themselves].

[Here ends the Second Part of the Treatise; the Third Part, which contains the practical application of the whole, follows entire, along with the remarkable "Prayer of Chaucer," as it stands in the Harleian Manuscript:—]

De Tertia Parte Poenitentiae. [Of the third part of penitence]

Now have I told you of very [true] confession, that is the second part of penitence: The third part of penitence is satisfaction, and that standeth generally in almsdeed and bodily pain. Now be there three manner of almsdeed: contrition of heart, where a man offereth himself to God; the second is, to have pity of the default of his neighbour; the third is, in giving of good counsel and comfort, ghostly and bodily, where men have need, and namely [specially] sustenance of man's food. And take keep [heed] that a man hath need of these things generally; he hath need of food, of clothing, and of herberow [lodging], he hath need of charitable counsel and visiting in prison and malady, and sepulture of his dead body. And if thou mayest not visit the needful with thy person, visit them by thy message and by thy gifts. These be generally alms or works of charity of them that have temporal riches or discretion in counselling. Of these works shalt thou hear at the day of doom. This alms shouldest thou do of thine own proper things, and hastily [promptly], and privily [secretly] if thou mayest; but nevertheless, if thou mayest not do it privily, thou shalt not forbear to do alms, though men see it, so that it be not done for thank of the world, but only for thank of Jesus Christ. For, as witnesseth Saint Matthew, chap. v., "A city may not be hid that is set on a mountain, nor men light not a lantern and put it under a bushel, but men set it on a candlestick, to light the men in the house; right so shall your light lighten before men, that they may see your good works, and glorify your Father that is in heaven."

THE CANTERBURY TALES

Now as to speak of bodily pain, it is in prayer, in wakings, [watchings] in fastings, and in virtuous teachings. Of orisons ye shall understand, that orisons or prayers is to say a piteous will of heart, that redresseth it in God, and expresseth it by word outward, to remove harms, and to have things spiritual and durable, and sometimes temporal things. Of which orisons, certes in the orison of the Pater noster hath our Lord Jesus Christ enclosed most things. Certes, it is privileged of three things in its dignity, for which it is more digne [worthy] than any other prayer: for Jesus Christ himself made it: and it is short, for [in order] it should be coude the more lightly, [be more easily conned or learned] and to withhold [retain] it the more easy in heart, and help himself the oftener with this orison; and for a man should be the less weary to say it; and for a man may not excuse him to learn it, it is so short and so easy: and for it comprehendeth in itself all good prayers. The exposition of this holy prayer, that is so excellent and so digne, I betake [commit] to these masters of theology; save thus much will I say, when thou prayest that God should forgive thee thy guilts, as thou forgivest them that they guilt to thee, be full well ware that thou be not out of charity. This holy orison aminisheth [lesseneth] eke venial sin, and therefore it appertaineth specially to penitence. This prayer must be truly said, and in very faith, and that men pray to God ordinately, discreetly, and devoutly; and always a man shall put his will to be subject to the will of God. This orison must eke be said with great humbleness and full pure, and honestly, and not to the annoyance of any man or woman. It must eke be continued with the works of charity. It availeth against the vices of the soul; for, assaith Saint Jerome, by fasting be saved the vices of the flesh, and by prayer the vices of the soul

After this thou shalt understand, that bodily pain stands in waking [watching]. For Jesus Christ saith "Wake and pray, that ye enter not into temptation." Ye shall understand also, that fasting stands in three things: in forbearing of bodily meat and drink, and in forbearing of worldly jollity, and in forbearing of deadly sin; this is to say, that a man shall keep him from deadly sin in all that he may. And thou shalt understand eke, that God ordained fasting; and to fasting appertain four things: largeness [generosity] to poor folk; gladness of heart spiritual; not to be angry nor annoyed nor grudge [murmur] for he fasteth; and also reasonable hour for to eat by measure; that is to say, a man should not eat in untime [out of time], nor sit the longer at his meal for [because] he fasteth. Then shalt thou understand, that bodily pain standeth in discipline, or teaching, by word, or by writing, or by ensample. Also in wearing of hairs [haircloth] or of stamin [coarse hempen cloth], or of habergeons [mail-shirts][11] on their naked flesh for Christ's sake; but ware thee well that such manner penance of thy flesh make not thine heart bitter or angry, nor annoyed of thyself; for better is to cast away thine hair than to cast away the sweetness of our Lord Jesus Christ. And therefore saith Saint Paul, "Clothe you, as they that be chosen of God in heart, of misericorde [with compassion], debonairte [gentleness], sufferance [patience], and such manner of clothing," of which Jesus Christ is more apaid [better pleased] than of hairs or of hauberks. Then is discipline eke in knocking of thy breast, in scourging with yards [rods], in kneelings, in tribulations, in suffering patiently wrongs that be done to him, and eke in patient sufferance of maladies, or losing of worldly catel [chattels], or of wife, or of child, or of other friends.

Then shalt thou understand which things disturb penance, and this is in four things; that is dread, shame, hope, and wanhope, that is, desperation. And for to speak first of dread, for which he weeneth that he may suffer no penance, thereagainst is remedy for to think that bodily penance is but short and little at the regard of [in comparison with] the pain of hell, that is so cruel and so long, that it lasteth without end. Now against the shame that a man hath to shrive him, and namely [specially] these hypocrites, that would be holden so perfect, that they have no need to shrive them; against that shame should a man think, that by way of reason he that hath not been ashamed to do foul things, certes he ought not to be ashamed to do fair things, and that is confession. A man should eke think, that God seeth and knoweth all thy thoughts, and all thy works; to him may nothing be hid nor covered. Men should eke remember them of the shame that is to come at the day of doom, to them that be not penitent and shriven in this present life; for all the creatures in heaven, and in earth, and in hell, shall see apertly [openly] all that he hideth in this world.

Now for to speak of them that be so negligent and slow to shrive them; that stands in two manners. The one is, that he hopeth to live long, and to purchase [acquire] much riches for his delight, and then he will shrive him: and, as he sayeth, he may, as him seemeth, timely enough come to shrift: another is, the surquedrie [presumption[12]] that he hath in Christ's mercy. Against the first vice, he shall think that our life is in no sickerness, [security] and eke that all the riches in this world be in adventure, and pass as a shadow on the wall; and, as saith St Gregory, that it appertaineth to the great righteousness of God, that never shall the pain stint [cease] of them, that never would withdraw them from sin, their thanks [with their goodwill], but aye continue in sin; for that perpetual will to do sin shall they have perpetual pain. Wanhope [despair] is in two manners [of two kinds]. The first wanhope is, in the mercy of God: the other is, that they think they might not long persevere in goodness. The first wanhope cometh of that he deemeth that he sinned so highly and so oft, and so long hath lain in sin, that he shall not be saved. Certes against that cursed wanhope should he think, that the passion of Jesus Christ is more strong for to unbind, than sin is strong for to bind. Against the second wanhope he shall think, that as oft as he falleth, he may arise again by penitence; and though he never so long hath lain in sin, the mercy of Christ is always ready to receive him to mercy. Against the wanhope that he thinketh he should not long persevere in goodness, he shall think that the feebleness of the devil may nothing do, but [unless] men will suffer him; and eke he shall have strength of the help of God, and of all Holy Church, and of the protection of angels, if him list.

Then shall men understand, what is the fruit of penance; and after the word of Jesus Christ, it is the endless bliss of heaven, where joy hath no contrariety of woe nor of penance nor grievance; there all harms be passed of this present life; there as is the sickerness [security] from the pain of hell; there as is the blissful company, that rejoice them evermore each of the other's joy; there as the body of man, that whilom was foul and dark, is more clear than the sun; there as the body of man that whilom was sick and frail, feeble and mortal, is immortal, and so strong and so whole, that there may nothing apair [impair, injure] it; there is neither hunger, nor thirst, nor cold, but every soul replenished with the sight of the perfect knowing of God. This blissful regne [kingdom] may men purchase by poverty spiritual, and the glory by lowliness, the plenty of joy by hunger and thirst, the rest by travail, and the life by death and mortification of sin; to which life He us bring, that bought us with his precious blood! Amen.

Notes to the Parson's Tale

1. The Parson's Tale is believed to be a translation, more or less free, from some treatise on penitence that was in favour about Chaucer's time. Tyrwhitt says: "I cannot recommend it as a very entertaining or edifying performance at this day; but the reader will please to remember, in excuse both of Chaucer and of his editor, that, considering The Canterbury Tales as a great picture of life and manners, the piece would not have been complete if it had not included the religion of the time." The Editor of the present volume has followed the same plan adopted with regard to Chaucer's Tale of Meliboeus, and mainly for the same reasons. (See note 1 to that Tale). An outline of the Parson's ponderous sermon — for such it is — has been drawn; while those passages have been given in full which more directly illustrate the social and the religious life of the time — such as the picture of hell, the vehement and rather coarse, but, in an antiquarian sense, most curious and valuable attack on the fashionable garb of the day, the catalogue of venial sins, the description of gluttony and its remedy, &c. The brief third or concluding part, which contains the application of the whole, and the "Retractation" or "Prayer" that closes the Tale and the entire "magnum opus" of Chaucer, have been given in full.
2. Jeremiah vi. 16.
3. See Note 3 to the Sompnour's Tale.
4. Just before, the Parson had cited the words of Job to God (Job x. 20-22), "Suffer, Lord, that I may a while bewail and weep, ere I go without returning to the dark land, covered with the darkness of death; to the land of misease and of darkness, where as is the shadow of death; where as is no order nor ordinance, but grisly dread that ever shall last."
5. "I have lost everything – my time and my work."
6. Accidie: neglectfulness or indifference; from the Greek, akedeia.
7. The pax: an image which was presented to the people to be kissed, at that part of the mass where the priest said, "Pax Domini sit semper vobiscum." ("May the peace of the Lord be always with you") The ceremony took the place, for greater convenience, of the "kiss of peace," which clergy and people, at this passage, used to bestow upon each other.
8. Three ways of ornamenting clothes with lace, &c.; in barring it was laid on crossways, in ounding it was waved, in paling it was laid on lengthways.

9. Penitencer: a priest who enjoined penance in extraordinary cases.
10. To be houseled: to receive the holy sacrament; from Anglo-Saxon, "husel;" Latin, "hostia," or "hostiola," the host.
11. It was a frequent penance among the chivalric orders to wear mail shirts next the skin.
12. Surquedrie: presumption; from old French, "surcuider," to think arrogantly, be full of conceit.

GEOFFREY CHAUCER

PRECES DE CHAUCERES.1

Prayer of Chaucer

Now pray I to you all that hear this little treatise or read it, that if there be anything in it that likes them, that thereof they thank our Lord Jesus Christ, of whom proceedeth all wit and all goodness; and if there be anything that displeaseth them, I pray them also that they arette [impute] it to the default of mine unconning [unskilfulness], and not to my will, that would fain have said better if I had had conning; for the book saith, all that is written for our doctrine is written. Wherefore I beseech you meekly for the mercy of God that ye pray for me, that God have mercy on me and forgive me my guilts, and namely [specially] my translations and of inditing in worldly vanities, which I revoke in my Retractions, as is the Book of Troilus, the Book also of Fame, the Book of Twenty-five Ladies, the Book of the Duchess, the Book of Saint Valentine's Day and of the Parliament of Birds, the Tales of Canter bury, all those that sounen unto sin, [are sinful, tend towards sin] the Book of the Lion, and many other books, if they were in my mind or remembrance, and many a song and many a lecherous lay, of the which Christ for his great mercy forgive me the sins. But of the translation of Boece de Consolatione, and other books of consolation and of legend of lives of saints, and homilies, and moralities, and devotion, that thank I our Lord Jesus Christ, and his mother, and all the saints in heaven, beseeching them that they from henceforth unto my life's end send me grace to bewail my guilts, and to study to the salvation of my soul, and grant me grace and space of very repentance, penitence, confession, and satisfaction, to do in this present life, through the benign grace of Him that is King of kings and Priest of all priests, that bought us with his precious blood of his heart, so that I may be one of them at the day of doom that shall be saved: Qui cum Patre et Spiritu Sancto vivis et regnas Deus per omnia secula. Amen.2

Notes to the Prayer of Chaucer

1. The genuineness and real significance of this "Prayer of Chaucer," usually called his "Retractation," have been warmly disputed. On the one hand, it has been declared that the monks forged the retractation. and procured its insertion among the works of the man who had done so much to expose their abuses and ignorance, and to weaken their hold on popular credulity: on the other hand, Chaucer himself at the close of his life, is said to have greatly lamented the ribaldry and the attacks on the clergy which marked especially "The Canterbury Tales," and to have drawn up a formal retractation of which the "Prayer" is either a copy or an abridgment. The beginning and end of the "Prayer," as Tyrwhitt points out, are in tone and terms quite appropriate in the mouth of the Parson, while they carry on the subject of which he has been treating; and, despite the fact that Mr Wright holds the contrary opinion, Tyrwhitt seems to be justified in setting down the "Retractation" as interpolated into the close of the Parson's Tale. Of the circumstances under which the interpolation was made, or the causes by which it was dictated, little or nothing can now be confidently affirmed; but the agreement of the manuscripts and the early editions in giving it, render it impossible to discard it peremptorily as a declaration of prudish or of interested regret, with which Chaucer himself had nothing whatever to do.
2. "[You] Who with the Father and the Holy Spirit livest and reignest God for ever and ever. Amen."

THE END OF THE CANTERBURY TALES

Printed in Great Britain
by Amazon